Gus the Great

BOOKS BY THOMAS W. DUNCAN

Novels

GUS THE GREAT
RING HORSE
WE PLUCK THIS FLOWER
O, CHAUTAUQUA

Verse

ELEPHANTS AT WAR
FROM A HARVARD NOTEBOOK
HOURS FROM A LIFE

Thomas W. Duncan

Gus the Great

A NOVEL

PHILADELPHIA
J. B. LIPPINCOTT COMPANY
NEW YORK

To
Actea

Gus the Great

And many horses weep when
their lords be dead.
—Bartholomew Anglicus.

1

Elephants had been buried on that land, and back in the glorious days on this country road you saw men in sweaters and caps leading the living elephants for their exercise in the sunshine of a spring morning. That pasture had once trembled beneath the hoofs of a hundred horses, and camels had munched hay on that farm. In those flamboyant years, a lazy hippopotamus had grunted in the Animal House, and if you walked those hills at night you heard lions roaring drowsily as they dreamed.

But that was over, now. The great days were dead. On the south slope of the hill the farm slept in the yellow autumn. The buildings marked "Paint Shop" and "Blacksmith Shop" and "Baggage Stock" stood silent in decay. Only sometimes you saw a girl hurrying into the house with a quick glance at the empty road, as if expecting somebody she did not want to see.

Southeast past the farm the valley ran; and once, along the base of the hill between the road and the farm, the stubby electric engine of an interurban line had clanged, dragging coal gondolas. But no longer. In these afteryears, weeds smothered the rotting ties, and long ago men had ripped up the rails and hauled them away to the scrapyards of cities.

On the flat ground between the road and the track, faded paint was peeling from a long, low barn where rats lived. From the gable a flagpole rose, whitely streaked by bird droppings and topped by what had once been a gilded wooden globe; and beneath the gable a sign, which the weather had nearly erased, said: Home of Burgoyne & Pawpacker's Great 3-Ring Circus.

Northwest, at the head of the valley, a few shanties huddled near the slag heaps of an abandoned coal mine. Several families dwelt cheerlessly there, because they didn't know where else to go. They were old men and women, Slovaks mostly, with garden patches and nanny goats; and they had lived there since those years in the early 1900's when a man named Oxenford owned the mine and the farm and the railroad spur which so foolishly had been constructed from the main line of Tamarack & Northern, some miles away.

One bright October afternoon a fat man came toiling along the interurban embankment a mile down the valley. His progress toward the

farm was slow, for he was not so young as in the days when steel rails
flashed through these woodland patches. Some need for caution—odd
in that sparsely inhabited valley—seemed to hold his big body on leash.
His gray eyes were watchful; and occasionally he halted and glanced
back, scanning the roadbed curving away with trolley poles askew
against the sky.

Despite the autumnal warmth, the man wore an overcoat. It was a
disintegrating garment, tinged in the sun with a faintly greenish patina.
Sere grass and bits of leaves clung to its back, as if it had been not only
worn but slept in. A single button latched it over his great belly, but
the buttonhole was so frayed that the coat kept coming unfastened,
revealing old tweeds in black-and-gray check.

Big as the man was, there was evidence that he had been bigger once.
A wattle of flesh dangled from his jawbone, and his heavy countenance
sagged beneath pouched eyes. His florid skin was specked with tiny
blood vessels, no larger than wisps of purple thread. He had gone un-
razored for several days, and his shoes were gray and cinder-scarred,
his hat dusty and stained.

But although he looked like a ragamuffin, something about him
hinted he would be able to deal with children jeering or dogs barking
that a beggar was coming to town. His mouth had a certain brutal
strength, and his eyes, although guarded, were fine and large and wise.
His hair was white, his profile bold and Roman; and if you had bar-
bered him and bathed him and sent him to a tailor he would have
looked more like a senator than most senators.

The man's hands were large, the fingers square and blunt; and now
that he was nearing sixty they were mottled with freckle-colored spots.
They looked like dominant hands that would serve their owner well,
bringing in money with large, easy sweeps and scattering it with sweeps
even larger. They were the kind of hands on whose left little finger
you expected a diamond ring. Indeed, he was the kind of man you
expected at one of the control posts of private enterprise, and you felt
that some very curious circumstances had brought him to this back-
country valley in the maddest season of the year.

He carried a stick broken from a tree, more club than cane; and
once, halting with the stick under his arm, he fished a cigar from his
pocket. As cigars went, it wasn't much. The tobacco was nearer yellow than brown, and the wrapper had rustled loose. He licked it into
place, then bit off the end and spat it out. Having lighted a match, he
waved the flame across the cigar tip and puffed with satisfaction. Then,
selecting a grassy spot on the embankment, he eased his weight to the
ground and rested against a sycamore tree. Breathing with the exertion,
he leaned over to unlace his shoes, but at the last moment he changed
his mind and lounged back, his cigar cocked at a prosperous angle. His

eyes, slitted against the sunlight, never roved far from the roadbed
along which he had made his cumbrous way.

After a few minutes he painstakingly snuffed out the cigar and returned it to his pocket. Sighing, he regained his feet and plodded on.
He held his head with almost senatorial nobility; he was cautious but
not hangdog. When the roadbed bridged a creek he hesitated, as if
reluctant to trust his weight to the worm-eaten trestle; but when he saw
that the creek could not be otherwise crossed he ventured forward. It
was as if he had business ahead whose urgency demanded that he take
risks.

Beyond the stream he encountered an elm sapling, taller than himself, which had sprung up where the rails had been. He stared, as if,
more than the debauched roadbed this slender tree spoke of the years
gone since he had passed this way. At last he tramped on a few paces,
then stopped and gazed back. But there was nobody else on the roadbed: only the mad scarlets and rotten golds of the decaying year.

Pushing ahead, he kept always to the embankment, following it up
the slow grades and through the cuts running bankful with sunlight.
The tall bleached grasses and thickets served the purposes of any man
who wished to move unseen through the countryside.

But presently as the farm came nearer the brambles thinned and the
valley widened out. The roadbed crossed another swaying trestle and
bisected a dirt road. Burgoyne stopped, standing as motionless as the
tattered milkweed in the ditches. And yet not quite motionless. His
eyes moved. At last he started on, walking faster now; but as the roadbed took him closer to the low barn his pace slowed.

To his right, the wreckage of lost years climbed the hill in the staring
sun. A high band wagon was canted precariously; a monkey wagon
lay upside down; and the gorgeously scrolled China wagon stood
neglected in a patch of thistle. Wind and rain had sabotaged its carved
and gilded lady and crouching tiger.

He turned slowly to his left, and in the paddock east of the low
Ring Stock barn he beheld the wooden horses. He stared, as men stare
at the secretive and familiar and strange faces of the dead. Then he left
the roadbed and made his way through the tangled ditch.

The wooden horses had been born first in his brain; in that curiously
expansive and shrewd and showy brain. They were slightly larger than
a merry-go-round team, and with their sleigh they were mounted on a
flat parade carriage. Necks arched, manes and tails rippling, they
possessed a hot turbulence that even their essential artificiality could
not quench.

He felt tired suddenly, and almost old. His gaze wandered to the
sleigh. He shouldn't have done that; he shouldn't have looked at the
sleigh. It brought back too much. He could imagine a blond woman

sitting there, on her lips that half-smile which in the beginning had piqued him, had tantalized him, till at last he had fallen ill of a fever to discover what waited behind it.

His palm touched one horse; its wood was soft. He withdrew his hand. Once those horses had been painted brilliant yellow, but the paint had vanished. Like the past. Days of sun had dried them gray, and wet weather had left brown stains dripping from their eyes, so that they looked like horses that were weeping. He turned away and started for the house, but not before he had swept the interurban embankment with a long, sharp scrutiny.

Where the driveway crossed the interurban he halted and gazed toward the house. It stood far back from the road in a yard that weeds had conquered, a two-story dwelling with a long kitchen wing. In the rich sunshine of midafternoon its white paint had a soft yellowish hue, and it looked as drowsy as an owl, waiting for darkness. He stood scrutinizing it with strict attention.

At last he advanced watchfully along the evergreen-lined drive, his stick ready for barking dogs. But he doubted that people lived here any more. They would starve if they did, for this valley had always been wretched for farming. Too many knolls and gullies, too many rocks. The soil was thin and sterile and sour, as if nature had borne it a grudge from the beginning; and even in the old days when the circus wintered here the land had refused to yield more than a fraction of the hay needed for the animals.

The driveway ended at a carriage yard, and his arrival sent a flock of sparrows whirring up from the deep dust. Then everything was quiet again. But it was a brooding quiet that filled him with uneasiness.

A picket fence separated the carriage yard from the house yard. It was a ramshackle thing with many teeth missing, and it would have tumbled down and rotted away save for the bushes that propped it up. Undisciplined by hedge shears, those bushes had grown exuberantly; and a grapevine had intruded there too, twining along the fence like some endless fantastic serpent.

The dust cushioned his movements with moccasin softness as he crossed to the gate. He squeaked it open and followed the path around to the kitchen porch. But when he reached the steps he came to an abrupt standstill, for a man was standing just inside the open kitchen door.

He was a small man, very old, and although the door commanded a view of the steps he gave no indication that any snapshots were flashing along his optic nerves. He had, however, the air of listening sharply. At last in a low voice he said:

"Eloise?"

Burgoyne did not respond.

The old man was moving now, his rubber-tipped cane guiding him across the sill. He reached the porch with great frugality of effort, his step weasel-soft; and he contrived to infuse that brief journey with enormous stealth and craft. When he inched to a halt he cocked his head forward.

Burgoyne turned, moving on tiptoe, and retraced his steps. His heart was pounding. The gate squeaked as he pushed it open, but he didn't look behind to see if Pawpacker had heard. He retreated down the drive to the low barn.

At the west entrance he stopped, and after what seemed a long time he caught sight of the old man, a small distant figure groping up the north hillside. Presently the foliage hid him, and Burgoyne stood scowling, asking himself why Pawpacker was here, why Eloise Sebastian was here. If strangers had been living at the farm it wouldn't have been good, but it wouldn't have been so bad, either. But Pawpacker. And Eloise. He hoped they would go to bed early and never hear somebody moving in the dark house.

And then without warning his nervous system jerked, and he was doing what he so despised himself for doing—glancing over his shoulder. He saw only the driveway joining the dusty road. Under the remote sky the valley lay silent as a country graveyard. Was he actually being followed? Was it all nerves, all shadow play? Of course! He had been under harrowing tension, these last days, making himself come back. He had erected psychic barriers and whenever he broke through one his tension increased. First the state line. Then the city of Tamarack. And now the farm.

He turned, moved into the low barn. All of it was here, all the memories of those roaring years.

A dusty passage ran the length of the barn, and he could hear a fly buzzing hopefully in the horse stalls. But today, only a thin odor of those horses remained. Ring horses. They had cost a fortune, but they had been beauties: magnificent Percherons, elegant Arabians.

Rungs ascended the barn wall to a loft above the stalls, and Burgoyne stared up at the aperture. He dreaded physical effort—his belly was like a large globe of the world, getting in his way—but up there he would be out of sight. He began climbing.

The rungs, afflicted with dry rot, creaked perilously, but they held. As his head rose through the aperture he heard a shrill squeal and the swift patter of retreating feet. A shiver cooled his spine, but he did not pause; and when he stood upright in the loft he gripped his stick and muttered:

"All right—come on, you damned rats."

He wished he had not spoken; the silence closed over his words with the finality of water engulfing pebbles flung into a pond. The rats had vanished into secret nests. He could imagine their pointed, whiskered faces as they came forth to investigate his sleeping body, and he shivered again. But he did not leave.

The loft smelled of hay that had been sweet once; and as he stood listening he grew aware of a new sound. Wheezing. It did not startle him but it exasperated him, for it issued from his bronchial tubes. He had fallen victim to asthma these last years, and the loft was rousing it. In the lances of sunlight invading the roof cracks he could see whole universes of dust motes whirling.

His gaze stopped at a bright slit in the north wall of the barn, and he started toward it. The floor complained. He envisioned his body plunging through a rotten patch of flooring, so he moved with the caution of an elephant in a jungle of sinkholes. When he reached the slit he found it too low for stooping; it would be necessary to kneel. He accomplished it slowly, with as many sighs and grunts as a locomotive.

Through the slit the day was very brilliant, very still. Not a person was in sight. Not a sound except his own breathing reached his ears. The windows of the Paint Shop stared at him blankly. Up the hill, through thinning bright foliage, he could discern the fat Baggage Stock barn with pigeons flashing about its ornamental cupola. That was the only movement. Otherwise he might have been gazing at a sun-flooded canvas daubed with October blues and golds by a painter drunk with the warm cider of autumn. His gaze moved west along the ridge, hunched up like a dinosaur's vertebrae. He did not see Pawpacker or Eloise. At last he labored to his feet.

Using his stick, he raked together a thin pile of hay, and he sat down, wearily and heavily. He fumbled with his shoes and pulled them off, sighing like a man who had learned to be grateful for humble comforts. Then from his overcoat he took a package wrapped in waxed paper. It contained thick beef sandwiches, and while he ate he thought of the future. It would be very fine. Till recently he had been quite without hope, a drifter along back streets. Then in the lobby of a cheap Denver hotel he had read a magazine. And suddenly hope surged through him. Instantly he knew he must return to this farm in the Middle West. He was his old self again, bursting with dazzling plans.

He found the half-smoked cigar and rolled it from side to side of his mouth. He wanted to light it, but he decided not to risk that. He lay back on the hay, stretching his toes, closing his eyes. He would wait here till nightfall. There would be a moon at eleven, but before that he would slip into the house and get what he wanted and be gone. Presently he dozed, and in his dreams he wore a prosperous suit and entered the Mirror Room of the Brown Palace Hotel with a vivid girl on his arm. They ordered cocktails and inch-thick steaks with the juice seared inside.

2

F OR SOME years the farm had been abandoned, the house untenanted
save for the mice who made merry in the puddles of moonlight on
the floor. Then ten days ago, in that autumn of 1938, old Mr. Pawpacker had come there to live, and with him this girl. Their arrival
stirred little interest up at the hamlet of Oxenford, for those Slavic
inhabitants were feudal souls with their own troubles. In the tiny store
that served the countryside, it was said that Mr. Pawpacker had adopted
the girl when she was a child, and that before catastrophe overtook
him he had deeded the farm to her.

Once in a while they saw her, when she walked to the store for
supplies. She was in her middle twenties, rather tall and striking.
Usually she wore slacks. She smoked a good deal, and she seemed pre-
occupied with her own affairs. Her hair was worn in a shoulder-length
bob, dark rust with an occasional crackling highlight. She used ample
lipstick, and without being in the least acrimonious her mouth had a
whisper of bitterness as if she had nibbled something—it might even
have been life—and discovered it contained too much alum flavoring.
Her voice was that way, too: disenchanted. A city voice. Her features
were very nice, but her expression seemed guarded, as if she didn't
wholly trust existence to remain on its good behavior if you turned
your back. That may have been because she had knocked around in
cities, where it is often wise for a girl to keep her own counsel. Sometimes at the store the old proprietor made a simple peasant joke, and
the girl smiled. The effect was fine. Once she even laughed.

She came of a family of troupers, and her father used to tell her
when she was a little girl that she had the makings of a good trouper.
Her father and mother had been married at eighteen, and when they
were twenty Eloise was born in Seattle. Her parents had wanted her,
planned for her, even though her birth was bad for their business. For
their art. That was how they thought of themselves, as artists.

Always their act either opened or closed the show, for they were
acrobats and ranked infinitely lower than entertainers like Sophie
Tucker and Thurston the Great. But they had faith that if they
worked hard and perfected their art they would come into their own,
someday. They called it getting a break. They were billed as "Sebas-

tian and Orika," and for several months at the time of Eloise's entry into the America of 1913 her father worked with a substitute whom a third-rate agent in New York recommended. The substitute was named Dixie Demming, and she did not have the interest of the act at heart. A floosie who was always running around with tinhorn sports and getting drunk. Her father was certainly relieved when Eloise's mother was able to rejoin the act.

By the time she was seven, Eloise had traveled thousands of miles back and forth across America, and there was scarcely a theatrical hotel in which she had not slept a few nights. She spoke in the jargon of variety houses, and when her mother taught her to read it was *The Billboard* that served as textbook. She loved trouping, and it never occurred to her or her parents that her view of existence was narrow and warped. She saw life through the speckled windows of chair cars and from side-street hotels.

Sometimes she made transient friendships with other theatrical children, but for the most part her association was confined to adults, so she was both wiser and more ignorant than most girls of her age. Many of the people she knew were cheap; but in some fashion her father and mother lived with cheapness, but escaped it. Their bodies were their livelihood and the instruments of their art, and they would as soon have abused their bodies as a violinist would abuse a Stradivarius. They avoided alcohol; they tried to get nine hours' sleep; they trained like athletes. Her father had a blond physique like a statue by Praxiteles, and although her mother was petite and weighed scarcely more than a hundred pounds the muscles beneath the silky skin of her legs and arms were like steel cables.

Till she was ten Eloise never stepped inside a schoolroom. Now and then in the cities where they played, the law made the halfhearted gesture of sending a truant officer to the theater or the hotel. On those occasions Eloise's mother looked exceedingly conscientious and explained she was teaching her daughter. She would ask Eloise to read for the man. There was seldom any difficulty, and if there was, the manager of the theater was always on good terms with some local politician who could fix things. And so if Eloise acquired a shaky knowledge of arithmetic and history her understanding of practical civics was excellent.

Those were the great years of vaudeville, and twice a day Eloise was to be found in the audience, watching the act from first row or back row or from the balcony in order to see how it appeared to customers in different parts of the house. The orchestra would crash into the overture and the curtain lettered "Asbestos" would rise and a page boy dressed in tight mauve trousers would walk to a gold-painted standard and shift the cards, and there would be the words: "Sebastian and Orika." Then the lofty dove-colored curtains swished apart and Eloise watched her bespangled parents and led the sporadic applause. Applause. It was what they yearned for, lived for, dreamed of, schemed for. When the act concluded the orchestra always played very loudly in order to give the illusion of a tremendous ovation. But it was never much.

If you cared for acrobats you would have been enthusiastic about Sebastian and Orika. But people did not attend vaudeville to see acrobats. They attended to laugh at the gag men and to watch the song-and-dance teams and to listen to the red-hot mammas. Sebastian and Orika were not stupid, and presently they realized that in vaudeville they had gone as far as they were likely to go. So they surveyed the show business and considered abandoning the stage for the ring. The circus. There were the disadvantages of a shorter season and lower wages in the beginning; but there were great advantages, too. In vaudeville acrobats were pariahs who were assigned the shabbiest dressing rooms, who were just tolerated by the gag men and ignored by the top liners. It was very differerent in the circus. They called you a kinker in the circus but they respected you as an aristocrat. And if some day you climbed to the payroll of the Big One—of Ringling Brothers—your salary would soar, too. On the Big One there were kinkers no better than Sebastian and Orika—or at least no better than Sebastian and Orika could become—who were famous the world over. You could perform in America during the summer and in the winter go to the famous indoor circuses of Copenhagen and Paris.

"It's this way, kid," Eloise's father told his wife. "They come to a circus for acrobats. Yeah, clowns too, and animals—but it's what goes on up in the top that makes 'em gasp. We don't want to be suckers all our lives, do we?"

No, Eloise's mother said, they didn't. So they got in touch with Gus Burgoyne.

That was in the fall of 1919, and Eloise would always remember the excitement that accompanied the writing of that first letter to Mr. Burgoyne. For days her parents discussed what they would say. They wanted Mr. Burgoyne to understand what wonderful acrobats they were, but they did not want him to believe them unduly egotistical.

"We can't give him the idea we've got a swelled nut," Ned Sebastian kept saying.

After their evening performance the Sebastians would go directly to their hotel, and while Lily (Orika) Sebastian sat at the writing table nibbling the pen, her husband paced about the room in the throes of composition.

"Dear Mr. Burgoyne . . . Um-m-m . . . The undersigned being

vaudeville artists of long standing and high repute . . . Um-m-m. No, better make that . . . vaudeville artists of refinement, long standing and high repute . . . respectfully submit herewith their qualifications for . . . um-m-m . . . for performing in your circus . . . um-m-m . . . better make that . . . um-m-m . . . your famous circus . . . and request the opportunity to talk with you about the same at some date suitable to the convenience of all concerned. Um-m-m . . . Now let's hear that, Lily, and see how it sounds."

And while Lily read the sentence aloud Ned stood rumpling his hair and frowning. And Eloise, lying quietly on the bed, hearing distant corridor doors opening and closing and the sound of a tap dancer practicing in the room above, would wonder why her father and mother took such pains with the letter. Why not simply tell Mr. Burgoyne what she fervently believed to be true—that they were the best acrobats in vaudeville?

After many evenings and many drafts the letter was ready.

"We've got to impress him," Ned Sebastian said. "I've got an idea."

So he visited a cheap printer, and a day or two later the Sebastians opened a brown paper package containing the stationery. It was as good as Christmas, opening that package. The letterheads were just about the most beautiful example of the printer's craft that had ever come from a press. Large type marched across the top of the page: "Sebastian and Orika." And in the upper left corner, "Ned Sebastian," and in the upper right, "Lily Orika." Beneath the name of the act the type announced: "Currently appearing on the Empress Circuit," and at the spot where you would date the letter were the words: "On Tour."

"Ah," Ned Sebastian said, "now we're getting somewhere."

Lily and Eloise were equally enthusiastic. Sight of their names in print always intoxicated them: it brought dignity and significance to their lives, to the frigid dressing rooms and the changing of trains at 3 A.M. and the fly-blown restaurants and the smells of cheap hotels. When they opened in a new town they were always nervous and restless till they could buy the newspapers containing their "notices." Often they were not mentioned at all, and sometimes the critic (usually a police reporter who wanted to see a free show) would dismiss them with, "Sebastian and Orika round out the program with the usual acrobatics," or "The program opens with Sebastian and Orika demonstrating that it's possible for man to walk on his hands." But now and then—ah—now and then the critic would be a writer of discernment, and he would devote a paragraph to their art. Red letter days, those! Happy cities, happy engagements! They were unaware that often the

critic had arrived at the theater too tardily to witness their act. Or
that his paper was needling an opposition theater for more advertising.
When gifts fell from heaven they did not ask why.

"Sebastian and Orika have brought their act as near perfection as is
humanly possible. They are young, enthusiastic, full of verve." (A
misprint for "nerve," the Sebastians thought.) "Their work on the steel
rings has a kind of aerial ballet quality, and they deserve a better spot
on the program."

True! A scholar and gentleman, that critic! They would buy a
dozen copies of that enlightened newspaper and send clippings to
agents and managers and friends in the profession. And Ned would
exclaim, "It's coming! It's bound to come! We'll get our break!"

A few such clippings they enclosed with their letter to Gus Burgoyne.
And the letter was typed. Ned typed it himself on a hotel office machine, using two fingers and ruining a dozen letterheads before he
produced a perfect copy. And in the lower left corner he wrote,
"NS:GL," so that Mr. Burgoyne would think he had a secretary.

"What does 'GL' stand for?" Lily wanted to know.

Ned laughed. "Can't you guess? It stands for what will bring us
our break. It stands for Good Luck!"

And when they posted the letter he insisted that all three should cross
their fingers.

After that the waiting began. Absurdly enough—and he knew it
was absurd but he couldn't help it—Ned started expecting a reply
the day after the letter was dispatched. On the second day he thought
they might receive a telegram from Mr. Burgoyne. Or a Special Delivery.

"I was expecting a wire," he would tell the desk clerk. "You're sure
nothing of the sort has come?"

The clerk was very sure, wearily sure.

A week elapsed and still no reply. Ned's enthusiasm was tempered
now, but he did not lose hope. He invented excuses for Mr. Burgoyne.

"Maybe he's out of town. Or sick. Or maybe he's just busy. We'll
hear. You wait and see. We'll hear when he gets around to it."

And then a second week went by. Lily thought they should write
to another circus.

"No," Ned said. "Let's play them one at a time. Burgoyne's show
is just right for us. Not too small, not too big. On a small one nobody
would ever hear of us. And if we started on the Big One we'd be
lost in the shuffle. What we want to do is start with Burgoyne and
get notices in *The Billboard* and then have the Ringlings come to us.
See the difference, with them coming to us? We'd say, well we don't
know. We're pretty well satisfied where we are, we'd say. We'd have
to have good billing, we'd say."

By the end of the third week even Ned was beginning to doubt whether they would hear from Mr. Burgoyne.

"Maybe we ought to write again," he said lamely. "Maybe the letter went astray."

But he knew it hadn't, and Lily and Eloise knew it hadn't. It was mid-November by that time, and they were trouping westward under the gray, cold skies of the central states; of Cleveland, Dayton, Akron, Toledo, Detroit. The old treadmill of cities they had played time after time. Low billing in second-rate houses. People beginning to whisper that there was an outside chance that the movies would kill vaudeville. Ha, a good one, that! Listen to that one and get a laugh! But then sometimes you would waken in the small, sterile hours of night and recall that doleful prediction and know panic.

It was in Grand Rapids that Burgoyne's letter caught up with them, after missing them by a couple of hours in Detroit. What a letter! What a day! They didn't dine at the Baltimore Dairy Lunch, that evening. They celebrated, went to a good hotel dining room with tablecloths and tipping expected.

"Look at that letterhead!" Ned exclaimed. "Classy! I'll bet ours impressed him!"

It was true that Mr. Burgoyne's letterhead was out-of-the-ordinary. Spectacular. Polychromatic. On either side of the two-line spread— Burgoyne & Pawpacker's Great 3-Ring Circus—an elephant trumpeted. The elephants and the name of the circus were in red ink. Down the left margin, in blue, ran a list of the attractions which Burgoyne & Pawpacker had given the public in the season of 1919. And across the bottom of the page, in red: "America's Favorite Circus, Because America's Best."

The letter exuded cordiality. Mr. Burgoyne said that he had not responded sooner because he had been turning over their proposition in his mind. (Picture of Mr. Burgoyne seated at a prosperous desk, pondering, pondering.) He was much interested in Sebastian and Orika. He had, naturally, heard of their act. (Oh, delirious line!) He wasn't, as they could readily understand, prepared to make them an offer in this first letter, but he did want them to know he was much interested. He noted on the route sheet which they had enclosed that they would be playing in Chicago between Christmas and New Year's. There was a strong possibility that business would take him to Chicago at that time, and if so he would certainly be interested in meeting them and talking further.

Sebastian and Orika labored hours on their reply. And three pairs of fingers were crossed when they posted it.

This time they expected a prompt response, but the days passed and no long envelope—embellished with a red elephant in the upper left corner—waited for them at the theater or at their hotel. But they had faith, now. He had said himself that he had heard of their act. In their thoughts he had become a great man, an executive busy at winter quarters directing preparations for next season. Turning their proposition over in his mind. Thinking, "And then there's Sebastian and Orika. If I can come to terms with them . . ."

November dragged itself to December, to the season of smoke and sooty snow and Fourteen-Shopping-Days-Till-Christmas. Their big theatrical trunk withstood the pummeling of baggage men in Green Bay, Milwaukee, Madison. It snowed and melted and snowed, and as they tramped to and from the theater their shoes were soaked and they all came down with hard colds. Flu. But they wouldn't recognize it as flu. There was the act to consider. Their heads ached and their bodies ached, but you would never have guessed it, the way they maintained the *élan* of their act. They hurried to their room from the theater and doped themselves with pills and liniment and moaned into bed. Feverish dreams. No reply from Mr. Burgoyne. No reply ever coming.

The weather turned bright and sunny on the morning they arrived in Chicago. A brisk wind grabbed the smoke pouring from stacks and hurled it up at the blue prairie sky. The streets were thronged with Christmas shoppers and loud with cab horns and the long hoots of traffic whistles. The tonic of that energetic city stabbed into their blood. The heaviness left their bones and they felt lighthearted. Faith returned. There was no letter from Burgoyne at the theater or at their hotel, but they would hear from him. Hunches told them. They felt that Chicago would be their city of destiny.

"By Christmas," Ned said. "We'll hear something by Christmas."

They were like children with the simple faith that Santa Claus would not pass them by.

"Well then, by New Year's Day," Ned said, when the last Christmas mail yielded no letter. "I know it. He's interested in us. We'll celebrate—"

So between shows they dined at Henrici's, feasting on turkey and dressing, and never mind the expense. It was Christmas, wasn't it? Their luck was about to turn, wasn't it? Eloise carried her new doll, fondling it all during dinner. She was bright-eyed, her hair falling in curls from her wise little head. The world was a vast place, filled with excitement and adventure. She loved sitting in the warm restaurant with Chicago hurrying past the windows; she took a deep sensuous pleasure in the crispness of the celery, the gleam of the olives, the verdant parsley, the thick deliciousness of mushroom soup sliding along her tongue.

Most of humanity experienced an afterholiday letdown on December twenty-sixth, but not Ned Sebastian. Great things were in the making. He knew. His hunches.

And then on December twenty-seventh it happened. A Western Union boy brought a yellow envelope to the theater and asked for Sebastian and Orika. It had been sent from Chicago. From Gus Burgoyne in Hotel Sherman. He would be pleased to see them at 10 A.M. next day.

"Think of it!" Ned exclaimed. "A telegram! He could have phoned. But he's no piker! A telegram!"

They took a cab to the Sherman. Extravagance! They could have traveled by common carrier, but that would be, Ned said, the wrong approach. They should meet Mr. Burgoyne in an aura of prosperity.

The morning was overcast with clouds spitting snow and wind blustering off the lake, but they were elated with a sense of high romance. Ned tipped the driver and escorted them into the Sherman as if he owned the joint. He strode confidently to the desk and asked the number of Mr. Burgoyne's room. And when he returned to his wife and daughter he grinned and said:

"Nothing cheap about him. He's got a suite!"

In the elevator they felt breathless, and in the upper corridor their legs went hollow.

"Ned," Lily breathed. "I'm scared."

"Why kid, you've just got stage fright. An old trouper like you! Remember—he sent us a wire. Asked us to come. He's heard great things about our act."

The door. The very door! Deep breaths. Bracing themselves. And Ned rapping.

The door opened wide and there he was—big, hearty, energetic; and it was like having the sun come up broad and red and jolly.

"Well look who's here!" he exclaimed. "Hello, troupers! Come in, come in!"

They floated into the living room of the suite; the carpet was a cloud.

"Sit down, folks, sit down. Take off your things. Hello, little girl. What's your name?"

"It's Eloise, Mr. Burgoyne," she said in that young voice whose inflections were like a parody of the vaudeville voices she had soaked up during so many performances.

"Well, well. Eloise. That's a pretty name. And how old are you, Eloise?"

"I'll be seven in April."

"Think of that!" he boomed. "You're coming right along!"

Eloise smiled up at him; she thought him enormous, ageless. He had turned thirty-nine not long before, and his weight had pushed well above two hundred. But he had a frame to carry it. The bright tan skin of his face showed scarcely a line. He wore a maroon dressing gown tied round his girth.

"Mind if I finish breakfast, folks?" He sat down at a table laid for one, poured more coffee from a silver pot. "I overslept. My wife's been up for hours and out buying me broke." He chuckled and went to work on the bacon and eggs, the oatmeal and toast.

Eloise sat quietly in an upholstered chair, looking as if she were made of sugar and spice and all things nice. But she was all ears and her thoughts clicked fast through her shrewd head, for she realized the importance of this interview. Her gaze moved from her parents to Mr. Burgoyne. He seemed to have a big appetite. Beside the table stood a cart made of bright metal from which he kept replenishing the food on his plate. The windows were gray with smoke and winter but the radiators hissed quietly and filled the room with comfort.

While he ate, he talked of inconsequential things, and many of his jovial remarks were directed toward Eloise. He asked her if Santa Claus had been good to her, and he told her she was lucky to have such nice parents, and then he added that they were lucky also to have such a fine little girl.

"This was my little girl," he said, bringing out his wallet and handing her a snapshot. "Her name was Barbara, but we lost her."

Eloise studied the picture. She couldn't see much of Barbara—just a baby in a carriage. Mr. Burgoyne and a woman stood on either side of the carriage, but what interested Eloise most was the elephant with its trunk on the carriage handle. She wanted to ask Mr. Burgoyne more about the elephant, but she decided she'd better not. She passed the snapshot to Lily, who passed it to Ned. They studied it and said that Barbara looked as if she had been a wonderful child.

"Oh, she was—a beautiful little thing. It was bad for Flora when we lost her. Flora's never been the same. That's why we like to get away from Tamarack at Christmas time. You know—other people have children and decorated trees. All we have is a lot of cat animals and bulls. So we come to Chicago or some place. I always have business to do, anyway."

He slid the snapshot back into his wallet and bit the tip from a fat cigar. Blew out a cloud of smoke.

"You know," he said, "we were here on Christmas Day, and I caught your act that evening."

It startled Eloise and she glanced quickly at her parents. On Christmas night Mr. Burgoyne had been in the theater, watching Sebastian and Orika! She could tell that they too were racking their memories. How had the act gone? How was the applause?

Ned smiled, tongued his lips. "Well. So you caught our act!"

"Yes sir, I caught it." He pursed his lips and stared at the ash accumulating at the cigar end. "And I liked it," he added.

Eloise could breathe again.

"We're glad you liked it," Ned said.

"We certainly are," Lily put in.

"Yes sir, you folks are all right. Of course, I don't need to tell you that the act would have to be changed if we produced it under canvas. You understand that."

Oh, certainly, of course, of course. The Sebastians understood that. (But changed—how?)

"In a theater there's one stage. Everybody looks at what goes on up there on the stage because there's nowhere else to look. If the act's bad they look anyway. Not, you understand, that your act's bad. Just the opposite. But you see what I'm getting at. Under canvas we've got three rings. Lots of competition for the crowd's attention. There'll be bulls performing in one ring, and Japanese tumblers in another and mutts in the third. And the Joeys will be getting laughs from the hippodrome track—Joey policemen—Joeys doing the Pete Jenkins act. They're all competing. See what I mean? An act has to be pretty spectacular to compete."

The Sebastians nodded, smiles frozen on their faces. Was he letting them down easy? Then why had he asked them to call?

"What I have in mind for you folks is aerial work. How about it— do you have cool heads for heights?"

Ned shrugged easily. "That wouldn't worry us."

"Good." He stood up, paced about the room, looking like a fat friar in that dressing gown. He stopped at a radiator, perched a foot on it, waved his cigar and talked while he gazed through the window. "You know, I'm always thinking of the future. Building my show—building my show! I'll tell you folks something—Burgoyne & Pawpacker's going to be the biggest in the business. It's the best already. I do a lot of dreaming. Just a dreamer—that's me. But look at that—where did all that come from?"

He waved a paw at the window pane, at the skyscrapers rooted by an inland sea and soaring cloudward in steel and stone.

"Chicago," he said. "Queen City of a Prairie Empire. Skyscrapers. And where did they come from? From men's heads! From their dreams, that's where! Practical dreamers built 'em. Gives you a thrill, eh? Makes you glad to be alive! Big things going on! Commerce! Business! Bustle! If I could take you high enough you'd look down and see railroads coming in from every direction. Steel rails from the cotton fields of the South. From the longhorn country of Texas. From the cornfields of Iowa and the wheat fields of the Dakotas. From the iron range of Minnesota. From the dairy country of Wisconsin. From Ohio, New York State, Pennsylvania. All steaming toward Chicago! By God!—it does something to a man, just to think of it!"

He turned from the window, puffed his cigar.

"Me, I started with nothing, you might say. All an idea in my head, all a dream. The circus. Nothing but a wagon show to begin with. And look at us now. And let me tell you one thing—those who started with Gus Burgoyne and stuck with him and climbed with him have never regretted it. Never!"

Impressive! The Sebastians had never thought of things in just that way. They felt molded and swayed by the man's flow of speech, the way grasses are swayed by wind. The man's fierce self-belief gave off vibrations; the room was charged with power. And suddenly they wondered why they had ever thought of merely starting with Burgoyne and eventually moving on to the Big One. Why not start with Burgoyne and stick with him? Grow famous together!

"Yes sir! People do the right thing by me and I do the right thing by them! Always! Ask anybody. Ask those in the know. They'll tell you where Burgoyne & Pawpacker's heading. It's the big time. The old Big Time Express—that's me!"

Suddenly he fell silent. His jaw protruded. His gray eyes narrowed to an intensity that was almost cruel, and he glared at the Sebastians— at Eloise, at Lily, at Ned. It was as if he thought they were doubting him. Their gazes dropped to the pattern on the rug. It took too much painful energy to meet his eyes.

And then he smiled. And said in a low, confidential tone:

"I like you kids. You've got the stuff. But you've been wasting your time. You tie up with me and you'll be stars. I'll put your names on billboards all over this country in letters a foot high. Red letters! You come to winter quarters a month ahead of the season and rehearse. I know what goes over with a circus crowd and I'll direct you. When will you be at liberty?"

"March," Ned said. "Early March."

"Good! Great! Where do you close?"

"Tulsa."

"Fine. You close and come to my winter quarters. How about it?"

Ned looked at Lily. She murmured, "It's up to you."

Burgoyne strode over to Ned Sebastian, dropped a big hand to his shoulder.

"How about it, Ned?" he demanded.

Ned said apologetically, "I was thinking of salary."

Burgoyne's eyes narrowed again. That gray intensity. Then he smiled. His voice was low, half amused, half offended.

"I'm a little disappointed in you, Ned. I'll tell you this frankly—I can't match what you're getting now. But in every man's life there comes a time when he has to think of his future. When he has to weigh great gain in the years ahead against a temporary loss in pay. But I'll tell you what I'll do. I'll give the three of you board and room. Figure it at two bucks a day apiece and that's forty-two dollars a week. And I'll give you thirty bucks a week cash money. How about it?"

Ned looked at his wife. She smiled, a neutral, it's-up-to-you smile.

Ned frowned. Then suddenly he smiled and said, "All right. All right, Mr. Burgoyne, it's a deal."

Mr. Burgoyne grabbed his hand, agitated it.

"Kids," he exclaimed, "you'll never regret it. You'll never regret joining out with Burgoyne & Pawpacker!"

And so one morning in March the Sebastians alighted from a day coach at the Union Station in Tamarack. It was a day of racing clouds and of railroad smoke and dust blown along the station platform. Mr. Burgoyne had promised to meet them, but he was nowhere among the crowd.

"He'll be along," Ned said. "Let's go inside and wait."

Their mouths were coated with sleeplessness and their hands grimed. So while Ned guarded their bags Eloise and her mother went to the ladies' room to freshen up. After years on the road the Sebastians had become as ingenious as hoboes in crisping up their appearance by using public lavatories. Often while they waited in a station to change cars Ned would disappear into the men's room and emerge a few minutes later with a fresh shave and a clean shirt and different tie. Sometimes even he would shine his shoes while the station porter glowered.

"No Burgoyne yet," Ned told his wife and daughter when they rejoined him. "I look like a bum. Wait here while I wash up and then we'll have breakfast."

Seeing them there on the red-varnished bench, nobody would have guessed that Lily and Eloise had spent the night on a slow train from Kansas City. Lily's appearance was impeccable, a small young woman with dainty features and an almost birdlike manner. You would never have guessed that she earned her living as an acrobat unless you had scrutinized her hands. Although small, they were as strong as a day laborer's, the wrists muscled and the palms thickly calloused. When she and Ned were performing, their safety often depended upon the strength in their hands.

Eloise was already nearly as tall as her mother, and she possessed an adult composure that made her seem older than her years. She was not one of those railroad station children who squirm and chatter and jump around on the benches and play on the marble floor. She had traveled so much and waited in stations so often that she accepted delays and inconveniences with urbanity.

Now she sat erect on the bench, her skirt primly below her crossed knees, her gray-green eyes on the lookout for Mr. Burgoyne. She was not offended or surprised that he kept them waiting. Agents and managers often treated you shabbily.

She didn't see Burgoyne, but as she watched the doors to the street her attention was attracted by a man who stood out from the rest of the crowd, not because he was physically large, for he was smaller than average, but because of his unusual appearance and of the distinction with which he carried himself. He was a man in his fifties, with a short trimmed beard that was bright cinnamon-colored and gray. His nose was a thin straight knife. His dark eyes surveyed the station and then with head erect and walking stick tapping the floor he paced to a door marked, "Station Master." After that Eloise lost sight of him for Ned returned, looking fresh and young and clean with health.

"No Burgoyne?"

"Not a sign of him," Lily said.

"Well, we might as well eat," Ned said; but at that moment a portly man in a railroad uniform filled the station with a foghorn voice. His words reverberated among the lofty arches:

"Sebastian and Orika. Paging Sebastian and Orika."

"Listen!" Ned exclaimed. "That's us!"

And he hurried off toward the uniformed foghorn.

Eloise observed the bearded man stepping forward and shaking hands with her father. They chatted a few moments before walking toward Eloise and her mother.

"Lily, this is Ivan Pawpacker. Mr. Burgoyne's partner. And this is Eloise."

He took Eloise's hand, his eyes twinkling, and he bowed slightly from the waist, like an Old World count. At close quarters his manner and his clothes seemed even more distinguished. He wore a Homburg hat and a Chesterfield overcoat with a white silk muffler.

"And are you part of the act, young lady?"

"They won't let me," Eloise grinned. "They think I'm too young."

Between the mustache and beard his lips quirked, and his eyes were full of humor.

"Aren't parents ridiculous people!" he murmured, and Eloise laughed. After that there was always a subtle bond between them.

"We didn't expect you, Mr. Pawpacker," Lily was saying, and that was quite true. In the Sebastians' thoughts it was Burgoyne who had loomed important; they had scarcely heeded the Pawpacker name in the partnership.

"Oh, well—you know how Gus is." Mr. Pawpacker smiled indulgently, as if he were speaking of a mischievous urchin. "He's so full of energy and enthusiasm that he gets all tangled up with himself. I tell him he's never quite as busy as he thinks he is. I happened to be in Tamarack on other business and he phoned my hotel from the farm. He was sputtering like a string of firecrackers. It seems that he had it in mind that you people were arriving tomorrow. Then he happened on a list of things he was to do today—he's always making such lists and misplacing them—and he saw he was to meet you. He asked me to come. I'm afraid my welcome isn't as—well—overwhelming as his would have been. He always makes people feel they've been greeted by a brass band."

Mr. Pawpacker chuckled softly. And then, as if realizing that his faintly mocking manner had made Mr. Burgoyne appear ever so slightly ridiculous, he added:

"But Gus is a good boy. A circus needs a man like him to pilot it. He's a good mixer—everybody likes him. And a born salesman. I tell him he could have made more money if he'd started a medicine show. And that enthusiasm—my! He paints with a broad brush. I just follow along and remind him of the details. And speaking of details—have you people had breakfast?"

"We were just going to eat," Ned said.

"I'm sorry! Here I've been talking and keeping you from coffee. And the before-breakfast world is a gray one."

He shepherded them into the station restaurant where they sat not at the counter but at a table. Mr. Pawpacker took the order blank and penciled their wishes in a small, neat hand. Then he sipped water from a tumbler and dried his lips with his napkin.

"Gus has told me about your act. He thinks it's very good."

The Sebastians murmured and beamed.

"But he has certain changes in mind. He probably talked them over with you. He wants you to concentrate on the steel rings and on trapeze work. And to lift the whole act up into the tent top. Gus is a good showman. It's an instinct with him—I tell him he plays by ear. You don't mind working heights, do you?"

"We're pretty steady in our nerves," Ned said. "We've never done much high work. But I can't see the difference between working eight feet up and thirty feet up. We'll expect our share of falls, but with a net . . ."

"Yes, of course. A net. I'd insist on the net, if I were you. At least till you get the hang of the thing. You know Gus. He'll want to do away with the net as soon as possible so he can bill you as daredevils.

Don't let him push you too fast. After all, it's your necks. If you take a stand and need backing, come to me."

Eloise thought: "They can't work without a net."

"You people are young," Mr. Pawpacker was saying, "and attractive. You ought to have a good future. Although how anybody can work heights is beyond me. Of course, Gus thinks I'm Old-Man-Caution himself. I'm really a country banker, you know. Only the Bankers Association thinks I'm a showman and the show people think I'm a banker."

Eloise returned his smile. But she was thinking: "They can't work without a net."

But of course they did work without one, eventually.

Eloise watched Mr. Pawpacker slide a leather case from his pocket and select a slim cigar. As he held the match to it he rolled it round and round so the tobacco would burn evenly. Then he picked up the check, making sure the waitress had added the figures correctly.

"The problem now," he said, "is getting you people to the farm. Gus said on the phone he was sending a truck in for your baggage. I could hire a car, but if you think you could manage in the truck—"

The Sebastians said of course they could ride in the truck.

The truck, it turned out, was powered by a Model-T motor and driven by Joe Griffin, the circus carpenter. Despite its square snout and workaday cab Eloise found it a romantic vehicle, for it had been painted bright red. Along the sides yellow letters marched: Burgoyne & Pawpacker's Circus.

Eloise and her mother rode in the cab with Joe, but there wasn't space for Ned. They laughed and told him he'd have to walk, and he offered to wager he'd reach the farm sooner if he did walk, from the looks of that truck. It was all very gay, and in the end Ned rode with the baggage, springing as easily into the box as a track champion going over a hurdle.

"I wish I could do that," Pawpacker said, from the curb. "It's wonderful to be young."

Whereupon Joe Griffin, who was squat and round as a beer keg, pushed back the cap from his bald head and said yes, he had been very powerful himself as a young man. He had been able to carry a hundredweight on each shoulder and think nothing of it.

And as if to demonstrate he was still a mighty good man, he tugged down his turtle-neck sweater over his expanded chest and waddled to the front of the truck and flipped the crank. The motor roared and raced while he trotted back and jerked up the gas lever.

"Take good care of them, Joe," Pawpacker shouted against the motor. "They're going to be our stars, you know."

The Sebastians had never played Tamarack, but to Eloise it looked like a dozen other cities of the Midlands—the new Union Station that appeared finer in contrast to the blocks of smoky old buildings near it; the pile of grimed masonry that was the courthouse; the corner cigar stores and the Yellow cabs. Ned had once asserted that every city in the Middle West aspired to resemble Chicago, and Eloise thought of that as the truck picked its way through the newer part of the business district.

"See that building?" Joe Griffin said, as the truck paused for traffic. "Gus Burgoyne's father-in-law built that. Named for him, too."

It occupied a busy corner and soared fifteen stories; and embossed over the main entrance were the words: Oxenford Electric Building. Eloise was impressed; they were going to work for a man whose father-in-law must be fabulously wealthy.

"Of course," Joe added, "he lost it when he went broke. But he built it, just the same. He was a pretty rich man. He built the interurban, too. The one that goes past the farm."

"Interurban?" Lily asked. "Why didn't we take it?"

"It's just a spur, lady. A spur from the main line. Goes to the coal mine up at Oxenford. He named that for himself, too. The mine don't amount to much, now. But them tracks are handy for us. When we want to move a train they run juice through the trolley wire and send in an engine."

He seemed to assume that they knew all about the geography of the farm, and he didn't explain further. But as the truck nosed through the residential district, he told them about himself and his work. A year-round employee, he was. There might be men handier with carpenter's tools, but he hadn't met up with them. No, he didn't travel with the show. He lived at the farm the year round.

"And Gus is all right to work for, at that," he said. "Always knows what he wants. Maybe in the summer I'll get a wire to meet him in Michigan or Ohio. 'Now what?' I'll think. But I'll go, and he'll have the plans all drawed for a new building on the farm. 'Joe,' he'll say, 'you get the material and start work.' So I do. That's one thing about him—he keeps his credit good in Tamarack. I've heard those stories—you know how people talk—but he's always paid me. Yes, sir!—right on the dot! And his credit's good in Tamarack. Maybe they'll have to carry him if he's had a bad season, but they get their money in the end. He's well thought of in Tamarack."

The wind was sweeping the sky clean of clouds, and as they drove through the northwest subdivisions into the rolling country the sun shone brightly. It was like a good omen. The air was sharp with early spring. In a hillside orchard Eloise sighted a robin flying with string in its beak, and the plows were out in the creek valleys. They drove north along a paved turnpike.

"Prosperous country, through here," Joe commented. "But see that ridge?" He pointed to a distant contour. "We drive along that and then we drop down into different country. The soil's no good for anything but grazing stock. And of course the coal under it—or that used to be."

The truck crawled across a wide valley and started up the ridge, sputtering and snorting like a balky horse. From the summit, Eloise could gaze back across miles of country and see the pall of soft-coal smoke hanging above the city. Then the pavement ended and they followed tan gravel through country over which a change had come without Eloise's being aware of the moment the change took place. It was a country remote in spirit. Thorn trees grew by the roadside and brambles went tanglefooting away into acres of woodlands. You could imagine foxes back in those timbered ravines.

"Now we're getting there," Joe Griffin said a few minutes later, as the road wound down into a valley. "It's about a mile."

After the uplands the valley seemed cozy. It had caught and held the warmth of the thin March sun, and on the south banks the grass was turning green. Down the middle of the valley a creek followed its wayward inclinations, with maples and willows peering at themselves in the water. And Eloise saw trolley poles walking up the valley from the southeast, holding a line of wire above rails on an embankment.

The truck throbbed west over a little hill, and Eloise caught sight of the circus farm. She felt a wave of excitement. She saw a house flashing through the trees; and basking in the sun on the south slope of a hill, big red barns were anchored. The road flattened out and crossed the interurban and the creek, and as the truck turned in at the gate it passed a long, low barn between the road and the tracks. An American flag was waving above the gable.

"Look," Joe said, halting the truck by the barn.

He pointed toward the west pasture where a herd of horses had been grazing. At the sound of the car one horse had lifted its head and neighed, and now the whole herd was galloping across the pasture.

"Not scared," Joe said. "Just frisky. Pretty, ain't it?"

Eloise thought she had never seen a more beautiful sight than the running horses. Some were gleaming black and some pure white; and there were horses with golden skins and Indian pintoes.

"Pawpacker can pick horses," Joe said, driving on.

They crossed the interurban, and on a long siding Eloise saw a score of railroad cars, as vividly painted as autumn leaves. And beyond the tracks, east of the drive, there were buildings marked "Paint Shop" and "Blacksmith Shop." Joe honked the horn and waved at several workmen who were greasing the axle of a cage wagon.

The truck halted in the carriage yard. A low building marked "Office" bounded it on the east. The door opened and a man bustled out. He wore a gray suit with a herringbone weave, and he roared cordially:

"Well! Look who's here. Hello, kids! How are you?"

As Ned Sebastian alighted nimbly from the truck Mr. Burgoyne grabbed his hand and pumped it. After that he wheeled to Eloise and her mother.

"Eloise! And Lily Orika! Beautiful as ever! Well, well!"

Then suddenly he exclaimed, "Say! You folks didn't ride out in the truck!"

They assured him that they had.

"Now I ask you!" he groaned. "Isn't that just like Ive Pawpacker? I told him to hire a car and he sends you in a truck! Always watching the pennies. That's Ive. Watching the pennies!"

During the next weeks Eloise had ample opportunity to explore the farm. The day after their arrival Sebastian and Orika began rehearsing in the Hippodrome Barn, a circular building up the hill, which was a cross between a gymnasium and a one-ring tent; and although Eloise theoretically studied while her parents worked, she didn't actually spend many hours on arithmetic and geography. There were matters of more pressing importance to engage her. She would begin conscientiously enough, at a table in the living room of the house, determined to memorize the boundaries of Paraguay or the exports of Brazil; but there were always interruptions. Perhaps it would be the voice of Wesley, Burgoyne's colored cook, singing about the old-time religion to the kitchen pans; or perhaps Burgoyne's wife would plod into the room and sigh into a rocking chair.

"I won't bother you," she'd say. "I'll just do my fancywork."

And she would push a lethargic needle through the cloth stretched over embroidery hoops. But after a minute this exertion seemed to weary her. With a long breath, she would permit the fancywork to float to her lap, and after that she would sit—just sit—the rocking chair squeaking. She seemed to possess an infinite capacity for doing nothing. The harder Eloise tried to concentrate on geography the more she was aware of the woman's presence; so presently she would snap shut the book and stand up, glad to leave that room and emerge into the sunshine and the air that smelled of early spring. She skipped up the hill to the Hippodrome Barn, opening the door a crack and peeking in at her father and mother. Dressed in white tights, Lily Orika was limbering her muscles on the horizontal bars, while Ned

Sebastian stood in the ring listening to Mr. Burgoyne explain the kind of act he wanted. Her parents never liked to have her watch them rehearse—it made them nervous to have an audience of even one little girl while they concentrated—so Eloise proceeded up the hill to the Animal House. It was a rectangular building whose bricks had been plastered over with gray concrete; and a rich, dark jungle odor uncoiled from the place. At the south end of the building open-air cages drank up the sunlight. Within that network of brightness and slim black shadows a score of monkeys were taking the morning air.

Eloise would have watched their antics longer had there not been so many other wonders to investigate. At the wide east door she peered into the building, discerning in the pungent gloom a row of cages along the north wall, with glowing eyes observing her. Signs muttered, "Danger! Not Responsible For Accidents," and "No Loafing!" In the center of the floor a concrete pit was sunk, filled with black water and surrounded by a steel fence. Nearly submerged like a dark-gray boulder a hippopotamus existed there, motionless, ponderous. A shivery place! A sign announced that this was the behemoth mentioned in holy writ. Whatever it was, Eloise was content to let it live its own slubbery existence unmolested. By contrast, the gray shapes of elephants hobbled along the far wall seemed genial. But they could be dangerous too, her parents had warned her; she must never enter the Animal House unless keepers were there. No keepers were there now, so she continued up the hill, turning west past the Camel Shed and climbing a fence into the north pasture.

Up there she discovered three huge mounds enclosed by a low picket fence. Somebody had erected a sign, "Elephant Graveyard," with an epitaph beneath:

> From India you came
> Glorifying Burgoyne & Pawpacker's name.
> Now your performing days are o'er.
> Rest in peace forever more.

Eloise stared pensively at the burying ground where a red ant was trudging through gray sand. It encountered another ant and they halted nose to nose, as if passing the time of morning. Eloise walked on up the hill.

From the ridge she could gaze miles in all directions. The air was brilliant, pellucid. Far to the southeast she could make out the smoke of Tamarack faintly staining the bright skyrim; and to the northwest the mining settlement looked very tiny, very still.

Then she heard the moan of a whistle and she peered to the southeast, her gaze following the bright lines of rails till they curved out of sight into a timber patch. The whistle moaned again, and she perceived an electric engine rounding the curve, pulling a long flatcar on which cage wagons were loaded. Their golden scrollwork flashed; but the whole thing—engine, flatcar, cages—appeared diminutive; and the clickety-click of the car wheels sounded like the sharp, distant footwork of a midget tap dancer.

As the engine clanged up the valley Eloise could see men leaving the Paint Shop to stare down the roadbed. By the time the engine halted near the Blacksmith Shop, Mr. Burgoyne had joined the group. Two men alighted from the flatcar. One strode to Mr. Burgoyne and there was a vigorous handshake. The other slouched in the background.

She left the ridge. At lunch she met the man who had shaken hands with Mr. Burgoyne. He was Captain Philip Latcher, the famous tamer of jungle beasts. The other man didn't eat lunch in the house; he lunched with the roughnecks in a barnlike building west of the Animal House which was labeled, "Hotel." He was a youth of about seventeen, Captain Latcher's cage boy. His name was Willie Krummer.

Where Captain Latcher had picked him up nobody ever asked, because in those days nobody had the slightest interest in Willie Krummer. Nobody, that is, except the authorities of a certain town in northern Wisconsin. And now after several years their interest was tepid. When he vanished from town they had been preparing to pack him off to industrial school, not because of any one great crime but because of a series of petty misdeeds. He was a damned nuisance; he got in their hair; maybe they'd teach him a trade and straighten him out in industrial school. But the sheriff and county attorney were not looking for a boy named Willie Krummer but Willie Parr. For that matter, you could not honestly say they were looking for him at all. No "Wanted" circulars; nothing of that kind. He was out of town, out of the county, and that was good enough.

At home Willie was not greatly missed. For one thing, the home was not commodious, and it was already rocking full of Willie's brothers and sisters and half-brothers and half-sisters. Three miles east of town, on the arm of a lake, the home had originally been constructed by a logging concern to serve as a bunkhouse. Having slashed through the timber and logged out what it wanted, the company forgot about the bunkhouse and the land. So Oscar Parr moved his family in. The porcupines and the wood ticks didn't care. Nobody cared. Willie was four years old at the time, a much yelled-at, switched-at child. Oscar Parr was engaged in killing his first wife then. He used a method of legal murder compounded of uninterrupted child-bearing, hard labor, abusive language, worry and occasional clips alongside the jaw. As a young man he had been a lumberjack, but now he followed the professions of trapping in winter, and in summer fishing and serving as guide for various paunchy he-men from Chicago and Milwaukee who made vacation forays into the North Woods against the lives of the muskies and pike residing in the lakes and streams.

When Willie, at fourteen, got wind of the education the authorities were planning for him (and heaven knew how he learned of it, except that he could sniff danger like a woods animal), Oscar Parr was at work on his third wife. Killing her wasn't going to be so easy, for she was a brawny virago who could give birth to a child one morning and cook a big breakfast the next. She had a tongue like a buggy whip and fists like sledge hammers, and when the two of them went after each other the kids tumbled out of the shanty and let them have the ring to themselves. The woods and the shore rocks roared. Their battles had a Brobdingnagian flavor not out of place in that vast land where Paul Bunyan had walked. Both fervently defended the adage that there is no bad whiskey, but the rumors were groundless that she could always drink him under the table. Sometimes; not always. Oscar was a pretty good man himself.

Willie had been gone three days before Oscar remarked his absence. Even had he been sober, which he was not, it is doubtful whether he would have been aware of the household's loss, for what was one child more or less in the multitude? It was a deputy sheriff who brought Willie to Oscar's mind. One afternoon the deputy drove his Ford through the sandy ruts to the Parr home and inquired for Willie.

Bleary-eyed, Oscar Parr fingered his stubbled chin and said:

"Damned if I know where the little son of a bitch is. Out in the woods, maybe. What's he done now?"

"We're going to send him off. Reform school."

"Vell, now," Oscar said, with his heavy German accent, "I don't know whether you are or not. Looks to me like you ought to talk to his Pa before you do that. If he's been into something I'll give him a going-over. Ain't that enough?"

"I want Willie."

"All right, all right," Oscar bellowed. "Take him. But you'll have to ketch him first. He goes off to the woods like a wolf an' stays for days. If you get him you'll have to ketch him. He's a slimery one, that Willie is. Slimery as an eel."

But they never caught Willie, for the good reason that by then he was occupying a boxcar on a Soo freight train, a hundred miles away. Much of his time during the next two years he spent in travel. He found it broadening. From other road kids he learned a dozen ways to hold body and soul together, none by working. He grew adept at materializing from a hedge, stealing a washing off a line and fading out of sight. He came to know which pedestrians on a city street were good for a touch. He learned to roll drunks for their cash, to live off the land by raiding gardens and orchards and chicken roosts; and he even worked up quite a business kidnapping pet dogs and watching the "Lost" columns for reward notices. ("He jus' follered me, mister, so I looks in the paper an' sees you want to pay ten bucks for the trouble of bringin' him home. . . .") After being returned to their masters, the dogs were skittish and unnerved. This wasn't surprising. Many of the complaints against Willie, back in Wisconsin, had concerned his treatment of animals.

By the time he was sixteen, if Willie had cared to offer himself as a laboratory specimen to a sociologist, he would have been informed that his chances of avoiding the penitentiary were slight. Indeed, the arms of the law were stretched out for him when he flung himself into the embrace of the circus.

His joining the W. W. Harris Circus & Menagerie took place one June midnight in the railroad yards at Worcester, Massachusetts. With two companions, Willie was engaged in breaking the seal of a refrigerator car containing fresh oranges when a detective of the Boston & Albany Railroad popped out of the shadows. There was a wild scramble as the three seekers after Vitamin C took to their heels and scattered. Willie fled west along the ties, darting in and out among freight cars and warehouses. Several times he heard a report behind him, such as a Police Postive might give forth, and something rattled into the cinders near his ankles. Willie shifted into high gear. He soared over a board fence enclosing the junkyard of M. Cohen and Son, snaked through the heaped blackness, mounted the fence on the street side and dropped to a sidewalk. He didn't run now, but strode briskly away from the railroad. After a couple of blocks, having sighted a patrolman, he worked back to the railroad and lay in a ditch. Presently the headlight of a westbound locomotive shafted along the right-of-way. Willie parted the weeds and scrutinized the blindingly lighted yards. The coast looked clear, so after the locomotive steamed past Willie darted out and trotted alongside the train. As deftly as a railroad man he swung up the ladder of a flatcar.

To his astonishment, he discovered that the flatcar was twice as long as the ordinary flat, and that it carried bizarre freight—cage wagons parked end to end, their wheels chocked. Beneath the wagons lay windrows of slumbering men. A circus! Hunched at the end of the car, sniffing the ripe odor of wild animals, Willie did some thinking. Why not try joining up with the show? He'd get travel, three meals a day, wages, and not be molested by railroad dicks. Though he refused to confess it, his encounter this evening had frightened him. He had never been shot at before, and he disliked it.

That was in 1918. A war in Europe and booming factories in Amer-

ica had diminished the labor supply. So next day when Willie applied
for a job the boss canvasman hired him without many questions.

From the first Willie enjoyed roustabouting. Food was plentiful;
you didn't worry about dodging cops; you were always on the move;
and after the tops went up in the morning you could lie on the grass
and doze or go downtown and look over the main stem. No more
work till evening. A fine life! Regular meals and swinging a sledge
hardened his muscles, broadened his shoulders; and now that he held
a job, some of the shiftiness left his manner. Often he would look you
directly in the eyes, now. He formed the habit of washing daily, and
that helped.

After a month on the show, he looked older than a boy who had
turned sixteen in early June. He was tall and hard. He wore his
wheat-blond hair clipped high and close (to lengthen the period between spending money for haircuts), and this revealed his strong
squarish skull. On either side of a thick-bridged nose his eyes were
pale blue. They were not his best feature. At times they had the hard
suspicion of an old detective's, and at times the look of a cat's when it
is having fun putting a mouse to death by slow torture. His jaw was
square and manly, but its forthrightness was corrupted by his mouth.
It impressed you as a slantwise gash, unamused even when he smiled.
Probably it was this unamused expression that caused other roustabouts
to mutter that Willie Krummer was meaner than hell. They should
have been more discreet about flinging stones from their glass houses.
Or perhaps it was because Willie always smiled when he began fighting. Growing huskier and more sure of himself, he fought a great
deal. He didn't fight like an Irishman, for the joyous sport of it, but
because he wanted to demonstrate that the other roustabouts were dirt
under his feet. After a fight he held a grudge. What was the use of
fighting if you were going to shake hands when it was over? You
fought as animals fought: to show who was boss. If you were beaten
you crawled away and ever afterward licked the winner's boots. There
was even a certain emotional pleasure in that.

Willie had changed since joining the show, but the reason was more
fundamental than regular work and meals. It was ambition. Soon
after becoming a roustabout Willie attended an afternoon performance.
The clowns left him cold; the bareback riders and acrobats interested
him only mildly; but then into a steel arena lions and tigers had been
driven, and Captain Philip Latcher entered with a whip and a pistol.
Willie snapped alert. Deep in his soul something stirred—an awaken-
ing half painful, half pleasurable. A tide of craving passed over him;
craving to wear a smart uniform like Captain Latcher's, to stride into
an arena looking hard and masculine and to subdue wild beasts. It
was the only thing he ever wanted to do, and he felt bewildered and

almost stunned that he had not thought of such a career before. He had always had a way with animals. The stray dogs he had taught tricks; the crow he had taught to speak after catching it and slitting its tongue. . . . A way with animals!

Willie couldn't attend the evening performance; his help was needed in tearing down the menagerie top; but the next afternoon found him again watching Captain Latcher's act. He liked it even better, and after that he slipped into the tent every afternoon. He stood by a section of the cheapest seats—the "blues"—waiting for the band to start blaring "Entry of the Gladiators." His gaze passed over the massed humanity, a curl to his lips and contempt in his eyes as he watched them washing down popcorn and peanuts with lemon pop. Gillies, suckers. Timid, soft people; stick-in-the-muds who would live out their days in one town. They didn't realize who was standing in their midst. They didn't realize they were brushing elbows with Willie Krummer, who was going to be the most famous animal trainer in the world.

Captain Latcher was a long rapierlike man of thirty-nine; intense, hard-bitten. His baldish head and angular face had been burned brown by many trouping seasons, and a toothbrush mustache bristled on his upper lip. His even teeth were very white, and in contrast to his brown face they flashed with spectacular incandescence when he smiled. He was not a captain, of course, and his name was not Latcher. He came from a good family in British Columbia whose name would have been embarrassed at finding itself on circus posters. As a youngster, after some trifling scrape or other, he had been sent to a military school where he won medals for rifle-shooting, boxing and fencing. He knew how to use a knife and fork, and he had a good deal of charm, although this was lost on his animals. His patrimony he had spent buying a wild animal act, because at heart he was a nomad and an adventurer.

Before entering the arena Captain Latcher snapped to attention and saluted the audience as if they were all generals. He handled his body curtly, precisely. This was not lost on Willie, who began going about his roustabout duties in a soldierly manner. Modeling himself after the Captain, he husked off his shifty movements as if they were the last year's skin of a snake.

Casual inquiries brought Willie the information that most animal trainers had served apprenticeships as cage boys. The duties were lowly and of the chambermaid variety, but Willie yearned for them. He soon discovered, however, that this position was occupied by another young man. This vexed him. His sense of proportion was not delicate, and he formed a cold hatred for Captain Latcher's cage boy, who was quite at a loss to explain why that roustabout was always glaring at him.

Willie had never spoken a word to him, but his balked ambition and acid loathing pictured the fellow as both a bungling idiot and a sinister miscreant. A threat to Captain Latcher and to the circus itself! And they seemed so unaware of their danger! Just to think of the situation filled Willie with righteous anger, and he brooded about it constantly. It would be an act of great magnanimity to rid the show of the villain. Willie spat, wiped his mouth with the back of his hand. Damn the fellow! But how to go about getting rid of him? How! He would be a vicious fighter, full of devilish craft. For by this time Willie believed passionately in the validity of the character with which he had endowed the cage boy.

At last, following an afternoon performance, Willie screwed up his courage to the point of climbing the steps to the dressing van of Captain Latcher. He paused at the sill of the open door. Although the outside of the van was scrolled in red and gold, the interior was severely plain. Whips dangled on the walls and lay in corners like nesting blacksnakes; and on the dressing table, with an opened box of ammunition, a couple of pistols glittered. But these details escaped Willie. What seized his attention was the sight of Captain Latcher lying face down and stark naked on a leather-covered table. And the cage boy—oh, villain!—was bent over that heroic man, kneading his muscles in a vigorous, injurious way. Willie had never heard of rubdowns, and when his coarse nose picked up the scent of rubbing alcohol there flashed through his brain a lurid scene: the cage boy getting Captain Latcher drunk and then killing him in some occult fashion. In order to acquire the act, of course!

Willie's mouth twisted in that dangerous smile and he pounced forward. He grappled the cage boy's shoulders and spun him round. Pure incredulity widened the cage boy's eyes and brought a yell from his mouth. Willie drew back a fist and was preparing to let him have it right in the kisser when Captain Latcher was resurrected from the near-dead. His hard brown body sprang from the table. The point of Willie's jaw jerked with pain, and then he was floating backward and downward. After a period of darkness Willie became aware of voices, and he lay without opening his eyes.

"Cecil, old fellow," Captain Latcher was saying, "run along and get me cigarettes. Two packs, please. And see here! You've been shirking on those uniforms, you know. You'll have to use petrol on those spots."

"Yes, sir," Cecil said.

"And what shall we do with that chap on the floor? Dump him to the cats?"

"I'd sure like to."

"You'd surely like to—what!"

"I'd sure like to, sir. He's been a-bothering me, sir."

"Molesting you? Why don't you report these things to me?"

"Weil—it ain't been much, sir. But he's been kind of glumming at me, sir."

"'Glumming?' Really, Cecil—"

"You know, sir. Looking. Like he was sore with me."

"You've never had any words with him?"

"No words, sir. No nothing."

"Interesting . . . Well, he'll be coming round presently and I'll put a few questions to him. It was a beautiful punch, wasn't it, Cecil?"

"It sure was, sir! Right on the button."

"That's science, Cecil. Nothing like it. Give me a lever, as the chap said, and I'll lift the world. My coordination was excellent, eh, Cecil?"

"It sure was, sir."

"And he's quite a husky fellow, you know."

"He sure is, sir. Are we going to dump him to the cats?"

Captain Latcher laughed shortly. "Run along, Cecil. I'll attend to him."

Willie lay very still as the cage boy stepped over him and departed. But he was not relaxed. Certain phases of the conversation had alarmed him. After a minute he heard Captain Latcher's voice, cool but streaked with amusement.

"You might as well get up, old fellow. You've come round."

Willie opened his eyes and sat up.

"How did you know that?" he asked, and then added, "sir?"

Captain Latcher was lounging easily at the dressing table, clad in slippers and a gray dressing gown. The likeness of a red lion was stitched over the heart.

"Observation, old fellow. Nothing like it. Your eyes were shut too tightly. What's your name?"

"Willie Krummer, sir."

"You're on the show?"

"Yes, sir. Canvas."

"Really! And may I suggest that you stand up when you talk to me."

"Yes, sir!" Willie scrambled to his feet and despite his slight dizziness and his sore jaw stood at attention.

"By jolly! Like a soldier!" Captain Latcher exclaimed.

"No, sir. Like you, sir. I've been watching you, sir. Every afternoon in the arena. That's what I want to do, sir. I want to be like you."

"Well, I'm damned!" Captain Latcher exclaimed, but he looked rather more pleased than damned. "You like my act, eh?"

"Only good thing on the show, sir. The rest is puke."

Captain Latcher closed his eyes and gritted his teeth in mock distress.

"Your comparisons, Willie! Enough to turn one's stomach. But I forgive you since you're such an ardent fan."

"I don't know about that, sir, but I sure like your act. It goes over big with the gillies. Only thing on the show."

Captain Latcher snapped a match, ignited a cork-tipped cigarette and blew thin, Turkish smelling smoke in Willie's direction. Willie remained at rigid attention. For half the cigarette Captain Latcher kept the conversation hovering around the virtues of his act. It couldn't be, really, as excellent as Willie thought. Oh yes it could, Willie responded stoutly. Even better! And that wasn't flattery; the words rang true as a silver dollar. Captain Latcher's manner became warm and friendly, and he said:

"At ease. And sit down, Willie. There—on the rubbing table."

"Is that what it is, sir? I never knowed what it was."

So the Captain explained how beneficial an alcohol rub could be after a few minutes in the arena.

"I sweat like a trooper," he said. "I'd be stiff as a broomstick if it weren't for the rubdown."

"I looked in," Willie said, "and never knowed what was going on. I thought—"

So he explained. The cage boy was not to be trusted. How did he know? Just knew, that was all. A bad one, that cage boy. Put him in mind of a road kid he had known, who had bashed in the back of a brakeman's skull with a rock. (This was fancy, but Willie was casting about for something resembling fact to buttress his suspicions.)

"You got to watch him, sir! Ain't to be trusted!"

And he went on to tell how alarmed he had been for the Captain's safety when he beheld what was happening on the rubdown table.

"I never meant to make no trouble, sir. But—"

"But you had my safety at heart," the Captain said, looking both amused and thoughtful. "By jolly! A guardian angel! Where did you come from, Willie?"

Willie was vague. He had joined up with the show somewhere back along the line. He'd forgotten the town. Albany, maybe.

"Look at me, Willie. You're lying, old fellow. If you and I are to do business you'll have to come clean."

Do business! Could the Captain mean—? So Willie poured out his history. That episode in Worcester. His road-kid days. How he had fled Wisconsin.

"Reform school, eh? What was the trouble, Willie?"

Well, Willie said, they had it in for him, that was all. Always picking on him. And then that final business about Mrs. Hanson's dog. He was simply attempting to teach the dog a few tricks, but it was very dumb. So what could he do but resort to a little force?

"Dogs!" Captain Latcher made an impatient, contemptuous gesture.

"Why waste your time on dogs? Any fool with a stick can teach a dog. You don't even need a stick. Just a twist of the ear—like that. But cats! Another matter entirely!"

"Oh, I worked out on cats too, sir!"

"Really, Willie!" The disgust in the Captain's voice brought hot chagrin to Willie's cheeks. "I'm speaking of big cats, of course. Jungle cats."

"I'd sure like to have you learn me about them, sir."

The Captain looked amused.

"Do I understand you're applying for a job as cage boy?"

"Sir, could I—?"

"No money in it, Willie. I'd toss you a copper now and then, that's all. And lots of work. Cleaning cages, cleaning uniforms, repairing whips, rubbing me down. A slave's life. You'd be my man Friday, you know."

"Friday—Saturday—any day," Willie exclaimed. "That's what I want, sir! To be your man!"

The Captain shrugged.

"We're talking dreams, Willie. Because already I have Cecil. But if he should ever leave, you're at the top of the list."

After Willie had gone—with a smart salute and a valiant attempt at an about-face—Captain Latcher sat blowing smoke at the ceiling. He paid Cecil four dollars a week. Willie would work for the joy of it. Cecil was stupid. Never a word from Cecil about the excellence of the act! Willie might seem stupid—certainly he was appallingly ignorant— but the Captain sensed in him a kind of wild, native intelligence, such as animals had. He could learn. It might be amusing to teach him. And he would be loyal. Smart enough—or possibly stupid enough— for that. The Captain knew his sort. Kick him about a bit and he would come back for more. Willie, he thought, was medieval; he had the soul of a loyal aide-de-camp. It appealed to Captain Latcher's romantic imagination to toy with the possibility of acquiring such a faithful follower: valet, bodyguard, servant, all in one. Of course, there was still Cecil. But after Willie thought the matter through, the Captain was sure he would devise some means of ridding the show of Cecil. It would be amusing to watch how Willie would manage. Spectacles like that amused Captain Latcher vastly.

Willie, however, had not inherited a subtle mind, and Captain Latcher's Machiavellian hint fell on stony ground. During the next week the only weapon Willie used against Cecil was that terrible glare. If looks could have killed, Willie's eyes would have been machine guns capable of slaying a whole regiment of Cecils. As it was, that baleful stare was not beneficial to Cecil's nerves. He developed a bad case of jitters.

Cecil was seventeen, a slightly built boy with a muddy blond complexion marred by pimples. He came from an old South Chicago family of steelworkers. He had entered Captain Latcher's employ the previous January in Blue Island where, in an abandoned factory, the Captain maintained winter quarters for his cats. There he broke in new animals, and from there he traveled to various indoor circuses to fill engagements which his booking agent in the Loop secured for him. When at liberty, the Captain liked to run into town to dine at a good restaurant and attend the theater. Wearing a dinner jacket and carrying a stick with which he hailed cabs, the Captain was the ultimate in punctilio. Dramatizing himself as an adventurer, he liked to pretend that the stick was a sword cane, which it wasn't, and that he was a tanned, hard explorer just back from far places of the earth. And, indeed, this harmless pretense gave him an air of dash which headwaiters and pretty girls often found irresistible. Nothing pleased him more than to be mistaken for an Englishman: one of those buccaneering yet gallant fellows from the pages of H. Rider Haggard. Inasmuch as he worked constantly at maintaining and adding to the accent his father had brought to British Columbia, this happened fairly often. He never missed the theater when the play was an English drawing-room comedy.

As the days passed and Willie failed to act overtly against Cecil, the Captain grew impatient. The more he thought about Willie as cage boy the better he liked the idea. One could always put four dollars to better use than wage-paying; and on droopy days when one's spirits dragged it would be heartening to have a Caliban like Willie who considered one absolutely tops as an animal man. During all these months never any comment from Cecil about the merits of the act! The lout! Moreover, it seemed to the Captain that day by day Cecil grew more inefficient and forgetful.

This was true. Worry had impaired Cecil's efficiency. How could a guy's mind be on his work when that roustabout glared at your every move? Enough to give you the shivers! In the mornings as soon as the menagerie top was erected and the cage wagons hauled in, it was your job to clean the cages. "To sweeten them up," as the Captain said. Okay, you drove the cats to the far end of the cage and closed the partition across the middle. You entered and started work. And then right away you felt that stare drilling the back of your head. You gave a glance out through the bars and there he was—that roustabout. Jeez! He'd be coming along the tent's edge, hooking up sidewall, but he managed to work and stare at one and the same time.

Or early in the afternoon you'd be sitting on the steps of the dressing van, repairing whips. And you'd feel it—that stare! There he'd be at the corner of another van, pumping that look into you. His mug put you in mind of an inbred cat. Eyes set too close. And anybody with any knowledge whatsoever about cats realized that a long-nosed cat with close-set eyes was a bad customer with a vicious disposition. Jeez! What had you ever done to the guy? It wasn't like as if you'd stole a dame off of him, or switched dice on him in a game of craps. You'd never had no truck with him whatsoever; never'd seen him till a couple of weeks ago. Fact! Then all at once there he was, like he'd dropped down out of a cloud, putting the buzz on you. Almost enough to make a guy want to duck the show. And on top of everything else, the Captain had started bearing you a grouch. The Captain had his good side and he had his bad side, like all guys, but when he started showing you the bad side that he showed his cats, it wasn't no fun. He used czarcasm—that's what. "Cecil—" he'd say, mispronouncing it "Cessell" —"Cecil, old man, do you think it would be too much of a strain for you to use that head of yours now and then? It *is* a head, isn't it, old fellow?" Jeez!

One morning on the lot the Captain strode up to the stake Willie was pounding and said, "Why don't you drop in and see me this afternoon? Let's make it a half-hour after my act."

Cecil had been sent on an errand, so the Captain was alone when Willie made his soldierly entrance. The Captain lightly echoed his salute and invited Willie to seat himself.

"Old fellow, I'm astonished at you. I thought you more resourceful."

"Huh, sir?"

"Don't say 'huh,' Willie. If you don't comprehend, say 'beg pardon.' "

"Beg pardon, sir?"

"I thought you were ambitious, Willie. I thought you wanted to be an animal trainer."

"I do, sir!"

"Then I'm astonished at you, Willie. Absolutely astonished. Afraid of a bit of chaff like Cecil."

Willie's mouth twisted and his countenance stormed over.

"Afraid! Sir, I'm not afraid of that—"

And Willie described Cecil with a string of lumberjack and road-kid terms, many of which were refreshingly new to the Captain.

"My dear fellow! Then what are you waiting for?"

"Waiting, sir?"

"You want to be my cage boy. Cecil is now my cage boy. If Cecil were gone, you would be my cage boy. Isn't it simple?"

Willie got it at last, and his grin accompanied his comprehension. He began pacing about, fists clenched, enumerating the damage he would wreak upon Cecil.

"Oh, dear, dear," the Captain sighed. "Let's be civilized about it, Willie."

"Civilized, sir?"

The Captain chuckled, because just then Willie's countenance was so very uncivilized-appearing.

"Why, yes, old man. Do it with a bit of imagination. Let Cecil frighten himself, eh?"

Willie's brow was deeply corrugated.

"Do you have a jackknife, old man?"

Willie produced it, a huge "toad-stabber" variety of pocketknife, the hilt decorated with the voluptuous figures of nude girls.

"Handsome affair, isn't it? Where did you steal it, old fellow?"

Willie colored.

"Never mind that, Willie. Now let me tell you how I managed to rid a school I once attended of a chap who was obnoxious to me. Just a threat—nothing more. And I want you to understand, old man, that if you so much as scratch Cecil with this blade, I'll chuck you to the coppers. No knifing, understand?"

The Captain flourished the wicked-looking blade, pretending he was addressing Cecil, announcing just how he was going to use the blade upon him. After a threat like that, the Captain doubted that Cecil would long remain on the show.

And the Captain was quite correct. It was that very evening following the show that Willie found opportunity to leave his roustabout duties and accost Cecil outside the dressing van.

"I want to talk to you," he said.

Cecil looked stricken. He opened his mouth several times and attempted to protest before he managed to rattle a few dry words out of his throat.

"Are you comin' with me," Willie said, very low, "or do I drag you?"

So Cecil accompanied Willie across the lot. The canvas of the big top lay on the ground now, and the center poles stood naked. High-perched floodlamps sprayed down white, garish light. Teamsters were shouting at the horses pulling baggage wagons, and now and then a work elephant swam across Cecil's vision as he stumbled along beside Willie.

They passed through bushes at the edge of the lot and halted in the weedy flatland beyond.

"I got some advice to pass to you," Willie said.

The advice was pointed. The circus, Willie said, was not large enough for the two of them. Willie's voice was pitched low, and in the distance Cecil could hear shouts and the barbaric chant of Negro roustabouts as they loaded poles onto a wagon.

"What did I ever do to you?" Cecil mumbled. "That's what I—" Willie grinned.

"You got in my way. And when a guy gets in my way, do you know how I fix him?"

There was a click, and in the dull light Cecil caught the gleam of a blade.

"I use this on 'im. I unbutton him with it. *S-s-sip!* Like that. Clean up to his tonsils . . ."

Cecil dropped back a step, and his hand floated to his Adam's apple. He was convinced he was dealing with a fellow not right in the head.

"I was leavin' anyhow," he mumbled.

"When?"

"Tomorrow . . . Maybe tonight . . ."

Willie grinned.

"If you're on the show tomorrow night . . . *S-s-sip!*"

"Don't," Cecil choked. "Don't keep speakin' about it."

Two days later, Cecil dropped off a freight train in South Chicago, determined to follow a career as a steelmaker and to forget as soon as possible that he had ever worked for Captain Philip Latcher.

It was in Chicago a year from the next December when Gus Burgoyne came to terms with Captain Latcher. Their haggling took place in a booking agent's office rather than in the hotel suite where the previous morning the Sebastians had agreed to join the show. Gus didn't much like the Captain. He was too supercilious, too frosty, too immune to bluff persuasion. And he was a phony—undoubtedly a phony. Yet as an animal man his popularity was growing. Recently a theatrical trade paper had published his picture on its cover.

At first they were poles apart in the matter of salary, but the booking agent kept spreading his hands and pouring balm on their differences, so after an hour everything was settled.

"Let's have a drink on it, old man," the Captain suggested when they emerged from the office. "I know an excellent place."

As they proceeded along Madison Street and turned a corner, the Captain swung his stick and remarked:

"There'll be a girl waiting for me. A pretty little thing. I might work her into the act."

Gus was instantly on guard.

"A contract's a contract," he said.

The Captain laughed against the roar of an elevated train.

"You misunderstand, old fellow. I wouldn't dream of touching you for more money because of her. She's very young, you know. Hardly more than a child. But she rather has me going. Odd the way the girlies can make a man spin, eh? I picked her up last month in St. Paul. A waitress. And she quite took to me. She had some dreadfully ordinary name—Swenson, Paulson, Jenson. . . . No good in the show business, of course. So I rechristened her. Rather fun, eh? Marybelle Monahan. Like it?"

"Sure," Gus said. "Fine name. Of course, Monahan's fairly common too—"

"Exactly! But common in an uncommon way, eh? And with the Marybelle—a nice effect."

They entered a restaurant and at the rear passed into a dusky room with booths and glowing lights. She sat in a corner booth, waiting. Years later when Gus tried to recall the impression she made on him that day it was all misty and vague. She was very young, as the Captain had said, and very blond. Her fine skin was washed over with blond coloring too, and her face had a still, sweet beauty. Her cheekbones were high; not too prominent, but prominent enough to give interest to a face which otherwise would have been that of merely another pretty girl.

Nor could Gus ever recall many of the details of that conversation. He carried away the impression that the girl was Captain Latcher's mistress, and he thought the Captain a reckless man to risk that with a girl who couldn't be more than sixteen. He also had the impression that she was quite in love with that phony person. Her manner was that of quiet devotion, of compliance and simple obedience. One remark Gus did remember. Out of the Captain's ready conversation it stuck with him down the years.

"I was telling Mr. Burgoyne," the Captain said, "that I may break you into the act."

The girl smiled. Half-smiled, rather. It was a smile sweet and yet mysterious, like a few tantalizing snatches from a melody by Tchaikovsky.

But what impressed Gus was the way the Captain had spoken of breaking her in, exactly as if she were a new animal he had acquired.

Considering that Marybelle Monahan would occupy an important place in his scheme of things, Gus thought about her surprisingly little during the next months. Perhaps he didn't think about her at all. When he looked back after a lapse of years and tried to remember his state of mind that spring he mainly failed. He was a busy man in those days; dozens of things on his mind. He was driving hard toward success—that enravishing word whose very sound always excited him and swayed him the way hidden riches in the earth pull at a throbbing divining rod.

He had actually reflected so little about Marybelle that he hadn't even wondered where she was when Captain Latcher and Willie arrived at the farm. It was the Captain who mentioned her when, after lunch, they crossed the carriage yard toward the office.

"Old man," he said, "I've been meaning to ask you. How about that girl of mine?"

"Girl? Oh, the blonde. Miss Flannigan—"

"Monahan, old fellow. Marybelle Monahan. How about her?"

"Thought we had that settled," Gus rumbled. "You want to use her in the act, that's fine, but a contract's a—"

"Oh, come, come! Of course that's settled. But I'm wondering about bringing her here. The situation might be considered delicate, eh? No marriage certificate, and all that."

"Where is she—Chicago?"

"Tamarack. I put the little bug away in a hotel room there. But see here! You don't run a Sunday School show. It would be capital if I could bring her out here and bunk her in with me. Quite all right, I suppose?"

Gus said, "Uh—yes. Suppose so. Of course, there's Flora. She might—"

"Exactly. Charming woman, Mrs. Burgoyne, but a bit of a moral filly, eh? But suppose I introduce the little Viking as my wife."

"Sure," Gus said. "Why not?"

"Excellent. As a matter of fact, there's a possibility she will be my wife. I've knocked around a bit in my time, you know. Sipped at every spring, as the Bard says. But look here. Why shouldn't I marry her?"

"Fine idea," Gus said.

"By jolly! The idea has possibilities, eh? Taking a wife. Marriage a great adventure and all that. And wouldn't it please the little chick! I'll stride into the room with a marriage license and chuck her under the chin and break the news in a blaze of glory. Romantic gesture, eh?"

"Think it'd please her, all right," Gus said. "Women like that sort of thing."

"By jolly, I believe they do!"

The Captain laughed pleasantly. He gave Gus a firm handshake.

"Thanks, old man, for bringing it to my attention. You know, it rather appeals to my dramatic instincts. I believe I'll run into Tamarack this afternoon. Is there a car I could use?"

So within the hour the Captain drove away. The idea of marriage had not come to him, however, quite as impulsively as he had led Gus to believe. In his heart the Captain possessed less derring-do than one might have supposed. He cut a dashing figure before the world, but he had been troubled by the warnings dropped by his booking agent. That gentleman had not wished to see one of his most profitable clients taken into custody, and he had asked the Captain to consider whether it was worth the risk, crossing state lines with a sixteen-year-old girl. "If you're smart you'll marry her," the agent had said.

And Captain Latcher was nothing if not smart. Next afternoon, when he returned with his bride to the farm, his spirit was once more untroubled by that worry. Now he could settle down to business and whip the act into shape. It didn't do to enter the arena with worry nagging you.

As for Marybelle, she was a serenely beautiful bride. She existed at the center of a golden cloud of lassitude, as if drugged by love, and she said little. But when the Captain introduced her as his wife, that queer little half-smile lingered on her lips, and she held tenderly in her arms the great, fragrant bouquet of roses which her groom had presented her.

One person was not invited to attend the wedding dinner in the house, nor did he participate in the joy and well-wishing that showered like rice on the bridal couple. His name was Willie Krummer.

Willie had matured in many ways since that evening nearly two years before when he frightened poor Cecil off the show. He was just as blond and square-headed and gash-mouthed as ever, but his muscles had hardened and his body had filled out. He had become a strapping, upstanding fellow. He was as strong as a young bullock and just as obstinate, and many of his moral and ethical standards were taurine, too.

Probably if Willie had returned to his home town—a visit he certainly was not contemplating—the sheriff and county attorney would never have recognized him as the ornery kid they had wanted to matriculate in industrial school. His shiftiness had been overlaid by the military manner he admired in Captain Latcher. But Willie's soldierly demeanor had in turn become less conspicuous. As he evolved toward manhood he realized that all that saluting and about-facing was kid stuff. His adolescent hero-worshipping had betrayed him into ridiculous deportment. It came to him suddenly that he had been acting like a jackass, and he almost never saluted the Captain again. When the Captain commented on this Willie forthrightly announced that his days of imitating a frightened orderly were over.

"Well, old fellow—feeling your oats, eh?" But a certain contemplation came into the Captain's eyes; such contemplation as might be observed in a hen discovering that the egg she had hatched had been left in her nest by a serpent.

No longer was the Captain a hero to Willie. For one thing, he was not a Captain; never had been. The medals he wore in a glittering row on his uniform were all military school medals. Nor was he very brave.

This revelation came to Willie with the force of a club blow on his hard cranium. For Willie admired courage. Not the soft courage of a lifeguard rescuing a drowning person, but the domineering courage of an animal trainer beating a furious brute into submission. The Captain told lurid stories of his experiences—how hard and ruthless and knife-brandishing he had been—but after Willie heard them several times and checked the various versions against one another he began to doubt that there was a grain of truth in them. But most disenchanting of all was the discovery that the Captain feared entering the arena.

This terrible knowledge of his hero's feet—and heart!—of clay cropped into sight little by little. For instance, after a few weeks' cleaning cages, Willie learned that the Captain's lions and tigers were not very ferocious. To the audience they seemed ferocious, but only because they were unfamiliar.

Of course, the arena was not as safe as an armchair by a fireside; with even the most mellow jungle galaxy accidents did happen; the Captain's hard body bore scars that proved this; but on the other hand striding from the safety cage to the arena was not much more hazardous than walking against a red light at a busy corner. You had to keep your wits about you and your nerves under control, that was all.

Nerves of the wrong sort were what Captain Latcher kept about him, and as season after season piled up behind him his dread of entering the arena increased. He had assumed his military manner to stiffen his courage. And the reason he perspired so copiously in the arena and had to be rubbed down could be ascribed to nerves.

Long after Willie had suspected this state of affairs, the Captain confessed his weakness, his tongue lubricated by whiskey. It was the winter following Willie's joining up as cage boy, and they were sitting in the office of the abandoned factory in Blue Island. For some time Willie had been urging the Captain to start breaking some new animals he had acquired, a couple of lions, three tigers. They were frisky, full of the devil.

"It's hard to make a start, old man. I dread it."

"Why? It'll be fun."

The Captain slipped off his bathrobe and with a forefinger traced a long, ugly scar on his left arm.

"Blood poisoning, old man. Just one sweep of a paw—and I was in the hospital for weeks. And this one." He indicated the scar tissue whitening his right thigh. "That was a month in a hospital bed. Damn it, old man—I hate hospitals. Smelly places."

"You mean you're scared?"

The Captain smiled and gazed at Willie over the whiskey glass.

"It's more complicated than that, old fellow. It has to do with this psychology stuff. It's called arena shell shock. It comes to us all sooner or later. Ask any animal man. Sometimes it creeps up on you gradually, like a damned tiger stalking you for days through the jungle, and sometimes it hits without warning and you go to pieces in the safety cage and are never any good after that."

He drank.

"Maybe, old man, it's a way the beasts have of evening up the score, eh? We cage them up and put them through their paces so that a lot of dullards can sit with their hearts in their throats. But it's all a damned unnatural business, eh? So old Dame Nature takes it out on us."

He drank.

"You look rather incredulous, Willie. Well, old son, you'll learn, you'll learn. More things in heaven and earth than are dreamed of in your philosophy, as the chap taught us at school. You're young now, old son, and you think nothing will ever break you. But it will, it will. If you keep on the jolly old cats will get you, just as they'll get me. I dream about it, you know. I'm in there without my whip and kitchen chair and gun. And they're all after me at once. By jolly!—I wake up in a sweat. Not a pleasant business!"

He drained his glass.

"But one thing you've got, old son, if you want to quit. You've got a trade."

"A trade?" Willie's mouth twisted scornfully about the words.

"What else, old man? A trade as a masseur. Haven't I taught you how to rub me down? I believe they pay rather well for that sort of thing at Turkish baths."

"A trade," Willie said. "For Christ's sake, who wants a trade! I want to go after them cats!"

"Ah," the Captain murmured, "in the bright lexicon of youth, and so on, and so on . . . Very well, old son, why not go after them? It's a great opportunity, Willie. I've had one sip too many or I wouldn't be making you the offer. The arena's out there, Willie, and the cats are there, and here I sit giving you *carte blanche,* as our French friends say. Proceed, Willie, old son! And may the better animal win, eh? And if you get a scratch, I wonder what will flow. Blood? I doubt it, old son. Ice water, I jolly well believe."

And so, with the Captain weaving along after him, Willie went from the office into the vast gloom of that factory which back in the 1880's had manufactured buggies. The long, grime-crusted windows

were set at infrequent intervals in the old brick walls, and thick walnut
pillars rose from the brick-paved floor to support the wooden ceiling.

"Light, Willie! You can't work in this beastly gloaming."

So Willie snapped a switch and a floodlamp poured a bright cone
into the circular steel arena.

"What part of the act, Willie? A couple of lions, as a starter? Kalem
and Nero?"

"Them!" Willie spat. "Them tame kittens! I want the new ones."

The Captain's brows went up. Then he shrugged.

"Very well, old boy. But just the three Bengals. No lions today."

While Willie hooked up the chute from the arena to the tiger den
the Captain glided back to the office and slipped into his training suit—
soft boots, light breeches, a light shirt. He snapped a wide leather belt
around the flat sinews of his stomach and checked the load of blanks
in both .32 revolvers. Out in the factory he found Willie impatiently
gripping a whip. He stood with legs apart, clad in some offcast boots
and breeches of the Captain, and he was gazing at the arena where
the three new Bengals were circling and hissing.

"Certain you don't want to work the old ones, Willie?"

"These!"

The Captain flipped one revolver, caught it expertly by the barrel
and gave it to Willie.

"I'll be in the safety cage, old boy. I shouldn't try much with them,
if I were you. If you're able to get inside for a yard or so it'll be a good
morning's work."

Willie laughed.

"I'm going to pedestal them."

"We'll see, we'll see," the Captain murmured. "Easy does it, old
man."

They entered the safety cage. Revolver in his belt, whip in one hand
and a kitchen chair in the other, Willie filled his chest and said, "Here
goes."

The Captain opened the door into the arena.

Willie didn't teach the new cats to leap to their pedestals that morning. The door had scarcely clanged shut behind him when a great
many confusing things happened. His gaze had darted momentarily
toward two of the animals at the far side of the arena when suddenly
something tawny loomed in the air before him and the kitchen chair
disintegrated as if by explosion. Willie staggered to one side just as
something brightly striped sprang past. Willie pivoted to the arena
bars, yelling lumberjack oaths, flailing the air with his whip and shooting. His courage plummeted from the boiling point to fifty degrees
below zero, and the shifty movements of his boyhood returned. He

forgot his career, the Captain, everything; everything save those slinking, flashing streaks.

He heard the Captain's voice; he heard the safety cage door clang; and then his courage oozed upward, for he discovered that by some miracle he was standing in the safety cage and the Captain had taken over the business in the arena.

It was possible to admire the Captain's virtuosity. His was the footwork of a boxer or fencer; he didn't shout. Two of the tigers were climbing the arena side and investigating with some panic the netting over the top; and when the third animal leaped at the Captain again and again he dodged, ducked, danced very neatly and lightly, fending the swatting paws with the kitchen chair.

"The door, Willie."

As easily as a man leading a dancing partner the Captain worked the bad tiger away from the safety cage; and when Willie snapped open the door the Captain stepped backward out of the arena. The tiger sprang and pounced shut the door.

The Captain's forehead gleamed and rivulets streamed from his cheeks.

"Rather wild, aren't they, old man?" he said.

Then he frowned, and as if from some inner compulsion he ordered Willie to clear the arena of the new animals and to hook up the chute to the cages where the old familiar cats lived and to bring them in.

Using a stream of water from a hose, Willie stood outside the arena and drove the tigers back into the tunnel.

The Captain went through his entire act that morning. He was like an aviator returning aloft immediately following a minor crackup. He even seized the jaws of lazy, sluggish old Nero and thrust his head inside Nero's mouth. At least, circus audiences supposed his head entered Nero's mouth. Actually, only his face went in. The Captain didn't like to do it because most lions suffered from bad breath, and Nero was decidedly not an exception. It wasn't a dangerous feat—not with Nero; but it occurred to Willie that it could be dangerous, after all. If Nero were to be startled.

When the time came for his rubdown, the Captain was quite exhausted. He lay with his face buried in his arms, legs twitching. Willie could tell he was all nerves. Mentally, he sneered at the man's cowardice.

As for Willie, he felt quite pleased with himself. He had made an excellent beginning. Very few young men would be brave enough to enter an arena with three unbroken cats. He would have pedestaled them too, if the lily-livered Captain hadn't interfered.

Willie was scarcely a past master at dissimulation, and during the next days his true feelings toward the Captain were apparent. He swaggered, and much of the time that ornery grin plastered his countenance.

Being a fairly shrewd judge of human nature, the Captain understood why their relationship was cracking up. He had treated the lad too well. As soon as he had allowed their officer-private caste system to fall into disuse, Willie's overbearing disposition asserted itself. He considered discharging Willie, but he decided against this because as an employee the boy had virtues. He was a good worker; even a dependable one. He kept the cages spick and span, the whips in good repair. He was a marvel at packing gear; and when they traveled with a circus everything in the dressing van had its place. Yes, a most orderly, industrious chap.

"When are you going to break them cats?" Willie kept asking, during the week after the episode with the Bengals.

"Soon, old man, soon. I'm planning my strategy with the kittens." Willie would grin.

The Captain's annoyance with the lad was growing, and then one morning Willie overstepped himself.

"I'd like to get another crack at them cats," he declared. "Let me go after them, if you're afraid."

The Captain smiled. He said icily:

"As a matter of fact, old chap, I'm going to start breaking them this morning. But first, there's another trifling detail to be attended to. Come, Willie."

The Captain led Willie from the office, and when they were in the gloom of the factory he explained his intentions in a matter-of-fact voice.

"Have you ever heard of insubordination, old chap? No? You've been the very picture of insubordination, old fellow, and I can't say that I like it."

Whereupon the Captain administered to Willie an extremely scientific and rather brutal beating. He had been an excellent boxer in military school and when, at first, Willie tried to defend himself with roundhouse blows it was most amusing. Willie's swinging fists, telegraphing their intentions, never came within inches of the Captain's jaw. When Willie discovered the hopelessness of fighting, he surrendered abjectly; he whined and blubbered and refused to get up from the floor. Kicks brought howls from the lad, but they didn't bring him to his feet. As long as he had embarked upon chastisement, the Captain thought it would be well to give Willie something to remember, so he seized a whip and finished the job with that.

And it was truly miraculous what the Captain accomplished that morning. He apotheosized himself in the cage boy's soul. The Captain was a great man, after all: a hero. He could respect him again. Of course, buried deep in Willie's being resentment burned, a determination to get even some day; but it was like heat generated at the bottom of a pile heaped with tons of coal. No flames were seen, and only a wisp of smoke now and then. On the surface Willie was respectful to the cringing point.

And his respect was the greater because as soon as the Captain stopped bringing howls and pleadings from Willie he ordered him to get up and drive the new cats into the arena. Not only the Bengals, but the lions as well. Willie was quite aware that it was stepping up the danger to mix untrained lions and tigers, but those were the orders. And he was in a mood now not only to obey every order to the letter, but to anticipate orders and wishes.

Of course, the Captain proceeded with the training more cautiously than Willie might have wished. For days he merely stepped into the arena and accustomed the animals to his presence. It was weeks before he managed to train them to leap to their pedestals.

Willie's insubordination was a weed which could be knocked down and broken, but not permanently destroyed. Twice during the next year the Captain was compelled to clean out the garden of their relationship so that Willie's orderly, virtuous onions could thrive.

It seemed the cage boy would never learn; and sometimes the Captain suspected that to Willie the whole business had the emotional beauty of a symphony's movements: a beating, cringing, respect, equality, arrogance, another beating.

"You're a queer chap, old fellow," he said, after the third punishment. "Rather twisted up inside, I imagine."

Willie learned more from his association with the Captain than either imagined. Not merely about animal training, although he was learning that too. Every now and then the Captain permitted him to enter the arena, always with the comfortable old cats. The Captain stood in the safety cage, ready to rescue him from a tight spot, while Willie got the act started. Once it was under way, a child could have taken over, because the cats knew the routine as well as the hands of a clock know the circle they travel. But the animals didn't like or trust Willie; he refused to fit himself into the regular rhythms of the act; he tried to hurry them; and instead of simply using the whip to cue them he couldn't resist snapping it into their hides. They would snarl and spit and pounce occasionally, whereupon Willie would discharge blank cartridges into their faces, and then a real mixup would ensue.

"By jolly, you need to learn restraint," the Captain told him repeatedly. "Cats have a bit of pride, you know."

"I'll pride them, all right," Willie snarled. "I'll show 'em who's got pride. If the act was mine they'd learn all about pride."

"Gracious, old chap! If the act were yours. Not thinking of buying me out, are you?" The Captain laughed and added half-humorously, "And certainly not thinking of sponsoring an accident! I've made my will, you know. Everything goes to my brother in British Columbia. You'd be out of a job, old boy, if the cats got me."

"Aw, quit the kiddin'," Willie protested.

And he turned to a theatrical trunk and became very busy arranging things inside. He could feel the blood in his cheeks and he didn't want to meet the Captain's gaze.

When they traveled to indoor circuses in the winter, they stopped at good hotels and ate in cafés, and this rolling-stone existence smoothed down and polished some of Willie's roughness. The Captain broke him of scooping food into his descending mouth with his knife, and he taught him to leave his napkin (only the Captain called it a serviette) on his lap instead of stuffing it into his collar. The first time they entered a hotel lobby with Willie carrying luggage, and a bellhop rushed to grab the grips, the Captain interposed just in time to prevent a scene. Willie thought the guy was trying to get away with something. Willie's boundless ignorance about the amenities of living always amazed and amused the Captain, and he spent many hours setting him right. He discovered that Willie's mind, beneath its rust of ignorance, had a hard, steel sharpness, and he even managed to patch up the more gaping holes in the lad's grammar.

"If you're going to be a famous animal trainer," he'd say playfully, "you'll have to learn to meet people. The outcast days of the circus performer are over. Sometimes it even amuses society people to invite a few top liners to their homes for dinner. Think how dismayed they'd be at the sound of your eating. By jolly! They'd think you were choking to death. Or if you sat next to a young matron of the Junior League, and dropped your hand on her knee—"

"Who are you kiddin'?" Willie inquired. "There ain't no girl players in the Leagues. Besides, I only follow the Majors."

The Captain laughed delightedly, and explained to Willie's corrugated brow all about the social order in the United States.

Under this tutelage, Willie's wood-rat and road-kid personality was gradually overlaid with the protective coloration of the ordinary traveler to be met in railroad trains or hotel lobbies. The Captain took him down to the Loop and purchased him a suit, shirts, shoes. Willie yearned to buy fabrics and ties that screamed, but since the Captain was footing the bill he had to content himself with tamer selections. Willie's wide shoulders and narrow hips were the dream-come-true of clerks in ready-to-wear stores.

"A beautiful fit, sir! Look at the hang of that coat!"

Sir! The coat tightened over Willie's chest and his chin came up as he admired himself in the long, three-winged mirror. But the clerk had let himself in for a good many sneering words by calling Willie, "sir."

"You know, old lad," the Captain said, when they emerged to the street, "you treated the fellow rather shabbily."

"Why not? That's what they're payin' him for—to wait on people."

Drill and hammer and blast as the Captain might, he could never inject into the cage boy's square skull the idea of equality in human relations.

Inspired by his new clothes, Willie began taking great pride in his personal appearance, and when their second autumn together came and they boarded a train for St. Paul, Willie could easily have passed for a college football player. He looked like a semi-pro in mufti. Jaws grinding away at chewing gum, chin cupped in his palm, he sat gazing out the window looking bored.

He had begun to do considerable reading, and although the range was narrow the quantity was vast, for every day he gulped down columns and columns of newspaper sports pages. He could tell you who pitched for the Yankees in 1910, and he was an authority on the current fortunes of a score of football elevens. Of them all, the aggregation which upheld the honor of the University of Wisconsin was his favorite. He held no grudge against his native state; quite the contrary. And he was ever willing to back up his high opinion of the Wisconsin team with a small wager. If the boys from Madison lost, a cloud of gloom descended upon him, but if they forged on to victory he grinned and crowed and rubbed it into the supporter of the other team. He despised Wisconsin's opponents, as if the coach and every member of the squad had insulted him.

Sometimes he daydreamed regretfully about what a spectacular halfback the world had lost when he failed to continue his education. How he would have plowed through the line! Old Powerhouse Krummer! Many a face would have carried his cleat scars for the rest of its days. Knees pumping high, he would have surged and stiff-armed down the field. Old Touchdown Krummer! Rah, rah, rah!

Still, you couldn't do everything, and a career as animal trainer remained his first love. Always he was tormented by the ambition that had crashed into flame on that long-ago afternoon when he beheld Captain Latcher saluting the audience and entering the arena. He pondered constantly how he could acquire an act of his own. He might, of course, go to work for a circus that owned a group of performing animals and wanted a trainer. But no! He wanted an act

that belonged to him. "Willie Krummer and His Trained Animals."
Only a more impressive name than that. King Krummer. Or Count
or Baron or Duke. Finding a new name would be much easier than
acquiring the animals. He hadn't been long in selecting a name to substitute for Parr. Jolting along on a Soo freight, he had seen a sign,
Krummer Lumber Company, in a village through which the train
hooted, and at once he became Willie Krummer.

Now and then Willie thought how simple it would be to foster an
accident when the Captain was rehearsing the cats. There were dozens
of possibilities. Since the world considered animal training so hazardous, nobody would be surprised to hear that a tiger had turned suddenly, or that Nero had closed his jaws with the Captain's head inside.
But damn it, what would be the use of arranging an accident when the
act was willed to the Captain's brother? Willie entertained a very
low opinion of the Captain's brother.

It was in St. Paul where they were playing at the Shrine Indoor
Circus that they met Mabel Swanson. On their second morning they
left the hotel and strolled along Wabasha Street, searching for breakfast.

"This will do well enough," the Captain said, so they entered a
quick-lunch joint and sat down at a white-topped table. Everything
ordinary and usual: paper napkins folded in a container, tinny-looking
silverware, the clatter of trays and dishes echoing from the white-tiled
walls. And then suddenly the place became out-of-the-ordinary and
exciting with the appearance at their table of this girl.

By this time Willie had had a number of girls, but there was something about this serene blonde with her just-right figure that stirred a
heretofore untouched nook of his being. He felt . . . well, a good deal
the way he had felt that afternoon when he first saw the Captain sub-
duing his cats. St. Paul had whetted his emotions anyway, for it was
simply alive with lovely blond girls, and this waitress with her smooth
skin seemed the summing up of all that fascinating pulchritude. Only
she had something that the others lacked. Her face was more complicated, more mysterious. Something silent and secretive and untouched brooded behind it, so that you felt like an explorer coming
over a hill and beholding vast leagues of northern white birch, rich
and virgin.

When she left menus and departed for glasses of water, Willie's gaze
followed her. She wore sheer, flesh-colored stockings, the seams running straight and intensifying the beauty of her well-turned legs.

While she took their orders, Willie detected a tiny smile playing
lightly about her mouth, and this roused and baffled him. What was

the joke, huh? What was so funny about him? His fingers stirred and tingled. If he had her alone and she kept mocking him like that, he'd slap that smile off her face. Nobody could laugh at Willie Krummer and not let him in on the joke.

He ordered bacon and eggs, the eggs to be fried sunny-side-up, but when she brought the food it was instantly apparent that she had willfully disobeyed the command of the future greatest animal trainer in the world. The eggs had been fried turn-over style.

So Willie acted like Willie. He pointed at the treacherously prepared eggs and with an arrogance of head and a few well-chosen words told the pretty minx his opinion of a waitress who flouted the customer's wishes. She quit smiling soon enough then. She looked bewildered and flushed.

It was at this point that Captain Latcher butted in on Willie's lovemaking. As usual at breakfast, the Captain had been lost in the pages of his morning newspaper, but as Willie's diatribe impinged on his consciousness he glanced up, took in the situation and put the paper down.

He flashed the waitress his most charming smile and said easily:

"Come, come, my girl. Don't let this chap disturb you."

"I'm sorry about the eggs," she murmured in her low contralto voice.

The Captain airily waved aside her apology.

"He's lucky to have anything at all to eat. I picked him up the other day out of a hobo jungle. You can't imagine how he looked. He'd never had a haircut, and I doubt if he'd ever had a bath. And look at him now. You'd very nearly think him civilized, wouldn't you?"

The Captain gestured easily toward his cage boy, and Willie found two pairs of eyes contemplating him as if he were a side show freak. His mouth twisted and the light in his eyes was sinister. And he felt hot crimson pumping up his heavy neck and into his ears.

"Willie's like fire. A good servant, a poor master. A simple fellow. He fancies himself quite dangerous, you know, but I give him a sound thrashing now and then, and that keeps him in line. I assure you he won't bite you—not while I'm present."

Willie's lips were moving, soundlessly echoing the venomous thoughts that milled and circled through his brain like cats in an arena. And he knew how a surly cat felt, facing the Captain. You couldn't break through his guard. His footwork was too nimble, just as his wordwork was too foxy. Many of Willie's thoughts wanted to pounce out of his mouth and claw the Captain, but he knew the Captain would dance aside and lash back worse than ever.

"See there?" the Captain said. "We have him tamed now, and

pedestaled. After a while he'll perform his tricks. He can use a knife and fork, you know. Really remarkable, eh?"

The air enclosing Willie's head was a pink-tinged, hot balloon. The plate where the eggs reposed (those damned eggs that had started it all) was thick and white, the edge chipped.

"Look up, Willie." The Captain snapped his fingers sharply, like a hypnotist. "Apologize to the girl."

Willie wasn't going to look up and he wasn't going to apologize. And yet, damn it, he did look up, exactly as if he were a hypnotist's victim, and his throat muttered something that sounded like, " 'pologize." He hated himself for it, and he hated the girl and the Captain —yes, and St. Paul and the world and the universe that had produced him without consulting his wishes in the matter. The girl was half smiling again, now, like a kid amused at the antics of a caged monkey.

"I didn't fix the eggs," she told the Captain. "It was the cook."

"Of course. Think no more about it. The incident's quite closed, eh? I say, what's your name?"

"Mabel. Mabel Swanson."

"Do you like a show, Mabel?"

"Sure. A good show—I like it."

"You're going to see one." He slipped a notebook from his pocket, tore out a sheet, dashed off a few words. "You present this at the gate, Mabel."

"Oh-h," she said, her low voice trilling up and down a tiny scale. "A circus." She frowned for a second, then smiled. "Your name signed here—I knew somewhere I had seen it. And you, too. In the news-papers."

Her voice and her diction had an engaging foreign flavor; not as pronounced as if she had been born in Scandinavia, but as if she had been reared in a household where a language other than English was spoken.

"Yes," the Captain said, "our advance notices have been very good in St. Paul. Charming city, St. Paul."

"Oh, yes—very nice. I like it."

"Lived here long, Mabel?"

"Not very long, no . . ." She glanced over her shoulder. "I must go, now. Other customers."

This time, it was the Captain's gaze that followed her departure.

"By jolly," he murmured. "An intriguing little creature."

And after that, his concentration upon his newspaper was not so complete. Willie chewed sullenly. He would have enjoyed escaping into the sports pages, but the Captain was prejudiced against splitting up a newspaper and sharing it. Always he read it through leisurely, passing it on to Willie after he had quite finished with it. It exasperated Willie, always accepting the crumbs and scraps of life. Everybody had forever been against him.

The Captain soared through that day in high spirits, but Willie's sullen breakfast mood remained. There was no matinee, so that afternoon he moped about town, staring into curio shop windows, spending a few cents in a penny arcade, and finally boarding a streetcar for the long ride to Minneapolis. He stared at a good many smooth blond girls—he guessed they didn't make 'em any color but blond, up here in Minnesota—but no girl affected him as Mabel had.

He tried to analyze his emotions about her, but they were such a tangle of shame and desire and jealousy and tantalization that he floundered about like a man trying to crawl through a thicket of brambles. He told himself that he hated her, but nevertheless he kept imagining what it would be like if she were to respond to his overtures the way she had to the Captain's. His daydreaming flourished uncontrolled, and it was lucky indeed that the other passengers couldn't know the thoughts that uncoiled in the head of that fellow who slouched in a seat, chewing gum and staring discontentedly out the window.

The car moaned across the Mississippi River, but it left Willie unimpressed. Just a lot of water. And the wide, bright, windy streets of Minneapolis left him unimpressed, also. In his present mood, he preferred the narrower, older streets of St. Paul. He boarded another car.

And that evening in the auditorium he attempted the impossible task of picking Mabel Swanson out among the thousands of blurring faces. He was hampered by the strong floodlights pouring brilliance into the ring. Willie wore a scarlet attendant's suit, the jacket scrolled with black, but of course nobody watched him . . . unless perhaps Mabel had come to realize . . . All eyes followed the Captain. He hadn't given an audience such a big money's worth in a long time. Elegant in a fresh uniform and highly polished boots (a result of Willie's elbow grease), he saluted the audience dashingly, and he put his cats through their paces as if they were expertly trained cadets. He had blended his new animals into the act, and they were still as unbroken in spirit as brand-new shoes. The Captain took chances that night which evoked Willie's grudging admiration; even the new cats had to step. The applause was thunderous; and in the dressing room following the act the Captain was as high as the statehouse dome. None of that arena-shell-shock stuff tonight.

"You run along, old boy," he said, patting his soft hat into place, adjusting his scarf, taking up his stick. "I have an appointment."

Willie stared. "Who with?"

"It's none of your business, old fellow, but if you must know, with the little Viking."

"Viking?"

"Don't be thick-headed, Willie. With Mabel. I dropped in for a cup of tea this afternoon, and suggested that we meet after the show."

Willie turned away, stricken. The next days were torment. And the worst blow of all bounced off his skull at the end of the week. For when they left St. Paul on the late Saturday night train, Mabel accompanied them. She and the Captain enjoyed Pullman accommodations. A stateroom. Willie dozed and twisted in his clothes amid the smells of orange peelings and garlic and the sounds of wailing infants in the day coach.

3

Years before, somebody had built the house at winter quarters. Not Burgoyne. He had come later. Whoever built it had gone bankrupt trying to farm the place, because the soil was so impoverished.

Back in the 1890's, in the city of Tamarack, a group of men had beheld visions. Financial and commercial visions. Like most men with idle capital they desired an investment that was both speculative and safe. They wanted their dollars to go adventuring and bring back alive great profits, but they were solicitous for the safety of their dollars while on the expedition.

The men thought: transportation. Ah! The country was growing. Roads were wretched and horses slow. Yet goods had to be moved and people were always yearning to be where they were not.

The men thought: electricity. Magic word! Thomas A. Edison! Modern wizardry! Profits!

So the men stroked their whiskers and organized an electric railroad and christened it Tamarack & Northern. As president they elected a man with more whiskers and more money and more stock in the company than any of the others. Mr. Samuel R. Oxenford. He had attained financial prowess partly by hard work and partly by great luck. As a stripling he had migrated west and secured employment at a general store in what was then the muddy pioneer village of Tamarack. He had no thought of becoming a financier or even a merchant. He wanted to be a farmer. So he slaved all day and at night he slumbered on the counter of the store in order to save the cost of lodgings. Presently he had hoarded enough money to begin buying a farm at the edge of the village. It was on this farm that Tamarack took it into its head to grow; by 1890, the most bustling corner in the Tamarack business district occupied the spot which Mr. Oxenford had intended as his cow lot. Nobody had been more astonished at this happy turn of events than Mr. Oxenford, but he pretended he had possessed great foresight all along, and people held him in awe.

Tamarack & Northern laid track, strung trolley wires, and for a few years it made money. When anybody suggested to Mr. Oxenford that these new horseless carriages might offer competition to his company, he enjoyed a hearty laugh. There were always, he said, Socialistic fools who would squander money on ideas like that. Why, he had even read in the newspapers about some idiots who thought they could build a flying-machine. Mr. Oxenford sometimes wondered what the country was coming to.

Mr. Oxenford was forever dabbling in various deals, and one of his side lines was the Tamarack Fuel & Ice Company. The concern operated several coal mines near Tamarack, but Mr. Oxenford, who always wanted more of everything, wanted more mines, so he employed a geologist to go poking about the country searching for land which might have coal beneath it; and one day the geologist drove his buggy into that valley northwest of Tamarack.

A week later, operating deviously, Mr. Oxenford began purchasing land in the valley. Not coal rights alone, but the land itself. For the land, being useless except for grazing, was priced so cheaply that he computed his possible profits as greater if he owned it outright. Moreover, if he started dickering for coal rights, the owners might suspect the existence of coal and shove up the price. In the privacy of his dingy office, many a chuckle rustled through Mr. Oxenford's whiskers as he thought how he was outfoxing the owners of the land.

Tamarack Fuel & Ice sank a mine shaft. Encountered coal. A settlement sprang into being, peopled by round-headed men with prodigious families who jabbered in a strange foreign tongue. The settlement was called Oxenford.

And then Tamarack & Northern decided to run a spur into the valley from its main line. The decision was not popular with the other stockholders. They howled. They saw ruin. But Mr. Oxenford owned fifty-one percent of the stock, and he had a streak of stubbornness as flinty as his small cold eyes. Profits which could better have been dispersed as dividends were poured into the construction fund. It was bad business for Tamarack & Northern but excellent business indeed for Tamarack Fuel & Ice to have other people's money lay track to its mine. That was in 1901.

Three years later a wedding occurred in Mr. Oxenford's great, showy wooden castle on Wellington Avenue in Tamarack. For better or worse his daughter, Flora, became the bride of that ambitious young fellow with the persuasive tongue, Gus Burgoyne. Burgoyne was a man after Mr. Oxenford's heart. A hustler!

For several years Mr. Oxenford had been watching Gus Burgoyne. Their first business transaction had taken place when, at twenty-two, Burgoyne was city editor of the *Tamarack Beacon*. That was soon after Tamarack & Northern purchased a controlling interest in the Tamarack Street Railway Company.

To Mr. Oxenford's slight dismay, the purchase had brought him into command of an amusement park. Amazing but true!—a park called Funland, complete with a roller coaster, a merry-go-round, a

Ferris wheel. For Funland was controlled by the streetcar company, which was controlled by Tamarack & Northern, which was controlled by Mr. Oxenford. Some years before, the streetcar company had put up the money for the construction of Funland Park away out at the edge of Tamarack, reasoning soundly that people who wanted to enjoy themselves at Funland would have to get there by riding the streetcars.

Mr. Oxenford was sapient enough to realize he knew nothing at all about the amusement park business, but so long as he had unwittingly acquired it he wanted to make a profit. And this much he did know: there would be no profit unless the citizenry could be lured there in droves.

How to lure them Mr. Oxenford couldn't imagine, for he had no interest in such tomfoolery. No showman's instincts. He could lean back in his swivel chair and rustle his palms together and hatch schemes for siphoning thousands of dollars from the bank accounts of other businessmen—dizzy mergers of companies which owned other companies and were in turn owned by still other companies; but how to inspire small fry to waste nickels and dimes at an amusement park was beyond him. He didn't understand the thinking processes of nincompoops who would pay to ride a merry-go-round. But he very well understood that ten dimes make a dollar: fortunes had towered up from the dimes of millions of spenders. Then it occurred to him that a newspaper man should have ideas on the subject, and he recalled that fellow Burgoyne, who had once interviewed him on his birthday and had written a very fine newspaper account about Mr. Oxenford's advice to young men who wanted to become successful. (Thrift, Industry, Integrity—those were the cornerstones of success, Mr. Oxenford had disclosed to the Leaders-of-the-Future.) So he summoned Burgoyne to his office, and when he learned that the reporter had been promoted to city editor he was certain he had picked the right man.

He offered Burgoyne what seemed to him the princely sum of ten dollars per week to act as publicity consultant. But Burgoyne laughed.

"I couldn't touch it for that. Too much risk."

"Risk?" Mr. Oxenford growled through his whiskers. "Where's the risk?"

So Burgoyne explained that a newspaper man occupied a position of public trust. He smiled when he said it and Mr. Oxenford smiled too: they understood each other. A newspaper man—and especially a city editor—was expected to permit news alone to enter the columns of his paper. That a city editor should hold a side-line job as a press agent was unthinkable, at least at a salary of ten per week.

"If my bosses found out what I was up to, I'd be fired so fast my head would swim. Of course," Burgoyne added, "I'd enjoy doing it— if the price was right. I've got lots of ideas on the subject, and anything I'd cook up would be sure to get into print. After all, I'm city editor."

"What would you consider a right price?"

"Oh, say twenty-five a week, as a starter."

"Great God, man!" exclaimed Mr. Oxenford. "Do you think I'm made of money?"

Burgoyne said, "Yes."

A promising fellow! Mr. Oxenford chuckled. And his rapid mind did some figuring. After all, twenty-five wasn't so much, if Burgoyne could deliver. Display ads would cost more than that, and they wouldn't be as widely read as news stories.

"You're hired," he said. And he thought: "You're smart, my young friend, but not as smart as you think. After you've taken that salary I'll have you where I want you. You'll have to take less then, or I'll tell your bosses what you've been up to."

Mr. Oxenford was neither the first nor last man who believed it possible to outsmart Gus Burgoyne. A year later Burgoyne left his job on the city desk to become manager of the park. And Flora Oxenford had fallen in love with him. She was a large, unbeautiful, cow= like girl, and some people were unkind enough to suspect that Burgoyne married her for her money. Burgoyne never suspected any such thing; he damned well knew it.

Burgoyne's first advice as secret press agent had been:

"Buy an elephant."

"A what!"

"An elephant."

"God Almighty!" Mr. Oxenford exclaimed. "What would we do with an elephant?"

"You're paying me for advice. If you don't follow it, don't blame me."

"An elephant," Mr. Oxenford groaned. "How much do they cost?"

"You might pick up a baby elephant cheap. Twelve or fifteen hundred."

The fellow was crazy! An elephant! Twelve or fifteen hundred! And yet . . . well, there was a certain fascination in the suggestion.

"What attracts people," Burgoyne said, "are superlatives. The best. The biggest. Of course, you could buy a whale—"

"Great God, no! Not a whale!"

"No, not a whale," Burgoyne agreed. "Because you can't exhibit a whale, unless he's dead and full of embalming fluid. But an elephant's different."

"How much do they eat?"

"Oh, well, you know," Burgoyne said, rather vaguely. "They're big. They have to be fed. Of course the kids would feed it peanuts and—"

He broke off. His eyes lighted. And he smacked his palm down on Oxenford's desk. "I've got it!" he exclaimed. "It won't cost you a cent! Not a red cent!"

"That," said Mr. Oxenford, "is more like it."

Burgoyne put his inspiration into words with such powerful and infectious enthusiasm that Mr. Oxenford found himself embracing the idea.

"It has everything!" Burgoyne kept interjecting. "It doesn't miss anywhere!"

And so it was that the children of Tamarack contributed their dimes toward the purchase of a baby elephant to be quartered at Funland Park. Wholeheartedly, the *Tamarack Beacon* sponsored the project. It became a crusade. Editorials were written upon the subject; civic speakers espoused the idea; the superintendent of schools declared the educational value of an elephant was beyond calculation; even a preacher or two said some fine things about elephants from their pulpits. The citizens of Tamarack began feeling keenly the lack of an elephant. People wondered how they had got along all these years without one.

Into the *Beacon* office the dimes began to tinkle. The tinkling swelled into a ringing torrent. The *Beacon* hired extra help. Human interest stories found their way into print. A story and picture of the little crippled newsboy contributing his dime. A picture of the little girl who did mother's dishes for a week to earn her dime.

On the day when the tide of dimes surged above the fifteen-hundred-dollar mark, the *Beacon* carried a banner headline: ELEPHANT ASSURED. And in the dining room of a country hotel, fifty miles away, a man sat reading that story. His name was Ivan Pawpacker.

Late the next afternoon, in the *Beacon* city room, the copy boy came to the city desk and told Burgoyne:

"Man to see you. Something about the elephant."

Burgoyne looked across the big dingy room with its long untidy tables and antediluvian typewriters. Beyond the railing he saw a small man with a gold-headed stick. The copy boy bade him enter, and Burgoyne watched him crossing the room. Pawpacker wore a short beard and his step was quick, firm, self-assured. His eyes were dark and keen. He extended a narrow, well-kept hand: the hand of a gentleman. Burgoyne's burly paw shook it heartily.

"Sit down, sir—have a chair," he boomed cordially.

In those brave days Burgoyne's zest for life was limitless; life was a melon he was going to carve up and find sweet and juicy. By his great energy and considerable ability he had bulled ahead in newspaper work, but he didn't want to spend his years chronicling the exploits of other men. He wanted to charge out into the arena where the sun was hot and a man could brawl and sweat and make a name for himself. Newspaper work introduced him to many men, and he shrewdly estimated them all and tried to impress those he might use.

As he talked with Pawpacker, excitement pounded in his blood. It was as if his highly developed instinct for self-advancement were crying out that here was a man who would be important in his life.

"I understand," Pawpacker said, "that you're in the market for an elephant."

"Well—yes. The *Beacon* has been raising funds. But Samuel Oxenford will make the actual purchase. With my advice. Any recommendation from me he'll accept. Do you have an elephant?"

"I have a half-dozen."

Burgoyne's excitement increased. The thought of elephants always affected him like a brass band. And he was excited too about the dazzling unpredictability of life. Five minutes ago he had been copyreading a dull story. And then this man appeared and calmly admitted ownership of a half-dozen elephants!

"Where are they?"

"In Missouri. Winchester. I have a circus brokerage business there."

Burgoyne felt as if he had quaffed champagne. Show business! He thought of Barnum. The Ringlings. Adam Forepaugh.

"I think you and I can do business," Burgoyne said. "How long will you be in town?"

"Till tomorrow."

"Good. Have dinner with me and we'll go over the deal. Then later in the evening see Oxenford."

They shook hands again, Pawpacker so laconic, so meticulous, so rapierlike; Burgoyne so big and well-met.

As soon as Pawpacker had gone, Burgoyne called Oxenford and made an appointment for nine that evening. He didn't mention the dinner engagement because already a scheme was sprouting in his mind whereby he might make a little money for himself on the deal. Moreover, he didn't want to share Pawpacker with anybody; he wanted to question him as to the cost of starting a small circus, and he knew that Oxenford would keep breaking in with pompous advice.

The *Beacon* was an afternoon newspaper, and except for odds and ends his day's work was over. He didn't bother to clean up those odds and ends.

"Tell anyone I won't be back," he instructed the copy boy. "Tell them I'm working on this elephant business."

At the door, he glanced back at the city room. How stifling it seemed, suddenly! A dusty bar of late sunlight shafted through the grimed windows, revealing the stained walls, the warped floor, the scattered wastepaper. At the copy desk a couple of men in shirt sleeves were laboring over long strips of paper, and a reporter was tapping out a feature story. Slaves! Visionless treadmill animals! In ten years and twenty years they would still be tapping away their lives, but he was going on and on. His faith in his own capacities had never given him such a boundless sense of power.

In his cheap lodging house he bathed and shaved and selected his favorite suit. A checked suit. He shrugged into crisp linen, hooked a starched collar round his heavy throat, knotted into place a blue tie with white polka dots. He was whistling.

The season was spring—balmy April weather—and instead of hailing a horse-drawn cab he walked to the General Grant Hotel. It was one of the happiest half-hours in his life. The sun had set but the streets were still light from the afterglow in the serene sky. He strode along past boys playing marbles, girls playing jackstones; he heard a robin singing. He stopped at a saloon and bought a fistful of cigars, but it never occurred to him to order a drink. He was intoxicated enough already. He was gloriously young, and out there ahead the entire future stretched. All he had to do was to make the correct moves in this fascinating game of getting along in life. He felt like a man who had suddenly fallen in love and who was keeping an appointment with the girl. That same light and exquisite delirium raced through his veins, and he viewed reality through the same tinted lenses of self-delusion.

In those days the General Grant was Tamarack's best hotel, and now at the dinner hour the lobby was full of aromatic cigar smoke and prosperous-looking men and handsome women and laughter and bustle and the sense of things happening. Burgoyne loved it. They were his kind of people, he thought. People upon whom fortune smiled. People who took what they wanted.

He found Pawpacker in a corner, smoking a quiet cigar, and he noticed then that trait which through all the afteryears the man never lost: his detachment. He seemed content to remain the shrewd spectator. To manipulate things silently in the shadows behind scenes. Well, every man to his tastes, but those were not Burgoyne's tastes. He was a born front man. In Pullman cars and cafés he wanted people to nudge one another and whisper, "That's Gus Burgoyne. You know, the big circus man."

"Well, Mr. Pawpacker," Burgoyne boomed, "see we're both on time. That ought to mean we can do business, huh?"

"I'm always on time."

"You bet! Punctuality's a wonderful thing. I'll fire a reporter quicker than scat if he's late to work."

Burgoyne had never fired a man for being late, but he wanted to impress upon Pawpacker the fact that his dinner companion was a man in authority around the *Beacon,* not some flunky.

"What's the fellow up to?" Pawpacker asked himself, as they walked into the oak-paneled dining room. He was puzzled, amused, interested. For after all, he was the man who had something to sell, and Burgoyne was the customer. Yet from the first Burgoyne had treated him with the deference and cordiality due a customer.

At the table, Burgoyne was the expansive host. Never for a second did the Negro waiter wonder which man was to foot the bill and provide the tip. He called the waiter George.

"How are the steaks tonight, George? Um-m. Are the planked ones good?" And to Pawpacker, "This place is famous for its steaks. Like a planked steak, Mr. Pawpacker?"

And after the order was given Burgoyne said, "I called Mr. Oxenford. Made an appointment for nine at his home. As I told you, he'll take my recommendation on the elephant."

"Good," Pawpacker said. And waited. He wanted to sell one of his elephants, but thus far the best tactics had been to remain aloof from the subject. His shrewd eyes studied Burgoyne. The fellow was big, hale, hearty; hardly handsome, but he had the good looks of youth and abundant animal spirits. A large head with a wide brow; a long thrust of jaw; a Roman nose.

"You say you're a circus broker, Mr. Pawpacker. Just what do you mean by that?"

Despite his preference for taciturnity, Pawpacker found himself drawn out by the genuineness of Burgoyne's interest. His actual profession was horse-buying, but some time ago a circus had played his town of Winchester. A small wagon show. During the evening performance the owner suffered a fatal heart attack. And it transpired that for months the show had been crawling along the brink of financial ruin. There was almost no money in the red wagon, and all the people on the show had been unpaid for so long that nobody had the price of a meal.

As a dealer in horses and mules, Pawpacker owned a farm at the edge of Winchester, with plenty of sheds and barns. And he had loose capital. He had found it wise always to have a sum of money in the bank—say four or five thousand—against which he drew checks only when an unusual business opportunity presented itself. His Opportunity Fund, he called it. False to believe that opportunity knocked but once! Opportunity knocked constantly. If you had loose capital.

This was opportunity. So he bought the circus. By the simple expedient of paying its debts. Actually, he had not wanted the wagons and canvas and wild animals. He had wanted the horses. The show possessed some wonderful draft animals. And several excellent saddle horses. The horses had lured out his checkbook. He would have bought only the horses, save that buying the whole outfit was no more costly than buying the horses alone. And he wasn't a man who avoided getting all a dollar could buy.

It was a good stroke of business. Better than he expected. Within a month he sold the horses and made a profit. And there he was with a lot of circus equipment on his hands. A cage of monkeys. Three lions. Canvas. An elephant. God knew what else.

The animals had excellent appetites. He feared they would eat him out of his profit. So, in an amusement weekly, he inserted an advertisement. He hardly expected replies. It seemed unlikely there were people willing to pay hard cash for monkeys. But a surprise awaited him. There were many people looking for bargains in monkeys and lions and snakes. Yes, snakes! Two boa constrictors. Imagine!

Men came to Winchester. His profits on that deal mounted. One man who owned some zebras offered to swap them for the elephant. His trading instincts rose to the occasion. He made the swap, and received a hundred dollars to boot. That was important in trading— always to get cash, even a little, to boot.

So without really intending to, he found himself in the circus brokerage business. One thing led to another. Hagenbecks' American representative called on him. The Carl Hagenbecks of Hamburg, Germany. Famous animal people. They were forever sending expeditions into Africa and India after wild animals. He imported a great many animals from the Hagenbecks, now.

Burgoyne thought he had never heard such a romantic story. He blurted out:

"I'm going to organize a circus. Could you outfit me?"

"Certainly."

"How much would it cost?"

"What do you plan—a railroad show or a mud show?"

"Mud show?"

"That's slang for a wagon show. A show that travels from town to town in its own wagons."

Burgoyne sighed. "I suppose that's the way I'd have to start. Start small, and grow."

"Like the Ringlings?" Pawpacker asked, with a smile.

"That's it! Like the Ringlings! How much would it cost?"

"Five thousand should get you started. In a small way. You wouldn't have much leeway, though. A week of rain would close you. You'd need luck."

Burgoyne's mouth hardened.

"If I ever get started nothing will close me."

And he thought: Five thousand! Five thousand! A monumental

sum. He didn't have even five hundred. But he would get capital. Somehow. It might take years, but he could be patient. He knew precisely what he wanted now, and he would go after it.

He said, "About this elephant. You've read how we put on a campaign to buy it?"

Pawpacker nodded.

"That was my idea," Burgoyne said. "The whole thing came from right here." He tapped his forehead. "Funland Park agreed to quarter the elephant and feed it if the kids would buy it. And the *Beacon* agreed to collect the money. You know—public service. When we get the elephant we'll have a big free day at the park, but after that the kids will have to pay admission to see their own elephant. That's smart, don't you think? Don't you think the whole idea was pretty cute?"

Pawpacker smiled; this fellow amused him. He was so blustery and so manifestly a scalawag; and yet when he talked about elephants and circuses his eagerness and enthusiasm gave him an air almost of naivete. Yet Pawpacker was an experienced enough judge of men to discern that he was not naive, really.

He said, "That's smart promotion. If you have many ideas like that, you're wasting your time in a newspaper office."

Burgoyne beamed. "I think so too!" he agreed heartily. "I'm full of those ideas. Full of them! That's why I want to get into the show business." And he added, "Now about your elephants. Do you have a young one? We thought it would appeal to the kids to get a baby elephant."

"Well, there's Molly. She's not very old. And she's a good bull."

"Bull?"

"That's more circus lingo. All elephants are bulls."

"I get it. Bulls. Good name for them. Seems to fit. How much do you want for her?"

"Fifteen hundred."

Burgoyne laughed. "You've read the *Beacon,* all right! Yep. We collect fifteen hundred so that's your price." He elbowed the table and spoke confidentially across the dishes. "Now listen, Mr. Pawpacker. It's Oxenford who'll make the purchase, but as I told you he'll take my advice. Because I cooked up this business and it's worked out fine, see? He trusts my judgment. But look here. Oxenford's a businessman. If we go out there and price this bull at fifteen hundred he'll smell a nigger in the woodpile. He'll think it's not worth that but that you're pricing it at fifteen hundred because we've got that much to spend. No, that won't do. He'll think you're slickering him."

"How high would he go?"

"I think he'd go to thirteen seventy-five. That'd leave him a hundred and a quarter to fix up a pen for the bull. Yes, if I'd advise him to buy at thirteen seventy-five he'd do it. But see here. A man has to watch out for his own interests and I ought to come in on the deal."

"In what way?"

Grinning, Burgoyne curled his fingers and scratched them against his palm.

"Catch on? If I recommend that we buy your bull that ought to be worth a hundred to you. You'd get thirteen seventy-five and pay me a hundred and that'd leave you twelve seventy-five. Think it over. Here, have a cigar."

Pawpacker took the cigar, and with a cutter neatly snipped off the end. Burgoyne bit the end off his and spat it out. Pawpacker settled back smoking quietly, watching his host puff like a locomotive.

"A good cigar," he said.

"Ought to be. They cost two-bits apiece."

The waiter cleared away the dishes and brought brandy. Pawpacker held his thin glass where the light could shine through and watched the bead. No, Burgoyne was not naive. An interesting fellow. But no nicety in an affair like this. Too blunt. Blurting out his proposal as if they were a pair of yeggs. Twelve seventy-five. Yes, he could make a profit at that price. And doubtless the fellow was correct in warning that Oxenford would find a price of fifteen hundred too damned obvious. He had overstepped himself there. He said:

"I'll price the bull at fourteen and a quarter. And if he wants to bargain I'll come down to thirteen seventy-five."

"And will you take care of me?"

"I can't give you a hundred."

And then it was that Pawpacker glimpsed another facet of Burgoyne's character. A slow flush crept over his face, and his eyes and jaw hardened. A tough face. Pawpacker thought: "He'll get what he wants. He'll go after it with a club. He'll knock hell out of anyone who gets in his way."

And he said:

"But I'm going to deal you in."

"How?"

"You say you want a circus. I'll give you two-hundred-and-fifty-dollars credit on my books. When you're ready to organize come down to Winchester. Pick out anything you want up to two-fifty and it's yours. And that five thousand I spoke about that you'd need to start a show. It wouldn't have to be all cash. I've been known to give credit."

Burgoyne's big fists relaxed. And his mouth's hard lipless look was replaced by a smile. A wise smile. His eyes were still hard and bright, gazing directly into Pawpacker's. He said:

"Why are you offering me credit? You don't know anything about me."

Pawpacker sipped his brandy. (Burgoyne's had vanished in a couple of gulps long before.) He said:

"I'd hold a mortgage on your show. I'd close you if you couldn't pay. I never take risks. You might as well know that, first as last. But as I size you up, I think you'd make a go of it. You're young and you've got a lot to learn, but you have plenty of brass. You'll need it. And if you do make a go of it, that's fine, too. For you'll want to expand. And I'll sell you more animals and equipment. I can't lose. Now do we understand each other?"

"You bet we do," Burgoyne said.

Mr. Oxenford's house stood on the north side of Wellington Avenue on a great lawn crowded with syringa and snowball bushes. At the front curb a cast-iron figure had been erected which Tamarack considered the apex of utilitarian art. It was a small replica of a Negro hostler wearing bright blue pants and a yellow vest. In its uplifted hand the figure held an iron ring to which you could hitch your horses. Dowagers riding sedately along the avenue smiled when they spied the figure and exclaimed, "Isn't that cunning?"

As for the house itself, a great service would have been done the Tamarack scene if the architect who designed it had been hit over the head with a hammer soon after birth. But that had not occurred, so out of the civilization of the mustache cup and the celluloid collar the house came into being. Upon the observer's retina it created the impression of simultaneously sprawling and towering. Around two sides of the house ran a veranda whose roof was supported by pillars as spindling as a spinster's leg, with a froth of wooden lace at the thigh. At either end of the house great wooden watchtowers rose, embrasured with round-bellied bay windows, and topped by roofs looking like enormous dunce caps.

Mr. Oxenford's wife had died suddenly ten years before, on the day the architect submitted his drawings, but no connection between the two events had ever been established so the fellow went scot free. Mr. Oxenford liked the plans and proceeded with the building.

Mr. Oxenford's only child, Flora, reigned over the house, but her reign was not happy. She was twenty-five years old, a big plump maiden obsessed by the awful fear that she was never going to be married. Her days were barren and empty, for she wasn't a girl who made friends easily, and most of the girls she had known in school had married and moved away or were busy managing homes of their own. After Flora conferred in the morning with the cook and gave the servants their orders she had nothing to do. So she spent long hours lying on her bed staring at the ceiling and daydreaming about a differently ordered existence.

In those dreams she was always the heroine, wand-slim and petite, and a half-dozen men flocked around her, and she was cool and lovely with brilliant *mots* tripping off her tongue, and in the end she and the best-looking man of all went strolling through the moonlight and on into velvet shadows, and then something delirious happened the exact nature of which she did not yet, at twenty-five, understand.

For the most part, in common with other men, her father ignored her. He was gone all day at his office, and at dinner he seldom spoke, for his thoughts were full of plans for acquiring more money and power. To him a meal was not a pleasant social interlude but a necessary nuisance, like furnace stoking, and he brought to the table the same eating manners that had come west with him as a young man. Before tasting a bite he salted everything, then dumped three spoonfuls of sugar into his coffee and bent nearer the table and ate like a hungry dog. He was inordinately fond of soup, and you could hear him consuming it all over the house. He was secretly proud of his lack of table manners, for he enjoyed thinking of himself as a self-made man who had never had time for the social graces.

A meal for him was no meal at all unless pie terminated it, and after swallowing the last mouthful he straightened and emitted three little belches. Never four; never two; always three. Then he pulled the napkin from his collar, rolled it into a neat cylinder and stuck it through his silver napkin ring. And finally, he brought a quill toothpick from his vest pocket and went to work with it. One of his little eccentricities was that no money should be spent for toothpicks. When he ate out at noon he pilfered several quills from the dish on the cashier's desk and brought them home. "I got where I am by watching the pennies," he would say.

He was stingy about his clothes too, wearing his black suits till the elbows shone and dots of grease gleamed on the cheap cloth. He bought them ready-made and they hung awkwardly from his big bony frame. Theoretically his hair and whiskers were white, but actually they were the yellowish color of old piano keys.

At home he passed most of his time in a room at the back of the house which was called the library. It had everything to deserve that name except books. For Mr. Oxenford was a practical man, and he had been heard to proclaim that people could find more useful ways to spend their time than by burying their noses in books. Where would he have got, if he had followed such a custom? He didn't exactly forbid his daughter to read, but if he caught her at it he rebuked her with his heavy-footed sarcasm. So Flora's reading was restricted to the newspapers. She didn't mind.

With the coming of spring that year her listlessness and despondency increased, and she had never felt more depressed than on that evening when she first saw Burgoyne. At dinner her father mentioned that two men were coming on business, but she imagined them to be older men, married men; and after the meal she left the house and with leaden feet moved about the garden. It was a lyrical evening, an evening for love, but all her argosies of hope had long since become rotting hulks in the Sargasso Sea of her despair. At the lower end of the garden, frogs were singing, and through the tepid air currents of sweetness flowed, but the scent of early blossoms and flowers meant nothing to her. It was an oppressive night, she thought; and she stood inert, staring at the shadows, and then her throat filled and big tears rolled down her cheeks. At last she plodded back toward the house and sighed into a rocking chair on the front veranda. Horses were clop-clopping along the avenue, and through the open window of a house next door floated the sound of a piano playing a sentimental ballad. The music drenched her with self-pity.

And once again she turned over and over in her thoughts the old problem of finding a mate. Her luck, she thought, had been very bad; God knew she had tried hard enough. She told herself that she was not actually homely, and that was true; and surely no young man would resent the fact that some day she would inherit considerable money. That was also true. Then why—?

But soon she grew weary of any realistic analysis of her troubles, for that demanded an intellectual vigor and honesty which she did not possess. She fell into daydreaming again, about the day when some foreign nobleman would visit Tamarack and sue for her hand. Sue for her hand: her thoughts were always garbed in such romantic clichés.

Then she became aware of two cab horses turning in from the avenue, hauling a closed vehicle along the driveway toward the porte-cochere at the east side of the house. That would be her father's friends, coming to drone on interminably about business. Her interest in them was scant, but because she was bored and had nothing better to do she arose and stood in the vine shadows where the front veranda curved into the side veranda. Light was falling from the side door, and her father emerged to greet his guests. She observed him distastefully, that bony, sharp-dealing, yellow-whiskered man.

The cab door opened, and there was a gleam of polished boots and dark cane as a small bearded man stepped out. She had never seen him before, but she knew instantly he was Somebody, and more than ever she was ashamed of her father's shabby clothes. Then a second man alighted from the cab, and although Flora's body remained breathlessly still her spirit fluttered and swooned.

He was a young man, big and broad-shouldered, with large hands and a deep chest and a noble head. A strong body. Powerful. Strong enough and big enough, she thought deliriously, to sweep you off your feet. He wore a gray-checked suit and a crisp tie, and his stalwart masculinity reminded her of those sterling young men whose exciting physiques loomed with so much virility in drawings by Charles Dana Gibson.

Then he spoke, introducing the two older men, and his booming voice, so hearty and powerful, produced in her a delicious shortness of breath. After her father led his guests into the house she tiptoed to the door, peering through the screen. She glimpsed the young man turning into the library at the far end of the long corridor.

Who was he? And was he married? No!—she couldn't believe that. Her heart told her he was single and that all these years Providence had been saving him for her. That he should suddenly appear at her home on this April night seemed to her marvelously romantic.

And suddenly she experienced annoyance and anger against her father, because he had known this young man but had been too self-centered and unimaginative to invite him here before and introduce him. But her anger passed quickly, crowded out of her thoughts by the plans she was making to meet him before he left tonight. First, however, she wanted to see him again; and filled with a sense of adventure she left the veranda and moved around the house to the library wing. Gone was her leaden-footed plodding; she tiptoed lightly.

The library windows were open, and as Flora approached she could hear voices inside. Near the house a lilac bush grew, and from that evening onward lilacs seemed to her the most romantic of flowers and April the most romantic of months. Long after she became Mrs. Gus Burgoyne she looked back upon this evening as a shining miracle.

Peering through the branches, she could see her father leaning back in his chair, his bony fingers stroking his whiskers as he listened to the man with the gold-headed cane. Then her eager gaze found the young man in the checked suit. He was sitting in a tipped-back chair, hands in pockets, hair rumpled, his countenance beaming.

"What do you think of the proposition, Gus?" her father asked.

(So his name was Gus! Wonderful name! Beautiful name!)

The young man stood up and put one foot on the chair seat and leaned toward her father, wagging his forefinger. She thought he looked masterful, commanding.

"Sam," he said, "it's like I've always said. There's nothing like elephants. You ask me, I think we're lucky that Mr. Pawpacker got in touch with us. You and I have a lot to learn about elephants, but he knows 'em. He knows the whole game. I think we ought to come to terms with Mr. Pawpacker."

So Flora realized that the deal was about to be closed, and panic touched her lest they finish the business before she had a chance to meet the young man. She turned and hurried through the back door, into the kitchen. A mirror hung there, and Flora studied herself. No, she was not actually homely. Her features were quite regular: nothing essentially wrong with them. Her hair was red. Not copper-colored or flame-colored; just red. She had the white, fine, baby-soft skin that sometimes goes with red hair, and her full mouth was soft and a bit babyish, too. Her eyes were reddish brown. Usually they possessed the soft, vacant expression of a dairy cow, but tonight her excitement and burning purpose had brought to them a hint of fire. Indeed, her whole countenance had an unaccustomed glow; if ever Flora had approached beauty, it was now.

With a beating heart she moved along the hall toward the library. Just before she reached the closed door she paused, doubting that she could go through with it. Her throat filled; her breathing had become shallow and choppy. She felt a vein pulsating in her throat, and suddenly she had a wild desire to flee. But it was now or never, so taking a grip on herself she rapped, and when her father said, "Come in" she opened the door.

Her tremendous effort at self-control saved her—saved her from banality, from coyness. It gave her a kind of dignity, not unbecoming; so that Gus Burgoyne's first impression was of a large girl whose Junoesque figure was somehow appealing to his robust appetites.

She did not look at Gus Burgoyne or at Ivan Pawpacker. She gazed straight at Samuel Oxenford and said in a level voice:

"Father, if you and your guests would like me to, I'll make coffee and serve you some cakes."

"Coffee?" blurted out Mr. Oxenford. "Why, it ain't been long since we et."

Flora blushed, and in her thoughts she consigned Samuel Oxenford to a thousand hells.

It was Gus Burgoyne who charged gallantly to her rescue. He had arisen when she entered, and now he beamed and announced heartily:

"Coffee? That'd be fine. Taste good."

Flora glanced at him and smiled.

"Don't believe we've met this lady," Burgoyne boomed. "Are you Miss Oxenford?"

Not trusting her voice, Flora nodded.

"I'm Gus Burgoyne. Old friend of your father. This is Mr. Pawpacker. . . . You just go right ahead, Miss Oxenford, and fix up those cakes and that coffee. And bring along some for yourself."

He wanted to know her better! As Flora retreated along the hall, her brain sang, her blood sang. She had come through the first skirmish victorious. She wanted to cheer and weep and laugh. What a man he was! How masterful! When her father's boorish stupidity bungled the situation, Burgoyne had taken charge, rescued it. She loved him. She had loved him from the instant she beheld him alighting from the cab. And she thought she would go on loving him till the end of her days; and she did; she did.

A. H. Burgoyne—that was how he signed his name. The initials stood for Augustus Howard. His mother, a maiden lady named Doll Burgoyne, had christened him in honor of two men, either of whom might have been his father. She was a judicious woman, and hence had bestowed second honors upon Howard Clancy, a fireman employed by the Chicago, Tamarack & Pacific Railroad. Poor Clancy never lived to set eyes upon his possible offspring, having been scalded to death in a wreck on the Omaha run in the spring of 1880, some months before little Gus was born. In her room above Mahoney's Saloon at the corner of Second Avenue and the railroad tracks in Clayton Junction, Doll grieved for Clancy. "There'll never be another Clancy," she always said. He was a big, black-haired Irishman with an Irishman's humorous tongue. He always had her laughing, even when they made love.

Clayton Junction was a smoky railroad town, a division point. It bounded the city of Tamarack on the west; Tamarack's back door; Tamarack's Jersey City. On the vaudeville stage in Tamarack, the hayseed comedians always said they came from Clayton Junction, and that line never failed to get a laugh.

The more probable father of little Gus was a railroad man also, but nothing so lowly as a fireman. Doll never could remember his exact position; it was something away up there in the economic scale. "He's a big man with the line," was how she thought of him. Physically, too, he was big, like a drawing of Capital in a cartoon. He wore black broadcloth suits with white piping on the vests; a big diamond sparkled in his cravat; and when he wanted to read he wore nose glasses on a cord. Class!

When they met he was in his fifties, his hair already salted with gray. He was standing at the bar in Mahoney's Saloon, his big fingers curled around a little glass of whiskey. In contrast with that shabby, beer-smelling place, he radiated prosperity. You could almost imagine tiny dollar signs stamped upon the links which fastened together his starched cuffs.

He had arrived from Chicago that morning on a tour of inspection, traveling in a private car which even now stood on a siding down by the freight warehouse, awaiting his bidding. The car, it was rumored, had a colored porter and monogrammed napkins and silver. In the saloon the other customers gave him plenty of elbowroom. They were

railroad men, mostly, wearing caps and overalls and bandannas at their
throats.

Because of his presence, the conversation was more subdued than
usual; monosyllabic. He drank slowly; and once, carrying his glass,
he paced leisurely over to the window and stood gazing through the
specked pane. Even in those days Clayton Junction looked old and
down-at-the-heels. The early afternoon was windy, and dust went staggering over the gray cobbles of Second Avenue. Whenever a switch
engine chugged over the crossing, a fine hail of cinders rattled against
the saloon windows.

He returned to the bar, paid for his drink; and then it was that he
heard footsteps descending a wooden stairway beyond the wall at the
north end of the room. A frosted-glass door opened and two young
women entered. They were Doll Burgoyne and her sister, Lucy, embarking upon a shopping tour to Tamarack, and they had entered the
saloon to get money from Tim. Tim Mahoney—he was Lucy's husband.

Doll was the younger of the two and the better-looking. She was
twenty, with flawless skin and violet eyes and dark hair which she
wore today in a cluster of short curls at the back of her pretty head.
She had style, a certain flair for clothes. Always had had. Even if she
did say so herself, she looked like a million dollars in that gray hat with
its purple plume, and in that French gray suit which molded so faithfully the curves of her lovely figure.

While Lucy and Tim whispered about family finances, Doll waited
at a discreet distance. A couple of yards separated her from the portly,
rich-looking man, and she surmised that he was the important person
from Chicago, a vice-president or something, of whom Tim had spoken
this noon. Traveled in his own railroad car. Her gaze wandered to
the mirror behind the bar, and by one of those interesting accidents in
human relationships his gaze happened to meet hers. He smiled.

Well, gosh, you didn't want to get the reputation of being stuck up,
did you? What else could you do but smile back? Besides, he was a
big man with the line, out here alone, and he'd think Clayton Junction
a mighty unfriendly place if its citizens didn't smile when they were
smiled at. It would be tantamount to insulting the entire Chicago,
Tamarack & Pacific Railroad not to smile; and she had a warm place
in her heart for the Chicago, Tamarack & Pacific, with Clancy working
for them, and all.

Her smile brought him along the bar to her, and what he said surprised her. You could have knocked her over with a feather.

"You look like Paris in that suit, Dolly," he said.

Those violet eyes widened as she looked up at him.

"How did you know my name?"

For a half-second his ruddy countenance showed surprise, too; then he chuckled. And in a confidential tone he said:

"A little bird told me."

"Now listen," she said, "don't give me that."

"It's the truth. A little bird perched right here on my shoulder and said, 'Mr. Phelan, when you get to Clayton Junction you'll see the best-looking girl in the world, and her name will be Doll.'"

"Oh—*you!*" Doll said, and although her words were depreciatory her tone was exceedingly genial.

"It's a fact," Augustus Phelan said.

"I'll bet I know how you knew my name," Doll said. "I'll bet Tim told you."

"Maybe he did. It's a nice name. It would have to be, for a lady like you."

"I think you're just blarneying me," Doll remonstrated. Her voice had a metallic, brash quality; but brash in a most amiable way. "You're Irish, that's what you are, and you're just laying it on."

"I can't deny I'm Irish," he confessed, "but you can't deny I've spoken the truth. Just look at your face in the mirror."

"Oh—*you!*" Doll repeated; and then this fascinating discussion was interrupted by the arrival of Lucy.

"I'm ready, Sis," she said.

At twenty-three, Lucy was not as pleasingly plump as Doll; she had high cheekbones and a thin face and long slender hands. Whereas Doll was poised and self-assured and confident that life would bestow good things upon her, Lucy was a bit apologetic. She was somewhat flat in the chest and round in the shoulders; in twenty years she would be a weary sharp-faced woman talking in a weary, thin voice. Not Doll. You felt that at forty Doll would still be erect and well-upholstered, a magnificent figure of a woman, good-natured and easygoing, riding through life on plush cushions.

"This is my sister," Doll said. "Mrs. Mahoney. Sis, this is Mr. Phelan."

"I'm glad to know you, Sis," said Mr. Phelan. "I'm always glad to meet a relative of my old friend, Doll."

Lucy genuflected like a fox terrier, and Doll grinned:

"'Old friends!' Listen to the man. Mister, you're a fast worker."

"I'd still be laying ties if I hadn't been. What are you girls up to?"

"We're going to Tamarack. Shopping."

"It's my lucky day," Mr. Phelan said. "For that's where I'm going, too, and now I'll have the company of two charming ladies."

"Oh—*you!*" Doll laughed.

Till Doll had mentioned Tamarack, Gus Phelan's plans had not included a trip there, but he was not a man to hold unwaveringly to a rigid course of action. Long ago he had discovered that life's most delectable experiences were those which occurred unexpectedly, so when adventure laughed in his ear and beckoned him to follow down some blossoming lane, he invariably accepted the invitation.

And he believed his habit of living spontaneously was largely responsible for his success with the Chicago, Tamarack & Pacific. He liked his work—what Irishman didn't love the movement and tooting engines and waving lanterns of the railroad business?—but he knew that fondness for one's work did not alone insure success. He had seen too many joyless fellows slaving-hopelessly away at clerk's jobs. No, something more was needed, and that something was adventure. And to Gus Phelan, adventure and pretty women were synonymous.

Adventure refreshed him, kept him alert and witty. It even contributed toward the success of his marriage. There were times when Nora and his eight children might have weighed him down with a sense of responsibility, save for adventure. To him domesticity seemed as unalluring as a safety pin, but because of such interludes as this one with Doll Burgoyne, he was a model husband and father.

He followed Lucy and Doll to the frosted-glass door. It opened into a narrow hall with steps climbing to the Mahoney living quarters above the saloon and with a door leading to Second Avenue. As the two women preceded him to the street, his heart was warmed by the lyric way Doll's bustled skirt trembled and swayed.

A few minutes before, Second Avenue had seemed a squalid street, littered and dirty, but not so now. Strolling along the board sidewalk, with Lucy on one arm and Doll on the other, he felt like a king of the earth. In his spirit, brass bands were playing and flags were flying, and he felt young again and free as a colt.

"How do we get to Tamarack?" he asked, and Doll told him a horse-car should be waiting at the next corner.

"Horsecar! Isn't there a livery stable where a man can hire a rig?"

There was; and while Gus Phelan strutted with the proprietor into the barn to select a team, Lucy and Doll waited in the office. Its air had a rich, horsy smell.

A dreamy smile veiled Doll's lips and eyes. Lucy observed her.

"You look about ready to purr," she said.

Doll smiled secretly.

"You ought to be ashamed," Lucy said, "just meeting him like that. Look how you've got him going."

"He's nice," Doll said. "Different."

"He's old enough to be your father."

"What of it?"

"You ought to be ashamed. Think of Clancy."

"Clancy's in Omaha."

"If **you** go skating around, Clancy will be sore. You ought to be ashamed. Clancy wants to marry you."

"I'll handle Clancy," Doll said. "You leave Clancy to me, Sis." And she added, "I've been thinking."

"Don't go to thinking," Lucy said.

"A girl marries," Doll said, "and what does she get out of it? A girl marries a fellow like Clancy, and there're kids and debts and a wash-board every Monday. No thanks. It's a big world, Sis."

"You're getting pretty high and mighty," Lucy said. "Just because a rich man looked at you."

Doll shrugged, perfectly good-humored and unruffled.

"There must be lots of men like that," she murmured. "Interesting men who have money."

"I don't know what Mamma would have thought, hearing you talk like that."

"What did Mamma ever get out of it? What do you get out of it?" And then, seeing a sudden glisten in Lucy's eyes, Doll put a hand on her arm. "I'm sorry, Sis. Tim's nice, and if that's the way you like it, that's fine. It's just that you and I are different, that's all."

"You'll get yourself into trouble, thinking things like that."

A merry twinkle came into Doll's eyes.

"No woman ever got herself into trouble just thinking," she said.

Despite herself, Lucy giggled.

"You're a case, Sis. You're really a case."

Doll wandered to the window, gazing out at the shabby façades lining the street, and when she spoke, very low, it was more to herself than to Lucy:

"I don't know yet what I want—not for sure. But it isn't Clayton Junction, and it isn't Tamarack. Maybe it's Chicago. Maybe even New York."

A thunder of hoofs on the stable floor interrupted her reverie, and she turned to see Gus Phelan in a bright-red phaeton, pulled by a team of spirited chestnut horses.

"Better than a horsecar," Doll thought. "Gosh, lots better . . ." And it occurred to her that this was what she wanted always: to ride in a phaeton instead of a horsecar, to walk in silks instead of calico, to drench herself in luxury, in a creamy, fluffy world of tinted lights and lace and champagne and mirrors and gilt and jewels and laughter. To roll in it, like a rapturous cat in catnip.

While the stableman held the horses, Gus handed Doll and Lucy up into the rig. He accomplished this with a flourish. The rig looked brand-new, its seats upholstered in light yellow. A delicious little sigh escaped Doll. Then they were out of the stable and off, the spanking team stepping high, the varnished wheel spokes glittering.

In those years, the eastern edge of Clayton Junction and the western edge of Tamarack had not yet reached out and embraced; marshland and brushland separated them. At the limits of Clayton Junction the cobbles ended and the phaeton rolled along a white, dusty road. It was September, the sky lightly grayed with clouds, the weeds lightly grayed with dust. Doll pointed to a thorn tree growing by the roadside.

"Look," she exclaimed, "red haws."

"Want some?" Gus Phelan reined in the horses. "Here Lucy, you hold the lines."

He eased his portly body out of the rig and bustled back to the tree.

Lucy gave Doll a half-amused, half-reproachful glance.

"The way you've got him going, Sis!" she breathed. "You ought to be ashamed."

Gus brought her a heap of the cherry-colored haws, cupped in his big hands.

"They're good," he declared. "I sampled one."

Sight of those haws, so autumnal red, brought a momentary nostalgia to Doll, for once when she was fourteen, back in her home town of Sioux Creek, there had been a school picnic and she and a boy had wandered off into the timber and had picked haws. She remembered the breathlessness in her lungs when she realized he was going to kiss her, and how when he did kiss her, her whole being burst into flower. She had been wanting that, more or less consciously, for a long, long time. Throughout her teens she had been crazy about the boys, always in love with somebody. After she was sixteen or seventeen, marriage proposals began coming her way, some very good too, but she turned them down because in the back of her mind a voice always said that out beyond the skyrim there were cities where life was shining.

The carriage rolled over a creek bridge and climbed a wooded hill. At the summit the brick pavement of Tamarack began, and as the horses' shoes rang against it Doll glanced back. She could see for miles and miles. South of Clayton Junction a river meandered through timbered lowlands, and a tiny-looking pumping station was puffing away, sending water to the railroad shops. From the east and from the west, steel tracks raced toward Clayton Junction, branching into an amazing number of sidings. Those rails had brought Gus Phelan from Chicago and they would bring Clancy back from Omaha tomorrow. Clancy. Yes, she could marry him, but she wasn't going to.

Phelan tickled the horses with the whip, and they went clacking briskly along the avenue.

"I've been thinking, girls," he said. "Why don't we all stay in town and eat supper together? You'll be hungry after your shopping."

There was a moment of hesitation. Then Doll spoke.

"Lucy couldn't. Tim's always cross if she isn't there to cook his supper. But she could go home on the horsecar, and I could stay. It sounds like fun."

"It will be," Gus Phelan said.

Doll and Gus had agreed to meet at six o'clock outside the Arcade Dry Goods Store, and when she arrived at five after six he was patiently waiting, holding a paper cone that wrapped a bouquet of sweet peas.

"Sweets to the sweet," he said.

She exclaimed delightedly and buried her face in the flowers, closing her eyes and inhaling their fragrance. Clancy never gave her flowers. She was sure such a thing had never occurred to him, but if it had he would have thought it sissy. Perhaps Clancy assumed that giving her himself was enough. He was a lusty fellow with thrillingly wide shoulders and biceps like lumps of pig iron, and he was such a jolly man; but sometimes she resented his assumption that she was his girl now, belonging to him alone.

"They're wonderful," she told Gus Phelan.

He beamed; and then like a small boy bursting with a secret too tremendous to keep he said:

"I bought you something else, too."

"Oh, Gus! What is it?"

"Now, now!" he said, patting her shoulder. "Let's wait a while for that."

"I'm just crazy to know what it is."

"Now, now, Dolly! You know the old saying—curiosity killed a cat."

He took her arm, and as they went marching along the street she remembered another old saying. Better an old man's darling, it went, than a young man's slave.

The sidewalk was crowded with clerks just released from their counters and bookkeepers just unchained from their high stools, and she compared them with Gus. Their faces were thin and gray and wore the meek look of men resigned to taking orders; men who would never set the world on fire. Gus Phelan's big countenance was florid, a garden where whiskey flowers blossomed, and his craggy nose and solid jaw were the features of a dominant man. His mouth was smiling now, but she could imagine it hard and authoritative as it shot out commands. She sensed that he could be ruthless. Maybe men who clubbed their way to the top had to be.

Shadows were gathering in the street; they passed a man who had mounted a short ladder and was lighting a benzene street lamp. A hint of frost edged the thickening air. Doll thought of Clayton Junction at twilight: dogs barking and mothers calling children in from play and the constant coughing and moaning and bell-ringing of locomotives, prowling in the yards. Sis would be in the kitchen, frying pork chops for Tim. Doll was glad she was here.

They turned down a side street; and darkness had changed the store fronts into cliffs of shadow by the time they reached Marlow's Restaurant. Before they even entered, Doll realized that she was about to enjoy a new experience. She had never eaten in such a fashionable place before. The front of the restaurant was not so much imposing as secretive with quiet luxury. You couldn't see through the windows because they were divided into many lozenge-shaped panes of red and blue glass; and the door was a great slab of heavy wood.

Ordinarily, she would have felt shy about entering such a place, but protected by Gus Phelan's masterful manner she felt composed and happy. He swung open the door and in they went, into that restaurant where your feet sank into a thick carpet, where waiters in black suits and boiled shirts hurried to and fro balancing trays on their palms, where lamps poured forth honeyed light and shadows enriched the paneled walls.

Rumor had it that the headwaiter was an Italian count; but rumor exaggerated slightly. He was Italian, but the son of a cobbler. To Gus it would have made no difference if he had been a crown prince; just another wop. So when the headwaiter decided they would occupy a table in the center of the room, and Gus preferred a table by the wall, they sat by the wall.

The bill of fare, an enormous card, confused Doll with its variety and its words in a foreign language, but she was a practical girl who had always side-stepped problems that she couldn't solve. So instead of letting the foreign words daunt her she said:

"I'll take what you take, Gus. Men know so much about good food."

"It'd take a Philadelphia lawyer to figure this out," Gus said. He looked up at their waiter and demanded, "Tony, you speaka da English, huh?"

"Yes, sir. My brother, he's Tony, sir. I'm Gabriele."

"Gabriele, huh? You ever work on the railroad? You know—hitta da spike with da sledge?"

"No, sir. No, I—"

"Your papa ever work for the railroad?"

"Oh, sure, Papa works for the Tamarack Line."

"All right, Tony—you tell your papa you waited on Gus Phelan tonight. He'll know who you mean. And here's something else—you tell the chef I'm here." Gus flapped a big hand against the bill of fare. "This stuff don't mean anything, Tony. So you tell the chef to send us in a couple of orders with soup and roast beef and all the fixings, and if it's not good tell him I'll be waiting in the alley for him. And bring us some wine, Tony. Make it dry, and the best in the house." And after the waiter had retired Gus clasped his hands on the table and confided, "Section hands or waiters, they're all the same. Have to keep after them."

And while they waited to be served he told her how he had begun working for the railroad when he was a young man. The job was laying track, but because he was a good fist fighter it wasn't long till he had been made a straw boss, and then a foreman; he knew how to handle men. The wine came, and the dinner, and he talked on, reliving his old triumphs. Sometimes Doll asked a question or made a brief comment but mostly she remained silent. Nobody had ever told her that the way to please men was to listen and listen and listen some more; she knew that instinctively.

She heard every word he said, but this didn't prevent her mind from working independently on a different level, so while he talked she observed the other people, comparing the women's clothes with her own and wishing she might have a pearl necklace such as one woman wore. But the necklace didn't spoil her evening, for she knew in her bones that some day jewels would come to her. She felt serene and warm with quiet happiness.

After the meal Gus brought out a fat brown cigar, putting it to his nose and sniffing the rich leaf.

"Mind if I smoke, Dolly?"

Her laugh tinkled merrily as glass chimes.

"Of course not, Gus. I'd like to have you. I like the smell of cigar smoke."

And that was true. All the odors and surfaces of the world of men were sweet to her. She liked the sound of their voices and the rough nap of their suits and their faces against her cheek; she liked their robust laughing and their zest. Men. She was so genuinely fond of them that it seemed petty to disappoint them when they desired her, and so although the world might have thought her a girl of easy virtue it wasn't that at all: she was just kindhearted.

"We could go to a theater," Gus said, when they emerged from the restaurant. "Of course, we have quite a drive back to Clayton Junction, and it would get you home late. But if you'd like to—"

He didn't want to; she could sense that. She would have enjoyed it, but she was too wise a girl to be gluttonous, so she said:

"There'll be other nights for that."

It pleased him. He gave her arm a squeeze, and as they walked toward the stable where he had left the horses, he said:

"Dolly, I like you. It's not just that you're pretty. You've got brains, too. You're one of the most interesting talkers I've met."

On the way to Clayton Junction he drove the horses leisurely. The wind had died at sunset and it was a fine night, the sky ablaze with stars. After they left Tamarack's last street lamp behind, the horses picked their own way along the dark road. Down there in the lowlands, mist was rising from the marshes. He slipped his arm around her and they kissed several times.

Fewer street lamps burned in Clayton Junction than in Tamarack; it was a poor man's town. The ugly little houses, begrimed by day, were heaps of shadows now; the livery stable was a larger heap of shadow, a whale-oil lamp weakly lighting the office windows, a smoky lantern hanging just inside the wide entrance. While Gus paid the stableman for the rig, Doll waited outside. From far to the west, up the long river valley, floated the wail of a locomotive, mournful and nostalgic.

Gus joined her and they groped through the darkness. Their evening together had an unfinished quality that disturbed her. Gus must have felt it too, for he said:

"Ever seen inside a private car, Dolly? Mine is pretty fine. Would you like to see it?"

"Yes," she murmured. "Yes, I would, Gus."

They toiled along the uneven board sidewalk of Second Avenue. Mahoney's Saloon was still lighted, and inside somebody was playing a lewd song on the tinny piano. As they approached, a man reeled out and stood swaying, in the middle of the sidewalk. He was a young man in workman's clothes, very drunk, and when they tried to pass he doffed his hat extravagantly and mumbled insulting words.

"Stand back," Gus told Doll; and then his big fist blurted out and smashed into the man's face. The drunk's knees buckled and he fell to the walk. Gus kicked him into the gutter. Then he dusted his hands together and took Doll's arm.

"I hate drunks," he said.

She felt strangely moved. He was old enough to be her father, Sis had said. Yes; but his body was still powerful. Clayton Junction was notoriously unsafe for a girl walking alone after dark; it was especially hazardous to linger around the railroad tracks, with so many hoboes. But now as they stumbled along the siding toward his car, she felt perfectly protected, and it was a fine feeling.

They passed the freight warehouse where by lantern light men were rolling great hogsheads into a boxcar; and in the darkness beyond they reached his car. He helped her up the steps to a back platform and opened the door. The observation end of the car had a rich red carpet; the woodwork was all curlicues and gilt; everything exuded luxury. As they entered, a dozing Negro in a uniform bestirred himself.

"I won't need you any more tonight," Gus said.

The Negro vanished along a corridor; somewhere a door closed.

Doll seated herself in a chair with blue plush cushions. Gus moved from window to window, pulling down the thin green shades.

"Do you like it?" he asked.

"It's wonderful. Wonderful," she repeated, stroking the chair arm.

"Maybe you'll like this, too."

He brought a small package from his pocket, wrapped in white paper, and while she opened it he stood huge and smiling. The outer box contained a second box, and it too was wrapped. Then she un-lidded the second box. Inside nestled a gold watch, small and finely made, with a thin lid that snapped open and shut. She would wear it on her shoulder. It brought an exclamation of pure delight from Doll. Her eyes were shining and she stood up and snuggled against him.

"Oh, Gus—how did you know I wanted one of these?"

They kissed, standing there, and gradually the gold watch receded into unimportance.

All during that fall and winter, business brought Gus to Clayton Junction, and they had jolly times together. He was always as welcome as Santa Claus on Christmas Eve. Many were the gifts she had from Gus; flowers and bonbons and jewelry of the less expensive kind. Sometimes he slipped her currency too, which she could exchange for clothes at the stores in Tamarack.

He told her about his wife and children in Chicago, but this didn't disturb Doll. Chicago seemed far away. Nor did she feel she was wronging his wife by being the other woman in his life. Doll's logic was flawless, although it was destined never to attain popularity among married women. She reasoned that if his wife loved him she would naturally wish to see him happy, and that if Doll's company made him happy, why then his wife should encourage his trips to Clayton Junction. Gus laughed when she told him these conclusions, and said he guessed she didn't understand Mrs. Phelan.

Those were happy months for Doll, but they were not without complications. She could not receive Gus in the Mahoney living quarters above the saloon, because Tim Mahoney had taken a dislike to him. Tim was an Ulster man, whereas Gus's forebears had lived near Dublin, and this was an instance of geography's being responsible for war. Tim was tall, lanky, sandy, dour, and he often told Doll and Lucy what he would do to that old rooster Phelan if he caught him on the premises. The premises included the saloon, of course, but that didn't count; that was business. So Doll and Gus met in clandestine fashion, but instead of detracting from their affair this secrecy gave it spice.

Then, too, there was Howard Clancy. He was South Irish also, but Tim liked him, perhaps because he was a bachelor with the honorable intention of marrying Doll and taking her off the Mahoneys' hands. In discussing Clancy, Tim would say, "Sure, he's a Cork Irishman, but what of it? You can't hold against a man the place where his parents were born." If Doll pointed out that this live-and-let-live spirit should also apply to Gus, Tim would freeze up and scowl and declare that was different.

Sometimes Doll laughed and told Lucy:

"Sis, I feel like a piece of meat in the middle of an Irish stew."

But she really felt more like a juggler that autumn, she was so busy not letting her left hand know what her right was doing. It was her hunch that if Clancy learned about Gus he would be hurt and perhaps annoyed, so to spare his feelings she did not mention those suppers in Tamarack and those evenings in the private car. She always managed things so that she would go out with Gus on the nights when Clancy was in Omaha.

And it was necessary to avoid wearing the gold watch or any of Gus's other gifts when Clancy called, and to guard her tongue so she wouldn't make references to Tamarack restaurants or shows she had attended with Gus. What a nuisance! Once she said:

"You know, Sis, sometimes I think I'll tell Gus and Clancy all about each other. It's too much work keeping them apart."

"Sis!" Lucy breathed. "Never do that!"

"Well, maybe not—but I feel like it. Turn them loose and let the best man win."

"Honestly, Sis," Lucy laughed, "I never know what you'll do or say next. You're the limit."

Lucy derived a great deal of vicarious enjoyment from Doll's escapades; in her eyes Doll was quite a heroine. Doll was so daring, so warm-blooded and fun-loving, such a believer in living while you lived. Things happened to her, and in her presence everything seemed colorful. On the mornings after Doll had been out with Gus, Lucy tiptoed about the house so as not to awaken her. Doll hated rising early. When she awakened about ten o'clock she always called out cheerfully, "Good morning, Sis—is the coffee pot on?" And Lucy would open her bedroom door and see her lying there looking as beautiful and comfort-loving as a pretty young cat. "I've got so much to tell you, Sis," Doll would smile. "What would you take to bring my breakfast in to me?"

Some of Lucy's happiest hours were spent sitting in that bedroom while Doll ate breakfast. They always laughed a great deal, but Doll's comments on Gus's foibles were never acid or bitter. "He's such a dear man," she always said. "So generous."

And Doll was generous, too. If Gus had given her money the night before she would say, "Hand me my purse, will you, Sis?" Then she would snap it open and rustle out currency and flip a bill or two to Lucy.

"I don't know, Sis," Lucy would say. "I don't know whether I should take it."

"Why Sis, why not? Go ahead. Easy come, easy go. And there's more where that came from."

But that idyllic state of affairs couldn't last forever, and late in February Clancy learned that Doll had been going about with Gus. Nearly everybody in Clayton Junction knew by that time, but nobody cared to risk Clancy's temper by telling him. As it was, a drinking pal told him, in Mahoney's Saloon, but instead of being grateful for the tip-off, Clancy went wild.

He roared the fellow had insulted Doll, and he lunged at him and knocked him down to the sawdust floor. He was about to stomp him, too, but one of the man's friends, Phineas O'Brien, sought to prevent this. So Clancy fought O'Brien. By this time the man on the floor howled to his feet and Clancy began getting the worst of it. Marcus Corrigan, who had gone to school with Clancy, couldn't permit that. So he joined the fray. A freight conductor, Red Murphy, who had never liked Corrigan, saw his chance now, so he too dived into the melee; and after that everybody joined the battle just for the hell of it.

The place might well have been wrecked, except for Tim Mahoney's clear thinking. He opened a drawer behind the bar and seized a leather frankfurter loaded with lead shot. Stepping into the brawl, he swung that sap lightly and expertly, delivering sleep-producing but not skull-fracturing taps behind each participant's ear. It was a shame and a sacrilege to ruin a beautiful fight like that, but Mahoney had his tables and mirror to think of.

Soon the floor was littered with loggy bodies; all except Clancy's. Because Clancy was his probable future brother-in-law, Mahoney didn't slug him. After his last opponent was floored, Clancy stood still waving his fists, looking dazed, his lips swollen and bleeding. Then he turned and stumbled to the frosted-glass door and climbed the stairs.

Mahoney wanted to join him, but he had work to do first. He sent his bar boy out to the pump to fetch pails of water, and he doused a full pail upon each knocked-out man. As they blinked toward consciousness, Mahoney dragged them to the door and rolled them to the sidewalk.

"If you bastards want to fight," he snapped, "fight outside." Then he told the bar boy to take care of the place, and he went upstairs.

When he opened the sitting-room door, he beheld an odd tableau. Clancy sat in a straight-backed chair, elbows on his knees, head in his hands. His drooping body looked heartbroken. Lucy stood at the window, gazing out at the night, dabbing her eyes. Only Doll seemed unruffled. Cushioned by pillows, she lounged on the plush sofa beneath the framed motto, "God Bless Our Home."

"Come in, Tim," she said. "Did the fight do much damage?"

"It's little enough you'd care if it did," he said.

Doll sighed and shook her head.

"I can't understand why everyone gets so upset about these things. Sis has the weeps, and I guess Clancy has, too."

From Clancy came a choked-up groan. He remained bent over, his fingers tenderly probing his sore skull, and he moaned, "God in heaven, God in heaven." Then he gazed up at Mahoney and said sorrowfully, "She admits it, Tim. Chasing around with that old buck. And I loved her, that I did. I worshipped her like an angel, and I thought I wasn't fit to kiss the hem of her skirt."

"You kissed more than the hem of my skirt," Doll reminded him.

Clancy's ears turned red. Creaking to his feet, he shuffled over to Lucy and put a hand on her shoulder. "Good-by, Sis." Then he shook hands with Mahoney. "Good-by, Tim. Take care of yourself." And without a glance at Doll he opened the door and clumped down the stair.

"See there," Tim snapped. "Now look what you've done, you little alley cat. He's gone and he won't come back."

"Oh yes he will," Doll said. "He'll be back, don't worry." And to Lucy she said, "Well Sis, at least I can start wearing my gold watch now."

A sudden giggle came from Lucy's tear-streaked face.

"Honestly, Sis," she said, "you're a case. You're really a case."

Despite her casualness toward Clancy that night, Doll felt sorry for him. She was not cold-blooded. But she hated scenes and she hated sentimentality and pettiness. She wanted life to move along smoothly, with everybody liking everybody else. Why, she asked herself, did people fuss so much about inconsequential things? She thought it selfish and little of Clancy to resent her going out with Gus. On the nights when Gus made love to her, Clancy had been in Omaha, hadn't he? Then why all the racket? Did he expect her to sit home and knit, when she could be enjoying restaurants and theaters? If that were what he wanted, she couldn't believe he loved her, because if he loved her he'd want her to be happy.

Clancy had attracted her because he had been laughing and witty and carefree and hell-bent. And strong. She admired strength. But that night when he stumbled up the stair from the saloon he had been blubbering and self-pitying. She found this revolting. Martyrdom disgusted her. It seemed obscene. Certainly she never intended making a martyr of herself for anybody.

Doll guessed that if anybody had the right to feel upset that night it was she, for she had consulted a doctor the day before and discovered she was pregnant. She had not yet told the news even to Lucy, for she wanted to think things through alone and make her decisions unaided. Although she was reasonably sure that Gus was responsible, she had been toying with the idea of congratulating Clancy upon his approaching fatherhood and allowing him to make an honest woman of her.

That would be the easy way. But it would also mean good-by to the life she had been planning for herself; good-by to silks, carriages, music, theaters. It would mean a smoke-discolored house in Clayton Junction with a perennial baby in her arms and a two-year-old tugging her skirts; she would be a woman hanging out washing on Monday and ironing on Tuesday and baking and canning fruit on sweltering summer mornings. Over-the-fence gossip with Mrs. McGinnis. Clancy clumping home from work, tired and cross. And some day she would stare into the dresser mirror and behold a woman with stringy hair and neglected skin, and that dowdy stranger would be she.

She would never be able to stick it. She would run off with a sewing-machine agent. Nobody expected a beautiful race horse to settle into dray harness. She was the person she was, and she couldn't marry Clancy. Even though she liked him.

She had reached that conclusion when he came stumbling up the steps and moped into the sitting room, punch-drunk from liquor and fighting. And when she saw him that way, hurt and sentimental and silly with jealousy instead of gay and witty, she didn't even like him very much. Lucy, always more emotional than Doll, caught Clancy's mood and waded with him into that bog of bathos. Lucy wept. Not Doll. She felt contemptuous of them both. And she was disgusted at the dramatic way he had said good-by to Lucy and Tim.

He would be back. She knew he would. And he was. The very next day.

He came back in a mood for argument, in a domineering mood. She was not, he announced loudly, to see Gus Phelan again. He became excited, stamping about the sitting room, and she fancied he wished he could win the argument by giving her a clip on the jaw. If she had been his wife he might have done just that. But she wasn't his wife. Thank God! Oh, how she hated scenes! Leaving him in the sitting room with Lucy, Doll went to her bedroom and locked the door.

Next time he returned he was contrite and sugar-tongued, but he was not the same good old Clancy. Everything he did and said seemed forced and unnatural. He was losing her—he had already lost her— and he had become obsessed with the notion of winning her back at

any cost. They could be married, he said, by the Presbyterian preacher.
And he had always been such a good Catholic. Doll shook her head.

"You'd regret it some day, Clancy," she said. "You know you
would."

Through the end of February and into the kite weather of March
that continued, Clancy all upset, never himself; and Doll began to
feel more concerned about her pregnancy. It was still a secret between the doctor and herself, but she'd have to tell Lucy soon. Then
one day Gus arrived in Clayton Junction. Luckily enough, it was on
an afternoon when Clancy was making the Omaha run.

Gus paid an urchin to deliver a note announcing he was in town; he
would meet her at the usual place. That was the livery stable. They
drove to Tamarack, eating supper and attending the theater, but
throughout the evening she felt dispirited. "Anything wrong, Dolly?"
Gus kept asking. She smiled, shook her head. But something was
wrong; everything was wrong. She had a dull headache and her body
felt heavy. Maybe, she thought, life was catching up with her. Maybe
it wasn't such a high lark after all; maybe you couldn't go along taking
what was agreeable from living and ignoring the rest.

Driving back to Clayton Junction she felt cold inside and depressed.
It was a windy night with a half-moon riding high and pale, and the
clouds racing across it had fantastic shapes as if they were witches on
broomsticks. Between the two towns the road curved ghost-pale, and
the roadside bushes, tormented by the wind, looked like bony fingers
clawing. After the horses thumped over a little wooden bridge Doll
said:

"Gus . . . Stop a minute, will you? I've got something to tell you."

"Whoa," Gus bawled into the wind. "Whoa, boy." His big arm
encircled her, and while they kissed she could hear the wind roaring
through the trees with a sound like waterfalls.

"Something to tell me," he said at last. "What is it, Dolly?"

"You know," she said, "how much fun we've had. Making love . . .
Well, I've found out I'm in the family way."

"Well I'll be damned," Gus exclaimed. "That kind of takes my
breath, Dolly. You're not worried, are you?"

"No. Not exactly."

He patted her. "Dolly my girl, you know me. I'll take care of everything. Nothing at all to worry about, Dolly. My wife's had eight and
there's nothing to it. You won't want for a thing, Dolly, I'll see to that.
You'll never want as long as I'm above the sod."

"Oh, Gus," she sighed, burying her face in his coat; and suddenly
she was sobbing. She wondered why. It wasn't like her. Then she
realized that deep beneath her unconcern she had really been worried

and frightened. But Gus was reliable, a pillar of strength. He patted her, murmured heavy endearments, and they drove on, to Clayton Junction, to the livery stable.

Gus was especially attentive and tender, helping her down from the rig. She waited by his side, in the dim lantern light within the stable, while he paid the stableman.

"Thanks," said the stableman. "Pretty windy night for you folks to be out drivin'. . . ." And then he asked, "Say, you hear about the wreck?"

"Wreck?"

"Oh, didn't you hear? Wreck on the Omaha run. Number Eighty-eight and Number Three-nineteen had a head-on collision."

Number Eighty-eight. Clancy was fireman on Number Eighty-eight.

"My God," Gus said. "That's awful. Anyone hurt?"

"The engine crew of Number Three-nineteen jumped," the stable-man said. "And the engineer on Number Eighty-eight. But the fire-man, he stuck with 'er. Guess the engineer tried to get him to jump, but he wouldn't. He stuck. Fellow named Clancy. He stuck and was scalded to death."

For a moment Doll felt numb, her tongue heavy and thick. Clancy wouldn't jump. He must have known what would happen to him when those two iron hogs collided, but he wouldn't jump. That moody wild-fisted Irishman knew he had lost her and he wouldn't—

The livery stable floor seemed to tip, and she thought black ink had been spilled over the lantern flame. Her knees buckled, the way a drunk's knees buckled one time when Gus hit him, and Doll realized that for the first time in her life she was fainting.

4

DOLL'S SON was born one evening the following autumn in her bedroom above Mahoney's Saloon. Old Doc Harvey attended her, and the delivery was wholly normal and speedy as if the child were eager to emerge into the world and be about getting ahead in life. To Doll the birth did not seem speedy, but even with pain streaking her consciousness her humor did not desert her. She remembered how Gus had said his wife had borne eight children and there was nothing to it, and she thought of a quip with which she would chide Gus. It seemed funny, the way jokes seemed funny when you were drinking, and she laughed aloud. Doc Harvey put a hand on her forehead and said, "There, there, my girl—easy does it," and then she was not laughing but sobbing.

Throughout the ordeal the familiar sounds of Clayton Junction reached her and comforted her. From the saloon downstairs she could hear somebody banging away on the cheap piano, and now and then through that bawdy music the whooping laugh of a drunk ascended. Her thoughts darted in and out among the upspurting geysers of pain, and in imagination she left the misery of her bed and went downstairs. It helped dull the agony to pretend she was entering the saloon, wearing that gray suit in which she looked like a million dollars. The sawdust floor was soft beneath her feet, and she could see the long bar and Tim wiping away the rings left by glasses.

She thought the saloon was empty except for him, and when he saw her he dropped the cloth and rounded the bar. She saw his lean body and dour countenance with the sandy hair and the discontented, brooding eyes. She felt his steely hands on her shoulders, and he tried to drag her against him and kiss her. She sensed his passion, but it was cold passion locked up within himself, and she placed her fists against his bony chest and pushed. Odd that she should imagine that happening in the saloon, because it really happened one day in the sitting room when Sis was out buying groceries. That was two years ago, only three or four weeks after Mamma died in Sioux Creek and Doll came to make her home with Sis. She pushed him away, and when he kept trying to embrace her she slapped him.

"Don't be a silly idiot," she snapped. "I'd just as soon have a jackass slobbering over me."

His face went white, then flaming red, and from that moment his attitude toward her changed. In her presence his lips tightened and his eyes were cold, and she knew he hated her with all the venom of desire turned back upon itself. Sometimes Doll was afraid of him. Although he was only twenty-eight, he seemed a bitter old man. Then from Sis, little by little, Doll gleaned information about their marital life, and she understood the frustration which always seemed to hagride those two. Sis had gone to him a virgin, and she had remained faithful to him, and hence to her making love seemed a vastly overrated pastime and she could not understand why Doll took to it so enthusiastically. Doll was a kindhearted girl and did not add to Lucy's discontent by describing the joys she was missing.

"We're different, Sis, that's all," she told Lucy. "Some people like oysters and some don't. It's just the way you're made."

She wondered whether Lucy suspected she was lying. She hoped not, for Lucy was without the fire and daring to find another man. Lucy was a person whom life shoved around. Most people were, Doll guessed. But she wasn't. Or perhaps she was. Perhaps life shoved everybody, but a few persons like Gus Phelan and herself shoved back. And if you shoved hard enough life yielded and you got what you went after.

Doll's remaining in Clayton Junction for the birth of her child was an instance of her shoving back, for as soon as the town learned that the stork was making reconnaissance flights over Mahoney's Saloon it became incensed. The town did not consider the bearing of children a proper occupation for unmarried women. Doll thought this a strange attitude. She could have understood such an attitude in Sioux Creek, for it was a prim village inhabited by staid people. They were kindly people too, not so much straight-laced as naive, and when scandal came along, such as the time the Presbyterian preacher's wife yielded to the blandishments of the choir tenor, they were genuinely shocked and sorrowful. Such an occurrence was so unusual they didn't know what to do. But they knew they must do something, so they fired the preacher. This was possibly not quite fair, for the preacher had been no happier than anyone else about his wife's frailty, but in the end a kind of rough justice was achieved, for the preacher left town immediately, taking his wife with him, and thus temptation was removed from both her and the tenor. The tenor, as it happened, was Doll's father.

Doll knew how Sioux Creek would have reacted if she had been living there pregnant but unwed. After the first shock the town would have been angry, but presently the anger would have cooled. The town would not have cast her out. It would have remembered that after all she was one of its daughters, a cheerful girl it had watched growing up. While disapproving such conduct in general, it would have made an exception in her case. "I guess it's no more than we could expect," the town would have said, "considering she's Bill Burgoyne's daughter."

None of that kindliness shone through Clayton Junction's attitude. It was such a rowdy town, so full of saloons and prostitutes and fighting, that Doll expected it to ignore her condition. She expected urbanity and indifference. Instead, the town turned upon her. That summer when she strolled along the street, men loafing outside saloons made insulting remarks, and sometimes the women drew aside to the edge of the sidewalk so their skirts would not be contaminated. Once in a dry goods store the clerk, a sharp-nosed spinster, refused to sell her material for a dress. Doll demanded to see the manager. He proved to be as gray-skinned and sharp-featured as the clerk, and he wagged a forefinger and ordered her from the store.

"We sell to harlots," he said, "but not to harlots that pretend to be ladies."

It was such an absurd utterance that Doll's indignation gave way to peals of laughter. Then she drew herself up and with dignity paced from the store. It was a July afternoon, and the town lay prostrate in the blazing heat. She knew how baking-hot her room above the saloon would be, and she didn't want to return there and upset Sis till the anger left her face. Doll's pregnancy had upset Sis enough already, for she was a conformist who abided by the conventions as naturally as Doll transgressed them. These last months had been unhappy ones for Sis, torn as she was between loyalty to Doll and fear of what the town would say and what Tim might do. Tim, as a matter of fact, had done nothing but scowl and curl his thin mouth when he learned of Doll's condition. Finally he said, "What can she expect, chasing around with that old rooster, Phelan?" He seemed to derive grim satisfaction from the worst's happening. Lucy had feared he might turn Doll into the street, but she didn't know her husband. She didn't know that sometimes he lay awake thinking of Doll, turning over and over his emotion for her, that choking emotion in which passion and humiliation and hatred were so entangled.

Leaving the store that afternoon, Doll felt more contemptuous than angry. She wanted to be alone to think over her situation, to make plans, to gain strength. For she had discovered it futile to seek strength and courage from outside herself, from other people. When troubles tumbled upon her she had formed the habit of going into solitude, of communing with herself. It was as if there were great reservoirs of power within her spirit, and if she groped humbly toward them she found them at last, and they refreshed and strengthened her. Then she could laugh again.

So through the heat she strolled along Second Avenue, past the livery stable where Gus had rented the phaeton that first day they drove to

Tamarack, away from the business district. The sun burned down on her shoulders, and she was grateful for the shade of the residential section. But even the trees in Clayton Junction were poor sick things, blighted by the soot that floated from the railroad yards. She hated the town that afternoon, and she wondered why she remained. Gus had suggested she go to Chicago or at least Tamarack to have her baby, where she was unknown. He offered to pay all expenses, but she said no. She foresaw too many complications. Landladies inquiring about her husband—that kind of thing. And besides, she wasn't going to give Clayton Junction the satisfaction of driving her away.

She made her way to the edge of town, moving slowly and cumbrously, scanning the board sidewalks for knotholes that might trip her. But this afternoon she did not attain the peace that solitude usually brought. Yet she had no regrets about the course she had taken. She wouldn't have traded places with any of the drudging women in those houses she had passed; she wouldn't have traded places with Lucy. She was glad she had not consented to marry Clancy.

In a way it was her fault that he had died: Tim openly blamed her, and she suspected that even Lucy shared his opinion. But in a larger sense it was not her fault at all. It was his own. A fatal weakness in his character, sentimentality. Because he loved her, he had selfishly thought she should shape her life to his. If she had complied and married him, it would have been she who would have died. Not physically, but her gay spirit would have left her. She couldn't marry a man just because he wanted her to.

Yet she had been fond of Clancy and she had grieved for him; not for the doleful Clancy he had become in his last days upon earth, when he realized he had lost her, but for the witty, devil-may-care fellow who said the most outlandish things when they were making love. She would have been glad to think the child in her womb was his, but she was gladder to feel the child belonged to Gus. For beneath his joviality Gus was hard as nails, and she thought a child of hers would need to be ruthless.

Clayton Junction was behind her now, and she felt tired. Deep with white dust the road to Tamarack curved away through the heat; heat flashed and shimmered in the vast cloudless sky. She stopped in the shade of a roadside tree. The sound of locomotives reached her, and to the south she could see their smoke puffing up in brilliant snowy mushrooms and dark plum-colored pillars. Some fine day she intended boarding a train and going away. East. Chicago. New York.

She turned back toward town, deciding to stroll along First Avenue. It looked shadier. A few minutes later she regretted that decision.

It began innocently enough when, deep in thought, she passed a dirty yard where three dirty children were playing joylessly. Two boys of ten or twelve, and a girl of the same age. One boy, who had red hair and whose face was plastered with red freckles, stood with legs apart and stared at her insolently. Some smart-aleck remark popped from his mouth and the other children giggled. Doll thought wearily that the town was full of brats and passed on.

She had walked a quarter of a block when she became aware of giggling behind her, and she glanced around. The children were there, with several others. They had the air of being up to no good. The redheaded boy dashed into the street and ran ahead, ducking behind a tree which she must pass. And suddenly she was afraid of passing that tree. That, she told herself, was ridiculous. Doubtless the children were engaged in some senseless game that did not concern her at all.

The giggling grew louder, and when she glanced around again she saw that several more children had joined the game, recruited from the yards along the way. There were several dogs, too, their tongues dripping out.

"What do you children want?" Doll asked.

They giggled harder, as if at some obscure joke, and one boy patted his palm against his mouth and hooted.

Doll marched on, and the tree where the boy was concealed came closer. He peeked around it, smirking, then ducked back. Her ridiculous dread of passing that tree increased. She told herself pregnant women were always foolishly nervous because they were carrying the whole future in their bodies. What she feared was that the boy would dash out and butt his head into her stomach.

Then she reached the tree and nothing happened. She breathed in relief and told herself she was silly.

Then she saw the redheaded boy again. Once more he was running down the middle of the street, and this time when he came abreast of her he yelled the word. The word was "whore."

She understood, then. This was no game, or perhaps it was a game, one of the oldest in the world. And in a flash she felt kinship for all the poor derided women in history, the women branded with the letter "A," the women beaten past the town's end in the Middle Ages, all those poor creatures who had yielded on spring evenings beneath the hedgerows.

And Doll did an odd thing. Odd for her, because she had never been very religious. She turned on that dancing mob of children and screamed:

"Let the one who is without sin cast the first stone."

They shrieked at that, and hooted, and the dogs barked, and then all the children took up the cry of the redheaded boy.

She hurried as fast as she dared along the board sidewalk. Their quarry was retreating now, and the pack was in full cry. A yard ap-

proached where a fat woman was hanging out diapers, and Doll
thought, "She'll make them stop. She'll make them behave."

But when the woman heard the words the children were yelling a
smile pasted itself over her face and she spat contemptuously.

"That's right, give it to her," the woman yelled. "She's got it
coming."

Doll felt sick in her legs, but she plodded on.

When she reached Van Buren Street she crossed it and turned west
toward Second Avenue. The business district was only a block away,
but still the children shrieked after her; she was at the center of a
moving tornado of hoots and yelps and barking dogs. Ahead she saw
a sign hanging over the sidewalk: "Clayton Junction Tribune." It was
the first business establishment on this side street, and as the noise
reached the place a man came out.

He was a tall man in his forties, round-shouldered, and because he
walked with a bad limp he carried a cane. He paused on the sidewalk,
gazing at the children; and then understanding crossed his face and he
limped fast toward her. His face was long and seamed, and his eyes
flashed angrily.

As he approached, the hooting ceased, and before it could begin again
he said:

"That's enough of this. Get along home."

The children glanced at one another.

The man brought paper and pencil from his pocket.

"I'm going to take down your names," he said. "They'll want to
know them at the police station."

"Not my name, mister," the redheaded boy yelled.

And he galloped down an alley. A few moments later not even a
dog remained.

"The little devils," the man murmured, staring after them. Then he
turned to Doll. "You'd better come into the office and rest. You must
be tired."

It was a good place to cry. The building was brick, and after the
bright heat of the street the dusky air seemed cool and damp. At the
editor's littered desk Doll buried her face in her arms and let the tears
come. Once she felt the man's hand on her shoulders and she heard
him say, "That's all right. It's a dirty town."

She didn't cry long. At first she was full of rage against the children
and their parents, but presently her fury turned cold and almost impersonal; it was like the helpless anger of a man shaking his fist against
the heavens after the destruction wrought by some great natural cataclysm.

And as her tears ceased and she sat quietly with her head cradled in her arms, she experienced a curious sense of shame. She was not ashamed of being pregnant without matrimony any more than a vixen fox would have been ashamed of that. Mortification warmed her cheeks because she had figured in a public spectacle.

She lifted her head and said quietly:

"Thanks for what you did."

The man sat tamping tobacco into a charred old pipe. His fingers were long, lean, alive-looking, with dirty nails.

"They're little imps of the devil," he said. "Except I don't believe in the devil. Bosh and rubbish. You ought to read Voltaire. And Darwin and Huxley. They've got the stuff." Points of fire gleamed in his gray eyes. "This is a stinking town," he said. "If I had any gumption I'd lock up shop and walk out. But I'll never do it. I know myself, see? I'll talk about it but I'll never do it. I'll rot here till I die, and then I'll really rot."

He grinned at that.

From a case of type another man called:

"Not if you keep yourself well pickled you won't. Old Mother Alcohol. God but I wish it was Saturday night, Frank. I'd be drunk if this was Saturday night."

He was a gnarled man of sixty-five perched on a stool, and while he spoke his right hand kept flying over the typecase, plucking out bits of metal and clicking them into the stick he held in his left. He wore straw sleeve-protectors, and dirt tarnished his silvery hair.

"You're Miss Burgoyne, aren't you?" the editor asked. "Well Miss Burgoyne, come back and meet Vince Fye. He's the best tramp printer I've ever had. That's not saying much."

Without a pause in his typesetting, Fye said:

"Pleased to meet you, Miss. And don't call me a tramp, Frank. Call me a boomer. A tramp's got more sense than me. A tramp won't work."

"How about it, Vince?" the editor said. "You've been around. Isn't this a stinking town?"

"I've seen better," Vince Fye said, "and I've seen worse. They all stink, Frank. Like the Good Book says. To the skunk all things shall stinketh, and to the rose all shall smell sweet. Or words to that effect."

Frank grinned. And he said to Doll, "You're feeling better now, aren't you?"

"A lot better," Doll said, and she smiled. It was that warmhearted, spontaneous smile which always made her so many friends among men. Its earthiness and abundance somehow reminded Frank Mac-

Gowan of his native Pennsylvania on a winey September afternoon. He asked, "Had those children been bothering you long?"

"It seemed quite a while," she said, and she told how it started and what the fat woman yelled and how the clerk in the dry goods store refused to sell her dress material.

"But if they think they're going to run me out of town they're wrong. I'll fight back. I used to play jackstones and I'm like the rubber ball. The harder they bounce me down, the faster I'll come up."

He chuckled, and Doll noticed a grin on the face of the old type-setter. Her heart went out to these men. They were different from any she had known; her experience provided no pigeonhole into which they would fit. She was grateful for the way they damned the town and clowned back and forth so she would feel that what had happened was beneath fretting about. They were nearly too good to be true, and a sudden suspicion flashed through her thoughts and she asked:

"You won't put anything in the paper about this, will you?"

Both men laughed, and MacGowan said:

"People who live in glass houses have to flock together. No, not a line. We go to press Thursday. If you're going to worry, drop in Thursday afternoon and read proof."

"I'm not going to worry."

"Then drop in anyway. Drop in when you feel like cussing out this town. That's the best thing we do."

"It's our safety valve," Vince Fye said. "We flatter the town in print and cuss it out in private."

When Doll rose to leave, MacGowan said he had an errand and he would accompany her to Mahoney's Saloon. She saw through that. He had no errand. What he did have was understanding and kindness; and she suspected he feared that after her experience she might have qualms about venturing forth alone.

They walked slowly to the corner and turned into Second Avenue. Their pace suited each other: she with her pregnancy, he with his lameness.

"I'm not much of a walking companion," he said. "This left leg is artificial. I lost it at Chickamauga in 'sixty-three."

"I'm not complaining," she said. "I'm spavined, too, for a while."

He chuckled, and as they moved along beneath the wooden awnings she stole glances at him. He had perched a dilapidated old hat upon his gray-sprinkled brown hair, and a streak of printer's grime ran across his cheek. He was as different as possible from Gus Phelan, Gus with his tailored suits and immaculate grooming; and yet in some fashion the men reminded her of each other. Perhaps it was because this man too, despite his lameness, gave her a feeling of strength. In his company she felt as perfectly protected as she had that first night with Gus when he knocked down an insulting drunk and kicked him into the gutter.

After that she often dropped in at the *Tribune* office, during those final months of pregnancy when she was incapacitated for love and her chief occupation was waiting, waiting. She grew fond of that dingy place with its odor of paper and printer's ink and burning tobacco, and she grew fond of Frank MacGowan, too. She saw him in many moods: tense and busy on Thursdays when the paper was printed; lazy and ready to talk for hours on Fridays. She watched him at his desk, working easily as he penned some trivial local item, scowling and gripping his pen as if it were a dagger as he wrestled with the syntax of editorials. These were sprinkled with references to Karl Marx and Herbert Spencer, for the established order did not delight him. If the few persons who read his editorials had understood them he might have encountered trouble, but Clayton Junction's ignorance was his guardian angel.

"Listen to this," he would exclaim, as his pen jabbed down the final period of an editorial. "This will show them."

And then, waving his hand, he barked out the sentences he had composed, while Vince Fye continued his endless typesetting and Doll listened without understanding a word.

"That's good," she always said. "Real good. It's pretty highbrow for me, but it sounds fine."

And Fye grinned and said:

"You've done it this time, Frank. They'll mob us Thursday night. Tar and feather us, and ride us out of town on a rail."

Frank scowled suspiciously.

"You don't mean that, Vince. You're having one on me again."

"Sure I mean it. The pen's mightier than the sword, ain't it? You know the old saying. He who takes up the sword shall gather no moss."

Frank put down the sheets, looking discouraged, and then a slow grin crept over his mouth.

"The town stinks, Vince," he said at last.

At the back of the office, beyond the typecases and composing stones and the old press, Vince and Frank batched it. Their untidy quarters would have horrified a woman with sterner housekeeping standards, but Doll didn't mind the unmade beds and unwashed dishes and the dresser littered with everything from *The Origin of Species* to Vince's sleeve garters. She herself was a bit careless about keeping house; often it was Lucy who slipped into Doll's room at midafternoon and made her bed.

But Doll realized there were certain inviolable conventions between men and women, and among these was the canon that a woman should express horror at the disarray of a bachelor's abode, so the first time she beheld that combination bedroom-and-kitchen she exclaimed:

"Frank, Frank! What a place! Something has to be done!"

She pitched in, making the beds, washing the dishes, and while she worked Frank sat watching her, conscious of an inner glow of happiness. He had never been in love. There had been a girl back in his native town about whom he thought while he was away at war, but she had married. Besides, with his leg gone he would have been too shy to mention marriage. And down-through the years in the presence of nice girls he was always conscious of that lost leg. So he had not known love. Passion he had known, not passion in its violent beauty but in violent tawdriness, and he expelled it like a good riddance in the cat houses on Rafferty Street, down by the roundhouse.

It would have given him a start to admit he was beginning to love a girl far gone in pregnancy with another man's child. But he did know that in her presence the world seemed more vivid. Between her visits the time stretched long and sterile, and when he was making up the paper or reading late at night he would think about her violet eyes and her brash voice and the way she wore her dark hair in short curls. His feeling for her was always shot through with a wistful ache.

"There now, that's better," Doll said, giving the bed a final pat. She turned to the kitchen portion of the room and sighed humorously. "Those dishes, Frank! Honest to goodness! And that stove! Do you really cook on it?"

"I go through the motions. The results aren't always digestible."

"What I ought to do," she said, "is to cook you a real meal."

"Would you?"

"Try me," she said; and that was the first of those occasions when Doll cooked a delicious meal for Vince and Frank, and they feasted together. Usually this took place on Friday evening, when getting out another edition of the paper was nearly a week away. They lingered long at the table while Frank expounded the doctrines of Herbert Spencer or Vince yarned about his experiences as a roving printer; and when they did the dishes they sang old songs.

Except for Vince and Frank, Doll might have found life lonely, because during that summer and autumn business did not bring Gus Phelan to Clayton Junction as it did before her pregnancy. He wrote now and then, but his letters did not sound at all like Gus. They were formal and impersonal; businesslike, really; and they always conveyed the same information: business was keeping him tied down in Chicago. Doll smiled at that; she was no fool. He avoided mentioning money in his letters—he was no fool, either—but when she tore open the envelopes, currency tumbled into her lap.

At the end of those Friday evenings in the printing shop, Frank accompanied her home. They would leave Vince Fye in the lamplighted bedroom-and-kitchen, and grope into the dark shop, where the machinery and typecases bulked black against the dim light falling through the front windows. One evening he suggested they take a stroll.

It was late September by that time, a sharp night with a frosty moon; and from the marshes outside town white mist had stolen in, ghostly silent. They moved slowly, Frank's cane swishing through dead leaves. For a long time they didn't speak, but the silence between them was the eloquent speechlessness of two people who had achieved understanding and trust. Finally he asked:

"When do you expect your child?"

"In about three weeks."

"Do you dread it?"

"In a way. I'll be glad when it's over." And she added, "I don't think anything will go wrong, do you, Frank? I don't think I'll die."

It stopped him. In a hushed voice he said:

"Don't even think about such a thing, Doll. Of course you won't."

"I wouldn't want to. It's such a big world, so much to see. It's such an interesting world, and there're so many things I want to do yet."

He experienced a pang. He could never hold her; he would never try. If death didn't take her away her restless spirit would. She was very close to nature, he thought; and he couldn't hold her any more than he could imprison a handful of sunshine. He said:

"I want you to remember one thing, Doll. If you ever need me, call me. If you're a thousand miles away and need me, you call."

She put her hand on his sleeve. "You're a good man, Frank."

Presently he asked:

"Whose child is it, Doll? Howard Clancy's?"

"I don't think so. It's Gus Phelan's."

Deep inside he cringed. He had seen Phelan in Mahoney's Saloon, and he could not imagine Doll in his arms. And then it occurred to him that probably Doll could not imagine him in the fat arms of a Rafferty Street trollop, either. In some odd fashion, he thought, his relationship with Doll had brought out what was best in each, the way April sun brought into bloom the shy, tender plants of the earliest springtide. In Doll there were probably impulses and determinations less lovely than he had beheld. And suddenly he was appalled at the complexity of human beings and at the vast tantalizing maze of human relationships.

Silently, they tramped back to Second Avenue. The railroad yards were noisy with tooting locomotives, and Mahoney's Saloon was noisy, too. Inside the vestibule at the foot of the steps, they could hear the piano banging away beyond the door, and men's voices reached them, husky and incoherent in various stages of intoxication.

Doll whispered:

"I've never had a friend like you, Frank. If you'd like to kiss me good night, I'd like to have you."

His body barely touched hers and he tried to keep his kiss tender, but behind it she sensed more than tenderness. Then he was gone, shuffling out the door. She watched him tapping away up the street, dragging his bad leg.

5

WHEN AUGUSTUS H. BURGOYNE was two minutes old, a woman fell in love with him. Her name was Lucy Mahoney.

That past year had been a difficult one for poor Lucy. She was one of those willing, patient, colorless little women who always seem to be begging everyone's pardon for being alive. Destiny had played a bad joke on her when it gave her a vivid sister like Doll and a dour husband like Tim. She should have married an earnest country parson and spent her life cooking him plenty of fried chicken and helping him do good works. And even with an evangelical husband, she should never have permitted Doll to spend a single night in the manse.

Lucy was eighteen when she married Tim. He was a native of Clayton Junction, where his father operated an esteemed saloon, but Tim fancied himself destined for higher things than pouring out drinks behind a bar. Occasionally in his father's saloon he had seen railroad officials in their fine clothes, and he thought that would be the life for him. So after his student days terminated with his graduation from eighth grade, he accepted a position with the Chicago, Tamarack & Pacific Railroad. It wasn't much of a job—cleaning spittoons in the station, sweeping out, heaving baggage—but the man who hired him said there was a future in it. He didn't say what kind.

Tim worked hard, groping for the bottom rung in the ladder of success, and after a few years he found it. He had learned the Morse code and the railroad sent him to Sioux Creek as assistant to the station agent there. He had the graveyard watch, working from dark till dawn, and the pay was small. Sometimes he considered giving up his career and returning to Clayton Junction where he would go into the saloon business with his old man.

The station agent in Sioux Creek advised Tim to make friends in the town, to foster good will for the railroad, so Tim attended the Presbyterian Church. There, he met Lucy. She fell in love with him: the Chicago, Tamarack & Pacific seemed to have a fatal fascination for those Burgoyne girls. At Tim's invitation, Lucy occasionally visited him at night in the station, and this was innocent enough except that the railroad didn't pay him to spark a girl on its time.

When the Widow Kritchlow learned of these nocturnal visits, God knew how, she immediately suspected that more was taking place at

the railroad station than the arrival of trains. She erred in her conclusions, for Lucy held virginity in higher esteem than her younger sister
ever would, but Mrs. Kritchlow's error was quite natural, for Lucy's
father had always assumed that Moses had misunderstood God when
he wrote down the Seventh Commandment. So Mrs. Kritchlow called
upon the station agent's wife, who was horrified that any breath of
scandal should touch the Chicago, Tamarack & Pacific. She repri-
manded her husband in a tone which suggested he was virtually as
guilty as Tim. The station agent, who was beginning to have grave
doubts that marrying meant perpetual happiness, became angry at his
wife, but he couldn't take it out on her, for occasionally in moments
of stress the woman threw things, so he took it out on Tim.

Nobody could talk to a Mahoney the way the station agent talked to
Tim. Not and get away with it, they couldn't. Years later, just thinking about it made Tim mad, and as time went on he kept recalling
more and more scathing things he said to the station agent. That
conversation was responsible for the railroad's losing a mighty good
man.

But the railroad traffic's loss was the liquor traffic's gain, and before
returning to Clayton Junction Tim asked Lucy to marry him. That,
he thought, would show the town a thing or two. It did. It proved,
Sioux Creek thought, that its suspicions had been correct and that Tim
had to marry Lucy. When months and then years passed without
Lucy's bearing a child, everyone felt badly let down.

Lucy felt let down too, for unlike Tim she wanted children. He
always said kids would be an expensive nuisance, but she possessed
deep maternal yearnings. As a little girl in Sioux Creek she had been
devoted to dolls, never happier than when on a summer morning she
could spread a quilt on the lawn and sit playing house.

"Lucy's never given me a minute's worry," her mother said. "She
makes the cutest dresses for those dolls and she talks to them like they
were real."

And as Lucy grew older her popularity among the women of the
neighborhood achieved spectacular heights, for she loved to take care
of babies. Not for hire: hers was a labor of love. When young matrons
wanted to attend afternoon parties Lucy was delighted to mind their
babies. She enjoyed rocking infants to sleep, and when the older children awoke from naps she held them on her lap and showed them
picture books.

Doll was different. Doll didn't give a snap of her finger about babies.
If there were nothing better to do she would play house, but she never
shared Lucy's pleasure in imagining herself a fond little mother. When
she played house she wanted to dress up in grown people's clothes, so
while Lucy sat on the lawn crooning to her china-and-sawdust children,

Doll went to her mother's bedroom and primped before the mirror, adorning herself in an old hat with a big plume, draping her body with a faded velvet dress, striking arch poses and making outlandish statements to the imaginary dukes and princes who kissed her hand—and not always her hand. When she and Lucy played house, they were really not playing the same game at all.

The games Doll liked best were those in which boys participated. Exciting games like kick the wicket or tallyho or run sheep run. Her most delectable childhood memories were of those long midsummer evenings when a score of children gathered beneath the great friendly maples in the Burgoyne yard. Because of the heat all rules about going to bed early were suspended, and as the long twilight crept over town the children argued about which game to play and chose up sides. Instinctively the gang always met at the Burgoynes', because they were an easygoing family; Mrs. Burgoyne never scolded if you happened to run through a flower bed. And Mr. Burgoyne was a delightful man. He operated the Burgoyne Produce Company, buying chickens and eggs and cream from farmers and shipping them off to cities. He was different from most men in that town, for after working all day he came home and spruced up in good clothes. Nor was he a man to get into a rut by spending his evenings at home. He liked to go downtown for a game of pool. The children would see him leaving the house, a handsome and somehow dashing man with a rich brown mustache, and he would pause and chat. Doll was fond and proud of him. She would skip over and they would stand together, his arm across her shoulders, while he made the children laugh with his airy persiflage. As a young man he had been an actor, filling the leading tenor role in a light opera that played Sioux Creek. He fell in love with Doll's mother, and when the opera closed a few weeks later he dashed back to Sioux Creek and made the town rub its eyes with his whirlwind courtship. The produce business he inherited from his father-in-law.

In those summer evening games, Doll always managed to be on the side with the most boys. She liked their company, and she played with them in a spirit of comradeship without any hint of tomboyishness marring her femininity. Boys liked her, too. All through the years Lucy was amazed at the effortless way Doll had boys and then men flocking after her. Lucy thought it typical of Doll to find a man to squire her around even when she was within a few weeks of giving birth to a baby.

Little Gus was a chubby baby with vast good humor. For hours he would lie in his cradle, waving his arms and kicking and cooing. When Lucy poked a playful finger into his ribs and exclaimed, "Cootchy-cootchy-coo," he laughed and laughed. About the only time he became angry was when Doll stopped feeding him before his big appetite was satisfied. Then he would protest lustily, and because he possessed an excellent pair of lungs you could hear him all over that end of town.

If there had ever been any doubt as to who was to take care of him, this was dispelled during the weeks following his birth. That honor fell to Lucy. And this was no more than a fair division of labor: after all, Doll had given him birth; why shouldn't someone else take up where she left off? No one could be equally competent at everything.

It was fortunate that Lucy enjoyed his company so much, because after being his constant companion for nine months Doll was a trifle weary of the infant. With her body slender again, she experienced a spiritual rebirth; she wanted to go places and do things. She made a shopping tour of Tamarack, buying new clothes. In other seasons Lucy had accompanied her on these purchasing expeditions, but this time Doll went alone, for somebody had to stay with the baby.

Once the child was born, business again brought Gus Phelan to Clayton Junction, and he and Doll took up their relationship where it had been dropped. They met as of yore at the livery stable and drove to Tamarack, dining out and enjoying shows. A girl with a meaner spirit might have held it against Gus that he had denied himself her company during her pregnancy, but Doll was blessed with broad understanding in such matters. Gus had behaved precisely as she would have behaved in his position. Besides, he had certainly not abandoned her when she was with child; his letters with currency demonstrated he had a great heart. She would never love Gus any more than she would love any specific man, for her love was infinite enough to include man as a species, but she liked him enormously.

Gus displayed no curiosity about his son, and when Doll described her sufferings he drummed his fingers and changed the subject. Doll let it go at that. Again, she understood. From his wife he had very likely heard that story before; and inasmuch as he had sired eight children you could scarcely expect him to consider a baby a novelty. Doll's instinct told her she had appealed to Gus because she was the very antithesis of his humdrum menage; hers was the ancient lure of beautiful women dedicated to love alone; to him she represented all the romance of sweet breath and smooth skin and soft, tinted lights. She was illusion; the dream woman running white and naked through the pearly mist of a glade at dawn. Realizing this, she told herself she had been a fool to loose the bull of reality in his china shop of illusion; and never again did she commit that error, with Gus or any man.

She was illusion for Frank MacGowan too, and during the months that followed she saw Frank often. Their relationship progressed beyond friendship, but even in passion it retained that tender, wistful quality which made it seem like an unimportant but sweet little melody a violinist might play for his own enjoyment between more ambitious numbers. Even after they became lovers they were still good friends. They never quarreled, and Frank never gave her money or gifts; only his humble love. She made no effort to conceal the fact that Gus came to visit her, but he accepted this with the same good grace that a man who drank from a spring of clear water might accept the fact that others quenched their thirst there, too. Once he said:

"I could easily be jealous. But I'm not going to. I might as well be jealous of the sun because it shines on other men."

Frank's attitude toward polyandry gratified Doll, but something told her Gus Phelan would not share it, so she never told him about the evenings she spent at the print shop. Gus was easily duped, for he walked in a cloud of thick egotism.

On one visit to Clayton Junction, Gus astonished Doll by telling her he'd like to meet his son. For months not a word about the child had been uttered between them, and she couldn't understand his sudden interest. She wondered whether somebody had dropped a word in his ear about poor Clancy, dead so long now, and whether he suspected there was a chance the boy was the scion of a long line of Clancys instead of Phelans.

That wasn't it at all. It was only curiosity. Doll had been so silent about the child that Gus began wondering whether he was healthy and sound, and he wanted to see for himself.

So that afternoon, risking Tim's displeasure, Doll smuggled Gus up the stairs to the apartment above the saloon. They found Lucy with little Gus in the sitting room. When they entered she jumped up, startled, for she remembered all Tim's threats about what he would do to that old rooster if he caught him here.

"Hello, Sis!" Gus boomed cordially. "How are you? You're looking fine. Haven't seen you for quite a while."

Torn between alarm and hospitality, Lucy smiled and curtsied and bit her lip nervously.

"How are you, Mr. Phelan?" she stammered. "I'm—it's nice to see you."

"Nice to see you too, Sis. Well, well! Look who's here!"

He beamed down at the floor, where little Gus was crawling.

"Say! He's quite a boy! Just look at him, will you! Look at that chest! He's a regular chip off the old block!"

Gus swooped and inserted his paws beneath the child's armpits, and little Gus went soaring ceilingward.

"Whoopsy-do! Whoopsy-do!" Gus bellowed.

All that noise combined with unaccustomed flight scared little Gus, and he started crying.

"Listen to him, will you!" Gus boomed delightedly. "I always say it's a good sign when a kid will cry. Shows he's healthy. Shows he's got a lot of power in his chest. Say! He's going to make a big man. Look at those fists. Bet he'll make a good fighter. Bet he'll work for the Tamarack line. Is that what you're going to do, Gus? You going to be a railroad man?"

Little Gus continued crying, so big Gus shoved him into Lucy's arms.

"You take him, Sis. Calm him down. Guess he's not used to his old Pa."

Lucy had a way with him, and safe in her arms little Gus ceased yelling. From the sofa where they sat, the child focused wondering eyes upon his father.

Gus seated himself in Tim's favorite easy chair.

"Yes sir," he kept exclaiming, "he's quite a boy. A fine boy."

Doll said, "Sis, why don't you make some coffee? I'll bet Gus is hungry."

"Oh, I can always eat," Gus said. "That's one thing about my appetite, it's never gone back on me yet."

So while Lucy trudged to the kitchen, Doll held the child. His lips had never yet formed a word, but for some weeks Lucy had been urging him toward speech. "You're Gus," she would say. "Your name is little Gus. Can you say Gus? Gus. Gus."

And now Doll pointed to big Gus and in honeyed tones said:

"You don't want to cry, darling. You want to be friends with the man. His name is Gus. Gus."

At that moment, when Lucy was puttering in the kitchen, her weeks of effort were rewarded. Without preamble the child looked at his father and said, "Gus."

It sounded more like "Goose," but it was a word. Speech! A delighted squeal left Doll, and she exclaimed:

"He talked! That's the first time he ever—! Sis! Come in here! Gus can talk!"

"By golly, yes!" big Gus was roaring. "I heard him too, Sis. He said my name! Now what do you know about that!"

Drying her hands, Lucy scampered in and knelt on the floor.

"Honest, did he? I've been trying . . . Talk for me, Gus. Gus. Gus."

The baby wrinkled his face and giggled.

"Come on, now. Talk. Can you say Gus? Gus. Gus."

"Goose," said Gus.

Doll screeched again, and big Gus swelled up in self-congratulation as if he had just been elected president of the United States. Lucy took the child and smothered him with kisses. Her eyes were damp, mostly from joy, but there was sadness about this moment, too. She felt a little resentful that, with no trouble at all, Doll had lured Gus into uttering his first word. All their lives it had been that way. All their lives Doll had had the best of everything. Usually Lucy accepted that as the natural order, and even when, as now, she wanted to rebel she knew that she never could; Doll's personality was too much for her.

A pungent odor wafted from the kitchen, and Lucy rushed out to rescue the coffee from boiling over. She had scarcely left the room when the hall door opened and Tim Mahoney entered.

Poor Tim was an unhappy man. He had boasted for so long about what he would do to Phelan if he caught him here that he had nearly hypnotized himself into believing he really would mop the floor with the man and kick him down the stairs. He had erred by barking about his intentions, and now he felt like a cur shivering on a rainy night with its tail between its legs.

A few minutes ago one of his cronies entered the saloon and reported seeing Phelan going upstairs with Doll.

"I knew you'd want to know it," the crony said. "Don't be too hard on him, Tim. He's an older man than you."

Tim blanched, possibly from anger, and snapped:

"Thanks. I'll fix the old rooster."

But he did not immediately rage upstairs. He kept doing what he was doing: washing beer mugs. Oddly enough, his fingers shook. And mutely he cursed his informant, for the fellow was moving among the customers, whispering that Gus Phelan was upstairs and Tim was going to deal with him. The saloon grew silent and everybody kept watching him. Damn them! They expected a man to fight whether he felt like it or not. And Tim didn't feel like it today. He was just getting over a cold and he wasn't in the mood.

As the minutes crawled past, the customers murmured to one another, and Tim knew he would have to do something. He kept thinking of his grudges against Phelan, trying to make himself mad, but damn it, when you had a cold you simply didn't feel like fighting. If Phelan had waited till his recuperation was complete then the old rooster would have had reason to beware! But no, he had to come today. Damn him!

Desperately, Tim flung bucket after bucket of kerosene on the fires of his hate, but the effect was as if the buckets had contained water. He thought of Phelan's fine clothes and how the old rooster strutted around self-importantly and how he was a vice-president of the Chicago, Tamarack & Pacific. Once Tim himself had hoped to hold a lofty position with the railroad, but the station agent at Sioux Creek fired him. That was really Lucy's fault. And in spite against the world at large he married Lucy, when actually her younger sister attracted him much more. Damn it, there was no fairness in the world!

Then Doll came to live with them, tormenting him with her attractiveness, but when he tried to do something about it she called him a jackass. How he hated her after that! Then she began going with Clancy and Tim hoped they would marry so her beautiful body would be out of his sight and he might know a little peace. But she took up with Gus Phelan and got herself in a family way, and now Tim had both Doll and Phelan's brat on his hands. A man needed his sleep, but could he get it with the brat yowling in the middle of the night?

Oh, he had plenty of reason for beating up Phelan, but with this cold . . . Yet his customers expected him to go into action and they would guy him forever if he didn't.

And so, scowling and squaring his bony shoulders, Tim paced to the frosted-glass door. Before closing it he turned and ordered: "You bastards stay down here. This is a private fight."

Then he climbed the stairs, his anger oozing from his heels, and by the time he reached the upper landing he would have traded half-interest in hell if he might have gone back downstairs. Why was he always getting himself into messes like this? Why did everything he attempted end in futility? Well, he couldn't stand out here forever. So at last he forced his fingers to curl round the knob and turn it, and he entered the sitting room. It was the bravest act of his life.

His arrival startled Gus Phelan. Gus had always been handy with his fists, and as a young man he had often fought for the sheer joy of it, but the passing of time had slowed him down. As a young cub he had fought anyone who wanted to fight, but in these later years he had selected his opponents carefully. It was one thing to fell a drunk man with a single, well-aimed blow, but quite another to engage in a battle that might stretch out for several minutes. He knew how his heart would pound and his breath would wheeze.

From Doll and from some of the railroad men Gus had heard about Tim Mahoney's threats against his person if he ever came here. Well, he had come anyway, and now here was Mahoney. Gus didn't know about Mahoney. Couldn't exactly figure him. Sometimes those cold ornery guys turned very dangerous in a fray. Sometimes they used knucks, even knives. Moreover, Mahoney had the edge on him in years.

Not that he was afraid of Mahoney! Perish the thought! If he were twenty-five years younger he would lick the bastard with one hand tied behind his back. But he wasn't twenty-five years younger. He was that much older than Mahoney, and a family man in the bargain. It would be unfair to his wife and children to mix up in a senseless fight that might injure him.

But although his flesh was on the weak side, his spirit retained its old shillalah virtues; even though an old bull he was still a bull, with a bull's instinct to attack. So Mahoney had no more than shut the door when Gus jumped up and blustered across the room and grabbed him by the collar.

"Now listen, Mahoney," he roared, "I like you—understand? But I've heard you don't like me. I hope I've heard wrong, because otherwise I'm going to beat you up within an inch of that God-damned ornery life of yours, and I hate to do that because there's ladies present, not to mention your poor little nephew. And it's ashamed of yourself you ought to be, coming up here and starting something before this sweet child and your wife and her sister."

"What do you mean, starting something?" Tim complained. "Can't a man come into his own home without being jumped on?"

Suddenly Gus felt braver than he had in years.

"Don't try to lie out of it, Mahoney," he thundered. "I know what was on your mind, and you do, too. By God, if you want to fight say so, and I'll kick your teeth down your throat."

"Now wait," Tim said. "Who said anything about fighting? I've got a cold today. I'm a sick man and you jump on me—"

"You'll be a lot sicker when I get through with you," Gus bellowed. "By God, you can't insult an Irishman this way. Do you want to fight it out and get your jaw broke, or do you want to sit down and behave yourself?"

"You started it," Tim pointed out. "I didn't say anything."

"All right then, sit down!" Gus roared, pointing to a straight-backed chair. "Sit down and cut out all this noise."

Releasing his prisoner, Gus steamed over to Tim's favorite chair and sat down. Miserably, Tim collapsed to the hard chair. His cheeks were burning. He glimpsed the amusement on Doll's face, and he saw Lucy in the kitchen doorway, nervously wiping her hands on a towel. She looked humiliated, ready to burst into tears. Phelan picked up little Gus and gave him a horseback ride on his knee. The brat screamed and laughed, damn its soul to hell.

Then Doll called to Lucy, "How's the coffee coming, Sis? I think we'll need some, after all this."

"It's ready now," Lucy said. "I'll bring it right in, Sis."

Little Gus's second word was "choo-choo," and his third was "train," and after that his vocabulary increased rapidly, for he had a quick mind that grabbed at things. But the word "Gus" remained his favorite; till the end of his life he considered it the most fascinating word in the language. Presently, however, "Burgoyne" ran a close second in his favor.

Till Gus was three years old, he was as good a child as anyone could hope for, chubby and sunny and bubbling with laughter. He never had many toys but he didn't need them, for in the curved window at the southeast corner of the sitting room he had a reserved seat for the most exciting performance one could imagine. It was continuous and never repetitious. The window overlooked the railroad yards where, over the bright steel rails, switch engines were always puffing; and a number of times each day passenger trains steamed past, and long freight trains. Because Clayton Junction was a division point, every train paused there for a fresh locomotive, and by the time Gus was three he became an authority on the type of engines used for limited trains and locals and fast meat trains and way-freights. And he drank in the sight of men signaling too, and presently he learned how to wave his arms to order imaginary engineers to keep backing or to halt.

By day the scene was cluttered with harsh ugliness, although Gus didn't mind that; but at night it possessed a wild beauty, with switch lights and waving lanterns and red flame flooding everything when the fireman opened an engine's firebox door to coal up. Gus loved it when an engineer let off excess steam in great clouds; and he loved all the other railroad sounds too. Those fussy locomotives of the eighties with their tall stacks seemed enormous to him, and he gave them names and thought of them as individuals. He learned to recognize their different-toned whistles and their different-sounding bells, and when a locomotive stood waiting and emitted from its innards a harsh, deep, coughing sound you never could have convinced Gus it wasn't alive and talking to itself about the run to Omaha.

When he grew up he was going to be a railroad man, of course. What occupation could possibly be greater? A railroad man—an engineer—was a powerful man. The locomotives were mighty, but they had their masters, and their masters were men; men in caps and overalls, with bandannas at their throats. It was disillusioning, later on, to learn that the masters of locomotives had masters, too; men like Gus Phelan who sat in faraway offices and gave orders. When Gus discovered that truth of practical economics, he lost interest in becoming an engineer.

The great change took place in Gus's life a couple of months after his third birthday, for in December of that year his mother deserted Clayton Junction for Chicago, and after that he never knew serenity any more. Under the joint control of Lucy and Doll, his existence had been pleasant and easy, for Doll was not a woman who believed in discipline for the sake of discipline. She had observed that people who

did were usually unpleasant about everything. She imposed few re-
straints upon herself and saw no reason to treat her son differently.
He seldom made her nervous or roused her ire, for in his reaction to
situations she detected traces of herself and Gus Phelan, and this
amused her. She wasn't one to take life seriously, and her sense of
humor was touched when she reflected that those nights of love with
Gus, when the last thought in either of their minds was increasing
Clayton Junction's population, had resulted in this by-product who
amused himself by waving his arms in imitation of railroad brakemen.

"He's a true son of the Tamarack line," Doll told Lucy. "You'd
think he was the son of a locomotive and a caboose."

And Doll would explore that idea further, dealing with all its
ramifications, while Lucy giggled so hard that tears came into her eyes.

"Honestly, Sis," she would protest, "you'll be the death of me. Honestly, you're the limit, Sis!"

And little Gus would join in the laughter too, not because he understood but because he was jolly and enjoyed laughing.

Frank MacGowan kept asking Doll about her son, so one day she
took him to the *Tribune* office, and the visit was such a success
that they often called there. As full of curiosity as a pup, little Gus
went nosing about that jumbled place. He touched things he shouldn't,
getting his hands dirty, and he conceived a vast admiration for Vince
Fye. That droll man's dexterity in handling type and his marksman-
ship with tobacco juice endeared him to Gus.

"Here, here—none of that," Vince intoned, when Gus tried to pull
out a typecase drawer. "Last little boy that did that I skinned alive
and sent his scalp to the chief of my old Injun tribe."

And Vince went on to spin outrageous yarns of his adventures in
the Wild West.

But even more than Vince, Gus liked Frank, perhaps because Frank
never patronized him or waggishly teased him but talked to him as
if he were an adult.

"He's a bright boy," Frank told Doll. "The way he's taking to the
newspaper business, we'll make a Horace Greeley out of him."

But other forces were conspiring to shape his career, and among
these was a heart attack suffered in Chicago by Gus Phelan. This
occurred one day in his office, and although he recovered, his life for
the next fortnight was a round of examinations by doctors, and self-
examination, too. For nearly half a century he had driven himself
mercilessly, the way he used to drive his men when he was a track-
laying foreman, and he had always relaxed vigorously as well. He had
swallowed too much hard liquor and helled around with too many
women. If he expected to go on living he would have to take better
care of himself.

So Gus decided to retire, and that would mean an end of his business trips to Clayton Junction. But he didn't want his affair with Doll to terminate, because he had grown exceedingly fond of her. Embracing her was like embracing youth and life, and now that he had lost one of those blessings and was threatened with the loss of the other she seemed more precious than all his attainments. Resting in a sickbed, Gus became introspective, and he brooded gloomily upon the madness of men in trading youth and self-respect and often honor for a success that once achieved was not enjoyed. Looking back, the things that had seemed important to him once—promotions, salary increases— seemed mere baubles now, and those things which at the time had seemed trifles—a pretty girl's smile, a gay trip to Tamarack with Doll —seemed the very treasures of existence.

During his long hours of rest he sketched a plan for the remainder of his life, and in it Doll loomed as the central figure. He would make it worth her while to come to Chicago, where he would set her up in a place of her own. Everything would be in the best of taste and he would spend long hours with her, not necessarily making love but perhaps only listening to her pleasant conversation and enjoying the beauty of her hair and skin and figure. He wanted a sanctuary to which he could go and forget that some day another heart attack would strike like an assassin. He wanted restfulness and quietude, and expe- rience told him that a three-year-old boy would not contribute to that. So the boy could remain in Clayton Junction, where his aunt would give him the best of care.

When Gus was able to travel, he made a final trip to Clayton Junc- tion and presented his plans to Doll. His appearance shocked her; he certainly looked as if he had been a sick man. He was thinner and there were pouches beneath his eyes and he carried a cane. But it was his mental attitude which betrayed his illness and his growing older. He took care not to walk fast and he avoided stairs. The cocky, perky bluster had vanished from his spirit, and Doll remembered that her mother used to comment that those big, vigorous men always seemed to break all at once and grow old over night. Only when they made love did Gus seem like his old self, and she remembered another favorite axiom of her mother: that even with one foot in the grave a man was never too old for monkeyshines. Living with Doll's father had made her mother cynical about men.

Doll listened in silence while Gus outlined his plan. They had rented a rig and driven north from town, but instead of turning east toward Tamarack, Gus drove west into the country where they could discuss their future without distractions. It was a raw afternoon, the sky packed with huge clouds like great rocks in different shades of gray, and the land rolling away to the horizon looked half-frozen already and the color of dead grass. The trees had lost their autumnal yellows and scarlets; they stood stark and bare, like the masts of sailing ships stripped for stormy weather. The bleak landscape depressed Doll; she hated winter. Even when she was a child its bobsled rides and skating parties had not compensated for her sense of panic at the fury of blizzards howling down across the continent. In winter, she thought, you saw the skeleton of existence, and she preferred the comfortable languor of summer when the bones of reality were gayly clothed.

Gus pictured their future together in smooth, glowing colors; hearing him talk was like swallowing the peach-tinted warmth of brandy. In imagination she saw Chicago as a romantic city and herself as a romantic person. She would be a woman of the world riding along a glittering avenue in a fine carriage, a faint scent of adventure lingering about her like perfume. She saw herself at a theater full of bright pastel gowns and jewels and gleaming shirt fronts, with the orchestra swinging into the overture; and she imagined the after-theater suppers with rich, exotic foods.

She couldn't imagine little Gus in that existence. He would be bewildered and unhappy away from his trains and his Aunt Lucy. In a few years, perhaps, after he was older, she would send for him. Meanwhile, Lucy would give him excellent care. Probably better care, she thought, than she herself would give him, for Doll cheerfully recognized her shortcomings as a mother.

Gus's offer seemed a great stroke of fortune. In gratitude and affection she linked her arm through his and snuggled against him.

"You've always been so good to me, Gus," she said.

And so for the next month Doll was busy making preparations for her departure. When Lucy learned what was afoot she experienced a jumble of contradictory emotions.

"I don't know what I'll ever do without you, Sis," she kept saying. "Gee, it'll be lonesome here. I'll miss you so much, Sis."

And that was quite true, but in a way Lucy was glad that once again she would be the only woman in the household. She realized that since Doll had come to live with them Tim had changed. Perhaps with Doll gone he would be more the way he was in the early days of their marriage.

Lucy was delighted that Doll was leaving little Gus behind. Without him, she would have felt bereft. Now he would be hers alone, hers to wait upon and sacrifice for. Already she thought of him almost as her own child, and perhaps as time passed and the memory of Doll faded he would come to think of her as his mother.

When Tim learned that Doll was going away he became angry.

This astonished Lucy; she guessed there was just no pleasing that man. He had been annoyed when Doll came to make her home with them; he had often privately complained to Lucy about her sister's presence; and now her leaving nettled him. Lucy told herself it all boiled down to his disliking Doll; no matter what Doll did, he would find fault. Tim said it was a disgrace that a sister-in-law of his should be going to Chicago and openly becoming Gus Phelan's mistress.

"If you go through with it," he warned, "you needn't ever come back here. You needn't ever darken this door again."

Doll laughed.

"Oh Tim, you're funny. You don't realize how funny you are."

That angered him and he stamped out of the sitting room to brood downstairs. His objections influenced Doll not one whit; she went right ahead with her plans, ignoring him for the inconsequential person he was.

And at last Doll was ready to leave. It was an evening a few days before Christmas when she boarded the Denver-to-Chicago express train. And a beautiful evening it was, the ground shining with silvery snow and more snow falling in great feathery flakes through the mild, windless air. With Christmas so near even Clayton Junction wore a festive look, and as little Gus accompanied Doll and Lucy to the station he kept prattling about Santa Claus and the sugarplums and red toys he hoped to discover in his stocking.

Doll was as gay as her son, and she had never looked more beautiful. Her eyes were shining and her smooth cheeks glowed. She held herself proudly, like a great lady, but there was a warm humanness and piquancy about her, too. Several snowflakes had become entangled in her hair, and these flavored her beauty with sauciness.

They entered the little wooden station. A potbellied stove glowed cherry-red in the waiting room, and the many-paned windows were smooth and black. A good many people were waiting for trains that night, and when Gus entered with his aunt and mother whispers ran around the varnished red benches.

"It's stuffy in here," Doll said. "Let's go outside, Sis."

So in the gently falling snow they waited on the brick platform. By and by a great flower of white light bloomed in the west, and as the train approached you could see snowflakes twisting down in its headlight shaft. People crowded from the station. The locomotive shook the ground, its balloon stack throwing out cinders, its big cowcatcher snooping along ahead.

Light from the cars shafted to the snowy platform, and finally the last passenger for Clayton Junction alighted. And then the people who were going away, as Mamma was, climbed the steps.

"Good-by, Sis. Take care of yourself."

Mamma was kissing Aunt Lucy.

"Good-by, Gus. Be a good boy."

Her lips pressed his; he was drawn against her soft body. She smelled sweet, as always; a fragrant odor of perfume and powdered skin and hair and clothes that would go with him down the years.

Good-by. Good-by. Wave good-by to Mamma, Gus. Good-by, darling . . .

The sight of her through the car window. The conductor waving his lantern. The gigantic sound of the locomotive beginning to labor. The car lights moving. The red lantern and the green lantern on the end of the train, going away down the track through the snow.

"Good-by, Mamma, good-by . . ."

But she couldn't hear him now, so far away.

Aunt Lucy took his hand; they trudged homeward. Gus felt odd. He felt as if something were inside his chest trying to come up his throat and get out.

They climbed the steps and entered the sitting room. Uncle Tim was sitting there. He scowled at them while Aunt Lucy helped Gus from his outdoor clothes.

And still that thing in his chest kept fighting to get out. Gus fought back. But he didn't like it.

He walked over to the window and gazed out at the railroad yards in the falling snow and then suddenly the lights began to swim and blur and the thing inside his chest was getting out and he was sobbing heavily.

Somebody said, "Shut up!"

But Gus couldn't shut up. He had tried to keep the thing inside his chest but it wouldn't stay there.

"I said shut up!"

It was Uncle Tim yelling at him but the more Gus fought to hold the sobs inside his chest the more powerfully they rose up his throat.

Uncle Tim said, "Now listen! When I tell you to do a thing you've got to learn to do it. You've been spoiled long enough. I'm going to start teaching you—"

And Tim seized little Gus and took him into the bedroom and gave him the hard whipping he had been needing for so long.

Lucy stood outside the closed door, wringing her hands.

6

ONE MORNING a few days after Doll's departure Tim climbed the steps from the saloon bearing a letter. Little Gus had been playing trainman in the living room, but when his uncle entered he stopped waving his arms and making train noises. He made his body small inside his clothes and edged to a far corner of the room, observing his uncle's every move with large round eyes. But this morning Tim wasn't interested in Gus. He stalked out to the kitchen where Lucy was washing dishes.

"From her," he said, holding up the letter. "It's about time she wrote."

The letter threw Lucy into great excitement. She dropped the dish-cloth and made a grab for the envelope, but Tim jerked it back.

"You fool! You'll get it all wet."

He paced into the living room, seating himself and staring darkly at the wall.

Drying her hands, Lucy hurried after him, and when she took the letter she noticed Tim's fingers shaking. She guessed that beneath his cold exterior he was as excited about hearing from Doll as she was.

The letter had traveled from Chicago in an exciting envelope. In the upper left corner the words "Palmer House" were printed, and there was a woodcut of a grand-looking building with flags flying and high-stepping horses drawing carriages along the street. Staring down at the envelope covered with Doll's large, free-flowing handwriting, Lucy experienced the same enchantment she used to feel when she carried breakfast into her sister's room and listened to Doll's recital of what had happened the previous evening.

"Aren't you going to open it?" Tim demanded.

So with unsteady fingers Lucy tore open the envelope. A faint scent of Doll's perfume floated up from the paper. The letter had not been dated except by the word "Tuesday," and it began, "Dear Sis."

It didn't contain much news, really. She said she had arrived safely in Chicago after a journey uneventful save for meeting on the train an interesting and charming gentleman named Mr. Schulze, a farm-implement salesman. By the time the train puffed into Chicago she and Mr. Schulze were like old friends, and he had invited her to dine out with him. Because of Gus Phelan she had refused, but Mr.

Schulze had given her his office address and urged her to get in touch with him if she should change her mind.

"Hated to turn him down," she wrote, "for he was so jolly and such good fun, but I thought maybe I'd better not. Honestly though, Sis, it's wonderful how nice everyone is, even in a big place like Chicago. It's not hard at all to get acquainted."

Gus had met her at the station with a nosegay in one hand and a box of bonbons in the other, and he had been so kind and wonderful that she felt at home instantly. In the letter Doll didn't refer to him as Gus. She called him "Mr. Phelan," as if writing his name demanded more dignity than speaking it.

She was staying at the hotel temporarily, till she found a suitable place to live. To tell the truth she had been too busy having a good time to do much about getting settled. She liked Chicago a great deal. Nothing dull about that town; something going on every minute.

"Some different from Clayton Junction," she wrote.

She sent lots of love to little Gus; she hoped he was being a good boy and not too much trouble. As for Sis, she admonished her not to work too hard and to get out and have a little fun. After all, one didn't live forever. She promised to write again soon. "Although," she added, "you know me and how hard it is for me to get around to writing letters. Don't worry if you don't hear from me too often."

After Lucy had finished, Tim growled:

"Is that all?"

"It seems to be."

He muttered a foul word and marched from the room. Downstairs, there were no customers in the saloon, and Tim stood staring out at Second Avenue. It was a gray morning and the town looked drab. Tim thought of Chicago—"some different from Clayton Junction." He thought of Doll in her bedroom at the Palmer House, her body smooth in a satin gown; and he thought of Gus Phelan calling on her there. Tim's blood was lemon juice that morning, and to sweeten it up he poured a drink of whiskey. After a while he poured another, and then another. He felt better then, and his self-respect came back. He told himself Doll had always been secretly attracted to him, but because of Lucy she had repelled him. He told himself that some day the Chicago, Tamarack & Pacific would realize what a good man it had lost when it lost Tim Mahoney. He swallowed yet another drink, and it occurred to him that he had been a fool all these years in keeping away from whiskey. Long ago his father had warned that a saloonkeeper should never drink, because that was a sure way to consume your profits and go into bankruptcy, but he realized now that like everyone else his father had been in a conspiracy against him.

He was quite drunk by noon, when Lucy came down to tell him his meal was getting cold.

"Let it," he said. "I'm busy."

While he poured more whiskey, Lucy stood watching with a worried look. But when he favored her with a hard stare she hurried out. He tossed down the whiskey and weaved to the door, climbing uncertainly to the second floor.

Instead of going to the table, Tim flopped into a chair in the sitting room, where he sat on the end of his spine, his eyes closed. Several times Lucy came to the door and watched apprehensively. Once little Gus started to speak, but she shot him a warning glance and put her forefinger to her lips and shook her head.

When she looked at Tim again she saw his eyes watching her. They had a glassy alcoholic gleam and his voice was hoarse.

"You ain't fooling me," he declared. "Not for a minute you ain't."

She didn't know what he was talking about.

"I know what you're cooking up," he said. "You and that sister of yours. You're planning to run away. You're planning to go to Chicago."

"Tim," she said, "I'm never. I'm never planning such a thing."

"A man has got rights," Tim said. "A husband has got rights. You can't get away with it."

Tears glistened on Lucy's face, and she leaned against the doorjamb, sobbing. Her shoulders looked thin and sagging like an old woman's.

Tim didn't stand up and go to her and put his arms around her. Except for closing his eyes again, he didn't stir. In the gray winter light his face looked lean and bitter.

Presently Lucy ceased sobbing and stood staring at her husband while she dabbed her eyes with her apron. His breathing had grown heavy and coarse. She watched him for several minutes before tiptoeing across the sitting room and picking up little Gus. She carried the child into the kitchen and softly closed the door. Since Doll's departure Tim had already whipped Gus three times, and she thought she couldn't bear to have it happen again today.

In the same mail with the letter to Lucy another letter arrived in Clayton Junction on Palmer House stationery. It was addressed to Frank MacGowan, and he sat now at his heaped desk in the *Tribune* office, reading it for the fifth time.

The letter was full of Chicago; not perhaps Chicago as it actually was, but Chicago as it looked to Doll, a place crowded with the excitement of hansom cabs and good-looking men and warm cafés and music.

"It's a great place, Frank," she wrote. "You ought to come in for a visit."

Frank let his imagination plan such a trip. He imagined attending the theater with Doll and eating midnight supper, and after that they would lie all night in each other's arms. But even while he planned it he knew he would not make such a trip. For years he hadn't ventured farther from Clayton Junction than Tamarack, and he doubted now that he ever would. Long ago when he purchased the *Tribune* he was full of ambition; he intended building the paper into a first-class sheet and then selling it and using the money to buy another paper in a better town. But gradually his ambition oozed away. He discovered it made no difference to Clayton Junction whether he published a well-written paper or a slovenly one. The subscription list and the advertising accounts remained the same. So little by little he fell into the habit of publishing the paper in the easiest way. Finally, his interest and pride simmered down to the editorial columns alone; and not one subscriber in twenty read his editorials. The indifference of the town had undermined his ambition.

Yet the paper made money. At the end of each year he was several hundred dollars to the good. But money didn't mean much to Frank. He seldom bought a new suit, because he preferred the comfort of his old ones; and he liked eating and sleeping in the back room of the office because it was convenient. So most of his profits went into his bank account.

Perhaps the chief reason for his lack of interest in money was Karl Marx. His copy of *Das Kapital* was a thumb-smudged, dog-eared, much-penciled book. Frank liked to sit comfortably in his swivel chair and daydream away the hours about the world of the future. And a fine shining world it was, with bright clean towns and poverty only a bad memory and human beings no longer selfish or cruel. After a session like that he would pull his chair closer to the desk and scratch out an editorial. But the editorial would alarm nobody, because always it stressed the delights of that Utopian future and ignored the means of bringing it about. He was more scholar and prophet than crusader, and any attacks on the social order of his day were buried deep within paragraphs and clothed in involved sentences. His editorials, people thought, were like the somnolent discourses of an old-fashioned preacher.

In the politics of his era he had such scant interest that he didn't even bother to vote. He realized vaguely there was corruption in high places and in low, but some day the Utopian future would come along and change all that and men would be honest and good. His was the large view, the long view. Clayton Junction and Tamarack were ruled by a machine, but it never occurred to him to attack it, not because he lacked courage but because that would have involved pen-lashing men he knew, little officeholders who were cogs in the organization. They were genial men who passed the time of day with him on the street, men with wives and children. He didn't want to write anything that would hurt anybody.

The politicians of the county misunderstood him. They thought he was being shrewd by keeping out of campaigns; he was a "safe" editor. They had never heard of Karl Marx, and they didn't care how often he mentioned *Das Kapital* so long as he didn't point out what group owned the houses on Rafferty Street. They rewarded the *Tribune* with political favors—such plums as county advertising—and for this Frank MacGowan courteously thanked them and never dreamed they thought they were buying him off.

Frank answered Doll's letter at once, but he didn't receive a reply for some time. As soon as he dropped his letter into the mail box he began feeling expectant, and all the next day he thought, "She has it by this time. Maybe she's reading it right now." He formed the habit of limping to the post office several times a day, but there was never an envelope covered with her handwriting. "Maybe tomorrow," he told himself; and when he wakened next morning he would think, "Maybe today."

He always forgave her not writing, just as he had always forgiven her everything. She was a natural woman, he thought; closer to nature than any person he had known. He told himself you couldn't blame her for her shortcomings any more than you could blame a brook for taking the easy way and meandering through flowery meadows; and you might as well blame the songbirds for flying away in the autumn as to censure her for leaving Clayton Junction.

After ten days he wrote her another letter, and two weeks later yet another, but still she did not reply. Finally he gave up hope of hearing from her at all. But she was often in his thoughts and as time went on it seemed he missed her more than he had immediately after her departure. Back in the days when she lived in Clayton Junction life had tang, for when he left the shop he never knew but that he would encounter her on the street, and she was always dropping into the office at unexpected times to tidy up his living quarters and to cook a meal for him and Vince Fye. It had been a long time now since the room where he and Vince batched it had been properly dusted. And they never sang any more when they did the dishes.

Vince had held his job with Frank longer than he had ever held a job in his life. Always before he had either been given his time for too extended a bout with the bottle or he had grown restless and moved on.

"I always had an itching foot," he told Frank. "Reckon I'd have been a hobo if I hadn't taken up the printing trade where I could drift when I felt like it. But I'm getting along in years now."

And that was very true; Vince had aged in the last year. He was bothered by pains in his legs and he shuffled more slowly from composing stone to typecase, and his fingers weren't as nimble as they used to be. He realized his roving days were over and he told himself he was lucky to find a good niche in which to work during his declining years. He and Frank were more like brothers than like employee and employer. Frank never gave him an order except in the mildest terms. "Maybe we ought to get that Fair Store ad set up first thing tomorrow," Frank would say, and Vince would deliberate the problem, his jaws working his tobacco, and finally reply, "Yep—then it'll be out of the way."

Vince knew that Frank would never turn him out, and now that he was too old to buck the current of existence he was content to remain in a backwater shop where nothing much ever happened. He had lived a full and even rich life, knocking about the country, working in Maine and New York and in San Francisco when it was lusty and full of hell; and he had plenty of memories to entertain him on the long evenings when he and Frank sat in the yellow lamplight of their living quarters. While Frank read, Vince sat rocking and chewing gently, and sometimes his eyes were merry and he would chuckle to himself about some escapade that had taken place thirty years before.

Vince missed Doll too; she was a fine woman. She was the kind of woman he had always taken a shine to in his younger days in frontier towns; free and easy and good-natured and generous. It had warmed his old heart when, after her child was born, she had taken to coming to the print shop of an evening to call on Frank. He used to vanish discreetly after supper, grinning wickedly to himself as he ambled to the nearest saloon. She made him feel young again and full of ginger; sometimes even he would give her a little pat or a gentle pinch. Now and then across the supper table she flirted with him, and that made him feel like jumping into the air and kicking his heels together and shouting, "Yippee!"

Yes indeed, a fine piece of female flesh, that Doll! Small wonder Frank had grown abstracted in the months since she had gone. One evening in March when they were sitting after supper Vince observed Frank for several minutes. His book lay open and he sat in a brown study. Vince cleared his throat but Frank paid no attention, so he cleared it again, very loud, and Frank glanced across the table and said:

"What's the matter?"

"I've been thinkin'," Vince said. "I've been thinkin' about you and what you need. You need female companionship."

Frank didn't reply for a long moment, and then with a smile he said, "Maybe I do, Vince, at that."

"Well," Vince said, "what are you waitin' for?"

So Frank got down his walking cane and limped to the front door and out into the early spring night. Vince followed him to the door and said, "I'd go with you if I wasn't so damned old." Frank tapped away down the sidewalk, toward Rafferty Street, and Vince stood watching till he turned the corner, his shadow narrow and jerky in the light from the oil street lamp.

And suddenly the sight of him, so derelict in spirit, brought a lump to Vince's throat, and he steamed back into the shop and wrote Doll an ungrammatical and profane letter, demanding what in hell she meant by neglecting her old friends.

A few mornings later Frank received his second letter from Doll. Vince knew something good had happened as soon as he heard Frank returning from the post office; his step was brisker, the tap of his cane sharper. When he came back to the stool where Vince was setting type he tried to appear casual, but his face was all smiles.

Vince peered over his glasses and said, "What have you been drinking? It must have been powerful."

Frank held up the letter. "From Chicago," he said.

Vince put down his composing stick and with the back of a hand swabbed at the trickle of tobacco juice running from the corner of his mouth.

"Well now, ain't that nice! Ain't that a surprise!"

He swabbed at his mouth again and spat copiously. It was really a nervous gesture, for he was uneasy lest Doll had mentioned his letter. He thought she had more sense than that, but he was uneasy just the same.

"I'll read it to you," Frank said, plucking the letter from the envelope. It was penned on lavender paper, faintly scented.

Doll began by blaming herself unmercifully for not being a better correspondent, especially in view of the many nice letters Frank had sent her. She wanted him to know, she said, that his letters were always as welcome as flowers in May, and if he would keep on writing her she would attempt to reply oftener.

However, she was certain he would forgive her if he knew how busy she had been. About six weeks ago Mr. Phelan had purchased and deeded to her a lovely little house in a nice residential district. But Frank was mistaken if he thought she hadn't been busy getting settled. The house had been new and unfurnished, and she had gone on countless buying forays, selecting carpets and lamps with colored globes and furniture upholstered in plush. Whew! She had hired a Negro woman named Minnie to help her get settled, and at Mr. Phelan's suggestion she was retaining Minnie as cook and maid.

"Oh, Frank," she wrote, "I'm so happy I feel like singing most of the time. The only fly in the beer is that sometimes I get a wee bit lonesome for somebody to talk to—you know, to *really* talk to. Mr. Phelan has been wonderful but I always feel I have to watch what I say more than I did with you and Sis and Vince. If only you three and little Gus could live here we'd have some good times, wouldn't we? Since he bought the house Mr. Phelan don't like to go out much in the evening, we haven't been to a show or a restaurant in ages. He's not very well, Frank, I think his heart's worse than he lets on. Sometimes when he's tired he looks quite old and it almost scares me. I feel so young, and he looks so old it's almost like he was my grandfather.

"But there I go talking about myself all the time. How are you and Vince, anyway? Do you ever see Gus and Sis and the rest of the Mahoney family? (Not that you're missing anything if you *don't* see the *rest* of it—ha, ha.) Sis writes me that the rest of the Mahoney family has taken up drinking, and I think she's worried. But you know how Sis is, she never complains, always afraid of worrying me. Sometimes I wonder if he's good to her and Gus. Maybe you'll call on that family sometime and give me the real news.

"Well, I guess that's about all for this time. I hope this finds you well. Do write me, and tell Vince Fye I'd *love* to hear from him! With love, Doll."

As Frank finished the letter Vince made his face expressionless.

"Now what do you s'pose she meant about loving to hear from me? You don't s'pose the girl's getting sweet on me, do you?"

Frank laughed and said he wouldn't bet that she wasn't; Vince possessed many lady-killing qualities. And he tapped off to the front of the shop where he spent the rest of the morning writing a reply to Doll. As Vince turned back to his typecase he was grinning wickedly.

The only serious disagreement between Vince and Frank took place the following autumn, and it provided a subject of argument for years to come. Vince always maintained that Frank had been a softhearted visionary to act as he did, whereas Frank said that if all men had been like Vince, blind to progress, the human race would still be walking on all fours.

"If you'd been there when the first man invented the wheel," Frank said, "you would have told him it never would work."

"Maybe I would and maybe I wouldn't. But if you'd been there when the first man thought he'd invented perpetual motion, you'd have invested in the damned thing."

It all began one rainy afternoon late in September. Frank had spent an hour in the office of the Fair Store, aiding Isaac Goldstein, the proprietor, in writing that week's ad. Most of the business establishments in Clayton Junction ran the same ad week after week from one year's end to another, mere stodgy announcements of the business and its purpose. Not the Fair Store. The Fair Store dealt in bargains and twice-a-year Quitting-Business sales, and although it always sold at a loss it managed, somehow, to prosper. Frank and Isaac Goldstein were great friends, possibly because although they lived in the town they did not consider themselves of the town. Their origins were far away, Frank's in Pennsylvania, Isaac Goldstein's in a Central European ghetto, and each in his own manner kept in touch with what was happening in the world. With his books and his magazines Frank knew what ideas people were discussing in New York and London and Paris; whereas Isaac Goldstein's quick brain knew what price traders in Chicago and New York and Liverpool had been willing to pay yesterday for a pound of cotton or a bushel of wheat, and what the current interest rate was in Wall Street.

Twenty years before Isaac Goldstein had trudged along the raw, new roads of the Middle West with a pack on his back, selling needles and thread and dress goods to farm wives; and then all at once he had a store of his own in Clayton Junction; and twenty and forty years hence there would be a Goldstein's Department Store in Tamarack, occupying half a city block, all sprung from the commercial acorn of a little, dark, energetic man who had bustled into farmyards and said brokenly, "Lady, you like bargains in thread, maybe, look the best thread at half-price."

Collaborating on an ad with Isaac Goldstein afforded Frank endless amusement, even though what should have been ten minutes' work took an hour. Isaac would dictate an item to be listed, but when it came to setting the selling price he would groan and exclaim, "It's terrible, Frank, to let it go at that. I'm losing money. It's killing me." But when Frank suggested a higher price Isaac would say, "And drive people away from my place of business? No, no—better a small profit than none, and I've been killed before." What troubled Isaac with his delight in bargaining, Frank suspected, was the necessity for setting down a definite price in irrevocable black-and-white.

On that afternoon, writing the ad had been particularly hectic, for with rain soaking their fields farmers had been unable to work and many had driven into town for shopping. The Fair Store had many customers—women who had bought dress goods from Isaac Goldstein's pack years before—and with such an influx of business Isaac verged on hysteria and kept scurrying back and forth between the office and the trade. But at last the job was done and Frank left the store.

Rain was drizzling from a low sky, and the boots of country people coated the board sidewalks with gleaming tan mud. The air had a rich smell of autumnal vegetation and of the steaming bodies of the horses hitched along the street. Frank limped with his head down against the raindrops, and as he passed beneath a wooden awning he heard someone call his name. He looked up and saw Lucy Mahoney, an umbrella in one hand and her other holding up her skirts from the mud. Little Gus was with her.

"Hello!" Frank exclaimed. "I don't see much of you folks any more. How's the young man?"

"I know you," Gus said. "You're Frank."

"Mr. MacGowan, honey," Lucy told him.

"Frank," Gus said.

Lucy giggled, and as always on such a social occasion she squirmed and wagged her tail like a delighted fox terrier.

"I'm almost four years old," Gus said. "I'm going to school next year."

Frank expressed astonishment. Really now, was Gus actually going to school next year?

"Sure," Gus said. "I can count. One, two, three, four—see, I can count. Five, six, seven—"

"He's awfully smart," Lucy said. "He picks up things fast."

"Sure," Gus said.

"You're quite a young man, aren't you!" Frank said. "My goodness, you're growing like a weed!"

And that was no mere pleasantry; it seemed to Frank that Gus looked twice as big as he remembered him. A big boy for his age with a large frame and chubby flesh. And it seemed too that Gus had changed in some other indefinable way. He was no longer a serene, almost dreamy child; something inside him had seemed to harden. He was not exactly defiant or insolent, but he was growing in that direction.

"Poor little devil," Frank thought. "What can you expect?"

He thought too that some equally indefinable change had taken place in Lucy. Now that the first smiles of their encounter had passed, he noticed that she seemed thinner and washed out, and deep in her eyes there lurked a look of perpetual worrying. Thin wrinkles—as fine as threads—were beginning to appear in her face. When he inquired after her health she said that as a matter of fact she hadn't been any too well lately; it seemed to be her stomach.

Frank asked:

"And how about Doll? Do you hear from her often?"

Lucy emitted her nervous little giggle and said:

"Well, not as often as we'd like to. But of course I'd like to hear every day."

"So would I," Frank thought; but aloud he said, "I've had three or four letters from her. She seems to like Chicago."

"Yes, she does. But you know Doll. She likes excitement."

Lucy urged Frank to drop in and see them; and then Lucy and Gus walked on down the street. Frank stood looking after them. Once, Gus glanced back and stuck out his tongue. Frank grinned and then Gus grinned too, as if he wanted it understood no rudeness was intended.

The encounter left Frank disturbed, and as he plodded on toward his shop a large melancholy enveloped him as the rain enveloped the town. He thought how swiftly time passed; it seemed such a little while ago that he and Doll walked the streets of Clayton Junction while she worried about the birth of her child. His thoughts were so wholly turned in upon himself that he didn't notice the man sitting in the office as he entered the shop and plodded back to the typecase with the Fair Store ad.

"What's he want?" Vince asked.

"Who?"

"Why damn it man, where's your eyes? That feller who's been waitin' for you the last hour."

Vince backswiped the tobacco juice from his chin and jerked a thumb toward the office.

"Oh," Frank said. "I don't know. I'll find out."

Vince scowled over his glasses as Frank moved away toward the office. Then he ran a smudgy forefinger down the sheet of Fair Store copy. But his mind didn't follow his forefinger; his mind followed Frank. The presence of that stranger filled him with uneasiness. The stranger had short legs and a stomach that looked as if he had just eaten a bushel of apples and swallowed a keg of beer. He had a deep double chin and a thick yellow mustache that drooped lugubriously. As soon as he had waddled into the shop and asked for the editor Vince had bristled with suspicion. He didn't know why. The man had spoken with a heavy Germanic accent, and something told Vince he was a printer. Maybe it was the professional way he sized up the shop or perhaps it was the type grime that had worked in deeply under his nails.

Vince kept peering toward the office where Frank had shaken hands with the stranger and where they now sat talking. He was almighty curious. Finally he put down his composing stick and went to a spittoon and cleaned out his mouth. Then he brought out his plug and bit off a fresh chaw and paced to the office.

Frank looked up and said, "Vince, meet Mr. Herman Bohnschweiger of St. Louis."

"*Ja*, we met already," said Mr. Bohnschweiger.

"But we ain't shook yet," Vince said tartly. He went to Mr. Bohnschweiger's chair and took a hand that was deeply fat-cushioned.

"Sit down, Vince," Frank said. "Mr. Bohnschweiger is inventing a machine that will set type."

That was like tossing a half-dozen cats at an old, fight-scarred dog. Vince could feel his short hairs rising; if there was anything that riled him it was this damned nonsense he had heard in recent years about the possibility of setting type by machine. It was contrary to nature. The only kind of machine Vince could envision was a Frankenstein monster that would stand before a typecase and pluck out letters and click them into a composing stick.

He plopped into a chair, chewing belligerently. The German had handed Frank some great sheets covered with drawings, and now he waddled to the desk and explained how the machine would operate. Vince stared at him with hostile eyes. The man was obviously an enemy of society, especially of that portion of society made up of typesetters. Probably at some time a typesetter had done him a bad turn, and ever since he had been hatching this scheme to throw all typesetters out of work. Not, of course, that the scheme would ever succceed!

"Don't you want to see these?" Frank asked.

"Nope," Vince said.

But he did want to see those drawings, despite his knowing very well that typesetting machines and perpetual motion were products of unbalanced minds. Yet he didn't budge from his chair. Outside, the rain had settled to a steady downpour and on the office panes the drops pursued one another endlessly.

Frank kept asking questions which Mr. Bohnschweiger answered at great length, struggling with the twin difficulties of the English language and technical elucidation. He seemed to have vast patience, and Vince guessed that time meant no more to him than to a hog. The low sky and the thick rain brought darkness early, and when Frank lighted a lamp he told Vince:

"You'd better look over these drawings."

So Vince yielded. He told himself that after all he should know something about that infernal invention, if only to be able to confute its heresies.

The intricate neatness of the drawings astonished him; the inked lines were as definite and sharp as the lines of an etching.

"Did you draw these?" he asked, looking at Mr. Bohnschweiger's thick fingers.

"*Ja,* who else?"

The first drawing depicted a machine that was as fat and squat as Mr. Bohnschweiger. An outlandish contraption! Vince wanted to laugh.

"Tell me one thing," he crowed. "Tell me just one little thing, Mr. Bohnschweiger. How can that thing walk up to a typecase and go to work?"

Mr. Bohnschweiger's scarlet face looked like a rubber balloon that couldn't withstand much more inblown air.

"*Nein!*" he exclaimed. "You do not unnerstand."

"Don't 'nine' me. Just show me. That's all."

So once more Mr. Bohnschweiger explained the operation of the machine. When he had finished he said, "Vell?"

Vince grinned. He felt better, now that he saw how insane the invention was. Mr. Bohnschweiger was manifestly crazy; a crazy inventor.

"I don't think it'd work," he said.

"Verk? But it does verk! In my chop in St. Looey it verks—"

"That's all right, mister," Vince said. "That's fine. You just go back to your shop and work it all you please."

Mr. Bohnschweiger had blue eyes, almost innocent blue, like a baby's. They looked now as if they might fill with tears. He turned to Frank.

"You don't t'ink it verks?"

"Yes, I think it works. But—well—there're so many parts. So many things to go wrong. And it'd be so expensive to manufacture. I'd want to think it over before I put any money into it."

"So," said Mr. Bohnschweiger. He looked from Frank to Vince and back to Frank. Then again he said, "So."

He heaved a hippopotamus sigh and at the desk patted the drawings into a neat square. He inserted them into an artist's portfolio and wrapped the portfolio in worn oilcloth, tying it with dirty old string. The office was quiet save for his breathing and the drip and splash of rain.

"Vell, goot-by," he said finally. "It is always the same. I need a leetle money to get started with it, but nobody believes it vill verk. So I start out on the road to show it to printers, but they laugh the hardest of all. . . . Vell, tonight I leaf for Omaha. Maybe somebody there vill not laugh."

The old office floor complained softly about Mr. Bohnschweiger's

tonnage as he waddled to the door. Frank had a last glimpse of him
as he passed the streaked windows on his way to Second Avenue.

Vince broke out laughing. "Cracked! Cracked as the old Liberty
Bell."

Frank did not reply. He felt troubled.

Vince felt troubled too, so while frying supper potatoes he reached
for his bottle and fortified himself with a couple of drinks. But instead
of smoothing his irritation the whiskey made that typesetting machine
loom with diabolical importance. Away back in a corner of Vince's
mind there lurked a suspicion that such a damn-fool machine might
turn out to be practical, and he tried to scare away that suspicion with
big talk. At the supper table he kept repeating his arguments against
the machine, but he couldn't get any response from Frank beyond an
occasional, "Maybe you're right."

"Of course I'm right! Settin' type is the most complicated thing a
man can do. Imagine the brass of that crazy old Dutchman!—thinkin'
a machine could do such work!"

Frank said nothing. He wasn't eating much—just pecking at his
food—and in memory he kept seeing the sharp black-and-white drawings of the typesetting machine and trying to follow the intricate mechanics of the device. And he kept seeing Herman Bohnschweiger too,
so gloomed by discouragement.

"Think I'll take a walk," Frank said, after supper. Vince eyed him
suspiciously and gruffed:

"Pretty wet night for that."

As soon as he emerged into the rainy darkness Frank knew he was
going to search for Mr. Bohnschweiger. He limped to Second Avenue
and south toward the railroad. The rain had driven other pedestrians
indoors and the store windows were black, but a light showed feebly
from far back in the Fair Store where Isaac Goldstein sat hunched
over a ledger. And as he passed opposite Mahoney's place he saw lights
burning in the saloon behind windows specked by last summer's flies
and crusted by last winter's smoke. He glanced up at the second story.
In the southeast window, shadowy against the lamplight, he made
out the figure of a small boy, observing from his low eyrie the world
of Clayton Junction. Frank paused. Little Gus was wearing a nightgown, and something in his stance suggested a diminutive cartoon of
a toga-clad emperor, surveying Rome from a balcony. Then a woman
appeared in the window. It was Lucy. She knelt, and Gus prodded
the pane with a forefinger, pointing at a locomotive that stood hissing
in the railroad yards. As the woman and the boy talked, a difference
of opinion seemed to develop, probably about going to bed; and at last

little Gus was lifted into her arms, not without protest, and carried from sight.

Frank sloshed on toward the station. The wind had risen, and in the headlight rays of the locomotive the raindrops were blown like translucent sand. The worn old bricks of the station platform gleamed emptily, and save for railroad men the station was empty, too. But of course the westbound train to Omaha was not due for an hour yet.

And as he left that place and brooded back along the platform Frank was thinking suddenly of Doll, of time gone and of letters she never wrote. The autumn damp had crawled into his bones; he wanted the warmth of whiskey; so he crossed Second Avenue and entered Mahoney's saloon. The first person he saw was Herman Bohnschweiger.

Mr. Bohnschweiger was sitting alone at a little bare table, nursing a mug of beer. A thick cloud of Teutonic gloom enveloped him; his heavy-lidded eyes flicked no recognition as he observed Frank limping across the sawdust floor.

"I was looking for you," Frank said.

"So?"

The monosyllable was not cordial.

"I want to hear more about your machine."

"Vell! Why didn't you say so?" The gloom cloud began to dissipate; Mr. Bohnschweiger removed his artist's portfolio from the extra chair and with sausage fingers waved an invitation to sit down. "I vill make you rich," he said.

And so for the second time that day Mr. Bohnschweiger launched into a discussion of the merits of his invention. He had just got under way when Tim Mahoney came from behind the bar and slouched to the table.

"What'll you have, gents?"

He had been drinking himself, and his apron looked as if a muddy dog had been sleeping on it. Black half-moons rimmed his nails and he could have stood a shave. Although he was still a youngish man his complexion was sallow; discontent had knifed two lines from his nose to the corners of his mouth; and his cold eyes held the bitterness of a man who had never contemplated peace or beauty in the world outside himself or the world inside. Frank watched his narrow legs as he shuffled away to the bar; and when he returned with beer and whiskey he slopped the drinks over the glass brims as he set them down.

As Frank sipped his drink Mr. Bohnschweiger talked on and on, piling fact upon fact, evidence upon evidence, until at last the type-setting machine lost its fantastic qualities and became a reasonable thing, and practical; and Mr. Bohnschweiger kept patiently elucidating even after four or five toughs from lower Rafferty Street came in and

ordered drinks and somebody sat down at the piano and banged out
a ribald song which drowned the sound of the rain pouring against
the windows and the long, sorrowing whistle of the evening train
which Mr. Bohnschweiger didn't take to Omaha.

The deal was virtually closed when, with midnight thick on the
town, Frank and Mr. Bohnschweiger left Mahoney's Saloon and labored homeward through the downpour. Vince Fye, with more rancor
than caution, had locked the front door, and Frank fumbled with his
key while water trickled down his spine. Mr. Bohnschweiger waited,
patient as a mountain.

Frank groped into the office to the lamp, and after bad luck with
several wet matches he struck a light at last, and the flame crawled
slowly around the wick. He fitted the glass chimney into its prongs,
peeled off his soaked coat and hat, and brought out whiskey. He had
invited Mr. Bohnschweiger to occupy his bed, but they had so much
to talk about that the half-hours slipped past and presently it was too
near morning to retire.

Except in mechanical matters, Mr. Bohnschweiger's mind was direct
and uncomplicated, and the company he had organized reflected his
simplicity. There were five thousand shares, each valued at twenty-five
dollars, but so few people had faith in his contraption that he held
nearly all the stock himself. In the end Frank agreed to purchase a
hundred shares, and next morning they boarded a horsecar and rode
to Tamarack to settle the affair in a lawyer's office.

The lawyer tugged his side whiskers as he studied the legal papers
Mr. Bohnschweiger produced from his portfolio. By and by he announced that the papers were quite in order, but he urged Frank to
reconsider his decision to invest money in a company whose assets
consisted so largely of patents on an invention which could never be
put to practical use. Mr. Bohnschweiger sat growing redder and redder.

"I've made up my mind," Frank said.

The lawyer shrugged. "It's your money, and I suppose if you want
to take a flyer it's your business. But I feel it's my duty to warn you."

So that morning Frank became the first person to buy any considerable number of shares in Mr. Bohnschweiger's company.

"You vill never regret it," Mr. Bohnschweiger assured him, as they
stood on the station platform in Clayton Junction that evening.

Nor did he; although after months elapsed and then years he wrote
his investment off as a complete loss. He admitted to Vince he had
put a little money into the thing, but he never confessed how much.
Vince assumed he had squandered perhaps a hundred dollars, and
sometimes he twitted Frank about it, good-naturedly now, for it had
become apparent to Vince that the talk about such machines was going

to die down and crazy inventors would turn their attentions to other fields.

Since Frank had no heirs, he comforted himself that he could afford to lose a good-sized sum on a whim. Sometimes he received letters from Mr. Bohnschweiger, assuring him that matters were proceeding satisfactorily although slowly. Other companies had been organized to manufacture such machines; companies with more resources than Mr. Bohnschweiger's; but they couldn't get around the fact that Mr. Bohnschweiger had invented and patented several devices essential to the success of a typesetting machine.

Letters from Mr. Bohnschweiger were not, however, what Frank hoped to receive as he waited in the post office for mail to be distributed. He always had the hope that a letter postmarked Chicago would come to him, and when such a letter failed to arrive he experienced a pang. But the pang lost intensity as the years rolled along toward the 1890's; and at last there was no pang at all. Sometimes he scarcely thought of Doll for weeks, and when he recalled his evenings with her he thought of the Frank who had escorted her about town as another person, a younger person distinct from the man with graying hair he saw in the mirror. And some evenings he would put down his book and ponder about that queer thing called time; that mortal foe of youth and beauty which men tried to drag down to the level of their understanding by fastening it to the clock and the calendar. He visited a secondhand bookstore in Tamarack and bought a number of volumes by the great philosophers, and gradually his conviction grew that man was an orphan in the universe inhabiting a planet that was itself a bewildered wanderer. And after much musing and reading he stumbled across a dictum that had to suffice as an answer to his questionings: the past existed only in memory and the future did not exist at all. Only the present had existence, and he began to think of life as a dream in the mind of some sound sleeper out in the wastes of space.

But getting out an issue of the *Tribune* each week was a very undream-like necessity, especially when he depended upon Vince to set the type. For the pains in Vince's legs persisted and increased, and one day a few years after Mr. Bohnschweiger's visit Frank realized that Vince was actually a very old man, and a feeble one. No longer did his fingers go flying over the cases; they moved painfully. It was necessary to hire another printer. Frank wanted to be tactful about it, so one evening he sighed and told Vince it was a fright how busy they were, and asked how he would like to become foreman in the shop with a printer working under him.

Vince sat rocking, his mouth so flaccid that the tobacco juice trickled from either corner unchecked. When Frank had presented the matter he said:

"There's too damn much work, and that's a fact. If I'm foreman I ought to have better wages."

Frank realized it was the old man's way of keeping up his self-respect, so he wrangled about it.

"You old owl," he said. "You've never been any good as a printer and you know it. And now asking—"

Whereupon Vince uttered a good many profane words. What would have become of the *Tribune* and its editor, he demanded, if it hadn't been for him? Why, that crazy inventor would have managed to steal everything Frank had, if Vince hadn't intervened with sound advice.

At last Vince was given a wage increase; and next day in relief Frank went to Tamarack and hired another printer, a young man named George who was told to humor the old foreman. But Vince didn't interfere with George's work; he took to sitting outside the shop when the weather was fine, lost in his memories.

It was about this time that Frank received a letter with a St. Louis postmark and the return address of a firm of lawyers. He had carried his big batch of mail—exchange papers, advertisements, bills—to the writing counter in the post office and was sorting through it when the long envelope turned up. He lifted it to the May sunlight and was about to tear it open when he heard a woman wishing him good afternoon. It was Lucy Mahoney.

She didn't, he thought, look well; the emery wheel of living so long with Tim had worn her down. The years had accentuated her tendencies toward thinness and round shoulders, and her features had sharpened, not into shrewishness but solicitude. She was still a smiling, tail-wagging fox terrier, eager to please, but deep in her eyes anxiety always lurked.

As they exchanged pleasantries, Frank slipped the letter from St. Louis into his pocket and gathered up the rest of his mail. Lucy glanced around at the other people in the post office and lowered her voice:

"I'd like to talk with you."

He nodded and suggested they walk to the corner together.

"Well," she said, when they reached the street, "I've finally heard from Doll again."

"How nice," he said. "How is she?"

"She's moved. To New York City."

It returned then—that nostalgic pang for the lost years; and his old sense of being wounded when he thought of her came back. And absurdly, he felt bereft because of the miles that had multiplied between them. In Chicago, she lived only an overnight journey away; tucked somewhere in his mind was the thought: "If I wanted to, I could get on a train and see her tomorrow." Chicago was close; the capital of the Middle West. But New York!

"When did she move?"

"I don't know exactly. I hadn't heard from her for a long time. At first she was pretty good about writing, but after while her letters came just now and then. And after that no letter at all for almost two years. Then yesterday I had this letter from New York. She tried to get me caught up on the news. Mr. Phelan died some time ago. He hadn't been well, you know. He was always such a nice man, too—so generous and jolly. I don't think it was really bad of Doll to go away with him like that, do you? He was more like a father to her."

They had left the hitching posts of the business district and were strolling along a residential street. Spring was at full flood, the air balmy.

"Doll was always such a case," Lucy said wistfully. "Even when we were girls I never could keep up with her. Well, she knew what she wanted, and I guess she's got it. She didn't like Clayton Junction at all. She used to say she belonged in a big city. Well, that's where she is now, and she loves it."

"Has she ever mentioned coming back for a visit?"

"Oh dear no! I'm sure she'd never do that. She didn't get along with Tim at all. And then the way the town treated her. No, I don't think she'll ever come back. But—and this is what I wanted to talk to you about. She wants me to go there for a visit. She even sent me the money."

"Are you going?"

Lucy's face and worried brow looked as if her decision would affect all humanity for centuries to come.

"I don't know," she said. "I just don't know."

"Would you like to?"

"Oh, I'm dying to go."

"Well then, you have the money for a ticket—"

"It's not that," she said.

They had reached the edge of town, and they strolled on along the white road curving north and east toward Tamarack. Thickets of wild plums were in blossom, their fragrance mingling with all the fresh, tender smells of loam and new grasses. Robins were chirping, and from a fence post a meadow lark sent forth liquid melody.

Lucy had withdrawn deep into her own problems, her lower lip between her teeth, her thin hands seeking each other for solace.

"I believe I'd go," Frank said. "It would do you good."

Lucy's lips trembled; she turned away. Her thin shoulders were in agitation, and she sank down to a stone by the roadside, her face in her hands.

"Don't," he said. "Don't cry."

But the floodgates were open now. Frank patted her shoulder.

"I'm sorry," he said.

Gradually the sobs subsided; she looked up and smiled wanly.

"I didn't mean to break down. But sometimes you can't help your-self, can you?"

"No," he said, "sometimes you can't."

"It's like Doll always said. You understand things, Frank. A woman wants a man to understand."

"Maybe it's what everybody wants."

"A woman especially. Tim never does. It just isn't in him. He's so —so bitter—and hard. It's been terrible, sometimes. Oh, I don't mean for me. I mean for Gus. He was such a good baby. But Tim—Tim's just about ruining him. You can't raise Gus that way. He's so smart— and he has a mind of his own. It's been bad for him, growing up in this town. He was such a sweet baby. Then Doll left. Doll would never have stood for Tim going after him the way he does."

"You mean he punishes him?"

"Sometimes I think I can't stand it another time." She began to sob again, then pulled herself together. "Gus has had a hard time. In this town. As soon as he started to school. Boys calling him that bad word. He's not the sort of child to take things like that without fighting. It's made him tough. Like a turtle with a shell. He's only eight years old, but he's tough. I don't want him to turn out bad, Frank."

"Why don't you take him with you to New York?"

She shook her head.

"I don't think . . . Don't blame Doll, Frank, but I don't think . . . She would have mentioned bringing him, wouldn't she? Maybe she'd have a gentleman friend and he'd see Gus. He's a big boy for his age. And Doll would want to look young and there would be Gus, growing like a weed. No, I can't take him, and I can't go, either. Because I wouldn't trust him with Tim."

"Is it that bad?"

"It was. But one time about a month ago—well, I couldn't stand it any more. That was all, I couldn't stand it. He'd have to whip me first, I said. He'd been drinking—he drinks so much, Frank—and he took hold of me and started to shove me aside, so he could get to Gus. I'm not very strong—my stomach's always upset—the doctor thinks maybe it's ulcers—but I fought back. Mamma always said even a worm would turn. It was easier, with Tim being drunk. He fell and hit his head. I was scared."

"You can't hurt a drunk man," Frank said.

"It did hurt him, though. Cut his scalp. You can't imagine how I felt when I saw blood. It knocked him out, and then Gus . . . well, don't blame the child, Frank, he's been through so much. Gus saw him lying there and he kicked him in the jaw. Tim never knew when he came to why his jaw was so sore. It was terrible, but he's laid off Gus. Except that he always nags the child. Goodness! It's a wonder to me he's as good a boy as he is. What time is it, Frank? Is it time for school to be out? I'll have to be getting home."

They were silent, walking back to town. When they parted Frank said:

"I have the beginnings of an idea. Maybe you can go to New York, after all."

"What is it?"

"Don't press me. I'll work on it."

And all the way back to the *Tribune* office he was lost in thought.

He found Vince Fye in his familiar chair outside, legs sprawled in front of him.

"Trying to block the sidewalk," Frank said. "There're ordinances to take care of fellows like you."

Vince's watery old eyes ignored him, but slowly the back of one hand floated up to his mouth and wiped at the brown juice. And still staring straight ahead Vince said:

"Report me, would you? Let 'em come after me. I'll shoot it out with 'em."

In the office, Frank reached into his pocket for his pipe, and his hand encountered that letter from St. Louis. He read it through once, then again. The law firm informed him that Mr. Bohnschweiger had died. The firm was representing his widow. A certain company was eager to acquire several patents which Mr. Bohnschweiger's company owned, and Mrs. Bohnschweiger had decided to sell out. Since she owned the majority of the stock, her decision was final.

The company making the purchase was willing to pay Frank Mac-Gowan a hundred dollars a share for his hundred shares of stock. Or it was willing to issue him an equal number of its own shares. In the legal firm's opinion, Mr. MacGowan might be well advised to take stock, because it appeared after all that machines to set type were practical, and there might be a considerable boom in the business of manufacturing such machines.

Grinning, Frank stood up and marched out to the sidewalk. But when he saw Vince Fye, so feeble, so far in the past, he slipped the letter into his pocket and turned back into the office. And until Vince died quietly in his sleep the next winter, Frank maintained the fiction that Mr. Bohnschweiger had certainly taken him for a trimming.

Frank could reach decisions fast when he had to, but he preferred operating in leisurely fashion. He liked to deal with problems the way an old dog deals with a bone: sniffing it, licking it, gnawing a little here and there, dozing over it, lying on his back and holding it between his paws and playing with it. Indeed, there was something reminiscent of a faithful old shepherd dog about him, shaggy, grizzled, lamed in a fight, dependable, easygoing; but still ready to scrap if that became necessary. And his office was about as unkempt as an old dog's yard.

But he never fretted about the lack of order. In the end things got done, somehow. It was his experience that often even the toughest problems dissolved when permitted to soak in their own juice.

At the moment, he had two problems under consideration: what to do about his typesetting stock, and how to arrange matters so Lucy might visit her sister; but he wasn't racing toward decisions. He pondered them while he puttered about at other things, between paragraphs of an editorial, while he filled his pipe and spilled tobacco crumbs onto the volume of Herbert Spencer he had been reading, while he fried pork chops for supper.

"What's biting you?" Vince demanded one evening. "The love bug?"

"Love? Oh no. Not any more."

"Why not? It's spring, ain't it? By crickety, maybe you need to go to Rafferty Street."

"Not tonight, Vince. I'm getting too old."

"Old! Listen to him! I'm old, ain't I? And what do you suppose I think about when I sit out there in front? Love—that's what!"

"Who's the lucky girl?"

"None of the floosies in this town! But there was a girl once in Frisco—by God, she was a woman! Make your eyes pop out! And who do you suppose she picked for a man?"

"Some handsome devil with a shiny rig," Frank grinned. "I'll bet she didn't know you were alive."

"By crickety!" Vince slapped the table. "I'll bet she did know I was alive! There was a lot of them knew I was lively alive! Not know I was alive—hell! Bet she's never forgot me. Oh, she was a woman. . . . It's a fact, Frank. A man goes through life and what does it all amount to? What does it get him? Just a pile of memories in the bureau drawer. And they're all about women. Women and liquor. They go together, the usual thing. When you get my age and look back, nothing else amounts to a damn. But sometimes a man wonders. Where did it all go to? All them years? You were right smack in 'em, and then they've gone on somewhere and left you. Where?"

"Where are the snows of yesteryear?" Frank said.

"Snow? Who said anything about snow? I was speaking about women. Always changing the subject on me. Never thought a son of mine would do that."

Frank pricked up his ears. "You never thought what?"

"I said," Vince snapped, "that I never thought a son of mine would change the subject on me."

And from that evening till his death, the delusion persisted in Vince's misting thoughts that Frank was his son. Communications between great areas of his brain broke down, so that sometimes he assumed he was living in San Francisco, and he would ask Frank to buy him a bottle of Bourbon in a certain saloon on Market Street. Frank bought it at Mahoney's, and through the evenings Vince nursed it, that warm milk of his second childhood.

Sometimes Frank arranged for Doc Harvey, very old himself now, to drop in for a "visit," and after he and Vince had exchanged yarns the doctor would examine him.

"Nothing wrong with me that any pills can touch," Vince snapped. "Just them pains in my legs. Rust pains—that's what they are. I'm rusting out. A nip of Bourbon is best for them."

In general, the doctor agreed with Vince's diagnosis and treatment.

With Vince failing so rapidly, Frank chided himself for having permitted the old man to work so long in the shop; and at other times he felt guilty for relieving him of his harness. Once he could sit and dream away the weeks, Vince seemed to deteriorate faster.

One evening a few days after receiving the letter from St. Louis, Frank sat at his desk scratching out a reply. He offered to sell twenty-five shares at a hundred dollars each, and to take seventy-five shares in the new company. Where business was concerned, he was not exactly the fool Vince thought him, and his native shrewdness told him to get back his original investment and then ride along with the remaining shares to see what occurred. During the next decade plenty occurred; by the turn of the century those seventy-five shares brought him the income of a well-to-do man; but he was not greedy and he never regretted selling twenty-five shares any more than he had regretted making the original investment when it looked as if his money had gone up the flue. The whole business always seemed dreamlike, anyway, and he was astounded at the accidental quality of the hinges on which human fortune turned. He never felt especially proud of his foresight; it was just good luck that Mr. Bohnschweiger hadn't been selling something worthless; and when the dividend checks grew fatter he lived on at the shop much as always. Often, fingering *Das Kapital,* he smiled ironically; and perhaps it was his knowledge of Marx which made him secretive about his good fortune. He didn't care to have Clayton Junction know his resources, so he opened a separate bank account in Tamarack to receive his dividends.

That evening he had just tucked the letter into an envelope when he

heard voices in the warm darkness outside: somebody talking to Vince.
At the open door, he saw Lucy Mahoney and her nephew.

"Well," he said. "Taking a walk?"

"That's just what we were doing," Lucy exclaimed. "It was such a
nice evening that Gus and I thought we'd get the air."

"That ain't it," Gus said scornfully. "She wants to make me stay
with her so I can't have fun."

"Don't talk that way, Gus," Lucy said. "You know what you'd do.
You'd get with those O'Brien boys and play in the railroad yards. It's
dangerous to hop freights, isn't it, Frank?"

"Great Heavens, boy," Frank exclaimed. "Don't tell me you hop
freights!"

"Sure. We ride 'em a little ways. Sometimes we talk to bums, too."

Frank whistled. "I don't think I'd do that."

"See there, Gus?" Lucy said.

But these splendid admonitions came to naught, for Vince spoke up.

"Hell's fires and pussycats!" he snapped. "Want to make a sissy out
of the young one? Ain't no harm in hopping freights. I've hopped a
good many, in my day."

"You have?" Gus said delightedly.

"Why hell, yes. In my booming days it was completely against my
principles to pay money to a railroad. Them robbers! I always went
from place to place by freight."

Gus said, "Gosh!"

And that was all Vince needed to launch himself on an odyssey of
memory; and when Lucy and Frank faded into the office and talked in
low tones they could hear Vince yarning on and on, and Gus saying,
"And what did you do when he pulled the gun on you?"

Lucy said:

"I thought if we walked by we might see you. I had another letter
from Sis today. She's just bound I'll go. I just don't know what to
write her."

"Have you mentioned it to Tim?"

"Oh, no! He doesn't even know I've heard from her. He used to get
my letters first and open them, so four or five years ago I told Sis to
address her letters to the Fair Store, with another envelope inside. Mr.
Goldstein's awfully nice—he understands how it is—and he lets me
know when I have a letter."

"*Sic semper tyrannis,*" Frank said.

"What?"

"The motto of Virginia," he murmured, "badly misused by Booth,
but true. 'Thus ever to tyrants.' What you've told me makes me
happy. The human spirit always finds a thousand ways to rebel against
tyrants."

"He's a tyrant, all right," Lucy said. "That's the trouble. I could up and go and he couldn't stop me, but he'd take it out on Gus. But you said you had a plan—"

"I have. It's practically complete. I'll put it into operation tomorrow."

"What is it?"

"You'll hear about it from Tim. I think it's better you shouldn't know anything about it. It will be easier for you to act innocent."

Outside, they found Gus trying to pin Vince down and get him to tell exactly how he had bested a famous gambler at his own game. Vince was acting nettled. To hell with unimportant details.

Lucy took Gus by the hand and their footsteps died away toward Second Avenue. The street grew silent. At last Vince said wickedly:

"Guess I was right at that."

"Right?"

"About you and the love bug and spring. But that Doll had more gumption than her sister. That Doll was a woman. Put me in mind of a girl I once knew in Cincinnati. Fine—"

"Oh, go to hell, you old owl," Frank said, turning back into the office.

"Where I'm headin'," Vince chuckled. "Yes, sir! Ought to be a big reunion one of these days."

Late the next afternoon Frank entered Mahoney's Saloon. The spring sun had sent the mercury climbing and Clayton Junction, down on the humid bottomlands, was steaming like an old booze-fighter in a Turkish bath. But the saloon was cool and dusky, the air pleasantly tinged with the odors of beer and liquor and the free-lunch smells of ham and dill pickles. At the cherry-red bar Frank swabbed his forehead and observed to Tim Mahoney that it was a hot day. Tim said it sure was, and asked:

"What'll you have?"

"Another quart of Bourbon for Vince."

Tim set the bottle on the bar. A couple of years before he had encouraged a mustache to bloom on his upper lip, in compensation for his receding hair, and now, pomaded and waxed, it curled thinly like a mustache brushed on in sand-colored paint. It was amazing how the departure of hair from his forehead and the arrival of the mustache had altered his appearance. He looked more foxlike; more the tinhorn sport.

Frank ordered a small whiskey for himself. Tim asked:

"How is the old man, anyway?"

"About the same."

"He'd died long ago," Tim said, "if it hadn't been for the whiskey. He was always a good customer."

Frank sipped his drink. They were alone in the saloon, for it was the off hour before the six o'clock whistle.

"It makes it hard for me," Frank said, "without Vince working. I've got this new fellow, but things don't go as fast as they did with Vince. What I need is a printer's devil."

"Printer's devil?"

"A kid to learn the trade. An apprentice. But you can't find a kid who'll do it."

Tim nodded sympathetically.

"All these modern kids want to do is raise hell. Lazy little devils. Always into something. Damned if I know what'll happen to this country when they grow up."

"It's terrible," Frank agreed solemnly.

"It sure is. Now take you and me when we were kids. We knew what work was. Up early, work hard all day—"

"That's the trouble," Frank said. "A printer's devil has a hard life. That's why they call him a devil—because he has such a hell of a time. Work from sunup to sundown—and then some. You can't find a modern kid who's willing to go through it."

"They're soft, all right," Tim said. "Coddled."

"That's it. Their parents don't want them to have to go through it. You know how ornery printers are. They kick them and cuff them around—"

"They do?"

"Oh, yes. Mean as hell to them. Take my man, George. He's a terror. If he had a printer's devil he'd skin him alive. And I couldn't do a thing about it. For that matter, the kid's parents couldn't either."

"They couldn't?"

"You know how the law goes," Frank lied. "Once you've signed up your kid to be a printer's devil, he's not your kid any more. The printer can work him to death, and if the kid doesn't step fast enough he can half kill him. Make him howl so you could hear him all over town. And that's exactly the way George would do it. But could you step in and stop it? No. You've signed him away—maybe for his summer vacation, maybe for five years—and you're helpless. Of course, you'd get his wages, and you wouldn't have to board and room him. But that wouldn't make up for the way the kid would suffer."

Frank finished his drink, picked up the bottle.

"Well, I'll move along. Vince was pretty thirsty when I left."

And he started toward the door.

"What's the rush?" Tim inquired. "Vince can wait for that drink. I'd like to ask you a question."

"Question?"

"Come on back to the bar. Here—have one on the house. Guess I'll have one myself."

"I really ought to be getting on—"

"Hell, let him wait for his snorter," Tim said, pouring two drinks. "What I want to ask you is about the wages a printer's devil gets."

"They're not much, when you consider all the hell the kid takes. George was telling me his last kid never was able to sit down. Had to sleep on his stomach."

Tim grinned. "He sure must know how to swing a paddle."

"Strap," Frank said. "With the kid's pants down. You can't blame George too much, though. He was a printer's devil himself, and he's got a lot of misery to pass on to the next generation."

"Blame him?" Tim exclaimed. "Who said anything about blaming him? That's what these modern kids need. Hard work and hard lickings."

"Spare the rod," Frank said, "and spoil the child."

"Now you're talking! What wages did you say the kid's folks got?"

"A couple of dollars a week. Not much, unless you figure in board and room."

Tim tossed off his drink, smoothed his mustache, poured another.

"What," he demanded, "would be wrong with that kid of ours?"

"Gus?"

"Sure, Gus! What would be wrong with him?"

Frank scowled.

"He's pretty young—"

"Not so young. He'll be nine in October. And he's big for his age."

"I don't know," Frank said. "I had in mind a kid about twelve."

"He's as big as lots of kids of twelve. Husky! And smart!"

"He probably eats a lot, if he's so husky."

"Well," Tim said, "the answer to that is yes and no. He don't eat so much as you might think. One thing I'll say for the little bastard, he goes for cheap foods. Take in the fall when the apple season comes on, he just hogs apples. And potatoes. No, I wouldn't say he costs much to feed."

Frank scowled in silence.

"How about it?" Tim demanded. "You said you were looking for a printer's devil. I'm offering you one on a platter."

"I don't know. What would his mother think?"

"Doll?" Tim's eyes went bitter, and he called her a string of names which made Frank wince. "Why, we never even hear from her. Haven't had a letter in years. Maybe she's dead, for all we know. She just ran out on us and left the kid on our hands. No, you'd never have no kickback from her."

"What would your wife think about it?"

"Damn my wife! She'd think what I tell her to think."

"She might always be running over to the shop and interfering when George went after the kid."

"Naw, naw—nothing like that. She's a mouse. George would have a free hand."

"I don't know," Frank sighed. "He's pretty young, but I need a kid and that's sure. I'll think it over. I might take him on for summer vacation and see how it works out."

"Why not for a year? Why not for five years?"

"I'll think it over."

"Now you're talking! Two dollars a week for five years."

"I'll sleep on it," Frank said. "If I decide to give him a try, I'll drop in tomorrow with the papers. It has to be all legal, you know."

"Oh sure. Of course." Tim glanced toward the door leading upstairs. "One favor. Don't speak of this to Lucy till it's settled. You and I could sign the papers, couldn't we, and then tell her?"

"I should think so."

"It's a deal," Tim said. "You come in tomorrow, and we'll sign it up all legal."

After the swinging doors ejected Frank, Tim permitted a smile of delight to suffuse his countenance. He turned to the heavy mirror behind the bar, and in the bright circle which was not soaped over he examined the smooth curl of his mustache with considerable satisfaction.

Next morning in a Tamarack lawyer's office Frank explained at length what he wanted and why he wanted it.

"I know the days of bound-out children are over," he said, "but if you could fix up something—"

"We can draw up a contract. It wouldn't hold in court, but you could make him go to court."

That afternoon, using the bar as a desk, Frank MacGowan and Tim Mahoney affixed their signatures to the papers. The lawyer accompanied Frank, and then he too signed as notary public. After that there were drinks, and everybody seemed happy.

Early one hot summer morning, about ten days after Gus entered the printing business, Lucy departed from Clayton Junction. Quite a delegation gathered at the station to see her off. The *Tribune* was represented by its editor, its printer's devil and its shop foreman, for when Vince Fye heard of Lucy's pilgrimage he insisted upon wishing her *bon voyage*. And at the last minute even Lucy's husband came.

Embarking for New York was the most daring undertaking of Lucy's life, and as she waited on the platform the whole adventure seemed unreal. She was aching to see Doll and excited at the prospect of travel, but she wanted to burst into tears at leaving Gus for three whole months.

Often she had told herself she would like to follow Doll's example and escape from Clayton Junction. Now she wondered. Last night in the sitting room she had felt a sudden love for the ugly haircloth furniture and the worn Brussels carpets and the huge steel engraving depicting the signing of the Declaration of Independence. The curtains hanging from a wooden rod between the sitting room and dining room —crimson plush curtains intricate with tiny plush balls depending— seemed as dear as old, trusted friends. Tears blurred it all and she sobbed to herself, "Oh, I don't want to go. I don't want to go to New York."

But it was too late to turn back, then. For days her preparations had gone forward. Frank MacGowan had duped Tim into releasing Gus into his care. She had spent Doll's money for new clothes, for railroad tickets. She had written Doll to expect her on a certain train. And then, with everything in readiness, with her bridges flaming, she had told Tim about her trip.

She made her announcement one morning at breakfast, and at first he treated it as a sour joke.

"But it's true," she told him. "I'm going. I was always tied down with Gus, but now you've sold Gus to Frank MacGowan I'm free for the summer."

"How about me?" Tim demanded. "It's always Gus, Gus. But how about me?"

"You won't miss me."

"That's not the question. You're my wife. A husband has rights. What are you going to use for money to get there? And what are you going to do in New York?"

She had withheld till now all mention of her sister.

"I'm going to visit Doll for three months. She sent me the money."

That brought the explosion. His face and lips looked as if his blood had turned to flour paste. His eyes were terrible.

"Doll!" And he called her only sister all those shameful names, and this made Lucy weep. "Doll!" He stood up so abruptly that his chair went crashing backward, and he stormed about the room. "So that's it. So she's behind it. I might have known. She wasn't satisfied to come into a respectable household and bring shame on it. That wasn't enough! She had to flounce off and leave her brat on our hands. And then work behind my back and lure my wife away. You never told me you were getting letters from her. How could you get letters without me knowing?"

"It doesn't matter. I got them. It doesn't matter how."

"By God! Women! Born deceitful!"

"No, Tim, no," Lucy sobbed. "It was just—well—her letters always upset you so."

"And why wouldn't they upset me? Why wouldn't letters from a life of shame upset a respectable businessman? Why that—that—!" He was at a loss to find a low enough epithet, so he repeated all the ones he had used before. "And now trying to lure my wife away into a life like that!"

"Tim—you know that isn't true. I've always been true to you."

"I wonder! By God, I wonder! Sure, I've always thought you were. But now—working behind a man's back while he works day and night to keep you!" He stopped at the window, glaring out at the railroad yards. Lucy sobbed and dabbed her eyes and sobbed more. At last he turned back into the room.

"All right, here it is straight. You aren't going."

"Yes, I am. I'm going, Tim. I'm all ready and I'm going."

He announced she was not, several more times, and she replied she was. So he roved about the room, inquiring of high heaven what the world was coming to when wives could go counter to their husbands' wishes. Finally he said:

"All right, go. If you're so smart you go, and see if I care. But you needn't come back."

"Tim! I'll come back. Of course I'll come back. It's just a visit—!"

"No, if you go I don't want you back. I won't be here anyway. You go ahead and find yourself a rich man like your sister did. That's fine with me. There're other women. You just go ahead and be a whore and see if I give a damn."

Lucy cried out a protest, but he stamped from the room and slammed the hall door.

She wept for several minutes, but after a time, recalling all the things she had to do, she stood up and cleared away the dishes. He didn't mean it about not being here when she returned. It was just his mouthiness.

They didn't quarrel again about her trip. Tim accepted defeat; coldly, and mainly with silence. But sometimes he made sarcastic remarks about the high old time she would have in New York while he slaved away in the saloon.

Lucy slept poorly the night before her departure. Sleep was a thin sheet against which all sorts of crazy magic-lantern dreams were projected. At last, toward daybreak, heavier sleep brought peace to her tormented spirit; and then she snapped awake and the clock said 6:25. And the train due at 7:01! Tim was not in bed; he was probably grinning about her oversleeping. She jumped from bed and raced about, hoping the train would be late. It would be just like the erratic Chicago, Tamarack & Pacific to bring its Chicago-bound train into Clayton

Junction on the dot this morning. But the Chicago train hadn't arrived on time in years, and this morning was no exception; so here she was on the station platform, finding it nearly impossible to believe that in a few minutes she would be sitting in a coach.

"By God, you're lookin' fine, Lucy," Vince Fye told her. "A fine figure of a woman! You tell that sister of yours to watch sharp, or you'll turn out the best-lookin' one yet."

Lucy flushed and wagged her tail.

"Better bring Doll back with you," Vince said. "Tell her this place ain't been the same since she left."

"Oh, she'd never come back."

"Well then tell her to write! You'd think nobody had never taught her her ABC's, from the few letters we've got."

"And you write, too," Frank said. "Let us know all about your trip. And tell Doll we've missed her."

"I'll tell her. I'll tell her everything. Gus—come back here! Gus!"

"I won't get hurt," Gus said.

Wearing blue overalls, arms extended, he was balancing himself barefoot along one of the rails.

"I'm a tightwire walker," he said. "Watch, Aunt Lucy. I'm a performer."

"He'll be a printer one of these days," Vince said. "We'll learn him to chew tobacco and hold down whiskey, and he'll be a real printer when you get back."

Lucy's giggle was not without concern, so Frank told her:

"Don't pay any attention to this old owl. He's corrupt. I caught him putting chewing tobacco in Gus's fried potatoes and whiskey in his milk."

Vince's expression did not alter. He stared straight ahead, brushed the back of his hand across his mouth, and spoke to the horizon.

"Always been my lot to fall in with rogues and liars. They've stole me blind and they've bore false witness against me. Myself, I've always led an upright, Christian life. But I've had to bear the cross of bad companions."

Still balancing himself on the rail, Gus faced the platform. He crouched, waving his arms, and cried, "Look, Aunt Lucy. Ooops!" And he made a flying leap to the platform.

"You be careful, Gus. You be careful while I'm gone."

"Sure. Feel my head, Aunt Lucy. Feel my head just once more before you go."

And Gus bent his round head where Lucy could finger it.

One of Gus's first requests from Frank had been to visit a barber shop and have his head shaved for the summer. He maintained that other boys found this not only refreshingly cool, but beneficial to the scalp. Gus had never before sat in a barber's chair; previously, Uncle Tim had clipped his hair. Where his nephew was concerned, Tim practiced rigorous thrift. Gus always dreaded these sessions when he had to sit with a towel choking his neck, for Uncle Tim's patience was not vast, and before he completed the job he usually worked in a bit of ear-pulling, light slapping and accidental jabs with the shears. Without training in the barber's art, Tim left his nephew's head appearing very slipshod, and Gus's companions guyed him about his weird tonsorial effects. So it was no wonder that he took so much pride in his fashionable tonsure.

"Ooo—it feels prickly!" Lucy exclaimed. "And you have such pretty hair, Gus."

"Healthier this way," Vince said. "It was all-fired bad, before. Every time he nodded his head you shoulda seen the fleas hop."

Lucy giggled; and then her face went serious, for she spied her husband coming.

He shambled along the platform looking as if he had eaten lemons for breakfast, his thin legs clad in sky-blue trousers, his narrow torso garbed in an unbuttoned fawn-colored vest and a purple-striped shirt. A hard straw hat with vertical purple-and-white stripes encircling the band protected his head from the sun.

"Quite a party," he said, and then, sighting Gus's head, he exclaimed: "You look like you'd been in the penitentiary."

Gus's jaw hardened and something snake-ugly gazed from his eyes. He sidled over near Frank and replied:

"Aw, go on. Guess they won't have to spend much time on your bald head when you go to the pen."

This allusion to the single flaw in his appearance distressed Tim; his mouth emulated the curl of his mustache and his hands twitched.

Vince broke into a laugh.

"Can't get ahead of that young one! No need to try. That young one's got a brain like a steel trap."

"He needs some manners pounded into him," Tim declared.

"Have to find someone who knows about manners to do it," Vince said. "With Lucy gone, there won't be nothin' but roughnecks left in this town. Well, I've always said the place stinks. I wouldn't never stayed a week if I hadn't fell into the clutches of bad company. I was a Christian man when I come here, and look at me now. I'm just about all tied up and packaged for hell. I can't lean over to pick up a collar button without the devil jabs me in the hind end with his pitchfork."

"Why aren't you at work?" Tim demanded of Gus.

"Frank's my boss. He said I could come. I do what he says. I don't have to do what you say."

"Oh Gus," Lucy breathed, and then she glanced in alarm at Tim, who had taken a step toward his nephew.

Vince's voice halted him.

"If I was in your place," he drawled, "I don't think I'd start anything. Take me—I've got a cane because I'm so damned old, and Frank there's got a cane because some flighty rebel shot off his leg. But if you want to tangle with us, take my advice and hand that pretty hat to your wife. Last time I smashed a fellow's head with my cane it just plumb ruined his straw. Got brains spilled all over it."

"You talk too much," Tim said.

"Maybe I do. But you know, I've heard lots of music in my day, but never any I liked as pretty as the sound of my own voice."

So Tim's throat made a noise that got by as a laugh, and he passed the whole matter off as a joke.

"The old man's still pretty witty," he said.

"There's been them who've found me so," Vince conceded soberly.

And then from far to the west a whistle moaned, and the river hills on the southern horizon caught the sound and tossed it back and forth among themselves until it evaporated into the shimmering blue heavens.

"It's coming," Gus yelled. "It'll be here in a minute."

The whistle sounded closer, accompanied now by the industrious chugging of the locomotive; and presently they saw it curving into view, vastly egocentric as locomotives have ever been, the tall stack expelling dove-gray clouds, the polished brass fixtures along its black spine burning in the sunlight. The bell clang-clanged and the platform trembled as the tired old iron horse galloped past and sighed to a halt, as if glad that Clayton Junction was a division point where it would be unhitched.

And now, although the train was scheduled to remain five minutes while a fresh locomotive was backed into place, a great bustling agitated the little group on the platform. Frank boosted Lucy's valises up the steps, and while passengers gazed from the wooden cars in boredom, Lucy bade them farewell.

"Good-by, Vince." She left a swift kiss on his cheek.

"Good-by, Frank. And—thanks—" She didn't kiss him, but her warm handclasp was deeply eloquent.

And then she swept Gus to her, showering him with passionate kisses. When she released him she was in tears.

Then she turned to Tim.

"Well," she said, "I guess I'd better be getting on the train."

She was thinking of Sioux Creek and her girlhood and of how interesting-looking that young man named Mahoney was. He was the new assistant station agent and he had a very nice voice when he sang hymns with the congregation at the Presbyterian Church and in memory she was standing in the vestibule after services one evening, her heart pounding as he stopped and asked, "Would you like to have me see you home, Miss Burgoyne?"

Now his eyes were bitter and old before their time and maybe a trifle sad, too.

"Yeah," he said, "it'll be pulling out."

"Good-by, Tim. I'll be back. Don't work too hard."

Impulsively, she put her arms around him and kissed his mouth that smelled of whiskey so early in the morning, and she felt his arms around her and she remembered fleetly a night on the porch in Sioux Creek when a gentle spring rain was falling and he took her into his arms for the first time and kissed her and she heard the rain dripping softly from the vine leaves.

She swayed away from him and kissed Gus some more and told him to be a good boy, and then she mounted the steps of the car and found her way along the blurring aisle to a seat by the window where she could wave good-by.

The fresh locomotive backed into the baggage car, jolting the roots of the passengers' teeth, and there was a great deal of tooting and bell clanging and waving of arms on the part of trainmen; and at last the Chicago Limited jerked and inched along the rails, slowly gaining headway, and the group on the platform watched the window where a woman was waving till the window was indistinguishable from the long line of other car windows, and the chugging of the locomotive receded down the rails.

Tim turned without a word and shambled away to his saloon. Then Vince sighed and said:

"No good waiting here. Might as well get back to the shop. I'm tired."

He looked tired, and he moved slowly. He had been buoyed up by excitement till he was very much like his old self, but now that the train had vanished and the sunshine lay bright and hot on the platform he sank back into feebleness and mental uncertainty.

One morning in mid-July Clayton Junction wakened to discover a huge sign adorning the front of Tim Mahoney's Saloon. "Under New Management," the sign announced. When the editor of the *Tribune* made inquiries he learned that for some weeks Mr. Mahoney had conducted secret negotiations for the sale of the business, and that he had departed the night before on a west-bound train. Everything had been included in the sale, even the furniture in the living quarters above the saloon.

The ticket agent reported that Mr. Mahoney had purchased a ticket to California; a one-way ticket; and ever afterward Clayton Junction was deprived of Mr. Mahoney's presence. And not for years did Clayton Junction hear even a whisper about his activities. Then in 1900 a man who had voyaged to the Klondike to search for gold returned to Clayton Junction (without gold) and reported that he had encountered Mr. Mahoney working behind the bar in a mining-town saloon. His mustache had grown to noble proportions; he had taken on weight; and he complained he was suffering from a kidney ailment.

Except for the man's report, nothing was ever heard about Tim Mahoney. He might have stayed in the Klondike, for all the town knew. He might have died there, for all the town knew or cared.

7

On a bright afternoon in February 1899, a young man left the electric car that had transported him from Tamarack to Clayton Junction and strode briskly toward the *Tribune* office. He was a large, well-built young man, bursting with good health and energy. He was scarcely handsome, but certainly he was attractive. A faint rosiness bloomed in his cheeks, and his gray eyes were clear and pleasant. His jaw was sturdy, his Roman nose resolute. He walked with shoulders squared, exuding self-confidence.

It was apparent that here was a young man who would amount to something. His was an aura of hustle, snap, success. Sharply creased gray trousers were visible beneath his reddish brown overcoat, and his large hands were encased in yellow kid gloves.

He lived at a moment most favorable for energetic young men. Progress vivified the air. Nobody wore bustles any more except smiled-at old ladies. Horsecars were clop-clopping into history. Carriages without horses were a demonstrated fact.

The young man had become an ardent disciple of progress—at his high school graduation the previous May he had delivered an oration entitled, "The Promise of the Twentieth Century"—and so it was that he held Clayton Junction in low esteem. The place lacked get-up-and-go. Only the Fair Store had revealed any evidence of modern business methods, but now it too had sunk into lethargy, for its proprietor, Isaac Goldstein, had sold out and founded a larger store in Tamarack.

The very sidewalk beneath the young man's heels was a specimen of the moss on the town's back, for it was constructed of wood. Last September, at his urging, the *Tribune* had crusaded for concrete sidewalks. Vigorous editorials signed "A.H.B." urged a bond issue. It hadn't taken the opponents of civic improvement long to deduce that those initials stood for Augustus Howard Burgoyne. Gus Burgoyne! Huh! He had his brass to advocate spending a great sum of the taxpayers' money. He was getting pretty uppity for a young man whose mother couldn't have scared up a marriage certificate if her life depended on it.

The crusade came to naught. Gus was disgusted. Not Frank. Frank just grinned and said it was necessary to cultivate patience.

Patience! As if that were a virtue! Not in Gus Burgoyne's book!

Now as he approached the *Tribune* office, where he would break the great news to Frank, it occurred to him that despite all this grumbling against the Trusts they represented progress. In the last decade, two great improvements had blessed Clayton Junction, both imposed upon the town by corporations. The Chicago, Tamarack & Pacific Railroad had erected a new depot, not, perhaps, from any urge to brighten up the town, but because an overheated stove had set fire to the old station and it had burned to the ground. Nevertheless, from whatever cause, the town had a new station.

Everybody recognized the need for the new station; but the second improvement, a beneficence of the Tamarack Street Railway Company, engendered a tempest of argument. When the mossbacks learned that electric motors were to replace the old nags that had pulled the horse-cars back and forth between Tamarack and Clayton Junction they were outraged. Electricity! Dangerous! Those motors were likely to explode.

Spearheaded by Gus, a few civic-minded persons arranged a celebration to commemorate the first voyage of an electric car from Tamarack. At the corner of Second Avenue and the railroad tracks (hard by a saloon once operated by Tim Mahoney), a speakers' stand was erected and decorated with bunting. A great crowd of two hundred people gathered, and while they waited for the car they kept entering the saloon for refreshments. Enthusiasm grew, and when the car, also bunting-draped, came clanging along the track a cheer rose from the throng. Music blared from the Clayton Junction Military Band. The car swayed with its load of politicians, street railway officials, Tamarack business leaders. There were many speeches and Gus feasted his eyes on these men who occupied positions of power. There was, however, one unfortunate occurrence. The chairman introduced a prominent Tamarack businessman with sharp eyes and copious whiskers, Mr. Samuel R. Oxenford. As he began to speak a switch engine chugged along the railroad, and the engineer, grinning wickedly, held down the whistle cord. If Gabriel had blown his horn there couldn't have been a greater racket. In Mr. Oxenford's beard every hair trembled. The noise quite obliterated the first minute of his short speech, and Gus regretted this. From a rich man like that you were likely to hear wisdom about getting ahead. As it was, the only audible portion of Mr. Oxenford's address concerned the virtues of Thrift, Industry and Integrity. Gus was disappointed. Virtues they might be, but they sounded very pedestrian. Gus was always alert for a short cut to wealth and power.

After the brilliance of sun on snow, the *Tribune* office seemed duskier than usual; and after he stepped inside Gus's nose and ears functioned better than his eyes. The homelike odors of printer's ink and paper and pipe smoke entered his nostrils, and the thump-thump of a job press reached his ears, operated by one of Vince Fye's long line of successors. After a moment, by squinting, Gus distinguished Frank at his desk, with that book he had been talking so much about which concerned the life of the ant.

Why any man should possess curiosity about the folkways of ants was laughably beyond Gus's understanding. Or about bees or birds, for that matter—subjects which had interested Frank in the past. Gus believed that the proper study of mankind was man: by learning the causes of man's actions, perhaps he could control the effects to his advantage. After receiving his high school diploma, when Frank suggested he enroll in the University of Tamarack, Gus declined. He did not wish to squander four of his best years slicing earthworms, scanning iambic pentameter lines, reading Cicero.

Frank put down his book as Gus entered.

"You're back early," he said. "I thought you were going to a matinee."

"I changed my mind."

Gus removed his overcoat, arranged it neatly on a hanger. He hung his hat on a hall tree in the corner. Then he looked for a place to sit. As usual, the chairs were piled with newspapers and magazines. He moved a stack to the floor and flipped his handkerchief over the chair seat. Then he sat down and tipped back, hands in pockets. His shoes gleamed, and his high linen collar with its blue cravat forced him to elevate his jaw. His brown hair was neatly parted on the side.

Frank by comparison looked as slipshod as an old shoe. His trousers hadn't been pressed since he bought them, and he wore a moth-chewed gray sweater beneath his old brown coat. In the interest of comfort he wore no collar at all, and his brass collar button gleamed dully in the neckband of his unstarched shirt. He was smiling, not at anything in particular: it had become a habitual expression. The years had seemed to lengthen his face, and both to strengthen and mellow it. Good-natured wrinkles had stamped themselves in half wheel spokes about his eyes. His eyebrows and hair had turned white. He was always forgetting to visit a barber, and a fringe of white hair bushed from the cracked tan skin of his neck.

At fifteen Gus had begun taking a sharp interest in his personal appearance, and from time to time he hinted to Frank that it might be well for the editor of the *Tribune* to look more prosperous. But it was no good. Frank was too occupied with such books as *Progress and Poverty* to think about clothes. It wasn't that he couldn't afford to dress well; Gus was certain of that. For Frank always seemed able to put his hands on ready cash. When Aunt Lucy died in New York back in 1892, he sent a check to help out with funeral expenses.

"How's everything in Tamarack?" Frank asked.

"Booming. That's a good town. It's growing fast." And then Gus broke the news. "I went after a job while I was there. And I got it."

"You did what?"

"Got a job. On the *Beacon*. Reporting."

Frank picked up a foul old pipe and tamped tobacco into the bowl. "That's quite a surprise," he said. "When do you go to work?"

"Monday."

"What do they pay?"

"Not so much. That's the only bad thing about it. They offered me four a week. I argued them up to six. They kept saying I was inexperienced, but I told them I'd had plenty of experience on the *Tribune*. Well, what do you think of the idea?"

"I hate to lose you here, of course. But I wouldn't stand in your way."

"I knew you wouldn't want to."

"I'm not so young any more, and I'd hoped you'd take over the *Tribune* some day. But you'll never want to, now."

"I might," Gus said quickly. "The way I figure it, a year or two on a daily paper will be good experience. I'll meet lots of important people."

"You'll move to Tamarack?"

"Almost have to. Be close to my work."

Frank said gently, "It'll be sort of quiet around here."

Gus grinned. "I guess it always has been quiet in Clayton Junction. I hate to leave you, Frank, but this damned town . . . I've never liked the place. It's too poky. You can't get ahead here. I want to live where things are happening. I want to make something of myself."

"You'll stay in the newspaper business?"

"Maybe. I don't exactly know what I want. I want to be—well, damn it—important. Like a politician making a speech. Only not that. But I want to have things happening and to be helping make them happen. I want my hand in the pie."

"Just one thing," Frank grinned. "Don't get your hand sticky or stained. You won't, of course. But remember, you can always come back here. You get a few years on a big paper, and maybe editing the *Tribune* won't look so bad."

Gus nodded. "It sounds like sense."

It didn't, of course, sound like sense; but he was grateful to Frank and he wanted to humor him; and besides, it was always well to have an ace in the hole.

Gus would work on the *Tribune* for the remainder of the week, so presently he left the office to visit news sources. Frank picked up his book, but he had lost interest in the manners and morals of ants. He sat smoking, smiling, but it was only the shell of a smile, for he felt sad and somewhat befuddled. In the past year Gus had relieved him of more and more editorial duties, and now he would have to hire somebody else, for he didn't relish going back to gathering news himself. As he grew older he found it harder to get around, with his bad leg, and as his mental world expanded his physical world contracted. The office, the shop, a little stroll to the post office—that was his life. The rut of living had become a deep canyon.

He had grown to love the familiar and to dread change; and Gus's leaving was a rockslide in the canyon of his life. But he didn't blame the boy. A frisky colt always wanted to kick up its heels and jump into greener pastures. For a long time he had sensed the boy's restlessness and realized he would be drawn to Tamarack. Gus's restlessness and bitterness against Clayton Junction had been intensified by that incident of the Junior-Senior banquet.

It was trivial enough—an older person would have shrugged it off— but Gus was only sixteen at the time, with all the self-doubts and sensitivity of adolescence. By sheer force of character and animal magnetism (and perhaps a little behind-scenes maneuvering) Gus had got himself elected president of his high school class, and this meant he would serve as toastmaster at the spring banquet the juniors tendered the seniors at a restaurant in Tamarack.

In March of that year a family named Bryant had moved to town, Cyrus Bryant having purchased the Fair Store from the man who owned it after Isaac Goldstein. The Bryants had a daughter named Norma who entered Junior Class. She was an attractive little thing, and sometimes Gus walked home from school with her, and he was forever dragging her name into supper table conversation. Frank was delighted to see him taking an interest in a nice girl instead of strolling down the railroad and into the woods with that section hand's daughter, Beulah Murray, who had quit school in seventh grade.

Some ten days before the banquet there was a hayrack picnic into the country, and Gus and Norma paired off, eating together and maybe discovering favorable qualities in the full moon. Usually at class parties Gus had been attentive to Madge Goodwin, daughter of a conductor who had served thirty years on the Chicago, Tamarack & Pacific. But since Norma moved to town, he had lost interest in Madge.

But Madge had not lost interest in Gus, so next day Madge's mother paid a social call on Norma Bryant's mother and filled her full of local history, devoting particular attention to the life and loves of Doll Burgoyne. This alarmed Norma's mother. She had no wish to awaken some morning and find herself an illegitimate grandmother. So Mr.

and Mrs. Bryant instructed Norma never to stroll from school again with the son of that hussy, Doll Burgoyne; and Norma wept and made bitter remarks about Madge Goodwin, but in the end she promised not to flirt with Gus any more. The situation was painful because she had promised to attend the Junior-Senior banquet as his partner.

Dissembling was foreign to Norma's nature, and next afternoon when she told Gus she couldn't allow him to escort her to the banquet, and he demanded to know why, she said her parents wouldn't let her. Gus's shrewd mind was instantly suspicious, and he pounded away for an explanation. Poor Norma went to pieces, and at last, blushing furiously, she confessed that Madge's mother had told her mother that Gus's mother had been fast.

Gus was furious, raging into the *Tribune* office, smashing his schoolbooks to the floor. His anger had an Olympian quality, as if only the anger of the gods were sufficient to arm him against the opprobrium of the world. He was not going to the banquet. He was quitting school. He would tie a few belongings into a bandanna and hop a freight for nowhere. If society insisted upon regarding him as its enemy, he would show it. Society would wish it had never started the quarrel. Gus swore horrible oaths that day, and he declared he wished he had never been born.

Wise old Frank permitted the storm to blow itself out. He realized this was a crucial hour in Gus's ascent toward manhood. As an urchin Gus had resorted to fisticuffs when some boy taunted him. But he couldn't do that now. Growing up had disarmed him.

Gus stamped out of the office, disappearing beyond the cases of type, and Frank found him back in their living quarters, face-down on the bed, fists clenched. Frank lighted his pipe, and at last he said:

"You're taking it too hard. There's no disgrace in being a love child. How many of those kids in your class do you suppose were planned for? I'd make you a bet that not one was, only there's no way to settle a bet like that. If we'd go around asking their parents questions like that they might think we were nosey."

Silence from the bed.

"You've got to take the long view. Your mother was never married to your father. What of it? If you'd been born a Mohammedan your dad would have had all the wives he could handle. And in some civilizations your mother would have had a dozen husbands. Either way, you would have been perfectly respectable."

Silence from the bed. But a listening silence.

"Well, just because your father and mother happened to meet in Clayton Junction you were born illegitimate. All that means is that this town has certain tribal customs, and your parents disregarded those customs. So the town is mad. Tribal law has been broken. That hasn't a damned thing to do with moral law—whatever moral law is. You ought to read Nietzsche. It would give you the long view."

Gus turned on the bed.

"I knew your father and mother. They were fine people. And they were strong. Did they let the tribal law of a stinking little railroad town hamper them? Of course not. They had passions and they satisfied them. They had courage. They were vigorous, healthy people and when nature told them to go into each other's arms they obeyed. And for my money that's a damned sight better than if your dad had sneaked off to Rafferty Street and your mother had withered up into one of these bleak spinsters."

Gus sat up. "You make me feel better," he said.

"I should think so! You've got the world by the tail, Gus. You were a love child, and that means you inherited a strong body from those strong parents of yours. And a strong will, too. The thing to do is to hold up your chin and face down the town. They can take you or leave you, and you don't give a damn which. You've got a brain and you're going places, and some day they'll point to that saloon and say that Augustus Howard Burgoyne was born up there."

Gus grinned. "By God, I'll show them!"

"Of course you will! Make them swallow their own medicine. If you'd go on the bum, that would please them. They'd know then they had you licked. And if you wouldn't go to that banquet they'd know you were licked. Well, are you going to let them lick you?"

"No," Gus said, "I'm not. I'll show them." He arose, squared his shoulders, stuck out his jaw.

Frank would have been the first to admit that he had presented his arguments from the furthest possible extreme. But he felt he had to use strong words to counteract the whisperings of the town.

From that afternoon onward Gus wore the armor of a conqueror. His jaw shouted he would show the town. But Frank suspected that inside the armor there lived a growing boy, wounded and troubled.

He didn't quit school and he attended the banquet and his quips as toastmaster made the long table giggle. Frank helped him prepare for the occasion, leaning heavily on a copy of *The Complete After-Dinner Speaker,* said to be endorsed by Chauncey Depew.

When Gus returned from the banquet he was glowing with success, and already he was planning further success: he would work up an oration to deliver next year at graduation which would sweep the audience off its feet. He remained bitter against the town, but never again did he rage into the office and explode about some cut. Sometimes, however, he returned from school in silence. And Frank was troubled to note that he no longer asked nice girls to be his partner at social functions. He began seeing Beulah Murray again, and during the spring of his senior year he went to Rafferty Street for the first time. Frank had grown to feel like a father toward Gus, with a father's protective instincts, but he scarcely felt himself in a position to forbid Gus's adventures on that rosy thoroughfare. However, he taught him to be careful.

On that long-ago day when Frank learned that Tim Mahoney had skipped out, a hunch told him Gus might live on at the *Tribune*. Immediately, he wrote Lucy, recounting her husband's departure and mentioning how furious certain people in Clayton Junction were. These people were Tim's creditors.

Business in that town was conducted in dawdling fashion, with businessmen maintaining charge accounts at one another's establishments that dragged along for an entire year. When the first of January arrived, a grand settlement took place. Ordinarily, Tim Mahoney might not have been considered a good enough risk to receive long-term credit, but inasmuch as he owned a business his charge accounts were never questioned.

The merchants whom he owed hundreds of dollars never dreamed he would secretly sell the saloon, including as assets the money they owed him; nor did the liquor wholesalers expect him to sell out so abruptly, listing as inventory unpaid-for cases of whiskey, gin, brandy.

All in all, it was a cunning stroke of chicanery. Tim had duped the purchaser, a lumbering German named Schmidt, by explaining that the negotiations should be secret so that his wife, who opposed the sale, would not get wind of it. Mr. Schmidt, who believed fervently that a woman should be kept in her place, was delighted to oblige. He was red-necked with fury when he learned that the liquor wholesalers expected him to pay Tim's bills, and that the merchants had agreed among themselves not to settle the accounts against them on the saloon's books.

As the news leaked out about how completely Tim had gulled everybody, Frank wrote further letters to Lucy, advising her to remain in New York till the scandal blew over. She needn't fret about Gus. He was enjoying himself at the *Tribune* office, and Frank would be delighted to have him live on there.

Lucy replied with bewildered, tearful missives, filled with such statements as, "It seems too terrible to be true, the way things have turned out," and "Oh, Frank, I miss Gus so much. You'll keep him from playing down along the railroad, won't you?"

And during the next years Frank even had a few secret letters from Doll. "I wasn't a bit surprised," she wrote, "to hear what Tim did. Isn't that just like that skunk?" And later: "Sis isn't feeling a bit well. She worries all the time and her stomach keeps bothering her." And later still: "I've had a doctor for Sis. He says it's serious. She looks terrible, Frank, and she's always worrying about Gus. Me, I tell her that's foolish. I know that Gus is in good hands as long as he's with you."

And then at last Doll wrote a long letter, describing in some detail Lucy's death and her funeral. "It would have been nice to take her back to Sioux Creek and lay her to rest in the family plot with Papa and Mamma, but I guess it doesn't make any difference to her now, where she is. It seemed so far back to Sioux Creek, and I would have had to go along, and I just didn't want to face all those people, Frank. Maybe I didn't even want to see you. You know what I mean. We're both older and I think it's better to remember each other the way we used to be. Maybe you think I haven't been all I should be, Frank, and I don't suppose I have, but I want you to know that I think a lot about the good times we used to have together. Wasn't Vince a jolly man? And now he's gone, too. It seems so sad that good people like Sis and Vince have to pass on, and skunks like Tim Mahoney are still alive. I'd like to get my hands on him! Sis told me the way he treated Gus. But wasn't it funny how you managed to get Gus away from him? I thought I'd die laughing.

"Usually I enjoy myself here, but sometimes I get the blues and I don't like New York at all. I think how nice it would be to live out there again, maybe on a little place in the country with you and Gus. Just dreams, of course. I guess we can't have everything, and I suppose it wouldn't be long till I'd want to see a good show again. I don't suppose I'd know Gus now if I'd see him on the street, and he wouldn't know me. Isn't life queer? It's hard to believe I have a twelve-year-old son. Gee, that would date *me,* wouldn't it? I've stopped telling my age. Most people think I'm about twenty-six."

Frank read that letter many times, and when he replied he enclosed his check for funeral expenses. He could afford gestures like that, for his stock in the typesetting machine was yielding phenomenal returns.

As gently as possible, Frank broke the news of Aunt Lucy's death to Gus. They were sitting in the office, and Frank was astonished at the calloused way Gus took it. "Uncle Tim's fault," he said. "He killed her. Always worrying her." Gus's young face was set in grim lines. Presently, with a "what of it?" manner, he tramped outdoors to play. Frank sighed. Gus was a hard little hickory nut. But a few minutes later, when Frank limped back to their living quarters, he discovered that Gus had sneaked in by the back door and was lying on the bed, weeping bitterly.

If child labor laws had been made retroactive to the 1890's, Frank would never have been punished for the hours he worked his printer's

devil. During those first years, Gus spent about as much time in the
shop as other children spent practicing their piano lessons. His quick
mind and chubby hands soon learned the typecase alphabet, and as
he grew older he took pride in his speed at setting type. By and by he
learned to work at the composing stone, to fill the forms and justify
a page. He had tremendous stamina: it was impossible to work him
hard enough to exhaust him. With his great store of animal energy,
he would doubtless have ventured into all kinds of scrapes had it not
been for his work in the shop.

By the time he was eighteen, he could have drawn better wages as
a printer than as a reporter on the *Tamarack Beacon*. But he wasn't
so much interested in present wages as in advancement. He realized
that a reporter associated on terms of equality with bank robbers and
bank presidents, with thieves and senators, with idiots and college
professors, and learned to distinguish one from the other; and he felt
that if he walked where the winds of opportunity were blowing he
would be bound to sniff the scent of riches. After he joined the staff
of the *Beacon* he worked like a drayhorse. And the question that
flamed day and night in his mind was how to get ahead.

His tastes were expensive; he liked to buy clothes at the best tailor's
and haberdashery at the smartest shops; and while he might snatch
lunch at cheap hashhouses he dined in style. He took to smoking cigars
rolled from rich Havana leaf. When he went out with young ladies
he liked to rent a dashing rig with matched chestnuts and drive about
the city on Sunday afternoons. He bought evening clothes, a top hat.
His only economy was his living quarters: when he moved to Tamarack he rented a room near the business district and he continued
living there. Having been born above a saloon and reared in the back
of a print shop, he was not dissatisfied with his small bedroom in a
district of raffish lodginghouses. He didn't spend many hours in his
room, anyway. He wanted to use money where it would show.

After six months as a reporter he demanded a salary rise, and another at the end of a year. These were granted, not because his copy
was so excellent but because he was a first-rate news gatherer. He
covered his beat exhaustively; he was seldom scooped; and every now
and then he nosed out a scandalous story that marched across page
one like a black-and-white polecat. In those days three newspapers
served Tamarack; it was dog eat dog; and to the managing editor any
reporter was dear who would dig out circulation-boosting news. Once,
with an election approaching, Gus cracked politics wide open with his
discovery of a shortage in the county treasurer's office. His method in
unearthing governmental disgraces was simple: he would consider a
certain official and ask himself what he would do if he were in that
official's shoes. Then he would start snooping, and often he turned

up something interesting. At the end of his second year he received his fourth salary increase. This helped anoint his conscience after the stab it received when, as a result of one story, a minor official put a bullet through his temple.

But even with his salary rising, he couldn't have lived in his dashing bachelor manner had it not been for other sources of income. One was Frank. Now and then Gus returned to Clayton Junction for a short visit, and when Frank asked how he was making out financially he always complained of the frightful time he was having. He emphasized his economy in living in a down-at-the-heels lodginghouse; he spoke of the expense one incurred eating out constantly. Frank usually gave him some currency to help him along.

After working on a city daily, Gus smiled at the *Clayton Junction Tribune*.

"You ought to get some new type faces," he told Frank one afternoon in 1901. "Or one of these typesetting machines. We use them exclusively on the *Beacon* now."

"Do you think they're practical?"

"Practical! They're as practical as a politician kissing babies."

"I don't know," Frank said. "Vince Fye never thought much of them."

"Vince Fye! My Lord! What did Vince know about them? An old tramp printer who couldn't hold a job in these times if he had to!"

"He was good company, though. Sometimes I miss him around here."

Gus never convinced Frank he should purchase a typesetting machine. Oh well, he thought, riding the streetcar back to Tamarack, maybe Frank was happier this way, operating a little shop in a one-horse town. He had great affection for Frank, more affection than for any other mortal. Taking him in when his own mother didn't want him. But he mustn't think about his mother or he'd start brooding. Slam the door on the past; that was best. It was the future that interested him, that shining land.

When Gus started as a reporter everybody liked him. But presently other reporters found he was so ambitious and hard-working that he showed them up. They were vagrant fellows who had worked on papers all over the country, and they had the souls of magnificent loafers, but while they yarned about famous beats and gigantic hoaxes Gus was hard at work digging up stories. It was damaging to their solidarity to have a reporter so damned energetic.

At first, Gus had been well liked also on his series of beats. But gradually the affection in which politicians held him was more sham than actual. His appearance in their offices was the signal for the skeletons in their closets to begin clog-dancing. Damn it, why couldn't he be easy-going like these other reporters? Everybody realized that to an officeholder elasticity of conscience was as essential as a firm handclasp, but this cocky devil was liable to sneak up behind you and snap the elastic of your conscience as if it were your suspenders. Damn him, you thought, smiling broadly and booming, "Hello, Gus! How's the boy?"

When Gus took over the city hall beat in his third year on the *Beacon,* insomnia became fairly common among the city fathers. In September 1901, the streets commissioner had an especially restless night. The commissioner's duties included the purchase of sewer pipe, and one morning a salesman called at his office. After a pleasant chat, the salesman pointed to a diamond stickpin he was wearing.

"What do you think of this pin?" he asked.

The commissioner thought it handsome.

Whereupon the salesman took it off and tossed it to the desk. "You can have it," he said. "I don't like it."

The commissioner protested mildly, but the salesman was adamant; he had experienced bad luck, he said, ever since he purchased it; if the commissioner didn't take it he was going to toss it into the river. Well! In that case—!

The salesman thanked him. It was surely a relief to be rid of the damned thing. Then the salesman arose, beckoned the commissioner to the office window and pointed to a fine horse and buggy hitched to a post.

"Just look at that," the salesman said. "A fellow offered me that rig at a bargain. I bought it, and now I'm stuck with it. I live in Chicago and think of the expense of shipping it. Want it?"

The salesman left the office with a huge order.

Gus was lingering in the outer office, and when the door opened he shielded himself behind a newspaper. He departed soon after the salesman, and followed him to his hotel. The commissioner's secretary had been so skillfully pumped that he scarcely realized he had informed Gus Burgoyne that the commissioner was about to purchase pipe.

A bar adjoined the hotel lobby and naturally, after such a sizable order, the salesman visited the place. And first thing he knew he was chatting with a young fellow who said his name was Gus Perkins and whose occupation was hardware drummer for a St. Louis house. Following their discussion of baseball and horse racing and women, they drifted around to talking shop. Gus spoke of the difficulties of his calling. You were always having to pass out quarts of Scotch to purchasing agents.

The salesman laughed. Compared with the difficulties he faced, Gus's tribulations were as peanuts. You can't mean it, Gus said. But he did mean it, the salesman said: he would tell Gus something that would open his eyes.

That afternoon, Gus dropped in for a chat with the commissioner. No, there was no news.

"I understand you've bought sewer pipe," Gus said. "Might use a story about that."

The commissioner didn't think it consequential.

"You got bids, I suppose?"

It amounted to the same thing, the commissioner said. He had talked to a number of salesmen and had given the order to the one whose product was cheapest when you considered quality.

"I see. And now I'd like a look at your new stickpin. And when do I get a ride in that new buggy?"

The commissioner had flowing mustaches, hard eyes. His mustaches didn't twitch or his eyes flicker. But he did change the subject abruptly.

"When's your birthday, Gus?"

"Next month."

"Drop in tomorrow morning. I've been planning a birthday surprise for you, and you might as well have it."

Next morning he handed Gus an envelope, and wished him a happy birthday. The envelope contained two hundred dollars. Gus thanked him gravely; it was nice to have one's friends remember one's birthday.

"By the way," the commissioner said, "about that sewer pipe. I hardly think it's worth a story."

Gus shook his head.

"No," he said, "it wouldn't interest the public. Just routine."

"That's right—just routine," the commissioner said.

Chances like that didn't come every month, but in the course of a year Gus's side-line pickings were considerable. Even honest politicians —and Gus thought of these as politicians who hadn't been caught— remembered him on his birthday and at Christmas. They considered it money well spent, like an insurance premium. And once the mayor tipped him off that a fine, wide street was to be cut through a certain shabby area, and guided by the mayor's forefinger on the city plat he bought some weedy lots. A few months later the city condemned these and Gus tripled his money.

After becoming a reporter he never dreamed of paying his way into a theater, for the managers saw to it that passes reached the newspapers, and when he was city editor it was his habit to sell six or eight of these to a scalper. He had an annual streetcar pass too; and when he visited Chicago he spoke to the traffic manager of the Chicago, Tamarack & Pacific and found it unnecessary to purchase a ticket. Nor was Mr. Oxenford the first man who paid Gus to act as secret press agent.

Perhaps the ethics of these extra trickles of income were open to question, but Gus's conscience gave him no qualms. Certainly the theater passes were legitimate enough, and it was an era when railroads showered passes on politicians and even ministers. And the most respected business leaders were glad to turn a quick profit when they received an inside tip that the city was to advance in an unthought-of direction. And if politicians wished to use a fraction of their boodle to buy him suits and boxes of cigars, who was he to injure their feelings by refusal?

Gus's work took him into a half-world where everybody was on the make, where his best friends were paying graft or receiving it, where the police themselves flouted the law in their methods of practical criminology. Nothing was ever as it seemed. Behind every big news story there was another story never printed. It was the fag end of the Victorian Age, and everybody was conspiring to give life a highly respectable air. It reminded Gus of the plays he attended at the Paragon: the plush-and-gilt seats, the showy boxes, the play full of lofty notions and punctilio; and backstage the bare walls and canvas flats. Well, he worked backstage.

Even if Gus had been endowed with a sharp ethical sense, he would have found it trying to determine which gifts were legitimate and which were bribery. It never occurred to him that he might be drifting into expediency and opportunism. He took life as he found it, and when, in June 1902, the managing editor offered him the city desk, at the very nerve center of the paper, he accepted with gusto.

He plowed into the job head down. He was getting places, now. At the first clang of his alarm clock he jumped from bed, gulped breakfast, bustled to the office. He sat in shirt sleeves, booming orders, cooking up stories with reporters. He was a skilled judge of local news, and his years as a reporter had given him precisely the recondite and irrelevant-seeming information that a city editor needed: whether the person involved was a power in town, whether he was an advertiser, whether the person's wife was a friend of the owner's wife. And of course his promotion did not cut off his side income; it augmented it. Now, instead of covering one beat, he covered in effect all beats. The *Beacon* was outstripping its competitors; it was Tamarack's great family newspaper; and everybody desired its city editor's favor. He had real power now, and he loved it, but—

But he found himself dissatisfied. After his first elation at getting the job, he looked back with yearning on his reporting days. A benumbing amount of drudgery accompanied his authority. He read copy till his eyes ached, and each day wave after wave assaulted the promontory where he ruled; reporters asking questions; people wanting news suppressed; people wanting unnewsworthy stories printed.

Till late afternoon he was a prisoner at his desk, bolting sandwiches while he worked and calling it lunch, making snap decisions that might mean a huge loss or gain in circulation or advertising. And there was the average amount of hell from the managing editor and the front office.

What did he want? He asked himself that, lying in bed at night, nerves exhausted. Well, he wanted to work for himself. Nobody over him. And he wanted work that would be lively and colorful. And he didn't, he realized now, want to remain a newspaper man. He sensed great capabilities lying fallow within himself, great energies frittered away in judging news made by other men. He wanted to make news himself.

During the last year he had gained weight and he looked older than twenty-two. He wasn't fat, but his frame had filled out. His eyes were wise and old beyond their years, they had seen so much: fires, arrests, hangings, the deft fingers of gamblers, the cheaply jeweled fingers of madams, stinking jails, smudgy political conventions, the cesspools and ash heaps and sewers of his era. All of it that had once seemed so amusing and significant flitted across his memory as he turned in bed, seeking sleep.

He was in this state of mind when he met a man from Winchester, Missouri, who owned a half-dozen elephants.

Elephants!

Despite his salary increases and his side income, Gus had saved no money. And so when, at that historic dinner with Ivan Pawpacker, he discovered that owning a circus was within possibility if only you possessed capital, he experienced momentary despair. But only momentary. He would get capital, somehow. Save it, if he had to.

As he sat in the General Grant Hotel, listening to Pawpacker talk offhandedly about zebras and elephants, Gus found himself gripped by tremendous excitement. A circus!

Why hadn't he thought of a circus during the past weeks when he lay sleepless and imagined leaving newspaper work for other vocations? How blind he had been! He remembered now the circus which visited Clayton Junction when he was a boy of ten. The night before its arrival he slept lightly, and at 3 A.M. he hurried into his clothes and left the *Tribune* office. Memory flashed that early morning back to him, the cool dew on the board walks, the brilliance of the morning stars, the stealth of the slumbering town, the velvety blackness of dust between his toes as he trudged along the road leading north.

He lingered where the road forked east and west, almost painfully happy with anticipation. Darkness had purified the air, and wild flowers and grasses and growing corn scented it. Night insects clicked and trilled, and up the valley far away a railroad engine moaned. At that unaccustomed hour even such a familiar sound was wrapped in mystery.

Presently darkness drained from the sky, and in the east gray light oozed upward, boldly contouring the wooded hills that bounded Tamarack. But Gus stared west, his heart beating at the thought of a circus approaching along that rooster-crowing road.

With the dawn other small boys arrived, chattering, boasting, daring, scuffling. But Gus stood apart and aloof, like a *religieux* in matinal contemplation.

The stars had vanished and the air was ruddy when he heard the faint truckling of distant wheels. He bounded west along the road, his shadow leaping wildly up the low hill over the rosy dust. At the crest he beheld it coming: a scene that ever afterward ornamented his memory. Spread out before him was the pastoral valley—the cool green of a meadow, miles of dew-bright corn. And ascending the road from a wooden bridge came the circus; wagons with golden wheels and glittering mirrors; wagons scrolled and gaudy, as if the designers had striven to outdo the opulent and ostentatious palaces of the merchant princes of the 1880's, and had magnificently succeeded.

As bedazzled as a beggar child at a coronation, he backed into the roadside weeds and stared at the procession flourishing past. He wanted to wave and cheer. But he just stood in his overalls, trying to swallow the lump in his throat, wondering why in this moment of overwhelming happiness he felt like tears. A driver grinned at him; a blowzy woman yelled something unfriendly from her buggy; it made no difference. The wand had been waved, the lamp rubbed, the dream born.

The day was a trance; a blue and sunny memory to hoard against dark winter afternoons in an ill-lighted schoolroom. Armed with the passes the *Tribune* received, he attended both the afternoon and the evening performances. He laughed, he caught his breath, he admired; but nothing inside the tent equalled that moment in the flawless morning. It returned to him bright and untarnished long after the rains of autumn filled the stake holes. Behind his spelling book, he was never a clown or a trapeze performer: he was an owner. It was not the ring alone that fascinated him; it was the circus complete. His Grandfather Burgoyne's yearning for the light-opera stage; Gus Phelan's love of the railroad business, with the excitement of clanging bells and tracks to far places; Doll's passion for freedom and splurge; the circus satisfied all those calls in his blood.

"Well, Gus—what are you going to be when you grow up?"

You didn't reply, "A circus man." Not after you entered your teens, you didn't; it sounded childish. Even Frank used to chuckle when he said it; so he stopped saying it; and after a time he stopped dreaming it. The world was a workaday place, and upon threat of ridicule it demanded that growing boys fix their eyes upon an occupation familiar and understandable. Whoever heard of becoming a circus owner? Might as well announce you were going to become a balloonist or a poet.

So Gus was going into newspaper work. Of course. He was learning printing, wasn't he?

But somewhere the dream lived on.

The dream was fine old wine that had gathered strength and flavor during its forgotten years in a cobwebby cellar, and tonight it ran sparkling through his arteries and set loose visions in his head. No circus could ever be so fine as the one that tinkled now between the hedgerows of his imagination. No elephant could loom so heroic; and never again would words whisper with such subtle lure as these that hung magically in the cigar smoke: the Hagenbecks of Hamburg . . . Bengal tigers . . . Borneo . . .

Gus looked at his watch.

"It's a quarter of nine. Shall we go on out to Oxenford's?"

They walked through the lobby, Burgoyne and Pawpacker.

Often Gus looked back on the evening he dined with Ivan Pawpacker and met Flora Oxenford as the most significant one of his life. He could never recall just when the idea of marrying Flora occurred to him. He hardly believed it was when they were sitting in Samuel R. Oxenford's library, drinking coffee and eating cakes, although his interest in Flora was already piqued.

He was elated that evening. The elephant deal was closed. According to plan, Pawpacker priced the bull named Molly at fourteen and a quarter. A growl fought its way through Samuel Oxenford's whiskers: too much. So they dickered. Both Pawpacker and Oxenford had highly developed trading instincts, and they enjoyed themselves immensely, flying at each other like sparrows disputing a slice of bread. At last, still according to plan, they settled for thirteen seventy-five. Gus couldn't help beaming. This meant he had two hundred and fifty dollars credit with Pawpacker, and it meant all the future excitement of the elephant's coming and being installed in Funland Park. And then Flora Oxenford entered the room, all bosom and hips in her white shirtwaist and blue skirt, and there was that instant of embarrassment when Oxenford said they didn't need coffee and cakes, and Gus galloped to her rescue.

She looked at him thankfully, and he did not find her unattractive. The excitement of having a young man in the house had dissipated her lethargy. Posterity's demand for life brought warmth to her face. Her brown, cowlike eyes did not seem stupid; they seemed innocent. And in the gaslight her hair did not shriek its redness; it had overtones of reddish gold and undertones of reddish brown.

He told her to go ahead and fix up the coffee and cakes, and to bring some for herself. She smiled and departed with a liquid swirling of skirts. Very feminine.

While they waited, Oxenford discovered that Pawpacker among his other accomplishments had a sound knowledge of the stock market, and this delighted him. He was never happier than when discussing money.

While they talked, Gus wandered about the room, too jubilant at the way the elephant deal had turned out to sit still. He stopped at the open window and drew the April darkness into his lungs; and he stood with hands in his pockets, teetering back and forth from toes to heels, musing about how far he had ascended the social scale since living in Clayton Junction. He remembered the time he had listened while Mr. Oxenford made a speech on the occasion of the first street-car's arriving from Tamarack. He had been a nobody then, and now he moved easily in one of the finest homes in Tamarack, smiled at by Oxenford's daughter.

He wondered why she had never married. Perhaps she was engaged. He would investigate. He considered inviting her to attend the theater with him. That indeed would boost his self-esteem: escorting the daughter of a leading Tamarack businessman when back in Clayton Junction the parents of some girls didn't consider him suitable for their precious daughters. He considered extending an invitation to Flora this very evening, but timidity—odd for him—held him back. He would proceed slowly. If she were engaged and refused him, he would feel like a monkey.

It was impossible for him to view Flora with ordinary objectivity. Even when she brought in the food-laden tray and smiled at him again he couldn't be certain whether it was a come-on or merely hospitality. He hurried over and helped her pass the coffee and cakes, but although he seemed to possess great assurance he had social self-doubts. She was more than a young woman: she was Samuel Oxenford's daughter. She lived in a fine house with servants. He had been born nothing; he was an adventurer; and she had been born into what the *Beacon* called (without a smile) Tamarack Society. Brilliant things coruscated about her face and hair: flashing dollar signs.

Somehow that evening Flora managed to tap into the great cosmic fund of feminine wisdom; she acquitted herself very well. After they sat down with plates on their laps she said:

"Tell me about this elephant matter. Have you really bought one?"

She didn't have to say much after that. She listened with admiration while Gus told how he had thought up the scheme to beguile the children of Tamarack into contributing dimes for the purchase of an elephant that would enhance the value of Funland Park. She said, "That's wonderful!" and "But how did you ever think of it?" Could he dream her stupid after such comments? He recounted the story in detail, with some boasting and a good deal of laughter. Mr. Oxenford grinned, and Mr. Pawpacker smiled quietly. And at one point he said:

"I think Gus is a natural-born showman. If he ever goes into show business he ought to make a killing."

Mr. Oxenford perked up. "Is there money in show business?"

"Do you think I'd be in it if there wasn't?"

Mr. Oxenford's eyes took on that intent, piggy look that always came into them when money-making was discussed.

"It's always seemed tomfoolery to me."

"Tomfoolery to the tune of thousands."

Mr. Oxenford lifted a saucer of coffee and supped noisily.

"We ain't showing a profit on Funland Park."

"You must have a poor manager then. You ought to find somebody like Gus to take it over. Somebody who would make it hum."

Mr. Oxenford frowned at the saucer and blew on it.

"It's beyond me," he said, "why crazy people will pay out hard money to ride a merry-go-round. What does it get them? Round and round. Their dime's gone and they're back where they started. I got where I am by watching my pennies. Thrift, Industry and Integrity. Those are the cornerstones."

"What's the fourth one?" Pawpacker asked.

"Fourth? There ain't no fourth."

"A building without four stones to support it?"

In Mr. Oxenford's whiskers a grin flicked, like a fox seen through brambles.

"Maybe you're right," he said. "Guess the fourth is getting up before daylight and outsmarting the other feller." He supped the last of his coffee, scrutinized his dollar watch. "Land o' Goshen. Talk about getting up. Look at the time. Hour past bedtime."

Flora wished for more lenient laws regarding murder. Mr. Pawpacker and Gus stood up.

"We're sorry," Mr. Pawpacker exclaimed. "It's been such a pleasant evening I hadn't realized—"

"Didn't mean to keep you up," Gus boomed. "But it's certainly been nice." He paused at Flora's chair. "And you helped make it perfect, Miss Oxenford! A man gets tired of eating restaurant food. Talk about bachelors' buttons! They ought to have home-cooked meals for bachelors."

She knew then. He was unmarried. She didn't look at him. She looked at the wall. She murmured:

"We always have something special to eat on Sundays. Maybe you'd like to come out for Sunday dinner."

"I certainly would! Next Sunday?"

She nodded.

"I'll be here. Johnny-on-the-spot!"

Perhaps it was while he slept that night that the thought of marrying her took shape in his unconscious. Certainly the thought of marrying him was in Flora's mind, and not her unconscious. She didn't sleep a wink. She lay in bed and planned and schemed and plotted. He mustn't get away. She must do the right things. He mustn't get away.

He almost got away, but that was far in the future on that sunny, warm April Sunday when he whistled out Wellington Avenue to break bread with the Oxenfords.

Shoulders back, he swung along briskly, thinking of the elephant that should be arriving within the month and of the credit he had accumulated with Pawpacker. More than money credit too, for he was certain he had impressed Pawpacker as a young man who knew his way about. Had not Pawpacker advised Oxenford to find a new manager for Funland Park, somebody like Gus Burgoyne?

The last few days he had been considering himself as a possible manager of Funland, and he liked the idea. He knew the present manager slightly, a bald, derby-hatted, cigar-chewing man who was the brother-in-law of the former president of the street railway. When Oxenford's Tamarack & Northern purchased the street railway the manager of Funland had been retained, but Gus was certain he had never had any qualifications for the job save nepotism.

Well, should he hit Oxenford for the job? He didn't think so. Let the present manager bungle along through another season. Let the seed Pawpacker planted have a chance to grow. If Oxenford broached the matter himself, Gus would be, he realized, in a better bargaining position. He must move adroitly, dealing with an old fox like Oxenford.

And he intended moving cautiously with Oxenford's daughter, too. She had invited him to Sunday dinner. That probably meant she liked him. But she wasn't like these girls you picked up on a saloon corner. She came from an important family. And he didn't want Oxenford to get any ideas that a fortune hunter was chasing his daughter.

In the late noon sunshine the avenue clattered and glittered with fine horses and shining carriages—people returning from church—and now and then from an open Victoria men nodded at Gus. Wealthy men, mustached or bewhiskered, wearing Prince Alberts and silk hats.

How solid and respectable they looked! But he knew facts in their lives about which their wives and families never dreamed. He returned their greetings, and he hoped he would be seen turning in at the Oxenford mansion.

As he moved toward the veranda he squared his shoulders to cover the odd stage fright that sifted through his kneecaps. He never experienced stage fright when meeting men like Oxenford in their offices; but this was different. This was a social occasion. He wished he could forget that Junior-Senior banquet.

A maid admitted him to the reception hall; and by daylight the interior of the house impressed him even more than it had the other evening. The ceilings were lofty, and sunlight shafted in through lace-curtained windows that were as tall as he. A grand staircase ascended to forbidden regions, and perched on a newel a voluptuous woman cast in bronze (but modestly draped) held a candelabra aloft in a Statue of Liberty gesture. Alcoves with bay windows opened off the hall, and everywhere space lay wasted, pretentiously wasted.

The maid ushered him into the parlor where he sat in a gold-brocaded chair and stole glances at himself in a huge mirror—tall enough for a giant—that was bordered in curling gold vines and whose top served as a perch for a gold American eagle. A minute passed quietly, save for faint sounds of dishes rattling in distant, muffled reaches. He sat looking at the dark, stupid oil paintings in heavy gold frames, at the chaste plaster busts of Diana and Juno, and his stage fright increased. Then again he glimpsed himself in the mirror: a wide-shouldered young man with an easy smile. He felt better. The hell with sitting like a guilty schoolboy. He stood up and moved about the room, scrutinizing the objects of what Mr. Oxenford's interior decorator had considered art.

Then muffled footsteps sounded on the stairs and the master's yellow whiskers entered the room.

"Hello, Gus. Why did that hired girl put you in here? Like a show-case, ain't it?"

He led the way back to the library, and in that less formal chamber Gus regained his self-confidence. Presently Flora appeared, wearing a filmy, high-collared shirtwaist adorned with lace flower petals. Gus went to her in greeting, and when he took her extended hand he couldn't resist pressing it, despite his resolve to proceed slowly. A flush came to her cheeks, but he could tell she was not displeased. He felt even more sure of himself after that; and by the time dinner was over his stage fright had vanished. Skillfully, without appearing to, he dominated the conversation at the table, bringing it to such subjects as Funland Park and the money-losing manager. And then out of a clear sky Flora asked:

"Papa, why don't you do what Mr. Pawpacker said and hire Mr. Burgoyne?"

Mr. Oxenford had been bent over his plate, eating greedily, but at that suggestion he quickly lifted his head, his chewing mouth full of food, his brows lifted, his eyes alert. Was there surprise and suspicion in his gaze? Gus couldn't tell. If there were he must quell it swiftly, so he shrugged and gave an easy laugh.

"I'm a newspaper man. I don't know a merry-go-round from a Mary-had-a-little-lamb."

Mr. Oxenford emitted a short guffaw. He swallowed the food in his mouth and said:

"Pawpacker seemed like a smart one to me."

"I think he knows his business," Gus said.

Flora was blushing again. After the words were out she realized that for some reason they were ill-advised. She must watch what she said.

But as Gus talked on about other matters he kept considering Flora's remark and it buttressed his self-assurance. To make a suggestion like that she must be more than a little interested in him. He would like to talk to her alone.

This was brought about without effort on his part. Following dinner, Flora mentioned that the yard looked beautiful at this time of the year, and asked if he would care to examine the garden. Out there, he suggested they attend the theater the following Wednesday evening, and she agreed without demur. And presently Gus was calling at the home on Wellington Avenue two or three times a week.

The elephant arrived in May, and on the front page of the *Beacon* this did not go unheralded. Gus wrote the stories himself, casting them in the form of "Molly's Diary." Considering that she was a baby elephant, Molly wrote very tellingly. In daily installments she told of her journey in a boxcar from Winchester to Tamarack. She gave her impressions of Tamarack (most favorable) and urged all the boys and girls to be good children and to obey their elders. She was, she said, living quietly and happily in her new home at Funland Park. She would not, however, be receiving guests till the first Monday after the dismissal of school in June, when all the children were invited to the park, admission free, to make her acquaintance.

"What's the idea of keeping her out of sight so long?" Oxenford demanded, one evening when Gus was calling on Flora. "Shadwell thinks we ought to show 'er off right away."

Shadwell was park manager, and Gus seized his opportunity.

"I'm afraid he missed on his showmanship when he said that. Don't

you see what we're doing by keeping her out of sight? Building up
curiosity. Making them want to see her. That's showmanship!"

"Uh," Oxenford admitted, "maybe you're right."

"Of course I'm right!"

And Gus plunged into a discussion of showmanship, revealing the
theories he had evolved about that spangled subject. Oxenford stroked
his whiskers and listened acutely. He said:

"I don't know much about such tomfoolery, but it sounds all right.
Wish Shadwell had more gumption."

"You just have to know human nature," Gus said.

"Then I wish he knew more human nature. Wish he was more
like you."

"Don't blame him. He hasn't had newspaper experience."

Mr. Oxenford clawed his whiskers. "I've been thinking. I've been
thinking it might be a good thing for the park if you'd take over."

Gus laughed easily.

"It might be good for the park, but how about me? No, I couldn't
afford to leave a job like mine to manage Funland."

"Maybe you could. You ain't given the matter enough thought to
know whether you could or couldn't."

"No," Gus said, "I wouldn't be interested."

Flora had been sitting placidly, and now she said:

"I've never seen the elephant. Is it big?"

"Not so big. But she's just a baby. She'll grow."

"Do I have to wait till June to see her?"

Gus looked at his watch. "It's early yet. We could see her tonight."

Flora thought that would be wonderful, so they strolled north
through the garden to a back gate that opened on Jefferson Avenue.
Dusk lay there in heavy fragrance, and fireflies swarmed like renegade
stars. The path was narrow and sometimes their bodies brushed. It
was the most intimate they had been, for Gus was adhering to the
broad strategy he had schemed out.

Steel tracks gleamed on Jefferson Avenue, and presently a westbound
car rumbled along. Gus's annual pass covered both their fares, and
they sat on the rattan seat with the acrid odor of the electric motor
in their nostrils. Funland Park had opened ten days ago, but apparently not many people were going there this evening; the car was
scarcely a quarter filled. Gus had visions of himself as manager with
streetcars loaded to their steps bringing customers.

Flora gazed out the window at the arc lamps sputtering past. On
their evenings together she never talked much, and what she said was
matter-of-fact. He had found that after a few hours in her company
an odd bleakness settled on his spirit. He couldn't understand it. He
would leave his lodgings with a high heart and return faintly depressed.

He didn't blame her. He blamed his strategy. It was unnatural for two young people to be together and not so much as hold hands. After their affair progressed to caresses everything would change. He could usually drive out his depression by telling himself he had been keeping company with one of the potentially richest girls in Tamarack. To-night, he found it stimulating to reflect that this streetcar was owned —or at least controlled—by Flora's father. The tracks beneath its wheels, the trolley wire above, the park to which they were going—all controlled by her father. And her father wouldn't live forever, and she was an only child. Fascinating, breathless thoughts! At times he un-shackled his imagination and let it run wildly into the future. He saw himself rich and powerful, holding in his big hands the streetcar company, Tamarack & Northern, Funland Park. Yes, and a circus. And ambitious boys in Clayton Junction High would muse how A. H. Burgoyne—the traction magnate and circus magnate—had attended this very school, had perhaps studied at this very desk.

The car was nearly empty when they left it. The park occupied a block on the south side of the street, and they crossed the tracks to a gate where electric bulbs spelled out its name. Another pass took them through the turnstile. The manager's office stood near the ticket kiosk, and Gus glanced in that direction. He knew he could occupy that office if he wanted to. His stand-offishness was succeeding with Oxen-ford. His spirits soared.

All the meretricious festivity of the park tasted like wine and meat to him. He stopped to light a cigar and he stood smiling, quaffing the festooned lights of the Ferris wheel, the pale glimmer of the skeletal roller coaster. In his ears were the faint click-click of the car wheels, the cries of the barkers, the tinny music of the merry-go-round. He smelled the porky odor of frying frankfurters.

"By golly!" he exclaimed. "You can't beat it!"

"It's nice," Flora said.

"Wonderful! Beautiful! It's like life ought to be."

And quite without warning his throat lumped, just as it had so many years ago when he stood in the roadside weeds and watched a little wagon circus wheeling toward Clayton Junction. He blinked, averted his head, suddenly ashamed.

"What's the matter?" Flora asked. "Something in your eye?"

"Cigar smoke. Got a little cigar smoke in my eyes."

"That's too bad. Maybe you want to leave."

"Leave! Oh no. We haven't seen anything yet. My eyes feel better. Just a little smoke."

"Do you smoke much?"

He laughed. "Not much more than a steamboat."

"I've heard it isn't healthy," she said. "I've heard it upsets the liver."

"Nothing wrong with my liver."

"That's just what I've heard. That it upsets the liver."

Irritation scratched him. Flora didn't sense it. She was a cow on a railroad staring unstartled at the steaming locomotive of his irritation. She mooed placidly:

"Maybe you ought to see a doctor about it. Find out whether it harms your liver."

He wanted to shout, "For God's sake, woman—we're at a park to enjoy ourselves! And we were enjoying ourselves till you started talking about livers. You take care of your liver and I'll take care of mine!"

But you didn't shout things like that at the daughter of Tamarack & Northern.

"Let's go see the bull," he said.

"Bull?"

"Elephant. That's what circus people call elephants."

"That's queer. Why do you suppose they do that?"

"Because it fits them. They're big and slow and powerful like a bull. Romantic name."

"Romantic?" she asked, not in argument but puzzlement.

He dropped the subject. He felt like a soaring balloon dragged back to earth. He felt depressed, alone. He had opened a door and invited her to share the beauty which he found in any phase of the entertainment business, and she talked about smoking too much and about livers. He was reminded suddenly of Frank MacGowan (old Frank— he ought to run out and see him oftener). Frank with his smiling pronouncements about the bourgeois mind.

He escorted her to a white barn at the northeast corner of the park. At their approach an attendant stood up from his tipped-back chair.

"Good evening, Mr. Burgoyne. Back again. You sure like this bull, don't you?"

"She's a good bull," Gus said. "Miss Oxenford would like to see her."

"Don't go to any trouble," Flora said.

The attendant took them within and snapped on a weak bulb. A partition between stalls had been knocked out to give the baby elephant more room. Molly was not much larger than a pony, and she stood swaying at her hobble, her loose hide the color of wet cement, her trunk weaving inquisitively. Gus walked over to her.

"Be careful!" Flora exclaimed.

"Why, this little girl and I are friends," Gus boomed. "Hello here, Molly! How's the girl?"

He scratched her broad, flat ears. Molly lifted her trunk and opened her yellow-white mouth and said, "Ah-h-h. . . ." Gus's laugh roared out. "Quite a girl! Quite a girl!"

He felt better, now. His sense of romance returned. Months ago as secret press agent he had had a brainstorm, and it had brought dimes to the *Beacon* and Pawpacker to Tamarack and Molly to this barn. And the end was not yet. His big nostrils dilated and contracted: already Molly had scented the barn with an elephant smell. That was fine with Gus. He loved the smell.

When he turned, he noticed Flora holding her handkerchief to her nose.

"And now," Gus said, when they emerged from the barn, "let's do the place."

He gestured largely at the falsely jeweled acres.

"How about the roller coaster as a starter?"

"Oh, I don't know. I don't believe so. They scare me."

"Well then, the merry-go-round."

"Do you think we should?"

"Why not? I've got passes."

"You know what Papa thinks about merry-go-rounds."

"He wouldn't care," Gus assured her, "so long as we don't spend money."

"He hates to see money squandered, that's for certain. But if you're sure you've got passes—"

The merry-go-round looked beautiful to Gus. Deep inside, he was as excited as he used to be when he stood at the sitting-room window watching trains. His eyes and his faintly smiling mouth did not look hard now.

They stood waiting for the next ride. The organ with its drums and cymbal filled the warm evening with lively tintinnabulation. Gus tapped a foot, and he drank in the lights and mirrors revolving past. When the merry-go-round halted he took Flora's elbow and hurried her toward it.

She started to enter a sleigh.

"Let's ride horses," he said.

"Oh, I don't know. I don't think I should."

"Why not?"

"I don't think it's very modest."

"Modest? Why, all the girls—"

The ride was beginning, so there was no time for further argument. They sat in the sleigh like a sedate couple of middle age, and as the ride took them round and round Gus felt like a small boy compelled by a maiden aunt to avoid the spirited wooden horses. But his jaw was set, and he said:

"We'll ride horses, next time."

"I don't know," Flora murmured, biting her underlip. "I don't think Papa—"

He could be diplomatic to a point, but only to a point.

"No, your papa wouldn't like it. But you're not here with your papa. You're here with me."

It struck her then that in some puzzling way she had angered him. She said hastily:

"Anything you want, Gus. I'll ride a horse."

So at the next pause they left the sleigh. The inside horse which Flora would ride waited with head flung impetuously high, and she approached it as tentatively as if it were a bronc.

"I'll help you on," Gus said.

She would ride sidesaddle so she backed against it, and Gus inserted his hands into her armpits and gave her a boost. Against his wrists her breasts were momentarily smooth and buxom, and Flora blushed furiously. Gus swung astride the outside horse and they were off, prancing on a gay trip to nowhere.

"Want another ride?" he called through the music.

"I believe I've had enough."

He helped her down, and she blushed again. Gus left the merry-go-round with many a backward glance. She didn't, she said, feel up to the exertion of the Fun House, that wicked place of distorting mirrors and swaying floors. The Old Mill? Yes, she guessed so.

They sat side by side in the gondola, carried on the narrow canal through mysterious blue-lit passages, and finally into the utter darkness which made the concession so popular with all the swains. Gus slipped his arm around her shoulders. She yielded against him, then stiffened away. He found her hand and held it. The palm was feverish and perspiring. When another blue-lit passage shone ahead she drew her hand away and he removed his arm, and by the time the gondola bumped into the incandescence of the loading platform they were as respectable as a good bank account.

After that they took passage on the miniature railroad, hauled by the shrilly tooting locomotive on a tour of the grounds, and then Gus hefted a rifle at the shooting gallery and popped away at the moving ducks. His aim was poor, and when he extended the rifle to Flora she drew back. Oh, no, she wouldn't want to shoot a gun. Besides, it was getting late.

They crunched along the gravel path, back toward the gate, the music of the merry-go-round tinkling farther and farther away. The manager's office was dark, the ticket kiosk closed. Gus paused and gazed back at the whirling lights. Again his eyes found a beauty in the garish scene that a more educated taste might have found in a Cézanne.

On the streetcar he experienced the melancholy which Flora's company was likely to evoke. The evening was an airy little melody played off-key. He made a decision. He would take her into his arms and see if that would help.

They left the car and fumbled through the gate into the dark garden. Fireflies still carried greenish lanterns through the perfumed air. Gus encircled her corseted waist and they walked slowly, hemmed together by the flowers on either side of the path. When they paused Flora was breathing heavily. Gus pulled her against him. His lips fought to her mouth. A long sigh escaped her; she swayed weak and heavy against him. After the kiss she moaned, "Oh, Gus. Oh, Gus." He kissed her again. She pulled away.

"You shouldn't, Gus."

"Why not?"

"People shouldn't kiss unless they're engaged."

So there it was where he could reach for it—Tamarack & Northern, the streetcar company.

"We should kiss," he said.

"Does that mean—"

"We should kiss," he repeated, and before she could pin him down he kissed her again.

Then he led her toward the porte-cochere, where thin light struggled through the darkness from a street lamp. He did not meet her gaze. His eyes might reveal his indecision. When they kissed at the door, her arms went around him.

"Gus," she whispered, "are we in love?"

"Are we?"

"I think . . . I am . . ."

A shining cool lamp of decency flickered on in his conscience, but he equivocated.

"That's your answer," he said.

He disengaged himself; he wanted to think.

"Gus," she said, "I hate to let you go."

"I know . . . I know . . . But tomorrow's a working day."

"Gus. Would you like to manage the park?"

"Maybe. I don't know."

"Papa would like to have you. I know he would."

"I don't know," he said. "Good night."

He crossed the lawn to Wellington Avenue. He would walk home. Think. He would have to decide soon whether he wanted an engagement. He had not thought the decision would be forced upon him. Maybe she had some of old Oxenford's foxiness, his acquisitiveness.

And so now indecision set up a tug of war in his life. When he went to bed he tasted the stale beer of insomnia, and more and more he grew to hate the confinement of the city desk. The problem which he alone could solve was always heavy in his thoughts.

No longer did he feel victory at going out with the daughter of a leading Tamarack businessman. It had seemed romantic and glorious for a young man from a seedy town like Clayton Junction to woo Oxenford's daughter, but it was devilish dull business. He continued writing "Molly's Diary," but his anticipation of the great day when the children would see their pet became tepid. He walked his treadmill, watching the day come closer without interest.

But the *Beacon* could not view the approach of that day without interest. As sponsor of the elephant, the *Beacon* felt duty-bound to point at itself with pride, to congratulate itself in print, to stuff its columns with comments from leading citizens about the service it had rendered the community. Feature stories were printed dealing with the lore of elephants: their longevity, their phenomenal memories.

If Tamarack had been elephant-conscious during the dime-raising campaign, it was elephant-delirious now. Barbers discussed elephants from the morning's first haircut to the evening's last shave. Dentists said, "Open wider. This won't hurt. . . . Well, are you going to see the elephant Monday?" And every politician scrambled for a chair on the speakers' platform.

The *Beacon's* rival newspapers discovered themselves in a lamentable position. They tried ignoring the whole affair—and watched their street sales plummet. They experimented with wry editorials—and received outraged letters. The *Chronicle* published what purported to be an interview with Molly, and the *Beacon* screamed fraud: only its own reporters were welcome at Molly's quarters.

Mr. Oxenford and the *Beacon* managing editor had agreed that Gus should serve as chairman of the arrangements committee, so by early June he was furiously busy. This pleased him: it provided excuses for avoiding the house on Wellington Avenue. Since that evening when Flora mentioned an engagement, he had called there only a couple of times. She gazed at him expectantly, as if at any instant he might go to his knees and ask her to become his wife; and embarrassment hung between them when he kissed her good night. She was plainly bewildered at the cooling of his ardor.

As chairman of the arrangements committee, it was necessary for him to attend the celebration at the park, so on that Monday morning he turned over the city desk to a copy reader and caught a streetcar. Above its cowcatcher, a brilliant placard announced: "Special To Funland Park." It was only nine o'clock and the program wouldn't begin till eleven, but the car was jam-packed with children and their parents, with uniformed members of a lodge band, with elderly men in full G.A.R. regalia. The Tamarack Retail Merchants' Association had agreed that this should be a half-holiday, and many stores had hung out flags. Even June had co-operated with deep blue sky, warm sun.

Hanging on a car strap, listening to chatter and laughter, Gus felt his excitement about the occasion return. He loved crowds the way a Fourth of July orator or a concession-barker loved them; they stimulated and revivified him. He liked their smell: starched dresses and popcorn and body warmth and powder. He reflected that none of them would be on this car if he had not served as secret press agent. His brain had brought it all about. He basked in the thought, in the sense of power it gave him.

And the warm dream of owning a circus came to him again. Every day from April to October would be like this: the crowds, the bands, the festivity. And always he would know it had all come from his brain. Oh, there was no doubt about it, he thought lightheartedly, marrying Flora Oxenford would bring its compensations.

The masses of humanity swarming into Funland Park exceeded his expectations, exceeded everybody's expectations. Already the hitching posts outside the park were tethering their capacity of farmers' buggies and lumber wagons. When Gus left the car he gazed back along the line: he could count five more over-burdened cars crawling along. People, people. All here because he had said, "Buy an elephant."

He stood in line, jostled through the turnstile. Although general admission was free the rides and concessions charged regular prices, and he could hear the spielers' voices rapturous at this bonanza. He could see the Ferris wheel with every seat filled, the merry-go-round tinkling joyously at its load, the tiny-looking people away up there in the roller coaster cars. You knew without looking when a car swooped down the first decline, because the girls always screamed.

Political dignitaries were gathering outside the manager's office: beards, long mustaches, Prince Alberts, black-silk summer suits. Great activity yeasted there: Good Morning, Mayor . . . You're looking well, Commissioner . . . Glad to see you, Congressman. Gus joined them and they all pumped his arm with that brief, mechanical handshake of politicians who knew their paws would have a big day's work.

Gus glanced into the office. Shadwell, the manager, was swiveled back in his chair looking pleased, as if he were responsible for the incoming tides of humanity. And another man was there. A fastidiously dressed man, sitting with a quiet smile, his gold-headed cane

gleaming. Ivan Pawpacker! Owner of elephants, tigers, spangled
wagons! Gus boomed into the office. Well, well! Mr. Pawpacker! An
unexpected pleasure!

"You'll sit on the speakers' platform, of course," Gus said.

Ivan Pawpacker made a depreciatory gesture. "That isn't necessary."

"Why certainly! If it hadn't been for you and me, they wouldn't
be having this celebration. And you came all the way from Missouri
to attend—"

"Not that far," Pawpacker smiled. "I'm on a horse-buying trip. I've
been reading about the celebration in the *Beacon*. And since my route
led through Tamarack, I thought I'd drop in and see Molly. I don't
know why I did it. Crowds tire me out."

"Me too," Gus said. "But on the other hand, you have to have 'em
in show business."

"It would seem so."

"Yes sir! Lifeblood of show business! Crowds!" Gus smacked his
lips. "Just look at 'em!"

They had emerged from the office and Gus waved his cigar at the
multitude flocking around frankfurter stands.

Pawpacker looked. Cool amusement sparkled in his eyes. He was as
detached from the throng as an aristocrat at a bear-baiting. He wore a
spotless white suit, a white Panama hat; he might have been an old-
fashioned Southern planter.

"It's worth a fortune to a man who knows how to draw a crowd
like this," he said.

"Think so?" Gus's blood coursed faster. And his manner became
more hearty. In Pawpacker's presence he quite involuntarily ripened
into bluffer and more staccato ways. Perhaps it was because Pawpacker
represented the circus business, and when he dreamed of being a circus
owner he saw himself as robust, expansive, a powerhouse, a cornucopia
overflowing with spectacular projects.

"Proof of the pudding," Pawpacker said. "This was your idea. And
look at the money it's making the park."

"Money—that's right! Thousands!" Gus sighed. "And no way for
us to cut in on it."

"You'll cut in. After this, Oxenford should make you an offer. It
might be good experience, managing a park."

Gus nodded. Yes, if he could get sufficient salary. They discussed
that, picking their way through the crowd.

The speakers' platform had been erected against the east fence. Built
of white pine, decorated with bunting, it had as much floor space as
a good-sized dance floor. At first a small platform had been planned,
but as the *Beacon* kept shouting about the celebration and it became

apparent that a large throng would gather, more and more politicians indicated willingness to occupy folding chairs where they could be seen. Steps climbed the north side, and a ramp slanted there also.

"Shall we sit here?" Pawpacker suggested, indicating the back row.

"No, no—let's sit up here. Where we can see."

And Gus led the way to seats in the front row.

There was a speaker's table, with a sweating pitcher of ice water. And already the lumber benches facing the platform were a mass of jack-in-the-box children and palpitating cardboard fans. In the pit a tuning-up band was giving forth bullfrog and tree-toad noises.

"You said you were on a horse-buying trip," Gus remarked. "Buying 'em for circuses?"

"No, I buy for companies in St. Louis and Chicago."

"Much money in it?"

"I've found it profitable."

"You must know horses pretty well."

"I got my start as a horse trader."

Gus laughed heartily. "Guess I'd better keep my hand on my watch and chain."

Pawpacker's smile was faint; he had heard that joke thousands of times.

"Just joking, of course," Gus added.

At that moment somebody said, "Why, it's Mr. Pawpacker!" And Gus glanced up to see Flora and Samuel R. Oxenford.

Flora didn't look bad at all this morning; in fact, she looked like a million dollars to Gus. Her copious figure was clad in a white muslin dress, and she wore a large white hat whose diaphanous brim shed soft, flattering light upon her face. She carried a folded white parasol. When the foursome seated themselves, Flora and Gus were side by side.

"My, but there's a crowd," she said. "And just think—you planned it all."

Her stock started climbing.

"My, but Papa's pleased," she whispered. "When he saw how people are spending money he said a lot of nice things about you."

Her stock broke par.

Gus radiated good nature. She was a pleasant girl, after all. The success of the celebration, meeting Pawpacker, the draughts of satisfaction his herd instinct drank from the crowd—these things brought peace to his warring selves. Life was good again, and he was going to be park manager and own a circus. The band began to play.

A few minutes after eleven, the mayor picked up the gavel and punished the table. He had goat whiskers, and he regarded the multitude with the amiability of an old goat gazing upon thousands of tin cans. He introduced the Reverend Welcome B. Shinn, pastor of the First Methodist Church, who had been selected to explain to the Almighty the meaning of all these goings-on.

With his flowing white beard, the Reverend Mr. Shinn looked like somebody right out of the Book of Revelation. In a rich voice he said, "Let us rise," and then there was silence save for the tinkling of the merry-go-round, the distant cries of barkers and the pop-pop of shooting-gallery rifles.

"Almighty God," said the Reverend Mr. Shinn, and you could imagine his resonant voice floating up and up, into the blue deep of sky, beyond the burning summer sun.

The Reverend Mr. Shinn spoke favorably of elephants in general and in particular of this elephant which the little children of Tamarack had purchased with their coppers. The presence of an elephant in this city would be a living refutation of the mad theories of evolution which unrighteous men had attempted to foist upon the world. He praised the *Beacon* for its signal public service in acting as trustee for the funds of the children, and he praised the rest of the Tamarack press for services rendered in other ways. That took care of the church editors on the *Chronicle* and the *Telegram*.

After the prayer, the mayor uttered a few well-chosen words. This consumed twenty minutes, for it would scarcely have been meet not to comment upon the beautiful equilibrium of the city budget. Then, one by one, he introduced the visiting dignitaries, asking each to rise and take a bow. They were glad to comply with his request.

"And now," he shouted, "by virtue of the power vested in me by the citizens of this great city, and upon behalf of the children who have so unselfishly given of their treasure, it is my high honor and deep pleasure to present this certificate of bestowal to Mr. Samuel R. Oxenford, president of Tamarack & Northern."

Limber and bony, his grease-specked black suit flapping, Mr. Oxenford arose and accepted the certificate. The ceremonies had lasted so long now that many children were whispering to their parents, and little journeys were made to the latticed and vine-clad buildings back among the whitewashed trees. And so it was that many of the rising generation missed the short speech delivered by Mr. Oxenford. This was a pity, for his yellow whiskers broadcast some beneficial hints about forging ahead. He advised Thrift, Industry and Integrity.

"Ladies and Gentlemen," the mayor proclaimed, "the committee will now retire to the quarters occupied by the pachyderm and escort her to the platform."

The band struck up "The Stars and Stripes Forever." The committee, consisting of Mr. Oxenford and seven politicians, crossed the platform, descended the ramp and disappeared toward the barn.

Suspense. Eagerness. People standing up. Fathers perching small children on their shoulders. Mustached and helmeted police brandishing billy clubs to warn small boys from the line of march. And all the while the band playing gallantly.

They were coming!

The committee had formed a hollow rectangle around the elephant and her temporary keeper. He carried a bull hook but he didn't seem expert in its use, for once when Molly decided to halt she halted and the entire committee representing so much achievement in government and finance had to halt too, till she decided to resume walking.

And a crisis arose when they reached the ramp. Out of sheer elephantine perverseness, or perhaps out of doubts about the trustworthiness of the carpenters who had erected the platform, Molly refused to mount the ramp. Ears and tail waving, trunk coiling, she came to a dead standstill. Her keeper spoke to her from the side of his mouth. She ignored him.

The band played and played and Molly stood and stood, and Mr. Oxenford ordered, "Giddap!" as if she were a horse, and the politicians offered gratuitous advice but all to no avail.

And then it was that a big young man bustled across the platform and down the ramp. He took the bull hook, and he smiled at Molly and boomed, "What's going on here, sweetheart? You're delaying the game! Can't do this!"

He hooked her lightly behind the ear and the immovable object moved. Together they ascended the ramp, Molly and Gus, and together they received the plaudits of the multitude. It was a high hour.

8

ONE MORNING the following November, at the corner of Tenth and Harrison Streets in Tamarack, more than a hundred human beings were staring at a hole in the ground. The hole was large, occupying a quarter of a block, and along the edge a wooden railing had been erected to prevent the human beings from tumbling in. At the bottom of the hole, other human beings were toiling.

The hole in the ground represented growth and progress. Less than half a century before, this portion of the earth's surface had been intended as a feeding lot for the cows of Mr. Samuel R. Oxenford. And then benevolent circumstances increased its value. A wooden building was erected there, soon replaced by a four-story brick building; and now the brick building had vanished and a loftier structure would soar from the hole.

It would be called the Oxenford Electric Building. Several months before the *Tamarack Beacon* had printed an architect's imposing drawing of this cathedral honoring the gods of business and finance. A likeness of the Prophet Oxenford had also appeared.

If you leaned there contemplating the hole, it was possible on occasion to glimpse Samuel R. Oxenford. This morning, the door of a little wooden structure opened and Mr. Oxenford stepped forth, accompanied by a man with a roll of blueprints. After gestures and confabulation the men parted, the construction engineer returning to his shack and Mr. Oxenford moving to the street. He glanced at the hazards of carriages and vans, then crossed briskly.

On the opposite corner he lingered in indecision. His bony fingers yearned to fetch out his coin purse. But the habits of a lifetime shuddered at spending money foolishly. He stood debating, the wind blowing his whiskers. His days were filled with these financial crises. At last his reckless impulse won, and he snapped open the purse and plucked out two cents. From the newsboy on the corner he purchased the first street edition of the *Beacon*. It was an improvident purchase, for the *Beacon* was delivered to his home. Now they would have two copies.

He rustled open the paper and peeked inside. The story and the picture were there; prominently there. He smiled. But he couldn't stand on a crowded corner reading. He folded the paper and slipped it into his overcoat. He would read it in his office. Since the old Oxenford Building had been torn down to make way for the new, he had taken temporary space in this building across the street, where he could watch the excavating. If any workmen seemed to be loafing, he reported them.

He turned to enter the building, then halted. Excitement was popping a block away on Harrison Street. Pedestrians stared; the loafers across the street shifted their attention from the hole to the street. The popping came closer, followed by barking dogs, preceded by horses rearing hysterically.

The pair of fur-coated men in the horseless carriage wore silly smiles. As the contraption exploded past, a laugh broke from the pedestrians and the loafers. Mr. Oxenford laughed as hard as anybody. Then he entered the building and the elevator cage.

Ten years ago he had sharp knowledge of how much he was worth, but that was before he organized Tamarack & Northern. Now his affairs were so tangled that when he attempted getting a clear idea of his position he ended feeling like a fly wading in flypaper. So he would spend an afternoon with his lawyer and get an approximation of where he stood.

Not that there was cause for worry! Land of Goshen, no! He held more financial power now than ever before: the goose was hanging high. The only reason he fretted was because during most of his business career he had conducted his affairs simply, like a small shop-keeper; and it was difficult to accustom himself to this financial super-structure he had built. But it was all legal! His lawyer had advised him at every turn. When Mr. Oxenford came forth with some sharp scheme, and the lawyer shook his head, Mr. Oxenford would demand: "Why can't I do it?"

"You can, Sam. Of course. But it would probably land you in jail." Jail! Whoa! Whoa-back! So he would follow his lawyer's advice.

Back when Mr. Oxenford caught the urge to own an electric rail-road, he heavily mortgaged his city property to get funds for a controlling interest in Tamarack & Northern. So far so good. That was simple and he could understand it. He already owned the Tamarack Fuel & Ice Company, and that too was simple. But the confusion began with his floating more Tamarack & Northern stock to get funds to purchase the Tamarack Street Railway Company.

There were wheels within wheels. He bought the land at Oxenford outright and then, after issuing stock in the Tamarack Fuel & Ice Company, he sold the coal rights to the company at a high price. By and by, using his majority voting power, he caused Tamarack Fuel & Ice to sell back to himself the coal rights at a much lower price.

Then he sold coal from his mine to the company at a smart profit. And presently he issued more street railway stock and more Funland stock. A mix-up!

But greater confusion followed when he decided to erect the Oxenford Electric Building. He presented all his stock in all his enterprises to the Merchants' State Bank as collateral for a whopping big loan. With the money, he bought a controlling interest in the Tamarack Fidelity & Trust Company. As majority stockholder, he approved a tremendous loan of depositors' funds to the Oxenford Electric Construction Company. He held fifty-one percent of the stock in this concern. Already, from deep in his financial labyrinth, he was considering using the construction stock as collateral for a loan from another trust company. And if he needed more cash he could use that loan to buy controlling interest in another trust company still, and then approve further loans. It was endless, bewildering.

But nothing to worry about! Not as long as his companies continued making enough money to pay the interest on his loans. He was not merely a rich man now: he was a financier. Well, you couldn't be a financier without cares. He wished the mine at Oxenford would yield more. He wished the profits of Tamarack & Northern hadn't dropped last year. He wished he could carry all these figures in his head. If he had become a farmer he could have done that. But he wasn't a farmer. He was a financier. But oddly enough, except for his home, the only property he owned without encumbrance was that farm near Oxenford. He wanted to keep the coal rights for himself, because the veins might suddenly grow richer. And as for the surface of the farm, no trust company except his own would lend money on that, and his lawyer wouldn't let him mortgage that farm to himself, because the land was poor and any fool would realize the loan had been rashly near fraudulence.

He left the elevator and stalked along the corridor to double glass doors flanked by panels of glass. Gold leaf said: "Tamarack & Northern; Tamarack Street Railway Company; Tamarack Fuel & Ice; Funland Park. Samuel R. Oxenford, Pres." Already his lawyer—a slick fellow who visited New York twice annually to learn how the big boys in Wall Street managed things—was suggesting that he amalgamate all his companies into one mammoth corporation. Call it something like Tamarack Electric & Guarantee. (Mr. Oxenford shared the lawyer's fondness for words like "guarantee," "fidelity," "trust.")

It was a daring idea with possibilities that made Mr. Oxenford dizzy. You could issue stock in the new company, always retaining fifty-one percent for yourself, and then you could begin the ring-around-the-rosy of putting up your stock as collateral for loans. Who said America was not the land of opportunity? By jingo! These Socialistic-horseless-carriage-flying-fool-radical-votes-for-women idiots made Mr. Oxenford's blood boil.

Mr. Oxenford flashed open the glass door and entered a large room with a long counter. On high stools at the bookkeepers' desks men sat. No women. He wouldn't have a woman in the place. Other firms might yield to the corruption of modernity, but not his! No sir! No immorality here!

At his entrance, the office became a place of industrious pen-scratching, of silence, of close concentration. Fear of authority glittered in the air; it was like a schoolroom when a stern superintendent enters. His cold little eyes scanned the place sharply as he passed through the gate and marched to a door marked with his own name.

Divesting himself of coat and hat, he creaked down at the old roll-top desk and opened the *Tamarack Beacon*. He read the story several times, as if determined to get his two cents' worth.

Last evening Gus had said the story would appear, and here it was on the page devoted to Society. Above a two-column cut of a young woman appeared the word, "Betrothed." And beneath the picture his daughter's name.

The headline over the story told the waiting world that Miss Flora Oxenford was engaged to marry Mr. A. H. Burgoyne. The story elaborated. Mr. Samuel R. Oxenford had announced the engagement. The wedding would take place next spring. The bridegroom-to-be had been employed for the past several years by the *Tamarack Beacon*. On January 1, however, he would accept a position as manager of Funland Park.

Mr. Oxenford put down the paper and sat absently rubbing his hands. He was not displeased. He knew all about Gus, for months ago when he realized that his daughter's intentions were serious he sent his secretary to Clayton Junction to make inquiries. Mr. Oxenford kept to himself the information his secretary gleaned. He was delighted to have it, because if he ever needed to he could hold it over Gus.

Not that he expected to be driven to that. He and his prospective son-in-law hit it off famously. Already they had been useful to each other. Throughout the summer Gus had tossed off a half-dozen money-making suggestions pertaining to Funland Park; and when the street-car company wanted to open a new line, Gus conferred with the council and the pay-off for the franchise had been much less than Mr. Oxenford expected. And during the heat of July when Tamarack Fuel & Ice raised the price of ice, and everybody kicked, the *Beacon* published an interview with Mr. Oxenford explaining why the increase was necessary.

Of course Mr. Oxenford did not approve all Gus's interests. His concern with showmanship was very well so long as it produced schemes beneficial to the park, but when he blustered off on a tangent and declaimed about owning a circus Mr. Oxenford thought, "Fiddle-faddle!" If that young man expected to use Oxenford money in such a nonsensical venture he was mistaken.

It never occurred to Mr. Oxenford to wonder whether Gus loved his daughter and would make her a good husband. Only a simpleton would marry without reckoning the financial advantages. A marriage was simply a contract, like any other. When Mr. Oxenford wooed his own wife he had not been unaware that her father owned three sections of land near Tamarack. Love? It didn't help balance a ledger, did it? Love was for women to fuss about, along with such nonsense as garden flowers and fancywork.

Gus's colleagues had not known of his engagement, so that morning when the copy boy fetched papers and distributed them about the city room there was a jovial and Rabelaisian uproar. Reporters and copy readers jostled around the city desk. Most of the remarks were based upon the cynical foundation that Gus had been thinking of Mr. Oxenford's money when he proposed. Since this was not wide of the truth, Gus flinched inwardly; but outwardly he enjoyed the jokes as much as anybody. He found candor his best defense.

"Sure I'm marrying her for her money. Think I'd pass up a million dollars?"

"I've heard that when a man marries for money he earns it," someone said.

"Pleasant work, though," Gus shot back, and they all roared.

"My, my—manager of the park," somebody else exclaimed. "Coming right along in the world, aren't we!"

"Yeah, and I want you buzzards to understand that when I come down here for publicity I want the best. Banner line page one. Won't settle for less."

They laughed, and the telegraph editor said, "Hell—we'll even extra for you, Gus."

They liked Gus, that morning. Sometimes under stress he had yelled at them, and when the opposition beat them he had blown up and called them lazy hounds, but you expected that. Men who sat at the man-killing city desk were not noted for sweet dispositions. But he was not basically mean. When the paper went to bed at midafternoon he relaxed, and he was likely to tell you to forget what he had said that morning; everybody got scooped now and then. And he always defended you to the managing editor, and he did what he could to get your wages raised. And if you got in a tight spot he'd get you out of it, and if you'd lost at craps he'd lend you enough to stave off your landlady.

Most of the men who had been reporters when Gus started had long since drifted on to other cities, and those who remained had forgotten how they used to hold his hard work against him. They weren't even jealous because a cub had climbed over their heads to the city desk. A bad spot, the city desk; they wouldn't take it as a gift. Caged up in the office.

After his engagement was announced and it was an accepted fact that he was leaving the paper, Gus became even easier to work for. If the *Chronicle* scooped the *Beacon* he shrugged and said you couldn't expect to beat the world every day. He wasn't on your tail all the time for feature stories; he left the office earlier; and one morning he didn't arrive till almost nine. Overslept, he grinned. That brought guffaws and speculation as to whether Flora Oxenford had overslept, also. Even the managing editor grinned. Indeed, he had been treating Gus with considerable deference of late. After all, Gus would soon be heir apparent to Tamarack & Northern; some day he would be an important man in Tamarack.

As the first of the year drew nearer, the more discerning reporters told one another they believed Gus had the blues about leaving newspaper work. On gray days when work let up for a minute you'd see him tip back and gaze out at the smoky sky. He wouldn't look his jovial self; he would look perplexed and melancholy. Maybe he was thinking that despite all the hell the newspaper game was a lot of fun. Or maybe he was just experiencing that human reluctance to close the books on one phase of life where the disadvantages were familiar and to begin another.

They decided to throw a party for him on New Year's Eve, give him a good send-off. Plans began taking shape in mid-December; they would rent a private dining room at the General Grant Hotel; make it a surprise party. But no, maybe not a surprise. He might have something planned with the Oxenford girl and be unable to come. So a few days before Christmas they revealed their plans. He was touched; you could tell that. He swallowed and grinned and said it was pretty damned nice of them to plan a thing like that. They asked if he'd like to have them invite Samuel R. Oxenford.

"No—not him," he said instantly; and he added, "He wouldn't come anyway. He goes to bed early. But there is someone I'd like to have."

"Not your girl! It's strictly stag."

"No, not her. But there's an old man named Frank MacGowan I'd like to have. Editor of the *Tribune* out in Clayton Junction. I learned the newspaper business from him."

So a reporter went to Clayton Junction, returning with the news that Frank would be delighted to attend; that when he was told Gus had asked for him tears came to his eyes.

It was very true that Gus experienced regrets as the end of the year brooded nearer. The *Beacon* city room had been his headquarters for nearly five years; he had come to the paper as a cocky, raw kid; he had triumphed there and met Ivan Pawpacker there. Now he was leaving; and when he returned in the future with publicity for Funland Park he would be an outsider. Newspaper men were cliquish; they considered life a spectacle taking place so they would have something to write about; and he knew the mingled envy and pity and disdain with which they regarded people who said, "I used to be a newspaper man myself."

They thought of them as men who had sold out. This was not quite fair, for Gus knew there were many young men like himself who became reporters because it was a quick way to meet influential people. Soon you were calling the people who ran the town by their first names, not only the puppets who held office but the bosses who manipulated them. Then in any city there was a group exerting quasi-official but very real power. Power more permanent than that enjoyed by the front men. Officials of corporations; officials of lodges and civic organizations. You met them, too; and from them any personable young man was sure to receive job offers. Samuel R. Oxenford was one of these.

Gus intended belonging to this group himself. Within the past months he had joined the Tamarack Commercial Club and several lodges, as well as St. Luke's Episcopal Church. That was the church of fashion; Flora attended there; and although Gus was a freethinker, belonging to such a strong, established church gave him satisfaction. In its respectability and authority he found compensations for being without a father. He figured attending would do him no harm; and the vestibule—crowded after services with silk hats and frock coats—gave him one more point of contact with important people.

On one visit to Clayton Junction, he encountered a boyhood friend who was now a railroad brakeman, and the friend informed him that somebody had recently snooped into town making inquiries about Gus Burgoyne. Gus suspected Oxenford; so next evening he told Flora the truth about his parentage and offered to release her from the engagement. She listened in silence, clasping his hand tightly, and when he finished she whispered, "That doesn't make any difference. Kiss me, Gus."

Astonishingly, he felt disappointment that she had not accepted his offer of release. He had thought his doubts about marrying her were locked permanently in the blackest dungeon of his mind. Last summer

he had debated the matter to its bitter conclusion: it was an opportunity he simply couldn't pass by. Having made his decision, he was
determined to give short shrift to his recurring incertitudes.

Besides, an engagement was not marriage; and even after he spent
his last dollar buying a bean-sized diamond for Flora he thought he
could still break up with her. She had been a believer in short engagements, but when he suggested that their marriage take place in April,
on the anniversary of the night they met, the romance of it instantly
appealed to her.

After the engagement was announced, Gus found himself greeted
more cordially by civic and business leaders; but the politicians withdrew to mere politeness. He understood but he didn't like it: since he
was abdicating the city desk they were no longer afraid of what he
might do to them in print.

On the day before Christmas it came to him afresh how much power
he was losing. Previously on that day when the spirit of Christmas
found its way even to the shabby cynicism of the city room, when
reporters returned from last-minute shopping tours with mysteriously
shaped packages, when everybody was a little more mellow and kindly,
as if suddenly made aware that man's journey was dark and that only
brotherhood could ameliorate it, Gus had always received many gifts.
Messenger boys brought them from the city hall and police headquarters and the courthouse. Oh, he had known that the gaily wrapped
boxes and the sealed envelopes with currency were tribute; of course
he had known. And yet in that season of joyful bells on frosty air
he suppressed the knowledge; he accepted them for what they pretended to be, freely given gifts, with the giver warm and human.

Today none came. Not a one. Not even the annual pair of cheap
suspenders from the ancient Negro janitor at the city hall, to whom
the knowledge must have trickled down that Gus Burgoyne should be
taken care of. Somehow Gus had supposed that woolly headed embodiment of rheumatic misery gave his poor gift from affection. As the
afternoon waned, and reporters were unwrapping their gifts and
chuckling, "What did the mayor give you? Gave me a quart of
Scotch," and the lamps were lighted in the street below, Gus experienced anger at the whole kit and boodle of those politicians, and then
depression. He knew he was unreasonable. Of course they would drop
him like a hot potato.

He wanted to get away from the office, so he shrugged into his coat
and strode through the gate, hat pulled low, his gift for Flora under
his arm. He was going out there to exchange presents with her tonight, for tomorrow he would work as usual: news didn't stop happening because the calendar was printed with a red "December 25."

He emerged to a street crowded and bustling. Everybody carried packages; most people were smiling, and their frosty breaths shone like silver. He stopped at a store and bought a bag of peanuts; the clerk gave him a cheery, "Thank you. And Merry Christmas!"

"Why—thanks," Gus said. "The same to you."

It was early yet; much too early for his appearance at the Oxenfords'; so he jostled toward the car line to Funland Park. The car was packed and jammed, only tonight people were not going to an amusement park to see a baby elephant. They were going home. Going merrily. In the car with its steamed-over windows the faces of pretty girls bloomed like flowers. Gus watched them. Their smooth cheeks, their red lips, their white teeth. Dark hair. Blond hair. Fur coats. Their girlish voices calling "Merry Christmas" when the car reached a friend's corner. He found himself wishing he were going to marry a pretty girl.

He speculated about the homes to which they were going. Ordinary houses, probably, and yet festive at this season with holly wreaths and hard-coal burners glowing at the stockings waiting for gifts. Homes of good people, kind people, located on quiet streets. People who didn't run the city and who were happy in not running it; who didn't know politicians or financiers; whose names would never be dragged across the front pages. He didn't know people like that, had never known them. Except maybe Frank. Probably the fathers in those homes would be like Frank.

And suddenly there came to him the large sense of experiences missed, experiences he would never have, and he felt homeless and bereft. For a fleet second he saw himself as an opportunist, a migrant from one class to another, a man who would never know peace, a man who would always want something beyond attainment. And he knew that what he wanted was gone and lost forever, had never, indeed, been possible. He wanted to be a little boy in one of those ordinary homes on Christmas Eve, peering out the window for his father coming home from work, a Christmas tree shining in the corner, his mother filling the kitchen with song and the scent of steamy broth. He wanted simplicity and goodness and pride in his father. ("My father can lick yours. . . . My father can drive a horse better than yours. . . .") Maybe he wanted to hang up his stockings and go to bed with the assurance that Santa Claus would not pass by that loving household. He had never believed in Santa Claus since he could remember. Uncle Tim had explained there was nothing to it. After he went to live with Frank he hung up his stockings, but he knew who would fill them.

The motorman was softly whistling "Silent Night," that song of simple shepherds honoring Mother and Child; and Gus thought of his own mother. What was she doing tonight? What did she look like? He remembered her dimly, a woman of beauty and fragrance with snowflakes in her hair.

Enough! He knew better than to do this, to look inside himself. The past was dead. Unalterable. The future was what counted. Think of the future.

"Merry Christmas," the conductor called as he left the car, and Gus returned the greeting.

He crunched through the snow to the park. Above the entrance, the electric bulbs had been unscrewed from the word, "Funland"; a sign said: "Closed For The Season"; and the iron gates were padlocked. He jingled out keys; the gate creaked on cold hinges.

Only a cadre of maintenance men worked here in winter; they had shoveled narrow paths through the snow. Gus unlocked the office; it held the clammy chill of unheated rooms. Shadwell had left the park last month, and Gus had been moving in a few of his things. The wall calendar was still turned to August. He put Flora's present on the desk and went outside.

A few lights showed dimly among the trees, silvering the snow that had drifted over the miniature railroad, over the entrance to the Old Mill, that lay heavily on the roof of the merry-go-round. Winter silence rose from the snow, and the distant city noises were muted. Gus walked toward the elephant's quarters.

A new, small barn had been built for her, with a pen outside. Faint light yellowed the window, and when he opened the door he found her keeper dozing in a rocker by the stove.

"Merry Christmas," Gus said.

"Well. Mr. Burgoyne. Merry Christmas to you."

Gus passed on to Molly's stall, and when he beheld her there, weaving at her hobble, his depression began lifting.

"Well young lady!" he boomed. "How's everything? Merry Christmas!"

Her trunk coiled toward him, toward the bag of peanuts. His laugh filled the little barn; and while he fed her he talked to her as if she could understand.

"Believe you're growing. Yes sir. Getting bigger. Be a big bull one of these days. Don't like winter, do you? Neither do I. Well, spring will come. New season. Lots of people here to see you."

Sometimes she opened her mouth and emitted sounds in a minor key, or said, "Ah-h-h." He scratched her ears and spine. Her hide was rough to his fingers but he liked it. He liked her smell. He liked her ponderosity, her absurd little tail, the way her hide sagged about her hindquarters like a man losing his trousers.

The keeper stood watching, and presently he said:

"She just weaves. All day long. Back and forth. She ought to stop it. It's bad for her front hoofs. Wearing 'em sore."

"Sore?" Gus exclaimed. "Let's see."

"Oh, she won't let you get near 'em!"

"Why, sure she will! What's the trouble, Molly? Huh? What's the trouble? Getting corns? Huh? Sore dogs?"

He leaned, grappled one leg. For a moment it remained rooted like a tree trunk; then she lifted it.

"Well I never!" the keeper said.

"Um-m," Gus murmured clinically. "Yep—they're sore, all right. Worn raw. Why do you want to weave so much, Molly?"

Molly said, "Ah-h-h . . ."

Gus stepped back, fingering his chin.

"Weaves, huh?" he murmured. "Weaves all the time?"

"All the time. Just weaves."

"She's not weaving now."

"No. We're here, now."

"Mean to say she stops weaving when someone's with her?"

"Usual thing, yes."

"By Golly!" Gus exclaimed. "Bet she's lonesome. Sure! You lonesome, old girl?"

Molly extended her trunk for a peanut.

"Wish we could buy another bull," Gus muttered. "But they cost so damned much. Oxenford would faint. Um-m. Maybe we could buy a pony. S'pose a pony would keep her company?"

"Might."

"Worth a try. Soon as I take over here . . ."

And so it was that when Gus installed himself in the office his first expenditure was for a Shetland pony, a gelding named Ranger. Ranger was a beautiful red-and-white animal, but it was a skin-deep beauty only. He lived for the moments when he could let fly with his heels or bite. But he never kicked Molly or bit her. They became fast friends. Molly ceased weaving and her hoofs healed. At first the two animals were not incongruously matched, but as time passed Molly towered over him. But their friendship persisted; everywhere that Molly went Ranger had to go; and when he died in 1910 she grieved noisily. But by that time she was part of the menagerie on Burgoyne's Circus & Hippodrome, and there were other bulls to keep her company.

That evening at the Christmas Eve celebration Gus did not mention Molly's weaving or his intention to purchase a stallmate. He knew what Mr. Oxenford would say: "Can't afford it." No matter how trifling or necessary the expenditure, that was always Mr. Oxenford's conditioned reflex.

Gus left the incoming car on Jefferson Avenue and approached the house through the snow-buried garden. Flora herself admitted him at the porte-cochere door, for the servants had been given Christmas Eve off.

"Merry Christmas, honey!" he boomed. And he threw his arms around her in a rough-and-ready hug.

Flora wished the hug had not been so brief. She would have enjoyed remaining in his arms all evening with his male odor of cold and cigar smoke. His winter-roughened lips pressed her mouth for only an instant.

"Oh, Gus," she sighed. "Merry Christmas. I wish you didn't have to work tomorrow."

"Have to though," he said, heartily, cheerfully. "You know. People getting killed, Christmas babies being born—"

She flushed dully. She thought it slightly improper for one's fiancé to mention the birth of babies. Babies were the result of whatever it was that happened in the shameful and delirious darkness ensconcing the marriage bed.

"Papa's in the library," she said.

Mr. Oxenford was laboring over figures. He sat on a high stool at an old-fashioned bookkeeper's desk. As a young man he had schemed his fortune at such a desk, and he felt more at home figuring there than in an easy chair. He glanced around, foxy-eyed and bewhiskered, as they entered the room. Gus thought he detected swift-vanishing worry on the old man's face.

"Merry Christmas," Gus called.

"Uh. Come in. Evening. S'pose I ought to wish you Merry Christmas too, but I don't know why."

"Papa doesn't believe in Christmas," Flora said.

"Not believe in it?" Gus laughed. "It's here, almost. It's a known fact. Got to believe in it."

Mr. Oxenford rattled his fingers through his whiskers.

"Ain't Christmas I don't believe in. A quiet Christmas is all right. A day of remembering Our Saviour. It's this damned present-giving!"

Mr. Oxenford appeared almost in physical agony, and Gus grew conscious of the package wrapped in holly paper he was holding.

"Who started it?" Mr. Oxenford demanded. "The Jews!"

"Jews?"

"Read the Scriptures! It's all there. The Three Wise Men started it. Jews, all of 'em. And these Jew merchants keep it up. Stores like Goldstein's. Crooks!"

"Wait a minute," Gus said. "Ike Goldstein used to run a store in Clayton Junction. Know him well. He's not a crook."

Mr. Oxenford muttered in his whiskers, sour and unconvinced. He turned back to his high desk.

"You shouldn't cross him, Gus," Flora whispered, after they left the library.

"Never heard of anything so crazy."

"Please don't cross him. He's worried with all these big deals. They're organizing a new company. He worries. He goes to bed early but I hear him up in the night walking the floor."

Gus's grumpiness persisted; conversation lagged. There was no Christmas tree.

"Maybe some day we can have one," Flora said. "Papa thinks they're foolish."

Gus felt restless, eager to leave. But he'd have to stick it a while yet. They wandered through the huge, shadowy rooms. In a front alcove they stood at the window, gazing out at the silvery night. Cold air leaked through the sash and the house itself lacked warmth; Mr. Oxenford kept a sharp watch on the coal pile. Then Gus thought of a pleasant way to fill the rest of the evening.

"Just thought of it," he chuckled. "I haven't eaten. Left work, went out to the park—"

The kitchen was enormous, with a coal range, a dripping faucet, a decrepit wooden refrigerator; everything had been arranged to give the cook miles of daily exercise. On the table before Gus, Flora set bread, butter, milk, cold roast beef. He made and consumed three big sandwiches, drank a second glass of milk. He felt better then, and lit a cigar.

"Nothing like food," he said. "Guess you know the way to my heart, at that."

When it was time for him to depart, Flora led him to the parlor. In lieu of a Christmas tree, she had placed her gifts on a gold-brocaded chair. There were only two packages. She handed one to Gus, and he gave her the one he had brought.

Unwrapping the package, he experienced anticipation; and when he saw it he was touched. It was a squat, lidded thing of hand-painted China. A cigar humidor. A sponge occupied a nook inside the lid, to keep the tobacco moist. And on the bottom of the humidor painted letters said: "Flora to Gus. Xmas, '03."

"Why this is wonderful," he boomed, knowing he would never use it. "Sponge and everything! How'd you ever think of it?"

"I just don't know," she smiled. "It just came into my head."

She exclaimed in delight over her present: a bottle of imported perfume. She closed her eyes and sniffed it like a cow sniffing clover.

"Um-m-m . . . I don't have much perfume. Papa thinks it's foolish. But I . . . love . . . it. . . . Oh, Gus . . ."

She embraced him, kissed him, nearly overbalanced him.

He pointed to the package remaining on the chair.

"Who gave you that?"

"It's from myself."

"You give yourself a present?"

"Oh, yes. Always."

It was like getting a glimpse of her childhood; probably with Samuel R. Oxenford for a father she too had not believed in Santa Claus. All at once he felt ashamed of himself for being bored in her presence. He experienced sympathy for her and pity; and he kissed her good night tenderly, almost as if he loved her.

In the autumn when Gus agreed to become manager of Funland Park, January 1 had seemed an excellent time to leave newspaper work and take another job. But during the week between Christmas and New Year's, he discovered that emotionally it was a deplorable time to make the break. The sun was a summer hobo that had gone South, and the days were short, raw, dark. Gus always loved hot, bright weather—circus weather; and when he sat in the noisy city room it gave him a chill to think that the following week he would be working alone in the stove-heated office at Funland Park. He enjoyed the company of people, and he wished he were taking over the park at the height of the season.

His spirits ebbed with the waning year, and his old doubts about marrying Flora returned. He even had doubts about a career in the entertainment business; owning a circus seemed remote. He wished Ivan Pawpacker would drop in, for that smooth, quiet man always excited him and made the impossible seem possible. Elephants and Ivan Pawpacker—they brought back his intoxicating dreams.

During that final week the *Beacon* really had two city editors, Gus and Bart Floyd, the courthouse reporter who was succeeding him. They worked together, Gus explaining the ins and outs of the job. Floyd was less than enthusiastic about his promotion; the managing editor had forced it on him.

Gus spent the last afternoon of the year cleaning out his desk; and he lingered in the city room long after most of the staff had gone. It was dark outside when he finally put on his coat and hat. Even then he returned to the desk and stood with his fingertips resting on it, remembering the miles of copy paper he had scrutinized there, the joyous hysteria of big stories breaking, the day he had looked up and seen Ivan Pawpacker. He turned away at last and tramped toward the gate, through the wastepaper on the floor, past the long tables charred with cigarette burns. At the gate he looked back once more, regarding affectionately that dingy room where he had poured out so much of his first youth. He thought: "I used to be a newspaper man myself."

He was glad the boys were throwing a farewell party; and indeed, New Year's Eve turned out much happier than Christmas Eve. He was with his own kind of people. In the General Grant Hotel the boys had rented a private dining room, and at an improvised bar white-coated Negroes served anything liquid you wanted, and all you wanted. There was a great deal of milling about, of improvised quartettes, of tall stories about the newspaper business. Everybody recognized Frank MacGowan as a kindred spirit; and they took a great liking to him, clustering about his chair. He was an elder statesman of journalism now, his hair white and shaggy, his eyes mild and honest, his face forthright. But the years had not dulled his brain, and when he talked about socialism in his mellow voice, predicting economic trouble for America, they listened attentively. By eleven o'clock when supper was announced most of them were Socialists—vinously. Not Gus, of course.

"Gus has never seen the light," Frank grinned. "He's an individualist. If this party weren't in his honor, I'd say he had the soul of an economic pirate."

"Yo-ho and a bottle of rum," somebody yelled, and there was laughter.

"But I like him, anyway," Frank said. "Pirates are often charming people."

"He's made us walk the plank!" a reporter put in, and there was more laughter.

Gus laughed with the rest. "You damned buzzards! After the things I let you get away with, to talk about me like this."

Supper was getting cold, a waiter told them, so they moved toward the long U-shaped table. Frank had difficulty in rising—his chair was without arms—so Gus seized his elbow and gave him a boost, and slapped his shoulders affectionately.

"Having a good time?" he asked.

"I haven't had an evening like this in years. I can't tell you how much I appreciate it." And he patted Gus's arm.

They ate enormously, drank enormously, sang an enormous welcome to 1904. Bart Floyd acted as toastmaster, and it was he who spoke of their affection for Gus ("Even if he is a pirate"—laughter) and presented him with a watch. Gus was quite overcome by the applause which greeted his taking the watch. He felt a wave of love for them all—for their runover heels and shabby clothes and keen brains—and it was a little while before he could speak.

"Gentlemen," he said finally, "I used to be a newspaper man myself."

They laughed and cheered.

"And sometimes by God I wish I still was!"

More cheers and laughter.

"But gentlemen, each of us has to follow our star of destiny, wherever it may lead. Yours is the gathering of news, and mine—"

He paused for a moment, his body swaying with too much liquor, but his brain like a clean June morning. And then the dream returned, the old boyhood dream of greatness and painted wagons truckling through an impeccable dawn.

"Mine," he went on with that Irish eloquence he had inherited from Gus Phelan, "is the show business. Elephants and crowds, crowds and elephants."

They thought he was talking about an amusement park, and he let them; even with his guard down he wasn't disclosing all his plans; but while he spoke about the virtues of elephants and the excitement of crowds he was thinking of Burgoyne's Circus & Hippodrome.

"And now in conclusion, I want to pay tribute to the whitest man and the best man I've ever known. He took me in when I was a dirty-eared kid. He taught me the newspaper business—guess I could hold down a job as a printer even now—and he taught me to hold up my jaw and to go after what I wanted. Gentlemen, anything I am or may become I owe to him—Frank MacGowan of the *Clayton Junction Tribune.*"

They gave Frank an ovation, and Gus helped him to his feet. After Gus's oratory, Frank was conversational and witty. He related several humorous stories about Gus's boyhood exploits, and he said he had known Gus's mother before him—a lovely woman. (Frank had been drinking, too.) And he knew, he said, that everyone here shared his hope that Gus would be successful in his new venture. But he had a feeling that Gus would return to the newspaper fold.

"If he does, we'll welcome him as the father of old welcomed the returning prodigal. And in any case, I know you join me in wishing him happiness. . . ."

And so at last the party broke up; and after the warmth and brightness the street was cold and nearly deserted now by the New Year's Eve merrymakers. It was snowing lightly, and a needle-sharp wind blew the snow in long serpentine streamers down the street. Gus and Frank labored slowly toward the car line, leaning on the wind; and on the icy corner they sought shelter in a building entrance.

At last the dim headlight of the car showed down the blocks, and Frank offered his hand.

"Lots of luck, Gus. Lots of happiness. I haven't had an evening like this since—"

He was going to say, "Since I knew your mother." But he changed it.

"Not in twenty years. I'm glad you remembered me. And do come out to see me. You'll have more time, now."

"Sure, sure! I'll be out often."

"Good night, Gus."

"Good night, Frank."

He limped slowly to the car, pulled himself up the steps. The car rumbled away toward Clayton Junction and Gus stood alone on the corner.

For fully three days after becoming manager of the park, Gus repined for the newspaper business; but then early in the new year the gloomy clouds gave way to bright sun and he felt more cheerful. Just as he had plunged heavily into his tasks as city editor, so now he crashed head down into his new work. He'd make things hum!

The maintenance men discovered at once that the lackadaisical era of Shadwell had ended. When Gus gave an order he wanted it executed instantly. Accustomed to city room tempo, he had little patience with delay. Every morning he arrived early at the park, and he demanded that a good fire be crackling in the stove when he blustered in.

The office was dust and cobwebs and debris, so by the end of his first week he had carpenters and painters at work. Commodious windows were embrasured in the east and south walls, giving him a managerial view of the park; and the interior was painted creamy ivory. In the furniture department of Goldstein's store he bought a new desk, new chairs, a good rug.

When the baby elephant was presented the summer before, a commercial photographer had recorded the event for future historians; so now Gus ordered a complete set of photographs and hung them in frames on the wall. His favorite was a likeness of himself with Molly.

By the end of January the office was no longer shabby but bright and interesting. The improvements were lost, however, upon Samuel Oxenford.

Gus had been unable to get a budget from Mr. Oxenford; and so, without consulting him, he had spent money as he saw fit, approving the in-pouring bills and sending them on to Mr. Oxenford's downtown office for payment. And so one morning in early February this brought the old fellow steaming out to the park.

"God Almighty!" he exclaimed, stamping into the office waving the sheaf of bills. "Are you trying to break me up?"

Gus had been expecting this; he remained at his desk, biting the end off a cigar.

"Sit down, Sam."

"Sit down!" the old man yelled. "What do you mean, sit down!

How can I sit down or sleep either with you spending money like water!"

He gazed in horror at the new rug, the new furniture, the sunny windows, the painted walls.

"Where do you think I'd got," he screeched, "if I'd squandered—!"

"Sit down!" Gus boomed it. And he jumped up and moved toward Mr. Oxenford as if he intended hitting him.

Something in this young man's burly personality caused Mr. Oxenford to take a backward step; and when he spoke he didn't yell but whined:

"It ain't moral to spend so much money. And a Shetland pony, too. Why you want a Shetland pony I don't know—"

"Sit down!"

Quite without intending to, Mr. Oxenford seated himself.

"Damn your stingy bones—listen to me! You hired me to run this park and I'm going to run it. Of course you don't understand why I bought a pony. But I understand and that's good enough. As long as I'm manager here I'm manager, see? Where would you be without me? I got you an elephant free, didn't I? Shadwell wasn't any good, was he?"

"Don't get excited, Gus. It's just—"

"I'll spend money, sure. But there's a purpose. Sure it's a fine office. It's got to be. Let's say I'm going to hire an outdoor act. They come out here to a shabby old office that I'm ashamed of, and can I dicker with them? They look at the broken-down old chairs and they feel above me. But now—!" Gus waved his cigar. "This is class. They come to a fine office and I'm in a position to beat down their price. I'll save you the cost of this furniture before the season's half over. And I'll show you a fat profit if you give me a free hand and keep your nose out of it."

Profit! Balm!

"Don't get so excited, Gus. It ain't that I don't trust you—"

"Now about this pony. I'll explain why I bought it but damned if it isn't the last expenditure I'll explain. I want a good budget and I want it now. I bought the pony so that bull won't wear her hoofs to the quick and then there'd be a big vet bill and maybe she'd die, and then where would you be?"

Gus stormed on; but he wasn't nearly as angry as he seemed. He was secretly amused; and he was delighted at the efficacy of his strategy. He knew how to handle people! Mr. Oxenford sat tapping a nervous foot and clawing his whiskers.

"Maybe so, maybe so," he muttered. "It was just that all them bills—"

When Mr. Oxenford took his leave they were on the best of terms, and they had agreed upon a fairly liberal budget. Gus had discovered that the old man's greed was more inordinate than his parsimony, and that the mention of profits had a magical way of unclenching his money-clutching fists.

Gus subscribed to all the trade papers of the amusement business and he gobbled them from cover to cover. He read and read again the pages devoted to circuses, and he dreamed of organizing his own circus in another year or so. How would he accomplish it? He didn't know. But accomplish it he would! Financial backing from Oxenford, credit from Pawpacker.

In mid-February, after a week of heavy snows, the temperature rose one sunny day and the park basked in the false spring of a winter thaw. The balmy air whispered of pussy willows, of robins in southern bayous preparing to fly north, of kites next month. The sun poured warmth through the office windows, and as Gus sat reading his trade papers he heard the spring music of melting snow dripping from the eaves and icicles tinkling to the ground. He thought of circuses all over America preparing to take to the long springtime roads.

He tossed the paper to the desk and looked at his watch. It said 4:29. That would be important tomorrow at this time, and on many afternoons in the future. A bewitching hour: 4:29.

As he slipped the watch back into his pocket he heard a knock on the door, and he called, "Come in."

She came in.

He stood up.

There was a long moment when neither said a word. The eaves tinkled and the sunshine ran through the windows in golden shafts. Gus's hands started toward his collar to arrange his tie, then stopped.

"I was looking," she said slowly, "for the park manager."

"Yes," he said, "sit down. I'm the manager. I'm Mr. Burgoyne."

"Thank you. I'm Miss Leslie. Carlotta Leslie."

He smiled. She smiled. He sat down at his desk.

"I hope I'm not interrupting—"

He lifted a hand. "Not at all. Glad to have you. Beautiful day, isn't it?"

"Isn't it!" she said, and her voice chimed as springlike as the tinkling eaves.

Gus felt strange. He couldn't remember ever feeling this way. And he was puzzled, too, for it seemed that somewhere or other he must have met Carlotta Leslie.

"Have we met before, Miss Leslie?" he asked.

"I—well it does seem—" She looked thoughtful and puzzled herself. "But I don't believe so."

"Have you lived in Tamarack long?"

"All my life," she said.

"Maybe then we've seen each other on the street."

"That might be," she said slowly. "I'm sure I've seen you somewhere. Did you go to the University of Tamarack?"

He shook his head. Till now, he had never regretted not going.

"I went two years," she said. "I thought we might have met there."

"No—but I was a newspaper man for five years. On the *Beacon*. I got around a lot. I must have seen you on the street."

The conversation lapsed. But by some miracle it was not an embarrassing pause. It was like the silence between old friends. Only different.

"You're probably wondering why I'm here, Mr. Burgoyne."

He nodded; but he hadn't been wondering. It had never occurred to him to wonder. Her entering the office had seemed natural and beyond the need for explanation, like the return of spring.

"I'm a schoolteacher. Third and fourth grades, Manning School. This is my first year."

Manning School. Yes, he remembered it. A new building on Forty-fourth Street in a good part of town.

"We're studying natural science and—well, perhaps it would be too much trouble for you—but I thought if some day I might bring the youngsters here—to see the elephant—"

"No trouble at all! That's what it's for."

"You're very kind."

"Any day! Why not tomorrow?"

"It would have to be on a Saturday. On a Saturday morning would be best."

This was Wednesday. Saturday seemed weeks away.

"Certainly," Gus said. "This coming Saturday? We'll make an appointment right now. How about eleven o'clock, Saturday morning?"

"I don't like to trouble you, but if that would be convenient—"

"Glad to do it, Miss Leslie!"

"Well, then, I'll meet the youngsters at school at ten, and we'll come here—"

She stood up.

He stood up, with alacrity.

"Wait," he said. "Don't go."

She glanced at him quickly. Her hair had the shining dark richness of pavement on a night of rain. She was the right height for him, neither tall nor short; and her figure beneath her inexpensive cloth coat was right, too; beautifully, gracefully right. He thought the pale-olive coloring of her skin exquisite, and her eyes remarkable. Fringed by dark lashes, they were a deep blue-violet.

"I mean," he said, "you'd like to see the elephant before you go."

"It's getting late, but perhaps—"

"Why, of course! You wouldn't want to leave without seeing Molly." And he added as further inducement, "There's a pony now, too. Shetland pony."

He told her about that as they emerged from the office and strolled toward the elephant barn.

The air was as subtly mild as early April. Rivulets of snow water sparkled along the path toward junctions with other thaw rills. The warm day had eaten great bites from the drifts and flashing planes of snow that only this morning had lain immaculate and seemingly eternal; the brown earth was showing itself like an animal stirring from hibernation. And against the cobalt sky the dripping branches of trees seemed already emancipated from the bitter sorcery of frost; you could imagine sap beginning to throb in deep roots.

He would remember this hour down the turbulent years; he would come back to it when he was tired. The westering sun sent gigantic shafts of hazy gold through the trees, painting the snow with rose and delicate mauves.

He had walked with pretty girls before; yes, with girls as pretty as this one. With girls even more spectacularly beautiful. But there was a difference.

In the elephant barn Molly lifted her trunk and greeted him with a delighted little squeal.

"Better move Ranger," Gus told the attendant; so the pony was led to a far corner where he could not repeat his past indignities of nipping and kicking.

"Well, sweetheart," Gus boomed to Molly. "Here's a pretty girl who wants to meet you."

"Isn't she darling!" Carlotta said.

Gus scratched Molly's ears and spine. Molly said, "Ah-h-h . . ."

"May I come closer?" Carlotta asked.

"Certainly. She won't hurt you."

With the graceful balance of an ice skater Carlotta came into the stall. She touched Molly's forehead and murmured foolishness as if she were talking to a baby; but to Gus it did not sound foolish. Her voice was sprigged with as many trilling notes as a bar of music.

When they left the barn the western sky was volcanic red beyond the black penciling of branches and the darkling shapes of the Fun House, the Old Mill. He walked through the gate with her; they stood waiting for her car. It came too soon, the trolley wires and the rails humming. She extended her hand.

"Thank you, Mr. Burgoyne. You've been very kind."

"Nothing at all," he said.

He watched her board the car. And he stood staring as it swayed off down the rails toward the violet smudge of the city.

"Carlotta Leslie," he murmured aloud. "A pretty name."

Custom had set aside Wednesday as an evening when he called on Flora. Tonight he did not want to go. He wanted to be alone, smiling a little, like a man remembering pleasant events.

But he went, arriving late, greeted by Flora's account of the worries she had suffered concerning his safety. She pointed out that by habit he was prompt, and she asked what had detained him.

"My watch was slow."

"The watch they gave you at the farewell party? A new watch shouldn't lose."

"I forgot to wind it."

"Still, it shouldn't lose. Does it have a guarantee?"

"I suppose so."

"Maybe you ought to take it back to the place they bought it. Have them look at it."

"It'll be all right. I just forgot to wind it."

Once in a path of thought, Flora had the slow bovinity of a cow plodding along a lane. And she had her father's concern with material things, with getting one's money's worth.

"But even if you forgot to wind it, a new watch shouldn't lose. You should have them look at it. Maybe give your money back."

"It was a present," he snapped. "Even if it started saying 'Cuckoo' I wouldn't take it back."

"Oh, it wouldn't start saying 'Cuckoo,'" she assured him. "They don't make watches like that. Just clocks."

"No!"

"Oh yes, Gus—that's true. I'm sure it is. Just clocks. Papa says though they're not practical. They get out of fix. Sometimes they say 'Cuckoo' and the bird never comes out at all. Or the bird comes out and doesn't say 'Cuckoo.' It's terrible—you can't depend on them. But they don't make watches like that. What's the matter, Gus? Does your head hurt?"

"That's right. I have a headache."

"Smoking too much, maybe."

"Maybe."

"Did you smoke much today? How many did you smoke, Gus?"

"Can't remember. Twenty-nine or thirty."

"Gus!"

"I mean nineteen or twenty. Or nine or ten."

"Well my goodness—can't you remember? If you can't remember any better than that there's no need trying to keep count at all, is there?"

"No."

"But you should keep count, though. I don't mean because of the expense—although it is expensive, isn't it?—but I mean because of your liver. What you ought to do Gus is start out the day with just so many in your pocket and then when they were gone there wouldn't be any more. Wouldn't that be a good idea, Gus?"

"Yes."

"Then why don't you do it that way?"

The words were out of his mouth before he could stop them.

"Oh, my God!" he groaned. "My God!"

"Gus, what—? You're not mad at me, are you?" Tears swam in her eyes. "You're not—?"

"No," he said. "No . . . No . . ." He jumped to his feet and strode about the parlor, his fingers fists and agony on his face.

"Why, Gus! What—?"

"It's my head. It's splitting. I think . . . I'll have a sick headache—"

She wanted him to lie down; she wanted to apply cold cloths to his brow. He shook her fingers from his sleeve.

"It's bed I need. A night's sleep. It's—I've got to leave. Bed . . ."

Bewildered, she stood at the front door watching him stride down the long walk to the street, his big shoulders bowed, his head lowered.

He wakened Thursday morning after a night of strange, troubled dreams. Usually he wakened refreshed and invigorated, glad to bounce from bed and plunge into the day's business. Not this morning. He lay with a forearm covering his eyes, wishing he might remain here opiated till Saturday morning.

He told himself he would feel better after breakfast, so he pulled on his clothes and dragged his body along the squeaking hall of the lodginghouse. Outside the morning was warm: early sun piercing the soft-coal smoke, the sidewalk veneered with patches of black ice frozen from yesterday's snow water. Along the street, carriages crunched through crusty snow and brittle ice-roofed puddles.

Children emerged from the doors of the cheap old houses, carrying schoolbooks. School. Probably at this hour she was on her way to school.

He went to his usual café and ordered his usual lusty breakfast, but he kept forgetting to eat. One minute his coffee was too steaming hot to swallow and the next it was stone cold. He drained his cup and sat blowing smoke at the scarcely nibbled toast, at the uneaten ham and eggs. Suddenly he realized he would be late at the park, but he didn't jump up from the table and bustle out. He heaved a deep breath and remained there scowling. When he stood up at last his movements were slow and laborious.

He caught his outgoing car, nearly empty at this hour, and sat staring through the window. Once he became aware of excitement on the street and beheld a horseless carriage chugging along. By this time there were several in the city; a motor club was to be organized; it looked as if the fad might take hold the way the bicycle fad had. People said that in the big cities they were becoming fairly common.

The car moaned past the garden gate to the Oxenford place, and Gus caught sight of the wooden turrets of the house. He was scheduled to dwell there after a certain date in April. A few weeks ago when that was decided, it had seemed a good idea. The place sprawled big with plenty of room for newlyweds; living there would save rent. And it had delighted him to think of Clayton Junction people driving past on Wellington Avenue, awed by the tremendous lawn and the stained-glass windows. But now the prospect seemed dreary. He wished he could dwell there without having Flora and Oxenford underfoot. He wished he could dwell there with somebody else as his wife.

By the time he reached the park he was feeling more himself. He had a job; the day's work must be done. Nevertheless, he still felt out of touch with reality. Last winter an attack of grippe had put him to bed with a fever, and he had experienced this same disengagement from the world of things. It gave him the disconcerting sense that material objects were unimportant; that the only place reality existed was within himself.

He left the car and crossed the tracks; and outside the gate he paused and gazed at the spot where yesterday afternoon two people had stood. It all came back to him then, the wrenchings within himself. It was as if his real self had never made its existence known before; as if it were a fabled giant, slumbering, bound, gagged; and now it was wakening, struggling against its fetters.

He didn't like that feeling, either. Always it had made him gloomy to look inside himself. This sense that there were momentous things in life—as mysterious and invisible as electricity—which you couldn't touch and see, gave him a feeling of being unmoored and drifting. If you couldn't put store by the visible, tactile, audible world, you were lost and lost. What was wrong with him, anyway? Why did he stand here staring at a place where a lovely girl had waited for a street-car? He'd have to take hold of himself!

So he took hold of himself, bustling into the park and into his office. The momentum carried him through his morning mail. Letter from Pawpacker! Good! Great! He'd written him a fortnight ago, breaking the news of the approaching wedding and inviting him to attend. Well! Pawpacker said he'd be delighted to come, if he could arrange it. Pawpacker wished him well with the park; and then, in a wonderful paragraph, reminded him of his two-fifty credit and said he hoped Gus would not give up his idea of organizing a circus. He would advise most young men against such a venture, but Gus had already shown himself a master showman. Pawpacker trusted his marriage would not interfere with his circus plans.

Interfere! Gus chuckled. Marriage would make his circus possible!

He crackled through the rest of his mail, letters from booking agents and concessionaires. He whistled. Show business. Promotion. Making things happen. He loved it.

He conferred with several maintenance men about routine matters; and after that he had nothing to do; his momentum was spent; and he sat at his desk aware that he was slipping back into his earlier mood. What was wrong with him, anyway? Was he catching a cold? Was he smoking too much, as Flora had hinted? Of course not! He was big, healthy, husky. Then why this predilection for sitting and day dreaming? Of course she was a pretty girl! But there were lots of pretty girls! It had even occurred to him that after marriage it wouldn't be absolutely necessary for him to cease joking with pretty girls. Of course it was a pretty name, Carlotta Leslie. But lots of pretty girls had pretty names. Damn it, why couldn't he think of other pretty girls he had known? Why did their remembered faces all go blank while Carlotta Leslie's remained vivid?

He found himself staring at the chair where she had sat. He remembered her saying that she taught at Manning School, and he realized that ever since then the Manning School section of town had glowed in his mind as an enchanted place. This very office was enchanted, as if the walls and furniture had absorbed her loveliness. And if he weren't virtually a married man, with his life all neatly charted, he would think that he too had come under that enchantment, bewitched like a character in a nursery tale. A vast, nameless pain existed in his chest; a delicious pain; and he kept taking deep breaths to get rid of it. But it wouldn't leave. Maybe at that he ought to see a doctor. But he was beyond a doctor's help.

By two o'clock he was invaded by a restlessness that kept him pacing about the office, that sent him to the elephant barn and back, that gave him no peace at all. Forty-five hours till 11 A.M. Saturday.

And then a fear hit him. It was so devastating, so cruel, that he stopped short on the office rug and exclaimed, "No!"

The fear was simply that there might be a change in her plans and she wouldn't bring her pupils to the park after all. But . . . that couldn't happen! Yet it might. If it did, what would he do? He had to see her again.

But of course she would come! If something changed her plans she would inform him. He dropped down at his desk, then immediately arose and paced the office. Finally he went outdoors and wandered along the path to the midway. A few minutes later he moved back toward the office, but instead of entering he passed through the gate and plodded along the car line toward the city. A bit of exercise would quell his restlessness, he told himself. He wasn't going anywhere in particular; just taking the air.

After a couple of blocks he cut away north and his pace quickened. Cigar smoke plumed back over his shoulder; he strode briskly like a man late for an appointment. Some minutes later he espied the Manning School on the west side of the street. It was a two-story brick building with a muddy playground, and he observed it covertly.

She was inside. Which room? As he approached he sighted a man leaving the building, obviously a janitor in overalls and an old hat. Gus followed him toward a cluster of neighborhood stores half a block away.

Grocery. Drugstore. Barber shop. The janitor was a short man with a black mustache. He entered the drugstore. Gus followed.

He was at the tobacco counter, purchasing Horseshoe Plug, discussing the benign weather with the druggist. As Gus peered into the showcase at the cigars the janitor was saying:

"But it can't last. A few days like this and it'll start snowing again."

The druggist nodded. Gus indicated a quarter brand and said:

"Six of those." And to the janitor: "You're absolutely right. It can't last."

"No, it can't," the janitor said. "We get these thaws, but they don't last."

"Lots of winter yet," Gus said.

"Yeah—lots of it."

The janitor knifed tobacco from the plug and tucked it into his cheek.

"How's everything at school?" Gus inquired.

"About the same."

"Friend of mine has a boy in that school. Third grade."

The janitor did not consider this remarkable.

"Let's see. Who teaches third grade? Miss—?"

"Leslie."

"That's the one. Hear she's a good teacher."

The janitor nodded. "Fine girl." He spoke with difficulty, owing to the size of the chew. "Not always jawing you like them old maids. Not complaining if the blackboards ain't washed."

"That so?"

"Sure it's so. You wouldn't believe it, the things they find to complain about. Too much heat. Or not enough."

"The kids like her?" Gus asked.

"Huh? Oh. Sure they like her. Sweet girl. Modest. Well, I got to get back."

He shuffled out. Gus spat the end from a cigar, ignited it at the counter flare. He found himself envying the janitor, because the janitor was employed beneath the same roof. He thought of something.

"Got a city directory?"

The druggist jerked a thumb toward the rear.

Gus nosed back through the thin medicinal odors to the prescription counter, ran through the plump book to the "L" section.

Leslie, Carlotta. There it was in print, her name. She existed; she was not something he had dreamed. Her occupation was given as a student at the University of Tamarack: the book had been compiled a year ago. Her address was on Mabis Avenue. That would be north and east of here. Yesterday upon leaving the park she must have taken the car downtown and transferred to the University of Tamarack line.

The book gave her a mother, Agnes Leslie, housewife. Her father was Herbert C. Leslie, clerk at the Tamarack Fidelity & Trust Company. For a moment that meant nothing to Gus, and then it came to him with a start: that was Oxenford's company. The trust of which he had gained control so he could borrow extravagantly.

Gus was troubled. He wondered why. Then he realized that all day he had been planning half-consciously how he could call a few times at Carlotta Leslie's home without letting Flora know. And now this! Herbert C. Leslie an employee of Oxenford! But Oxenford had hundreds of employees. Probably he didn't know Leslie even by sight.

His watch showed 3:15. School would not be dismissed till four. He wasn't going to accost her when she left school. He craved doing that, but even in his agitation he perceived the arguments·against such a course. It would be pushing things too fast. Of course, if he could make it appear a chance encounter . . . No. Better wait till Saturday. But he wanted to glimpse her.

He left the drugstore, entered the barber shop. Slack business had stretched the barber out asleep in his chair.

"Any chance to get a shave?" Gus boomed, and the fellow jumped as if stuck with a needle.

"Sure. You're next. Fine weather."

Gus removed his tie and detached his linen collar.

"Can't beat it," he said.

"It won't last, though," the barber said.

Gus closed his eyes, floated toward a half-doze under the bliss of the warm towel. Sometimes he sighed. Maybe out at the park they were wondering where he had gone. Damn the park. Yesterday the park and his future in show business had seemed the most vital things in the world. Now they were not exactly unimportant but certainly they had been jostled from the forefront of his thoughts. A girl had entered his office, and it was as if an innocent-appearing chemical had been added to a solution and brought about turbulence. The barber talked without expecting replies from the folds of the towel. And as he slapped on lather he mentioned a rumored rise in streetcar fares.

He flourished his razor, moved it across Gus's cheek.

"It's that damned highwayman Oxenford," he declared. "He's got his hands on this town's throat!"

Gus didn't consider this the time for rebuttal. And after a few minutes, when the barber dusted powder on Gus's velvety cheeks, he was discussing prize fighting.

Gus killed time with a haircut he didn't need, and it was nearly four when he stood at the mirror and hooked his collar to his shirt. His face had matured in the last year or two: he might have been twenty-six, twenty-eight. His eyes were shrewd, and so many years of determined thinking about getting ahead had brought a habitual protuberance to his jaw. His countenance had a solid quality. He paid the barber with a five-dollar bill and tipped him a quarter; he despised niggardliness.

Gaining the street, he beheld children marching from the school entrance. At the sidewalk the lines burst out in all directions: boys running, scuffling, hooting. The scene might have been the Clayton Junction school when he was a boy; it might have been any school, anywhere. He entered the drugstore and stood by the front windows, gaze fixed on the school. Most of the children had vanished. A little girl came out and dusted two blackboard erasers. Yes, in Clayton Junction there had always been such a teacher's pet who remained after hours to help with chores. The girl disappeared and minutes passed; and then, at 4:20, Gus saw Carlotta Leslie leaving the building and turning toward the neighborhood business district. A young man walked by her side.

Gus stared. He had lighted another cigar and he never realized how furiously he puffed. In his overcoat pocket his right hand was a fist, and in imagination he left the store and strode across the street and smashed his fist into the young man's narrow, eyeglassed face.

Now they had reached the opposite corner. They paused. She was talking to him soberly; he nodded—the educated fool!—and said some-

thing; and then she smiled and continued north alone. Gus drank in
her loveliness; but his emotions were mixed, for the educated fool came
across the street and entered the store. Narrow shoulders, pasty face.
Gus eyed him through clouds of cigar smoke. He made a purchase
and left, his narrow legs scissoring off toward the west.

"That fellow looked familiar," Gus told the druggist. "What's his
name?"

"Harold . . . Somebody. Can't remember his last name. He's principal over at the school."

"Guess I don't know him," Gus gruffed.

He left the store, stared north. The tree-lined distances had taken
her away from him. He strode back toward the park, telling himself
it would be natural for a teacher to talk to the principal. But damn it,
she didn't need to smile at him. Maybe she knew other men, went out
with them. It was a supposition as devastating as it was likely.

On Friday and Saturday mornings upon arriving at the office he
grabbed his mail and shuffled through it fast, but on neither morning
did he find the envelope he dreaded: a note from Carlotta Leslie
telling him her plans for a visit to the park had changed.

So she was coming! This was Saturday at last, and at eleven she
would arrive. Gus sat staring through the window.

The sky had clouded over in the night, and the air was the color of
gray water. Light coming through the window filmed Gus's countenance with gray, too, and shadows whispered about his eyes and mouth,
as if he had been missing sleep.

He heaved a breath and gazed down at the desk. For three days he
had neglected his correspondence; it was piling up on him. He'd have
to attack it, he thought, gazing at the cumbrous typewriter on a little
table beside the desk. He really needed a secretary, but such a suggestion would throw Oxenford into apoplexy. Always before he had
answered his letters promptly, using two fingers to jab out the replies.
A sheet remained in the typewriter, a half-written publicity story about
how Funland had acquired a Shetland pony to keep Molly company.

He stood up and prowled. Once he straightened a picture on the
wall and once he rearranged a chair. Last Wednesday afternoon seemed
weeks ago, weeks since he had been able to look ahead and plan his
moves; marriage, money, a circus, more money, a bigger circus, renown.

He wished she had never come knocking on his office door. No he
didn't. Yes he did. What did he wish? He sighed and smiled faintly:
he guessed he wished it were eleven o'clock.

But it was scarcely nine. He left the office and pushed through the
leaden morning toward the elephant barn. The black ground was a
frozen crust daubed with unclean snow, and the park buildings looked

bleak. Impossible to believe that one summer morning thousands had swarmed here, or that ever again the place would be festive on a warm evening. He crossed the narrow gauge of the miniature railroad with its tiny crossing sign: "Watch Out For The Cars." On a siding the little locomotive and coaches were hidden by a dirty tarpaulin. And suddenly the whole park seemed cheap and tawdry, a catchpenny enterprise beneath his capabilities.

He didn't like that. It was a way to make a good living, wasn't it? It was a springboard to bigger things, wasn't it? Why these soul-searchings? Perhaps, he thought consolingly, all men experienced such misgivings, at times. Maybe on gray days lawyers gloomily thought of themselves as hired participants in a dog fight, and perhaps merchants asked their hearts why they were piddling away their lives with fifteen-cent sales. Possibly all men, in youth at least, had high dreams of themselves as bigger than life, illustrious heroes striding forth to slay dragons or drive lion-pulled chariots. And then, tricked and trapped, they compromised.

He fisted his hands. He wouldn't compromise, by God! He knew what he wanted and he'd get it. He'd bull and push and bawl his demands, and life would yield. He'd come a long way from Clayton Junction, and he had only started.

And then again Carlotta came into his thoughts. He was astonished she had been out of them for even an instant. He had halted, and he was staring out across the park, and for the first time he faced candidly the problem of two dreams in his life now. The circus. And Carlotta. A little house on a quiet street, with children joyful on Christmas Eve.

He recoiled from the choice. He was moving pretty fast, he told himself. Maybe he wouldn't like her when he saw her again. Maybe she was deeply in love with somebody else, going to be married. Maybe if he saw her a few times the shine would wear away, like cheap jewelry turning green with use. And maybe—maybe he could have her and the circus both.

That was an instant of happiness distilled pure. He beheld the two of them riding down the years together, and every day would be circus day and every instant would be ecstasy. Suddenly rage stormed through him because he had permitted that vision to be born. How could he buy a circus without Oxenford's backing? Well, Pawpacker had offered him credit. Bah! Hadn't Pawpacker frankly said he'd close him if things went bad? He'd need a backlog of capital. He wasn't a fool. You didn't organize a circus with hopes and dreams. Capital. He had saved nothing. Money ran through his fingers. He didn't have Oxenford's tightwad disposition—wouldn't want it. He wasn't the type to scrimp and save, penny by penny. He was the type to seize a big hunk of capital and toss it at Pawpacker and tell him what he wanted. He had two-fifty credit with Pawpacker. Pin money! He'd need several thousand. Where could he get it except from Oxenford? Frank MacGowan? Nonsense! Frank wouldn't have much saved. His dinky weekly paper supported him, and that was all. No, he mustn't admit that vision to his thoughts again.

He strode on to the elephant barn, and as always the sight of Molly soothed his troubled cortex. He ordered the pony moved a safe distance away, and then he approached the coiling trunk and boomed a greeting. How glad she seemed when he visited her! Some kind of bond existed between them: almost made you believe that stuff about transmigration of souls. He had a way with her, understood her, as if in some previous existence his spirit had resided in an enormous gray body, or as if now a burly elephant's soul inhabited the chemical entity men called Gus Burgoyne.

"Well, sweetheart! How are you? You'll have to behave this morning. Yep—have to mind your p's and q's. Going to have visitors."

After instructing the attendant to herd the pony and Molly into the outside pen, he returned to his office. Ten o'clock, now. She had said the children would gather at the school at ten. He could imagine them over there across the gray blocks. Some children would be early, some late, and all excited. No more excited than he!

He saw them coming when they were a half-block distant, a long and not very regular line of children marching in twos, led by Carlotta Leslie. He saw them from his desk through the shrubs and steel pickets of the fence rimming the park. He jumped up, not waiting to see the end of the line.

His heart was thumping, and the pain in his chest had been replaced by breathlessness, as if the atmosphere had rarefied and he wasn't getting sufficient oxygen. He made himself wait in the office to give them time to reach the gate. At last he opened the door.

The line of march was breaking up inside the park, the children whirlpooling. Carlotta was saying:

"Now wait, children! Wait!"

As Gus walked toward her, smiling jovially, all the restlessness of the last days left him. Pain left him. He was quite himself again; he felt completely in command.

"Well!" he boomed. "Look who's here! Good morning, Miss Leslie!"

Her young face had been concerned with the problem of herding the children, but now she looked up at Gus and smiled.

"Yes, we got here. Finally!"

For an instant he enjoyed the electrifying experience of staring into her blue-violet eyes.

"Told Molly you were coming," he grinned. "Told her to be on her good behavior."

"The youngsters are *so* excited. They—"

He didn't hear the rest. His gaze had chanced to the gate, admitting the last of the children. And he was turbulent again. For somebody was bringing up at the rear of the line. A pasty, eyeglassed face.

The educated fool!

Perhaps she detected the change in his face.

"I asked Mr. Henderson to come along," she said easily. "It's such a responsibility to take a group of children through the streets—I needed somebody to help. Oh, Mr. Henderson. Would you come here and meet—?"

His narrow shoulders knifed through the swirling children. His face was oval, his hair mouse-colored; and the hand he extended was soft.

Gus felt as masculine as a stallion. He shot out his big paw and seized the schoolmaster's hand, shaking it so bone-breakingly and vigorously that the fellow's eyeglasses threatened to hop off his thin nose.

"Mighty glad to know you, Henderson," he boomed.

Henderson said, "How do you do." His hand escaped the inquisition, and while he massaged it he asked, "Haven't I met you? Or seen you?"

"Don't think so."

"I'm sure I have. My memory seldom fails me. I never forget a face." Oh, insufferable braggart!

"Neither do I," Gus declared stoutly. "In my line of work—"

"I have it," Henderson exclaimed. "I didn't meet you, but I saw you. It was Thursday afternoon in the Square Deal Drugstore. I had just left Miss Leslie after agreeing to attend her on this expedition. You were standing by the window, looking out. Smoking a cigar."

"Thursday? Couldn't be. I was downtown all afternoon."

"I never forget a face," Henderson insisted, with a schoolmaster's passion for precision and details. "And I'm sure—"

He stopped. Perhaps the look in Gus's eyes stopped him, or perhaps he realized that his scholarly instincts were carrying him close to disputing Mr. Burgoyne's honesty.

"It might have been somebody who looked like you," he conceded lamely. But he sounded unconvinced and puzzled at this instance of unwarranted deceit.

"It doesn't matter, anyway," Carlotta sang out. "Let's get on to the elephant barn. The children are so eager."

This was understatement.

"Better form a line," Gus said. He cupped his hands and bawled, "Listen, you kids! We're going to see the bull, now—the elephant.

Don't want any nonsense. Line up, just as you were. Henderson will be behind you, and Miss Leslie and I will lead the way."

That put Henderson in his place.

And so, like a cigar-puffing, cigar-waving Pied Piper—a prosperously dressed and self-assured Piper who had embroidered legend by acquiring a lovely companion—Gus led the slow snake dance of children toward the elephant barn. It lifted his spirits. He loved leading a parade.

The children were too anticipatory to observe how amiably Miss Leslie and Mr. Burgoyne were striking it off. Her laugh kept ringing out, and she was constantly glancing up at him in a cordiality that on occasion was almost coquettish. They looked well together, as if they were walking along to music that nobody else could hear.

"Uh—Miss Leslie," Gus said, just before they reached the barn. "After this is over would you drop into the office for a second? Want to ask your advice about a matter."

Far to the rear, Mr. Henderson shambled along like a humble scholar at the end of an academic procession. You could almost imagine him garbed in cap and gown.

In the outdoor pen stood Molly and Ranger, and when the children glimpsed them they broke ranks and surged to the fence. They shouted; they exclaimed. Gus kept bawling instructions: stand back, not too close! One intrepid boy attempted climbing the fence, but when Gus strode toward him he dropped to the ground and danced away into the throng. Other children asked if they might ride the pony, and a half-dozen negatives exploded from Gus's lips: Ranger's gentleness was illusory. Molly gazed at the small fry with eyes that were sapient and almost ironical, as if divining how many times down the circus years she would be stared at, gasped at. But always her gaze returned to Gus; she waved her trunk at his imperial figure and trumpeted affection.

"Can they do tricks?" one boy shrilled. "Can the elephant and pony perform?"

" 'Course not!" Gus replied. "They're just babies. But they will. I've got several trainers on the string who want the job. You come back next year at this time and they'll do tricks."

Next year at this time. He winced secretly, wishing he had not mentioned the future, as if already he sensed the decisions his ambition would force upon him. And so, as always when attacked by doubt, he buckled on robustness, great assurance, armor he would wear oftener and then perpetually as he plunged on into the chaos of the twentieth century.

"Yes sir!" he boomed. "You won't find a smarter elephant anywhere. She'll do tricks the like of which have never been seen!"

Impressive words, when buttressed by his persuasive power. There was a moment of round-eyed silence as the children stared at the beast whose tricks would some day be fabulous.

At last the children had remained long enough—according to their elders—and the procession wound back toward the gate.

"You said you wanted to ask me—" Carlotta said.

Gus gestured at the office. "Yes. Come in."

She called to Mr. Henderson, asking him to keep an eye on the youngsters; she would return immediately.

Gus followed her into the office, closed the door. It was an island of cubic silence, distantly assaulted by the surf roar of young voices.

"Sit down," Gus said.

"I can't stay."

"Do sit down."

She obeyed. He preferred that arrangement—the other person sitting, himself standing—when he conducted an interview that would yield him advantage.

"I'm writing a publicity story," he said slowly, waving at the typewriter. "About our buying the pony to keep Molly company. I'm having trouble with it. Want it to appeal to children. You know children well—teaching them. I'd like to have you read it and give me your advice."

"Well—of course. But—"

"I know, I know. You don't have time now. But if—if I could drop in at your home some evening—get your advice—"

All futurity waited for her reply. The children were yelling, laughing, whooping.

"Why . . . yes," she said.

"Tonight?"

"No . . . not tonight. I couldn't . . . tonight."

"Tomorrow night?"

He would go on forever through the calendar.

"Yes," she said. "Tomorrow night."

"About eight?"

"Yes." She stared at the rug. "Or . . . well, we always have a Sunday night picnic in the living room. After a heavy meal at noon, we have . . . popcorn and apples. Why don't you come for that? At six."

"Why, that's great," he said. "About six. Great!" And he chuckled. "Better pop plenty of corn, Miss Leslie. When it comes to popcorn, I eat like an elephant."

He floated through the rest of the day. Only one moth gnawed at the rich fabric of his happiness, his obligation to call on Flora that evening. Wednesday and Saturday evenings she expected him.

"How are you feeling, Gus?" Flora asked, as soon as the door opened.

"Me? I'm feeling great. How are you feeling?"

"I've been worried about you. You weren't feeling good the other night."

"Oh. No—guess I wasn't. But I'm feeling fine, now."

"How's your watch?"

"It's all right."

"Has it lost time any more?"

"No—keeping fine time."

"I'd take it back, anyway. Have it checked."

"Sure. I will if it loses again."

As they reached the library Mr. Oxenford hopped up and strode toward Gus, hand extended. He was smiling knowingly.

"Evening, Gus. Have you saw the paper?"

"Paper?"

"The *Beacon*. Have you saw it?"

Gus hadn't. No news could have competed that day with the momentous events in his life.

"Just looky here," Mr. Oxenford crowed, snatching up the newspaper. "Just read this."

From page one Mr. Oxenford's bewhiskered countenance peered out at the world, and a long news story accompanied the picture. It announced the organization of a new corporation, Tamarack Electric & Guarantee. The public was being permitted to exchange its dollars for pieces of paper known as stock in the corporation.

"And they're snapping it up," Mr. Oxenford chuckled.

Assets of the corporation consisted of other pieces of paper, stock certificates in such enterprises as Tamarack & Northern, Tamarack Fuel & Ice, Tamarack Street Railway.

"Congratulations!" Gus said. "Didn't realize you had this iron in the fire."

"Lots of irons," Mr. Oxenford said, rustling his palms together. "This is the smartest deal yet. That lawyer of mine's a sharp one. Sharp as a tack."

"Uh," Gus said, "you still control everything?"

"Control! You bet I do! That's the point. It ain't important to own all the dollars that work for you, Gus. Just control 'em. Take Electric & Guarantee. I hold fifty-one percent of the stock. The other forty-nine dollars out of every hundred belong to the public. But I vote the majority."

"That's pretty cute."

"Cute as a dollar sign! Cuter! For between us, I ain't actually put up dollars for my majority in Electric & Guarantee. I put up my stock in other firms."

"But it amounts to the same thing," Gus said. "You paid for your stock in those firms."

"Well—yes and no. That's my answer there—yes and no. When you start trackin' it down, Gus, it makes you dizzier than following rabbit tracks. Take Oxenford Electric Construction Company. Our funds there are a loan from Tamarack Fidelity & Trust. I sort of own that trust. Got control by borrowing from the Merchants' State Bank. They hold stock of mine as collateral—but I can still vote it. It's kind of mixed up, as I say. But it's all legal! Don't forget that! Never get Sam Oxenford to break a law!" He grinned and added, "Might bend 'em a leetle mite, but never would break 'em."

Both men had forgotten Flora. She sat admiring Gus as if he were a bale of clover hay.

Gus looked puzzled. "But where's the catch?"

"What do you mean—catch?"

"You can't get something for nothing. And it looks to me—"

"Something for nothing! Land of Goshen—you sound like a Socialist! Ain't something for nothing at all! I control the whole shooting match because I use my head—that's why! Ain't a man's brains worth something?"

Gus grasped the point at once. "I'm a little slow tonight," he grinned. "Of course."

"Yep—brains is what does it. And when my brains ain't smart enough I hire brains. That lawyer's. Once you're in the saddle you can control brains and vote 'em, so to speak, just like you control a company. Of course, I s'pose there could be a catch."

Gus waited.

"Nothing's perfect," Mr. Oxenford philosophized. "And if say a Democrat would get elected—say they'd put up some wild-eyed fool like Bryan and elect him. And the country would go into a panic. But it ain't likely. I'm gambling it won't happen. We got heavy interest payments to meet, you know. We got to keep showing profit. But we will. I'm gambling that we will."

Gus was gambling that way, too.

At midafternoon Sunday, snow began to fall and dusk came early. The air was damp and raw, and Gus rode in a hack toward the Mabis Avenue address. All day he had been full of anticipation and elation, but now uncertainty took hold of him. It was like the stage fright that had assailed him that first Sunday when he dined at the Oxenfords'.

Only then he had been awed by wealth and power, but tonight it was the memory of Carlotta that agitated him.

The closed hack smelled like a livery stable and the cushions were slick and cold beneath his drumming fingers. His breath and the animal warmth of his big body steamed over the windows; with his sleeve he swabbed the glass. The snow was falling more thickly now, swarming around street lamps like summer insects.

The hack wheeled more slowly as the driver puzzled out addresses, and at last it halted before a tall house where a gas porch light was burning. The shallow front yard was rimmed by a low snow-sparkling hedge. After his money sent the cab wheels squeaking off through the snow, Gus stood looking at the house, trying to forget the saloon in Clayton Junction and the diamond he had given Flora.

As he reached the porch something told him he was embarking on a new experience with people different from those he had known well. It was a tree. A Christmas tree, still on its standard, moved to the porch in the vain hope that the wintry air would help it retain its needles. A red-and-tinsel star still decorated its tip, and although the branches looked dry and woebegone Gus imagined them green and heavy with presents on Christmas Eve.

And in a flash he remembered his own sterile Christmas Eve; and he thought of Flora and of Beulah Murray in Clayton Junction and the Rafferty Street girls. He remembered the girls he had gone out with when he was a newspaper man, pretty girls met in a dozen casual ways. Some lived with their families in the wrong part of town, but most lived as he did in the lodginghouse district, girls of the night and the half-world, laughing on the road to nowhere.

Curving out from the front door was a cast-iron lever. He shoved it down, bringing a loud peal from the bell attached to the other side, vibrating a summons through the rooms of a happy home.

"There he is," Carlotta sang out. "I'll go."

She lifted her skirts and glided from the sitting room. Tonight she felt full of the devil and laughter, perhaps because of her new dress. It was a lovely thing of tulip-yellow, and the skirt swished like a tree full of leaves as she hurried along the hall from the back sitting room.

On her right, double doors closed off the parlor. The Leslies were not parlor people. They would as soon have put guests into stocks as entertain them in that stiff room. Had they owned the house instead of renting it, they would have abolished the parlor. Modern people, the Leslies.

Light was hissing from a gas globe in the hall, and at the mirror Carlotta gave herself a final survey. The girl in the glass had a smooth and almost regal loveliness, with all that brunette darkness and smolder. She made a little face at herself and opened the door.

"Hello—come in," she called. "My goodness! Look at the snow!"

"Well," the young man boomed, "I got here! Yes, quite a snow!"

She watched while he heaved out of his great, expensive overcoat and hung it on the hall tree. His suit with its tiny gray check was expensive, too. A sense of winter night had entered with him, and of male gusto in shouldering through cold and dark. He was smiling broadly, and his Roman nose sniffed.

"Golly, Miss Leslie, but that popcorn smells good! Smells like a circus!"

She laughed and told him to come along and meet her family.

The Leslie sitting room was a snug place with rose-colored curtains drawn across the windows. A coal fire glowed in the grate, and there wasn't an uncomfortable chair in the room. No professional decorator had furnished this house; it couldn't compare in fashionable tastelessness with the Oxenfords', but the room sinned in its own lighthearted way. There was too much furniture; too many knickknacks; and the walls were nearly hidden by pictures. There was a dark old oil of a setter with a wild duck, but most of the pictures were photographs. Some years before the family had given Mr. Leslie a camera on his birthday, and these shots of dogs and children and picnics were the fruits of his hobby.

Carlotta's mother was a plump woman with laughing eyes and a section of white underskirt showing beneath her dress. To look at her was to think of pumpkin pie and turkey dressing.

"We're glad you could come, Mr. Burgoyne," she told Gus, and within a few minutes he felt he had known the family for years.

Herbert C. Leslie, in his fifties, was a Dad-looking man with gray hair and mild eyes. Gus classified him at once as one of the great number of men who made a livelihood not by giving orders but by taking them.

Mr. and Mrs. Leslie had produced five children: Carlotta's older sister, Florence, married now; Herbert C. Leslie, Junior, aged fifteen; and the twelve-year-old twins, Alice and Chalice. They were identical possessors of dark pigtails, and Mrs. Leslie told Gus he could distinguish them by Alice's wearing a red hair ribbon and Chalice a blue.

"Dad can't tell them apart except that way," she said. "And sometimes they even fool me. They're so full of Old Nick, Mr. Burgoyne. Sometimes they switch ribbons and plague their poor father something awful."

The twins giggled, bringing a scornful sigh from Herbert C. Leslie,

Junior. He had a soap-shining face and water-plastered black hair. They called him Herbie.

When the mantel clock chimed eight, Mrs. Leslie declared it was time for the twins to retire, and for Herbie to complete his homework in his room. And since tomorrow was Monday, Mr. Leslie announced that bed seemed the logical destination for himself.

"I believe you and I work for the same man," he told Gus. "For Mr. Oxenford."

"Sure. Sam Oxenford. Quite a fellow."

Sam! Mr. Leslie swallowed.

"I'm with Tamarack Fidelity & Trust Company," he said.

"A good bank."

"Not really a bank. Everybody calls it a bank, but it's a trust company."

"Amounts to the same thing, doesn't it?"

"In practice. But we're not subject to as many regulations as a bank, and we don't have to keep such a big cash reserve."

Gus laughed. "Sam would like that, not being regulated. Cash reserve or not, guess with Sam behind it there's no danger of its going broke."

Mr. Leslie managed a smile. A faint one. He was an old employee at Tamarack Fidelity & Trust; he had witnessed its growth. No danger of its going broke!

"Just joking, of course," Gus boomed.

At ten o'clock when the Leslie front door closed behind Gus the snow was still falling in heavy, damp flakes, and as he picked his way down the drifted steps and gained the silent street he felt proud of the way he had resisted temptation. All evening temptation had been present in the guise of Carlotta, and all evening he had yearned to suggest that they dine together soon or attend the theater. But he had stood firm against her lure; he kept reminding himself that with Mr. Leslie's working for Oxenford there was danger that Flora might learn of his taking Carlotta out; and now he congratulated himself upon his discretion and the power of his will.

Through the snow he tramped north toward the University car line, remembering her dark beauty, so spectacular in the yellow gown with the tight bodice and lusciously full skirt. "Loveliest girl I've ever known," he thought; and suddenly the memory of her face and figure ran sharply through him like a lance, and he stopped in the snow and half-turned.

But of course he couldn't go back now and ring the door bell and say, "Forgot something. Would you like to take in a show some night?"

He plodded on, but he no longer felt happy about his tremendous will power.

He had liked not only Carlotta but her family and the cozy sitting room, and the great bowl of popcorn, and the apples, and the feeling that this was a home: a collection of warmhearted people who belonged together, loving and quarreling but mainly loving, backing up one another when trouble came, a warm little fortress. And yet—

Well, even as he basked in enjoyment he kept thinking that life held more for him than that. He liked Herbert C. Leslie, but it chilled him to picture himself at fifty, a man taking orders and a salary. He wanted to be out there in front, up there at the top, a man giving orders and making things happen. When he entered a famous restaurant he wanted people to whisper, "That's Gus Burgoyne."

Toward that goal he was well on his way. He was engaged to Flora. He called Mr. Oxenford Sam. If he started taking out Carlotta where would it lead? Certainly not to Tamarack & Northern.

So he resisted temptation. So he had will power. So he was still safe on the highroad to spangles and elephants. So he ached.

No streetcar was in sight when he reached the University line; no hacks. He decided to walk to his lodginghouse. It was a long way, but he would have a chance to think. He brooded along, his feet damp and cold, past the dark houses of the middle class. It comforted him to reflect that he could still drop Carlotta a note, asking to see her again.

In her bedroom Monday evening, Carlotta sat at the table by the front window, attempting to write a love letter.

The room had been to college, once. Pennants decorated the walls, and favors from parties dangled by the dresser mirror. On a little stand reposed a box that had contained bonbons, a two-pound box that Jim Wheeler had once given her. Now it contained programs of the Atheneum Literary Society at the University of Tamarack. She and Jim had belonged to that, and it used to seem consequential for the Atheneum to win silver cups in debating and oratory over the rival Delphian Society. There was also a large album with "Post Cards" in gilt on the cover.

Nibbling the pen, she gazed at Jim's photograph on the writing table. He was a pleasant-looking young man with alert eyes and a mouth that had been ready to smile when the picture was taken. She remembered how brilliantly he had argued on the Atheneum debating team. He had been a campus leader, active on committees, president of the student council, a member of the men's honor society.

Last spring in the university she and Jim had become engaged.

Now he dwelt in Chicago, where he had entered a solid, old law firm. He received a salary for briefing up cases, and he was saving to buy her an engagement ring, and in another year they would marry, and someday the partners in the firm would invite him to join them in their crusade to bring justice to the world.

This evening, Carlotta assured herself that she was in love with Jim. Of this there was not the slightest doubt. And just as indubitably she was not in love with Gus Burgoyne. How could she be? She had been in his company on only three occasions. He was an interesting young man—although certainly not as handsome and socially smooth as Jim—but she could never love him. The only reason she had thought about Gus today was because he had annoyed her by not asking to see her again. Had he made such a request, she would have refused. Indeed, she had composed a high-minded little speech of refusal, with the information that she was engaged to Jim Wheeler.

She sat staring at the sheet on the table. Except for the date line and the salutation it was blank. Gus was certainly different from anybody she had known. An amusement park manager. And planning to organize a circus. He seemed more mature than Jim but at the same time more boyish. Were she not engaged, it might be interesting to spend another evening in his company. If he should ask her. It puzzled her that he had not.

She dipped the pen into the bottle and began to write. But after a few sentences the words piled up like a log jam in the ink flowing from the pen. She read what she had written. It sounded all wrong. She tore up the sheet and started over. But again, after the date line and the salutation, she couldn't think of anything to say. She would have enjoyed writing about this different young man who managed an amusement park, who was excited about elephants, who referred to the great Mr. Samuel R. Oxenford as Sam; but she feared this might disturb Jim. Needlessly! For she certainly could never love Gus Burgoyne.

That week, for a girl in love with Jim Wheeler, Carlotta thought about Gus more than was necessary. As she walked to school she wondered what would happen if she should encounter him around the next corner. She was always imagining the conversation that would take place.

And after school she played with the possibility of finding him waiting outside the building. She knew this was absurd, but as she walked along the corridor she was aware of excitement in her blood. When she did not find him there, she experienced disappointment and pique.

She found reasons for going downtown after school instead of walking home. The nearest car line was that linking the business district with Funland, so what could be more natural than traveling that route? Waiting on a corner, slender and attractive, she gazed along the tracks toward the park, picturing him out there in his office; and when her car came rocking along she thought perhaps he would be on board. It was odd and a bit exasperating to reflect that he worked within a few blocks of her school, that he rode this car line, that possibly this morning he had occupied this very seat, and yet she never encountered him.

As the week crawled by her puzzlement deepened. She was such a beautiful girl it was possible she had been spoiled. Since she started going out with boys she had never experienced anything remotely like unrequited interest. At the university she was one of the campus beauties, and seldom indeed did she walk home alone from the library, or attend chapel unescorted; and her week ends were crowded. Since Jim moved to Chicago, she had remained faithful, and perhaps she had missed young men calling more than she realized. In any case, she didn't enjoy Gus's failure to implore seeing her again.

The long week ended. Sunday afternoon was fine, so Carlotta and Herbie went for a stroll. Carlotta chanced to mention last Sunday evening and Gus Burgoyne, and that led to a discussion of the elephant, Molly.

"I saw her last summer," Herbie said. "Wonder if she's grown. I'd like to see her again."

"Mr. Burgoyne would let you. If I'd drop him a note and ask him."

"Would you?"

"Why, yes," Carlotta said. "I might."

And suddenly she felt lighthearted.

She made quite a ceremony of writing the note. That evening she went upstairs early, lingering in a warm bath, and then in slippers and kimono she stood at her dresser mirror, touching her hair with perfume, smiling, feeling on the verge of momentous events.

Composing the note was a daring and pleasant experience. First she scribbled it in pencil, then copied it in ink. It said:

> Dear Mr. Burgoyne:
>
> It was certainly pleasant visiting with you the other evening, and now I have another favor to ask. My brother Herbie saw your elephant last summer, and he would like to see her again. He wonders if she has grown. I don't like to bother you with a request like this, but I'm sure it would make him very happy if it could be arranged.
>
> Sincerely,
>
> Carlotta Leslie

She addressed the envelope to Funland Park, inserted the note, and then kept taking it out again, imagining herself in his place, receiving it. Leaving the envelope unsealed, so she could reread the note in the morning, she propped it against the books on her writing table. She kept gazing at the name on the envelope. Mr. Gus Burgoyne. Sometimes she read it in whispers, so her ears could share her eyes' pleasure.

She slept sweetly and wakened happily. Even before breakfast the note sounded very good, so she licked the flap and pressed it evenly against the envelope. On her way to school she entrusted it to a mail box. According to the collection schedule, the envelope would be picked up at noon. That meant he would receive it tomorrow morning.

After school the regular Monday teachers' meeting was held in the principal's office, and although she sat trying to look prim and academic her thoughts were elsewhere. Harold Henderson presided with as much formality as if it were a conference of world powers instead of a meeting attended by a pretty girl and five tired old spinsters. Harold lived for these gatherings. He called them "faculty conferences," and everything had to proceed according to Robert's *Rules of Order*. He was not more than twenty-five, but he had been born with a school-book in his hand, and probably he would die clutching his Phi Beta Kappa key and his Ph.D. Not that he had yet attained that degree, or even his Master's, but it was wearily inevitable that he should. For in his own odd way he was ambitious, spending his summers at the University of Chicago, saving his salary so by and by he could leave public school work and eat his gray bookworm path through volume after volume, crawling always toward his Doctor's Oral and his dissertation concerning "The Influence of Plato's *Republic* upon Sir Thomas More's *Utopia* and upon the *Works* of Francis Bacon."

The meeting was less concerned with curriculum than with deportment. It seemed some of the youngsters had been pilfering chalk and scrawling bad words on the building. Miss Dodge, who reported this, had not trusted her heart sufficiently to investigate the inscriptions, but had accepted the janitor's recital as veracious.

"None of my children was involved," Miss Dodge declared. "But I understand Everett Whitcomb was one of the boys."

And since Everett Whitcomb was enrolled in fourth grade, Miss Dodge's long nose managed to hint that Carlotta had put him up to it.

"If Everett did it," Carlotta said, "I'm sure the older boys must have told him the words."

And she in turn managed to imply that Miss Dodge, who instructed fifth and sixth grades, had whispered the words to the older boys and commanded them to induce Everett to deface school property.

The other teachers now joined the fray. Only this morning, Miss Stoffel reported, she had erased a bad picture from the wall of what she called the Girls' Locker Room. It was a picture showing considerable talent in art, and everyone knew that the only girl in school who could draw well was Gladys Wabash of sixth grade.

Miss Dodge flushed. It was by now apparent she was corrupting the young. She said icily:

"I'm sure I don't know anything about such a picture. Why didn't you report it to me, Miss Stoffel?"

"I thought this meeting the proper place to report it if action were to be secured," Miss Stoffel said.

Little Miss Benson, always the peacemaker, suggested:

"It is my thought that the children should be lectured upon these matters. I'm sure they don't realize what they're doing. Mr. Henderson could lecture the boys and one of us could lecture the girls."

Mr. Henderson looked troubled.

"I suggest," he said, "that a committee be appointed to confer with other schools and with the central office to learn whether they have faced a similar problem, and, if so, how they have handled it. Do I hear a motion to that effect?"

Miss Benson so moved; Miss Stoffel seconded it.

So Mr. Henderson appointed Miss Benson chairman of the committee, to be aided by Miss Stoffel and Miss Dodge. Another matter settled!

After that the meeting took up the problem of boys and girls trespassing on lawns; also the snowball problem. When the meeting adjourned at five, it was the concensus of these experts on children that the younger generation was the worst in history.

Mr. Henderson hurried into his overcoat so he might accompany Carlotta from the building. She didn't dislike him, for he had been kind to her in a dozen pedagogical ways since her appointment to this school, an appointment mainly resulting from her father's friendship with a school board member. Although he had never asked to call at her home, she sensed that he might. For professional reasons she would have to grant that request, but she foresaw a stuffy evening. Thus far, she had fended him off with casual references to her fiancé.

The late afternoon looked like March, with craggy red clouds in the west and slate-colored clouds dashing eastward. On the playground boys were untangling kite strings.

"Rather a heated meeting at times," Harold Henderson said, and Carlotta laughed.

"Miss Dodge and Miss Stoffel have been at each other's throats for years."

He smiled.

"I trust that my gingham-dog-and-calico-cat strategy in that committee appointment will be effective."

He might, she thought, be amusing, if you accepted him on his own terms.

They paused on the corner opposite the drugstore. And all at once she was alert, for something told her he was edging toward personal matters.

"I'll have to get on," she said. "I'm expecting a letter from Jim. He's in Chicago, you know, but business may bring him to Tamarack this week."

"How interesting."

"I think so," she smiled.

She had saved his feelings, for after sending that note to Gus Burgoyne she was keeping her schedule clear.

He said, "I must be getting home, too."

He lifted his hat from his narrow skull with the dry, mousy hair. His colorless lips smiled. But she was most aware of his eyes. Behind his glasses they were warm and friendly. She felt ashamed of lying to him, but it was a charitable lie.

"Good afternoon," he said; and she wanted to laugh. If he weren't so dignified!

Carlotta spent that evening in preparation for Tuesday. Tomorrow morning he would receive her note and tomorrow afternoon he would be waiting outside the school. What should she wear? All during supper her thoughts flitted like a moth among the clothes in her wardrobe. She wanted to look her best, but on the other hand she felt it unwise to look unduly ornamented. The problem was complicated by the modest size of her wardrobe. The Tamarack Independent School District paid her a monthly check of only two figures, woebegone little figures when compared with the price tags on the clothes she desired. And the clothes she needed! A new winter coat, for example. She would not—certainly not!—have traded her immortal soul for a fur coat; but she would have been tempted.

She was not free to spend all her salary for clothes. Part of it she contributed toward the upkeep of the household. After Mr. Oxenford had purchased control of the Tamarack Fidelity & Trust Company, his first act had been to slice ten percent from all salaries. He did this to strengthen his employees' characters by teaching them thrift.

Thrift! Mrs. Leslie could have written a definitive encyclopedia on thrift. Peel the potatoes thin; round steak instead of T-bones; and the twins would look so cute in those new dresses—but no. . . . Herbert C. Leslie was also acquainted with the subject. When the cut came, he stopped smoking cigars. It nearly killed him, but he stopped. He bought a cob pipe and puffed at that, even though a pipe bit his tongue. He allotted himself ten cents for lunch instead of twenty. When the weather was decent, he walked home from work instead of riding the streetcar. It was several miles, but maybe it would decrease his waist-line. (A health benefactor in disguise, Mr. Oxenford!) And the Les-lies had a creaky buggy and a creaky old horse named Ned. These they sold. No more Sunday afternoon rides, but the saving in oats and hay was considerable. When Ned departed from the stable behind the house, the twins cried. Not Herbie. He was too old to cry. Not Mr. Leslie. Men didn't cry. Mrs. Leslie didn't cry either; not until the house was empty and she had the kitchen to herself. But she was a sentimental woman who disliked imagining Ned bony between the shafts of a junk dealer's cart. Besides, they had purchased Ned in their early days of marriage when Mr. Leslie was younger and had a great future; Ned was a link with youth. Ned had known her as a slim, pretty young matron, back when the buggy was new and he trotted briskly. Carlotta remained at the university all that day when Ned was sold. Upon returning home her eyes looked red-rimmed. She surely hadn't been crying about Ned, had she? Mrs. Leslie laughed. Pooh-pooh! That old nag. He'd be dying soon, anyway. Better sell him while they could!

It was also in the interest of thrift that Carlotta stopped school after her second year at the university. That would have especially pleased Mr. Oxenford. Money spent educating women was money down a rathole. This also held true for money spent educating men, unless the man studied something practical like law, dentistry, medicine. No frills about Sam Oxenford! All this stuff they learned young people at the university! Latin, French, Economics, Philosophy! Nonsense! Waste! Cluttered up their brains so they couldn't think straight about making money!

Carlotta had planned studying Counterpoint, Harmony, Piano, dur-ing her last two years. How fortunate that during her first two some premonition had matriculated her in "Education" courses leading to a teacher's certificate! And how lucky her father knew a school board member! Yes, the Leslies had fared better than most families who learned thrift from Mr. Oxenford.

When the salary cut was announced, Mr. Leslie had been guilty of thoughts disloyal to Tamarack Fidelity & Trust. Behind the closed bedroom door he even voiced these to his wife. Maybe, he said, he ought to make a change. A new job. But what? Where? It was frightening to think about. All very well for these young fellows to pull out. "Damned if I'll let that old tightwad do this to me!" they said. "I'll get a better job!" Understandable! Young men were more flexible. Often they welcomed, not dreaded, change. Not Mr. Leslie. You couldn't expect an old milk horse to become a fire-engine horse. Besides, jobs were not plentiful. A man with gray hair. Why are you leaving your present position? Because of a salary cut. Ha! A trouble-maker!

Moreover, there was the retirement fund. At the moment, the money in the fund was on loan to the Oxenford Electric Construction Company. Where better? Up from the corner of Tenth and Harrison Streets you could virtually see your money rising in steel and stone.

Mr. Leslie remained with the company. Bird in the hand. But it was certainly a blessing that Carlotta was receiving a salary. She thought so, too. Even more heartwarming than new clothes was her ability to ease the financial stresses of the household. At the supper table this evening she thought her father looked tired; her mother looked tired. She wouldn't permit Mrs. Leslie to do the dishes.

"No, you go in and sit with Dad. The twins and I will do them."

With her hands in soapy water, she continued combing her wardrobe, and finally she narrowed her choice to either a skirt and shirtwaist, or her black wool dress with white collar and cuffs. She decided at last on the dress. It was both casual and smart. Stirring up the cookstove fire, she put the irons on to heat; and presently she pressed the dress. A happy task.

Then in the bathroom she washed her hair, returning to the kitchen to dry it in the heat pouring from the oven. It was long hair, falling nearly to her waist. She sat idly ruffling it, dreaming about tomorrow.

The children in third and fourth grades felt lucky to have such a pretty teacher, and Tuesday she seemed prettier than usual and more vivacious. She looked queenly in her long black dress, its starched collar and cuffs flashing as white as her teeth when she smiled.

February had been a good month, with a red slotted box on St. Valentine's Day, and programs on the birthdays of Washington and Lincoln; and now with March so near Miss Leslie advised them to be on the watch for pussy willows and spring birds. She said they would set aside one freshly washed square of blackboard on which she would chalk the name of the pupil who spied the first robin, the first bluebird. She seemed happy about the return of spring.

After morning recess Everett Whitcomb reported seeing a wren, but this brought jeers from his schoolmates, who maintained that what Everett had seen was a young sparrow. Miss Leslie shared their doubts, but because she was in such a gladsome mood she inscribed Everett's name on the board, followed by "wren." However, in the interests of science, she wrote a large question mark beside the word.

Carlotta carried her lunch to school, and when noon came she sat at her desk eating, wondering what he thought of her note, thinking that in four hours she would see him. After the jostling morning, the schoolroom was unnaturally silent, so that the usually drowned-out tick-tock of the wall clock sounded large and fateful. When she brushed the crumbs from the desk blotter it was only 12:15, so she decided to go to the drugstore for dessert. In the corridor it occurred to her that Gus might be lingering outside the school now, and her heart beat wildly. But only the sunny noon waited outside, melting away the fag-end patches of winter.

In the drugstore she saw Harold Henderson sipping root beer at a wire-legged table. He stood up smiling and beckoned her to an opposite chair. After she ordered a chocolate sundae sprinkled with nuts, he asked if she had received her letter. For an instant she didn't know what he meant, but just in time she remembered her fib about Jim's coming. She had thought so little about Jim lately.

"No, I didn't. I'll probably have one today."

"If he comes, when do you expect him?"

"Tomorrow. Thursday, maybe. I don't know."

Her sundae arrived and her tongue was blissful with the delectable mixture.

Harold was scrutinizing the glistening circles his root beer glass had left on the table. He spoke in a painfully strained voice.

"*Hamlet* is coming, you know. To the Paragon. The New York cast. I had thought of inviting you to attend with me Friday night, but of course if your fiancé is coming . . ."

Carlotta watched the bright spoon with the little round bowl go dipping into the swirling chocolate syrup specked with tan nut gratings. Jim, Gus, Harold. It never rained but it poured. The fashionable Paragon Theater. She could refuse Gus if he asked to see her Friday evening. It might whet his ardor. She could wear her new yellow dress to the Paragon, the one she had extravagantly bought to wear that Sunday for Gus. Harold had been nice to her. He was principal. Her fib had not stopped him. He must like her. You couldn't help liking somebody a little bit when he liked you. *Hamlet!* Dull memories from high school English. Harold was certainly intellectual. She glanced up and flashed him a smile.

"Jim should have let me know before this," she said. "I'd love to go."

She was always amazed at the effects her smile produced. It transformed Harold from a scholar suffering anxiety into a young man revealing evidences of being human.

"Splendid," he said.

And when they left the drugstore he insisted on paying for her sundae.

The early afternoon dragged, but when the clock hands reached three, time speeded up and Carlotta found herself in a state of nerves. When she was a girl of sixteen she used to feel this way as she waited for a boy to call at her home. To sit still was difficult, and the air she drew into her lungs left her with a smothering sensation. Four o'clock came; there was the usual confusion of children struggling into rubbers and squirming into overcoats; and then they were sitting at their desks. She opened the corridor door; the fifth and sixth grade children marched past. She turned back to her charges.

"Turn. Rise. Pass."

They filed through the door, all but two little girls who lingered to attend to their apple polishing. To their redundant questions she rattled off quick answers, shooed them out.

What she beheld in the mirror fastened to the inside of her cloak-closet door heartened her. A pretty face. Even the mirror's wavy imperfections couldn't detract from the bright lips and the warm olive coloring of the cheeks. Her hands primped at her hair; she held a hatpin in her teeth while she arranged her hat. The final effect was so strikingly beautiful that she smiled at herself. Then, serious again, she stepped back and turned her lovely countenance to the right, to the left. Her heart was in her eyes. She lowered the richly fringed lashes, then swept them up. The result was startling, ravishing.

She brushed her coat, slipped into it. The lining was coming loose, and again she yearned for a coat of fur. She thought of the displays of coats and gowns at Goldstein's; lovely colors and fabrics created for girls like her. She buttoned the coat over her curving bosom, surveyed herself again. She was ready.

She took a breath, crossed to the door, moved through the sweeping-compound gloom of the hall. At the head of the short flight of steps to the door she paused, her slim glove resting lightly on the newel. Within their underskirts her legs were troubled by uncertainty. Turmoil clouded her windpipe, her lungs. Over her heart her ribs vibrated.

She descended the steps, and looking casual she pushed open the outer door. She faltered. Gus was not there. Nobody was there.

She was unbelieving. He should have received the note this morning. She had assumed that of course he would do the direct, natural thing: walk from the park to meet her here. Her gaze swept the street. Except for loitering children the south-going sidewalk was empty.

With the air of having forgotten something she turned and entered the building. The clock in her schoolroom said 4:22. She would wait ten minutes.

She waited in puzzlement, apprehension, vexation. Maybe the letter had gone astray. Or maybe he had a business appointment at this hour. Possibly he would write her a note. She wished they had a telephone at her home. More and more people were installing them. Her father and mother had discussed getting one, but the expense . . . She stood up, wandered about the room. She couldn't view the street from the windows: wrong side of the building. Ten minutes passed. She de-

cided to wait five more. They crawled. In the end she made herself
wait seven more. Seven was supposed to be lucky. When she left the
room the janitor was sweeping the corridor.

"You're here late," he said.

"Yes. Things to do."

Her hope was guttering as she descended the steps, and it snuffed out
when she opened the door. No Gus. She couldn't return to her room
and wait longer. The janitor would think it odd. She moved to the
sidewalk, cast a long glance to the south. She didn't see him. Men!
Men! They had everything their own way. A girl was expected to be
demure, modest. To wait. You never knew where you stood. Always
you had to guard against being too forward. A man could sow the
wildest of oats and then turn around and marry a lovely woman, but
let a girl so much as smile once too often and the whispers began.
Maybe these suffragettes were not so crazy. She was full of miserable
anger and antagonism against the whole male sex. She was going
home and write a nice long letter to Jim. That would show Gus Burgoyne whether she cared a snap of her finger about him.

She marched north, her pretty chin tilted. She crossed the intersection at the neighborhood business district. And then she heard
somebody call, "Miss Leslie."

She flashed her gaze across the street, toward the drugstore, and
there Gus was coming toward her. All this time he must have been
waiting at the store. Her anger vanished. She was smiling.

"Well," he boomed, lifting his hat. "Thought you were never coming. Must work you hard at that school."

"Mr. Burgoyne!" she exclaimed. "This *is* a surprise!"

It was the loveliest of late afternoons. March would soon be here.
Dull old weathermen said that spring began on March twenty-first, but
tadpoles and pussy willows and two people strolling slowly in the
nimbus of their own enchantment knew it would begin March first.
The air was still and the late sunshine tender. Trees were bare but
they had a look about them of things going to happen. They knew
that nests would soon be woven in their branches and that buds would
swell. Carlotta and Gus passed a house where the curtains were down:
a woman was washing windows and a boy was beating carpets. In the
distance the street was lightly hazed.

"Mighty glad to get your note," Gus was saying. "Glad your
brother's interested in the elephant."

"Oh yes, he's interested—very."

"Bring him over any time." Gus paused to light a cigar. "I've been
sick since I saw you," he said.

"Oh! I'm terribly sorry."

"Just a hard cold. It was snowing that night—remember? I decided to walk home. Got my feet soaked—and the air was raw. Next day I woke up with a terrible cold. It put me in bed. Stayed in bed till Thursday."

"Do you feel all right now?"

"Oh, wonderful! Feel fine, now . . . Then Thursday morning I had a letter from a bull man. You know, elephant trainer. I'd been trying to find a good one. This fellow said he'd be in Winchester, Missouri, on Friday. Man named Pawpacker has a circus brokerage business there. So I hopped a train Thursday night and went to Missouri. I stayed over the week end. Didn't get back till last night. Interesting place. I could hardly pull myself away. I hired the trainer. Good man, I think. He had some monkeys and high school horses he was selling Pawpacker. That's how he happened to be in Winchester."

He didn't look as if he had ever been sick. He was wearing a new-looking spring overcoat of light tan twill and a felt hat of pale turquoise. His oxfords were polished tan. From her schoolroom drudgery his life looked romantic: getting a letter from an elephant trainer and hopping a train to Missouri.

"What's a circus brokerage business?" she asked.

He explained with an enthusiasm that carried them along for several blocks. He told her about the sleepy town of Winchester that seemed to belong in the deep South instead of northern Missouri.

"Settled by Southern people. Except Pawpacker. He came from New York State. And he's quite a fellow." Gus chuckled. "Got his fingers in a dozen pies. But between ourselves he's not much of a showman. He ought to go into business with someone like me. I'd make him a million."

Gus puffed his cigar, looking as if he had already made several million. And he remarked that in Winchester, a couple of hundred miles south, early spring had arrived.

"Hard to believe, but it's a fact. I left winter here and ran right into spring. Down there robins are thicker than hair on a dog. Great life, isn't it!"

It seemed so to Carlotta. She thought it intensely romantic, his voyaging south to meet the approaching springtime. He seemed to smack his lips over the deliciousness of life, as if it were juicy canvasback and rich plum pudding; and in his presence existence seemed a corking adventure, crammed with surprises and glowing colors. This afternoon he seemed to exude a kind of elemental joy, as plenteous as electricity from a dynamo. With him, it seemed anything might come true.

When they turned east their shadows capered ahead of them on the bright gray sidewalk, hers shorter and slimmer, his big and full as a Chaucerian monk's. Crossing a street, he glanced at his half-smoked cigar, took a final puff and tossed it extravagantly into a gutter. When he made his fortune, she thought, he would be the fabled millionaire lighting cigars with ten-dollar bills.

His visit to Winchester had left him as intoxicated as a bumblebee that had drunk rose-dew. He couldn't stop buzzing about the wonders he had beheld. You went north, he said, from the Courthouse Square and there you were at the edge of town. You saw great mustard-colored barns with "Pawpacker" painted in blue under the gables. A railroad siding curved in, crowded with circus cars. It took your breath. One barn was full of mules. Missouri! And lanky farmers with twangy voices were dickering for teams. And another barn housed great work horses and glossy carriage horses. But best were the animal barns. Panthers! Elephants! And flashy circus owners were there to buy, and they mingled with the farmers and it was all rich in comedy, contrast, gustiness. And at the center of the enterprise Ivan Pawpacker reigned, quiet, smiling.

"Makes running a little park with one bull seem like peanuts," Gus said. "But I'll have a show of my own. By golly, though, it's hard to wait!"

He lifted his big nose, filled his lungs with a great whiff.

"How've you been?" he asked. "Seems a long while since I saw you. What have you been up to?"

"The usual things. Teaching. Nothing exciting like a trip to Missouri."

"Well look here. Why don't we take in a show together? Would you like that?"

"Yes," she said. "I would, Gus."

"Tomorrow night?"

She nodded.

"That's great," he said. "Wonderful!"

They didn't attend Shakespeare. They attended vaudeville. When the cab discharged them at the marquee, Gus ignored the line at the ticket window, escorted her directly to the door. He brought out his wallet and exhibited a card to the young man taking tickets. The young man smiled.

"Good evening, Mr. Burgoyne."

"Evening, Chet. How's business?"

An usher hurried up.

"Good evening, Mr. Burgoyne."

"Evening, Harry. Got something nice for us?"

"Yes sir, Mr. Burgoyne. This way."

They followed the usher down the sloping carpet to a lower box. Carlotta had never before sat in a box. From English literature she remembered that in the Elizabethan theater plumed and sworded gentlemen sat on the stage; the box must have derived from that custom; and she knew that if privileged patrons still sat on the stage she and Gus would be sitting there tonight.

"Do you have a season ticket?" she asked.

"A pass. I know all the theater managers. Give 'em passes to Funland, and they give me passes." He grinned. "Of course, I get the better end of the deal, but they don't mind. We're all in show business together."

The theater was filling, and Carlotta gazed out over rows of heads. She even glanced up at the cheaper balcony, where she usually sat, and at the murky heights of the gallery. People were looking at her, just as she always scrutinized the fortunate and obviously wealthy people who occupied boxes. She felt like a countess.

Through a little door from under the stage the orchestra crawled into the pit, and after a tuning-up cacophony the leader flicked his baton and the overture sent up the asbestos curtain. For five minutes the audience listened to Neapolitan street music and gazed at the scene painted on the canvas curtain, a Venetian canal done in outlandish pinks and gaudy blues. A gondolier with black curly hair and gold earrings guided his craft with its romantic couple; and from an upper window, where doves fluttered, a girl in peasant's costume leaned eagerly out and flung flowers to a man who clutched his side as if he were suffering indigestion but who was probably only singing a love ballad.

"Good picture," Gus said. "Always liked it."

Memories of her college course in Art Appreciation told Carlotta that the canvas was scarcely a masterpiece, but she didn't dispute him. However, even after the curtain had risen on a trained-dog act, she kept pondering the manner of person he was. Her professor in that art course had said most people preferred bad pictures because they were obvious, easy, familiar. She didn't think that accounted for Gus. He was attracted by the theatrical, the gaudy, as if in that tinsel world he found a beauty he had searched for and never discovered in reality.

And she wondered again why she was so attracted to him. The dog act was over and he was clapping lustily. He liked the next act just as well; he liked them all. From time to time she stole glances at him; he drank in what took place behind the footlights with the delight of a small boy. When a joke pleased him his chair creaked with laughter; his applause smacked heartily. Perhaps, she thought, she was drawn to him by his tremendous vitality. Perhaps the attraction between two people was as chemical as a laboratory formula, and love was the bright explosion. The problem of exactly what love was had occupied her thoughts a great deal lately.

The program ended with spangles flashing on the tights of acrobats, and although many of the audience were stirring from their seats Gus did not budge. And when the act was over the performers acknowledged his appreciation with a bow toward the box. This made him so happy that he applauded harder than ever.

"Good show," he said as they left the theater. "Always like vaudeville. Now how about something to eat?"

It was growing late and she had to teach tomorrow, but she didn't want the evening to end. She slipped her hand through his arm and they strolled along blithely past lighted show windows. He stopped on a corner and bought tomorrow morning's paper, folding it and thrusting it into his pocket without more than a glance. The newsboy thanked him by name. Gus lit a cigar and asked how business was. "Slow," the boy said. At an alley a beggar in dark glasses stood with pencils and a tin cup. Gus's trousers pocket tinkled as he thrust after change; he clanged a quarter into the cup. He asked the beggar how he was doing. "Terrible till now, Mr. Burgoyne," the beggar said.

"By golly, I'm hungry," Gus exclaimed. "Think I'd like a steak. Ever been to Marlow's?"

She hadn't.

"You'll like it. Used to be a fashionable place. They still serve good food."

To reach Marlow's they left the newer part of the business district for a section of pawn shops and secondhand stores. Windows were black, and the old buildings looked secretive with dingy memories of the 1880's. Feeble light seeped through the lozenge-shaped red-and-blue panes of Marlow's Restaurant, and beyond the heavy door the carpet showed gray paths worn by generations of waiters.

"Let's have that table," Gus told the aging headwaiter. "Over there by the wall."

No longer did Marlow's waste money on linen cloths; the shining dark wood of the table was bare; but this gave an effect not of poverty but of all fripperies stripped from the business of serving good food.

Their waiter, an old Italian with a head as brown and bald as a buckeye, wore a boiled shirt, a threadbare black suit with a shiny badge on the lapel.

"Good evening, Mr. Burgoyne."

"Evening, Joseph. Got any good steaks?"

"Sure, Mr. Burgoyne. Always good steaks."

Gus ordered two heavy T-bones with French fries, as well as an appetizer of blue points and cocktails.

"You tell the chef Gus Burgoyne's out here, Joseph. He knows how I like steaks. Sear 'em brown on the outside and broil the juice in."

Blue points were strange to Carlotta, and a cocktail stranger. She watched Gus fork an oyster, swill it in red sauce, gobble it. She managed to swallow two.

"Going to eat the rest of your oysters?" he asked. "If not, I'll trade you."

They exchanged plates; he attacked the remaining blue points gustily. That made ten for him.

"Ah," he grinned. "They give me an appetite!"

She sipped her cocktail, glanced at the other patrons. In the years since Gus Phelan took Doll Burgoyne there, Marlow's had lost vogue with the best citizens of Tamarack; and the people Carlotta saw were as far beyond her experience as the exquisite drink on her tongue. Many of the women were young, but not in wisdom of the world; they were as buxom as popular actresses and beautiful in a painted way. Plumed hats rode on their intricately dressed hair, and they wore clothes a shade too stylish for good taste. Many of their escorts had attained middle age and pouched eyes, and the younger men's faces held knowledge from race tracks and baize-covered tables.

As she finished her drink, the restaurant glowed bewitchingly. The paneling acquired rich depths, the cigar smoke hung dazzling white. Third and fourth grades at Manning School receded into a long-ago dream; Gus's face blurred pleasantly. She thought, "I'm in love with him. I went to an amusement park to ask about an elephant and I fell in love."

She had not confessed it so frankly to herself before. She felt awed. And she felt apprehension, too. She sensed bewildering complexities in his character. With Jim or with Harold Henderson you knew where you stood, where you would go: a home with children and Jim's becoming a corporation lawyer or a judge. Harold Henderson getting a Master's, a Doctor's, joining a college faculty. But Gus. With him the future was all tangled. A marriage march played on a calliope.

Love. The word lay shining in her mind. To her it was not the common word that millions had spoken, the old coin worn smooth by usage, its edges clipped. It was new-minted from gold, still warm, sharply milled. Gus was talking, gesturing, and she listened and smiled and nodded, but all the time she thought her secret thoughts. The steaks sizzled to the table and she picked up knife and fork, thinking how hazardous life was, how unprotected you were. You were engaged to a nice boy and then you went to an amusement park expecting the manager to be an ancient in his forties, but he turned out to be Gus Burgoyne and after that everything grew jumbled.

As his knife bit into the thick steak, Gus yarned about Winchester and Ivan Pawpacker.

"You ought to meet him. He knows showmanship when he sees

it, but he doesn't have the knack himself. By golly, if I had his equipment I'd put a show on the road that would . . ."

The wave of his hand was eloquent.

Brandy came with coffee, and Gus slipped the gold band from a rich cigar.

"A ring," Carlotta said. "Let me see it."

He dropped the band into her palm. She tried it on her engagement finger.

"My father used to smoke cigars," she told him. "When I was a little girl he gave me the bands. I had a collection."

She saw at once that this band, heavily embossed with Spanish, had probably cost as much as the cigars themselves her father smoked. She tucked it into her purse.

"I'll start a new collection," she smiled.

When the waiter brought the check, Gus tossed a twenty-dollar bill to the table, and he tipped generously. The waiter was all smiles and bows; and as the winged memory of brandy carried them to the door he scurried to open it. The street was cold, with a stray wind sneaking from alleys to sniff their ankles. A helmeted policeman labored from door to door, testing locks, and as they passed he said, "Hello, Gus."

"Evening, Lieutenant."

When they were beyond earshot Gus chuckled, "He's not a lieutenant, of course. But it makes a cop feel good to call him that."

Carlotta's legs felt dreamy; her brain felt dreamy. When they found a hack she sank into the cushions, her chin snuggling into the cheap fur collar of her coat. The interior was a little dusky world, with Gus sitting closer than necessary and the clopping of hoofs sounding muffled. Presently he took her hand, and she guessed that was all right. Usually she kept a boy at arm's length, but he was not a boy and he was different. His big arm encircled her shoulders. She did not object. Her will was sweetly benumbed; she sighed and rested her head on his shoulder. Her eyes closed and with the cab rocking and the rhythmic clopping of hoofs it was like wandering through the drowsy meadows leading to slumber. She wondered why he didn't try to kiss her. She wouldn't let him, naturally; she was a nice girl not in the habit of spooning.

Then suddenly she sensed it coming, and before she could duck her chin he was kissing her. She wanted to draw away but she was bedrugged and enchanted. Then she didn't want to. Her left hand pressed the back of his shoulder. She was engaged to Jim; she was a schoolteacher supposed to set a high moral example for the young. She had never been kissed before, like this. At last she drew away, averted her face. Blood coursed through the veins of her throat; night reeled past the cab—shadow-wrapped houses, stark black trees, lonely street lamps. She felt bad and bewitched and glad.

Very close to her ear he murmured, "Tomorrow night?"

"Yes," she heard herself saying. "Yes, Gus. Tomorrow night . . ."

"And Friday and Saturday and Sunday . . ."

"Yes. All of them. But not Friday. Don't be mad, Gus. I can't Friday. Not Friday. But Saturday . . ."

"Why not Friday?"

"I promised. I promised Friday. To go to Shakespeare."

"Shakespeare!"

"*Hamlet.* I promised . . . to go with Harold Henderson."

"The educated fool!"

As he blurted out the words a passing street lamp showed her what opposition could do to his face: hardening it.

"I know," she whispered fast. "He's strange. But he means well. He's my boss. He's made things easy for me. I don't want to, but I promised. I don't want to . . . now. Just one night. All the rest for you . . ."

Suddenly he was kissing her again, so vigorously that it choked the breath from her lungs.

"Oh, Gus," she whispered when he released her. "I'm bad . . . to let you . . . so much. No, no. Not again. Oh, we're crazy . . ."

"Yes," he said, "we're crazy. We couldn't help ourselves, could we? What happened to us . . . that first day at the park?" Another street lamp revealed his bewilderment, and when he spoke he seemed to be beseeching the cloaked forces that charted man's perplexing journey down the years. "I missed you," he added, and there was astonishment in his voice, as if the strangest thing about the whole experience was his discovery that separation could bring hunger to the heart. "When I had that cold I lay there thinking of you. And in Missouri. You seemed to be with me—on the train and when I talked to Pawpacker. It seemed part of you and me were down there. Maybe always will be down there, walking through those barns. . . . It makes a man wonder," he muttered. "Makes you wonder if it's—love. . . . Only I never believed in that."

And now for the next weeks Gus and Carlotta became mad people, and there was no cure for their affliction save being together, and that was not a cure after all but a sedative. The mad month of March blustered in, a mischievous flute-player clowning through the streets of town, peeking under skirt hems and making fat men chase their up-spiraling hats; and all through the countryside solid conservative rabbits turned daft and heedless as bankers at a burlesque show. Up from the thawing pond bottoms came bullfrogs to sing their Rubaiyats to the windy stars; and cats wandered much abroad, those bawdy jongleurs of back fences.

Thursday, Gus spent the evening at Carlotta's; and when she kissed him good night she regretted bitterly her engagement to witness *Hamlet* with Harold Henderson because it meant she wouldn't see Gus again till Saturday evening. Two whole days! She wondered how she could pass the hours till then.

All day Friday she was moody; even the prospect of wearing her new dress to the theater couldn't lift her spirits. And when Harold called for her he was scarcely more welcome than tonsillitis. But she was essentially kindhearted and she told herself she had got herself into this evening with him, and it would be wise to make the best of it. So she greeted his narrow black overcoat and oyster-colored face with a happy smile, but she deplored throwing away the evening.

Instead of traveling to the theater in a cab they rode the streetcar. She despised the snobbish thoughts that sneaked into her head. After all, she and Jim had always journeyed by streetcar, and when she went out with her family they rode Mr. Oxenford's common carriers. She told herself she should be grateful to Harold for dipping into his meager stipend to take her to the theater. Nevertheless, she couldn't help comparing his way of doing things with Gus's way. Gus gave the impression of scattering money—more where that came from—but she could imagine Harold taking out a little account book at the end of the evening and carefully noting down what he had disbursed.

They did not occupy a box at the Paragon. They did not even occupy orchestra seats. They mounted carpeted stairs to the balcony. Again the snobbish imps taunted her. Pretty cheap of Harold! Useless to argue with the imps! Useless to confront them with maxims spoken by every philosopher of thrift from Poor Richard to Mrs. Herbert C. Leslie! A penny saved. Waste not, want not. The imps snickered. How dull! If you were a successful young man like Gus, the imps said, you disregarded such threadbare and humble maxims.

She had to admit, in fairness, that their seats—in the center of first row, balcony—were about the best in the house. In a box, without craning your neck, you couldn't see more than half the stage. In the orchestra seats your neck suffered a crick from gazing upward. From here, visibility was unexcelled. Sitting in a box was ostentatious. This argument didn't confute the imps. They merely pointed out that in a box her new dress could be seen to better advantage by more people.

On the way to the theater much of Harold's conversation had concerned William Shakespeare's well-known abilities as a playwright, and as soon as they seated themselves he brought from his pocket a small volume entitled *Shakespeare's Tragedy of Hamlet.*

"It will be interesting," he said, "to follow the text and see what lines are cut."

In his quiet way he was as excited about attending Shakespeare as Gus had been about attending vaudeville. His lips—the least ascetic feature of his oval face—were smiling, and behind his glasses his eyes were bright. He continued discussing Shakespeare, pointing out that after his death literary fashions changed and people preferred the metaphysical poetry of John Donne and the dreadful conceits of Donne's imitators.

"Dryden recognized the master's greatness," he said, "but even Dryden thought him lacking in literary elegance and rewrote him. And I've never been able to forgive Dr. Johnson in the eighteenth century for his lukewarm praise."

Carlotta thought: "I'll bet that upsets Dr. Johnson's ghost."

She said, "That's interesting."

"Isn't it! It shows how literary fashions change. Very probably in another generation such writers as Clyde Fitch and Augustin Daly will be forgotten."

"Really?"

"Oh, yes. And such poets as Ella Wheeler Wilcox and novelists like Mrs. Humphry Ward."

She didn't argue, although she knew he was overstepping himself there.

Throughout the performance, Harold held the book open, now and then leaning forward to peer at the print in the dull light from the stage. Sometimes he smiled to himself, as if amused at the deletion of some line too ruggedly Elizabethan for modern ears. The company was billed as an original New York cast, but it seemed probable their closest approach to Broadway had been Syracuse or Albany. Between acts Harold commented that although this Hamlet and most Hamlets were emaciated tights-wearers, scholars agreed that the original man who acted the title role had been plumpish. Hence the line about the too, too solid flesh. This information he delivered in tones fraught with high significance. He was a born teacher.

The audience tonight was not the audience of vaudeville. Except for the coaching staff, virtually the entire faculty of the University of Tamarack was present, as well as teachers of English from little towns for miles around. The theater was as full of brains as the variety-meat showcase in a butcher shop. After the performance the foyer was crowded with rusty black evening clothes and the smell of mothballs. Harold nodded good evening to his various old preceptors from the university, and to Ellis Higby Bartholomew, professor of philosophy, he spoke a few well-chosen words.

And as they walked toward the streetcar line, he told her:

"Dr. Bartholomew is considering an instructorship for me. As soon as I get my Master's."

"That would be wonderful!"

"I'd have my foot in the door," Harold said. "Then every summer I'd work toward my Ph.D. And perhaps eventually take a sabbatical to complete my studies. Dr. Bartholomew seems interested in me. He retires in ten years, and if all goes well I might attain a professorship."

They did not visit Marlow's, or any café.

Two weeks later Harold once more screwed up his courage and invited Carlotta to spend an evening in his company. Although her refusal was bandaged in kindliness and tact it was still a refusal. Wounded, he dragged himself home to his furnished room; and that evening instead of continuing his reading in modern philosophy he went back to the Stoics. But even Epictetus failed to comfort him, and so at last, yielding to the temptation of light reading, he took down his worn copy of Ovid and read about love.

At last he went to bed but he lay sleepless, his thoughts filled with Carlotta's lovely face and figure. And gradually determination shaped itself in his will. If he believed anything, he told himself, it was in the power of the intellect. The mind could conquer circumstance and matter! So he made a resolve. Some day he would marry Carlotta Leslie. She was already engaged. What of it? Before this engagements had been broken.

He doubted that she took her engagement seriously, because he knew for a fact that she had recently been much in the company of that amusement park manager. Burgoyne! On several afternoons, glancing from his office window, Harold had seen the fellow striding toward the school to meet Carlotta and stroll home with her. What in heaven's name did she find in him to attract her? A blusterer. Someday, Harold was sure, she would come to her senses.

During late February and the first half of March Gus's visits to the house on Wellington Avenue became infrequent, and finally they stopped altogether. The more he was with Carlotta the more he wanted to be with her; he saw her every night, and on Sundays he hired a team and they drove into the country; and when they were apart he was given to long periods of daydreaming. He was like a poet struck with celestial madness. All his values changed; nothing mattered much except being with Carlotta. When humdrum affairs intruded he was as irritated as a poet at the knock of a creditor.

He reached a point where even to think of Flora set his teeth on edge. All his old disgust with her returned doubly intensified. Yet every sunset brought their marriage date closer, and he knew that soon he would have to make a decision. This he dreaded and postponed.

Never had he mentioned Flora to Carlotta. At first he fully intended to, and then suddenly it was too late. He had held her passionately and told her he loved her more than man ever loved woman. He meant it. At that instant he determined to break off cleanly with Flora the very next day.

But next day he realized what would happen if he broke his engagement. Flora would moan to her father and old Sam would fire him. That appalled him. He was just getting a start in the amusement business; he thought of Ivan Pawpacker, of elephants. If he lost his job what could he do? Crawl back to the *Beacon* and ask for employment? Or return to Clayton Junction and the *Tribune*? Those alternatives left him sick.

On the other hand, when he saw himself as Flora's husband, with Carlotta lost to him, he experienced panic. Without Carlotta he wouldn't want to go on living.

It was a problem so vast and insoluble that he locked it out of his thoughts. But now and again he sensed it, a black thundercloud forming below the horizon to rise presently and devastate a serene spring afternoon. It frightened him. But he told himself that somehow everything would turn out all right. "Things will work out," he thought, over and over.

He wished that time would stop, that he could go on like this always, walking with Carlotta through the enchantment of earliest spring. But deep in his mind he had the shrewdness and hard wisdom to know that time had never waited on the wishes of poor mortals, and never would.

Flora Oxenford was not perspicacious, and hence long after most girls would have grown suspicious she smelled no mouse in the castle of her dreams. The date of her marriage was set, and it never occurred to her there might be danger of her husband-to-be becoming her husband-who-was-to-have-been. She would have been delighted to have Gus call every evening, but when he told her that business prevented this she did not doubt his honesty. Indeed, his great concern with business gave her the comfortable feeling that everything was as it should be, for as long as she could remember her father had passed his evenings poring over figures.

Even when March arrived and many days passed without sight of Gus her suspicions were not roused. Probably one reason for this could be marked to the credit of the Bell telephone.

In his campaign of modernizing Funland Park, Gus had ordered a telephone installed. The expense of this distressed Mr. Oxenford, but experience had taught him to proceed cautiously in rebuking Gus, so he hadn't grumbled about it more than a couple of hours, and for him this was practically enthusiastic endorsement.

Of telephones Mr. Oxenford had been long suspicious. Years before when he first heard of this invention he had dismissed it as an impractical plaything, a money-waster and time-waster. But the juggernaut of progress refused to halt because of Mr. Oxenford's bewhiskered figure in its path; it would as soon have run over him; so at the last moment he climbed aboard the juggernaut to the extent of installing telephones in his offices. To do business at all, he almost had to.

But he still disliked the contraption with its alarmingly high toll charges. And he never learned its proper use. He held the receiver awkwardly against his ear, and he fairly screamed into the transmitter, for unconsciously he still doubted its efficacy and thought the dry-cell batteries should be augmented by lung power.

He had steadfastly refused to install one of the things in his home. Therefore, he was astonished but not delighted on that day in late winter when, upon arriving home, he was ushered by Flora into the kitchen.

"Look, Papa. A surprise."

There it was screwed to the pantry wall, a telephone!

Mr. Oxenford started and cried out as if he had beheld a skunk with tail lifted for business.

"Great God in Heaven! What's that!"

"It's a telephone, Papa."

Mr. Oxenford replied vociferously that he was profanely aware it was a telephone. During the next minutes he referred to the telephone company as a gang of robbers out to pauperize unsuspecting citizens. He wouldn't have the thing in the house. First thing next morning it must be removed.

This outbreak aroused no visible emotion in his daughter. She stood gazing at the instrument, stolidly chewing her cud, as pretty as a picture on a can of condensed milk.

"It'll be nice for me to call up Gus," she said.

"Gus! Ain't you got better use for your time than calling up Gus and keeping him from work!"

Flora chewed on. Presently she opined, "It'll be real handy to have."

Mr. Oxenford stormed out of the room, and before breakfast next day he called the company and ordered the telephone removed. However, as soon as he left for work, Flora countermanded the order. After this went on for several days, Mr. Oxenford surrendered. In another week he even used the instrument himself. And in the end, despite its unholy expense, he was gladder than not that it was there, for it provided him with a never-failing subject of complaint.

At least once a day Flora called Gus at his office, asking, "Do you know who this is?" Gus always knew. To get her money's worth from the telephone, Flora believed in long conversations. Sometimes Gus's voice seemed to fade into the distance, and she would say, "Hello. Hello, Gus. Can't hear you."

"I'm still here."

"That's good. What was I telling you?"

"About your new brown dress."

"No, I told you about that five minutes ago. I know. I was telling you about my wedding dress."

Near the end of the conversation Flora would ask:

"When am I going to see you?"

This query provided Gus's imagination with a great variety of calisthenics. Every day he invented a new reason why it would be impossible for him to call that evening. By and by his opinion of the telephone sank to the level of Mr. Oxenford's. Nevertheless, in fairness to Alexander Graham Bell, he admitted that had it not been for the invention it would have been more difficult to keep Flora unsuspicious in her pasture.

With the wedding approaching, Flora's energies turned to assembling a trousseau, and to aid her a woman named Minnie Pond came to the house several times each week. Minnie was what Flora thought of as a widow-woman. In her middle fifties, she was a thin, energetic, little hyperthyroid, with black little eyes.

By nature Minnie had been endowed with the abilities of a gossip columnist, but by profession she was a seamstress. For years she had been going from home to home along Wellington Avenue, gilding lilies, and her mind had card-indexed more facts and near facts than you could find in an almanac.

Even when pins bristled from her mouth she could out-talk an Edison Phonograph; but she knew how to phrase a leading question, too, and when to listen. Her ears were sharp, and she could outdo Sherlock Holmes in deducing a shocking corollary from meager evidence.

For years Minnie had served Flora and her mother before her, and hence she had been electrified by the news of Flora's engagement. During a dressmaking bout last autumn, she heard the whole romantic story from Flora's own lips. Privately she concluded that this Gus Burgoyne from Clayton Junction had purchased the engagement ring as an investment, and she yearned to learn more about him. Minnie always had her sources, so one afternoon she boarded a car for Clayton Junction and spent several profitable hours with a school friend who had moved there years ago after marrying a livery stable proprietor. The friend's husband had inherited the business from his father, and as a young man he had worked in the stable at the period when Doll was meeting Gus Phelan there. With much head-shaking and tongue-clucking Minnie listened to the delicious saga of Doll; and the very next day, while fitting Mrs. Jason Cadwallader, wife of the patent medicine king, she poured out the whole story.

"Well!" panted Mrs. Cadwallader. "So that's the kind of young man he is!"

"Just what I said. So that's the kind he is! Lift your arm, honey."

Within twenty-four hours, all the leading families of Tamarack were relishing the shocking information that Flora was to marry a man whose mother had been a high-stepper. Heretofore, interest in Flora's marriage had been slight. Dowagers had talked it over for only a few hours, concluding finally that Flora's fiancé must be either a fortune hunter or a glutton for punishment. Now, however, their curiosity was whetted; they wanted to behold this Burgoyne person with their own gimlets; and during the autumn and winter most of them managed to catch sight of the fellow, either after church or at the theater or at some party to which Flora and Gus had been invited with this purpose in mind.

They weren't quite as shocked as they pretended, for with Queen Victoria's death moral disintegration had set in; and some members of Flora's own generation shrugged and remarked that you couldn't blame Gus for what his mother did. This brought rebukes from be-whiskered fathers, who in self-protection had to evince outrage lest the world suspect them of moral turpitude and discover their mistresses. But all in all, Tamarack was much more urbane about Gus's parentage than Clayton Junction.

"Honey," Minnie Pond asked, one fine spring morning, "does Mr. Burgoyne have a double?"

Flora stared down at her. "Double?"

"You know what I mean, honey. Somebody who looks like him."

They were in the sewing room, a small second-floor chamber over-looking the garden. Scraps of dress material and thread littered the carpet, and a stack of patterns from bygone years towered up from the golden oak table. Against the wall a foot-powered sewing machine stood ready, with Minnie's help, to convert the raw material from dry goods counters into fetching creations.

Flora stood wearing a dress in the penultimate stage of completion. It was part of her honeymoon wardrobe, a thing of sober black silk, as bridelike as a raven. But it would be handy to wear in the after-noons. Moreover, being a practical girl by heredity and training, she had planned her trousseau for service long after her bridal days had passed.

Mr. Oxenford had been complaining lately about his daughter's extravagance in preparing for marriage. Land of Goshen! When he repeated the marriage vows he had committed no such sacrilege as wearing a new suit. He had worn his three-year-old Sunday suit. Didn't Flora already have enough clothes to outfit her?

"But Papa—I can wear these new clothes a long time after I'm married."

"That don't mean any nickels in my bank. After you're married, Gus'll be buying your clothes."

The wedding would take place at 8 P.M. in the Oxenford parlor, and already Flora was addressing scores of invitations. Oddly enough, Mr. Oxenford offered no objections to a large wedding, even though it meant expense. Instead he encouraged it. The motive behind this apparent extravagance was the same that had caused him to build and furnish such a pretentious house: advertising. Within the fastnesses of his heart he harbored secret uneasiness about his enterprises. He admitted to himself that the ice was a little thin. So it would do no harm to splurge. He knew the wedding would garner lavish newspaper space, and prospective stockholders would be reassured. Depositors in the Tamarack Fidelity & Trust Company would sleep soundly on. After he had erected his fine house, he had been instantly aware of increased respect from other businessmen; the house had aided him in organizing Tamarack & Northern. Smart business to spend dollars foolishly now and then, where they showed! It pained him, naturally, but at the same time it suckled his ego. He thought how well he had done and how sharp he had been, coming west with nothing and working hard, observing the copybook maxims, and now living in a mansion. It just went to prove that if you worked hard and held onto the right land and hired a slick enough lawyer you could get to the top. Mr. Oxenford thought of himself in the great Log-Cabin-to-President tradition.

Following the wedding, Gus and Flora planned to catch the night train to Chicago, where they would honeymoon. Already, Mr. Oxenford was fretting lest Gus buy Pullman space instead of spending the wedding night in a day coach. (Gus hadn't told him he intended renting a compartment.) And Mr. Oxenford kept mentioning a cheap hotel in Chicago which would be inexpensively ideal for a honeymoon. "Ain't nothing wrong with it at all," he insisted. "No fancy do-dads, but it's a good family hotel. Reasonable rates, too." Gus, of course, intended stopping at Chicago's best caravansary.

So everything was moving smoothly toward the April wedding, except that the bridegroom wasn't participating in the planning as enthusiastically as Flora might have wished. And now Minnie Pond had asked that odd question about Gus's having a double.

"I don't think he has a double," Flora said. "I've never heard him speak of it."

"Um-m-m," Minnie replied. She had been kneeling, trying to get the skirt to hang right; and now she arose and viewed it from a few paces away. She removed the pins from her mouth, stuck them into her dress. "I think that will be all right now, honey. You can take it off."

Flora houdini-ed out of it. Several layers of underskirts still guarded her virginal legs; a tatted corset cover shrouded her bosom; only her freckled arms were bare. With elbows cupped in opposite palms, she stood staring at Minnie.

"Why did you ask that?" she demanded.

"Ask what, honey?"

"If Gus had a double."

"Oh—that! Don't worry about it, honey. You just get into your dress and don't worry about it."

"I'm not worrying."

"Of course you're not! Gladys Campbell was mistaken. And Mrs. Woodley, too. Lots of people look like other people. Maybe not really doubles, but they look like each other from a ways off."

Absently, Flora scratched her arm. Two vertical lines appeared above her nose.

"Aren't you going to put on your dress?" Minnie asked.

Flora pulled it on. After she had arranged it she asked:

"What about Gladys Campbell and Mrs. Woodley?"

"Now, honey. I fixed them. I told them Gus was here night and day. I told them of course he was with you those evenings."

"What evenings?"

"Why, goodness me—the evenings they saw his double with that girl. Let me see what evenings. Gladys Campbell saw them in a box at some show last Saturday I believe it was. And Mrs. Woodley was eating in the General Grant dining room last Monday evening and thought she saw them. They don't know Mr. Burgoyne very well, do they? Might easily be mistaken. Was he with you last Saturday and Monday?"

"No," Flora said. "He wasn't. What did the girl look like? Who was she?"

"She wasn't anybody, honey. Not anybody who amounted to anything. They didn't know her."

"What did she look like?"

"Well, for that matter they said she was pretty enough. Dark-haired. One of these dark beauties, honey. I always say you have to watch those dark quiet ones. Still waters run deep, I always say. Now you're not going to worry, are you? You're engaged to him, you know.

I always say men aren't worth worrying about. Goodness me, the things they put us through. Awful!"

Flora stood rooted to the floor, arms dangling. The lines in her forehead had deepened.

"The same girl?" she asked. "Both times?"

"The same one, honey. The dark one. But now don't you go worrying. It was probably another man who looked like Mr. Burgoyne."

"I don't think there're any who look like him," Flora said.

"Well then, it might have been some relative he had with him."

"Might."

"Don't go jumping to conclusions," Minnie advised. "Of course, it might be just as well for you to ask him about it. Have it out with him. You're engaged to him and just the same as his wife now, except for certain things. Not that that would make any difference, honey, the way men are. If I'd tell you the things Mr. Pond put me through when he was alive, poor man, you wouldn't believe it. They're all alike, honey. Let a pretty skirt switch past and they're off like a tomcat. Ain't it awful?"

"Awful," Flora said.

"Yes it is! It's just that—awful! A good respectable woman don't seem to appeal to them, somehow. I don't know why we fight for them the way we do. But that's what you'll have to do, honey. Fight for him."

"Fight? But how?"

"Listen to your heart, honey. It'll tell you how. Every man's different, so the way you'd fight for one wouldn't work with another. You listen to your heart, honey."

The perplexity stamping Flora's brow had invaded her eyes. And when she left the room her feet moved in heavy bewilderment.

After the door closed, Minnie's solicitous expression was replaced by a beatific one. Not much happened to Minnie Pond except needle pricks. Most of her joy in living derived from observing the validity of the truism that money did not bring happiness. She always did what she could to help the truism prove itself.

Flora's bedroom was situated at the southeast corner of the house, under one of the great wooden dunce caps which Mr. Oxenford had found so appealing in the architect's drawing. Flora closed the door and sat on the bed, staring at the marble-topped chest of drawers against the wall papered in golden mustard.

She tried telling herself it wasn't true, that Gladys Campbell and Mrs. Woodley had been mistaken, that perhaps Gus actually had a double. She tried to remember what excuses he had given for not calling last Saturday and Monday evenings. But she couldn't sort out the excuses he had used to cover those evenings. There had been so many excuses lately. And suddenly she stopped pretending it wasn't true. It was true.

Her fingers clenched and she leaned slowly forward. Her body shook. Then she flung herself into the center of the bed. Terrible choking sounds left her throat, and she pounded the counterpane. The agony of weeping seized her whole body, and she pulled a pillow against her mouth to muffle the wails leaving it. Her sorrowing had the forlorn, hopeless quality of a cow's bawls when men have led away its calf.

She didn't know what to do. She had nobody with whom to share her problem. She had never had any close friends. Her mother was long dead. She knew she could find no sympathy or understanding in her father. She was alone . . . alone.

She wept till from physical exhaustion she could weep no more. Then she lay quietly, save for an occasional moan. Her nerves were limp as old string. Her body was torpid. She felt life had cast her into a deep pit, breaking her courage, and she was too weak and heart-sick to stir. Her thoughts were as formless and viscid as a puddle of molasses. She was beaten. Minnie had said to fight. But how?

From the yard outside she could hear the sounds of springtime. At the house next door a workman was removing storm sashes, putting up screens. This had been going to be a deliriously happy spring. She lay remembering last spring, the night Gus had first come to her father's house. Now he was going out with another girl, and she was losing him. And she didn't know what to do.

At last she heaved a great sigh and found strength to stand up and plod to the mirror. Her hair was mussed, her eyes red-rimmed and puffy. She went to the bathroom and bathed her eyes; she did what she could to her hair. Now and then, without warning, a sob jerked her diaphragm. She moved along the upper hall to the stairs. As she passed the sewing room she heard the machine humming inside, and she knew that Minnie would be wanting her for another fitting. She wouldn't be here. She didn't want Minnie to see her grief-puffed face.

Downstairs she put on a large hat with a gray veil that would mask her sorrow from the world. She picked up her alligator-hide purse and left by the side door. Without destination, she walked through the balmy garden, along that path where Gus had kissed her the first time. On Jefferson Avenue she caught an outgoing car, seating herself on the Funland Park side.

As the park approached she peered through the window. She glimpsed a workman burning leaves, but she didn't see Gus. She rode on to the end of the line, through an area that till recently had been meadow land. Once Funland Park had been at the very edge of town, but now the city had spilled beyond it. She saw surveyors' stakes and graders cutting new streets. Bricklayers and carpenters were erecting houses.

On the return trip the car halted at the park to take on a man in overalls, and she stared at the little building where Gus had his office. The workman was still burning leaves and the sunny white smoke was filtering thinly among the budding trees.

As the car left the park, she tried to marshal a plan of action, but the only idea that came to her was negative: she wouldn't call him on the telephone any more. Let him call her. Would he? She doubted it. Everything was over between them, she thought; he had found some-body else and now she would never be married. Tears slid from her eyes, and she had to bite her lip to keep from wailing aloud.

The car was approaching her home, but she didn't signal a stop; the garden gate whisked past. She had no idea where she was going; she guessed she'd just ride for a time; the mechanical noises of the car and its swaying soothed her a little, and she was grateful for any comfort no matter how slight. As the business district came closer noon whistles were blowing, and Flora stared at the office workers and clerks thronging the sidewalks. Once the car halted in midblock; up ahead a drayhorse had fallen down; and there was a terrible snarl of traffic: buggies, hacks, wagons. Lost in the mixup was an automobile, and of course its motor had gone dead and it refused to budge, so after the horse had regained its feet the automobile tangled everything up all over again. Men pushed it to the curb. People were laughing at the befuddled driver. A man ahead of Flora told a companion he favored a law prohibiting automobiles the use of downtown streets.

The car clanged peevishly and crawled ahead. A block away Flora caught sight of the girders of the Oxenford Electric Building. The lower stories were already clothed in brick; but up above the steel ribs clawed for greater heights. She experienced a grudging admiration for her father: it awed her to think that this towering building was the result of those evenings he spent at his old-fashioned bookkeeper's desk. She had not the dimmest conception of his affairs, his elaborate financing, for Mr. Oxenford belonged to a generation that believed Almighty God had reposed financial and political wisdom exclusively in the male sex. If she had asked him about his affairs, he would have quoted something like "Whistling girls and crowing hens, always come to some bad ends." She had a child's belief that he was fabulously rich and that like a wealthy king in a fairy tale he kept his money hidden in a great heap somewhere.

She remained with the car through the older part of the business district. It crossed the river into dingy East Tamarack, where small factories and great warehouses and great bawdy houses flourished. She

saw a policeman accosting a bewhiskered stumble-bum, and although
the feeble old fellow offered no resistance the officer whacked him with
his billy club and he dropped to the walk. The car clanged on; but
Flora carried from the scene a sudden horror. It came to her that the
world was full of things she had never known about, living on Wellington Avenue.

The car squealed around a corner and gained speed along a street
of decaying brick apartments. A placard caught her eye. It was
propped against the pane of a lace-curtained window in a smoke-
blackened frame house. It said: "Madam Thale. Clairvoyant."

That the sign might offer her comfort did not occur to Flora for
several blocks. And when the idea of consulting Madam Thale burst
upon her she thought: "Oh, no. I couldn't do that!" But she kept
thinking about it all the way to the end of the line, all through those
precincts of wretchedly housed humanity, past the factory with the
gold-lettered sign, "Cadwallader Medicine Company," past the Woodley Stove Works, past the weedy lots bordering the sidings of Tamarack & Northern, past brickkilns and a washing machine factory and
a lumberyard and all the other enterprises that bought carriages and
dresses and mistresses for Wellington Avenue.

As the car nosed back toward the city, Flora toyed with the idea of
going to Madam Thale; but not till she thumbed the stop button and
descended from the car did she believe she was actually going to do it.

Upon closer inspection, the house looked more slatternly than it had
from the car; and Flora lost courage. But desperation conquered her
fear, just as desperation was beginning to whet her mental faculties;
so she turned in at the short brick sidewalk and climbed to the narrow
porch. The door was opened by a boy whose face was a stranger to
soap and water.

"Is Madam Thale here?"

The boy invited her in.

She stepped into a small front parlor, and as she crossed the sill she
was assailed by an odor of fried pork. And underneath that odor was
another more permanent one. To Flora it was unfamiliar, because it
was the odor of poverty. After telling her to wait, the boy disappeared.
Flora sat on the edge of a sofa upholstered in velour. The doorway to
a second room was decorated with hangings of strung wooden beads.
The cracked window shades were purple, and they tinged the room
with unhealthy light.

She became aware of her racing heart, and she wished she had never
come to this dreadful house. In her lap her hands were clenched.
Then Madam Thale walked slowly and portentously into her room,

the beaded hangings clacking. A sleazy black dress rustled about her thin figure. Her blond hair looked twenty years younger than her hatchet face and her sharp eyes. Jet earrings dangled alongside her powdered cheeks. Before Flora could utter a word, Madam Thale exclaimed:

"You—are in trouble. Already I sense that much."

"How did you know that?" Flora blurted out.

An occult smile revealed Madam Thale's gold teeth.

"I was born with a caul."

"What's that?"

"Haven't you ever heard of a caul?"

"I can't say that I have."

"You are wearing one now. A veil. Only mine was of flesh."

"Well I never!" Flora exclaimed, amazed, believing, her timidity gone.

Perhaps Madam Thale was not on intimate terms with occult forces; but what she lacked in second sight she made up in first sight. Her powers of observation were excellent, and she deduced that a good bank account had purchased her visitor's clothes.

Troubles about money and love brought people here. She felt sure that in Flora's case financial worries could be discarded. That left love.

Those troubled by love divided themselves into two great classes: the married, and the wanting-to-be-married. Within these divisions endless subdivisions existed, but at the moment Madam Thale wished only to place this customer into one or the other category.

"Throw back your veil," she said. "And take off your coat. Sit down here."

She seated herself at a little table, and Flora took the opposite chair.

"Your hands, please."

Flora's hands, never roughed by scrub water, confirmed Madam Thale's deduction that money did not worry her customer. The engagement ring pigeonholed her as unwed. The swollen eyes spoke of recent distress.

"You are in trouble because of a man."

Flora nodded.

"A man you love."

"That's right."

"I see him as—" (This girl was large—she wouldn't be cavorting with a midget.) "—as a large man. Handsome. Successful."

Flora nodded.

Madam Thale groped on, feeling her way, and within a few minutes she had told Flora a great many things Flora already knew. She blundered badly in describing the woman who was threatening Flora's happiness, for she saw her as blond. But when no affirmative came, she backtracked neatly.

"I see them together . . . in shadows. Perhaps her hair . . . yes . . . the brightness about her hair is a headdress of some kind. Silvery. Underneath . . . yes . . . the hair is dark."

"One of those dark, quiet kind," Flora said. "What's her name?"

"I want you to concentrate on her name," Madam Thale said. She pushed a pad and pencil across the table. "To help you concentrate, write her name. Do not let me see it."

Madam Thale had various ruses to get possession of anything Flora might write; but she was unprepared for Flora's response.

"I don't know her name. That's what I want you to tell me."

"Um-m-m," Madam Thale murmured, "this is going to be more difficult." And she added, "If she has a good soul, I'll get her name fairly fast. But if her soul is evil . . ."

Madam Thale closed her eyes and struggled to pluck from infinity the name of a dark-haired girl. At last she confessed:

"I don't get a single impression."

Flora's lip quivered. She leaned forward, head on her arms, and cried.

A speculative light showed in Madam Thale's eyes.

"Now, now," she exclaimed. "We won't help ourselves this way. What you need is my Complete Service. I guarantee success."

Flora lifted her head.

"What is it?"

"It's advice. Based partly on clairvoyance and partly on my knowledge of the world. It costs five dollars. But many people have found it invaluable."

"I want it."

Madam Thale smiled. "I see your situation very clearly. But I want to hear your story in your own words. Suppose you begin at the beginning."

For twenty minutes Madam Thale listened. She cursed herself inwardly when Flora revealed her name: she might just as well have asked ten dollars, fifteen. When at last the recital was over, Madam Thale said:

"The first thing to do is learn the girl's name. And the best way to go about that is to find where she lives."

"How can I do that?"

"You'll have to follow Mr. Burgoyne."

"Follow him! What if he'd see me!"

"He won't, if you use ordinary care. Hire a hack and wait outside his roominghouse tonight. When he comes out, follow him and let him lead you to the girl. Be sure to remember her address. Once you have it, bring the house number to me. And I'll find out everything about her—that is, if you want to hire me to do that."

"Oh, yes—I want you to help me all you can! I just didn't know what to do, till I came to you!"

Madam Thale smiled.

"There have been many who have found me helpful."

The vibrations she received from the occult deceived Madam Thale when they told her Flora's purse was stuffed with currency, for after forking over five dollars Flora had less than two dollars left. Getting cash from Mr. Oxenford was about as easy as converting a dog to vegetarianism. He didn't consider it wise to trust money with a woman, for she was as likely as not to spend it. He maintained charge accounts at all the leading stores, and when Flora brought up the painful subject of cash he always said, "If you need something, buy it and have 'em put it on the books. But be sure you need it!" The bills from the stores provided him with an efficient check upon his daughter's expenditures. If a foolish purchase were listed, he sounded and acted as if he were walking on hot coals.

The money Flora paid Madam Thale had been carefully hoarded for months. She had acquired it by indirection. The trick was to purchase a small item, charging it, and then turn around and sell it for cash at a greatly reduced price. Often one of the servants would see something she wanted at a department store and ask Flora to buy it for her. The servant obtained the article cheaply; Flora got the cash; and everybody was happy except Mr. Oxenford.

On the streetcar toward town, Flora realized she faced a fiscal emergency. Hiring a hack to follow Gus would consume money. Further advice from Madam Thale must be paid for. She needed more money than the servants could afford to spend.

Twenty-four hours ago she would not have been as bold as now. She guessed that when life made demands you found the strength and means to satisfy them. She left the car in the business district and marched into Goldstein's Department Store. At the silver counter, she ruthlessly swelled Mr. Oxenford's debt to Goldstein's by seventy-five dollars.

Carrying her purchases, she left the store and strode toward the older part of the business section. She turned in at an entrance beneath three gold balls. She emerged from the pawn shop with thirty dollars. She was ready for battle.

Throughout the day a mounting excitement took possession of Flora. She bathed, and dressed in black, because she felt that tonight she would be an adventuress and a woman of mystery, and clad in black she would blend into the shadows. She was still deeply troubled at Gus's deception, but she no longer felt impotent and hopeless. She had a plan of action, now. Just where it would lead she wasn't sure, but at least she was doing something, not just moping around waiting for things to be done to her; and with her implicit faith in Madam Thale she felt that her woes would end in victory. With a psychic telegraph operator like Madam Thale as her adviser, she felt the entire zodiac was working to drag Gus to the altar.

Although she harbored murderous sentiments toward the unknown dark girl, she found it easy to forgive Gus. He was only a man, with all the weaknesses that masculine flesh was heir to, and certainly he could not be blamed if by bad luck he had encountered a hussy who duped and entranced him. But she would surely like to get her hands on that girl!

Her dresser mirror held the image of a very different Flora from the one who had sobbed out her heart this morning. Her eyes no longer had the placidity of a cow's. Determination gleamed in them; and her jaw had hardened. It was as if all along she had possessed qualities she had never used because she had never had to.

Supper as usual was a nearly wordless—although not silent—meal. Mr. Oxenford sat at one end of the table, Flora at the other. He bowed his head and returned thanks rapidly, then fell to. The sound of his eating soup had an epic rhythm, like waves on Homeric beaches. When his spoon had scraped up the last drop, he glanced at his daughter.

"Gus coming tonight?"

She shook her head.

"Ain't been here much lately, has he?"

"He's been busy at the park."

With the amenities thus disposed of, Mr. Oxenford plunged back into thought. The percentage of slate in the coal from the Oxenford mine was mounting alarmingly. Last month Tamarack & Northern had shown another decline in receipts. The total income from all his enterprises was tremendous, but the outgo was gigantic, too. He simply had to maintain bond interest and dividend payments, for if the public ever lost faith there would be a crash like the walls of Jericho. Worried him, sometimes. But things would get better. Soon the Oxenford Electric Building would start yielding rent. Tamarack & Northern would pick up.

He yanked the napkin from his collar, belched three times, brought out a quill toothpick and shambled off toward the library.

Flora arose and tiptoed along the hall. In the vestibule she put on her coat and hat; and again tonight she wore a veil. She slipped from the

house and caught a streetcar. It was early yet: just barely dusk. Downtown, she hurried toward the General Grant Hotel, where a line of
cab horses always waited. She selected an older driver.

"I want to hire you for an hour or two," she told him.

"Yes, mum."

"I want to drive to a certain address. We'll wait outside. A man
will come out and I want you to follow him."

"Well, mum—I wouldn't want no trouble—"

"There won't be. Just you follow him, that's all."

Darkness had settled when they reached the vicinity of Gus's lodging. Flora told the driver to halt three houses away on the opposite
side of the street.

They waited. Sometimes the horses stamped or blew darkly. A
block away children were playing shrill games, and farther yet away
an occasional streetcar clanged. Once a door opened and closed, and
a sporty-looking man whistled toward town. The driver lighted a foul
pipe. Carriages clopped by. Flora sat forward on the seat, her gaze
fastened on the lodginghouse. Her nerves were alertly keyed. Lemon-
colored light fell through the downstairs windows, and after a few
minutes she saw a woman with a plumed hat turning in at the lodging.
The door opened; voices rang out in greeting; the door closed. Later,
a man left the house. An older man in a derby hat; portly. She had
never seen him before; she would never see him again; and she was
dimly aware of the romance and mystery of existence. Then the door
opened and Gus emerged. Flora whispered something to the driver.

Walking briskly, Gus turned toward town; and then, spying the
hack, he angled across the street toward it. Flora thought she would
collapse. With her heart in her windpipe she oozed off the seat and
crouched on the floor.

"Cab?" she heard Gus say, very near.

"Sorry, mister. This here one's took. Just waiting."

His footsteps died away. Before she regained the seat the cab began
moving. The driver swung it around and holding the horses at a walk
followed Gus. On the seat again, Flora peered out. She glimpsed him
striding along half a block ahead.

On one of the lighted avenues near town he hailed another hack with
more success; it drove off west. Flora's driver followed at a safe distance through evening traffic.

"That was a close one, mum," he called back, chuckling.

"Don't lose him," Flora ordered. "But don't let him see us. Wherever he's going, I want the address."

"Easy. Ain't nothing to it, mum."

Some minutes later, on Mabis Avenue, Flora beheld the other hack pulling to a stop. Gus stepped out and approached a tall house in a narrow front yard. Her own hack halted.

"I'll get the address," the driver mumbled. He tethered his horses with a round iron weight to which a strap was attached. Then he shuffled away toward the other hack and spoke to the driver.

"Nothin' to it," he grinned, upon his return. "Told him I was hunting an address. Asked him that house address. It's 3818 Mabis Avenue. What do we do now?"

"Keep following," Flora said.

Presently two people left the house and entered the hack. Gus and a girl. Flora strained forward, eyes pin-pointed. In the illumination from an arc light Flora discerned that the girl was dark-haired.

The vehicle they were following clopped along to the west and southwest. Once it paused at a corner, and Gus and the girl descended. She glided to a mail box and posted a letter. Then they re-entered the hack.

Flora remained on the edge of the seat, staring. Her hatred for the girl was cold and sharp. She had to admit that the girl was graceful and pretty, but she was convinced it was beauty of the epidermis only. What injured Flora most was seeing the girl and Gus together. Nevertheless she kept straining her eyes to see them together. Her mouth was grim, and she knew that after her experience tonight she would never again be quite the same.

The trail led to Jefferson Avenue and then west along the car tracks toward Funland Park. Flora's driver followed expertly, reining in his horses when the other hack stopped at the park entrance. Flora breathed hard as she witnessed Gus and the girl entering the park. Gus must have paid off his driver, for the horses trotted back toward town.

"What now, mum?"

"Pull closer to the park."

The vehicle creaked ahead.

"This will do," Flora said, when they were nearly opposite the gate. "You wait for me here."

The springs complained as she shifted her body and stepped down. Her breath choppy, she crunched across the cinders between the car tracks. To the east, the lights of town cast dim radiance against the sky. Flora reached the concrete esplanade outside the entrance; she grasped the cold iron gate. It jangled against its chain and padlock.

Locked! After entering, Gus had snapped shut the padlock.

Flora stared between the perpendicular bars. Scattered about the park, lonely bulbs shone weakly. Her gaze followed the gravel path that wandered toward the elephant's quarters. Down in the glade she could distinguish two figures strolling slowly. As she watched they halted, embraced. Minutes later they moved languidly on, toward the elephant barn.

Flora shivered, and her teeth wanted to chatter. She clamped her jaws. A faint sickness curled inside her stomach, and the surface of her brain felt numb as if from a series of blows. But she was aware of activity taking place on some distant level of her being: a gathering of titanic rage as she realized how monstrously and ignominiously she had been deceived.

She waited a long time, clutching the gate; and at last she made out two shadows returning. She knew she ought to clear out of there, but she couldn't tear away her gaze. And then they were ascending the path very near, and it was much too late for her to trundle to her hack. She shrank back, pressing her body into the angle of the wall and gate. When they left they would be sure to discover her.

She hardly breathed. She heard the rumble of Gus's voice, followed by the girl's bell-clear laugh. Sweat sprang out on Flora's brow and she closed her eyes tightly. Any moment she expected to hear the jangling of the padlock chain.

It didn't come. Again she looked. The office door was opening; a light flashed on inside. The door closed. And presently the office was plunged into darkness.

Flora wavered back toward her hack. She heard her voice ordering: "Drive back down Jefferson Avenue. I'll tell you when to stop."

She creaked inside. The hack rocked away. She paid off the driver at the garden gate. She entered the house at the porte-cochere door, and as she fumbled along the hall Mr. Oxenford came from the library.

"Where you been?"

Flora blinked at him.

"What's the matter?" he shrilled. "Cat got your tongue? Where you been?"

"Walking. It's—a real nice evening. So I went for a walk."

"Well why didn't you say so in the first place?"

He turned back into the library; she had a glimpse of his book-keeper's desk covered with papers. Slowly, she pulled herself up the stairs. She closed the door of her room and flung herself to the bed, strangled by sobs.

Next morning Flora rode the streetcar across town to Madam Thale. She poured out the whole story of what had happened the night before. Madam Thale scribbled down the address.

Flora broke into tears as she related those terrible events, and Madam Thale went to her chair and slipped a comforting arm around her.

"Don't cry. Everything will be all right."

"Oh, I don't know," Flora wailed. "I love him so much, and that girl's so pretty—"

"Don't you trust me?"

"Y-yes . . ."

"Then don't worry. You do what I tell you and it will come out all right."

"How will we find out the girl's name?"

"I'll go into a trance."

"You'll do what?"

"After you leave I'll enter the trance state. I dread it. It is very wearing. That's why I have to charge ten dollars. But when I'm in the trance state I always get lots of information. You come back to-morrow morning—"

Two hours later, Mrs. Herbert C. Leslie answered the doorbell. Her caller was a hatchet-faced blond woman who said she was engaged in a survey sponsored by the Retail Merchants' Association.

"I haven't anything to sell," the caller said, flashing a gold-toothed smile. "But I would like to gather some information."

"Why yes—come in," Mrs. Leslie said.

The caller was a good listener, and Mrs. Leslie loved to talk about her family.

"Her name," Madam Thale told Flora, the following morning, "is Carlotta Leslie. She's twenty. She went to the university two years, and now she teaches at Manning School. She's engaged to a man named Jim Wheeler who lives in Chicago."

Flora stared wide-eyed. She would have believed anything now.

"Her father," Madam Thale went on, "works at the Tamarack Fidelity & Trust Company, and her brother—"

"Where?" Flora exclaimed.

"Tamarack Fidelity & Trust."

"That's Papa's bank!" Flora's eyes glinted. "Maybe Papa would fire him! Maybe if that girl won't stop bothering Gus, Papa would—"

"I don't think that will be necessary. Not if you follow the plan I outline."

"I'll follow it. Anything!"

"First, you're to call Mr. Burgoyne and invite him to your home for dinner next Sunday."

Tears threatened Flora. "Maybe he won't come."

"He'll come. Don't give him a chance to refuse."

"I'll call him this morning. Then what?"

Madam Thale pressed her forehead against her knuckles and with eyes closed sat meditating. At last she shook her head.

"The rest isn't clear. I'll have to enter the trance state. That is, if you feel like spending the money. I'm sorry this is costing so much, but when I use up my strength in the trance state—"

Flora opened her purse. "How much?"

"The same as before."

Flora brought out ten dollars. "It's worth it," she said. "Every cent. I think you're wonderful. I wish I could hire you permanent. I want to keep seeing you till Gus and I are married."

Madam Thale smiled. "Perhaps it can be arranged."

At that hour, the skies above Chicago were gray, and a young man named Jim Wheeler, an employee of the law firm of Hibber, Marks, Kloppe, Johnson and Hibber, sat in the law library of the suite, staring through the window at pigeons wheeling over the Loop.

The letter which Carlotta had posted night-before-last had reached him this morning. It was a five-page letter, the gist of which was that absence did not after all make the heart grow fonder, that what they had shared in college was not true love, that now she was experiencing true love, and that it seemed only fair to inform him and break their engagement.

The young man, despite the pain it gave him, kept reading this letter over and over. He was supposed to be briefing up that railroad case for Hibber, Senior, but the calf-bound volumes stood uncracked on the table. At last he folded his arms on the table and his head sank.

"Well now, Wheeler, what's this?" exclaimed Hibber, Senior, when he entered the library a few minutes later. "Are you sick, my boy?"

Wheeler said he was very sick.

So Hibber, Senior, sent him home for the day, but Wheeler did not go home. He stopped at a saloon. The next year he married a Chicago girl.

That afternoon, obeying Madam Thale's instructions, Flora boarded the Jefferson Avenue car and rode toward Forty-fourth Street. Madam Thale had told her that if she felt any inclinations toward anger to encourage them.

"It would do you good to get mad," Madam Thale said.

By the time she left the car and plodded north toward Manning School, Flora was good and mad. Not at poor helpless Gus, but at Carlotta Leslie. Ever since leaving Madam Thale, Flora had been brooding. Her face was flushed, and as she hoofed along she kept clamping her fists. Hers was the righteous anger of the innocent and injured, of the duped. All her grievances against life fueled it. Old animosities and humiliations swarmed through her thoughts as she strode along the sidewalk. In grade school she had been the fat little redhead at whom boys jeered and whom the little girls excluded from their secret societies. It was she who received the worst comic valentines. Her brain had been slow to grasp the schoolbook lessons, and in consigning her to the foot of the class, teachers had held up her exercises as horrible examples. The terror and shame of not being promoted haunted her childhood, and the other children audibly deduced that only her father's place in the community was responsible for her progress from one grade to the next.

As she grew older she did not suddenly grow slim and attractive, as did many chubby little girls. She remained Flora, sluggish, clumsy-footed. She was not invited to birthday parties, unless the fathers of the little hosts wanted something from Mr. Oxenford. And when she attended, the other little guests found ways to torment her and make a fool of her. She was the butt of every joke. She would always bite on every conundrum.

High school was even worse. The lessons offered more difficulties, for one thing. And there were the social ordeals. Boys took girls to parties. She was a girl. But no boy took her to parties. She attended school functions alone. Alone! She had always been alone.

With girlhood behind, her interest in men intensified. She stared at men on the street, and in her bedroom she dreamed about them. She took odd fancies to men in social orbits far below hers. She had reached the point where she would have married anybody male and Caucasian. That nice floorwalker at Goldstein's, the iceman who always—significantly!—said, "Good morning." And then—Gus!

Gus! She had asked a crust from life, and life had sent her roast turkey with dressing. She would have been content with vinegar, and life had given her wine. Gus!—handsomer than any male from the ink bottle of Charles Dana Gibson. And they were engaged to be married in April, and then what happened?

A pretty little chit named Carlotta Leslie tried to steal him, that was what! Small wonder that rage filled her as thunder fills sky. Oh, she knew the habits of these pretty girls! She knew, she knew! Luck had given them everything, but were they satisfied? Not them! The dirty little sluts had to sneak around and try stealing the man you were engaged to!

She strode faster through 4 P.M., and by the time she reached Manning School her rage was a leviathan threshing within her, driving her on.

From the drugstore up the street, Gus Burgoyne beheld her, not without concern.

The central office of the Tamarack Independent School District, like so many educational systems, considered pedagogical organization more important than teaching the young; and hence it required every school within its jurisdiction to turn in endless reports. These were due at noon Saturday.

Harold Henderson didn't mind. As academic as a stick of chalk, he enjoyed making out these reports. The task filled his orderly soul with the snug sense that all was well with the world. Like a bureaucrat in the passionate embrace of red tape, the more complicated and preposterous the report the better he liked it. It satisfied a craving in his soul to know that in a thousand years any interested person could thumb through the school district files and discover that during such-and-such a week a certain number of absences and tardinesses had occurred at Manning School, Harold Henderson, principal.

Harold had discovered that he must fill in subsidiary reports daily if he hoped to have the master reports completed by Saturday noon. He sat at his desk now, concentrating on the sheets. His legs were neatly crossed and his eyeglasses flashed as he gazed from the slips turned in by various teachers to his own sheets.

So hard was the shell of his concentration that even any untoward disturbance in the building could not have cracked it. But at this hour no disturbance could possibly take place. Ten minutes ago the lines of children had marched out, leaving the halls full of bad air and peace. Even the playgrounds were silent, deserted by the potential presidents of the United States.

Nevertheless, despite his concentration, Harold afterward fancied that while he worked he had been aware that all was not as usual in the building. Along the hushed halls, through his closed office door, a distant turmoil wafted to nudge the edge of his consciousness. Unheeding, he worked on.

His concentration, of course, had limits; and it could not be expected to withstand the swift knocks that presently assaulted the door, and the voice of Miss Benson in distress.

"Mr. Henderson! Mr. Henderson! Are you in there?"

"Yes, Miss Benson. Yes, I'm here. Come in."

The door burst open, revealing the horrified countenance of little Miss Benson.

"Mr. Henderson! You must come at once!"

"Are you in some difficulty?" Harold inquired.

"Difficulty! Can't you hear it?"

Now that Miss Benson mentioned it, Harold did hear it. From down the hall came the sound of voices. The voices of school teachers and of the janitor. But they were mere murmurs compared to the voice they fringed. This voice was lifted in anger.

Dumbfounded, Harold glanced at Miss Benson.

"What under the sun is taking place?"

"It's some terrible woman," Miss Benson exclaimed. "She's reading the riot act to Miss Leslie."

"Miss Leslie!"

Harold snapped through the door ahead of Miss Benson. She hurried after him.

Harold gained speed down the hall. He had heard of such things as this happening: some parent outraged by a child's punishment or low grade coming to school and tearing into the teacher. But as he neared Miss Leslie's room, he concluded this was no irate mother. Certain hysterical words screamed by the voice told him otherwise. The voice was accusing Miss Leslie of larceny, of kidnaping, the victim being Gus Burgoyne.

The janitor and the teaching staff were clustered about the door to Miss Leslie's classroom.

"What's this!" Harold exclaimed sharply. "Why haven't you stopped it?"

"Did try," the janitor said. "I'll take wildcats. Any day!"

"Let me through!" Harold commanded. Reluctantly, the teachers made space for his passage. He noted fleetly the pleased expressions on the faces of Miss Dodge and Miss Stoffel.

Upon gaining the arena, Harold's first emotion was pity for Carlotta Leslie. He had never seen her face so white; and her eyes looked stricken. She had retreated to the far row of windows.

"I just won't listen—I won't!" she was saying, and her hands went up and she plugged her ears with her forefingers.

The person she addressed was a large, loutish girl with red hair. Her face was flushed.

"You'll see! I'll have your father fired! I'll tell Papa to fire him. If he's a thief like you—"

With a long, precise forefinger Harold tapped her shoulder.

"That's enough!"

The girl's jaw swung round.

"I said that was enough!" Harold declared. "You are leaving! This instant!"

For a moment the issue remained in doubt. The redheaded girl looked brawny enough to turn Harold over her knee and paddle him. This would have been the icing on the cake for the Misses Dodge and Stoffel, but it didn't occur. The girl's lip curled.

"I've had my say," she said. Halfway to the door she turned, eyed Harold with distaste.

"A schoolteacher!" she expectorated.

Then she plodded out the door.

"Back to your rooms, all of you," Harold ordered the teaching staff,

exactly as if they were erring pupils. They were amazed at this un-
guessed steel in Mr. Henderson's spine, but they obeyed.

"Carlotta," Harold commanded, "you come into my office."

She also obeyed.

With the office door closed, Carlotta collapsed at the desk into heavy
weeping; and the steel in Harold's spine (whose presence had astonished him as much as anybody) melted away into embarrassment.

"Now, now," he said. "Please don't."

But Carlotta did. Harold might as well have been advising Niagara
Falls to call the whole thing off. Uneasily he kept clearing his throat.

"It really doesn't matter," he said once. "Unfortunate, but of no
consequence. The woman was obviously a virago."

Carlotta's whole body wept. Her arms and head mussed Harold's
desk, spattering the reports with tears, and one hand clenched spas-
modically, crumpling the papers. Unfortunate, but unavoidable.
Harold paced uneasily to the window, gazing out at late afternoon
creeping across the playground. The sky was blue, the trees budding;
and when a lull came in the weeping Harold cleared his throat.

"A beautiful afternoon."

She lifted her wet face. He thought she looked as lovely as a spring
flower after a shower.

"What?" she asked.

"I said it was very nice outside. Beautiful weather."

She emitted a sound that was half-laugh, half-sob; and then the
weeping began all over again.

"Really," he said, "the incident was quite unimportant. Not worth
the attention you're giving it."

He moved to the desk and put a hand on her shoulder. Suddenly
it occurred to him that this would be as good a time as any to broach
a subject that had been much in his thoughts. Perhaps it would take
her mind off the recent unpleasantness.

"I've been meaning to ask you," he said, "whether you would marry me."

Her face snapped up.

"Did I hear you right?"

"I have no way of knowing. I asked whether you would consider
marrying me."

She dabbed at her eyes, softly blew her nose. She arose and went to
the window. At last she said:

"I think you'd better take me home now, Harold. Would you mind
—walking with me? And what you just asked me. Yes, I will consider it. I will."

"Do I understand," he asked, "that you will marry me, or that you
will consider it?"

"That I will consider it."

"Thank you," he said. "That is very gratifying."

Inside the drugstore, Gus stuck a cigar between his teeth and frowned at Manning School. Flora Oxenford had just gone steaming through the door.

He did not have an appointment to meet Carlotta outside the store; he never met her there by arrangement but only when his schedule at the park allowed him to get away and stroll home with her. Although they were together nearly every night, they welcomed any additional hours they could spend in each other's company.

The past weeks were a blur in his memory, a period when time had gone mad, racing when they were together, crawling when they were apart. They had dined together and attended the theater and driven with picnic baskets into the country; and Gus had grown to resent even the demands of the amusement park because they took his thoughts from Carlotta. Twice they had quarreled about trifles, suffering a day or two and then making ecstatic peace.

The separation of those quarrels had taught him how intensely they had grown together, and he had become increasingly alarmed when he thought of his wedding date and of Flora. He realized that by temporizing and procrastinating he had floundered into a dreadful tangle, and he worried about extricating himself.

Time and again on the evenings with Carlotta he had made up his mind that next day he would break his engagement. But he never did. He knew what that would mean: the wrecking of the future he had planned.

Sometimes in his office he decided to tell Carlotta the whole story, but when evening came he couldn't bring himself to that, either. Life without Carlotta would be unbearable.

Yet he knew that soon he had to make a decision; things couldn't go on this way; but he put it off and put it off, and all the time his position became more impossible. And then the other evening she had dropped an envelope into a mail box, afterward telling him it had been a letter to Jim Wheeler breaking her engagement. The next move was plainly his. He had sworn so often he loved her that it was natural for her to expect marriage, now she was free. But he wasn't free; he was all tangled in his own folly. He could see no way through his difficulties; he couldn't imagine how it would end.

And now he had beheld Flora striding toward the school. Such an occurrence he had never anticipated. Somebody must have tattled. And Flora was forcing the issue, just as she used to keep forcing the subject of marriage.

He stood chewing his cigar, staring at the school, his nerves jumpy, his thoughts dark and profane. Damn it, he wished he had told Carlotta about his engagement, so she would have been more prepared for this. He wished the world were ordered differently and that Carlotta's father owned the park. He wished he knew what was taking place inside that school.

After what seemed a long time he perceived Flora coming from the building. At the street she paused and glared back. Then she plodded south. Till her figure receded from sight Gus stared after her. She was his future.

No! He couldn't bring himself to marry her, not even for a circus. He'd resign from the park and marry Carlotta and they'd go away somewhere. At once! He'd write his resignation tonight. This afternoon!

Several women were emerging from the school now, and Gus thought they looked like teachers. There were four large women and one small, and they clustered on the sidewalk, heads together. Sometimes they glanced at the building. Finally the group broke up, two walking south and the others coming in Gus's direction. He observed them pass on the other side of the street, their skirts sweeping the sidewalk, their tongues going lickety-split.

Gus dropped his soggy cigar and brought out a fresh one, biting off the end but neglecting to strike a match. What was keeping Carlotta? He compared his watch with the drugstore clock. Both showed five. He returned his gaze to the school, and after a few more minutes he espied the person he was waiting for. Only she was not alone. The educated fool accompanied her.

Henderson! Why did she want to walk from school with him? And the nerve of the fellow! He had his hand on her elbow, guiding her.

As they moved closer, Gus noticed that Carlotta walked as if she were tired. She kept her gaze on the sidewalk, and once her handkerchief went to her eyes. Crying! What had that fool Flora done?

From experience Gus knew that on the corner opposite Henderson and Carlotta would part company. So he waited for that.

But it didn't happen. The educated fool accompanied her past the corner. You'd think he intended walking home with her. Gus plunged out the door, crossing the street at an angle. He called.

They stopped. Forcing a big smile, Gus bustled up to them. But his smile was not answered. Henderson's gray face looked judicial, passionless. Carlotta's eyes were flashing with enmity.

"What's wrong?" Gus asked.

Carlotta spoke deliberately and distinctly.

"I've just had the great pleasure of meeting the woman you're going to marry."

"You have, huh? Well now look here. Hope you aren't upset. I can explain—"

"Upset! Oh no, not in the least. She practically wrecked the school, that's all. And as for explanations, I've had everything explained very clearly."

"Carlotta! Look here! You—"

"And as for you," she said, "I hope I never see you again. I wish I'd never met you in the first place."

Biting her lip, she wheeled around and struck off down the sidewalk. Henderson had to hurry to keep pace.

Gus stared after them till their figures were far away.

Feeling utterly at loose ends, he ambled back toward the park, his shadow elongated by the low sun. Once he stopped to light his cigar but he had chewed it to a pulp that wouldn't draw. He cast it away, lit a fresh one, moved on, dully watching the sidewalk cracks advancing under his feet. He knew he was in for a bad time, but at the moment he felt nothing save a vast emptiness. He had nothing to do tonight, tomorrow night, the next night. All that time which somehow he must fill loomed formidably ahead. She had said she never wanted to see him again, and her manner convinced him she meant it.

Perhaps even Flora wouldn't welcome him now. Then he remembered. She had called him this morning and invited him for Sunday dinner. Even then she must have known about Carlotta, must have been intending to accost her at the school. Inviting him had been her way of letting him know all was still well between them. He found himself surprised she had been intelligent enough to figure that out. You never could tell about women, he thought. Who would have thought Flora had it in her to go to the school and raise hell?

He brooded through the park gate, went to his office, dropped down at his desk. He didn't sit there long, for terrible restlessness seized him. He paced the office, finally emerging into the twilight and wandering toward the elephant barn. He remembered that Saturday in February when he walked this path by Carlotta's side, leading the children. He remembered the nights they had come to the park and had paused to embrace here at the miniature railroad crossing. She was everywhere, he thought, with panic. My God, he thought, I'll never escape.

Heavily, he moved on to the barn. Molly's trunk was stretched at full length, welcoming him.

"Hello, old girl," he said tonelessly. "How's everything, huh? How're things going?"

She murmured, talking to him in her own language. He scratched her; she sighed blissfully.

"Growing," he told her. "Yep, you're growing. Be a big bull one of these days."

He felt better.

During the next days, a number of persons in Tamarack experienced unhappiness.

One was Flora. Having ridded herself of anger, she felt as deflated and sunk in despair as the gas bag of a balloon in a swamp. She feared that once again she had done the clumsy thing, that Gus would be angry, that he wouldn't appear for Sunday dinner. She moped across town and consulted Madam Thale, but even when that woman assured her she couldn't have acted more effectively Flora was not entirely consoled.

Another was Carlotta. Indeed, the whole Leslie family found itself distressed as little by little Mrs. Leslie coaxed from her daughter an account of what had happened. Mrs. Leslie didn't, however, tell everything to the rest of the family. To prevent worry, she kept to herself the threat Flora had brandished about having Herbert C. Leslie discharged. Mr. Oxenford would never do that, Mrs. Leslie told herself, as she prepared broth in the kitchen to carry to Carlotta's bedside. Herbert was a valuable employee; Mr. Oxenford (whom she considered very nearly as all-wise and remote and all-powerful as God) would have too much common sense to permit his daughter's love problems to interfere with business. Nevertheless, she worried. You were an easy victim of worry when the welfare of your family depended upon the whims of one man.

Nor was Harold Henderson completely serene during the remainder of that week. With Carlotta ill at home, somebody had to assume her duties. Harold requested a substitute teacher from the central office, but none was available. So he taught third and fourth grades himself. But that was not the worst. The worst was the summons he received to appear at the central office. The summons came from Clarence Beeley, superintendent of schools. It seemed that news of Flora's visit had flashed through the entire Tamarack educational system, and Mr. Beeley wished to get to the root of the scandal.

So Saturday morning Harold repaired to the central office, where he was closeted for an hour with Mr. Beeley. Leaving, Harold looked flushed and annoyed. In his opinion, Mr. Beeley possessed the mental powers of a gnat. For Mr. Beeley had flouted logic and held Harold partly responsible for that unfortunate incident. Moreover, Flora's outburst and the repercussions which followed had instilled in Mr. Beeley's mind grave doubts about Miss Leslie's suitability as an instructor of the young. Plainly, he considered her far gone in immorality. Where there was smoke there was fire, he kept insisting. Never again would he hire a good-looking, normal girl as teacher. He was asking Miss Leslie to resign at once.

On the street, Harold sizzled like a firecracker fuse. He told himself that Clarence Beeley was a timid simpleton, afraid that the faintest breath of scandal would blow him out of a job. Well, Harold thought, what could you expect of a man who had taken his Ph.D. in "Education"?

Without Carlotta, Manning School was going to be dreary. Harold supposed he could stick it for the rest of this year, but he couldn't imagine returning next fall. By frugality he had saved seven hundred dollars toward continuing his studies. Perhaps he might get a job of sorts at the University of Chicago. So he went home and wrote one of his summer school professors there, requesting a teaching fellowship.

Unhappiest of all were Carlotta and Gus. He didn't take to his bed as she did, but he felt like it. He spent his days in gloom, and he discovered that only a stiff drink of whiskey at bedtime would bring the surcease of sleep.

At his desk he found it hard to focus his thoughts on business. He wandered out into the sunlight of late March, moving aimlessly about the park, observing carpenters and painters at work preparing for the new season.

He felt as if some invisible weapon had pierced his vitals, leaving a wound that bled secretly in the dark. Only Carlotta could heal him, and she had sent him out of her life. Dozens of times, of course, he considered going to her or writing her. But supposing he did. Instantly all those old complications would entangle him, and once again he would be confronted by the decision he must make. He didn't feel up to it. He felt a sense—odd for him—of having been bound hand and foot by life. He felt defeated, confused.

And yet sometimes as he floundered through misery a sudden elation would lift him, and for a minute he would feel that things would still turn out all right. He didn't know how; he knew only that they must. Other people's lives might go awry, but he was different. He was Gus Burgoyne. He was something special in the universe. He would have Carlotta and fame as a circus owner too. But the moments of elation passed.

Everything spoke to him of Carlotta, restaurants where they had eaten, streets where they had walked. He would stare from a streetcar window and, seeing a certain corner, remember how they had laughed as they passed it. Looking back, it seemed they had laughed a great deal. And strangely, the memory of their laughter hurt most of all. Conversely, remembrance of their quarrels soothed and salved him, possibly because those other quarrels had turned out all right.

He spoke of his sorrow to no one. Carlotta had her mother; even Flora had Madam Thale; but Gus had only himself. Long ago he had formed the habit of keeping his own counsel. But when he found his loneliness and pain unbearable he would wander to the elephant barn and talk to Molly.

The only thing of consequence about Sunday dinner at the Oxenford's was that nothing of consequence occurred. Coached by Madam Thale, Flora greeted Gus cordially and never mentioned Carlotta Leslie. To Gus this was such a relief that he very nearly enjoyed himself.

During the meal Gus talked business with Mr. Oxenford, divulging the spectacular publicity stunts he was planning for the park. He warmed to the subject, and presently his occupation as park manager seemed colorful and exciting again. Astonished, he realized he hadn't thought of Carlotta for several minutes.

When they left the table Flora led him outside to the garden. Now she would certainly upbraid him. Again he was pleasantly surprised. As they strolled she talked cheerfully about her trousseau and plans for the wedding, but never did she rebuke him for neglect. She was a pretty good sort after all, he thought. Not one woman in a million would have welcomed him back this way. Blowing out cigar smoke, he surveyed the spacious garden, the stable which was larger than many people's homes, the massive, sprawling house. Only two things separated all the wealth represented here from his fingers: a wedding ceremony, and Mr. Oxenford's health. He wondered whether he was going to be a fool and let a passing attachment to Carlotta prevent him from becoming a wealthy man.

As they sauntered back toward the house he patted his stomach. "That was a wonderful meal. But I ate too much. Made me sleepy."

"Why don't you take a nap?"

He grinned. "Wouldn't be very polite, would it? Going to sleep on your hands?"

"If you're sleepy you sleep. You could take a nap in the library."

But when they went to the library they discovered that Mr. Oxenford had appropriated the couch. He lay with his mouth open, snoozing off his big meal. In sleep he looked older. He was only mortal, Gus thought; and again it occurred to him that any young man would be a fool to turn his back on the wealth Mr. Oxenford had spent a lifetime accumulating.

They tiptoed from the library.

"You could take a nap in Papa's bedroom," Flora whispered.

"Oh, I'll be all right."

"After a meal like that you need sleep. Come on, Gus."

So she led him up the carpeted stair, past the bronze woman on the newel, past the great blue floor vase on the half-landing. He had never visited the upstairs before, and the unfamiliar spaciousness impressed him.

Mr. Oxenford's bedroom occupied the corner beneath the great south-western dunce cap. The bedstead was carved walnut, dating back to the early years of Mr. Oxenford's marriage. In this gigantic bed Mrs. Oxenford had conceived her daughter.

"I'll shut the door," Flora said, "and you take a good nap. You look kind of tired, Gus."

He was touched by her concern for his well-being. She was almost motherly.

He did not lie down at once. Roving about the room, he paused at the tremendous walnut dresser that matched the bed. Photographs stood on the marble top. One was brown with age, the wedding picture of Mr. and Mrs. Oxenford. Mr. Oxenford was a bony young man with a mustache but no beard. His sharp eyes were staring at the camera as if he expected the photographer's bill to come popping from the lens. He was seated on a plush chair, his legs thin and his shoes glued to the carpet. His bride stood beside the chair with one hand resting on it. She looked about Flora's size.

Gus went to the bed, sat on its yielding feather tick, removed his shoes. He sighed and was about to recline when he noted sheets of paper on the bed table. He picked them up.

They were covered with figures, penciled in Mr. Oxenford's chirography. Their import was unknown to Gus, because no explanations accompanied them. What excited him was their size. Those figures represented millions, but only Mr. Oxenford understood whether millions he hoped to acquire or had acquired or owed. Gus optimistically assumed they represented wealth Mr. Oxenford had salted away.

He lay down. Millions. He had only to reach out his hand.

Sleep was rolling over him like sea and fog engulfing a whale. Nice of Flora not to jump on him. Nice of her to insist on a nap. He felt comfortable, taken care of, peaceful. With a little sigh, he dropped into unconsciousness.

He slept dreamlessly for hours. Once, with twilight stealing through the windows, Flora opened the door and tiptoed to the bed. She gazed down at him tenderly. While he slept he was hers, all hers. His breathing was deep and regular; his hair was mussed; he looked relaxed but very tired. And suddenly she experienced a kind of maternal pity for him, lying there so defenseless, so mortal, wrapped in the little death which was slumber.

It was after nine when he wakened. He felt like a new man. Vastly refreshed. Oddly happy.

"Well, well," he boomed, thumping down the stair, "I certainly slept. Look at the time!"

It was a great joke; Flora giggled, and even Mr. Oxenford seemed amused. He approved of sleep; nobody ever squandered money while sleeping.

"Ain't long till my bedtime," he grinned. "Thought I'd have to roll you onto the floor."

"Are you hungry, Gus?" Flora asked.

"You bet I am. Any of that chicken left?"

Mr. Oxenford had already supped; so Gus and Flora raided the icebox. Consuming food at the kitchen table, Gus was elated at feeling so natural and normal again. Once he had gone to bed with a toothache, and when he wakened in the morning it had vanished. He felt now as then, amazed and thankful that the pain had left him. Perhaps the human spirit could suffer only so long without respite; perhaps pain would return; but in the meantime he would enjoy himself.

Riding home in a hack, he still felt pretty good; and he slept soundly that night. But Monday brought the pain again.

However, its bite had lost sharpness. He was able to work. And he still felt happy, because he thought the interlude of painlessness proved that at last it would wear away altogether. In time, in time.

He rode downtown for lunch, and for some reason the pain increased. Returning on the streetcar, he sat in gloom. And at the park the familiar restlessness sent him about the grounds. But even as he brooded he had to acknowledge that the park looked bright and cheery. Tree trunks had been newly whitewashed, fresh gravel scattered, the roller coaster painted. Men were greasing the machinery of the merry-go-round and polishing its brass fittings; and a mechanic was overhauling the miniature locomotive.

Gus entered the Old Mill, groping along the dry canal into light-tight depths. Presently he heard voices ahead and saw light glimmering. Workmen were mixing cement and patching cracks in the waterway. When he emerged the daylight blinded him. He stood squinting. And he made out a figure leaving his office.

Excitement sent Gus hurrying toward the visitor.

"Mr. Pawpacker!" he bellowed. "Here I am!"

"How about dinner with me?" Gus suggested, after he had given his guest a cigar. "I've got a matter to discuss with you. Want some advice. Shall we meet in the General Grant?"

Pawpacker assented.

"Fine," Gus said. "Now let me show you how we've fixed up the park."

They strolled along the paths with Gus gesturing and pouring out ideas for attracting customers.

Once he said:

"You know Ive, it's struck me you and I ought to team up. Organize a circus. We'd make a cool million!"

"We might. But why don't you organize your own show and make the million for yourself?"

"Capital. That's all that's stopping me."

"After the wedding," Pawpacker smiled, "you shouldn't be troubled by lack of capital."

Gus frowned.

"Did you find your letter?" Gus's landlady asked him that evening, as he thundered down into the hall, dinner-bound.

"Letter?"

"It must have got here after you came in. I didn't think you were home yet. It's there on the table. A Special."

Gus grabbed it. Carlotta's handwriting.

He thrust the envelope into his pocket; the front door slammed after him; he swung off down the street. Once excitement began, he was thinking, it didn't stop. First Pawpacker, and now this.

His heart beat faster at the thought of the letter, and he wondered why he postponed opening it. What did it contain? More of the sarcasm she had used against him that afternoon opposite the drugstore?

Flora wasn't so bad. Yesterday at the Oxenfords' had turned out pretty well. After his nap he had faced losing Carlotta without agony. Today he had suffered again, till Pawpacker came. Even talking to Pawpacker he hadn't exactly forgotten Carlotta, for his suggestion that they go into partnership had sprung from the wild outside chance that Pawpacker would agree, and then both Carlotta and a circus would be his. But Pawpacker had refused. Of course! Couldn't blame him! A young man without capital was doomed to a job.

He entered a cigar store and purchased the quarter brand. A half-dozen. He guessed his tobacco bill alone would keep a family in groceries. He stowed away the cigars, brought out the letter, weighed it on his palm. It didn't weigh much. It didn't weigh as much as a million dollars. Or two million, or whatever the old man was worth.

He tore open the envelope, and there in the cigar store with its hard bright lights and the noises of traffic yapping in from outside he read the note.

Dear Gus:

I'm so miserable I don't know what to do. And something terrible has happened, and I'd like to talk to you.

Carlotta.

Something terrible. What? It worried him; but he drove worry from his thoughts as he entered the General Grant. He might have owned scores of elephants already, from the imperial way he marched through the crowded lobby. With its marble pillars veined with rose, its gigantic spittoons, it seemed a hotel for herculean men.

"Uh—want to send a wire," he told Pawpacker. "Just a minute."

He bustled to the telegraph counter. Since the Leslies had no telephone, this was the fastest way of communicating with Carlotta.

"I will call at eight Tuesday evening," he wrote. He hesitated, then added: "Lots of love. Gus."

After eating, Gus felt better; and when the liqueurs arrived he blew out cigar smoke and leaned forward.

"Um-m-m. Now about this matter I mentioned. Feel I need advice from an older head than mine. Fact is, I'm sort of involved."

And he told Pawpacker everything.

"Let's sit in the lobby," Pawpacker said, "and talk it over.

They sat in a remote corner and lit fresh cigars.

"Of course you realize," Pawpacker said, "that it isn't easy to give advice in a matter like this."

"Realize that. You bet I do."

"I've told you before what I think of your future in show business. How much does that future mean to you?"

"Why, it means—" Gus waved his cigar. "Means everything . . ."

"I thought so."

"Uh—then you think—"

Pawpacker shook his head. "I can't advise you, Gus. Either way you jump, you'll have regrets. Of course, if you marry Flora you'll do your regretting in luxury."

"Something to that," Gus said. "Uh—one question. Do you believe in love?"

Pawpacker didn't reply immediately, and it was as if he saw faraway visions in the cigar smoke.

"Yes," he said, "I believe in it. But the question is whether you believe in it."

"Sure I believe in it. Of course I do. What you say, though, about regretting in luxury—there's a lot in that. Let me ask another question. Can you think of any way a man like me could start a circus without capital? I mean without any capital."

"Offhand I can't."

"Neither can I," Gus said.

He slept badly that night.

In the hack next evening Gus felt jumpy, his stomach queasy. From high school physiology he remembered a chart of the nervous system, and he felt like the chart: every fiber pen-lined tight, every ganglion quivering.

The Leslies' porch light was burning; he told the driver to wait. Facing the house, he had an impulse to duck back into the cab and tell the driver to whip up his horses. He squared his shoulders, took a deep breath; and going to the house he bustled.

The doorbell pealed. Almost at once Carlotta opened the door, as if she had been waiting in the hall.

"Well," he exclaimed heartily, "hello here!"

"Hello, Gus. Come in."

The hall was full of embarrassment, but he fought its tortures courageously. He said it was a nice evening; yes sir, fine evening. A little cool, but mighty nice. You could certainly tell spring was here, he said.

Carlotta looked tired. He watched her at the mirror arranging her hat. There was a droop to her shoulders and she didn't say much. She was like a girl preparing to attend a funeral. And the house had a chill funereal quality. The doors to the other rooms were closed on silence. He'd be glad to get out of there.

When she turned and gave him her coat to hold, her face looked drawn. Her eyes looked hurt. He couldn't help but remember the other evenings he had called for her. She had been girlish and dashing, then. She had been laughter.

And suddenly he was wrung by nostalgia and regret, and he remembered that long poem she had read aloud on one of their picnics about an old Persian who saw life as a phantom and a madness to which only love and wine and poetry could bring a measure of sanity. The lines hobbled brokenly back to him now, something about shattering this sorry scheme of things and remolding it nearer to the heart's desire. When she read it the philosophy had been too oriental for his tastes, for he was the flower of Western Civilization in the twentieth century, full of the sturdy American virtues of getting ahead, of progress; and the poem had left him uneasy and troubled by the sense of great forces loose in the universe which were not especially concerned with the welfare of Gus Burgoyne.

When they reached the street Carlotta said:

"You have a hack. Can't we walk a while, instead?"

"Tell you," he whispered, "I had him wait. Hate to send him off now. We'll ride a while and then walk."

He directed the driver to Funland Park; and as the hack swayed

along she sat on the far side of the seat, silent. He tried to make conversation, without success.

Clopping toward Jefferson Avenue, the cab passed Manning School,
and he grew aware of a change in Carlotta. Her head was more
averted than ever, her shoulders hunched, and he realized she was
fighting tears.

"Why honey," he muttered, slipping his arm around her, "what's
the matter?"

She wept then as he had never known a girl to weep. And he wept
too, in spirit. And he knew that even for the Oxenford money he
couldn't cast her aside like a burned-out cigar. He guessed he was
soft, but he couldn't. And suddenly he felt both trapped and glad.
He spoke his mental farewells to Flora and Sam Oxenford and Ive
Pawpacker and to the dream of elephants parading through band
music. He'd get a job. Some newspaper. It wouldn't be so bad; not
with Carlotta trimming a Christmas tree and himself donning false
Santa Claus whiskers. Yes, someday they would have children and
he'd take them to a circus and the clowns would make everybody
laugh except himself.

"Tell me about it," he said. "You can tell me. Sure you can."

But she couldn't, then. She could only cry.

When the hack creaked to a halt at the park she staunched her tears,
and with her handkerchief at her face she stepped to the shadowy
esplanade where they had stood together that first afternoon while she
waited for a streetcar that came too soon. Gus embraced her while
the hack clacked away toward the city. Then he jangled out keys and
guided her to the gate.

Regret wrenched him as he reflected that he wouldn't be opening
this gate many more times. Flora would bellow and old Oxenford
would fire him and people would crowd through this gate on summer
evenings, but he wouldn't be present to hear the music from the merry-
go-round. He'd be hearing presses thundering out another sort of
music from the basement of a newspaper shop. Fire and graft and
flood and sudden death. And when a circus press agent visited town
he'd probably astonish the fellow by taking him to lunch.

Maybe he could crawl back to Clayton Junction and take over the
Tribune. The last few times he had dropped in there, he had noticed
how old and tired Frank seemed. Yes, he could do that; only he
couldn't. People would say that although Doll Burgoyne's son had
flown pretty high for a time, they noticed he had come back. Back to
the dirty railroad smoke and the sorrowing of trains. And he couldn't
bring up children of his in Clayton Junction. Memories were too long.

From inside the gate he reached through the bars and snapped shut

the padlock; and then with Carlotta he wandered along the path toward the miniature railroad and the elephant barn.

"Let's not go in there tonight," she said. "Let's sit down somewhere."

Faint irritation pricked him, because it seemed they were being untrue to Molly, not visiting her. Poor Molly had her troubles, now that
the trainer had arrived and started schooling her. It seemed to Gus
he used the hook too much and too cruelly, but he said the first weeks
were the hardest. Sometimes Gus wished that she didn't have to be
trained, but if she weren't the kids would clamor eternal questions as
to why she didn't know tricks.

They walked among the ghostly whitewashed trees to the bandstand
in the center of the park, climbing the steps and sitting down and
talking a long time.

Next June a famous band would present a week of free concerts beneath the pointed roof of this octagonal pavilion. At least, Gus planned
to announce in his publicity that the band was famous; and the music
would certainly be free to those who had paid admission to the park.
Within the last week he had signed a contract with the band leader,
who, at Gus's suggestion, had promised to compose a piece of virtually
original music to be called "The Funland Park March."

"Be great publicity," Gus had declared.

But now, Gus thought regretfully, he wouldn't be here when the
band played the world première of that composition. He sighed. A
march rendered by a brass band was his favorite music. He preferred
it even to a merry-go-round organ or a calliope.

Tonight the pavilion was shadowy, lighted only by the distant bulbs
burning among the trees. They sat on the wooden bench encircling
the bandstand, Gus leaning back with his arms outflung along the
railing.

"I've never had such a shock," Carlotta said at last. "I mean that
awful woman coming to school."

Her shoulders shivered at the memory; he drew her against him.

"Must have been bad," he agreed.

"You don't know how bad. You can't know. She just screamed and
yelled. Everybody heard. All the other teachers."

"Yeah, pretty bad, all right. Must have been."

Carlotta pulled away and faced him.

"Why didn't you tell me you were engaged to her?"

"I did intend to, honey. But I never seemed to get around to it."

Carlotta expelled a snort of disgust.

"How did you ever get mixed up with her?"

"Uh—well—tell you. It just sort of came about. I got to doing business with old Sam, and Flora was always around—"

"And you couldn't miss seeing her, I suppose. At the Oxenfords' they keep an elephant in the parlor, and you like elephants."

Gus felt his ears burning. He knew Flora's shortcomings as well as anyone, but it seemed hardly fair for a girl as lovely as Carlotta to keep clawing her. He forgave Carlotta, for Flora had picked on her first; but nevertheless Flora was a pretty good old lumber wagon, and he experienced an odd loyalty to her.

"I don't know what you see in her," Carlotta said. "If you like her —and you must or you wouldn't have got engaged—then I don't see how you could like me."

Gus shifted his position on the grill.

"Yeah, funny thing, all right. Just the way things happen."

"Or maybe," Carlotta said, "you were cold-blooded about it. Maybe you liked her money."

The temperature rose in Gus's ears; he didn't want to get mad.

"Let's not talk about it," he said.

"Not talk about it! What do you suppose I've been thinking about all these days! The trouble with you Gus, you don't like to face things. If something unpleasant comes along you turn your back. The reason this mess came about is because you wouldn't play fair. That's what's wrong with you."

That anything very serious was wrong with him came as news to Gus. And he didn't enjoy hearing it. Why couldn't Carlotta be like Flora in just one respect? Why couldn't she welcome him back without hooking it into him? Last Sunday Flora had been wonderful to him. A fine meal, a restful nap.

"Well, why don't you say something?" Carlotta demanded. "I guess it's because you know you're in the wrong."

"Oh hell!" Gus muttered. He stood up and paced around the bandstand.

"Swearing won't get you any place. That's what's wrong with you —you won't face things. You'll swear and bluster but that's all it amounts to."

"Oh, Carlotta," he groaned. "Why do you have to be this way?"

"What way?"

"I mean dragging me over the coals—"

"I didn't used to be this way. I used to be happy. I was getting along fine till I met you. I was engaged to a nice boy. Then you came along and—"

"You started it. You came to the park. I was doing fine till then, myself."

"Yes," she snapped, "I came to the park. On perfectly legitimate business. And what did you do? You started moonshining up to me and urging me to go out with you and made me fall in love with you. And I broke my engagement with Jim Wheeler, and—"

"I didn't tell you to do that."

"No, you didn't. That's not the way you do things. You play three or four at the same time. I'm not like that. You told me you loved me, so naturally I broke my engagement. I've never known anyone so unfair as you."

She began to cry.

Gus trundled over and muttering heavy endearments fumbled an arm around her shoulders. She shook it violently off. He frowned, resumed pacing. He was more than a little angry and disgusted himself. He'd been in the wrong—sure. Ought to have told her about Flora. But he didn't think he had been as far gone in duplicity as Carlotta thought. He could find valid excuses for himself. And he'd decided to do the right thing, hadn't he? She had broken her engagement, and he loved her and he would marry her. My God, didn't it occur to her what he would be giving up by marrying her? Did she think the Oxenford empire was just a lot of wastepaper? Who in hell did she think she was, anyway? Queen of Sheba, or somebody?

Well, he knew what he was giving up! And he had a damned good notion not to do it.

Carlotta had stopped crying now, and Gus sat again by her side. But this time several inches separated them, and his arm didn't encircle her. He gruffed:

"You said in that letter something terrible had happened. What is it?"

"I wondered if you'd forgotten that. I wondered if you cared enough—"

"Oh, stop it," he growled. "Stop picking on me, can't you? And come to the point."

She was venomously silent.

"My God," he said finally. "Are you going to tell me, or aren't you?"

"Yes," she said crisply, "I'm going to tell you. I've been fired."

"Fired?"

"Yes, fired. Haven't you ever heard of somebody getting fired? The superintendent of schools has fired me."

"He can't do that."

"You might tell him that. He'd be glad to get your ideas, I'm certain."

"I mean—well, don't you have a contract? And what did he fire you for?"

"Why do you suppose? Because of the things that awful woman said. After the scene she made I was in disgrace."

"Why that's—that's silly. Crazy."

"You don't know much about school systems, do you? Teachers are supposed to set good examples. If there's any scandal they can fire you. There's a paragraph about that in my contract. I didn't pay any attention to it when I signed. Of course, that was before I knew you."

Suddenly he was very angry, and he knew he was going to say things he would regret.

The battle continued intermittently the rest of the evening. In the hack going home they were silent, exhausted, wounded. But there was a difference between them. Carlotta sat in dejection. She hadn't intended to say such bitter things. It was just that for days her anger had mounted and once she got started she couldn't check herself. But she wasn't angry, now. The tears that rolled down her cheeks were not tears of rage.

Gus's was the silence of grumpiness. Tonight his self-esteem had taken a bad beating. It didn't help to tell himself he deserved what he got. She needn't have stooped to personalities. Tomorrow was Wednesday, and on Wednesday evening he used to call on Flora. He guessed he would tomorrow evening. He'd phone her in the morning.

When they descended from the hack Gus told the driver to wait. They walked slowly to the porch and climbed the steps. The porch light was out.

"Gus, I'm sorry," Carlotta murmured.

He sighed. "That's all right. I'm sorry, too."

"Am I going to see you again?"

"Sure. I'll get in touch with you."

"No," she whispered. "I don't think you will."

"I said I would, didn't I?"

"You're mad. Aren't you?"

"No—not very. I'm tired. I'm all mixed up."

"I want to know," she said slowly, "if you're going to see me. Because if you're not—well—Harold Henderson has asked me to marry him."

"The educated fool."

But he didn't say it in anger, or even with much jealousy. And suddenly his heart wrenched and he pitied Carlotta. And he realized then that whatever his decision he could never entirely escape her. He took her into his arms and kissed her and at last they were at peace. He was always glad afterward they had not parted in anger.

"Sure," he mumbled, "I'll get in touch with you. You don't have a phone—I'll write you—or wire—or just drop in—"

He kissed her again and finally he left. She watched him fumbling down the steps and ambling toward the hack, big, bewildered, his head lowered. She heard his voice rumbling directions to the driver. He started to enter the hack, then turned, as if he had a notion to come back. Instead he lifted an arm in a clumsy wave. Then the hack door slammed and the horses started walking. And a wave of pity for him overtook her, because she had seen him at his best as well as his worst, and she knew how wistful and ingenuous he could be, and how confused and how lost.

9

AFTER THE wedding of Flora Oxenford and A. H. Burgoyne more than two years passed before Ivan Pawpacker saw Gus again. He didn't greatly miss him, for he was exceedingly busy with his own affairs. He was in his forties now, a period of expanding prosperity. Already well-to-do by Winchester standards, he saw the opportunity to become actually rich. His dealings in horses and mules brought him good income, and his circus brokerage business had developed surprising profits. But banking attracted him most.

After buying stock, he had gained a seat on the board of the Farmers' National Bank, and he was scheming to elect himself president. Then he would exert his energies toward absorbing the only other bank in Winchester. He wanted to become a financial power in the state. Sometimes he thought of himself as a general and his dollars an army. As a strategist he was never a heedless raider but a commander thinking first of defending what he had and only then reaching out to capture a new position.

Not often, of course, did he philosophize about his purpose in expanding his financial duchy. To make more money whether you needed it or not seemed the natural thing to do. He was grateful that civilization had advanced to the place where dollar power exceeded every other power. Somewhere back in the centuries men with brains had outwitted the big slow fellows who thought with lumpy muscles. Physical strength had been enslaved by the power of finance. It didn't make much difference any more, he told himself, if you were not a big strapping fellow; the sources of power had passed from body to brain.

He was born in upper New York State at Larkin Corners, a hamlet in a land of meadows and stone quarries. Its population could never quite reach the hundred mark, for always when a new baby was due somebody would die unexpectedly, foiling the community's ambition for a census in three figures. The place had the quiet spirit of a Currier & Ives print, with a village green where a town pump stood by a watering trough; and in the tan dust of the street dogs slept in perfect safety.

Few business establishments faced the green, and only two were important. One occupied a building of native stone with a wooden awning shading the wooden sidewalk. A sign told the villagers what they already knew: this was Pawpacker's General Store.

Ivan was the fifth child of Vermont parents who considered they were migrating west when they moved to Larkin Corners. His father, a taciturn, wiry man, had quit school after a few terms and worked hard to get money to buy a store. The older children worked dutifully there, but all Ivan wanted to do was hang around the other important business enterprise, Kronkmeyer's Livery Stable. It stood on the east side of the green, a stone building whose dusky interior was enriched by the odor of horses. From earliest youth that aroma pulled him like a tropism. On Saturdays he could scarcely wait to finish his wood-splitting and weed-pulling so he could hurry to the stable.

Try as they might, his parents couldn't keep him away. They worried about his propensity for the stable not because it was disreputable, for Herman Kronkmeyer was a respectable citizen, but because they felt Ivan was falling into the habit of loafing.

When he was eleven Ivan convinced Mr. Kronkmeyer he needed a boy to help around the stable at real wages, so after that his parents couldn't object. In those years, no matter how vigorously he scrubbed, a faint scent of horses always emanated from Ivan. He couldn't understand why it was distasteful to his sisters and the girls at school; he loved it.

Kronkmeyer's stable was his high school and his college with the entire curriculum devoted to horses. Kronkmeyer and the hostlers were his teachers; from them he absorbed vast information about the vices and diseases and virtues of horses; and by the time he entered his teens it almost seemed he gleaned knowledge from the horses themselves by a kind of mental and emotional osmosis.

To possess a horse became his passion, but that was far beyond his resources because he turned over his wages to his father. But Ivan would not be balked. To attain a horse he developed the trading instincts inherited from his father. Beginning with a collection of birds' eggs, he traded and bargained with urchins of his own age; and presently he owned a rifle. He cared nothing about hunting, so now he began a series of trades with grown men, and after a year he owned a buggy. It was far from new, but he greased the axles and polished the body; and then came the opportunity to sell it to a farmer for real money. Ivan insisted that the farmer throw in some old harness. The money he banked and with the harness he embarked on another series of trades. His reputation as a trader was greatly admired, and by the time he was fourteen grown men would sometimes commission him to conduct their trading. But trading always played second fiddle to his ruling passion: horses.

And that same passion ruled another person in the community, a
man forty years Ivan's senior. The leading citizen and the richest, his
name was Major Adam Redmond, and he dwelt in a stone house on a
farm a half-mile west of the village. His title he had attained while
serving in the cavalry during the Civil War.

In the meadows of the Redmond farm many fine horses grazed, and
Ivan used to stop by the fence and stare yearningly at the horses and at
the house with its iron grillwork in a pleasant maple grove. The
stone barn was enormous, and a weather vane with a trotting horse
topped its cupola. Sometimes he would see a buggy flashing down the
drive, pulled by a spirited pair of matched blacks. Major Redmond
would be holding the reins.

As a little boy that was the closest Ivan ever got to Major Redmond,
but he admired him breathlessly. But after he began working at the
stable he saw more of the major, who would sometimes drop into the
office while his horses were being shod at the blacksmith's next door.
He was a full-blooded man with a beard like General Grant's; and
he carried a gold-headed cane. He never seemed aware of the boy in
nondescript shirt and trousers; but of him Ivan was very much aware.
He thought it would be pretty fine to become a carefully dressed man
with a beard and a gold-headed cane.

One day when Ivan was fifteen, the major's visit to the stable co-
incided with the arrival of a horse trader. Everyone gathered on the
green to look over the horses, and the major's fancy was taken by a
roan saddle mare. After examining her teeth he rode her, and when
he trotted back to the green you could tell he admired her to the buying point.

Swinging from the saddle, the major stood looking very judicious,
sometimes backing a few paces to get an over-all view of the mare,
sometimes slowly encircling her. When somebody plucked at his
sleeve, he glanced around with irritation. Concentrating on the roan's
points, he didn't like being interrupted.

It was the stableboy.

"Could I say something to you, Major?" Ivan asked. And when
the man seemed about to wave him away he added in a whisper:
"About the mare."

So they entered the office, the major so fashionably immaculate, the
stableboy in patched pants.

"Don't think I'd buy her, if I was in your place," Ivan said.

The major frowned at this thin-faced boy with dark eyes and brown
hair that needed cutting.

"Why not?"

"Think she's a stump-sucker, Major."

The major's frown deepened, for he prided himself upon being an excellent judge of horseflesh, and he hadn't seen a horse in a long time that he admired so much.

"You know the animal?"

"Never saw her before."

"I like her."

"She's sweet. But I think she's a stump-sucker."

"What makes you think that?"

Ivan couldn't put his suspicion into words. Something told him, that was all.

"You've never seen her eat wood?"

"No."

"Never seen her till today?"

"No."

"You're wasting my time," the major gruffed. He stalked from the office and bought the mare.

A few days later the major's groom came to the stable and told Ive he was wanted at the Redmond place. Ive rode out in the buggy with the groom. As they turned in he saw the major pacing back and forth in front of the house, his cane jabbing the sod. And when the buggy halted in the side yard the major stamped over, looking angry.

"You're Pawpacker's boy, aren't you?"

"Yes, sir."

"Why didn't you tell me the other day you'd known that mare before?"

"I'd never known her before."

Scowling, the major led Ive into the barn.

The mare's name was Goldie, and when they reached her stall Ive saw she had gnawed a splintery U-shaped hunk from the manger.

"Stump-sucker!" said the major.

"Yes, sir."

"Somebody must have told you."

"No, sir."

"You're lying."

"No, sir."

"Then how did you know?"

"Just knew."

"Come, come!"

"Just knew. I could tell."

"How?"

Ive made an uncertain gesture. "I don't know how."

"Likely story! By gad, I ought to have you discharged. Stump-sucker!"

The major acted as if Ive had sold him the mare. Men hated to be bested in a horse deal.

Ive said, "You were in the war. An officer."

"What's that got to do with it?"

"You could judge men."

"Of course I could judge men!"

"Knew which ones you could trust. Which ones would be scared, Which ones would carry out orders."

"By gad!" the major exclaimed. "What's the war got to do—?"

"You judged them by looking at them. Maybe talking to them for a minute."

"Certainly."

"Well," Ive said, "that's the way I judge horseflesh."

Gnawing the edge of his mustache, the major led the way along the stalls. He halted and pointed at a heavy Clydesdale.

"All right, judge him."

Ivan looked him over.

"He's between five and six. Like him pretty well in the withers. But—" Ivan frowned. "Not a buy," he added. "Subject to the heaves."

"My groom told you!"

"No, sir. Nobody told me."

"By gad!"

Ivan was silent.

The major tramped on to the next stall.

"Judge her."

Ivan took his time. At last he said:

"She's three. She likely broke hard. Maybe still shies to the right. Think she'll get over it. Kind of headstrong yet, but she's got a gait like a rocking chair."

"By gad!"

A few minutes later, the major ushered Ive into the library of his house. Ive had never seen a room like that. The major had more books than a lawyer.

"You don't drink?"

"No, sir."

"Admirable!" The major poured a stiff jolt of Bourbon, downed it without a wash. "You needn't sit on the edge of that chair. It won't nip your hind end."

Ive grinned, leaned back.

"You don't look at their teeth, even," the major said. "Why not?"

"Don't need to."

"By gad!"

"You can tell a man's age without looking at his teeth. Well, I can tell a horse's. Sometimes I miss."

"You didn't miss today."

"Sometimes I do."

"By gad!" The major had another drink. "It's a gift," he declared. "Like a baritone. Like one of these artist fellows."

"I've always liked horses."

"Like one of these child prodigies. On the fiddle."

"Sometimes I miss."

"By gad! Must speak about this to your father."

"He knows about it. But horses don't mean much to him." The major poured more Bourbon.

"With a gift like that," he said, "you've got a future."

"I like horses. Always have. I like to work with horses." The major pursed his lips. Scowled. At last he said: "What am I going to do with that stump-sucker?"

Ivan didn't know.

"By gad! I can't abide a stump-sucker. Never could. And that damned trader . . . Look here. Do you want her?"

Ive grinned. "I don't have much money."

"Money! Where're your wits, boy? Do you want her as a gift?" Ive expelled a long breath.

"That's handsome of you. Real handsome."

"Can't abide a stump-sucker. Messy! Splinters! But look here. I want a good saddle horse. You buy me a good saddle horse and I'll pay you a commission. Five dollars. But she's got to be good. Perfect."

"They don't come perfect."

"Say ninety percent perfect. But by gad! No stump-sucker!"

"Yes, sir," Ivan said. "No stump-sucker."

Three weeks later Ivan swapped the mare Goldie to a horse trader for a chestnut pacer. He demanded ten dollars to boot. He got six.

Five weeks later he heard of a saddle horse owned by a farmer. He called at the farm, looked her over. Then he got in touch with Major Redmond. The major paid him five dollars commission. And never regretted it.

During the next months Ive was a frequent guest at Major Redmond's. The major told him about the great world beyond Larkin Corners. If Ive were to become a famous horse judge—maybe an expert at society horse shows—he should acquire more learning. He should know how to speak correctly. The major lent him books from his library, and because Ive was a serious young man who desired someday to have a nice home like the major's, he dutifully read the books. He read Addison and Shakespeare and Byron without too much understanding or enjoyment. But he gulped Fielding and Dickens.

And during the next two years he continued trading; and the major spoke to his friends about that boy's ability to judge horses, and other people began paying him to render expert opinions.

At seventeen, he owned a team and a wagon and three additional horses. And early one spring morning when the eastern sky was beginning to pink he drove from Larkin Corners along the road past the pleasant meadows of the Redmond place and on toward the West to seek his fortune. A few years later, richer by several thousand dollars, he drove south across the Iowa line toward Winchester, Missouri.

In Kansas City and St. Louis, the great neckless men who pilot the Republican Party and the Democratic Party in Missouri agree upon one thing: that it would be political waste to send campaign orators into a certain tier of counties. Little Dixie, they call these counties; and the safest prophecy under heaven is that in any election they will turn in thumping Democratic majorities.

Northernmost of the county seats in Little Dixie is Winchester, but Ive Pawpacker soon discovered that to the town geography meant nothing. Architecturally and emotionally it was a town in the deep South: the farthest northward push the South ever made.

The town was built around the Courthouse Square, and in the hot summers old men lolled in the humid shade of the courthouse lawn and drawled about the virtues of various flea-pestered hound dogs. Or, if they were talking business, their conversation concerned mules. Usually somebody's Negro man lingered at the edge of the group, perhaps Judge Southwick's Ed. Judge Southwick would be telling how his bitch hound holed a fox last week, and he'd say in his charming, liquid voice, "Isn't that right, Ed?" And even though it was the greatest whopper a man ever told, Ed would exclaim, "Yes, sir, Jedge—that's just how it happen!"

Of course by the time Ive Pawpacker reached Winchester the Negroes were technically free, but the town went on year after year as if the Emancipation Proclamation had never been signed. The early settlers had brought their slaves with them, and during the Civil War most of the young men had gone away to fight for Jeff Davis. So far as Winchester was concerned, there had been only one important war in history, The War. And after it was lost the town was a defeated town. It turned its back on the future.

It was a languid town in a country of rolling hills, and it seemed older than General Lee's grandmother. The courthouse was not a great domed structure, but a little building of slate-colored stone with corridors that smelled of musty documents and tobacco juice. Away from the Square the streets dozed in dank shade, and the dwellings were of time-blurred brick or wooden houses with galleries and pillars that needed paint.

Life was easy there, because everybody believed making a living a necessary evil, and nobody was in a hurry to have truck with that evil. The women were mostly beautiful and lazy, and the hounds were beautiful and lazy, and the men were charming and lazy. Nearly everybody was related to everybody else. In the daytime the Negro women sang at their work, and at night you could hear the nostalgic music of hounds baying in tangled valleys.

On Saturdays the farmers who drove to town were not the plump, thrifty peasants of the Middle West. They were gaunt, raw-boned men, lean as squirrel rifles. Hound dogs flopped along in the shade of the wagons, and the wagons were pulled by mules. While the women-folks bought calico and corn meal the men gathered in feed lots to buy and sell mules. In that town the principal industry was the breeding of mules. It was an ideal occupation for Winchester, because the horses and jacks did most of the work.

He was not like other horse traders. Most of them were thieving men who needed shaves and baths, and their eyes were shifty beneath the brims of slouch hats. They creaked from town to town in filthy wagons covered with canvas, camping by the roadside and sometimes lifting a chicken from a farmer's henroost. Dealing with them you were on guard. They were full of tricks, and you might find you had bought a horse stolen from the next county, or a horse doped.

He was not as they. He drove an ordinary lumber wagon without a canvas cover, and he never camped out. He was shaved and clean and respectable, wearing a neat suit and blacked shoes; and when he entered a town he drove to a livery stable and demanded the best for his horses. They were always well-fed and glossy. And he inquired about the best hotel and took a suitcase from the wagon box and strode into the place with great assurance. He was not big, but wiry and supple. His lean face was weather-browned and intense vitality burned in his dark eyes.

He was shrewd enough to know the power of words, and hence he never announced himself as a horse trader but always a horse buyer. It threw the smartest men off guard, for they began scheming how they could sell him their horses at extravagant prices instead of worrying about protecting their pocketbooks from the tricks of a horse trader. He had been commissioned, he said, to buy horses for Major Redmond of New York State. It sounded impressive and somehow official.

Before he tried to sell or trade he bought a horse or two. Always his routine was the same. In the paddock of the livery stable he stepped back a few paces from the horse up for sale, scrutinizing it sharply. Then with slow deliberation he paced around it, his concentration in-

GUS THE GREAT

By Thomas W. Duncan

GUS THE GREAT is an outstanding piece of workmanship, head and shoulders, in my private opinion, above any fiction which the judges of the Book-of-the-Month Club have examined this year—and yet its inherent soundness defies many critical tenets. It is devoid of brilliant literary style in the academic sense, and still it has its own narrative power, and that unanalyzable quality which can move its reader effortlessly from page to page. Except by broad indirection, it preaches no social sermon — an obvious black mark against any novel in these enlightened years, though to some this may be a blessed relief. In construction it is not conventional, for Mr. Duncan, its author, has a Tolstoian way of breaking his many narratives at crucial points to introduce whole new platoons of characters. A great many readers, however, will intensely enjoy and be very grateful for *Gus The Great* because of the vitality and glamour it gains through its own strong individuality.

Gus The Great is primarily the story of a circus and one so true and so complete as to make it the last word in our long shelf of circus fiction. At the same time, in its three-ring frame, with something doing in every ring every minute, it contrives to tell the tale of the rise and decline, the loves and ambitions, that had made up the life of the typical American town from which this circus started. In its broadest sense, it is a tale of the manners, the weakness, and the strength of our American way of life, as it bloomed in the earlier part of this century under the older free enterprise system. And a circus, with its crises of boom and bust, its moments of dubious moral compromise, and its occasional bursts of sacrifice—the show must go on, you know, and the rubes aren't going to stop it—is not a bad vehicle with which to explain certain American philosophies.

In Mr. Duncan's broad and restless stream of plot, you will be introduced to many remarkable people in *Gus The Great*, with and without the glitter of a sideshow barker's verbiage. You will meet the acrobatic Sebastians, who swung on rings, at the very apex of the big top, without the benefit of a net to catch them, and who died because a ring once broke. You will meet their daughter Eloise, and the neat, cool lion tamer, Captain Philip Latcher, and his dangerous cageboy, Willie Krummer, who finally brought the Captain to his death because he coveted the Captain's wife. You will come to know Ive Pawpacker, the small town banker and entrepreneur, who loved horses and who put up money for the show. You will be introduced to roustabouts, gamblers, small businessmen and news editors, and to all their women. You will smell sawdust, and at the same time hear small town gossip of loans and love and business.

One figure will loom above all these others, giving them a unity through his own ebullient and meretricious expansiveness. He is Gus Burgoyne, head of the whole show, a shoddy but at the same time occasionally magnificent parody of a Mr. America, a product as purely American as plug tobacco. He is Gus the Great only out of courtesy, because of his dreams rather than his actions, but he is someone you will understand, just as you will understand his associates. They are people you have met before. They walk today on every Main Street.

Gus, you will see, was an up-and-coming small town boy, imbued with American ambition, who turned down the girl he loved, in spite of real mental anguish, to marry the rich man's unattractive daughter. He had a turgid conscience. The lure of the fleshpots and the flesh usually got the better of his feeble ethics. His dreams themselves had the tawdry quality of the circus poster, consisting mostly of visions of himself as head of the greatest show on earth and the godlike center of the show. Yet Mr. Duncan will make you realize that Gus was not such a bad man, either. In spite of failure, he could always get up again, with an undiminished faith in himself and in the order that made him—even when we leave him, a broken asthmatic old man of sixty, moving westward, full of belief in a better day and glad he is alive.

Gus The Great is done on a broad sort of mural canvas with large sure strokes and generous splashes of clear color. It is a tribute to Mr. Duncan's skill that he gives all his many characters roundness and reality. Every one of his pages reflects some part of his country's courage, or vitality, or faith. Anyone who starts *Gus The Great* will not leave it without a new affection for the land we live in and its people, despite the tragedies, the stupidities and weaknesses so ably and often so devastatingly described. There is an optimistic sweep to *Gus The Great* that never falters even in the darkest hours of Gus Burgoyne. It is an American novel, in the best sense of the word, humorous, brave, and tragic. No one will leave it without being wiser, though all the lesson it teaches is that most people are both good and bad. No one can leave it without a sense of having lived in a changing, restless period, in the company of men and women adapted to their time. Perhaps some such impression as this is the best test of a good novel, and to the tens of thousands who will read it, *Gus The Great* will stand this test.

JOHN P. MARQUAND

In accordance with a suggestion made by a number of our subscribers, this monthly reprint from the Book-of-the-Month Club *News* is printed in this format so that it can be pasted, if desired, to the flyleaf of the book.

tense. He could judge weight within a few pounds, and through the years all the lore and knowledge of horses had steeped his very bones. He didn't like a draft horse that was too ready to prick up its ears, although in a trotter that was the very trait he wanted. He preferred a Roman nose to a dish face. A Roman nose was hard to break, but once broken he was reliable, whereas a dish face was easy to break but you never knew what he would do. Of all markings he was suspicious. A white star on a black forehead might be a natural marking, but sometimes it meant the horse had been stolen and the star bleached there by applications of hot potatoes.

These and a thousand other scraps of knowledge swayed his judgment. It never took him long to make up his mind. His decision resulted from the total impression he received, never from individual points, for you were likely to deceive yourself if you fancied too much the curve of a crest or the line of a back.

Sometimes he made a bad buy, for he relied somewhat on hunch. Perhaps ten percent hunch and ninety percent knowledge compounded his judgment. But usually he was right. When he wanted a horse he made a single offer. If the owner refused and started haggling, Ive shrugged and turned away.

"If you can't afford to sell him at that," he said, "keep him. I don't want to cheat anybody."

Usually the owner ended by accepting the offer.

After he had finished buying, somebody always asked if any of his horses were for sale.

"Certainly. I've never owned a horse I wouldn't sell if I got my price."

In selling as in buying, he refused to haggle. He set a price and they could take it or leave it. Usually they took it. With his trader's soul he would have loved to haggle, but from experience he learned that arrogance in a horse deal was more impressive and profitable.

He made money. Knowing values, he offered to buy for slightly less than the horse was worth, and he had the cash in his wallet to make full and instant payment. Experience told him that most men who offered a horse for sale needed money and were prepared to sacrifice a few dollars to get it. On the other hand, a man in the market for a horse almost always had spare cash, and if the horse took his eye he would pay a little more than its actual value. He never tried to make killing profits on a single deal. He preferred to make money by lots of buying and selling with small profits.

And so gradually as he worked his way west, through Pennsylvania and Ohio and Michigan and Illinois, his capital grew. He took care of it, opening accounts in three banks, for he was too cautious to trust his money to a single institution. And he took care of himself too, buying good clothes and living well and often spending his evenings reading. He had never forgotten Major Redmond's advice about improving himself.

More than he realized he modeled himself on Major Redmond. Someday he wanted a nice home like the major's, and he wanted to be looked up to as a leading citizen and carry a gold-headed stick. He didn't want to spend his life wandering about the country. The time would come when he'd find a livery stable for sale in a town he liked, and he'd take root. He'd hire hostlers to operate the stable and with it as headquarters he would go out on buying trips.

By the time he was twenty-two, he had a pretty shrewd knowledge not only of horses but of men. And travel had taught him a good deal about the world. Sometimes he granted himself a vacation and spent a week in Milwaukee or Chicago, eating at the best restaurants and attending the theater.

And so in many ways he was more self-reliant and experienced than most young men, but in one way he was still callow and adolescent. He didn't know much about girls. Driving from town to town, he had little opportunity to become acquainted with what he thought of as nice girls. And caution kept him away from the other kind. Desire tormented him more and more, and when he was falling asleep at night he thought of the pretty faces and bosoms and hips he had seen on the street or in the lobby, and he felt fever hot. One evening in Chicago desire led him to the shadowy levee district, but he was too shy to knock on the doors of the more fashionable houses. And the women who accosted him on the sidewalk turned his desire to disgust. They were blowzy, cheaply jeweled, ostrich-plumed, and he suspected they were diseased. He was too fastidious for adventures of that kind.

In his thoughts all girls were either nice or not nice. The not-nice he abhorred. And like a schoolboy daydreaming about a lovely face, he thought of all beautiful and nice girls as shining creations, pure and gentle and angelic. He had reached marrying age without the hand-holding and kissing parties and preliminary skirmishes that prepared most men for the battle of life. Then he met Georgiana Kelvin of Winchester, Missouri.

At midafternoon as he drove south toward Winchester a thunder-shower sent him to a farmer's barn, delaying him more than an hour, and now at sunset the town was still several miles away. It was May, and the scent of springtime bewitched the land. He drove through grazing country with hills rolling away to the horizon and long valleys where creeks meandered and brush grew thick. The broad rays from the low red sun projected wagon and horses in a grotesquerie of moving shadows. Then the sun vanished and Ive drove along in the re-

flected fire of a west that had become salmon flame. That soon died
and the air cooled. And with dusk came the mist.

He was winding along a ridge when he noticed it first, rising silently
down in the creek valleys. He knew the habits of quiet country at
twilight, and he assumed that the mist would remain down there
where it belonged, hanging above the rills and brooks like the ghostly
spirit of running water. In the east a rising moon was swimming in
lavender sky, and somewhere a whip-poor-will began its melancholy
and repetitious song.

The cooling air was still damp from the shower, and perhaps that
explained why the mist came stealing upward, filling the valleys, until
finally from his wagon seat Ive gazed out on lakes of spectral froth.
Above the ridge road the sky was clear, the moon white as a plum
blossom and the stars yellow. Not of the sky was the mist born, but
of the damp mysterious earth.

The team plodded on, and the road dipped. Ive glanced back. His
trading stock, three untethered horses, were not straggling now to
munch the tender grass. They followed close, as if uneasy.

Down in the hollow the wagon was engulfed so thickly that he
couldn't make out the horses' rumps. Then the road climbed and gradually the mist thinned. But not completely. As it had taken the valleys
by stealth, so now it was taking the ridge.

He wondered how far it was to Winchester. Not a great distance,
likely; on a clear night he would have driven on; but he didn't like
wandering blind down an unfamiliar road. Halting the team, he
fumbled in the wagon box for a lantern. In its rays, the mist glistened
and moved like smoke. While the team waited he groped along the
road, discovering presently a grassy turnout. Returning, he grasped
the bridle of the off-horse and led the team to the camping spot.

The whip-poor-will was silent now, but other sounds invaded the
roadside hush. Frogs were croaking somewhere; and off in a valley
he heard the forlorn bonging of a cowbell. And once, far away and
nostalgic, he heard a hound yelping on the tracks of a fox or raccoon.
It was like the voice of the legendary South, bringing to mind all the
lazy mystery of that possum-sleepy land: hot bread and fiddle music
and yellow wenches laughing.

He unhitched, kindled a fire; and sitting on the wagon tongue, he
munched what remained in his lunch pail, a pork sandwich, a hard-
boiled egg, a square of ginger cake. In the firelight his brown hair
looked black and his face sober. His eyes were moody. His straight thin
nose and lean jaw and thin mouth gave his countenance almost an
ascetic cast. His hands were dark tan and well shaped, the fingers lean.
He looked too well-dressed to be sitting at a campfire. His vest was the
hue of creamed coffee, checked with red-brown lines and pearl-

buttoned. His shirt was still crisp after a day of travel, his cravat buff-colored; and his jacket and trousers had been tailored from leaf-brown fabric. But sandy mud stained his shoes.

He scraped off the mud with a stick, considering as he worked the problem of water. By morning the horses would be restless with thirst; even now he was thirsty himself. He stood up and listened to the night, attempting to isolate the direction of the frog voices. But it was no good: they croaked everywhere. On a dry night frogs would mean a brook or pond, but probably in this dripping mist they were bouncing all over the place. It seemed ridiculous to be thirsty when every leaf and blade glistened and the air was so crammed with moisture, and he wondered whether he'd get lost if he went exploring for water. He decided to chance it. And then, coming far down the road from Winchester, he heard galloping hoofs. A saddle horse, he decided, as the sound drew nearer. And its rider must be mad or drunk to be plunging pell-mell through a night like this.

He stepped into the road, swinging the lantern and calling. If the fellow weren't too drunk perhaps he could direct him to water.

Through the wet air the hoof beats sounded as sharp and definite as whip cracks. As they came closer he shouted louder and poised himself, ready to leap aside if the drunken fool failed to heed his lantern and voice. When the sound was very close he detected a break in the horse's stride. A yell cut the mist, and then looming bigger than life he saw a black horse rearing. He jumped to the roadside and the horse's front hoofs landed where he had been standing. It caracoled on a few yards before wheeling back into the radiance of fire and lantern, its glossy coat streaming mist and sweat.

"I declare!" the rider exclaimed gaily. "Were you trying to suicide yourself?"

The rider was neither mad, drunk nor male. The rider was a girl with shining yellow hair falling to her shoulders from under a gray campaign hat. She swung easily from the saddle.

"I didn't see that lantern till I was near on you. I might just as well have killed you."

Ive saw then that, hard as it was to believe, she was wearing not a ladylike riding skirt but rawhide-colored breeches and black boots. Her blouse was open at the throat, and she wore a man's jacket snugly buttoned over her breasts.

He felt the blood coursing up his neck. She must be a wild hussy to deck herself out like that, but she was a hussy very exciting to the eyes. She didn't look more than eighteen, and in the firelight the smooth skin of her face and throat was overwashed with a golden tint. And despite her boy's getup, there was no mistaking that a girl's curved body occupied those clothes.

"Reckon when your eyes are full," she drawled, "you'll wish to fill your pockets."

But he could tell she wasn't offended because he had stared, and suddenly his embarrassment left and he felt more at ease than usual with girls.

"It's a fetching getup," he said.

Her smile was teasing.

"You ought to try wearing a riding skirt. Then you'd know why I hate them. But if I'd go garbed in pants in broad daylight, they'd lack smelling salts enough. 'Goodness alive!' they'd say. 'There goes Georgiana Kelvin in her pappy's hat and her cousin Stuart's britches! Goodness alive!' "

"So you ride at night."

"Near every night. Except when I ride afternoons with my cousin Stuart. This fog sure bewitches things something terrible."

"You were covering the road."

She puckered her nose. Her face was saucy, her mouth and chin willful, and Ive judged that once she took it into her head to ride in pants nobody could stop her.

"Blackie, he was just lazying along tonight. That horse has got no use for fog, nohow."

Her warm voice flowed slow as honey, so that what she actually said sounded like, "Blackie, he was jus' lazin' 'long tonight. That hoss got no use fo' fog, nohaow."

"How far is this from Winchester?"

"Mile and a half, I reckon. Maybe two."

Her hand fussed with her hair while she gazed at the wagon and the horses. When she wasn't smiling the willfulness of her chin was more pronounced, her full mouth almost sullen.

"You don't look like a horse trader," she said, "but reckon you must be with all this stock. What's your name?"

He told her.

Smiling, she crinkled her forehead and cocked up a blond brow.

"How come you have a name like Ivan?"

"My mother found it in a poem."

"I never did get much understanding out of poesy. But my cousin Stuart can recite it by the mile. You're from up North, I reckon."

"I'm a horse buyer. I buy for Major Redmond of New York State. That's where I'm from."

"Goodness, you've come far. I hear tell that Yankees are smart traders. Sharp as their voices, I hear. Daddy's a lawyer. He was in the legislature once. The wages the state pays are real generous. Do you make much money trading about the country?"

"I do all right."

"I declare!" She grinned hoydenishly. "You're the first man I ever hear confess to it. Daddy says there's no money in the law. But my cousin Stuart *would* read it. In Daddy's office. It's an occupation fit for a gentleman, he says. Are you a gentleman?"

Before Ive could reply she drawled on:

"Reckon not. You never hear tell of a gentleman trading horses about the country. Or making money. My cousin Stuart has passed himself over the bar, now. He'll go off to St. Louis soon to practice. He's marrying a St. Louis girl. Are there flocks of handsome girls in St. Louis?"

"I've never been there."

She stood idly snapping her crop against her boots. Sullenness had returned to her face, but in the firelight her hair was angelic. Ive didn't know what to make of her. He felt he should classify her as a nice girl, yet those riding pants made his blood race as if she had been wearing only boots from the waist down.

"I'd like to lay sight on St. Louis," she said. "My cousin Stuart's been there twice. How come you've never been there?"

"Just never have, that's all." He felt he had lost caste with her because he hadn't seen St. Louis. "I've been in Chicago. Lots of times. I've eaten oyster stew in the Palmer House."

It left her unimpressed.

"How long do you aim to be in Winchester?" she asked.

"As long as trading's good."

She turned to go.

"Well, if you find yourself in law trouble, you call on my Daddy. W. C. Kelvin, south side of the Square. Everybody knows him. They all call him W.C."

"I'm in trouble now. Not law trouble. But I need water for these horses."

"Well goodness alive! Why don't you move down to the branch and fetch it?"

"Branch?"

"Tucker's Branch." She waved at the brambles. "It's not much farther than you can throw a nigger."

He looked where she pointed, but all he could see were mist-dripping bushes.

She gave an exaggerated sigh.

"Goodness alive, but menfolks are helpless! Give me that lantern and I'll show you."

"I'll get buckets," he said.

As he rummaged in the wagon, he felt attracted to her and stung by annoyance. Her conclusion that he was not a gentleman—a word which seemed to have an odd technical meaning—piqued him; and he didn't like her saying that menfolks were helpless. Maybe the men she knew—maybe this Stuart person—but not him! And he was nettled by her stubborn clinging to a geography so hazy that she believed St. Louis the world's leading city. He discovered he had taken a dislike to St. Louis. And he wanted to impress her in some way; so when, carrying buckets, he rejoined her he succumbed to the temptation to boast. Never before had he boasted to anybody. It wasn't his nature, with his streak of caution; and besides, it was bad business for a horse trader to seem too smart. But now he told her how he had pulled himself up by his bootstraps till he possessed five horses and money in three banks.

"I declare," she grinned. "Ain't it a fright the tales a man will spin for a girl!"

"Don't you believe it?"

She put a consoling hand on his arm.

"Don't look so down in the mouth. It was a real noble attempt. A girl likes to hear big talk."

A senseless urge to prove himself right and conquer her stubbornness took hold of him.

"I can prove it."

"No doubt. But I reckon you wouldn't bet on it."

"I reckon I would."

"The horses maybe," she conceded. "Maybe you own them. And maybe not. Maybe you're just this Major Redmond's hired hand. Reckon that's it."

He felt heat in his cheeks and ears.

"But money in three banks," she went on lightly. "Nobody ever had money in three banks."

"I have, and I'll bet on it. And I'll prove it."

She half closed her eyes and gazed dreamily into the mist.

"There's a bracelet in Grove's Store," she murmured, "that I'm near dying to own. The price is something terrible. Near five dollars. Would you bet that much?"

"Against what?"

She pouted her lips. "Reckon I don't own anything of value to bet. Lest I'd bet a kiss. A kiss against the bracelet?"

As he went to the wagon and opened a suitcase, his palate was dry and his lips feverish. Excitement pulled him quivering tight. His fingers shook as he found the bankbooks tucked in a corner of the suitcase. He was kneeling in the wagon and he glanced toward the fire. She stood gazing into the flames, her profile toward him, a smile playing with the end of her mouth. She kept snapping her riding whip against her booted legs. The firelight threw them into round contour, and he could see the lazy rise and fall of her breast. She had taken off her campaign hat and her hair was lustrous.

"My goodness alive," she murmured as she fingered the little calf-bound bankbooks. "It sure does look like—"

She rustled the pages, scrutinizing the deposits. Her countenance was sober, interested, impressed. And when she returned the books her eyes were puzzled and speculative.

"I never did know there was that much money tied to one man's name."

Ive pocketed the books. His breath was swift and shallow.

"Time to pay bets."

She smiled ravishingly and teasingly; she extended her hand.

"We didn't say what kind of kiss," she purred. "You can kiss my hand."

He felt outraged, duped. He took her extended hand; and then before she could pull loose he seized her in his arms. The kiss from her full, pouty lips telegraphed itself to his toes. The fragrance of perfume bottles and girlish skin was in his nostrils. She struggled at first, then gave herself against him. When at last she pushed him away he thought she might cut him with the riding whip. In Vermont and in Larkin Corners girls didn't submit lightly to caresses. Instead she flashed him that teasing smile.

"My goodness alive," she drawled. "Reckon that bet was sure paid off. But I do wish I'd won. I do fancy that bracelet."

"Maybe," he said quietly, "you'll get it anyway."

Her eyes widened and her smile was brilliant.

"Sure enough?"

"I don't guess it would break me up."

He felt suddenly adult, masculine. Masterful. And never before had he been so sharply conscious of the power in dollars. All at once, more than ever, he wanted to make thousands and millions, and dress in finery and carry a walking stick and show the world he was a gentleman.

Carrying the lantern, she led the way into the brambles on the search for water. Ive followed with the buckets. In the fog the lantern's orange smudge and the moon-flooded translucence dislocated reality. They fumbled through shining, pearl-gray myopia. The mist drifted between them and swarmed into their ears. Tree trunks swam past, bulging with fog-produced corpulence. Underfoot the wet earth and grasses were slick as grease, and once Ive miscalculated, assuming a jutting shadow to be part of the hillside. He regained balance just in time to avoid a fall. The buckets banged to the ground.

"Goodness!" Georgiana exclaimed. "Hurt yourself?"

"It's slippery. But I'm all right."

"You be careful how you break your neck."

She had turned back to him; in the lantern rays the air fizzed like soda water. They had stopped in a patch of hazel brush.

"I *thought* there was a path," she said. "Where do you reckon it vanished to?"

"You've been here before?"

"Ofttimes. Hazel-nutting when it comes fall."

"Don't get us lost."

"Lost! Reckon I know Winchester County blindfolded. I've never been out of it, except when Daddy was in the legislature. But I was too young then to recollect much about Jefferson City."

"If there's water," Ive said, "it's likely down in the gully."

"Anybody knows that. What I want is to find the path."

She moved on, resuming an obstinate search among bushes that slapped wetly and low-hanging branches that clawed. Sometimes she halted and frowned at the steaming woods, her mouth turned down and her chin stubborn.

"That old path!" she exclaimed, in vexation. "It's just hiding itself away on purpose!"

"Maybe you're mixed up about where we are."

"I'm not!" Her face stormed over and she stamped a foot. "I know where we are just as well as anything."

He did not argue further but he concluded that the mist had completely befuddled her. Probably she had mistaken his camping spot for another place along the road. At last Georgiana started down the slope.

"I didn't care about that pesky path, anyway," she said. "But I do think it's right mean of it to hide away like this."

Damp sand curved along the gully basin but no water gleamed there. The far wall rose steep, with acrobatic bushes and saplings climbing out of sight into the fog.

"This wouldn't be Tucker's Branch," she said. "It's the next one. This is Cave Hollow. I knew it all the time. There's a spring along here somewhere. I know this hollow."

As they followed the sandy gully there came again to his ears the baying of a hound from lonely distances, mournful and haunting as a threnody. And he wondered about this country of willful and beautiful girls and bewitched hollows.

Once the gully narrowed and a limestone cliff towered up, smooth as a wall. They paused, and he thought he might steal another kiss. But she backed nimbly away, holding the lantern between him and her seductive body.

"No you don't," she smiled teasingly.

"Please. Just one."

"Is kissing all you ever think about?"

It was all he was thinking about at that moment. Beyond the hot lantern her skin was golden smooth; he was dazzled and tantalized.

"Reckon that's all you do, journeying from town to town. Just kiss the pretty girls and leave their hearts broken."

She spoke lightly, tauntingly. She baffled and roused him. Her words stung him into feeling both wickedly experienced and ineptly adolescent. Her jeering smile and coquettish eyes seemed to be daring him to take what he wanted.

He took a step toward her. Graceful as a ballet girl she smiled out of reach, at the same instant moving the lantern so its bright glass brushed the back of his hand. An exclamation of surprise and pain broke from his lips. He stopped in his tracks, his hand going to his mouth. For a second he hated her.

Then she was beside him, seizing his hand and showering the burned skin with kisses.

"Honey! I'm right sorry! Oh, look at it—all red and burned! That's an awful shame! Honey, I never meant—"

"I know you didn't. It's all right."

He forgot he had suspected her of burning him deliberately. Her hair was soft as a kitten's; and bending over his hand she murmured words that soothed like ointment.

"Such a shame," she said, looking up.

He kissed her then, longer than before. His senses were warm delirium, the pain in his hand far away.

"No—not any more," she said finally.

"One more."

"Then *just* one. And do you forgive Georgiana for being so awkward with that old lantern?"

He had forgiven her kisses ago.

She untangled herself from his arms and took up the lantern.

"We'd best get to that spring," she said. "Your *poor* thirsty horses!"

They found the spring bubbling clear and bright from the hillside. She put down the lantern and went to her knees to drink. When she arose her lips gleamed with the water. Then Ive drank. He could hear the water purling softly; it was icy, with a mineral tang; and he thought again of the witchery of these Southern hills.

He filled the buckets, and with Georgiana going ahead to light his way he started climbing the gullyside. He felt winged and exalted. The mist smelled sweet and his hand didn't hurt so much now. He breathed the magic night into his farthest lung cells. His thoughts dreamed high above the mist, into the moon-haunted sky. But his feet were ground-chained. And the ground here was steep and slippery. Suddenly where there should have been solid earth under his right foot there was the treachery of a gopher hole.

It caught him by surprise and before he could catch himself he fell, the buckets spilling, quick agony wrenching his ankle. He must have yelled as he went down, for in an instant Georgiana had returned to him, kneeling.

"I'll be all right," he said. "I—"

He moved his ankle then, and he clamped his teeth on an outcry of pain.

"Honey, let me see—"

Under her light fingers, his ankle felt as if a knife were being twisted into it.

"You poor honey child! It's starting to swell. Reckon it must be sprained."

She helped him up. His teeth were gritting most of the time, now. He experimented with easing his weight on the ankle. It brought sweat to his forehead.

"No," she said, "don't step on it. Maybe you could sort of hop. On the good foot. Back to the wagon. You poor child—I'll hitch up your wagon. You can lay down in back and I'll drive. You're coming right home with me. We'll put you to bed there and get a doctor."

The house in Winchester where W. C. Kelvin had begot his beautiful daughters was a Southern planter's mansion whose growth had been stunted by the winters of northern Missouri. It stood on Jackson Street, its gallery facing the South, where its heart lay. Small square pillars rose two stories to support the roof, which needed reshingling nearly as badly as the house needed paint. When January piled the yard with snow, the house looked bewildered and out of place; but in the humid summers the gallery attracted what breeze might be stirring, and after a day in his office W. C. Kelvin liked to repose there in an easy chair, smoking his long, slim cigars.

He was rather like his cigars, long and slim and slow-burning. In his late fifties now, he looked a distinguished man. You might have mistaken him for a judge or a governor-general of some unimportant colony. His narrow head was mainly bald, but what hair remained was pure silver and neatly brushed over his almond-colored scalp. His eyes were a liquid, swimming brown, the upper lids drooping, and even in late middle age they gave him a languishing, romantic expression which still fluttered the hearts of the cracked old belles of the town.

With his parents he had migrated to Winchester from Virginia back in the 1830's. Friends preceded them, and the letters telling of opportunities in the West tempted the Kelvins to pack up their slaves and other chattel and make the move.

W.C.'s grandfather had been a moneymaker, a prosperous breeder of slaves and horses, but his abilities to persuade the silver eagle to hatch eaglets accompanied him to his grave. In the strictest sense he had not, perhaps, been a gentleman; but his son and grandson were, so that evened things up. If offered his choice between talking about hunting all day or working, W.C.'s father always preferred conversation, so his bank account dwindled and his debts rose. But a gentleman he undeniably was. It was his enjoyable lot to proceed through the pleasantest phase of the fine old shirt-sleeves-to-shirt-sleeves tradition.

As a boy W.C. was fond of rhetoric. He loved to mount the platform at a schoolhouse entertainment and in imperative tones command the deep and dark blue ocean to roll, or to inform admiring ears that the mountains looked on Marathon. People assumed that their souls were stirred by W.C. alone, instead of W.C. in collaboration with Byron; and everybody said he should become a lawyer. So he entered Judge Hablett's office and read the law, and after his admittance to the bar he became the judge's partner. With the judge to keep him at work he made a little money, enough to marry Eliza Gregory. She too was a migrant from Virginia, a great beauty.

Then war came along, and as went Virginia so went her sons, W.C. and his brother, Arthur. They rode away south to offer aid, comfort, encouragement and—if it came to that—even a little fighting to President Davis. Both boys became lieutenants. Arthur perished in a Southern fever camp. Exactly what W.C. did to help the Confederacy lose The War remained always obscure, but doubtless it was exactly the right thing. When he returned to Winchester he was gallantly and tatteredly weary, and he always lacked energy thereafter. It was as if the deep South had thinned his blood.

After an absence of several years, W.C. found his affairs jumbled. Bills had mounted. Arthur's wife had died—from grief, it was said—so their son, Stuart Kelvin, had gone to live with W.C.'s wife and three daughters. Judge Hablett had died; and without the judge to direct him, W.C. floated languidly on the backwaters of the law. At home, he fathered a fourth daughter. She was christened Georgiana, in honor of the state through which Sherman trekked.

If W.C. could have spent his time as a court attorney he might have been successful, for juries liked his leisurely ways and his drawl. But in Winchester County not many cases came to trial; sometimes several terms of court were convoked without W.C.'s trying a case. There remained the dull, musty, unromantic details of his profession, wills to be probated, titles to be cleared, deeds drawn, documents notarized. On the side he wrote hail and fire insurance, if people came to his office and asked for it. He was unsuited by temperament to this kind of thing; his yen for the law had been that of an orator for the platform.

In the early 1870's he became a statesman, serving two terms in the legislature, and for a time it looked as if he had found himself and would go on to higher honors. But even in legislative committee rooms there was work to be done—statesmanship was not all speechmaking—and sometimes W.C. overslept or whiled away the afternoon in a bar instead of on the house floor. During one of his absences a bill which his county wanted passed did not pass; it lost by his vote. So at the next election his constituency retired him; but in print he was still called the Honorable W. C. Kelvin. With a career in marble halls blasted, he sank deeper and deeper into the lethargy of the law. If only he could have discovered an occupation where no work was required he would have gone far.

With the waters of bankruptcy always awash in its hold, how the Kelvin ship of family managed to sail rather proudly was an example of spirit victorious over matter. Socially they were among the first families of Winchester. Their daughters grew and were gowned. Stuart Kelvin grew and was suited. The house and lot occupied a quarter of a town block; and in the stable dwelt two riding horses and a cow. In a shack fronting the alley lived Maggie Penbrooke and her husband, Harmon, the Kelvins' Negro servants. Also residing along the alley were chickens and ducks and pigs. The financial arrangement between the Kelvins and their servants had never been stated, and little cash was involved. What Maggie needed for her own larder she took from the Kelvin pantry. When she wanted a collection-plate dime for the Calvary Afro-Methodist Church Mrs. Kelvin could usually find one somewhere. W.C. gave Harmon tobacco money.

Eliza Kelvin kept Maggie happy by telling her she was the best nigger in Missouri. Eliza didn't know what she would ever do, she said, without her. This praise was true and sincere. Without Maggie nobody would have eaten in that house, and in the sitting room the dust would have obscured the plaster-bust features of General Lee and President Davis and Lord Byron. Eliza had never learned to cook, and she would have had scarcely any more idea how to use a feather duster than a chronometer. In her early fifties now, she was a woman sweet as sugar and water. Her hair was the pinkish white of an apple blossom and her skin as velvety textured. She was tall and willowy, with delicate wrists and ankles, and in spirit, at least, she had never lost her youth.

Two of her daughters had married, Virginia to a bank clerk in New Orleans, and Cordelia to a Winchester youth who had taken his bride off to Texas. The eldest daughter, May, had reached thirty several years before; it was too bad about May. At twenty-five she was engaged to an upright young man, son of a livery stable proprietor, such a jolly boy. They would have made a wonderful couple, for they loved

devotedly and May was in many respects the most beautiful daughter
of all, willowy like her mother, auburn-haired and fawn-eyed. Then a
queer thing took place. One summer dusk the young man called and
found May sitting on a garden bench, lost in contemplation of the fireflies and other natural wonders. Being so jolly and full of fun, the
young man tiptoed up behind her and suddenly shot out his hands,
grabbing her shoulders and exclaiming, "Now I've got you!"

All in fun, of course.

But May leaped to her feet and whirled, trembling violently. Then
she lifted her skirts and fled to the house, and ever after that she hated
the young man, and reality receded beyond a soft gentle haze. "May
isn't herself," was the way the family alluded to her condition. Dr.
Bennett examined her and could find nothing wrong, physically. He
said they had better observe her closely to make certain she didn't set
the house on fire. But that was a concern they had long ago dismissed;
she cared nothing about playing with matches. She was lamb-gentle,
and her mental cloudiness was not cyclonic but like the great floating
clouds of a summer day that dissolve harmlessly at twilight. In many
ways her interests were like her mother's: flowers and trees and birds
and butterflies. Only when May wandered about the garden and talked
to the trees they replied, telling her beautiful stories. Spinsterhood had
not brought angularity to her features, but only a sweet and faintly
melancholy beauty, like a weeping willow. Sometimes she seemed very
lucid, but at others the haze thickened between her and the world and
she went wandering off into the fields and woodlands to hear new
stories from the trees growing there. So far as her family could gather,
she no longer thought of Harry Nodamoore, her former fiancé.

Harry, naturally, felt simply terrible about the entire business, blaming himself for setting May off like that. Nobody else blamed him, but
after a few months he couldn't stand it any longer, so he left Winchester for the distant Pacific Coast. His father, Prentice Nodamoore, had
always counted on Harry's taking over the livery stable, but it didn't
look now as if he ever would. Lately Prentice Nodamoore had been
talking about finding a good buyer for the stable and moving west to
join his son.

Georgiana was different from anyone else in the family. More energy
and blaze. She was a yellow-haired dandelion thrusting gaminely up
among the moon-colored lilies and orchids of a hothouse. Seven years
younger than Cordelia, the next oldest, she had mildly astonished Eliza
and W.C. by being born. When Georgiana was a little girl, W.C.'s
mother had still been alive, and she declared that the young one put
her in mind of W.C.'s grandfather, the long-dead slave breeder and
horse breeder, the last of the moneymaking Kelvin men. Old Arthur,

he was, as distinguished from W.C.'s brother, Young Arthur, who died in The War. It seemed Old Arthur had been quite a hell-raiser, willful and hard-riding, tempery and wenching and always sure he was right even when he knew he was wrong. Yes, indeed; Georgiana was like him; very like.

You never knew what she would decide to do next, but one thing you did know: whatever she decided would be done, else there would be trouble. Even as a little girl she was unpredictable. Once when she was seven she wrote Santa Claus a letter, telling him to bring her a doll cradle, and on Christmas morning when the family gathered in the sitting room the cradle was there, red beneath the green boughs of the tree. She emitted a sharp cry of delight and scampered to the cradle and dragged it to the center of the room, not waiting for W.C. (who distributed presents with great wit and charm) to announce that it was hers.

Everybody indulged her eagerness, for she was the baby of the family, and they had neither the heart nor the fortitude to cross her. They stood beaming: W.C. and Eliza, younger in those days and a handsome pair; Virginia and Cordelia, pretty girls in their teens; Grandma Kelvin, a slim old lady with a cameo pinned on her black-taffeta dress; May, who had not yet been startled by Harry Nodamoore; and Stuart Kelvin, handsome and even at seventeen very courtly. Maggie and her husband were there, grinning at the edge of things; only at that time Maggie was married not to Harmon Penbrooke but to Fabius Thompson, her third husband, who was discovered a few years later razored to a corpse down in the railroad weeds. (An unsolved murder and an odd one, for Fabius was a preacher and apparently on excellent terms with the Lord.) No matter how often Maggie changed husbands, her occupation and her Kelvins' Alley address remained unaltered.

On that bright Christmas morning when the house was full of excitement and the odor of a turkey roasting, Georgiana found not only a cradle but a doll reposing inside, lying under a quilt that Grandma Kelvin, whom Santa Claus sometimes employed at piecework, had made with her own hands.

Then without warning Georgiana's face clouded and the tip of her blond nose turned red. A storm signal. Nobody had any idea what was angering her. Then they saw she was holding the letter she had written to Santa. He had placed it on top of the cradled doll, as if to indicate that he had received hers of December 3rd inst., and was complying with her request. It transpired he had sorely offended her by returning her letter. A deed no gentleman would commit! Even at seven Georgiana understood decorum, for she had listened endlessly to Grandma's yarning about glittering Virginia society where if a careless remark so much as nicked a gentleman's honor he pranced for his dueling pistols. People in Virginia, to hear Grandma tell it, oozed gentility the way a grasshopper oozed tobacco juice.

When angered, Georgiana always fell into a tantrum, kicking her heels and squealing like a sinner getting religion. As a baby she used to hold her breath when enraged, and while that was alarming it certainly was easier on the ears. Her performance this Christmas morning attained new peaks. As always, W.C. and Eliza stared at each other helplessly, Eliza's hands describing vague circles of mild despair. Grandma simply ignored the histrionics, the way any Southern lady ignored the unpleasant and the sordid. With Georgiana holding center stage, Virginia and Cordelia sighed incapably, and Virginia murmured, "I declare! I do believe she's gone into one of her tantrums!" And May added: "Now I wonder why. But I do think she's a charmin' little sweet potato."

Fabius Thompson and Maggie held their own opinions about child rearing, derived straight from the Book of Proverbs; but they kept their ideas about the hazards of rod sparing to themselves, for after all Georgiana's hair was spun golden silk, not kinky black, and her skin peaches and cream, not chocolate.

It was Stuart Kelvin who quieted Georgiana. Even then she adored him; he could do anything with her. He was as tall and blond and handsome as a curly-headed statue of youth and gallantry; soft-spoken and gentle, romantic as a ballad.

He lazied over to her now and knelt, stroking her forehead and hair. "Did old Santa Claus insult my Georgiana?" he asked.

Her heels ceased battering and she sat up, her pretty face all tear-streaked.

"He didn't want to keep my letter!" she wailed. "I wrote it to him and he didn't want to keep it!"

"Reckon he just didn't know better. I'd sure keep any letter you wrote me. Reckon he's varmint-stupid, not to keep a letter from the prettiest little girl in creation."

At that her mood changed; she smiled sunnily. Then her face turned sulky again and she declared:

"Reckon he's no gentleman!"

" 'Course not, honey. He's from 'way up north. They don't know better, up there. You want me to, I'll send the cradle and doll back to him. And I'll write him a scorcher."

She pondered a moment. Then she said:

"Reckon I'll keep what he left. But write him the scorcher."

The crisis over, W.C. strolled to the Christmas tree and distributed gifts. With each one he quoted an appropriate line of poetry. Georgiana's tantrum was soon forgotten; but that afternoon she reminded

Stuart of his promise to write Santa a scorcher, and he smilingly complied. She helped him, and the most cutting remarks in the letter were from her little tongue. Not till she had put Santa in his place could she relax and bask in the spirit of Christmas.

For as long as she could remember Georgiana had been devoted to Stuart, and when she was eight and ten and twelve she had numberless bad evenings when he attended parties with girls of his own generation. He was a most eligible young man; Winchester was full of beautiful girls who were delighted to go out with him; and Georgiana hated them all. Lying in bed on a prurient summer evening, thinking of him under the Japanese lanterns of a lawn party, she wandered toward sleep along a tormented road. She would resolve to put him into his place next day and keep him there; to ignore and disdain him. But never for long could she maintain the pretense of despising him.

In those years he spent much of his time around the house, for since completing his secondary education at the Winchester Public Academy he had not quite decided upon his lifework. Once he contemplated becoming a doctor, but after a visit at Dr. Bennett's office, where he leafed through the closely printed pages of Gray's *Anatomy,* he experienced doubts. The doctor told him about the arduous study required of a medical student—the dissecting and memorizing and stern devotion to science—and after that Stuart dropped the whole idea. Picturing himself a doctor, he had not considered the study-lamp midnights. He had thought only of how respected he would be and of how handsome and romantic he would look, driving along in a polished rig, and of how it might be necessary to comfort a beautiful patient by holding her hand.

He thought of entering the clergy, too, for the poetry of the Episcopal service appealed to him, but after discussing that career with the rector he decided the Call he had heard had been directed at someone else with a similar-sounding name. For the rector explained that unless he wished to become one of these brimstone-spouting, self-ordained preachers like Fabius Thompson, he must study Latin and Greek and Hebrew, all of which smelled like a lot of hard labor.

After that he thought of attending West Point; letters concerning his possible appointment passed between W.C. and the congressman from that district. Stuart thought of himself in the uniform of a young officer, dashing and valorous and witty like Captain Absolute in *The Rivals;* but here again he discovered that a conspiracy of learning existed against a talented young man. Once he heard of the entrance requirements at the Academy and realized he must study at least a year before he could hope to pass the preliminary examinations, he concluded he had not really wished to serve the flag.

For a week or two he played with the idea of entering finance, but there was no opening in either Winchester bank. Moreover, he deduced that mathematical skill was sometimes helpful to a financier. And alas, in school mathematics had been his weakest subject.

Those were all careers which a gentleman might follow, and the only other was the law. W.C. was pessimistic about anybody's chances to make money in the legal profession, but he could understand Stuart's reluctance to enter any of the others. So at last it was decided that Stuart should go each day to W.C.'s office, reading Blackstone and studying the Code of Missouri. It seemed the only thing left, for certainly Stuart—a Kelvin—could not be expected to go into trade.

Stuart rather liked studying the law, because he worked under an indulgent taskmaster, himself. W.C. never interfered, never demanded that he brief up a certain number of cases each week. And certainly W.C. would not have dreamed of requiring him to perform the menial duties usually expected of an apprentice lawyer, sweeping and spittoon-cleaning. Once every month Maggie and her current husband came to the office and tidied up.

Stuart wanted to acquire a deep, solid knowledge of the law, not merely to skitter over the surface, so months and years passed while he studied. W.C. taught him the legal Esperanto used in drawing up documents, and he learned the meaning of those words that smelled like ancient yellowed papers and calf-bound books, words like replevin and writ and torts and probate.

For some unknown reason not connected with industriousness, W.C. was a fairly early riser; he breakfasted at eight and drifted to his office at nine. Not his nephew. Stuart had learned that the most restful slumber sifted over him between midnight and ten in the morning, and he was not one to lose sleep and perhaps undermine his health by getting up at seven. His mind worked better in the afternoon, anyway. So usually he left home about eleven, strolling along the wooden sidewalk toward the Square, perhaps stopping to chat a few minutes over a picket fence with some girl or lady.

In his late teens he had been handsome but rather thin, almost gangling. The years had remedied this. Nearing twenty-seven, his body had filled out, and he had grown a silky straw-yellow mustache. Once a girl had told her mother that Stuart Kelvin looked like a Greek god but that he lacked the conceit usually present in a handsome man. This was very nearly true. Long ago he had accepted the fact of his good looks and his charm, and he didn't think about his appearance unduly. He thought about girls and horses and hunting and hounds and the law; and at the heart of his daydreams two contradictory yearnings persisted. One showed himself as a plantation owner, a vast place in the South of imagination, with a company of pink-coated ladies and gentlemen—his guests—riding to the hounds through frosty sunlight. The other yearning dealt with the Open Road beckoning on and on through a land equally imaginative, and himself a gypsy lad with gold rings in his ears. Every poem which he could find—and they were numerous—about the Open Road and the gypsy life he committed to memory, and sometimes he recited these to Georgiana. She was seventeen now, a young beauty. Both enjoyed riding horseback, and in the afternoons you would see them cantering into the country. Their relationship had changed, for with Georgiana a young lady he could no longer treat her like his baby cousin.

In midsummer the deep South shambled north over the Missouri hills and embraced Winchester, like a sweating Negro mammy smothering a long-lost child with affection. The town lay motionless in yellow heat, and the leaves of the great old shade trees looked as heavy and still as vegetation in the tropics. Now for the first time since January the Negroes thawed out, their spirits becoming lively as bedbugs in a tick with a warming pan. All day the hound dogs slept in shadows, and during the afternoons ladies like Mrs. Kelvin napped behind closed blinds.

At this season, the summer before Georgiana met Ivan Pawpacker, a visitor from St. Louis journeyed to Winchester, along the branch line that ran one train each way every twenty-four hours. Her coming was the social event of the summer, for she was Eulalia Delacroix, daughter of Colonel Hubert Delacroix of St. Louis, a lawyer who had added to his inherited wealth by investments in steamboat lines and warehouses and mercantile establishments.

The editor of the *Winchester Enterprise* heralded this visitor with every favorable adjective whose meaning he knew, and some whose meaning he didn't. Winchester was honored, charmed, enraptured, enthralled: in short, glad to have her.

Eulalia's hostess was Penelope Trevelyan, a young lady equally beauteous, resplendent, sublime and pulchritudinous, according to the *Enterprise*. The editor knew what his public expected, and to give it to them he labored like a farmer pitchforking manure. If he had merely said both girls were beautiful, the town might have lynched him for insulting Southern Womanhood.

Both girls were twenty, so naturally a girl of seventeen like Georgiana was excluded from the parties and teas and collations that honored Eulalia. Cordelia Kelvin attended (she had not yet married and moved to Texas), and so did Stuart. And he made the exhilarating discovery that Eulalia deserved all the adjectives with which the *Enterprise* had gilded her.

"She's very beautiful," Cordelia told Georgiana, the morning after the first party at the Trevelyans'. "Slender as a squirrel and raspberry blond. They say she traveled with a whole trunkful of clothes. And are they ever fetching! Soon as Stuart laid eyes on her he began wandering in circles."

The girls were lingering over breakfast in the dining room; Cordelia lifted her coffee and sipped.

"And if I'm any judge," she added, in a tone that announced she deserved the Supreme Bench, "I'd say that Eulalia was much taken with Stuart. The way she used her eyes on him was scandalous."

She smiled at the memory. She didn't notice the effect of her words on Georgiana; she was merely reminiscing.

"And wouldn't she be a catch for Cousin Stuart," she went on, in a voice as warm and sugared as the coffee. "They say her Daddy's frightful rich. Must be, the way she's turned out. He's an attorney, too. If Stuart ever reads his way through all those law books, and gets himself legalized to practice, he might enter her Daddy's office in St. Louis. Yummy yum! Not that I'd want Cousin Stuart to wed for money, but I do think it would be mighty sweet if he'd fall in love with a girl of means."

Georgiana's pale blue eyes looked like a cat's following the overhead flight of a redbird.

"You came home first last night," she said. "Stuart came later."

"Why honey, 'course he came later. Although how you knew that! Mean to say you were lyin' wakeful all through the night hours?"

"He stayed with her?"

"He wasn't out coon huntin', honey. Why shouldn't he linger behind after the party? The Trevelyan garden is sweet-beautiful this season. And that full moon last night was silver-luscious. It was indeed."

In the midst of this chitchat Georgiana arose unexpectedly and left the dining room. She didn't reply when Cordelia asked, "Where you goin', honey?" Feeling as if nettles had lodged beneath her skin, she went to the front veranda and flopped into a chair. Angry tears were seeking to pry themselves into her slitted eyes. Her fingers clenched and her foot tapped the floor. She looked moody and waspish. Presently she left the porch and wandered into the garden, not to admire the marigolds and petunias, but to sit tight-mouthed on a bench, boiling with resentment.

Not yet had she seen this Eulalia Delacroix, but already she hated her. And she hated Penelope Trevelyan for inviting her here. She hated them separately and she hated them together, for girls like that had everything she wanted, clothes and money to travel away from a stupid town like Winchester.

Money. That, she thought, was what counted in this world. For a long time now she had nursed a grudge against her family because they didn't have it. With money you could go to St. Louis and board a steamboat for New Orleans and wander with a young man beneath the live oaks while snows blew across Winchester. Or in July you could travel to French Lick Springs or to Cincinnati and thence to some fashionable watering place in the Virginia mountains. You could be attended by a personal maid and travel with trunks of beautiful clothes. Eulalia Delacroix had brought one trunk to Winchester. One trunk, indeed! Georgiana's mouth curled. With Eulalia's money she would have brought a half-dozen. She would have changed dresses every hour and filled with envy every girl in Winchester.

Money. She thought of her family. Her mouth curled again. She was a clear-headed girl with a steel-trap brain, and for a long time she had seen through them. Her father was too lazy to live. A gentleman; oh yes, a gentleman. But a gentleman without money was a general without a sword. Her mother was utterly inconsequential, as simple as a child. Since she could walk Georgiana had been able to pull the wool over her mother's eyes. And May; moon-struck May! The state maintained institutions for girls like May, where they were kept hidden so they couldn't drift in when you had guests and tell what some sycamore tree had said. As for her other sisters, she supposed they were all right, but they accepted penniless gentility as their lot. Grandmother Kelvin had died five years ago; she no longer counted. There remained Stuart.

Her mood softened. She reckoned she had loved him as long as she could remember, but when she was a little girl it was a different love from this she had experienced the last few years. This was love that wanted moonlight and passionate kisses. He used to kiss her, long ago, but she had been a child then and they were playful caresses. She was no longer a child, despite the way the family treated her. She was a woman.

Eulalia Delacroix was a tall, graceful girl whose hair and skin were tinted with the most subtle palette colors. Her hair was neither red nor yellow, but a mouth-watering blend of both. Stuart thought of it as golden beach sand flushed warm with the glow from an orange sunset.

Instantly she attracted him, and he lingered on after the party to walk with her in the Trevelyan garden and suggest that they go horseback riding the next afternoon. She agreed at once. When she had accepted Penelope's invitation to visit Winchester, she had expected to rusticate for two weeks. She supposed the Winchester young men would be country bumpkins. But here was Stuart Kelvin, handsome as an oil painting, witty as any St. Louis man, courtly, exquisitely mannered, and given to quoting gypsy poetry. It was a balmy July night with a brilliant lovers' moon reflecting itself in the lily pool; spicy scents from the flower beds sifted through the windless air; and as they sat on a stone bench and gazed at the silver-tipped trees she found herself already half in love with him.

Strolling homeward, Stuart bared his head and pulled the summer darkness deep into his chest. He felt moon-struck and intoxicated. Even if she had not been the daughter of a wealthy lawyer he would have loved her, but certainly her father's position did not irk him. He resolved to settle down and study the law in earnest, so he could pass the bar and enter her father's firm as a junior partner and ride horseback through St. Louis parks. And he was glad and glad again he had eluded Georgiana's determined pursuit. He told himself he would indeed be in a pretty pickle if he had yielded. But he had battled triumphantly and she had no hold on him.

During the next fortnight Eulalia and Stuart wandered deeper and deeper into the mists of love. To every party in her honor he escorted her; and on the evenings when no party was held he called at the Trevelyans'. Almost every afternoon they rode horseback. Unlike Georgiana, she preferred a gentle horse, so he mounted Blackie and she rode Princess.

They were secretly engaged by the time Eulalia had spent ten days in Winchester. Soon she must return home, but they planned that Stuart would visit St. Louis in September and meet her family; and he would study hard and pass the bar and they would be married the following June. Where would he practice? St. Louis, of course.

"I think Winchester is a most charming little village," Eulalia said, "but I just don't believe I could bring myself to live here. Not after St. Louis."

She went on to say that she would speak to her father about Stuart's entering his firm. She called her father Papa and she pronounced it Pa*pah*.

"Papa will love to have you. He just dotes on me so sweet he'll do near anything I ask."

Winchester suspected that an engagement would ensue from all Stuart's courting, and these suspicions lifted not only Stuart but the entire Kelvin family in the town's estimation. To his astonished delight, W.C. discovered that his nephew's romance had improved his credit rating with tradesmen, for the financial standing of Eulalia's father was well known, and the butcher and grocer and clothier assumed that out of Stuart's union with Colonel Delacroix's daughter some financial benefit would surely accrue to the Kelvins. W.C. himself assumed as much. The assumption was not sharp and mercenary and schemed-out, but he did find himself filled with a vast sense of financial well-being. All things come to those who wait: that had long been W.C.'s favorite maxim, and from long practice he had perfected the technique of waiting. Taking advantage of the credit transfusion which Colonel Delacroix had unwittingly given, W.C. purchased a new linen suit and a planter's straw hat and another of the narrow, black string-ties that he liked so well. Wearing his new clothes, pacing leisurely around the Square, he felt virtually on intimate terms with Colonel Delacroix already, and he mused how pleasant it would be to run down to St. Louis for a rest from the legal wear and tear and spend a few weeks as the colonel's guest.

Georgiana alone disapproved the match. Day by day she became harder to live with. Her temper was a six-gun trigger filed to explode at a touch. Oftener than ever she burst into tears and ran upstairs to her bedroom. She was stinging as a hornet with her father and mother and Cordelia and poor May, and most of the time she refused to speak to Stuart. She called Maggie a lazy nigger, and Maggie confided angrily to her husband that the child was a caution, as full of poison-sap as an ivy plant. Georgiana brooded and went riding alone, taking her spite out on Blackie till the frightened animal shied at her approach.

In September, Stuart visited Eulalia in St. Louis, and their engagement was announced the next spring, after he passed the bar. They were to be married in June.

Georgiana was moody and unhappy that autumn and winter and spring. She continued pestering Stuart, but fortified by his love he resisted her adamantly. Every evening he went to his office and worked hard behind locked doors. He wrote a daily letter to Eulalia and received a daily reply.

After Cordelia's marriage in October, Georgiana found life duller than ever. More and more she hated the town and yearned to escape. But how? She was without funds; W.C. was without funds. She possessed no skills, and if she managed to raise the railroad fare to St. Louis what could she do? Starve along as a shopgirl? No thank you. Unlike the rest of the family, she couldn't even look forward to visiting Colonel Delacroix at the time of Stuart's wedding, for Eulalia was not fond of her. When the girls met the fur had flown, and Eulalia had plainly stipulated that Georgiana should not attend the wedding.

It was the blackest period she had ever known. Sometimes even the joy of riding Blackie palled, and she took long solitary walks, cutting across the Square and going north past the Farmers' National Bank. The last house she passed belonged to Prentice Nodamoore, a red brick dwelling on the west side of the street. He had lived there alone since his wife's death and his son Harry's moving to Oregon to forget how he had startled poor May. Poor May bosh! Georgiana's mouth curled. May could have been mistress of that house today if she hadn't gone to pieces.

That was an exciting night, when Georgiana brought Ivan Paw-packer to the Kelvins'. Lamps came on all over the house, their rays shafting out into the swarming fog. A lamp was lighted in Maggie's cabin, and presently Maggie herself bustled into the house, flinging up the windows of the downstairs bedroom, smoothing clean sheets on the bed, tucking the fat pillows into crisp pillow cases. By and by, Harmon came inching along the path, accompanied by his floppy-eared hound. Sensing the unusual, the hound now and then elevated his muzzle and released an enormous bay that floated heavenward in a great blossom of sound.

Harmon couldn't be sent for Dr. Bennett; his heels were not the winged ones required in an emergency; so Stuart went. Meanwhile, W.C. and Georgiana aided Ivan Pawpacker toward the house. Harmon accompanied them with a lantern. Using W.C. and Georgiana as crutches, Ive hopped along slowly.

In the bedroom, pain-sweat gleamed on Ive's forehead. His ankle felt as big as a stovepipe and as red-hot. He wanted to get into that inviting bed as quickly as he could. So the women retired and W.C. helped him out of his clothes and into his nightshirt. Then Dr. Bennett and Stuart arrived.

The doctor's fingers were agents of torture, but his verdict was gratifying.

"Nothing broken. But a bad sprain. You won't be using that foot for a while."

There were basins of water and more pain. As Ive lay grimacing he thought of his horses, and he asked about a stable. He wanted the best.

"Reckon Nodamoore has the best," Georgiana said. "Stuart will drive your wagon down there. Don't you worry. We'll take care of everything."

Ive smiled, full of gratitude. He swallowed the sedative which Dr. Bennett gave him, and presently the pain drifted out of his ankle. The doctor had gone; somebody turned down the lamp and blew it out.

"Reckon you'll feel better in the morning," a voice said. "Good night."

It was the girl's voice. Georgiana Kelvin. A lovely, bewitching girl.

"Good night," he murmured. "And thanks."

"You get a good night's sleep," the young voice said, sounding far away in the darkness. "Then you'll feel better."

His eyelids were heavy; he smiled. These people were Samaritans.

His horses would be taken care of. He had no worries. Through the window the scent of flowers drifted from a garden. And now that his ankle was sprained, he would have a good excuse to carry a cane. He had long wanted to. Like Major Redmond.

Those days of illness were the most pleasant in his life. For half a decade he had been an itinerant, a stranger among strangers. Usually he had been lonely, but till now he had not realized how acutely so. Wandering and loneliness were the prices an ambitious young horse trader had to pay while he accumulated capital. He had been willing to pay, for he wanted money more than comfort and friends. You couldn't, his harsh Vermont wisdom told him, get something for nothing. He might have remained in Larkin Corners and married a country girl and never known homesickness, but opportunity was limited there and that meant making money was limited. And making money was his passion. After he acquired it he took care of it, naturally; that was horse sense; but he wasn't abjectly stingy. He bought what he wanted, within reason.

As he lay in bed at the Kelvins', the thought of his capital comforted him. He had enough money to marry and settle down, to own a business and a home, to live in one town and become respected. Those three bank accounts gave him a quiet sense of power. He could make any move he pleased. He was master of his life.

During those first days when he remained in bed, he saw much of Georgiana. Presence of a young man in that downstairs bedroom awakened her more efficiently than any alarm clock. The lordly Kelvin roosters had scarcely bugled up the sun before Georgiana opened her eyes. She lay smiling. She loved having a man all to herself, lying helpless in the room below where no other girls could have at him. He was rather attractive, too. Rather nice. And three bank accounts! Whew!

He was not the man she would have chosen in a perfectly ordered world. He was not Stuart. He was not tall, wide-shouldered, blond. But she had lost Stuart anyway, the idiot. She consoled herself by assuming that Stuart had fallen in love with the Delacroix fortune. Someday he would realize how he had ruined his life when he cold-shouldered Georgiana. That would be a sweet day for her. She'd break his marriage so wide open Eulalia would think a cannonball had struck it. And it would serve Eulalia right—that bag of bones!—for excluding her from the wedding. People just couldn't expect to go through life being mean to other people, Georgiana philosophized, without getting repaid.

But that was in the future and meanwhile she didn't intend becoming a spinster. She knew a good thing when she saw it and three bank accounts were a good thing thrice over. Married to Ive Pawpacker, she would have funds to visit St. Louis, watering at a fashionable hotel, and she would be on hand when Stuart realized he loved her. She might even hasten the coming of that great realization. Perhaps Eulalia Delacroix assumed that excluding her from the wedding was a slight soon to be forgotten, but if so she was mistaken.

Having begun her day with these charitable thoughts, Georgiana sprang from bed, stretched like a silky cat, dressed, and descended to the kitchen. That room was angelic with the odor of Maggie's hot biscuits mingled with the aroma of coffee and sizzling bacon. Georgiana arranged linen and silver on a tray; she even skipped outdoors to pick flowers to decorate it. During her absence, Maggie snorted. If that young white man were wise, he would dispense with Dr. Bennett and call in a good voodoo doctor. Not to cure his ankle; the Lord would do that. But to fix up a charm to fend off Georgiana. "Need the Lawd *and* the devil *and* voodoo," Maggie thought, "to wall him away from her."

During his days in bed, Ive's great concern was not for his ankle but for his horses. Georgiana assured him Nodamoore's stable was the best in town, and Stuart reported the horses seemed in excellent spirits, but he wanted to see for himself. So when on the fourth morning Dr. Bennett brought crutches and told him he could get up, Ive determined to visit the stable.

"You'd better come along," he told Georgiana, who couldn't have been kept home with leg irons.

"Should I?"

"I may need your help. Besides, I promised you a bracelet."

"Oh, Ive! I do relish that bracelet. Are you sure enough going to buy it for me?"

"If you want it."

"I'm just dyin' for it!"

Early that afternoon he and Georgiana set out for the Square. He couldn't have selected a better day to see Winchester for the first time. Rain had fallen the night before, washing the town clean. Now the sun shone cheerfully and the balmy air smelled of mock oranges and peonies.

He thought Winchester the prettiest little town he had ever seen, and Georgiana the most charming girl. He loved her drawl and the odd way she used words. Beneath the silk of her parasol her face and hair were radiant. She chattered happily by his side, warning his crutches against the knotholes in the sidewalk.

They cut across the courthouse lawn, and when Ive sighted Nodamoore's Livery Stable he paused, interested as always in anything concerning horses. It was a long, commodious building. Even the big, solid horse trotting on the weather vane looked prosperous.

"That's a nice layout," he said.

"Best in town."

"Nodamoore must make money."

"Reckon he does. He's getting old now, though, and wants to sell out."

Ive said nothing further because he wanted no one—not even Georgiana—to guess how much he admired the stable.

Prentice Nodamoore was a portly old man with white chin whiskers.

"I'm Pawpacker," Ive said. "I've come to look at my horses."

Nodamoore led the way from the office into the stable, and as Ive followed he passed swift and favorable judgment upon the construction of the building and the number of horses housed there.

His own horses he found in excellent condition, and he told Nodamoore he would be keeping them here a few more days.

"Till this ankle heals. Then I'll move on."

"You're a horse trader?"

"A horse buyer. For Major Redmond of New York State. I've just about finished a buying trip for him. I'll go back to Peoria soon. I'm thinking of going into business there."

"Horse business?"

"That's right."

He started back toward the office, where Georgiana had waited.

"I've got a good business here," Nodamoore said.

Ive said he didn't doubt it.

"But I'm getting old. Reckon I'll be selling out one of these days."

Ive nodded.

"As a matter of fact," Nodamoore added, "I'm putting the business up for sale."

"I'll remember that," Ive said. "If I hear of anyone who's in the market, I'll mention your name."

"Maybe you'd be interested."

"I might have been, two months ago. But I like that layout in Peoria. The deal's still in the dickering stage, but I like the layout."

When Ive moved back toward the Square with Georgiana, Prentice Nodamoore stood in the stable door, reflectively stroking his whiskers.

Grove's General Store where the bracelet was on sale occupied a big building fronting the west side of the Square. Ive and Georgiana stopped at a showcase just inside the door. At a bench facing the front window, a little man sat on a stool, scrutinizing the works of a watch through a jeweler's lens. Georgiana peremptorily tapped the showcase.

While she examined the bracelets, Ive glanced about the store. Ten thousand dollars' worth of stock in the dry goods department alone, he estimated. Winchester might be a small town, but to support a store like this it must be a prosperous trading center. A county seat. Farmers driving in to court and to pay taxes. Driving in. That meant business for a stable.

He imagined himself owning the stable; he'd hire a good man to manage it when he visited neighboring county seats to buy and sell. Tomorrow he'd go to the stable again—merely, of course, to check up on his horses—and perhaps Prentice Nodamoore would set a price on his business. By using his wits he had placed himself in an excellent bargaining position. Whatever the price, he'd beat it down. He doubted whether he had enough capital to buy the stable outright, but when the time came he would go to the Farmers' National Bank and swing a loan. The stable would secure the loan. It was good business to hire a thousand dollars to work for you at wages of sixty dollars a year. That was what the mumbo jumbo of borrowing at interest boiled down to: hiring dollars the way you hired men. He liked to keep everything simple.

Of course, to hire dollars you had to convince their owner you were trustworthy, but he didn't anticipate difficulty there. The money he had saved would do that. Long ago he had figured out that the way to get rich was to save diligently till you had a sum to use as working capital. After that, you could borrow. After that, you could scarcely help becoming well-to-do.

Georgiana was plucking his sleeve.

"Ive—you aren't listening! Look."

She held a bracelet in each hand.

"This old thing," she said, waving the one in her left hand, "was the one I told you about. It's four ninety-five. But this one," she beamed, lifting her right hand, "this one I do relish. It costs more, but I sure enough like it best."

Ive could see no difference between them. Trinkets. But it appeared that girls—those fascinating, mysterious creatures—liked such things. He took the bracelet from her right hand and asked the jeweler:

"What's this worth?"

"Eleven-fifty."

"What will you take for it?"

The jeweler said frostily:

"The price is eleven-fifty."

"I'll give you nine dollars."

The jeweler stared at Ive. Ive stared back. At last the jeweler said: "I might let you have it for eleven."

Ive pursed his lips.

"It's a big price, but I'll give nine-fifty."

The jeweler flushed. He said Grove's Store wasn't in business for its health. Ive replied he had gathered as much. And he offered:

"Nine seventy-five."

The jeweler shook his head.

Ive crackled a ten-dollar bill to the counter.

"That's as high as I'll go. If you don't want to sell for that, we'll take the four ninety-five one."

The jeweler said:

"I'm losing money, but you can have it for ten."

When he took it to his bench for wrapping, Georgiana gazed at Ive with mirth and amazement.

"You're wonderful!" she whispered. "I do declare! I've never seen the like!"

"Do you mean you always pay the first price they ask?"

"I just never did dream you could buy for less."

"The easiest way to make a dollar and a half," he said, "is to save it."

She touched his arm.

"Reckon Daddy wouldn't think it gentlemanly to buy that way. But he wouldn't have the money to buy me a bracelet. It's right handsome of you to give me such a nice gift."

When the jeweler returned, Ive asked whether the store sold canes. They were referred to the men's clothing department. There Ive selected a dark stick with a gold head.

So now he owned a cane. Like Major Redmond. It aided him greatly, once his ankle was well enough so he could discard the crutches, and he continued carrying it after his ankle was completely healed. In a town like Winchester, a cane-swinging young man would ordinarily have been jeered at; but while he needed its support people grew used to seeing him with it, and when he kept on using it they assumed his ankle had been weakened by the sprain and that he must occasionally find it necessary.

Walking home that afternoon, Georgiana warned Ive against mentioning the bracelet to the Kelvins. She explained that her mother and father harbored old-fashioned ideas; they would doubt the propriety of a young lady's accepting jewelry from a young man to whom she was not engaged.

"They think I'm terrible anyhow," she said. "They don't think I should wear riding pants even at night."

Actually she was quite unworried about her parents' reaction to the bracelet: it was only her fondness for deception and intrigue which prompted her to keep it a secret. Moreover, this seemed a good opportunity to dangle an engagement before Ive.

His cheeks warmed at her mention of the pants, and in imagination he saw her as she looked by the campfire. And he tingled with the realization that if all went well he might take this girl as his bride.

"But I'd like to see you wear the bracelet," he said.

She flashed him a brilliant smile, and her eyes were as full of promise as a harem.

"I'll wear it next week. Next Tuesday they're leaving for St. Louis. Daddy and Mamma and Stuart. For his old wedding. That will leave just you and me at home. And May, of course. But she won't mind."

Excitement filled him as he thought of being alone in the house with Georgiana and May. May didn't count: already he had heard her tell about her fascinating conversations with trees. This was Friday. Four days till Tuesday.

"I'd like to see you wear it before that," he said.

She smiled secretly.

"Maybe you will."

"When?"

"Now don't tease."

"When?"

"Maybe tonight. Reckon I might come down and show it to you after the rest have gone to bed."

Her words were innocent enough, but her manner flavored them with enigma and promise. The remainder of the day, resting in his bedroom, he wondered whether she meant more than she said.

It was late. In the Kelvin house only the youngest daughter and the guest were wakeful.

Even Ive was not very wakeful. He lay on the bed drowsy but somewhat vexed, for by this time he despaired of Georgiana's coming. Then his gaze chanced on the door to the hall and he beheld the knob turning. It made no sound, for Georgiana's movements were as sly as a cat's in the night. As the door inched open she held a forefinger on her lips.

The door closed and she slipped over and sat down beside him on the bed.

"See?" she whispered, lifting her wrist and displaying the bracelet.

Ive saw the bracelet, and more too; for just as Georgiana was ahead of her time in the matter of riding costume so did she hold advanced ideas as to what a girl should wear when calling on a young man in his bedroom. She was attired in a white nightgown.

"I thought you were never coming," Ive said.

"I had to wait till they were all asleep, didn't I? Reckon they wouldn't like it if they knew I was here."

In the lamplight her hair and skin were flawless. Ive's breathing was swift and his very tonsils quivered with excitement. She seemed unaware of his perturbation as she sat with her wrist aloft, twisting it slowly and admiring the bracelet.

"It was sure enough nice of you to buy it for me," she whispered. "You won the bet. Why did you buy it for me?"

"Maybe because I like you."

"Do you, Ive?"

"You know I do. Do you like me?"

Her glance slid toward him from the corners of half-lidded eyes, and her smile curled teasingly.

"Maybe."

"Don't you know?"

"Maybe."

"Don't you know any other word but maybe?"

"Maybe."

She laughed then, like a child delighted by some foolish game. He slipped an arm around her waist, under her arm.

"I'd best go," she said.

"Don't go yet."

"I'd best."

He kissed her.

"Honey," she whispered at last, "you're sweet. But I'd best go."

"No. Please not yet."

"Yes."

He kissed her again.

She pulled away and stood up. But he still clasped her hand.

"I'd best go," she said. "Let me go."

"No."

He had remained seated because of his ankle. She smiled poutingly down at him.

"You'd best let me go."

"No. Please not yet."

"I'll do something bad if you don't."

He misunderstood her meaning and gripped her hand harder.

"I warned you I'd do something bad," she smiled, and kicked his sprained ankle.

Ive yowled.

She clapped a palm over his mouth.

"Sh-h-h! Do you want to wake the house?"

Pain-sweat had broken out on his forehead, and he glared at her.

She removed her palm and pressed her lips against his. After that kiss the hostility left his eyes.

"You shouldn't have kicked my ankle," he said.

"You shouldn't have held my hand when I said I had to go."

"But it might be bad for my ankle."

"It might be bad for me to stay, too," she said, witchery in her smile.
He was gripping her hand again.

"One more kiss," he pleaded.

"No."

"One more."

"No."

"Please."

"Well—just one."

She sat by his side and Ive lost himself in the kiss. He thought it was
like diving from a dizzy height through warm golden air.

She stood up abruptly.

"I'm going now," she said crossly. "If your hands can't behave I'm
going."

Ive looked down at his offending hands.

"Don't go. Please, not yet."

"I think I'd best."

"Please, not yet."

"You're bad," she said.

"You're beautiful."

"You're very bad."

"You're very beautiful."

Her face lighted.

"You're nice," she smiled. "I like you."

"How much?"

"Very much."

"Enough," he heard himself asking, "to marry me?"

Her eyes widened.

"Ive!" she whispered.

"I love you," he said.

"Reckon that's what you tell all the girls."

"No! Georgiana. I love you. Will you marry me?"

She sank to the bed.

"My goodness! Reckon you've taken my breath."

"Didn't you know I cared that much?"

"I had no idea."

"I think you're lovely," he whispered. "And beautiful. And sweet."

She smiled dreamily.

"Will you marry me, Georgiana?"

"Maybe . . . I don't know."

"Why don't you know?"

"I'd want to think about it."

"When will you know?"

"I'd want to think about it a few days. I'll let you know—next week. I'll let you know Tuesday. After the folks leave for St. Louis."

"If your answer's yes, could we be married right away?"

"Maybe."

"The day you tell me yes?"

"Maybe."

He kissed her. At last she stood up again.

"Those hands! Those bad hands!" But she smiled when she said it. He grinned.

"I reckon," she said, "they think we're married already."

"I wish we were."

"Well we aren't. And I'll have to go."

"I wish we were married tonight."

"You're terrible," she said.

"I can't help it. I wish we were."

She laughed softly. "Don't you, though!"

And she leaned forward and brushed her lips across his mouth and then darted out of reach before he could grab her.

"You'd pay for that," he said, "if it weren't for this ankle."

"Would I?" she smiled teasingly.

And once again she leaned forward. This time he caught her and pulled her down beside him. After a few kisses she said:

"Let me go now."

"No."

"I'll kick your ankle."

"Darling," he said, "you wouldn't do that."

"I'm going to," she said impishly.

Instantly, he released her. He was learning.

She jumped up.

"Good night," she said.

"One more."

"No."

"Just a good-night kiss?"

"That last one," she said, "was our good-night kiss. And here's another."

She kissed her fingertips and blew.

"That's your good-night kiss," she smiled, opening the door and disappearing into the hall.

Ive lay awake for hours.

The following Tuesday morning, after Stuart and Eliza and W.C. boarded the train for St. Louis, Ive hitched his team to a light buggy rented from Prentice Nodamoore. With Georgiana he drove to a neighboring county seat, and that afternoon a judge married them.

After the ceremony, Georgiana dispatched a telegram to her parents in St. Louis. It pleased her to think of Stuart's face when he heard the news and realized she had outdistanced him into wedlock by four days.

Their bridal night they passed in a wooden hotel near the courthouse where they were declared man and wife. Neither slept well, owing to the unfortunate presence of bedbugs in the room. Upon returning to Winchester, they found May and Maggie beside themselves with worry about Georgiana's disappearance.

"Married?" May gasped. "Well I never!"

"What do you mean by runnin' off and lettin' us worry ourselves gray?" Maggie scolded.

Georgiana tossed her head.

"I'm married now. I don't have to answer to anybody, now."

" 'Cept your husband. You'll answer to him."

Georgiana laughed.

Ten days later, after hours of bargaining with Prentice Nodamoore and more hours of consultation with the president of the Farmers' National Bank, Ivan Pawpacker came into possession of the livery stable and feed lot, as well as various traps and four-wheelers and an amorous stallion and an even more amorous jack. By the same deal, which mortgaged Ive up to his eyebrows but left him a good sum of working capital, he acquired Nodamoore's house, completely furnished. He even acquired responsibility for a Negro couple who had served Nodamoore as Maggie and Harmon served the Kelvins. Their names were Uncle Meredith and Aunt Acacia; and although Ive didn't feel that a young couple just getting started needed servants, it was fortunate for his stomach that Aunt Acacia remained to prepare meals. Georgiana, of course, knew nothing about cooking; and she evinced not the remotest interest in learning.

Their first violent quarrel took place the Saturday following their marriage. It concerned nothing at all, but it ended with a flung shoe clipping Ive's ear. It was quite coincidental that the quarrel brewed itself at 4 P.M., the hour of Stuart's wedding in St. Louis.

From the beginning Ive made money with the livery stable. The burden of debt rested lightly on his shoulders, probably because he continued to think of borrowed dollars as hired dollars. As soon as possible, of course, he wanted to pay off his bank loans, so he worked hard; harder than any three men in Winchester; harder than five hundred W.C.'s.

Ruthlessly he reorganized the livery stable, discharging two hostlers, hiring others at less pay, hiring a responsible manager. Soon after taking over he informed the lazy hangers-on who cluttered up the office that they would have to loaf elsewhere. These moves roused some ill-feeling against him in Winchester; people said he was a cold, calculating, money-getting Yankee; but he didn't care. He wanted money and lots of it. He knew that loafers in the office would impair his efficiency as he sat concentrating on figures; so out went the loafers. He had little time for anything but business. In those first years while he was getting out of debt people learned it was useless to invite him to go hunting or fishing; he was too busy. After slightly more than three years he paid the last of his loan at the bank.

"Mr. Pawpacker," the president said, "you're the best risk I ever had. You can have anything you want at this institution."

"Thanks," Ive said; but it never occurred to him to ask for happiness from the bank, because he realized banks did not keep happiness locked in their vaults.

Yet there were times during those early years of marriage when he was not unhappy. Now and then, even, he was not unhappy at home. But for the most part he found it wiser to spend more and more time at the livery stable, returning in the evening to sit at his desk and plan his business forays.

As soon as he became convinced that the stable manager could be trusted, Ive resumed his horse-trading travels. A couple of months after marriage he drove from Winchester in his lumber wagon, several horses following. At that time he still had hopes that the marriage would turn out well after all, and he invited Georgiana to accompany him. Her mouth curled.

"Reckon I don't relish traipsing around the country in a wagon," she said crossly. "I don't see why we can't visit St. Louis."

"We have to stick to business. Till we're out of debt."

"Business. That's all you think about."

He didn't argue further, for he had learned that anger came easily to his wife, and often she threw things.

He set out lightheartedly on that first trip, but by evening he found himself lonely for Georgiana. The farther he drove from Winchester the more unimportant their quarrels seemed. He remembered the times when she had been good-natured. So he returned home ahead of schedule and rushed into the house.

"Well, my goodness," she said. "What are you doing back so soon?"

"I was lonesome for you."

After permitting him to kiss her she said:

"Reckon it's a good thing you came back. You didn't leave me near enough money."

So they were arguing again.

Indeed, money inspired many of those early battles, so at last Ive opened a separate bank account for Georgiana. Often she overdrew. This distressed him. He told her she had no money sense, and they were at it again.

Presently Ive's trips were lasting ten days, two weeks. Both were happier when he was gone. He knew more about women now, and sometimes when a girl smiled at him on the street of a strange town he considered making her acquaintance. But he didn't. He was still hoping for the miracle that would turn a bad marriage good.

At the end of one trip he found not Georgiana waiting for him, but a note. It announced that she had taken the train to St. Louis for a short visit.

She returned enthusiastic about St. Louis; she would enjoy living there. She said she had looked up Stuart Kelvin; he was fine. From the city, Georgiana brought back many newfangled notions. Most significant was the fashion for a husband and wife to occupy separate bedrooms. Never one to lag behind the times, Georgiana instituted this custom in her own household, moving all Ive's belongings from the large front bedroom where they had made love as a bridal couple to a smaller bedroom at the back of the house. Ive could discover nothing commendable in this vogue, but Georgiana was not to be dissuaded. The lock on the front bedroom was excellent, and she used it. Next time Ive made a horse-trading trip he struck up an interesting acquaintance with a pretty chambermaid.

Georgiana's visits to St. Louis became more frequent and longer as the years went by. At last she rented a flat there. She was really a St. Louis woman then, who made short visits to Winchester. This took more money, but by that time Ive considered money well-spent if it kept Georgiana away. He had stopped loving her, had stopped hating her. She had become only an annoyance, the embodiment of a mistake he had made as an inexperienced youth. He had not, however, stopped loving. In a county seat fifty miles away he met a widow a few years his senior, and presently she moved unobtrusively to Winchester, occupying a small house a block from Ive's. After the town went to bed he called on her. They were lovers. More important, they were great friends. She wasn't even very pretty, but Ive no longer believed in the essential goodness of beauty. She never stamped her foot. She never burst into tears and threw movable objects. She never nagged him for more money. She possessed an abundant good nature and an astonishing ability as a cook. After making love they returned to the sitting room, where she served him cold chicken and bun-bread and cookies. Then he lighted a cigar and they sat behind drawn shades, playing checkers. It didn't bother her when he won.

Sometimes he thought of divorcing Georgiana, but divorce was a disgrace in the most quiet circumstances, and he knew that if he began action Georgiana would fight it tooth and claw. There would be scandal. And probably Georgiana would even ferret out his relationship with the widow, Etta Rogers. He discussed it with Etta, offering to marry her once he was free. But she shook her head. They were happy as they were, she said. Why should he risk the agony of a divorce case? Let things drift. He had grown his mustache and short beard by that time, and he stroked them as he listened to her counsel.

His renown as a judge of horses spread, and presently a great firm of horse dealers in St. Louis commissioned him to buy for them. So occasionally business took him to St. Louis, and he called several times at Georgiana's flat. Not that he wished to see her, or that she wished to see him. But he knew she would feel slighted and be furious if she learned he had been in town without paying her a call.

The small flat seemed stuffy to Ive, with its raspberry carpet and plush furniture, its cuckoo clock and its cluttered whatnot, its voluptuous cushions and its oak center table bearing a dish of artificial fruit. But she seemed to enjoy living there with her high-yaller maid. On the mantel Ive noticed Stuart Kelvin's picture. He looked well-fed and well taken care of.

Evidently Georgiana and her cousin were on the best of terms, for Ive's keen eyes detected a number of Stuart's belongings in the flat. Several law books. A brief case with his name stamped in gold. A half-empty package of the pipe tobacco he preferred. Ive smiled with that quiet irony which was becoming his companion.

Years of toil in the Inns of Court had wearied W.C., so late in the 1890's he retired. To this event the *Winchester Enterprise* devoted a great deal of space. Headlines on page one said: Hon. W. C. Kelvin Retires from Active Practice. Prominent Barrister Will Devote Time to Study. The news story occupied more than a column; the editor let himself go, recounting how W.C. had served in the Confederate army and in the legislature; and after reading the story, people felt that a great man had been living in their midst.

Those sundown years were pleasant. Stuart and Ive agreed to share in the Kelvins' support; but off in St. Louis, Stuart had big expenses, keeping up with Society, rearing three children; so most of the Kelvin livelihood came from Ive's checkbook. He didn't begrudge the money, for he grew fond of his family-in-law. Nearly every Sunday he dined with them, and after the meal he and W.C. would sit on the gallery, smoking and discussing Shakespeare and mules and national affairs. Far from dimming W.C.'s memory, the passing years brightened it: he kept recalling more and more battles in which he had participated during The War, and more and more important pieces of legislation which he had helped shape.

Georgiana's visits to Winchester had long since ceased, and Ive was just as glad. He settled deeper and deeper into his money-making routine; into his routine of calling on Etta Rogers. The Boer War came along; agents of the English government visited the United States, booming the market in horses and mules; and Ive made money hand over fist. He bought the pasture stretching north from his house and erected big barns, for his livery stable could no longer accommodate the great number of animals he assembled at Winchester for shipping. And at this time a shabby little circus wandered into town and expired.

Wanting the horses, he acquired the show. That was the beginning of new adventures. And then one day in a St. Louis paper he read of a circus that had gone broke in Illinois and was to be sold under the sheriff's hammer. He made a quick trip to Illinois, and when he returned he owned a fairly large circus, complete with railroad cars. Side track was laid into his pasture from the branch line serving Winchester, and presently a string of gaudy circus cars stood there, waiting to be sold to showmen.

But he didn't let his new adventure interfere with his business in horses and mules. He still made buying trips. And now he actually was a horse buyer and not a horse trader. He was known and respected by farmers and livery stable proprietors in several states. Before he visited a town he sent an advertisement to the weekly paper, announcing he would buy horses at a certain stable on a certain day. Farmers brought in their horses and gaped at this quiet, fastidiously dressed man who carried a walking stick and sized up an animal without even examining his teeth.

It was on such a trip when, in a county-seat town, he read how the *Tamarack Beacon* was sponsoring the purchase of an elephant. Next day he met Gus Burgoyne.

From the first, Burgoyne amused him, puzzled him, tickled his vanity. Was he a rogue? A mere bag of wind? What was he up to? Why did the mention of elephants always make him sputter and bluster? Ive liked him. He began to smile as soon as he sighted Gus striding like a serio-comic emperor through a hotel lobby. All at once life seemed a robust affair. A grab-bag full of surprises. Romantic. Something to be enjoyed to the hilt. Ive found that even if he were weary from travel, a few minutes with Gus acted like a strong tonic. You had to brace yourself lest his enthusiasm sweep you off your feet. He was a born showman; and when he puffed his cigar and grinned infectiously and outlined some earth-shaking project you felt a conspirator in some comic and mouth-watering adventure, as if you were a pair of small boys planning a raid on a melon patch.

It might be, Ive thought, that he could use Gus someday. First let him take out a show and get experience (on his own money) and then hitch up with him in a partnership. If he could be trusted. Well, he had married money now; perhaps that would steady him.

But for more than two years after attending the wedding, Ive lost touch with Gus. Once in passing through Tamarack he telephoned Funland Park, but a workman answered and said Mr. Burgoyne was out of town. So Ive returned to Winchester without seeing him. And as the months passed, busy as he was with his own affairs, he forgot him.

And then one autumn afternoon in 1906, at his desk in the livery stable office, Ive heard the door burst open, and a familiar, hearty voice boomed greetings.

"Well, well! Ive Pawpacker! How are you, Ive?"

He turned and beheld Gus striding in, bigger than ever, exuding prosperity and good health and powerful laughter.

Gus seized Ive's hand and pumped it.

"Here I am! Just like I said I'd be when I was ready for a circus! By golly, but it's good to see you! Here! Have a cigar!"

10

Funland park had prospered under Gus Burgoyne's brisk management. No longer did Mr. Oxenford's clerks uncork the red ink when they prepared a financial statement at the end of a season. Indeed, the park was showing more profits on capital invested than any dominion in Mr. Oxenford's empire. This bewildered the old man, for he still could not comprehend the improvidence of people shelling out money for merry-go-round journeys. Where did it get them?

But it delighted him, too, although he concealed his joy behind yellow whiskers and flinty eyes.

"Ain't a bad showing," he told Gus. "Maybe next year you can do better. Your expenses are a caution. If you could just pare them down!"

"What do you want?" Gus growled. "A hundred dollars profit on every dollar I spend?"

And although Mr. Oxenford realized this was sarcasm, his eyes lighted and his dry palms rustled together.

"That's it! Ain't a bad goal at all! Keep it in mind when you're tempted to spend money."

The 1905 season at the park had closed, and they were sitting in Mr. Oxenford's private office on the fifteenth floor of the new Oxenford Electric Building. The battered old desk and seedy chairs looked beggarly in the bright, fireproof office.

"Ain't no need at all to buy new furniture," Mr. Oxenford had declared, when he moved in. "Lots of wear left in this desk."

His thrifty fondness for old things, Gus thought, went to fantastic lengths. Why couldn't the old man buy a new suit, or at least send this one to a cleaner? With its shiny elbows and grease-specked vest it looked like something a secondhand dealer had cast aside. Nor were Mr. Oxenford's shoes the proper footgear for a business leader. A network of cracks crisscrossed the cheap leather. They had been blacked and blacked again, not at a shining establishment, but in the kitchen at home. Mr. Oxenford was his own valet, and every morning he energetically buffed them. Not vanity but economy directed his purchase of blacking. "Preserves the leather," he said. "Polish is cheaper than shoes."

Soon after Gus moved into the house, Mr. Oxenford advised him to form a similar habit. Eying Gus's oxfords, he observed:

"Them shoes of yours have a nice polish. Do it yourself?"

"There's a kid downtown I usually hire," Gus said.

"What do you pay him?"

"A dime."

Mr. Oxenford clawed his whiskers.

"Now look here, Gus. This is a lesson in practical thrift. Say you hire him five times a week. That's fifty cents. And say you have it done fifty weeks in a year. That amounts to—Land o' Goshen—that amounts to twenty-five dollars!"

"The kid has to make a living," Gus said. "He quit school when his old man was killed in an accident."

"Twenty-five dollars a year! That's the interest on five hundred dollars at five percent. See how money gets away from a man if he don't watch sharp?"

Gus was more amused than annoyed, for he was still a newcomer under Mr. Oxenford's roof. But as the days passed and the old man continued nagging him, his amusement evaporated and his annoyance boiled into anger. A scene ensued, the first of many, for Mr. Oxenford considered it his duty to plug the leaks in his son-in-law's purse. Gus roared and boomed, and finally Mr. Oxenford retired sullenly behind his whiskers and grumbled:

"I was just trying to advise you. Land o' Goshen! Don't know where I'd got if I'd gone scattering money like a drunken sailor."

After that, his references to shoe-polishing were oblique.

"Been up for hours," he would announce at breakfast. "Gave my shoes a good polish. It'd surprise you how long shoes will last, if you ain't too proud to use a little elbow grease."

Before marriage, Gus had been enticed by living in the great house on Wellington Avenue, but in practice it disturbed his domestic tranquillity. Mr. Oxenford remained head of the house, and Gus felt like a guest. Mr. Oxenford thought he smoked too many cigars and hired too many hacks. If Gus bought a copy of the *Beacon* instead of waiting to read the copy delivered at the house, Mr. Oxenford pointed out that two pennies had been squandered.

"Gone forever. You'll never get 'em back. Two cents may not seem like much, but it's a year's interest on a dollar at two percent."

Or the old man would comment:

"New necktie you're wearing, ain't it? What did it set you back? How much? A dollar? Land o' Goshen! What's wrong with all them ties you've got already? Lots of wear in 'em yet!"

When Gus bought a new shirt or hat, Mr. Oxenford looked as if he were suffering indigestion, and if the purchase were a new suit the poor old fellow writhed and exclaimed:

"God Almighty! Why I ain't bought a new suit since 1902. And I could buy and sell you a thousand times!"

Gus did not permit these outbursts to go unanswered, and after a quarrel both men were grumpy.

Flora worried about the friction between her father and husband. That first summer of marriage, she would sit for hours rocking and chewing gum, attempting to find a solution. In bed at night she whispered:

"Gus."

"Uh?"

"You asleep?"

"Uh . . . Just dropping off, I guess."

"Gus, I'm worried."

"What about?"

"About you and Papa."

"What about us?"

"About the way you spat. You shouldn't, Gus."

"What do you mean, *I* shouldn't? He starts it. I can't spend a penny without—"

"I know. But you shouldn't cross him. It makes him mad."

"Well, by God! It makes me mad, too."

"It's just his way, Gus. He hates to see money wasted."

"I don't waste it."

Flora did not respond.

"I suppose you think I waste it," Gus said.

"I know Papa's careful about money," Flora said, "but you do spend a lot, Gus. You know you do."

Gus sat up and swore. "Now you're starting it. You're as bad as the old man."

"Don't swear, Gus. Please don't swear. I love you, Gus. And I'm not as bad as Papa. I'm sure I'm not."

"You think I smoke too much," Gus said.

"It's just because I don't want your liver upset."

"Hell and damnation! There's nothing wrong with my liver. What ever got it into your head my liver was upset?"

"Because you smoke too much. Smoking too much upsets the liver. That's true, Gus. Everyone knows it's true."

They went round and round, till Gus was fuming. Not Flora. She seldom lost her temper. Sometimes Gus wished she would. But she had the even disposition of a milch cow, and about the same abilities at logical reasoning.

At last Gus found his slippers and left bed.

"Can't sleep, now. All upset. Damn it, why did you want to upset me?"

"I didn't, Gus. Smoking does it. Smoking upsets your liver."

Not trusting himself to respond, he groped to the door and padded along the upper corridor, kitchen-bound. At the head of the stairs he snapped a switch that lighted the downstairs hall. But no light came. So he felt his way down, and in the black lower hall he barked his shins. Swore. Then a terrible suspicion entered his thoughts, and he pawed till he located the light fixture depending from the hall ceiling. The bulb was loose in the socket; he twisted it; light came on.

"Well I'll be damned," he muttered.

The old man had hit upon another device for saving money. He had unscrewed the bulb against the careless servants and his careless son-in-law; he wasn't going to have a light burning needlessly in the hall. Some time ago, a dishonest salesman from the public utilities company falsely told Mr. Oxenford that he would save money by having the gas fixtures wired for electricity. He exhibited figures to prove his contention, and Mr. Oxenford yielded. But when the first electric bill came he found he had been tricked. The world was full of robbers and thieves. Preying on honest men! After that bill, Mr. Oxenford preached the gospel of turning off lights. Flora was converted and preached the gospel also, but Gus did not heed.

Leaving the light burning, Gus entered the dining room, switched on the chandelier, pushed through the swinging door to the kitchen. From the icebox he brought milk, butter, cheese, cold beefsteak. Food always cheered him. After swallowing a great quantity, he went to the veranda and sat smoking. The July night was so warm that he felt comfortable clad only in his nightshirt.

He thought of Funland Park, of how successfully he was operating it this first season. And his thoughts dreamed ahead to next year. He would have a circus, then. He had been biding his time, proving he could wrest great profits from the amusement business. He was certain that once the season's profits from Funland were computed, Mr. Oxenford would be glad to back him in the circus venture.

Gus had never been lazy, and that first season he worked as obstreperously as a locomotive. He thundered gladly from bed, as zestful as a 6 A.M. whistle. At the open window he stripped off his nightshirt and cleansed his lungs with great draughts of fresh oxygen. His fists thumped his enormous chest and then—a true believer in Theodore Roosevelt's Strenuous Life—he launched into setting-up exercises. He was persuaded that the calisthenics benefited him more when accom-

panied by audible testimonials of their rigor, and hence Flora was
awakened by vast puffings and grunts and groans as her husband
sought to touch the carpet without bending his knees.

Although a large girl, Flora was scarcely more muscular than a
hundred and fifty pounds of jelly; she had never sought to develop her
sinews; and on that first morning in a Chicago hotel room, upon awak-
ening from love-opiated slumber, she was startled by her husband's
groans. She blinked and gazed toward the window. Then suddenly
she emitted a cry of shame and buried her face in the pillow. In spirit
she was still a maiden, and the glimpse of her unclad groom shocked
her.

But now, after several months of marriage, she was used to Gus's
morning gymnastics, and she lay watching with interest and admiration. Sometimes she asked:

"How many times did you touch the floor?"

"Hoo! Huh? Oh. Fifteen. Hoo!"

"You seem to work awful hard at it, Gus. Think it's good for you
to strain yourself that way?"

"Hoo! Ah-h-h! Huh?"

"I said you seem to strain awful hard. If you strain so hard something might snap."

"Huh-uh. Good for me. Start the day right."

"It might put a strain on your liver."

But by then Gus—stretched face-down and shoving himself up and
down with bulging biceps—was too engaged to respond.

The calisthenics over, he thudded along the hall to the bathroom.
Recently some sadistic wretch had published an article advocating icy
showers, and so presently from beyond the bathroom door came bel-
lows and howls. You would have thought it Mr. Oxenford just discovering his error in purchasing Brooklyn Bridge.

Gus's morning toilet did not include shaving, for every afternoon
he went to a downtown barber shop patronized by Tamarack business
leaders. A regular customer, he was accorded the honor of a private
shaving mug. It stood in a cabinet along with those of other consequential men, a handsome white mug with "A. H. Burgoyne" lettered
in gold.

"Ever considered growing a beard?" Mr. Oxenford once asked.

"Beard? Not for me. Too old-fashioned."

Mr. Oxenford bristled.

"May be old-fashioned but it's practical. Economical, too. Whiskers
will come back. You wait and see."

"Don't think so," Gus said. And some jovial imp made him add,
"People are driving automobiles now. Whiskers get in the way."

"Automobiles!" Mr. Oxenford nearly shouted the word. "That ain't no argument at all! Automobiles! Nothing but a fad. Won't last. Too much expense. A dying fad."

"See more of them all the time, though."

That, Mr. Oxenford pointed out, was because the manufacturers had sought out all the fools who happened to have money. The supply of fools would soon be exhausted. Then automobiles would vanish into bad memory.

"Ought to ban 'em from the public streets," Mr. Oxenford declared. "A common nuisance—that's all they are. Just a common nuisance." Having thus disposed of the gasoline engine, Mr. Oxenford returned to whiskers. "A man spends a lot of money buying shaves. Even if he shaves himself the outlay is considerable. Razor and strop and soap. If I was in your place, Gus, I'd give a beard serious thought."

"I like a smooth face."

"Well then, why can't you shave yourself? Land o' Goshen! Barbers run into money fast. Now I realize a good razor's considerable expense too, but once you've got it you've got it. Something to show for your money. You buy a shave and what have you got? A smooth face. But you ain't got it tomorrow! You're right back where you started, tomorrow. And your money's gone. Ain't that logic?"

"Sure. But I like a barber shop. You get on friendly terms with important people."

"Fiddle-faddle! Important fools! They're looking out for themselves. They ain't looking out for you. You save your pennies, Gus, and pretty soon they'll be flocking around you. Don't have to seek them. They'll seek you. Flies will always buzz around molasses, and if you've got money they'll come buzzing."

Mr. Oxenford stroked his whiskers, and hard humor gleamed in his eyes.

"Take me, Gus. When I come to Tamarack there was plenty of young dandies who wouldn't have thought I was good enough to harness their horses. And plenty of flibbertigibbet girls who wouldn't have let me pick 'em out of a mud puddle. Did it fuss me?"

Mr. Oxenford snorted.

" 'Course it didn't. Leastwise not much. I just minded my p's and q's and saved my pennies and kept my eyes peeled and my mouth shut. I worked from sunup to dark and I got my sleep. Let them dandies with their fancy vests take them flimflam girls to dances! I saved my money."

"Guess you did, at that," Gus grinned.

"You bet I did!" Mr. Oxenford exclaimed, warming to his favorite subject. "I saved and I scrimped and I was industrious. Industry, Thrift and Integrity! Them's the cornerstones. Can't beat 'em! And I lived to see a lot of them dandies hired out to me. Didn't used to

notice me, but they notice me now! It's 'Good morning, Mr. Oxenford,' now. They speak it as pretty as you please. And they call me
Sir, now, like I was a Dook or one of them English nobles. And me
not good enough to dance with them flippity girls that used to make
eyes at them!"

Mr. Oxenford's eyes hardened, and he said heatedly:

"And what did it? Being economical, that's what! A penny here
and a penny there. Pretty soon you've got a dollar. And that dollar
goes to work and brings interest. Before long you've got a lot of dollars. And the word gets around! You bet it does. Flies will always
smell out molasses. So they come to you with propositions. Most of
them are crooked, but after while a good thing comes along. Like
with me when I organized Tamarack & Northern. You bet! Then
you've got money and you can call the tune. They're dancing now
to your fiddling! Once you've got money you can do anything with
'em. Crack 'em like hickory nuts!"

Gus grinned broadly.

"Get the gold right out of their teeth!" he said, with stingo.

"That's it! Right out of their—" Mr. Oxenford stopped abruptly,
eyes flashing shrewdly. "Well now Gus, not hardly that. Nothing
crooked. I ain't one to break any laws. You got to respect the law.
It's the law that protects a man from them Socialists and Anarchists
and whatnot. The law's your best friend, I always say. But on the
other hand, I say a man's a fool not to take every last advantage the
law allows him. If them lawmakers didn't mean a man to do that
they would have legislated different. That's just horse sense. So I
say walk right up to the edge of the law. Maybe push on it a little.
It'll give, the usual thing, without actually cracking. Get my meaning? And now don't you think it might be wise to shave yourself?"

Always one to be overwhelmed by genuine enthusiasm of any kind,
Gus heard himself saying:

"Sure. Sounds like a great idea. I'll think it over."

But that afternoon he purchased a store shave, as usual.

Funland Park opened late in May and closed early in September.
Since the open season on the public was so short, Gus felt he must
make every minute count, so during the summer his working day began at eight and lasted till midnight. He didn't spend every hour of
this long day within the park; he came and went at will; but even
when he rode downtown or returned home for dinner he ruminated
about park business.

Except for his prompt arrival at work and his remaining till the
last customer left, his schedule was exceedingly flexible. He liked this.
Routine was not for him. Just as he had hated the confinement of the

city desk but had enjoyed his freedom as a reporter, so now he loved
this job where he accounted to nobody—not even Mr. Oxenford—for
how he spent his time.

At first Mr. Oxenford rebuked Gus for this erratic schedule. But
he didn't rebuke him a second time.

"I'm manager," Gus told him. "I'll run things in my own way. You
keep out of it."

"Don't seem businesslike," Mr. Oxenford complained, "for a man
not to be in his office when you ring him on the telephone."

"Shadwell was always in his office, wasn't he?"

"Yep. He stuck to business."

"And he lost you money, didn't he?"

"Land o' Goshen, yes! It was a caution."

"All right! Now look here, Sam. I'm going to make you a fat profit.
But I've got to do it in my own way. I get my best ideas on a streetcar
or in a saloon. Either I run things my own way and make you a good
profit or I quit!"

Profit! Mr. Oxenford cried:

"Now wait, Gus. Hold your horses. Don't get mad. It was just
that I—"

"Don't even think about the park," Gus advised him. "Leave it to
me. It's in good hands."

And this was quite true: never had the park been in better hands.
All through that first summer Gus was forever hatching new schemes
to remind the public of Funland. He organized trolley picnics whereby
some company would sponsor an employee party and take over the
park for an evening. He convinced lodges and patriotic organizations
that they should hold outings at Funland. The fact that the park
owned an elephant was a bargaining weapon of great power. Once
when a lodge held its state convention in Tamarack he permitted
Molly to march in its downtown parade provided the lodge would
designate one day as "Funland Park Frolic Day." And the Tamarack
Police Department held its annual picnic at Funland, greatly to the
uneasiness of the ex-convicts who operated concessions.

Gus faithfully attended the weekly luncheon of the Tamarack Commercial Club (not for another decade would it be known as the
Chamber of Commerce), and when they sang "Tamarack the Beautiful," a composition borrowing extensively from "America the Beautiful," his strong baritone led all the rest. He always sat next to Mr.
Oxenford: they might have been Allah and Mohammed. Other businessmen thought, "Smart young fellow, old Sam's son-in-law. He'll
take hold of things and keep them going when Sam dies."

Once Gus delivered the luncheon address. His subject, "Merry-Go-
Rounds and Eugene Debs," filled the organization with the uneasiness

which any mention of unrest among the lower classes always engendered; but he hadn't spoken two minutes before he had them in
the palm of his hand. Gus did not advocate socialism; his thesis was
soothing and optimistic. The ordinary worker, he said, was a fine,
loyal American whose native horse sense had been clouded by doctrines
from foreign parts. What this victimized American needed to flush out
these ideas was plenty of entertainment in the fresh air. Where better
could he find such entertainment than at an amusement park? Tamarack could consider itself fortunate to have one of the most up-to-date
amusement parks in the land.

Gus had heard Frank discuss socialism so often that he buttressed
his speech with catch-phrases that made him seem a profound student
of sociology. His interest in socialism, of course, was as faint as ever:
it didn't worry him. He felt he could get on very well in any social
order. His intention that noon was simply to speak in praise of Funland, and in casting about for some means of masking his real purpose
he hit upon socialism.

He built better than he had dreamed. As he stood at the speakers'
table he looked stalwart, solid, commanding. His natural eloquence
was great; sentences came readily to his tongue; he drove home points
by smacking his fist into his palm. When he mentioned Washington
and Lincoln his voice quavered.

The Commerical Club nearly rioted when he finished. Applause
thundered; some people even cheered. Whiskers swarmed round the
speakers' table and hands jabbed toward Gus in congratulation. He
couldn't have stirred them more if he had been sincere. One old fellow
even said they ought to run him for Congress.

Reporters always attended the luncheon, to get a free meal, so that
afternoon Gus purchased all the papers. His address had landed him
on the front pages, for the city desks knew that any attack on socialism
would delight patriotic advertisers. BURGOYNE'S BIG GUNS ROAR AT
DEBS, the headlines ran; and PARK MANAGER RAPS MARXISTS. The
Beacon even used a one-column cut of A. H. Burgoyne with the stirring overline: RADICALS' FOE. And it proudly terminated its story with
the information that Mr. Burgoyne was a former city editor of the
Beacon.

Gus folded the papers and caught a streetcar for the park, where in
his office he could feast his gaze without interruption. It was the going-
home hour for the little people, the people who worked for the men
he had addressed that noon. The car was jammed; late afternoon heat
flowed through the windows with a hot-asphalt smell; Gus swayed
from a strap.

He didn't mind the heat and the packed car; he was gregarious as a
sardine; and under his breath he whistled "In The Good Old Summer

Time." And he smiled. He knew it was absurd to be so elated about his name on the front pages; newsprint fame was brief and often ill-deserved. But absurd or not, he loved it. Only a few years ago he had been a nobody in Clayton Junction; he had come far.

Clutching the newspapers, Gus left the trolley and strode through the park gate. He stopped outside his office and gazed at his domain. It was 5:45—an off-hour—but business was better than fair. Families were unpacking picnic baskets under the trees; children had gathered round the pen where Molly and Ranger lived; ecstatic screams came from the roller coaster; and the merry-go-round whirled and tinkled.

Gus spread the papers on his desk, lit a cigar, enjoyed himself. The photograph the *Beacon* used had been snapped several years before. Gus examined it critically, his cigar angling upward. The photograph's jaw and nose were aggressive, but the eyes were not quite as wise as the eyes gazing upon it.

"Still look a little damp behind the ears," Gus thought. "Guess I should have a new picture taken for the papers."

He smoked and read the stories over and over, glowing as if from whiskey, remembering the applause at the Commercial Club and the old fellow who had nominated him for Congress. He considered a career in politics, rejected it. Some opponent would dig up his illegitimate birth and start a whispering campaign. He wasn't feeling sorry for himself, but merely being realistic: he understood the manners and morals of his age. Giving up a political career didn't distress him in any case; he wanted a circus.

Idly, he leafed through the *Beacon*. When he came to the Society page he stopped. For a long moment he stared, nonplussed. The office was very still. In the distance the merry-go-round organ was playing "After The Ball."

Below the word "Bride" a two-column picture of a girl looked out at him. Only Gus saw more than a likeness badly reproduced on newsprint. He saw hair the color of gleaming pavement on a rainy night, and violet eyes. Somewhere in an echo-chamber of his brain he heard her saying, "Gus, I'm sorry. . . . Am I going to see you again?"

Beneath the picture, they had printed, "Mrs. Harold Henderson." And in a column beside the picture they had printed other things. Married Thursday afternoon. That was yesterday afternoon. A quiet wedding at home. The couple left at once for Chicago . . . where Mr. Henderson . . . teaching fellowship . . . will study for higher degrees . . .

The cigar had gone cold in his fingers; absently, he cast it into the spittoon. The merry-go-round played its entire repertoire. Screams came from the roller coaster. The shooting gallery said pop, pop, pop.

Dusk crept through the windows, gathered in the corners, inked the floor. Outside the lights came on.

That was a big evening at the park. It didn't matter much. Perhaps the front page stories had brought Funland Park to people's minds. Perhaps they said, "It's a fine night. We haven't been to Funland yet this year. Let's go out there." Yes, that was how publicity worked. Not that it mattered.

The educated fool. Great God. The educated fool, of all people.

He left the office, moved through the tepid evening. Hello, Gus, people said. Good evening, Mr. Burgoyne. . . . Hello, he said. Hello, there. Glad to see you.

But he wasn't glad.

He ventured along the path that dipped to the miniature railroad. He didn't bustle. He moved like a man recuperating from a long illness. Only he wasn't recuperating. He had made his decision and there had been a great wedding with tremendous publicity, and since then he had hurled himself into work. Hadn't allowed himself to think—very much. When he thought of her he told himself she was still living in Tamarack. Might bump into her on the street some day. Yes, he was a married man now but . . . well . . . old friends, weren't they? Let's drop into this café for coffee. How've you been, Carlotta? I've missed you, you know that? Uh—s'pose you could drop over to the park some evening? Like to talk to you. Ask your advice about . . . about . . . a publicity story. . . .

He stopped at the railroad crossing; the locomotive came tootling, dragging cars loaded with yipping children. Some waved. Gus lifted a halfhearted paw. The train clattered away down the rails.

He slowly mounted the rise toward the elephant pen. Molly spied him coming, lifted her trunk.

" 'Lo, Molly. How are you, old girl?"

And again in that mental echo-chamber he heard a voice chiming, "Isn't she darling!"

Presently he tracked back to the office, fumbled through the shadows to the couch and lay down. He told himself he would get over it. Once long ago he had sorrowed when another woman with violet eyes left him on a silvery night, for Chicago. He had got over it. "Get over these things," he mumbled. And it occurred to him that man's faculty for burying such loveliness beneath the trash heap of passing years was the saddest thing in existence. But the kindest, too. He drew a long breath, wondering whether he could compel himself to go home tonight and crawl into bed with Flora.

The Tamarack papers were delivered in Clayton Junction, and

Frank MacGowan subscribed to all three. That evening he sat in the *Tribune* office, amused as he read of Gus's ascent to fame on a journalistic skyrocket.

In a quarter of a century not many changes had come to the *Tribune*. Electric lights had replaced the kerosene lamps, but the chairs were still stacked with magazines and papers, and the desk hadn't been cleaned in years.

Back in the shop, a new job press had been installed, but type was still set by hand. There were two printers now, and a reporter, for Frank was too busy reading and pondering to have time for work. His stock in the typesetting machine yielded such good dividends that he could afford these luxuries.

Frank told himself that once he might have been irked by Gus's blast against socialism, but tonight he was amused and pitying.

"Poor Gus," he thought.

Although Frank had advocated socialism at the New Year's Eve party, he was no longer certain he should call himself a Socialist. He had never, of course, been a party member. That was just as well, for now he would have been considered a backslider. What perplexed him was the nature of the territory into which he had backslid.

But even though Gus's attack did not irk him, he was troubled by the opportunism inspiring the attack. Somewhere he had read that a conservative young man had no heart, a radical old man no brain. Frank hedged this sentiment with his usual reservations, but he would have felt more comfortable if Gus had now and then flung himself headlong into some cause—any cause—besides the cause of Gus.

Frank spent the remainder of the evening scratching out a light-hearted editorial refuting the theory that amusement parks would cure a sick society. A socialist would have realized instantly that the author of the editorial had more than a passing acquaintance with *Das Kapital*.

Next morning Frank awakened feeling as chipper as a man in his sixties had any right to expect. Hot weather agreed with him. When winter came he ventured out little, because he feared that his bad leg and treacherous ice might lead to broken bones. His stuffy indoor life brought on colds; he suffered neuralgia and he felt and acted old. But this was August, and since spring he had walked every day to the post office and basked in the sun. He felt a decade younger; young enough to visit Rafferty Street again. The last year or so he had considered selling out and moving to a warm climate. California, possibly. But he was unacquainted on the Coast, and he dreaded loneliness.

In his office after breakfast, he read the editorial he had penned the night before. It still seemed amusing, so he took it back to the shop and gave it to Mark Hare to set up.

Hare had come to the *Tribune* a month before. A lean man of
thirty, he had sharp features and sharp eyes behind steel-rimmed
glasses. Frank always had the vague sense that he suffered from
stomach ulcers.

Frank returned to his office, and a few minutes later Hare appeared.
His dry skin was cracked in an unaccustomed smile.

"It's about that editorial you gave me. Best thing I've read in a long
time."

"Glad somebody liked it," Frank said. "You know, I tried an experi-
ment once. I published the same editorials three weeks running.
When nobody mentioned it to me, I began to wonder if they were
being read."

Both men laughed.

"Years ago, I had an old tramp printer named Vince Fye. I used
to write something red-hot—full of Spencer and Karl Marx—and old
Vince would tell me they'd ride us out of town on a rail. But they
never did, damn it."

Both laughed again. Then Hare ventured:

"Read that story in the *Beacon* last night. It burned me to a crisp."

"Bosh. That was just Gus blowing his tuba to draw attention to
Funland Park. Gus doesn't give a damn one way or the other about
socialism. Of course, if the Revolution would come tomorrow he'd
jump on the band wagon and grab the reins and start driving. No,
don't let that story get under your skin. I suppose I'm as much a
Socialist as I am anything, but—"

"You're a Socialist?" Hare sighed. "I've been a party member for
years. And to think the day would come when the boss would be a
Socialist. My God! We really must be growing."

"I'm not a party member," Frank said.

"Why aren't you?"

"I've never been sure I could join with a clear conscience. I've
reached my conclusions independently."

"You're just the kind of man we want," Hare exclaimed. "Our
Local meets Monday evening. Why don't you come?"

Frank considered, eyes twinkling.

"I might," he said, "say something that would stir up the animals.
I'm not a pure Marxian by a long shot."

"My God! Who is? We've got every shade in the Local. From
pale pink to red-crimson. How about coming?"

"All right," Frank said. "Why not?"

Monday evening Frank debated riding in a hack to the meeting,
but he decided this might appear too plutocratic, so he journeyed from
Clayton Junction in one of Mr. Oxenford's trolley cars. He left the

car at the University of Tamarack and limped along a middle-class
street.

After nearly a block he sighted a small brightly lighted house. The
porch light was burning, and several bicycles stood in the yard.
Through the open windows he heard excited conversation. Mark Hare
had said tonight's meeting would be held at the home of Mrs. Beatrice
Webster, an English instructor at the University of Tamarack.

As he knocked he gazed through the screen door at a dozen persons
in the sitting room. Since most of them were talking, he had to knock
a second time to make his presence known. Then a plump woman in
her fifties answered. Her round face and brown eyes were friendly.

"I'm Mr. MacGowan," Frank said.

"Oh yes. Come in. The meeting's just warming up."

Mark Hare hurried across the room and shook Frank's hand. Then
he lifted a palm for silence.

"Comrades, this is the man I mentioned. I'll introduce you."

First, Frank met the woman who answered the door. She was Mrs.
Webster, the hostess, and instead of merely bowing and murmuring
she held out her hand and gripped his firmly.

"I'm glad to know you, Comrade," she said breezily. Her voice had
the warm friendly texture of home-baked bread. She looked as if life
delighted and amused her.

The others were more serious, as if working for the Revolution were
after all no laughing matter. Frank shook great calloused hands that
had groped toward socialism from humble occupations, and he shook
the soft hands of persons whom the hired wags of capitalism were
calling parlor socialists. He met Jews, Gentiles and a Negro.

The business meeting did not differ materially from the business
meeting of a commercial club. The secretary—a German carpenter—
read the minutes, and old business was argued into limbo. Frank sat
studying the members and musing how delighted he would have been
fifteen years ago if he had chanced upon this group. In those days
socialism had crackled like a pitch torch in his brain.

But the years had made him less sure of truth, and certainly much
less sure that the Revolution was within even telescope range. He
sensed the futility of this little group—a handful in the Tamarack
population area—and he thought it comic that men like Mr. Oxenford
should be so exercised about the dangers of socialism. He glanced
across the room at Mrs. Webster's good-natured, intelligent face. What
path had led her from a university classroom to this group?

When the discussion was thrown open to new business, a knotty
blond man arose and delivered a Swedish-American diatribe against
certain views recently uttered by one A. H. Burgoyne. Presently his
attack shifted to Mr. Burgoyne's father-in-law. His countenance red-

dened and his speech thickened, for he was employed in the streetcar company's barns. The wages were niggardly, and his problem of making both ends meet was complicated, he blurted out, by his old woman's getting pregnant every time he hung his overalls over a chair.

At the revelation of this biological phenomenon, the meeting broke into laughter. Mrs. Webster fairly shook.

"Yah, almost dot bad," the speaker declared.

And he went on to advocate that this meeting pass a resolution of protest against Burgoyne's remarks, and dispatch it to the press.

Aaron Bergheim, a young attorney, took the floor to opine that the press would refuse to print such a resolution.

"I read those news stories," he said. "They were utter nonsense. Beneath our contempt. But I agree with Comrade Pearson's remarks about Samuel Oxenford. He's getting this town by the throat." Comrade Bergheim illustrated the process with his hands. "Squeezing it. But I've been prying and watching, and I think he's spreading himself too thin. It wouldn't surprise me if there'd be a crash some day. If anybody here has any money in an Oxenford bank, I'd advise him to get it out fast."

Whether the resolution should be passed occupied the rest of the meeting. Many Comrades rose and spoke, all attacking Mr. Oxenford. He had raised the price of ice; he had raised streetcar fares; one workman had been killed and three injured during the construction of the Oxenford Electric Building. All the speakers assumed Gus Burgoyne an unimportant figurehead. Old Oxenford, they implied, had prompted his son-in-law to attack socialism. Frank held his tongue, but the thought of Gus as anybody's figurehead amused him.

At last Mark Hare gained the floor.

"Comrades, I've got something to read you. It's a perfect answer to Burgoyne's attack. It will be printed as an editorial in the *Clayton Junction Tribune,* and with Comrade MacGowan's permission I'll read it."

They looked at Frank. He felt embarrassed; and as Hare read the editorial his discomfiture mounted. Most of the faces here were pretty grim; doubtless they expected an editorial skinning Gus alive. What they heard was irony and gentle humor. Feeble humor, Frank decided, observing their lugubrious faces. Then he glanced at Mrs. Webster. She was smiling broadly, and when Hare finished she declared:

"That's delicious. There's no weapon like humor. Simply delicious."

An intelligent woman!

She was. And she was that bird of rarest plumage, a teacher of freshman composition with a sense of humor. Also she was a lonely woman. Perhaps loneliness as much as intelligence sustained her membership in the party. She had joined back in the days when Charles was living. The Reverend Charles Webster. Charles. Thin-faced, brown-haired, intense; the gentlest of men, till roused. Poverty roused him. Men railroaded to prison roused him. Urchins kicked into the bull pens of jails; old women shot gleaning coal along a right-of-way; lynchings; sheriffs who received fifty cents a day to feed each prisoner and spent two cents; phrases like unearned increment; all roused him. Then how he preached!

Born a Pennsylvania Quaker, he had found Unitarianism at Harvard. And he had found Beatrice in Old Main on the campus of the University of Tamarack. The Atheneum Literary Society had considered itself daring to invite the new Unitarian minister to address it that January evening. That was the evening of the great blizzard and not many attended. Beatrice attended, Phi Beta Kappa key and all. The new Unitarian minister lived up to firebrand expectations.

She remembered the ribs of the old building creaking in dark wind; window panes plastered with snow; and she wore red velvet. She was secretary of the Atheneum, not because Uncle Timothy was president of the university, but because she had attained popularity in her own right. She was a senior; twenty-one; and she could have married almost anybody. Tall; dark-haired; buxom. But not a haughty beauty. She couldn't manage aloofness. Things always amused her; all kinds of things. Besides, haughtiness demanded unfriendliness, and it happened she liked people.

She sat on the first row and he talked at her. You felt injustice had lighted a hot fire inside him. Not like the senior boys. He wasn't very old. He wasn't much taller than she. Maybe she ought to attend Unitarian church some Sunday. When he spoke she caught a sense of vast forces gathering, out in the beyond-the-campus world. Industrial Revolution. Workers rising. Machines. Bought legislatures. Wall Street. Wage slaves. His voice was vibrant. He had gentle eyes. His face was thin. She was such a good cook. "I enjoyed your speech, Reverend Webster. Do you speak of such things in the pulpit?"

They were married the following summer. And there were many churches in many cities the next twenty years. The congregations always the same. Such a wide divergence of opinion in Unitarian congregations. Always the atheists who still felt the need of Sunday morning communion. The agnostics. The believers in God who denied the divinity of Christ. The religious liberals but economic conservatives; the religious conservatives but economic liberals. Poor Charles. And he so hated contention . . . "They don't think I should march in picket lines. Well, we can move on."

Charles contracted smallpox while investigating jail conditions; and grief was a great tide sweeping you out and out on solitary oceans.

But you must fight your way back to the reality of land, because of
Charles, Junior. Uncle Timothy was no longer president of the University of Tamarack; honorably dead these fifteen years; but possibly
because he was your uncle, or because you attained Phi Beta Kappa or
because you were an Atheneum and Uncle Timothy's successor was an
Atheneum, you became instructor of English and blue-penciled comma
splices. And Charles, Junior, was furious about the *Maine* explosion;
and fever was prevalent in Cuba, but a very sympathetic letter arrived
from the war department. And this time the ocean flashed with more
terrible loneliness, but life must go on. Freshman composition classes
must go on. "A comma splice? I have explained that many times.
Oh yes I have—but you were probably thinking about the freshman
picnic." Laughter from the class. "A comma splice is very wicked—
nearly as wicked as a split infinitive." Laughter. (They know I'm
talking nonsense. How they would gasp if I'd tell them they're thinking too much about other kinds of splicing.) "Only one 'A' in this
course. To Harold Henderson. A very fine student, Harold. Conscientious." (But oh Lord, how dull!)

So grief had a double edge, slowly blunting. Corsets were uncomfortable; she hadn't bought a new one in several years; this one was
comfortably sprung in the right places. She wore it even to the theater,
to that second-rate performance of *Hamlet* at the Paragon. (Those infrequent trips to New York with Charles. John Drew!) And of all
things! There in first-row balcony sat Harold Henderson and Carlotta
Leslie! And Carlotta supposed to be in love with Jim Wheeler.
Harold was certainly not the young man one would imagine Carlotta
choosing.

Then one August afternoon the *Beacon* came (the *Beacon* with the
idiotic outburst from A. H. Burgoyne) and in the Society section you
read an account of a wedding. Carlotta. Gave her a "B." Mrs. Harold
Henderson. Life was strange.

And now the Monday evening meeting of the Local had ended, and
she stood alone in a house suddenly stilled. "Frank MacGowan. It
pleased him when I wanted a copy of the *Tribune* containing the editorial. He promised to bring one to me Thursday evening. What goes on
here? I like his eyes. Gentle, like Charles's. The poor man has a bad
limp. And his face is thin. Must bake Thursday. Apple pie. All men like
apple pie. And this corset is such a comfortable old friend, but I really
must go down to Goldstein's tomorrow and buy a new one."

Thursday evening Frank took a hack to Tamarack. Mrs. Webster
hung up his hat and settled him into a comfortable chair.

"Now let's see the *Tribune*," she said.

"It isn't much of a paper."

As she unfolded it, a queer humility overtook Frank, and he wished he had heeded Gus's suggestions and purchased new type faces, a new press, perhaps even a typesetting machine. The paper was off-size: too wide for its length. The serifs of the Old English nameplate had worn fuzzy; the column rules wandered crookedly; the print paper was flimsy. The old press, always erratic, had grown quite unpredictable with age, printing some lines faintly and others in startling boldface.

As he watched Mrs. Webster, Frank had the feeling that in unfolding the *Tribune* she was unfolding and scrutinizing his life. There he was: shabby, gray, aging, deep in his rut. And he experienced sharp discontent with the *Tribune* and with his life; both might have been of more consequence.

And yet, despite its shortcomings, he loved the *Tribune,* perhaps because it was his only offspring, the only projection of his poor mortality. And it was the past. Some of those stodgy ads on page four had doubtless been set years ago by Vince Fye. At least the type printing the ads had been handled by Vince, scrubbed with gasoline by Vince. And he seemed to recall Vince's admiring that woodcut of a horse which ornamented a livery stable ad.

Frank glanced about the sitting room. He liked it. The other evening, crowded with people, the room's personality had been eclipsed, but tonight its comfort, its mellowness, its sense of having been wept in, laughed in, read in, thought in, rose from the carpet, flowed from the bookcases, from the comfortable chairs, from the reproductions of Renoir and Manet on the walls. The gas chandelier was dark tonight; soft light came from two old kerosene student lamps with green shades. One pooled illumination on the table by Frank's chair, the other on the table by Mrs. Webster's. She put down the paper, chuckling.

"It's a good editorial. I like it even better than I did Monday evening."

"Then you and Mark Hare are my public," Frank smiled. "The Local didn't seem to care for it."

"They take their socialism very seriously. It's castor oil and elixir of youth. They think it will cure everything."

"Don't you think so?"

"No. Do you?"

"I used to," Frank said. "But I've concluded we're going about it wrong-end-to. Society will change when human beings change."

"You pessimist," she grinned.

"Not at all. Human beings have changed. For the better. In another thousand years we'll be ready for socialism. But if it would come now, and somebody like Gus would take it over—"

"Gus?"

"Gus Burgoyne. A. H. Burgoyne."

"You know him?"

"He grew up in my shop."

She wanted to hear about that. He told her. He told her how he had outwitted Tim so Lucy could visit Doll in New York, and he told her about Doll. Never before had he put the whole story into words, and he wondered why he was doing so now, unburdening old desires to this woman he had met only three nights before. Perhaps he sensed in her the understanding that had come from much experience. He knew she must be a dozen years younger than he, but as he unearthed those relics of time gone it seemed she was older in wisdom than he could ever be.

As she listened he watched her. Very little gray had intruded into the smooth black braids wound on her head. In the lamplight the only wrinkles in her face were laughing wrinkles; her eyes were merry. She must have been very beautiful once. Her full body—which for some reason seemed more svelte tonight—looked as full of comforts as a feather bed.

"So you didn't visit her in Chicago," Mrs. Webster said. "You never saw her again."

"No, never."

"Do you regret it?"

He thought a moment. "I think it was better that way. She would have changed. I never blamed her for anything. I think she was the most natural woman who ever lived."

Mrs. Webster's eyes twinkled.

"My dear man—all women are natural women."

And she thought briskly: "This man needs somebody to bring in his tricycle and guard his marbles. Doll! Imagine his mooning for years about a little slut like that! He's taller than Charles. But that same gentleness. That same goodness."

She said:

"I baked today. Pie. Would you like some?"

"Why yes, what kind is it?"

"Apple."

His face lighted. "My favorite!"

In October of that year, as a result of the terrible quarrel between Mr. Oxenford and his son-in-law, Flora and Gus established a home of their own.

"It'll be better now," Gus told himself. "Guess I was a fool to try living with old Sam."

After inspecting many flats and houses, they rented an unfurnished house in the new real estate development that had sprung up west of Funland Park.

"Be close to my work, this way," Gus said.

"I don't know, Gus," Flora said. "The rent seems awful high. Maybe we ought to buy. You pay rent and the money's gone. Gone forever."

But Gus's resources did not empower his making even a down payment on a house. He was, unfortunately, almost broke. The five hundred dollar check Frank had given him last April as a wedding present had been spent. His salary had flashed through his fingers. Whither all those dollars had departed he did not know. Hacks, cigars, cocktails, dinners, tips, shirts, ties. He was not one to waste time accounting for pennies.

Part of the money he had given Flora, for unlike some husbands who spent freely Gus did not become suddenly thrifty in his wife's presence.

"How're you fixed for cash?" he asked.

"I guess I'm all right, Gus. I've still got that twenty you gave me last week."

"Better have some more. Here's another twenty. Person always ought to have cash, in case of emergency. Let me know when you need more."

This bewildered Flora. It even made her uneasy, for after years with Mr. Oxenford it seemed contrary to nature. She took the money, but she didn't understand. And whenever she made a purchase she noted it down in a little book, just in case Gus should revert to what she considered masculine type and suddenly demand an accounting for all the money he had showered on her.

The house Gus and Flora rented was exceedingly modern. None of this stained-glass stuff. It was the pride of 1904, what the real estate salesman called "a story-and-a-half job, hardwood floors throughout, oak finish, six rooms and bath, not a lot of extra space for the missus to clean, know you'll be mighty happy there."

It faced the east, and it still smelled of paint and plaster when the Burgoynes moved in. The clay yard had not yet been sodded, and the concrete front walk had been so recently laid that one gained the porch by treading on planks. The real estate development where it stood gleamed with other equally new and modern houses. The loftiest tree in the "addition" towered to only seven feet.

They bought furniture at Goldstein's, on credit extended by the store-owner himself. While Flora wandered about the furniture department Gus sought out Isaac Goldstein in his office.

"Want to buy our stuff from you, of course," he said. "But the fact is, I'm a little close run just now, and I'd like to stretch out paying for it."

Isaac's beard had turned patriarchal white, and he wore a black skullcap, to the amused chagrin of his five dapper sons who returned one by one from Harvard with knowledge of Chaucer's sources for *Troilus and Cressida,* and with merchandising hints from the Boston stores.

"Sure, Gus. Sure. You can have unlimited credit, within reason."

After Gus departed, Isaac telephoned his son Morris in the credit department and instructed him to keep a sharp eye on the Burgoyne account. For Isaac remembered an occasion years ago in his Clayton Junction store, when Frank gave Gus a dime and Gus promptly spent every cent of it for candy. And last spring at the wedding Gus had told him of Frank's handsome gift. Five hundred dollars. And now Gus was close run. Oi! Nor was Isaac impressed by Gus's relationship to Samuel R. Oxenford. Isaac was not among the investors in Mr. Oxenford's enterprises. Nor was he a depositor in any Oxenford trust. He should live so long and entrust his funds to Oxenford!

Flora and Gus bought chairs upholstered in figured velour and a bedroom suite of bird's-eye maple. The clerk who served them was a girl of twenty-five, with hair the color of the bedroom suite and a trim figure. At first she was smoothly professional, but presently Gus made her laugh. In discussing price and quality she and Gus found it necessary to smile at each other. And once when Flora bent heavily over a chair to examine the construction Gus winked at the clerk. Ever so slightly, she winked back.

Next day Gus returned to the furniture department, and late in the afternoon he telephoned Flora that some old newspaper friends were throwing a party which he must attend. If one wanted publicity one must remain on good terms with the press. Flora was disappointed, for this was their first day in the new house, and she had purchased T-bone steaks to broil for her husband's dinner. Nevertheless, she understood. Business came first.

A few weeks later the girl, whose name was Inez, resigned her position at Goldstein's and took a flat. Her means of support were not visible, except to Gus. But she was not Carlotta. She was the first of many who were not Carlotta. This puzzled Gus. Why did Carlotta keep returning to his thoughts? Why did he wonder what she was doing on Thanksgiving and Christmas and on the anniversary of their meeting in February? One of life's imponderables! And he hated imponderables! Sometimes in his office he wrote her name and sat staring at it. Sometimes he dreamed of her at night. And gradually in a secret part of his brain there evolved a series of imaginary events. In that existence he had married Carlotta and acquired a circus and they were forever gallant and young. Sometimes he wondered whether other human beings lived double lives. Sometimes he wondered if the actual world were not that phantom world. Perhaps he was asleep by Carlotta's side now, in that other existence, dreaming he had married Flora. Never having read a line of philosophy, Gus thought he had come upon an original idea.

Despite his excursions into the rosy half-world of Inez and her successors, Gus had a certain fondness for his wife. She tried hard. She cooked what he liked. Their occasional quarrels resulted from her sluggish perceptions rather than from any shrewish outcroppings. She was loyal, taking his part in the quarrel with Mr. Oxenford, even though her better judgment told her Papa was right. When Gus spent an evening at home she mooed with happiness. He was not unkind to her, save for the unkindness of many absences. Marriage agreed with her; during the first two years in their own home she gained weight; and when, now and then, Gus kissed her with a certain significance she remembered from honeymoon days she trembled with delight. She even wished he would kiss her that way oftener. Once she said as much, but he laughed and said they were old married people now, grown beyond that foolishness. She believed him. She believed anything he told her. She thought his wisdom vast.

Although it often resulted in monetary loss, Flora didn't mind when Gus entertained male friends at an evening of poker. After preparing stacks of sandwiches and making sure the beer bottle opener was where he could find it (Gus never could find anything even if it were in plain sight; he would accuse her of hiding things), Flora went upstairs so the men could swear if they wished as they played at the dining-room table. Lying in bed, she heard their voices rumbling, and she dozed off feeling exceedingly married, exceedingly contented.

As their first Christmas approached, Flora seized courage by the horns.

"You know, Gus, I feel kind of sorry for Papa. He'll be all alone on Christmas. I feel kind of sorry for him."

"You do, huh?"

"Yes, I do, Gus. I don't know. I feel kind of sorry for him."

"Well, maybe we ought to invite him over for Christmas dinner, at that," Gus rumbled. "Let bygones be bygones."

"You won't start fussing with him, will you Gus? You won't ask him to buy you a circus again?"

"I didn't ask him to buy me one. Just wanted his backing. Just wanted him to sign my note."

"Well, anyway, you won't, will you, Gus? Christmas doesn't hardly seem the time to fuss with him."

"Guess it wouldn't do any good if I did. Although I don't see why he won't back me."

"He wants you to run the park, Gus. You're such a good manager he doesn't want to lose you."

"Well by God! If I'm a good park manager I'd be twice as good with a show. All I wanted him to do was back me. And he said a circus was tomfoolery. By God!"

"Don't swear, Gus. Please don't swear. Papa means well. It's just that he don't like to spend money."

"No!" Gus snorted.

"Oh yes, Gus—that's true. He don't like to. I thought you realized that. He's always been that way. He's careful with money. But he means well. And he's getting old. Maybe—well—maybe when he passes on you could have a circus."

Flora spoke as if such a thought had never entered her husband's head. Gus sighed.

"But I want a circus now. Damn it. If I could just buy a small one —take it out in the spring—"

"Then it's all right if I invite Papa, Gus? You won't fuss with him again?"

"No," Gus said, "I won't."

So Mr. Oxenford came, striding from the car line through bright snow. Living alone, he had grown even more thrifty, and recently he had dismissed his combination handy man and coachman and had sold his team. He had reduced the staff of servants to a lone house-keeper. Much of the house remained shut off in winter, to save heat. Thrift was his Crackerjack: the more he tasted the more he wanted.

As Mr. Oxenford climbed the porch steps Gus flung open the door.

"Well, well! Sam! Glad to see you! Merry Christmas!"

A grin flicked through the old man's whiskers.

" 'Lo, Gus. Same to you."

Since their quarrel they had not, of course, refused to speak, for park business had to be discussed, but the atmosphere when they met would have given a polar bear pneumonia. By the time cold turkey was eaten Christmas evening, however, they were on the best of terms. Flora had judged her husband correctly; observation had told her he was never so good-natured and expansive as when acting as host. Realizing it took two to make peace, Mr. Oxenford also did his part. When he sighted the Christmas tree, decorated with all sorts of expensive do-dads, he very nearly cried out. A tree in the house! How much did it cost? Waste!

But he restrained himself. It was hard, but he did it. After all, Gus had shown a smart profit with the park.

One morning after the close of Gus's third season at Funland, Frank MacGowan called him.

"I'd like to see you, Gus. I have a couple of important matters to talk over with you. Could you run out?"

"Be there in an hour."

Gus hung up, consulted his watch. It was attached to a heavy gold chain looped across his vest. The chain had been a birthday gift from Flora, purchased with funds saved from thrifty management of grocery money. A single ornament dangled from the chain: a large lion's tooth. Gus had discovered it in a novelty shop the winter before, when he and Flora spent a month in New York. He prized it highly. If he couldn't have a circus he could at least accouter himself as he imagined a circus owner should.

Lighting a cigar, he left the office and strolled toward the miniature railroad. It was a sparkling morning in mid-September. Workmen were boarding up the dance pavilion and lugging park benches inside for storage. A faint melancholy touched Gus, as always at season's end. Good-by to crowds and whirling lights. This morning the melancholy was intensified by his feeling of marking time. Three seasons as park manager, and a circus as far away as ever.

His desire for a circus never strayed far from his thoughts. But alas! Samuel Oxenford kept refusing to back him. And also alas, Mr. Oxenford's health remained good. To Gus it seemed likely the old fellow would run a close second to Methuselah. Last winter, because of low temperatures in the Wellington Avenue house, Mr. Oxenford had contracted bronchitis. But did it turn into something more serious? No! After Mr. Oxenford regained his feet, Gus called on his physician. Mr. Oxenford had often referred to him as a highway robber—making so many unnecessary calls—but the man turned out to have an honest face.

"Just wondering about old Sam's health," Gus told the doctor. "My wife and I've been worried. Anything serious wrong?"

The doctor beamed a negative.

"He's as organically sound as a man of forty. A wonderful specimen. Unless he freezes to death in that cold house, he has a good chance to live to a hundred. You can stop worrying."

But Gus didn't stop.

Despite his calisthenics, Gus was putting on weight. Around his middle, there was a hint of the huge girth to come. Beneath his jaw-bone, there was a whisper of double chin. "He'll be a fat man some-day," strangers thought.

But his face had strengthened, too. Determination for a circus had tightened his mouth and thrust out his chin. His eyes were harder, more calculating. When he was alone he brooded more than in other days. He fretted about his lack of progress, and he still thought of Carlotta. A few weeks ago the *Beacon* had carried a brief story announcing that Mr. and Mrs. Harold Henderson and son Harold, Junior, were returning to Tamarack after two years in Chicago. Mr. Henderson had been appointed assistant professor of philosophy at the University of Tamarack.

Harold, Junior. That hurt. Perhaps, he thought, he and Flora should have a child. A. H. Burgoyne, Junior. A kid to toddle excitedly toward a lighted Christmas tree. Perhaps through a son he could recapture—and alter!—his own childhood. No Uncle Tim to scare A. H. Burgoyne, Junior. No kids at school to chant, "Yah, yah, yah! Gus is a bastard, Gus is a bastard!" Things would be different for Gus, Junior. And someday he would inherit the vast Oxenford enterprises. Only by then they would be the Burgoyne enterprises. And chief among them would be a circus. Organically sound as a man of forty! Bah!

Assistant professor of philosophy. That must mean an advancement over being a public school principal. So the educated fool—even more educated now and, Gus hoped, more foolish—was getting ahead. And he was standing still. If he chanced to meet Carlotta she might ask, "What ever happened to all your big plans for owning a circus?"

He mounted the rise to Molly's pen. She lumbered to the fence, trunk aloft. He scratched her ears. Only now he had to reach up to scratch her ears. The hay she had consumed had not been for naught. For with all living things Molly shared the mysterious power permeating the universe. She ate. Drank. And within herself the mystery operated, converting water and hay into this huge gray bulk.

South of the pen stood a long building, built last spring. For that building a girl named Ruby was responsible. Ruby had come into Gus's life as a ticket seller. She reminded him a little—a little!—of Carlotta, and he inquired one day how she would like to live a life of ease, a flat of her own, sleeping late, possessing pretty clothes. She could discover no drawbacks to such an existence. So presently Ruby was toiling not, but spending much. Mr. Oxenford refused to give Gus enough of a salary increase. He needed money.

One day an idea came to him, and immediately he called at the Tamarack newspaper offices. But on these trips, instead of yarning with reporters and city editors, he sought higher authority. Managing editors.

"I've got a move in mind," he said, "but before I start I want to talk it over with you. I'm absolutely in your hands. I know the power the press has."

"What's the move?"

"Between ourselves," Gus lied, "Funland isn't doing so well. Unless I can boost profits, we might close. That wouldn't be good for me and it wouldn't be good for Tamarack. An amusement park draws people to town."

Undeniably, said the managing editor.

"Well now, look here. We both know this town's wide open. Lots of gambling. Must be a dozen houses. Notice you've laid off them—and I agree with that policy! Don't think I don't! The public gets sick of campaigns against vice. Well, I was thinking we might have a few games at Funland. It would boost our revenue. Give us just the margin we need to keep operating. Nothing rowdy, you understand. Just a few quiet games. Discreet. But as I say, it's up to you. If you say no, I'll drop the whole idea. But if you'll promise you won't mention the matter in print, I'll go ahead."

Gus obtained three promises of silence.

Next he visited the sheriff. Next the public safety commissioner. He told of the promises from the press. And then he started speaking language the sheriff and the commissioner understood.

Thus armed with co-operation of the Fourth Estate and the Law, Gus called upon an old friend from his reporting days, one "Honest Jack" Dennison. Their discussion of terms occupied two hours. Once Gus boomed:

"What's the advantage to you? Hell's bells, Jack! Don't give me that stuff. I know your business falls off in the summer. And I'm offering you a pitch where there're suckers. Crowds and crowds of suckers. Advantage to you, for God's sake! I wasn't born yesterday."

So lumber was hauled to Funland Park; south of Molly's pen a building rose. Mr. Oxenford became curious, but from Gus he had received such excellent training in keeping his nose out of park business that he didn't interfere. He couldn't resist asking a few questions, however.

"Now listen, Sam. You keep out of this. You don't know anything about it. You'll be happier that way."

"I know, Gus, but all them bills for lumber and nails and whatnot. Land o' Goshen! Like to break me up!"

Gus grinned. "Wait till you see how our profits go up."

"Profits! Why didn't you say so! Land o' Goshen, I ain't one to turn down a little profit."

But Gus did not account to Funland for all the profits from those quiet summer games. One had to look out for one's interests, and in view of all the extra trouble he went to, and Ruby's penchant for jewelry and sending money to her mother in Kansas City, it seemed only fair that some profits should slide into his own pockets.

By August, Honest Jack Dennison was sending six and eight of his employees to the park to operate the games. Once more, Gus had proved to himself that he possessed genius at separating the public from its excess cash. Oh, for a circus! But he made up his mind to one thing. On his show he would carry no grift. Run a clean show. Sunday School show. Like the Ringlings. Honest Gus Burgoyne— that was how people would think of him.

When Gus boarded a trolley that morning for his appointment with Frank, he discovered the conductor to be one of his old Clayton Junction schoolmates. As a boy, the conductor had taunted Gus, but today he didn't taunt him.

"Mr. Burgoyne!" he exclaimed. "Good morning!"

"Hello, Ira. How's everything?"

"Fair. Guess it's pretty good with you. You've sure gone to the top, Mr. Burgoyne."

"Oh, I can't complain."

"Guess you can't! Clayton Junction's mighty proud of you, Mr. Burgoyne."

Gus took a seat in the center of the car. Clayton Junction mighty proud of him. Hogwash! Nevertheless, the conductor's greeting touched him with well-being. His melancholy left him. His decision against marrying Carlotta had been wise, after all. As the car sped along, he even ridded himself of his worry about Ruby. All that girl thought of was money. Once he had wearied of Inez, he had extricated himself fairly easily, but sometimes he wondered whether Ruby would accept his cooling passion so cheerfully.

All the way to Clayton Junction, the conductor was politer than usual to passengers, and he even rang up every fare. And when Gus left the car he called:

"Good-by, Mr. Burgoyne. Glad to have saw you."

Clayton Junction! How long since he had visited the place! How it had contracted!—a town seen through the wrong end of field glasses. Only it hadn't really contracted. He had grown.

The railroad yards still puffed and moaned and flung cinders against the windows of what had been Mahoney's Saloon. Now it called itself Finnegan's Bar. And above the saloon, that southeast window still overlooked the tracks. Memory stabbed his ribs. Aunt Lucy. His mother. Mustn't think about the past. Let it remain buried back there in the nineteenth century—their century. This was the twentieth. His!

As Gus thundered into the *Tribune* office, he noticed an amazing change in Frank.

"You look great!" Gus bellowed. "Yes sir!—looking wonderful! What's happened?"

Frank smiled. His angular face was shaved slick as a whistle; his hair had been recently trimmed. Possibly even shampooed! No printer's grime in it, today. It crested his head in a distinguished shock, as vividly blue-white as only Scotch-Irish hair could be. He wore an open-gate linen collar, a dark tie with a pearl stickpin. A white handkerchief peeked from the breast pocket of his dark suit; his shoes gleamed.

"All right, Gus," he said. "Grab your chair and hold tight. I was married last night."

"Married! Why, you old devil!"

Gus roared. He laughed. He slapped Frank's shoulders. He pumped his hand.

"Married! My God! Tell me about it!"

So a little later, after Gus had spluttered and rumbled and blown himself out, Frank told how he had courted Mrs. Webster.

"Remember," he asked, "that time a couple of years ago when you attacked socialism at the Commercial Club?"

Gus laughed.

"Lot of bull. You know what a commercial club likes. Got myself in the papers, though. That's what I wanted. They all swallowed it hook, line and sinker. Damn near swallowed the pole, too. But hope you understand there was nothing personal in that speech."

Frank understood. And he told how the speech had indirectly led him to Mrs. Webster.

"Like to meet her," Gus said. "Is she here?"

"She's at her house in Tamarack. I'll be commuting for a while. But as soon as I dispose of the *Tribune* we're moving to California. And that brings me to the other matter. Do you know a man named Louis Rink? I believe they call him Curly Rink."

"Moving to California!" Gus exclaimed. "Well I'll be damned. Bet you'll like it out there . . . Uh—Rink? Sure, I know Curly. He's a county supervisor."

"What do you think of him?"

"Fine fellow."

"I mean—is he a crook?"

"Oh sure, he's a crook. I said he's on the board of supervisors, didn't I?"

And Gus laughed.

"Rink wants to buy the *Tribune*."

"He does? What the hell for? Uh—wait! I get it. He lives in the other end of the county. He probably wants the *Tribune* to build himself up politically in this end."

"That's how I figured it."

"Uh—wait a minute, Frank. Let me think. Seems to me I heard a rumor . . . Let me use your phone."

Gus called the *Tamarack Beacon* and talked to the city editor. When he hung up he was grinning.

"I thought Curly must have something up his sleeve. Seems there's a fight under cover between the sheriff and the board of supervisors. Lot of bad blood. Something about county funds. Rink controls the board, so it boils down to a scrap between him and the sheriff. They expect Rink to put up his own man against the sheriff at the polls. Rink's after control of the county."

Slowly, Frank filled his pipe. Socialism seemed far away. He said: "You seem to know what's going on behind scenes."

"Have to."

"What sort of person is the sheriff?"

"Oh well, you know. Run-of-the-mill. Nice fellow."

"Is he crooked, too?"

"I wouldn't bet he wasn't. . . . Uh—now about Rink and the *Tribune*. Take my advice and ask him a good whopping price. He'll pay. He's got plenty salted. If he's after control of the county, he'll—"

"Damn him!" Frank said suddenly.

"Sure, damn him all you please, but ask him a good big price."

"He can go to hell. I've owned the *Tribune* for too many years to let it get mixed up in a dogfight with a lot of crooks. After you've run a paper as long as I've run the *Tribune,* you get pretty fond of it. It's an old friend. You know its faults but you love it anyway. Maybe you love it because of its faults. It's an old-fashioned paper, Gus, but at least it's honest."

"No doubt of that."

Frank's forefinger tamped his pipe. Suddenly he asked: "Would you like to have the *Tribune?*"

"Me!"

"Why not? Would you like it?"

Gus was about to say: "Hell, no! Why would I want the creaky old sheet? Think I want to spend the rest of my life in Clayton Junction? I've got other plans. Circus!"

But he checked himself. A vast wild plan flashed through his thoughts. He said:

"Of course I'd like it. Every reporter has a notion he'd like to run a weekly. And I'm sick of Funland. Sure I'd like it. But I don't know what I'd use for money."

"If you want it," Frank said, "you can have it. Free. Or maybe I'd better charge you a dollar. That would make it a legal sale. My lawyer will know about that when we draw up the papers."

"Now wait! Hold on a minute, Frank! Didn't think I was a slow worker, but you're too fast for me! You mean—?"

Frank meant it.

Gus walked to the window. Could he do it? Frank loved the *Tribune*. Could he take it as a gift and then sell it to Curly Rink? No! Damned shabby trick!

"If you give me the *Tribune*," he asked, "what would you live on? Did the woman you married have money?"

"I've made a few investments. I'll have plenty. Do you want the *Tribune?*"

Gus turned from the window, still not knowing whether to say yes or no.

One fine frosty evening three weeks later, Mr. and Mrs. A. H. Burgoyne accompanied Mr. and Mrs. Frank MacGowan to the railroad station in Clayton Junction. Gus carried Frank's grips. After the two women had been ensconced in the station, the men went outside and stood on the platform.

In a quarter of a century the Clayton Junction yards had changed little. Except for the new station—which was no longer so very new— and the larger switch engines, and the lean steel towers of the automatic block system, the yards looked the same as on those long-ago evenings when a small boy stood in the window above Mahoney's Saloon and waved to signal the trains of his imagination. Switch lights still glowed in the darkness, and when a fireman coaled up, the rails and cinders still were bathed in hellish red flame.

As they stood beneath the stars Frank kept poking at the platform bricks with his cane, and now and then his hand explored his pocket to make certain he had not lost the tickets.

"How're you feeling, Frank?"

"Homesick."

"Now wait a minute! None of that! Wonderful thing for you— California."

Frank said:

"I've cussed this town for half a lifetime. Vince Fye and I used to cuss it before you were born. We used to say it stank. Well, Vince left it in one way and I'm leaving in another. And damn it, I'm homesick. I'm leaving a lot of years behind. A human being's a queer animal, Gus."

"Be great thing for you though—California."

"One thing I've meant to mention, Gus. About Vince's grave. I always buy flowers and decorate it on Memorial Day. Sentimental, I suppose. Vince would probably like it better if I'd decorate it with a plug of tobacco and a quart of whiskey. But when you get older, those

gestures mean more. I'd appreciate it if you'd look after Vince's grave.
Make sure they keep the grass cut, and buy flowers on Memorial Day."

"Bet I will! I'll look after it."

"And keep sending me the *Tribune*. As soon as we have a permanent address I'll let you know. And—oh, damn it, I'm a nosy old man!
—but there's one other thing I'd like to speak about."

"Not nosy at all! Go right ahead."

"Well—it's not my business—but if I were you and Flora, I'd think
about children. When you're an older man you'll wish you had a child
or two. I've been lucky, of course. I've had you."

A lump came to Gus's throat. He would not, he resolved abruptly,
sell the *Tribune* to Curly Rink. From low in his throat he gruffed:

"Guess I should have kept in closer touch with you, after I left Clayton Junction. But damn it, I was always so busy—"

Frank touched his arm. "Sure you were, Gus. I understood."

One other subject remained. An unspoken subject. Doll. Frank
thought of her. Gus thought of her. It was as if her gay, unfettered
spirit were there on the platform with them, beautiful, laughing, easygoing, always young in both their memories.

Gus wanted to say: "Tell me about her, Frank. Tell me about my
mother. I remember her as—as beautiful. She always smelled sweet.
When I didn't mind her, she laughed. I remember her as—as the most
beautiful woman I've ever known. You must have slept with her, you
old devil. Did you sleep with her? Would she sleep with just anybody? I've not been all I should, but I hope—I kind of hope—she
wouldn't sleep—with just anybody."

But he didn't say it. He said:

"You've been mighty good to me, Frank. Want you to know I appreciate it."

"You're a good boy, Gus," Frank said.

An hour later, Mr. Louis (Curly) Rink hung up the receiver of the
telephone on his dining-room wall and, swearing a blue streak, rejoined his wife in the sitting room.

"It ain't right for you to use such language," she said, "and you a
supervisor. Maybe it was okay when you was working at the brickkilns,
but it don't sound right for a supervisor—"

Mr. Rink continued taking the Lord's name in vain.

"Well," his wife sighed, "what is it?"

"It's that damned Gus Burgoyne. I was fixing to buy the *Clayton
Junction Tribune* from an old goof who didn't know straight up, and
now Burgoyne's bought it! That was Burgoyne on the phone."

"Maybe you could buy it from Burgoyne."

That possibility threw Mr. Rink into another spasm of profanity. At
last he shouted:

"Buy it from him! Sure! That's his idea. He told me it was for sale! But the bastard will make me pay through the nose. I know him. Knew him when he was a reporter. He had every politician in this county scared silly. He's crooked as a dog's hind leg. Oh, damn it to hell, anyway!"

"Do you have to buy that Clayton Junction paper?"

Mr. Rink scowled. Thought. Sighed.

"Wish I didn't, but I ought to have it. I've always been weak in that township. Need them roundhouse workers. And with the *Tribune,* I could club them Rafferty Street landlords. Make 'em shell into the kitty. Yeah, with the fight that's coming in this county I need the dirty little sheet. Damn Burgoyne! Trouble with him, he's nothing but a crook!"

Beatrice MacGowan had been at the grocery store when the mailman came. She was still at the store. Frank sat at a desk by the window, staring out at the copious sunshine of southern California. The sunshine fell from low clouds in gray streaks, soaking the lawn, dripping from the eaves.

Once more Frank read the story in the *Tribune,* announcing the paper's sale to Mr. Louis Rink, the widely known supporter of the full dinnerpail.

At last he drew ink and paper toward him and scratched furiously. In the letter he told Gus exactly what he thought of him, and what Frank thought of Gus that morning would have given the postmaster general a heart attack. He boasted. He told of his stock in the typesetting machine company. Who had been going to inherit that stock, after Mr. and Mrs. Frank MacGowan passed on? Gus Burgoyne, that was who! And who would inherit it now? Damned if Frank knew, but certainly not Gus Burgoyne!

"I'm disappointed in you," Frank wrote. "Bitterly disappointed in you. This instance of barefaced crookedness—"

He broke off writing. He stared out the window. The sunshine splashed down harder. At last, with a long breath, he picked up the letter, tore it across the middle, tore it again, and then again. He dropped the pieces into the wastebasket.

"Who am I?" he asked himself. "God Almighty? Who am I to judge? Maybe if I'd been born above a saloon—and had Tim for an uncle—and had been called bastard—"

He drew another breath. Stared at the torn letter in the wastebasket. No letters would ever be sent from this house to Gus Burgoyne. He must find a lawyer. See about changing his will. Find some worthy cause.

He picked up the *Tribune.* He read the story a third time.

"Poor Gus," he thought.

11

Editorial appearing in the *Tamarack Beacon,* April 22, 1907:

Good Luck, Gus!

About eight years ago a likeable young fellow named A. H. Burgoyne came to our office from Clayton Junction and asked for a job as reporter. In the newspaper business as in every occupation many are called but few are chosen. However, there was something about this young man that convinced us he was a hustler, so we took a chance on him.

Our judgment proved correct. A. H. Burgoyne—who right away was "Gus" to everybody—turned out a top-notch reporter. In his covering of police and then the courthouse and then the city hall he made a host of friends. Before long, Gus's energy and ability caused us to promote him to city editor.

Gus could have carved out a great career for himself in the newspaper professon, but his interests lay in other directions. He left us—with mutual regrets and good will—to manage Funland Park. Under his able direction Funland has become one of the snappiest amusement parks in the country, a place where young and old may enjoy good, wholesome entertainment.

By virtue of honesty and thrift, Gus has prepared himself for a new venture. Throughout the past winter he has assembled circus equipment and trained animals at Funland, and today this fine little circus—Burgoyne's Circus & Hippodrome—took to the road. By special arrangement with the interests controlling Funland, the elephant, Molly, and the pony, Ranger, are accompanying the show.

In these days when kickers and whiners complain that there are no longer opportunities for young men, we submit that the career of A. H. Burgoyne refutes such talk. We believe that from this beginning Burgoyne's Circus & Hippodrome will grow into one of the important shows of the land, and we do not need to point out what a fine thing for Tamarack it would be to have a large circus wintering here.

God bless you, Gus, we believe you will go far. Lots of luck!

*

Feature story appearing in the *Tamarack Beacon,* April 22, 1907, with several illustrations and appropriate headlines:

Your alarm clock begins banging and you tumble from bed and turn it off. The hands point to 3 A.M. But you aren't sleepy. You're wide-awake with an excitement you remember from boyhood. Circus day excitement!

You grab a hasty breakfast and catch a trolley for Funland Park. It is not yet 4 A.M. when you arrive. But inside the park great activity is going on.

A circus is being born this morning!

Tamarack's own circus—Burgoyne's Circus & Hippodrome!

This isn't the first time in recent months your reporter has visited Funland. In fact, your reporter has spent many spare hours there since last November, observing the gradual accumulation of wagons, tents, horses, wild animals. In recent weeks, your reporter has met many of the performers who will entertain and delight circus crowds during the coming months. Your reporter has attended rehearsals of the show, held in the big top that has been pitched in the open space near the bandstand.

Nor is this your reporter's first acquaintance with Mr. A. H. Burgoyne, owner of the show. A few years ago your reporter served under Mr. Burgoyne—whom his countless friends know as Gus—when he was city editor of this newspaper.

Gus has brought the same boundless energy, the same enthusiasm to his circus that he brought to his duties as city editor. As soon as your reporter entered the park he caught sight of Gus, hurrying to and fro, issuing last-minute orders.

To your reporter's layman's eyes, this show looked like a winner. There are eighteen wagons, gay with paint and gilt. The band wagon—which will accommodate fourteen musicians in the parade—is pulled by six beautiful white horses.

On the show—and Gus explained you are always "on" the show, never "with" it or "in" it—on the show there are a number of interesting animals. In addition to the many performing dogs and ponies, there is a striped hyena, said to have been captured in Tibet, as well as a great boa constrictor. A zebra, a northern timber wolf, a pair of red foxes and a ferocious cougar, captured in the Rocky Mountains, round out the interesting menagerie.

And of course there is Molly, the elephant which Tamarack children know and love, as well as her friend and companion, Ranger.

"I'm convinced," Mr. Burgoyne declared, "that the American public in our smaller cities and towns is ready for a circus that will bring first-class, clean entertainment at popular prices. My policy can be simply stated: never break faith with the public."

It is 5 A.M. The circus is ready to leave for Graham, a town ten miles west of Tamarack. (Today will be spent in setting up and in final rehearsals—the first performance will take place tomorrow afternoon.)

Mr. Burgoyne lights a cigar, climbs into his light buggy, lifts his hand. The procession starts, leaving the park by the northeast wagon-gate.

Your reporter watches. Teamsters order, "Giddap." Wagons rumble. Dogs are barking and the cougar lets out a blood-curdling shriek. Directly behind Mr. Burgoyne's buggy Molly and Ranger march.

A circus is born!

*

From the journal of Harold Henderson, assistant professor of philosophy at the University of Tamarack:

April 22, 1907

. . . and during our conversation I mentioned to Dr. Bartholomew my projected textbook, *The History of American Philosophy,* explaining I hope to make it the definitive work in its field. He was most encouraging.

Carlotta isn't well this evening. Immediately dinner was over, she retired with a headache. Hence, I have been minding the infant this evening. He grows more alert every day. But I discover that unlike Dr. Bartholomew and myself, he is a follower of the pragmatists.

*

Editorial in the *Tamarack Morning Chronicle,* April 23, 1907:

Something Rotten In Funland

A few years ago the children of Tamarack bought an elephant! THE CHILDREN bought it, with THEIR OWN DIMES. Where is that elephant today?

The elephant has departed from this city to travel with a circus. HOW COME?????

A certain newspaper sponsored the purchase of that elephant. Now this same newspaper publishes a laudatory editorial about the circus AND GLOSSES OVER THE DEPARTURE OF THE PACHYDERM!

The little children of this community and their parents have a right to know by what high-handed monkey business a privately owned circus can abscond with the children's elephant. They bought it to be quartered at Funland Park.

NOW IT HAS GONE!

HOW COME?????

*

Telephone conversation between Mr. Samuel R. Oxenford and a reporter for the *Tamarack Beacon,* April 23, 1907:

Reporter: You read that editorial in the *Chronicle* this morning?

Mr. O.: I read it over a feller's shoulder on the streetcar. I ain't a subscriber.

Reporter: Do you have any statement to make?

Mr. O.: It's all legal! There ain't nothing wrong about it. We own the critter!

Reporter: What sort of arrangement did you make with Mr. Burgoyne?

Mr. O.: Young feller, that ain't none of your affair.

Reporter: I'm sorry, Mr. Oxenford, if I seem to be prying, but I want you to know the *Beacon* is on your side in this matter. We want to show up that scare sheet down the street.

Mr. O.: Well, there wasn't any arrangement about it. Gus said to me, "Sam, I've been meaning to tell you, that bull's eating up a lot of park profits. The kids have all saw her now, and she ain't bringing no extra trade to the park. Why don't I take her out with my show," Gus said, "and take the expense of feeding her off your hands?" So I said for him to take her, and that pony, too. Never did see the use of buying that pony. Land o' Goshen! Like to break a man up, buying ponies and feeding elephants!

Reporter: As I understand it, the children purchased the elephant and presented her to the park. Is that right?

Mr. O.: Sure it's right! We own her, lock, stock and barrel. Guess a man has a right to do what he pleases with his own property. You'd think them Socialists were in control, the way things—

*

News story appearing in the *Tamarack Beacon,* April 23, 1907, under the head: OXENFORD REPLIES TO *CHRONICLE'S* CHARGES:

Declaring that permitting the elephant, Molly, to travel with Burgoyne's Circus was in every sense legal, Samuel R. Oxenford, head of the interests controlling Funland Park, today struck back at the editors of the *Tamarack Chronicle*.

"I very much regret the *Chronicle's* attack," Mr. Oxenford stated. "If before writing the editorial the editors had consulted me, I could have explained."

According to Mr. Oxenford, after the elephant was purchased by school children in 1903, she was presented to Funland Park as a gift.

"It was perfectly understood at that time," Mr. Oxenford said, "that the elephant was to become park property with no strings attached.

"Nobody has absconded with the elephant. She is temporarily on loan to Burgoyne's Circus, that is all. As a matter of fact, observations of park officials have shown that the children are no longer as interested in the elephant as they once were."

Mr. Oxenford went on to say that it was thought the elephant's absence from the park for a brief period might whet and renew the children's interest in the animal.

"We proceeded on the theory that absence makes the heart grow fonder," Mr. Oxenford smiled. "We were thinking of the best interests of the children. The *Chronicle* is completely in error in suspecting anything underhanded about the affair."

Mr. Oxenford indicated his belief that such irresponsible attacks are dangerous, playing into the Socialists' hands by undermining respect for private property.

*

Editorial in the *Tamarack Morning Chronicle*, April 24, 1907:

What Kind Of *Beacon*?

Yesterday the *Chronicle* published an editorial asking some questions.

Questions about the disappearance of the elephant, Molly, from Funland Park to travel with a circus.

Questions that were evidently embarrassing in some quarters.

Yesterday the *Beacon* published what purported to be an interview with Mr. Samuel R. Oxenford, allegedly answering our questions.

The gist of that interview was that the children of Tamarack have wearied of the pachyderm which they BOUGHT WITH THEIR OWN DIMES.

The further gist was that the *Chronicle* has turned Socialist.

The *Chronicle* refuses to believe that Mr. Oxenford made any such accusations or offered any such thin excuse as to why the elephant has vanished.

The *Chronicle* believes the public will recognize that interview as a TYPICAL EXAMPLE OF THE *BEACON'S* UNRELIABLE REPORTING OF THE EVENTS OF THE DAY!

Nobody is questioning Mr. Oxenford's high integrity or the high integrity of Mr. A. H. Burgoyne.

BUT THE *CHRONICLE* DOES QUESTION THE *BEACON'S* STEWARDSHIP OF THE MONEY IT COLLECTED FROM THE CHILDREN OF THIS COMMUNITY.

Doubtless Mr. Oxenford had a legal right—as the interview claims—to lend the elephant to Burgoyne's Circus.

BUT THE *BEACON* HAD NO MORAL RIGHT TO COLLECT DIMES FROM LITTLE CHILDREN, TO BUY A PACHYDERM AND THEN TO GIVE HER FREE GRATIS TO A PRIVATELY OPERATED AMUSEMENT PARK!

No, gentlemen of the *Beacon,* your thin explanations will not do!

The *Chronicle* will continue turning its fierce, clean searchlight of publicity upon the activities of the *Beacon,* to ferret out the SHINING TRUTH from the maze of HALF-TRUTH AND OUTRIGHT FALSEHOOD!

We repeat what we said yesterday.

THE ELEPHANT HAS VANISHED FROM FUNLAND! HOW COME?????

*

Memo from the business manager of the *Tamarack Morning Chronicle* to the editor, 12:45 P.M., April 24, 1907:

Suggest you lay off. Jimmy has just landed a series of ads from the st. car co.

*

News story appearing in the *Tamarack Beacon,* April 24, 1907, under excusably rapturous headlines:

A free circus!

That is what Tamarack children were promised today by A. H. (Gus) Burgoyne in an exclusive long distance telephone interview with the *Beacon.*

"When Burgoyne's Circus & Hippodrome comes in off the road in the fall," Mr. Burgoyne declared, "we are going to present two absolutely free performances for the kiddies of Tamarack."

Mr. Burgoyne stated that he had been holding back announcement of the free circus as a surprise. However, due to what Tamarack people are calling a "tempest in a teapot" about the elephant, Molly, Mr. Burgoyne decided to make his announcement at this time.

"Not only will both performances be free," Mr. Burgoyne said, "but Samuel R. Oxenford has promised that streetcar transportation to the circus grounds will also be furnished free. Burgoyne's Circus & Hippodrome is proving a sensational success, and the Tamarack kiddies can look forward to the best circus of its size in America."

Officials of the *Tamarack Beacon* announced today that all children attending the circus will receive free balloons, peanuts and lemonade with the compliments of the newspaper.

Date for the free circus has not yet been set, although it will probably take place on a Saturday late in September or early in October.

Inasmuch as the date will be announced in the *Beacon* as soon as it is known, it is suggested that parents restrain their children from telephoning the *Beacon* to inquire as to the date.

*

Comment from Mr. Samuel R. Oxenford upon learning from the *Beacon* news story that he had promised free transportation to the circus grounds:

God Almighty! Why that—that—robber! Break me up! That crook! That—that—!

*

Portion of advance publicity sent by Burgoyne's Circus & Hippodrome to editors of weekly newspapers:

When a man bites a dog, that's news.

And when a great newspaper like the *Tamarack Beacon* comments editorially upon the merits of a circus, that's bigger news.

In a recent issue, the *Tamarack Beacon* did just that, singing the praises of Burgoyne's Circus & Hippodrome which will show in ——————— on ———————.

"We believe . . . Burgoyne's Circus & Hippodrome . . . one of the important shows of the land," the *Beacon* said. "We do not need to point out what a fine thing . . . to have a large circus wintering here."

In a recent news story, the *Tamarack Beacon* went even further.

"Burgoyne's Circus & Hippodrome is proving a sensational success," it declared, "and the . . . kiddies can look forward to the best circus . . . in America."

And in a feature story the *Beacon* announced, "This show looked like a winner. The American public . . . is ready for a circus that will bring first-class, clean entertainment at popular prices."

After such praise from a newspaper of the *Beacon's* standing, further comment is needless. However, a rapid glance at some of the startling and amazing features offered by America's newest and brightest circus is in order.

Burgoyne's Circus & Hippodrome offers tons of mirth and merriment in Molly, the only elephant in the world that has trained a Shetland pony to mimic her own tricks.

Burgoyne's is the only show where you can watch a monstrous boa constrictor crush a live chicken in its mighty toils and eat the same.

Burgoyne's is the only show . . .

Burgoyne's is the only . . .

Burgoyne's . . .

Burgoyne's . . .

Burgoyne's . . .

*

After-notice of Burgoyne's Circus & Hippodrome in the *Weekly Excelsior,* Huntsville, Iowa (Pop. 783), issue of June 6, 1907:

Last Tuesday evening we took our "better half" and our three "chips-off-the-old-block" to the circus. The kids seemed to enjoy it, but we'll have to " 'fess up" that we ourselves were a little disappointed.

Maybe we're just an old "grouch," but after the advance publicity and the statements attributed to the *Tamarack Beacon* we expected something pretty novel in the way of circuses. Doggone it, guess we expected a small edition of Ringling Brothers.

The circus was pitched in Blackmer's pasture down near Fox Creek, and from the scratching we've been doing ever since we estimate the mosquitoes were impressed by that advance publicity, too.

The show consisted of some eighteen wagons and a little "top" with one center pole. Seated around four hundred, we'd say. The "menagerie top," through which you entered the "big top," was a mite bigger than the tent we used on our camping trip to Spirit Lake last summer.

Guess we expected monkeys and tigers and such-like. There was a pair of foxes, but heck!—a man can see those any day if he wants to get himself a hound dog and go rambling through Uncle Charley Johnson's timber.

Guess we expected to see that boa constrictor eat a chicken. But it turned out they only feed the "big worm" twice a week, and this wasn't a feeding day. That snake impressed us as almighty lazy—he just lay there in his canvas pen "snoozing his head off."

The same laziness seemed to afflict the northern timber wolf and the Rocky Mountain cougar. The latter sort of reminded us of our office cat, except somewhat more sizable. But then maybe we would be lazy too if folks would hand us our food without any work.

After the big circuses we have seen, the performance struck us as kind of tame. We liked the bareback riding act, and the clowns cracked some jokes we hadn't heard since boyhood, but the trapeze work didn't quite come up to the acrobatics we saw last summer when the kids of our neighborhood staged a "circus" in Thompson's barn.

Most of the performance consisted of trained dog and pony acts. We've always had a dog around our house, and we think we know a good deal about "man's best friend," and these trained dog acts always make us uncomfortable. Maybe we're wrong, but the dogs always look "scared to death" with their tongues lolling out.

The show was climaxed by the performance of the elephant, Molly, and the pony, Ranger. We didn't care much about the tricks, but it's certainly fascinating just to watch an elephant moving. At the very end the trainer set off a firecracker in a wooden cannon, Molly waved "Old Glory" in her trunk and the show was over.

During the day we had the pleasure of meeting and visiting with A. H. Burgoyne, the show's owner. He struck us as a mighty nice young fellow, full of energy and enthusiasm. Mr. Burgoyne—who is known in the show world as "Honest Gus"—gave us the best cigar we have smoked since the governor spoke here in his 1904 campaign.

Honest Gus served as equestrian director—what we ordinary folks call "ringmaster"—during the show, and it seemed to us he enjoyed the performance more than the audience. He got a good laugh from the clowns, and when Molly performed we thought he looked pretty proud.

We liked Honest Gus, and we're sorry his circus fell short of what his advance publicity led us to expect. We don't think he

meant to deceive the public. Probably his own enthusiasm for his
circus led him to overrate it in his publicity.

One thing about Burgoyne's Circus & Hippodrome—it's a
"clean show." Honest Gus lived up to his name. In these days
too many circuses shortchange the public at the ticket window,
or carry gamblers. Honest Gus told us he operates what is known
in the show world as a "Sunday School show." We approve of
that, and we will be looking forward to Honest Gus's next visit
to our little city.

*

From the journal of Harold Henderson:

Chicago, Illinois
June 20, 1907

Here we are at the University of Chicago again, where I shall
continue my studies toward my doctorate during the summer
session. I am growing more and more interested in my project,
The History of American Philosophy. I hope to be able to rework much of my dissertation material and use it in my *History.*

This is a decidedly humid evening, and one feels like a limp
rag. The weather causes Harold, Jr. to be fretful, and I fear he
is a great trial to Carlotta, who is pregnant again.

My courses this summer include . . .

*

Editorial in the *Tamarack Morning Chronicle,* June 24, 1907:

Many Happy Returns!

This is the birthday of one of Tamarack's leaders!

Seventy years ago today, back in Maine, Mr. Samuel R. Oxenford was born.

In the life story of Samuel R. Oxenford you can read the
pageant of America! The westward migration—hard work—
honesty—achievement—all are there!

Mr. Oxenford himself has often stated that his success can be
ascribed to all that is embodied in three words. They are:

THRIFT! INDUSTRY! INTEGRITY!

Ponder those words well, ye lads of today!

At this time, owing to the unsound policies of a certain gentleman occupying the White House, the nation is in the throes of a
depression. Beginning with the collapse of shaky financial institutions in New York, there has been a wave of bank failures.

TAMARACK HAS COME THROUGH THIS "BANK-
ERS' PANIC" UNSCATHED!

WHY?

BECAUSE OF MEN LIKE SAMUEL R. OXENFORD!

Our banking institutions rest upon firm foundations. We sleep well o' nights.

Congratulations, Mr. Oxenford, upon your many splendid achievements! May your period of Service to your city and your country be long!

*

Telephone conversation between the editor of the *Tamarack Morning Chronicle* and his wife, 11 A.M., June 24, 1907:

Wife: Hello, Scoop?

Editor: Yeah.

Wife: I read your editorial, Scoop. About old Oxenford.

Editor: Yeah.

Wife: Listen, Scoop. Is the Tamarack Fidelity & Trust an Oxenford bank?

Editor: Not a bank. It's a trust.

Wife: Don't quibble, darling. Does Oxenford own it?

Editor: He controls it.

Wife: Well honey, reading your editorial about Oxenford made me wonder. Is he honest?

Editor: Honest! Hell, no! Whatever gave you that idea?

Wife: Do you think there's any danger of Tamarack Fidelity closing its doors?

Editor: You're damned right there is. Last few days there's been a lot of scurrying going on behind scenes. Every banker in town is scared. They'll try to save Oxenford because if he goes they'll all smash together, but—

Wife: Listen, Scoop. I didn't tell you. I thought I'd save it and buy you a nice birthday present, but—

Editor: What are you talking about?

Wife: If you wouldn't keep breaking in I'd tell you! Last week Aunt Hattie gave me a hundred dollars, and thinking I'd save it I deposited it in Tamarack Fidelity, and—

Editor: Tamarack Fidelity! For God's sake, woman, you get right downtown and pull out that dough!

*

Telephone conversation between the *Chronicle* editor's wife and a friend, 11:15 A.M., June 24, 1907:

Wife: Gladys?

Friend: Oh hello, Josephine!

Wife: Listen, Gladys! I don't have time to talk. But I remem-

ber you said you banked at Tamarack Fidelity, and I just
talked to Scoop and he says . . .

*

Portion of a letter from Mrs. A. H. Burgoyne to Mr. A. H. Burgoyne, June 25, 1907:

. . . and with this hot weather I'm kind of glad we closed our
house for the summer and I moved in with Papa, it's so much
cooler in this big place, although it seems a shame to keep paying
rent on our house when we don't use it.

Saw the doctor again today. He says I'm doing all right. He
said again I shouldn't wear a corset. Don't know why he always
says that, I sure wouldn't think of it, I think it's awful to wear a
corset when you're in the family way.

Yesterday was Papa's birthday. Had fried chicken, but he
didn't eat much. He don't seem very well, Gus, sometimes I wonder if it's his liver. He seems kind of jumpy, he's cross, and he
thinks I see the doctor too often. Says the day before he was born
his mother hoed potatoes in the garden, the doctor never got
there at all, just a neighbor woman. I don't know, sometimes I
think he's too careful with money, I don't think it's wasteful to
see the doctor. Guess Papa's working on a big deal. Last night
several prominent men came and they talked in the library till
way past his bedtime, and when I went to the bathroom at three
in the morning there was a light in his bedroom. Kind of odd,
don't you think, he was never one to sit up late.

Oh yes, I knew there was something else. The other day Papa
and his lawyer came out to the house with a lot of legal papers
I didn't understand and had me sign. Anyway, what it was, he
deeded this house to me, except there was a paper that said he
could live here till he dies. Deeded me the coal mine at Oxenford too, and that farm that won't grow good crops. Seems kind
of funny to me because when he passes on I'll inherit anyway.

Well Gus, glad to hear business is better now the rainy spell is
over. Do you think you'll make as much as you did managing
the park?

Yours truly,
Flora Burgoyne

*

Telephone conversation, 9:30 A.M., June 25, 1907:

Woman: . . . and Sally said that Mary had told her that Gladys

said the Tamarack Fidelity might close its doors and
I thought I'd better tell you . . .

*

Editorial in the *Tamarack Beacon*, July 1, 1907:

A Time For Cool Heads

In its news columns today the *Beacon* is publishing a symposium by such financial and business leaders as Mr. Samuel R.
Oxenford and Mr. Jason Cadwallader. We recommend it to the
thoughtful attention of our readers.

The disturbing fact is that during the last few days a series of
quiet runs have been taking place on the trusts and banks of this
city. Why these runs should occur against institutions whose integrity and stability are unimpeachable is a mystery. The only
possible answer, as our leaders point out in the symposium, is
that the financial flurries of last spring in New York are having
a belated effect in Tamarack.

An entirely different situation exists in the country today than
existed last spring. Only a rash and ignorant man would dare
impugn the impregnability of the Tamarack banking system.

Of course, as everyone knows, no bank or trust ever keeps all
its assets in liquid form. A bank could not exist if it were to do
so. Business could not go on if banks were to do so. The money
you deposit in a bank is lent to enterprising businessmen, who use
it to produce new wealth, to provide jobs which in turn produce
more purchasing power. That is the way to economic health and
prosperity.

As it happens, the financial institutions of Tamarack have been
able to convert a great share of their assets into liquid form, and
they are prepared to meet requests for withdrawals to almost any
amount. If you want to let yourself be swayed by foolish fears
and vicious rumors, if you wish to withdraw your funds, they
will be waiting for you. But in a few days, when you return your
funds, you will have lost interest and feel, in general, rather
foolish.

So the *Beacon* suggests that you retain your faith in these leading men of Tamarack, and turn a deaf ear to the gossipmongers.
This is a time for stout hearts and cool heads.

*

News story in an extra edition of the *Tamarack Beacon*, July 2,
1907, beneath a banner proclaiming, FINANCIER PLUNGES TO
DEATH:

Samuel R. Oxenford, 70, widely known Tamarack financier, plunged to his death at approximately 2:15 P.M. today from his office on the fifteenth floor of the Oxenford Electric Building.

Police believe the fall was a suicide, although investigation is still going forward.

Dr. W. L. King, county coroner, has not yet announced an opinion.

The Tamarack Fidelity & Trust Company closed its doors at 12:45 today in the face of a line of depositors a half-block long. (See other columns for this story.)

The Merchants' Trust Company, the Farmers' and Mechanics' Trust Company and the Guarantee Savings and Trust Company all closed their doors at approximately the same hour.

Mr. Oxenford was heavily interested in these institutions.

Witnesses report that Mr. Oxenford's body came hurtling without warning into the traffic of Harrison Street. It landed in a dray owned by the Schwartz Transfer Company.

The force of the fall caused the body to bounce from the dray into the street, in full view of horrified spectators.

In the confusion the dray horses were frightened and a runaway resulted. Several pedestrians narrowly escaped injury. After about a block the driver of the dray brought his team under control.

Patrolman Oscar J. Terwillinger, traffic officer on duty at Tenth and Harrison Streets, promptly brought order from the confusion resulting from Mr. Oxenford's fall.

He covered Mr. Oxenford's body with gunny sacking from a wagon belonging to the Tamarack Grain and Feed Company. Then Patrolman Terwillinger called headquarters for a police ambulance.

Officials believe that Mr. Oxenford's fall can be ascribed to mental distress resulting from the closing of Tamarack Fidelity & Trust Company, and other institutions.

Employees in Mr. Oxenford's offices on the fifteenth floor of the Oxenford Electric Building report he returned from lunch at approximately 1:30 P.M.

He left an order not to be disturbed and went to his private office, closing the door. Employees maintain they had no intimation of what was to take place.

Mr. Oxenford is survived by his daughter, Mrs. A. H. Burgoyne.

This summer Mrs. Burgoyne has been residing in her father's home at 2609 Wellington Avenue. Mrs. Burgoyne's husband is on tour with Burgoyne's Circus & Hippodrome, now playing in southern Minnesota. Prostrated with shock and grief, Mrs. Burgoyne would make no statement.

Funeral arrangements have not been completed.

(See later editions of the *Beacon* for full story of Mr. Oxenford's life, artist's drawing recreating the plunge, interviews with witnesses, and up-to-the-minute developments.)

Want to sell? Want to trade? Want to buy? Try a *Beacon* Want Ad for results!

*

Telegram from Mrs. A. H. Burgoyne to Mr. A. H. Burgoyne, care of Burgoyne's Circus & Hippodrome, Wheatland, Minnesota:

PAPA PASSED AWAY FALL FROM OFFICE WINDOW CAN YOU COME

FLORA

*

Story in second extra edition of the *Tamarack Beacon,* July 2, 1907, under a banner, EYEWITNESS DESCRIBES OXENFORD'S PLUNGE:

I saw Samuel R. Oxenford leap to his death at 2:15 today.

I am Royal Washington Ealey, a colored window washer, living at 1781 Calkins Court.

Shortly after noon today I resumed work washing windows on the tenth floor of the Metropolitan Exchange Building, directly across the street from the Oxenford Electric Building.

At approximately 2:10 P.M., from my perch where I was safety-belted to a window ledge, I happened to look upward at the Electric Building.

My heart was in my mouth.

For I saw an old gentleman with a white beard sitting on the ledge of a fifteenth floor window with his legs dangling.

I yelled at the top of my lungs. I don't think he heard me because it is always windy at that height even though it may be calm on the street below.

But he might have heard me because after a moment he withdrew his legs and disappeared inside the office.

I breathed easier. But I was still looking up at the Electric Building.

Then all at once through the open window the old gentleman came plunging. It appeared to me he had made a running dive through the window.

I was transfixed with horror as his body went hurtling downward, turning over and over.

I could see wagons and buggies and tiny-looking people on the street far below. I thought he might crash into a crowd of pedestrians.

It was terrible.

I breathed with relief when he averted the pedestrians and struck the dray.

*

News story in *Tamarack Beacon,* July 3, 1907, under the head, FUNLAND TO REMAIN OPEN FOR HOLIDAY:

Funland Park will be open for business as usual on the Independence Day holiday, Henry Worthing, park manager, has announced.

"Although the entire staff of Funland is grief-stricken because of Samuel R. Oxenford's death," Mr. Worthing stated, "we feel he would want us to carry on."

A number of organizations have planned Fourth of July picnics at the park, Mr. Worthing said.

"Interest is high," he declared, "in an act brought to Funland for one day only. Speed Marvelli, the daredevil motorcyclist, will ride his cycle in an arena with three prowling Nubian lions."

*

Series of headlines appearing in various Tamarack papers during 1907:

TAMARACK BANKERS HOLD EMERGENCY
INDEPENDENCE DAY MEETING

ATTORNEY GENERAL TO INVESTIGATE
OXENFORD EMPIRE

MANY BANKS WILL REOPEN TODAY

TAMARACK ELECTRIC & GUARANTEE
STOCKHOLDERS WILL ORGANIZE
PROTECTIVE ASSOCIATION

RECEIVERSHIP FOR TAMARACK
ELECTRIC & GUARANTEE

BAR ASSOCIATION BEGINS
DISBARMENT PROCEEDINGS
AGAINST OXENFORD ATTORNEY

OXENFORD CARRIED $50,000
LIFE INSURANCE FOR DAUGHTER

3 OXENFORD EMPIRE OFFICIALS
TESTIFY BEFORE GRAND JURY

ATTORNEY GENERAL SAYS OXENFORD
INSURANCE CANNOT BE ATTACHED

BURGOYNE DENIES KNOWLEDGE
OF OXENFORD ACTIVITIES
Circus Man Says He Was
Merely An Employee

GRAND JURY FAILS TO INDICT
OXENFORD OFFICIALS

BAR ASSOCIATION ABSOLVES
ATTORNEY OF BLAME IN
OXENFORD DEALINGS

GOVERNOR DECLARES LEGISLATION NEEDED
TO CONTROL ACTIVITIES OF TRUST COMPANIES

GOVERNOR SAYS MANY OXENFORD
ACTIVITIES "LEGAL FRAUDULENCE"

*

From the journal of Harold Henderson:

Chicago, Illinois
July 4, 1907

Since this is Independence Day no classes are being held, and I
had anticipated a day of study despite the heat. This morning,
however, a letter reached us by special delivery from Carlotta's
mother which has distressed us both.

The Tamarack Fidelity & Trust Company, the institution with
which Carlotta's father has been associated for many years, closed
its doors July 2. Soon thereafter Mr. Samuel R. Oxenford took
his life by leaping from the top floor of the Oxenford Electric
Building.

Mother Leslie was unable to state how these events will affect
Father Leslie, but she fears the ultimate results will be adverse.
I share her fears. She reports that the closing of Tamarack Fidel-
ity has been a great blow to Father Leslie.

It is possible, of course, that after those in authority have in-
vestigated the situation Tamarack Fidelity will open its doors

once again; but I fear the possibility is remote. One deduces that if all had been honest and well with Mr. Oxenford's affairs he would not have found life too great a burden to bear.

I never, of course, knew Mr. Oxenford save by repute; but from his public statements concerning matters of moment, and from snatches of gossip, it is not impossible to imagine the kind of man he was.

Mr. Oxenford, I believe, must have been representative of the more than ordinarily successful business man of the nineteenth century. He was a product of his environment and his time. Driven by an urge to acquire, he put his faith in material things; and his inner life—the life of the spirit—withered into atrophy.

When adversity overtook him, when the material structure he had erected collapsed, he found himself unable to turn anywhere for consolation. Doubtless the great poetry of the ages— the noble tragedies of Sophocles and of Shakespeare—were unknown to him. The Greeks attended the theater because they found that great tragedy purged them of the pettiness of workaday life. They left the theater cleansed and ennobled. Tragedy lifted them outside themselves and gave them perspective, causing them to realize how small and yet how divine a being is man. Tragedy gave them tolerance and pity and understanding and love for their fellow man.

It is a terrible thing for a man to be without the consolation of philosophy.

Mother Leslie is especially concerned about the future of the Tamarack Fidelity retirement fund. For many years five percent of Father Leslie's salary has been withheld and placed in this fund at two percent interest. At age seventy he was to begin receiving a monthly check double the amount withheld, the company contributing the same amount as that withheld. Now Mother Leslie fears the retirement fund has been looted and squandered.

Probably her fears are justified. She is bitter; Carlotta is bitter.

I am not bitter. Only saddened. I cannot but remember that after all Mr. Oxenford was only a poor, misguided, foolish mortal. He must have been sorely tormented in his last days. One can only imagine the suffering which will cause a man to go counter to the most basic instinct of self-preservation and take his own life. I cannot help thinking it ironical that the vainglorious structure Mr. Oxenford built—the Electric Building—should have at last served him only as a means for ending his days upon the earth.

I think I might rework some of today's entry in this journal and use it to chastise the pragmatists in my *History of American Philosophy.*

*

Letter written by A. H. Burgoyne:

2609 Wellington Ave.
Tamarack, Iowa
October 28, 1907

Mr. Ivan Pawpacker
Winchester, Missouri
Dear Friend Ive:

I've just finished trying to call you long distance. They tell me you are out of town on a buying trip and don't know your exact whereabouts or when you will return to Winchester. So I'm writing you. When you read this letter will you give me a ring long distance? I want to come to Winchester to do business with you, but don't want to make the trip and find you gone.

Well Ive, a lot has happened since our paths crossed last. Maybe you've heard how everything went to hell all at once last summer. Old Sam went smash all at once, and he ended it all by jumping out of his office window. I was out on the road with my show at the time. I hustled back for the funeral. It was a bad time for it to happen—just before the Fourth of July. We were booked to play a town where they were celebrating the Fourth, and I wanted to be there, but of course the show went on just the same. Good gate.

It's a damned shame about Sam, but guess there's no use crying over stale beer. Sam was pretty foxy, even at the last. Just before he cashed in his chips he deeded this house to Flora, as well as the coal mine at Oxenford and the farm. He owned those clear, in his own name—they weren't mixed up with any of his companies. Also, it turned out he had carried a life insurance policy for a fairly good amount, so Flora and I aren't in such bad shape.

There's been a hell of a stink here. A lot of people lost their savings, and all the suckers who owned Tamarack Electric & Guarantee have howled their heads off. There have been investigations and God knows what all. Even had me up before the grand jury, but I was absolutely in the clear. I was able to prove that I just worked for Sam as park manager and had nothing to do with Electric & Guarantee and all the subsidiary companies. Also, I was able to prove that I started Burgoyne's Circus & Hippodrome with my own funds derived from the sale of the *Clayton Junction Tribune.* So I came through it all with a clean slate. The boys at the Commercial Club are pretty mad at Sam, but they're friendly to me. Glad of this, for a circus owner ought to keep his reputation spotless and his credit gilt-edged in his home city. Then if you run into trouble on the road you can always give leading men in your home city as references.

Had a pretty good season with the show, despite all the financial troubles in the country. Think it's just temporary. Any man's a fool who will bet against this country's ability to recover from a little financial bellyache brought on by a lot of crooks in Wall Street.

I learned a lot about show business this summer. Molly went over biggest of all. Incidentally, I've bought her from the wreckage of Electric & Guarantee, which owned the streetcar company, which owned Funland. (Didn't old Sam have everything mixed up and complicated!) They were glad to sell the bull, and I was glad to buy her. Bought that little devil, Ranger, too.

As I say, I've learned a lot, and I know now that nothing goes over with a circus crowd like a bull. Bulls—you've got to have bulls, Ive. A lion's just a big house cat, and a zebra's only a horse gone convict. It's bulls that make a show. I want a herd, and I want to put my show on rails next season. Maybe not a lot of cars, but at least enough to be known as a railroad show. That's why I want to come to Winchester—to look over what you've got on hand in the railroad car and bull line.

Say! You licked the living hell out of me when you sold me those foxes and that timber wolf and that cougar. Nobody gave a damn about them. You might as well have sold me a jackrabbit! But this will give you a laugh. I sold them all—and at a profit!—to the Amazon Exposition, a dinky little carnival that played day and date with us at the end of the season. Had to talk my head off to sell them, but I did it! Know that will give you a laugh.

I had intended wintering my show at Funland, but with old Sam gone I couldn't very well do that. (The lawyers and receiver and stockholders in Electric & Guarantee are still wrangling about who in hell does own Funland. I want to keep out of it.) Well, at the end of September when we closed I brought the show to that farm near Oxenford. The land doesn't amount to a tinker's damn, but it's going to work out fine for winter quarters. I kicked out the tenant and will remodel the house. Also, am fixing up the farm buildings.

It's a hell of a good spot for winter quarters even if I go on rails, for that branch to the mine from the main line of Tamarack & Northern will work out fine to carry our cars. I have big plans. Took a trip over to Baraboo recently and looked over the Ringling quarters, and ran on down to Peru, Indiana, and met

Uncle Ben Wallace and looked his farm over. I've got a layout
on the farm near Oxenford that has them both beat. I've hired
a handy man named Joe Griffin to be my year round carpenter.
I've got him doing repair work and I'm planning more barns, a
Blacksmith Shop, a Paint Shop—with a sail loft for repairing
canvas—an Animal House, etc. I'm small yet, but I won't always
be small.

Kept the show Sunday School this year. Good policy, don't
you think? I wouldn't carry grift for love or money, although
sometimes when you think of all the cash you're passing up by
being Sunday School you wonder who's the sucker—you or the
gillies. They're calling me Honest Gus—had you heard? I had
a visit with Chas. Starrbuck of the Great Starrbuck Circus—we
showed in towns ten miles apart in August—and he thinks I'm
a sucker to stay Sunday School. He not only doesn't pay his
ticket seller—the guy's an expert at holding back change and
double-counting currency—but he also—now get this!—he also
sells the pickpocket privilege on his show. Not bad, eh? Of
course, he admitted this leads to all kinds of fights and clems,
and he can't book himself back through the same territory next
season, so there're disadvantages, too. Guess I'll string along Sunday School, although as I say, you wonder sometimes if you're
a sucker. But I kind of like the sound of Honest Gus.

Well Ive, give me a ring when you get back to Winchester
and I'll run down to see you. Will probably come by rail, although recently I bought a nifty automobile—Cadillac. Man,
how she tears up the road! I've had her up to forty! Really need
it to go back and forth between Tamarack and the farm. It's
good advertising, too. I had them paint Burgoyne's Circus &
Hippodrome along the sides.

Guess that's about all. I'll tell you more about my first season
when I see you, as well as my future plans. I'm headed for places
and places, Ive! Now don't you wish you'd hooked up with me
in a partnership?

Sincerely tho' merely,
A. H. (Honest Gus) Burgoyne

P.S. Wife and I are "expecting" next month. Figured I needed
a son and heir to carry on the show!

*

From the journal of Harold Henderson:

November 2, 1907

I am laboring endlessly on my dissertation. Dr. Bartholomew
is a great help. Having completed my residence class work at

the University of Chicago last summer, only my dissertation and my Doctor's Oral remain between me and my Ph.D.

Mother and Father Leslie called on us this evening. They were in high spirits. Father Leslie has tried without success to find a position in an office or bank. However, at last he has found a position as a clerk in the Bargain Grocery. He begins work next week. I am happy that they are happy, although it seems an economic waste for a man of Father Leslie's bookkeeping and accounting abilities to clerk in a grocery. I am happy, too, for Carlotta's sake. She has worried a great deal about her family's financial future, since it was announced that the retirement fund has evaporated along with other assets of Tamarack Fidelity. Carlotta should be unworried just at this time, for we are expecting our second child in January.

*

News story from the *Tamarack Beacon,* November 12, 1907, under the head, DAUGHTER BORN TO BURGOYNE, CIRCUS MAN:

Mr. and Mrs. A. H. Burgoyne, 2609 Wellington Ave., are the parents of a daughter born early this morning at Presbyterian Hospital. Mother and child are doing well.

Mr. Burgoyne, a former reporter and city editor of the *Beacon,* is proprietor of Burgoyne's Circus & Hippodrome.

*

Notice in vital statistics column of the *Tamarack Beacon,* January 24, 1908:

Births

Henderson, Mr. and Mrs. H., a son, Presbyterian Hospital.

*

From the journal of Harold Henderson:

January 24, 1908

Another son! And a fine, healthy child he is. One is reminded of the Roman mother who said, "These, my children, are my jewels."

I do hope I shall be able to send both my boys to Harvard. I have never confessed it, even to myself, but one of my great disappointments was in being financially unable to attend Harvard. How stimulating it would have been to sit under Santayana!

Carlotta is doing well, and I have never seen her more beautiful than she looked this morning, lying in bed suckling my son. She is a good wife. In the early days of our marriage I sometimes wondered whether she were as happy as a bride should be, but we have built a good marriage and I no longer wonder, now. Before she left for the hospital she made me very happy. She told me she loved me deeply, and that she considered me the kindest of men. I was oddly embarrassed, and I fear I acquitted myself as clumsily as usual where human relations are concerned. I replied simply by saying, "Thank you, my dear. I have always loved you devotedly." Then I kissed her. She smiled, and her eyes were moist, and I believe that mine were hardly dry.

Now that the boy is safely delivered, I shall return to the completion of my dissertation . . .

12

Those were great golden years for Gus, those years when the nation was half horse and half gasoline; when Theodore Roosevelt discovered a jungle river of no vast consequence and William Howard Taft ruled the land like a benevolent Republican Buddha; when more and more electric lights blessed the American Commonwealth and playgoers were shocked ecstatic by the great climactic scene in *Bought and Paid For*. Halley's Comet swooped and missed and swished its tail away into the outer universe, grumbling it would return some day; and people laughed at Buster Brown and were properly impressed by learned editorials about the Panama Canal.

Gus wore goggles and a linen duster when he piloted his motor car, and his circus expanded and prospered, and more barns were erected at winter quarters, and people were excited about Luther Burbank and Thomas A. Edison and Henry Ford's motor car for the millions. Newspapers spelled airplane "aeroplane," and the *Titanic* would surely have broken a speed record, and the band played "Nearer, My God, To Thee" while the water rose about their knees. The call of the Bull Moose was heard in the land, and thousands of sinners would have fried everlastingly save for the intercession of the Reverend Billy Sunday.

William Jennings Bryan thrived on grape juice and became Secretary of State, and Harry Houdini escaped twice daily on the Orpheum circuit, and thousands of policemen chased thousands of pie-stealing tramps across the sheets of thousands of nickelodeons. Patty went to college, and some people thought *The Sky Pilot* concerned aviation, and Irene and Vernon Castle danced. America danced. Orchestras played "Everybody's Doing It," and for fourteen years the twentieth century struggled to be born, an unruly Gargantua freed at last from the Victorian womb by the sword's Caesarean.

"I had that dream again last night," Flora told her husband at breakfast.

"Uh?" Gus said, looking up from the *Morning Chronicle*.

"I said I had that dream again."

"What dream?"

"That dream I'm always having. About that girl."

395

"What girl's that?"

"Don't you remember, Gus? That girl who tried to steal you."

"Uh. Well, don't let it worry you."

"It does though, Gus. It always worries me."

"Forget it."

"I can't, Gus. I always think about it. The dream's always the same. I dream I go to that schoolhouse, but then it's different from the way it happened. The way it happened, that man schoolteacher made me leave. You know, that Henderson she married."

Gus helped himself to another fried egg.

"Always like breakfast," he said. "Best meal of the day. Have another egg?"

"Don't believe so, Gus. Well, maybe I will. Now about that dream. In the dream, instead of Henderson it's you who makes me leave. What do you suppose that means?"

"Doesn't mean a thing. You know how dreams are. Why, last night I dreamed I was an elephant. Doesn't mean a thing."

Gus laughed and returned to the sports pages.

It was a November morning in 1910. Gus occupied the master's place at the head of the table, the very place where Mr. Oxenford used to dog his food and belch three times. Gus was heavier than in the days when Mr. Oxenford lived. The promise of a double chin had been fulfilled, and his belly was expanding toward hemispheric solidarity and greatness. No longer were his cheeks faintly rosy; his skin was tan. Not long ago he had attained thirty, but his eyes were not that young.

In essence, Flora had not really changed, but certainly she had agglomerated. Gus possessed a great deal more wife than in the early days of marriage. During pregnancy she had lost her figure, and in the years since Barbara's birth she had never found it again. Her hair was still the color of a fireman's nightmare, and her expression was that of a mighty intelligent cow.

Masticating the egg, Flora studied her husband. Sometimes she worried about his color. He told her his tan skin was the result of wind and sun on circus lots, and this was true; but sometimes Flora thought it indicated a faulty liver. She didn't know, but she thought so. Several years before, he had discontinued his calisthenics and his icy showers. Now he maintained his great good health by Turkish baths and massages. But just the same, Flora wished he had not discontinued his calisthenics. Cost less than Turkish baths, and in the health column of the *Beacon* she read that bending exercises were stimulating to the liver. The same health column informed her that the liver was virtually a charter member of the Anti-Saloon League; nothing annoyed it more than cigars, rich food, beer, late hours. Despite his penchant for joining, Gus had never evinced the slightest interest in the Anti-Saloon League. He loved cigars, rich food, beer, late hours. This worried Flora. She didn't mean to be a nagger; it was only that she considered the best interests of his liver.

Now, as her husband turned the newspaper page, she said:

"Gus, I think maybe I ought to see Madam Thale."

"Uh? Why?"

"About that dream."

Gus chuckled. "Don't fall for her hooey. Leave that to the gillies."

"Oh, but she's good, Gus. She's psychic."

"You've been listening to Butch."

He was referring to Butch Strollo, a man with tough vocal cords who stood on a platform outside the side show of Burgoyne's Circus & Hippodrome and urged the public to spend one thin dime for a ticket. Within the side show, which Gus called the grind show, one could receive occult intelligences from Madam Thale, the celebrated seer who had often advised the Emperor of Germany and the Czar of All the Russias.

Ever since the days of Carlotta's grand larceny, Flora had maintained her friendship with Madam Thale, for after snatching a matrimonial prize like Gus, she did not want to lose him. Madam Thale had never told Flora about Inez and Ruby, possibly because she was unaware of those light ladies; wire trouble would occur on the line between the Madam and the zodiac. She had, however, given Flora a great deal of common-sense advice about how to annoy her husband as little as possible. Gus was only hazily aware of the professional relationship between the two women; and when, upon the Madam's prompting, Flora suggested that he hire her for his circus, he realized instantly the merit in this idea.

That was back in 1909. Flora brought Madam Thale to the house, ushered her into Gus's presence and left them alone to discuss terms. The interview took place in what had been Mr. Oxenford's library. When that financier was among the quick, the room had had a dark, sober quality. Gus had changed all that. Converting it into his den, he ordered the walls painted cream and the woodwork pale yellow.

"Liven the place up," he told the workmen. "And take all this junk up to the attic."

The junk at which he waved included Mr. Oxenford's high book-keeping desk and various decrepit old chairs.

In Mr. Oxenford's time, few pictures decorated the walls. High priest among these was a steel engraving of Benjamin Franklin, with whose opinions on early-to-bed and thrift Mr. Oxenford agreed hysterically. By the time Madam Thale visited Gus, Poor Richard had been exiled. Now, brilliant lithographs splashed the walls. The lithographs mentioned Burgoyne's Circus & Hippodrome, and there were likenesses of yellow tigers and kingly lions. One poster showed countless circus cars in a railroad yard, with several elephant herds. Another depicted a big top with eight center poles and numerous smaller tops.

"I didn't realize your show was so big," Madam Thale said.

"Uh—well—tell you. We're not quite as big as all that. But we will be. We're growing."

In the years since Flora had first consulted her, the Madam's skin had grown drier and more cracked, but her hair was as blond as ever, her teeth as gold. She read Gus's palm, predicting a long life and tremendous riches, and then they discussed terms.

"I'll give you your feed and a berth on the train," he said, "and you can charge what you please for fortunes."

"Charge?"

"Of course you'll charge. And all you take in above fifteen a week we'll split fifty-fifty."

"Let me get this straight, honey. I thought if I gave readings in the grind show, and you charge admission, I'd have to do it free."

"Not that at all. That entrance fee is just the beginning. Once they're inside we charge 'em for everything we can. Life story of the midgets, life story of the wild man, pamphlet on how you can eat fire—"

Waving his cigar, he halted before the fireplace. It crackled cheerfully with hickory, as it had never burned in Mr. Oxenford's fuel-hoarding days.

"Of course, I run a Sunday School show. Want you to understand that. Matter of fact, they call me Honest Gus. My advance men always mention that when they get a license. Sometimes, though, when I think of the pickings I might take—"

Gus sighed, eyes wistful.

"Why, we could charge 'em for the grind show and have a few games inside. Not that I'm thinking of it, understand. I'm just telling you why they call me Honest Gus. We could have three card monte, and the shell game—oh, that's a game, Madam, that's a game! Thousands in it. I was talking to Honest Jack Dennison the other day. He'd work it any way I wanted. Pay me a flat sum for game privileges, or split with me. Think a flat sum would be better, because you can't trust Honest Jack.

"I refused, of course. And know what Honest Jack said to me? 'Gus,' he said, 'who's the sucker now? You or the rubes?' What could I say? No answer to that one. Honest Jack has some pretty good connections. He knows one of the slickest little dips. . . . Met him at Honest Jack's. A little guy named Deacon Charley. Know what the Deacon did to me? Just while we stood talking he pulled my watch and roll slick as a whistle."

Gus laughed and added hastily:

"Gave 'em back to me, of course. All in fun between friends. But it just goes to show. . . . Best thing, I think, would be to sell the pickpocket privilege outright. Those dips are such damned crooks you'd never get your split. Not that I'm thinking of quitting Sunday School. You start running a crooked show and you run into all sorts of trouble. On the other hand, dips will follow a show. Kept us busy last season chasing them off the lot. But we couldn't chase them off the parade route. It makes a man wonder. You'll have pickpockets either way. Sometimes I think it would be more practical to sell the privilege and be done with it. Then your dips would chase off outsiders. That way, the thing would be controlled. All open and above board, so to speak. The other way, you've got a lot of outside dips that are no better than parasites. A farmer gets his pocket picked and he blames you even if you don't know the dip and aren't getting a cut. No justice in that."

After they came to terms, Madam Thale gazed at the railroad-yard poster and asked:

"How many cars do you have?"

"Uh," Gus said, "let's see. I'm adding some this season. Hope to add at least one. Would add more, except I'm building up my bull herd. Bulls are more important than cars. Had three bulls last season. Hope to get a couple more this year. Buy 'em from a fellow named Pawpacker. I like the little devil, but he's a close bargainer. Banker. Sort of tight. Don't know why it is, I'm always getting mixed up with tightwads. No pockets in a shroud—that's my motto. . . . Uh, as to the cars. Mine are better than the average show's. Bigger, safer, more commodious. Let's see. Last season I had—uh—six. I'll keep adding, though. First season I was in wagons. Next season on rails! Growing! Got the Ringlings worried already!"

So Madam Thale joined the show in 1909, and that stirred Flora's interest in the enterprise. Till then, she had accepted her husband's owning a circus in a matter-of-fact spirit, as if it were an occupation as commonplace as selling sausages or tombstones. Flora's observation told her that most men worked at something or other; Gus had entered show business; and that was that.

"Guess I'll go out to the farm and see you off," she said, a couple of mornings before the season opened.

"Uh—sure you want to?"

"Guess I will. I kind of want to."

"Thought you might rather catch the show when we open in Tamarack."

"Guess I'll go out to the farm."

"How about Barbara?"

"I'll take her along."

So Gus drove to Ruby Woeckener's flat and broke the news that she could not after all accompany him to the farm that day. She didn't like it. She stated it was bad enough, his refusing to take her on tour. But now—this!

"But honey—"

"Don't 'honey' me! You're tired of me, that's what. You don't care for me.any more."

Gus sighed. And he resolved that once he was through with Ruby he would desist from these extra-matrimonial adventures. Where did they get you, anyway? Took your thoughts from building your show.

"Now Gus," Flora said, "don't drive too fast."

Carrying Barbara, she had emerged from the house and stood regarding the new Apperson beneath the porte-cochere.

"Huh?" Gus called from the tonneau, where he was stowing luggage.

"I said I wouldn't drive too fast, Gus. It's dangerous."

"Safer than horses. Faster and safer."

"I don't think it's safer than horses, Gus. It may be quicker but I don't think it's safer."

"Statistics prove it."

"I don't think it's safer, Gus. And I hope you won't drive too fast. Might scare Barbara."

Gus roared with good humor as he puffed to the porch.

"Why, this little lady wouldn't be scared of her dad's driving. Look at her! Smiling all over the place!"

Barbara was a little beauty. She looked not like Flora, or Gus, or Mr. Oxenford, or a railroad vice-president named Phelan. More vivacious chromosomes had patterned her. Her eyes with their thick curving lashes were the color of woodland violets; her skin was pale olive, her hair dark brown.

"She'll be a heartbreaker!" Gus sometimes announced. "It's a scandal the way she flirts with me. Fifteen-twenty years from now, there'll be a line of beaux from the front door to the street."

"I don't know, Gus. I don't think you should say that."

"It's the truth."

"Maybe so, but I don't think it sounds refined."

This afternoon, Barbara gave her father a bewitching smile and said, "B'loon."

"Want a balloon ride? That what you want?"

Barbara extended her hands and Gus inserted his great paws beneath her armpits.

"Whoopsy-do, whoopsy-do!" he roared, and Barbara soared high, screeching with delight.

Flora watched dubiously, like a cow that disapproved jumping over the moon. She least understood her husband when he romped with Barbara. Didn't seem dignified. Mr. Oxenford had not been given to frolicking. In motoring costume, Flora looked matronly. A duster encased her ample figure, and she wore a large hat with a heavy veil.

"You be careful, Gus. Don't drop her."

But neither husband nor daughter heeded. Sometimes when they played together Flora felt excluded.

"Think that's enough, Gus. You're puffing. Don't want to wear yourself out. You'll tire out Baby, too."

"Hoo! One more. One more ascent. Parachute jump, this time. Big crowd watching. Daredevil Barbara and her balloon. Hoo! Here we go. Whoopsy-do!"

"Don't think you ought to call her Daredevil Barbara," Flora muttered to her veil.

After Daredevil Barbara yipped earthward by parachute, Flora picked her up and carried her to the car. The top was down, and as Flora entered the back seat the car swayed. She harbored a faint suspicion against the internal combustion engine. Just a toy, Papa had said, an impractical toy.

Despite Papa's descent, without parachute, from the Oxenford Electric Building, Flora remained loyal to his memory and many of his ideas; she still believed he had been a great financier. Say what you wanted to about Papa, he had built a fortune from nothing. At times he might have been too careful with money, but that was how he got rich, by being careful. Better careful than spendthrift! Sometimes she worried about the way Gus was going through the insurance money. He said you had to spend money to make it. Maybe. Papa had never said that.

Nearly everybody blamed Papa, but she thought they misjudged him. In her opinion, Papa had been betrayed by his lawyer and by those other businessmen. After his death people snubbed her—as if she had had anything to do with starting those bank runs!—but she was able to bear their ostracism fairly well. After all, it was hard to ostracize her from Wellington Avenue Society when she had never been in it. Moreover, Madam Thale remained a staunch friend. When Flora became lonely she invited the Madam to Wellington Avenue for the day.

Flora had fretted lest the businessmen ostracize Gus, but they had proved broad-minded and charitable. When It had happened ("It" was Flora's euphemism for Papa's swan dive) Gus had been traveling with his circus, and—luckily enough!—Papa's money had not backed that first circus. Things had a way of turning out for the best.

Even if the businessmen had wished to ostracize Gus, it wouldn't have been easy: about like ostracizing a tornado. Her husband was a great good mixer. The world never knew it when a gloomy mood overtook him. Being his wife, she knew it, and she would ask:

"What's the matter, Gus?"

"Nothing. Got the blues, I guess. Must be something I ate."

"I think it's your liver, Gus."

Certainly he didn't have the blues this afternoon. Having donned goggles, duster and gloves, he bustled to the front of the car and gripped the crank. After herculean effort he was rewarded by a cannon roar from the exhaust. He hurried to the front seat and calmed the motor. Some men cranked a car unobtrusively, but when Gus urged combustion there was a large, fateful air about proceedings.

Gaining the avenue, he sped along at a good clip. Most of the teams past which he whizzed were blasé animals, accepting the transportation revolution with good grace; but now and then a farmer's team took a few steps on hind legs. Gus drove principally with accelerator and horn, and his journey across town to Madam Thale's did not pass unnoticed. In the business district the letters announcing that this car belonged to Burgoyne's Circus & Hippodrome caught many glances.

"There goes Burgoyne," he imagined people saying. "The circus man."

This put him in fine spirits.

Gus's arrival at winter quarters loosed stores of energy in his employees. Even if workmen had nothing to do they did it anyway, with great dispatch. They knew he loved bustle.

All this industry did not stir Flora to emulation. The nervous wear and tear of motoring with her husband had exhausted her, so she was glad to sit in the living room and recuperate.

"Don't you want to look around?" Gus asked. "Been lots of building going on since you were here."

"Don't believe so, Gus. Kind of tired. Think Madam and I will just sit here. Have a stick of gum, Madam?"

"Thanks, honey. But maybe Mr. Burgoyne has work for me to do."

"No," Gus boomed, "that's all right. Guess you don't need to rehearse your pitch. I'll show Barbara around the place."

"Now you be careful, Gus. Don't let Baby get close to those cages."

So, carrying his daughter, Gus left the house and crossed the carriage yard. On the east side a low building had been erected, and a sign said: "Office." Lorenz, the general manager, was waiting outside. He was a big man of fifty-five with suspicious eyes, and he hailed Gus.

"It's about Pete Nesbitt," he said.

For two seasons Pete Nesbitt had served as general ticket seller, and Gus wanted to know what about him.

"He fell off a bridge last night."

"Did what?"

"Fell. Or maybe jumped. Happened in Tamarack. Seems Pete was liquored up, celebrating the new season, and he was showing some guys how tightwire walkers work, and he fell off the bridge railing."

"Uh. Shouldn't have done that. Hurt him?"

"Didn't do him no good. He lit on the bank. Broke both wrists."

Gus swore about this piece of ill fortune, and asked who they'd get to sell tickets.

"That's what I want to talk to you about. I know a guy we could get cheap. He'd work for the love of it."

"Now wait a minute! You know we're Sunday School."

"That's right. We're Sunday School. But just thought I'd speak of the guy."

"Who is he?"

"Well now Gus, matter of fact he's my brother-in-law."

"Brother-in-law. Uh." Gus spoke in a tone that suggested this changed things somewhat. "Nice fellow, I s'pose?"

"A prince of a fellow, Gus. One of the nicest fellows you'll meet anywhere. He's got a smile like an angel. Everybody likes him. No rough stuff. A gillie gets shortchanged, this guy will smile and everything's dandy."

"Smile means a lot," Gus said. "Keep smiling—that's my motto. Uh—where's he working now?"

"Well now Gus, that's a long story. Walt—his name's Walt Ambrose —Walt ran into some hard luck a few years ago. He was on the Indio World Shows, and when they were playing Illinois there was some trouble. Upshot of it was, they put Walt in Joliet. But he's out now, and looking for a connection. You'll never regret taking him on."

"What kind of trouble?"

"Nothing serious, Gus. Nothing to do with the treasury wagon. Think there was a roughhouse and some punk was killed. One of those things. But nothing to do with ticket-selling."

"Where is he now?"

"In Tamarack. He could join out there. You'd never regret taking on Walt. He can count change from a twenty-dollar bill so you'd swear it was right, and yet he'll hold back ten. Think you might be interested in Walt?"

"Might."

"If you are, let me know soon. Walt's got a couple of other good offers, but of course he'd rather travel with us, account of him and me are brother-in-laws."

Gus nodded thoughtfully. Evidently there was considerable good in Walt, if he were swayed by such a strong sense of kinship.

"I'll think it over," Gus promised. "Let you know in a few minutes. Want to show Barbara around the farm just now."

Lorenz leaned close to Barbara, his broad grin revealing his missing back teeth. Her tiny hand closed over his extended forefinger and she regarded him coquettishly through half-lowered lashes.

Gus had the instincts of a builder, and many improvements had blessed the farm since he appropriated it. The Animal House had been completed recently, and inside, Barbara renewed her acquaintance with Molly. Full-grown and huge, the elephant murmured with delight when she spied Gus.

"Well, old girl!" he boomed. "How's it go?"

"Ah-h-h-h . . ."

Gus reached up and scratched Molly's ears. Her hobble clanked as she swayed with affection.

"This old girl and I are pals," Gus announced. "Old pardners, that's us. She knew me back when I didn't have a cent."

Barbara regretted bidding good-by to Molly, and after they had left her and climbed the ridge Gus chuckled and told his daughter:

"You're like me. You like elephants. Bet a man could take out a show with nothing but a bull and make money. The biggest—that's what attracts the public. Your grandpa didn't understand that. Even Pawpacker doesn't, way he should. But I always say what did Hannibal use when he crossed the Alps? Bulls! And by golly we'll cross the Alps some day ourselves. Tour Europe with the show."

And although Barbara didn't comprehend all this she listened wonderingly, riding along on Gus's arm like a princess on an elephant, and suddenly she flung her arms around his neck and kissed him.

"Love you, Daddy."

"Well now," he bellowed, "guess that goes double. Yes, sir! Guess I love you more than I love Molly even."

On the ridge he put her down, and they stood in the late sunshine. Off to the northwest the hamlet of Oxenford was a cluster of weathered houses, mainly deserted. Work had stopped at the mine, owing to the increasing quantities of slate. As he gazed at the high tipple he scowled. It seemed there should be some way to cash in on the mine. He couldn't figure how, but it was a problem that now and then engaged his attention.

His gaze swung along the valley to the tents in the pasture, to the new Ring Stock barn, long and red-painted between the interurban tracks and the road. On the siding near the barn his railroad cars were strung, pumpkin-yellow and chocolate-brown. He had enjoyed giving the cars names, as if they were argosies. The car with his office and stateroom he had christened "Clayton Junction."

What should he do about the ticket seller? He wished he didn't have to make the decision. But circumstances had a way of forcing decisions. Oh, the hell with it! Guess he'd tell Lorenz to try hiring another ticket seller. And if none were available, then let Walt Ambrose join the show. For a few days. See how it worked out. If the gillies complained they'd been shortchanged it wouldn't be his fault. Circus was a big organization. He couldn't control the actions of every employee.

Barbara was plucking his coat, wanting to go down and see the tent. He picked her up, and her smile was heartbreaking. He had never known how a smile could twist you inside till he had begotten a daughter. He had never known what love was. By God, nobody would ever harm her! Always he would stand between her and the corruption of the world. Things would be different for Barbara. Her life would be high and shining.

At the rehearsal next afternoon Gus lost his temper many times, for the performance was as poorly synchronized as a thousand-legged worm suffering locomotor ataxia. Nearly all the acts were independent units hired from booking agents, and each maintained its individuality instead of molding itself into the complete performance.

The rehearsal began at 1:30 and it was still going strong at five. And the whole show should run only two hours! Gus paced up and down the hippodrome track, lacerating and discarding cigars, shedding coat and vest, rolling up his sleeves, shoving his hat farther back on his head. He roared and rampaged. By God, he'd whip the show into shape or burst a blood vessel. Opening tomorrow in Tamarack, and look at the damned thing. Suppose Carlotta should attend the performance tomorrow!

No longer was Gus equestrian director; he had grown beyond that; but from experience he knew just how an equestrian director should keep things moving.

"Pace!" he bellowed at the new equestrian director. "Pace it! Pace it! Keep it moving! They don't come to a show for a nap!"

In its expanded form, Burgoyne's Circus possessed two rings and a wooden stage, and the tent was much larger than in wagon show days. The audience at rehearsal included all the grind show freaks and geniuses; and the roustabouts and razorbacks were there, and the candy butchers.

Madam Thale did not watch the show from the blues. In a roped-off box near the band, she sat on a folding chair beside Flora and Barbara. Whether Flora shared her husband's perturbation it was impossible to tell. To the rehearsal she brought the matter-of-fact equanimity that only such emotional holocausts as Papa's passing and Carlotta's theft and Gus's chauffeuring could disturb. By motion of her jaws alone did she betray the dramatic influences of the circus: her gum-chewing kept time with the band. She did not gasp at the trapeze performers, or cheer the tumblers, or laugh when clowns wheeled in a buffoon automobile that kept smoking and exploding.

Now and then she told Madam Thale:

"I'll sure miss you, Madam. I'll miss your advice when you're gone with the show."

"I'll miss you too, Flora."

"You've been a good friend to me, Madam. Best friend I've ever had. I'll sure miss you."

Sometimes Gus returned briefly to the box, where bottles of beer reposed in a tub of water and ice. Continuing to watch the performance, he snapped off the cap and tilted the bottle, letting half its contents slide down his throat. Sweat runneled his cheeks and drenched his shirt.

Toward the end of the afternoon the general manager entered the tent, and the corner of his mouth told Gus:

"Couldn't locate any other ticket seller, so I phoned Walt Ambrose to join us tomorrow."

Concentrating on a pony act, Gus merely nodded. And he yelled toward the ring:

"Have to pace that faster. You're playing too long."

And thus did Burgoyne's Circus & Hippodrome forsake all that Sunday School nonsense.

The rehearsal lasted till 5:30, and when it was over Gus ordered all performers into the tent. They were lugubrious, perching themselves on the blues. Gus stopped pacing, flung away his cigar, grinned broadly and boomed:

"All right, kids. Let's not have any hard feelings. If I've lost my temper forget it. You're pretty good. All of you. Pretty good bunch of artists. Don't think the Ringlings have anything that can touch you."

The bleachers were a withered flower garden revivified by honeyed rain.

"We're making history, you and I. Yes, sir! Before this season is over you'll all be famous. I can tell. You've got the stuff."

For five minutes he flattered them, collectively and individually. Living to please, they had to please to live, and his words were salve and cocktails. This was the A. H. Burgoyne they had liked so well when they arrived at the farm.

He jollied them and he joshed them; he told the story of the color-blind Irishman in a red-light district. He had them hysterical. He had them in his two big paws. He was God for a little while, and he loved it.

"All right, kids. Want you to eat and rest and act on the suggestions I've made. Want you back here ready to roll at eight o'clock on the dot. We're going through the show again, and by God if we don't keep it down to two hours I'll break your necks. We'll zip through the whole thing, and then see how fast we can get loaded. All right, beat it."

Flora had not remained for his speech, and Gus lingered in the tent after everybody else had gone. The late sunshine had turned the canvas golden. The trapezes hung motionless. The red wooden tubs and the blue-painted bleachers, waiting for crowds and crowds, looked beautiful to him, as much the essence of the circus as names like Fore-paugh and James A. Bailey and P. T. Barnum. Someday a new name would be a household word in America. A. H. Burgoyne. Honest Gus. In the twilight Carlotta would tell her children that once she had known A. H. Burgoyne. Reluctantly he left the tent and crossed the pasture, his shadow before him, and for a second it seemed he was walking like a young god in the fires of the setting sun. And it seemed that Carlotta was out there in futurity waiting for him. Somehow, they would meet again. That was a hope that trouped ever with him during those years when he was young.

That was a fat season for Burgoyne's Circus & Hippodrome, the first summer of the big money. Gus felt like a hog in a corn crib, like a janitor in a United States mint. It seemed he couldn't make a wrong move that summer: it was like poker when the cards were running right. His roll of bills grew bloated, and no matter how fast he spent the stuff there was always more. It was like walking in a sleet storm of five-dollar gold pieces.

Once he left the show for a quick train ride to Winchester, where he bought more animals and equipment.

"I'm glad you're doing well, Gus," Ive Pawpacker said.

"Doing well!" A rich chuckle flowed up Gus's throat. "Why Ive, we're shoveling it in. We don't miss anywhere. Now don't you wish you'd joined up with me?"

It was a sweaty afternoon, and they were sitting in the livery stable office. Ive was adding a column of neat figures, and he didn't reply. His silence brought a hearty laugh from Gus.

"Ive, you old devil," he roared. "I can tell you wish you had. Didn't I tell you we'd make a cool million?"

Ive smiled, and Gus laughed harder.

The pencil finished its work. Burgoyne's Circus & Hippodrome owed Ivan Pawpacker $13,993.27.

"There it is, Gus," Ive said, handing over the bill.

Gus didn't check the addition. Lips pursed, heavy eyes jovial, he gave the paper a cursory glance. Then he pawed out a thick checkbook and a fat fountain pen.

"Oh, hell," he said, as he started writing. "Let's make it an even fourteen thousand. I hate piddling with odd numbers. Besides, thirteen's unlucky."

Ive heaved a mental sigh. And as always, he experienced both admiration and disapproval at Gus's largess. He observed him making out the check. Gus used a blunt-pointed pen, and the ink flowed freely. He wrote with broad strokes. Prosperity was puffing his hands, puffing his body. In today's heat his huge face was red and sweating beneath his shoved-back straw hat. He ripped out the check and flipped it to Ive's desk as if it were a cigar coupon.

"There you are, Ive. Easy come, easy go." He tipped back, stretched, thumped his meaty chest. "I'm doing some building this summer at winter quarters. That farm makes a nice layout."

"Isn't there coal under it?"

Gus nodded. He was about to say, "But it's no damned good. Too much slate."

But such talk was defeatist. It was like mistrusting your poker luck when you were scooping in every pot.

"Sure there's coal. That's why old Sam left the place to me and Flora. Some of the richest veins in this country run under that farm."

"Are you working the mine?"

"Matter of fact, I'm not. Too busy raking in the wampum. Way I figure it, that coal's been there a long time, and it's not likely to walk out on me."

And Gus rumbled on about other things, but the fact that rich coal lay beneath the farm stuck in Ive's brain.

If Walt Ambrose had remained in Joliet, Gus might have showed even fatter profits that summer. Between them, Walt and Lorenz made a very good thing out of the circus. Despising details as he did, Gus was content to let Lorenz keep the accounts, and this was like hiring a hungry wolf as a sheep herder. Gus enjoyed watching Walt work, and when the boss climbed into the red treasury wagon Walt was right on the job. He was a lean, round-shouldered man in a hard straw hat, and a never-ending stream of metallic words left the side of his mouth. His expression was as dead-cold as the tip of his half-smoked cigar.

The ticket counter was higher than the eye level of customers, and a thin strip of wood had been tacked to it. When Walt wanted to hold back silver he would openly count it from his right hand to his left and then slap all that chicken feed down to the counter behind the strip. When he pushed the change toward the customer the strip detained part of it. Gus had to fight back a laugh.

The customer grabbed the change and squirmed through the jam of people crushing toward the window. Now and then, of course, some suspicious tightwad would count the change for himself. When that happened, one of the roustabouts stationed by the wagon would shoulder the fellow off into the mob. And when the sucker elbowed back to the window, five minutes later, Walt would be unable to recall him. "I'm sorry, brother," he'd grin, "but I can't remember you. Too many people. You shoulda squawked when I gave you the change."

And if the customer turned out to be a troublemaker, the roustabouts asked him a few questions. They inquired what he was trying to get away with. They asked him what he was attempting to pull. How would he enjoy a fast one in the snoot, they asked.

But Walt was at his best when some idealist expected correct change from a ten or twenty. Right under your eyes he could count the same bill twice or three times: he accomplished this miracle by folding the roll of change around his forefinger.

When business was high the money rolled in so fast there was no time to sort it, so Walt shoved it into a bushel basket beneath the counter. Gus enjoyed picking up the basket and feasting his gaze on that green currency. Sometimes he plunged his hand deep into the basket, like a bear pawing wild honey.

When the circus was at winter quarters Gus did not always wish to drive every day to the farm, so he established offices in town. These were nothing spectacular, but he furnished them comfortably, and gold leaf on the door announced that this was the city headquarters of Burgoyne's Circus & Hippodrome, A. H. Burgoyne, Owner. The offices were located in the Oxenford Electric Building, a few floors below what had been Mr. Oxenford's quarters, and the windows of Gus's private sanctum looked directly on that part of the atmosphere through which the old fellow had whizzed. But Gus was not sensitive about this; never thought of it.

Needing a secretary, he employed Beryl. Some of the applicants were pretty droopy specimens, but as soon as Beryl smiled to a chair and unbuttoned her coat Gus realized that here was a superior amanuensis. And as far as that went, the girl actually could type. Not, perhaps, ninety-six words per minute, but speed wasn't everything. She took shorthand too, if Gus spoke slowly. He was satisfied; and since he was paying her, whose business was it?

Not Ruby's, certainly, although that girl acted as if she owned him. He didn't tell her he had rented an office, but she learned about it somehow, the way the Rubys of this imperfect world always learn things like that, and first thing you knew she was dropping into the office at embarrassing times, wanting money and seeking information as to why he never called at her flat.

Ruby and Beryl never hit it off very well. When Ruby swept in with her furs and plumes you would have thought the place a power plant, from the electricity in the air. Once when Gus had left word he didn't wish to be disturbed—he was talking serious business with Honest Jack Dennison, arranging things for next season—Ruby flipped across the outer office, anyway. Beryl sought to bar her, and trouble of a more or less physical variety ensued. Looking tousled, Ruby flung open the door. Gus and Honest Jack settled the gambling part of their arrangements, and were discussing pickpocket privileges. Ruby wept and spoke in a shrill voice and even descended to profanity.

Scenes like that can be embarrassing. Luckily, Honest Jack was broad-minded, but Gus's visitor might just as well have been the president of the Greater Tamarack Association or the secretary of the Commercial Club. Gus had recently been elected president, and the secretary often dropped in for counsel.

"Gus," Honest Jack said, after Ruby departed, feathers soothed by a gold-back, "let me give you some advice. I'd get rid of that twist, Gus."

"You would, huh?"

"Yes, I would, Gus. A woman who can't respect a closed door is a bad egg, Gus."

"Something in that, all right."

Honest Jack was a medium-sized man of sixty, with carefully brushed gray hair. He wore a salt-and-pepper suit, a snowy shirt, a blue four-in-hand with a quiet stickpin. His hands were small and beautifully manicured. He always kept his voice confidential, and he had the air of knowing many facts that would accompany him to his grave.

"Now," he said, "about this business of the dips. If you prefer a flat sum, that's satisfactory with me, Gus. I think—"

Honest Jack had got his start in Western mining camps, but for years now he had operated the Eagle Cigar Store down near the Union Station, and on the rolls of the Commercial Club he was listed as a tobacconist. Outside the store, a battered old wooden Indian menaced pedestrians with uplifted tomahawk, and as far as that went it was possible to purchase cigars in the front room. But it was the back room from which Honest Jack derived a snug income. It was a large blue-aired chamber with subdued lights and a long bar, and the walls were decorated with oil paintings of such classical subjects as Venus in her bath. The air was fragrant with excellent tobacco and liquors and the perfume of the lighter ladies of the town. As you entered you heard the click of roulette balls and the voices of dealers at the crap tables announcing that eight had just been achieved in the hard way.

A leather-bound door separated the front room from the back. This was kept locked, not in a spirit of inhospitality but because of convention. Actually, you were very welcome there, as you discovered if you thumbed a button on the door-jamb.

Only when a raid was due did they leave the door unlocked. Newspaper readers could count on those raids twice a year; they were as regular as the autumnal and vernal equinoxes. This did not mean that Honest Jack and the police were at odds. On the contrary, everybody agreed that the raids were a fine, healthy thing. They satisfied the church element and gave the police commissioner something at which to point with pride. Honest Jack wouldn't have had it any other way. He and the police talked it over, deciding upon a raiding hour convenient for both, and Honest Jack gave his dealers the afternoon off and told customers the place was closed for the day. Equipment was hidden and then the police arrived, often accompanied by some self-appointed vice crusader. Once a year they found the place empty and once a year they found a half-dozen men playing cards. With gong clanging the patrol wagon carried these criminals off to jail. They were out on bond in an hour and a few days later Honest Jack paid all fines. Editorials and ministers commended the vigilant police, and the whole business could be forgotten for six months.

Several afternoons a week Gus dropped in there for poker. You were always meeting interesting people at that round, baize-covered table. Often you found Pud Myra there, for although he headed the detective bureau of the police department he liked a game of stud as well as anybody. Between him and Gus existed the warm friendship possible between two men succeeding in noncompeting fields. When Gus was a police reporter Pud had been a sparrow cop, and now each was forging ahead. Gus always predicted Pud would be chief some day.

"Gus," Pud said one afternoon, "I've got a favor to ask."

"Favor? Sure. Have a cigar."

"I'm on the committee for our police benefit ball, and we're looking for entertainment. Do you have a circus act you could lend us?"

"Uh—don't see why not. Where'll the ball be?"

"Civic auditorium."

"Uh. With that good concrete floor looks to me like a bull turn would be all right."

"A what?"

"Elephant act. Might bring Molly in."

Pud thought that would be splendid, although he said the guests might wonder about the punch, if they started seeing elephants. Gus laughed and looked at his hand and the game went on.

But presently he wasn't paying much attention to his cards, for some idea kept tiptoeing to the threshold of consciousness and darting back. He'd make a grab for it, but it would escape. Then it didn't escape, and he rumbled:

"Uh—Pud. Mind sitting this hand out? Matter I'd like to discuss with you."

The two men shouldered through mauve haze to a far corner. Both looked dim and huge, heads inclined confidentially. Gus did most of the talking. Pud listened, smoke dribbling from his lips, and once he chuckled and poked Gus in the ribs.

"Sure," he was heard to say. "Glad to. Glad to take care of it for you. Know how those things go. Glad to."

Two mornings later the doorbell rang in Ruby's flat, and four men in plain clothes entered, flashing badges. They informed Ruby they might well toss her into the can, for she had sinned against the laws of the commonwealth, but inasmuch as they were weary of testifying on immorality charges and hearing judges pronounce sentences, they would let her off easy. They were giving her till midnight to leave town and keep going.

"Farther you go, better we'll like it," one man said. "Like the nigger says you go so far it'll cost four dollars to send a post card."

The men laughed.

Not Ruby. Ruby was scared sick. She tried to find Gus at his office, but Beryl said he was out of town. She even tried to find him at his home, but both he and Flora were absent. So that evening Ruby boarded a train. During the following months Gus received letters from her, postmarked Louisville and Cincinnati and Baltimore. She wanted money. After a time the letters stopped coming and he never heard of her again.

For several years after marriage Carlotta and Harold were very poor. Even at a large, rich university a young man who expects a teaching fellowship to support him must live frugally. Carlotta and Harold soon discovered that a teaching fellowship is an erudite name for an academic sweatshop. At Chicago, Harold worked a sixteen-hour day, and sometimes an eighteen- or twenty-hour one.

They lived in a tiny flat on the South Side, a cell in the monstrous honeycomb of Chicago. Harold was both student and teacher. Part of the day he sat under learned men, filling his notebooks and his brains; and part of the day he occupied the instructor's desk in section meetings.

Hundreds of undergraduates were enrolled—and occasionally even mildly interested—in such courses as Philosophy A and Logic 1. Twice a week these droves of tyro Aristotles listened to lectures by associate professors and awesome full professors. But in a large class like that, how can one be sure that each and every student is retaining the wisdom flowing from the podium? One cannot: that's one's answer. Hence, one breaks up the course into sections. Students whose surnames begin with letters from "A" to "E" are channeled into a section. Those from "F" to "J" into another section. This goes on right through the alphabet, to Xenophen, if there is a Xenophen, and Yohomakawa and Zchovitch. Each section contains about thirty earnest—one trusts— young men and women, and the sections meet with such pedagogic chore boys as Mr. Henderson. Mr. Henderson devotes part of the section meeting to general discussion, clearing up such matters as the difference between an idealist in philosophy and an idealist in life. Then he gives a quiz.

But one must not fancy that his labors are thereby at an end. They are just beginning. After collecting the papers he must correct them, grade them, record the grades and leave the grades in one's box. On the basis of these grades one determines, at semester's end, whether Mr. Zchovitch is to receive an "A," a "B," or possibly an unfortunate "F."

It is gratifying to have these details attended to by persons like Mr. Henderson. However, one will readily comprehend that if one were to hire this work done on a full-time basis the budget of one's department would suffer. So the trick is to offer teaching fellowships whereby persons like Mr. Henderson receive free tuition and a modest honorarium. It is advisable for the recipient of a fellowship to have saved a certain sum to aid him in discharging his pecuniary obligations.

Chicago was hot and sticky when Carlotta and Harold arrived by day coach. And flat-hunting was a disheartening business, because the only places you could possibly live were operated by landlords who had no understanding of the finances of graduate students. So finally you moved into a place where you could not possibly live.

Not for years could Carlotta look back and find her honeymoon tinged with romance. In those early weeks the marriage was saved only by her will power and by the astonishing fact that Harold was a skillful and understanding lover. (He had read Ovid.) During the long days when her groom was meeting sections and worming through tomes in the library she was bitterly homesick. And Gus-sick, too. Tears dripped off her chin as she dried breakfast dishes. She hated Chicago with a black, unreasoning hate. It frightened her. Those end-

less ash-colored streets! Those swarthy inhabitants jabbering and jabbering! Those hooting whistles of traffic officers in the Loop! The
growl and roar of the place, trying to pull you into some polyglot
nightmare!

Not only did she think of Gus. She thought of Jim Wheeler too, a
lawyer in one of those massive Loop blocks. If she had married Jim she
wouldn't be living in a flat where people and parrots and phonographs
were always screeching. Why had she married Harold! Oh, why!
Marrying on the rebound was about the most senseless yielding to
pride and emotion that she could imagine.

But after September, Chicago weather turns very nice. When asked
about the weather in July or February, even the Chicago Chamber of
Commerce has to change the subject. But in October and early November you really have something. You have yellow sun on an intensely blue lake, and the air is as crisp and sweet-smelling as washed
clothes on a line. In October Carlotta stopped abhorring Chicago and
began tolerating it. Presently she was embracing it.

There were Sunday afternoons on the lake front with Harold. There
were Saturdays when they lunched in the Loop and visited the Art
Institute or bought cheap seats for excellent plays. There were hours
browsing in bookshops. And that winter there were concerts.

Harold made friends among the graduate students, and pretty soon
you were invited to the flats of other young couples. Living on a shoe-
string seemed like fun, when you laughed about it with other graduate
wives. It seemed like adventure. You were young, and you caught the
feeling of struggling joyously toward a lofty goal. Pretty soon you
weren't thinking so much about Gus.

Chicago. Englewood and Jackson Park and Wabash Avenue and
Dearborn Street. In later years those names were synonymous with
youth. You remembered that electric feeling of Michigan Avenue, the
feeling that you were clipping briskly along one of the streets of the
world in one of the cities of the world. You remembered the cavernous
sleeping power of the financial district at night, brass gates barring the
entrances to banks and the sight of a watchman in shining marble
vistas. You remembered the city fighting a blizzard, yowling and
scooping right back at stinging snow. You remembered spring nights
when those specks of light far out on the lake were ore boats from
Duluth.

And at some time during that first year you began loving your husband. Love didn't roar into your life this time . . . and out of it. It
came quietly, like the changing of a season, stealing in so softly that
you couldn't name the hour when it arrived. You began feeling sorry
for him when you saw him late at work by his study lamp, he looked
so industrious and so thin and tired. Sometimes he removed his glasses

and closed his eyes and with thumb and forefinger pinched his nose where the glasses had clamped it.

He was good, that was one thing. He tried to be like the Greeks. Not the fruit-stand Greeks but the Greeks in the Golden Isles when the world was at its morning. He thought the Greeks were good because they were wise, and he doubted that the great Greeks ever lost their tempers, so he didn't. And the Greeks were patient, so he was patient.

Maybe you changed, too. At first you didn't know why he was so enthusiastic about the Greeks, but pretty soon you caught some of his bright vision of that sun-flooded, rocky land where olives grew, where you might hear Pan fluting in the hush of daybreak and Zeus rumbling above the clouds of a summer storm, where the bluer-than-blue Aegean creamed and swished among the shore rocks. You caught his vision of Socrates as a tremendous shining intellect, Socrates in flowing robes with the young godlike men listening while he went hoboing through the sunny land of the mind.

And maybe he changed. Became—well—more human. Maybe he grew to realize that all the golden hours of life were not ensnared in the books. Maybe you taught him to splash around in life as it was now. To laugh at vaudeville slapstick as well as at Shakespearean slapstick. To savor the taste of sherry. To fill his lungs with the smoky, power-charged air of Chicago.

Yes, that was it; you both changed, each growing toward the other. You were in the same boat, in marriage together. It was both of you against the world. Chicago could roar and rumble outside, but it couldn't get at you in your little flat, because you were marriage. You had something that a lot of people didn't have. And so perhaps you were not so poor, after all.

When you returned after two years in Chicago and Harold became assistant professor, Tamarack seemed pretty small. But then almost any city would have seemed a frog to Chicago's crocodile. Omaha, Kansas City, Minneapolis—any of those Mississippi Valley cities in Tamarack's population bracket would have seemed tame.

You lived in a house now and went into debt for furniture and you were busy with the baby. You worked hard and liked it, and the hours and weeks and months elapsed, and it was Thanksgiving before you knew it with all the Wednesday evening excitement of singeing pinfeathers off the turkey. Such a big turkey! You were having the folks over for Thanksgiving dinner and you were scared silly you couldn't cook that enormous bird to taste like anything. So in the kitchen on Wednesday evening you and Harold pondered the problem and he thumbed through your cook books and read aloud the various advices about rendering a turkey fit for human consumption. You both laughed a good deal.

Harold was looking better since he became assistant professor at the University of Tamarack. You cooked him appetizing meals and his face was filling out. His skin didn't look so gray. He loved his work: if ever there were a born teacher it was he. He was a Master of Arts now and well on his way toward becoming a Doctor of Philosophy. Dr. Harold Henderson, assistant professor of philosophy. And the head of the department had promised that year after next they would promote him to an associate professorship. In the academic world those ranks meant a lot. To the public any man on a college faculty was a professor. Ha! Little did the public know, little did they know! It was like feudal society. A mere instructor was nothing. Less than the dust. An assistant professor was a young man to be watched. An associate—that was getting somewhere. And when you became a full professor—well! That was nearly as good as a dean. They couldn't fire you if you were a full professor, unless, of course, you started impregnating co-eds with something more than learning. But no worries about Harold on that score. Thank God he wasn't in music or dramatic art!

Yes, that first year on the Tamarack faculty slipped fleetly past, and when the time came to return to summer school in Chicago you dreaded going. You liked your house, even if it was only rented and none of the closet doors fitted correctly into their frames. Harold said you'd start buying a house, after he took his doctorate.

A better flat, this time, but Chicago summer nights weren't anything to write a travel folder about, especially with the wind off the stockyards. But Harold didn't mind the smell. He said it was the smell, in a slightly different form, of the deep soil of the richest river valley in the world. Great civilizations often emerged from great river valleys, he said. The Euphrates. The Nile. And now it was the Mississippi's turn. He said he would try to work that idea into his *History of American Philosophy*. One evening he elaborated the idea, and he made it sound epic and stirring. In your mind you saw the great lazy Mississippi on a living map, beginning its journey among the pine smells of Minnesota, and as it flowed it grew broad, as the waters of the Rocky Mountains came pouring into it from the yellow Missouri, as the Ohio joined it with waters that had fallen on the Appalachians. And you saw the measureless empire of Middle America where farm boys were studying by lamplight to become the judges of tomorrow, the engineers, the philosophers, the painters, the poets. Nevertheless, the stockyards still smelled like stockyards.

Ellis Higby Bartholomew, professor of philosophy at the University of Tamarack, was a plump, rosy little man who had never done any harm to anybody, except maybe flunking football men. Even that didn't happen much any more, because in advising the squad about what courses to take the coach steered the boys clear of philosophy. Oriental Art and History of Architecture—those were the courses to take. You'd have to be virtually a Juke or a Kallikak not to come through those courses with a gentleman's "C."

By 1911 Dr. Bartholomew was one of the grand old men of the Tamarack faculty. He had come to the school away back in the 1870's, when it was a small college in a small city. Old Main was a new building when he arrived with the ink still damp on his Yale Ph.D. He had lived to see Tamarack become a good-sized city and the college a good-sized university.

Dr. Bartholomew kept his promise in the matter of an associate professorship, and when Mr. Henderson became Dr. Henderson he became also an associate. And Dr. Bartholomew gave Dr. Henderson a great deal of sound advice about the book he was slowly writing, *The History of American Philosophy.*

One April morning in 1911, a month after Dr. Henderson became the father of a third child, a daughter, Dr. Bartholomew didn't feel so well at breakfast. He felt dizzy and he suffered a headache. He didn't meet his classes that morning, because of losing consciousness, and that afternoon he went wherever good philosophers go.

"Dr. Bartholomew passed away from a stroke," Harold informed his journal that evening. "This is a terrible blow. I do not know how I shall carry on without him. Only yesterday we discussed the chapter in my book concerning the transcendentalists, and he seemed in excellent health."

The *Tamarack Beacon* splashed the news all over page one. The editors were neither philosophers nor sons of philosophers, but they had the journalist's intuitiveness that senses the significance of events without necessarily comprehending that significance. Dr. Bartholomew had been a hawser linking the nineteenth century with the twentieth. He had heard Lincoln speak and he had seen an airplane fly. In his boyhood men had been scalped on the prairies by Indians, as well as on the stock market by traders. He had lived in Emerson's day and in Billy Sunday's. Of course, many men older than Dr. Bartholomew were still alive, but they were dropping away, one by one, and it began appearing inevitable that someday nobody would be walking the American earth who had walked it when Lincoln wore a shawl and Grant chewed cigars. America had entered the twilight of the celluloid collar.

In the newspaper business it's feast or famine, and that day there was more news than you knew what to do with. Not only had Dr.

Bartholomew died; the police had raided the Eagle Cigar Store and bagged seven men playing cards for money.

Because of these events, a news-feature yarn with pictures was crowded off page one, back to page nine. It concerned Burgoyne's Circus & Hippodrome, opening its fifth season that day in Tamarack. Few persons regretted Dr. Bartholomew's death more than A. H. Burgoyne.

The old one about an ill wind held good in Harold's case, and that June the trustees of the University of Tamarack endorsed his appointment as full professor and head of philosophy. (This was the same week that a shakeup occurred in the police department and LeRoy (Pud) Myra became chief.) Although Harold was only thirty-three, he brought great dignity and erudition to the post. That summer he labored tirelessly, outlining the new courses he would teach and even getting in a few licks on *The History of American Philosophy.*

Harold had lost his bean-pole thinness, and no longer did his austerity and flashing nose-glasses seem slightly absurd. It was as if he had been to the Ph.D. born, as if at seventeen and twenty-five he had actually been a full professor in spirit. He was like a youth who had once worn clothes too big for him, but who had now grown into them, and they fitted perfectly.

The year before, he had purchased a house a few blocks west of the campus. It had a full third floor—his study—and a large shady back yard where Harold, Junior, and four associates were excavating an underground house. Sometimes Carlotta sat out there with three-year-old Leslie and three-months-old Portia. Carlotta enjoyed the services now of a maid. They could afford such luxuries, for Harold's salary had mounted to $3,500 a year. Nothing spectacular, but a comfortable amount and a steady one. They were even talking about buying a motor car. Again, nothing spectacular: it would have to be a Ford. Harold doubted that he could learn to drive, but Carlotta said she would do that. That would probably be safer, for often Harold's thoughts strayed far from the immediate present. Wondering how best to deal with Margaret Fuller in his *History,* he might push the wrong pedal or move the wrong lever.

Getting along toward thirty, Carlotta was still the prettiest faculty wife at the university. Childbirth hadn't devastated her figure, and her skin was still glowing and smooth. When Harold held open house for his students on Sunday evenings, they thought it remarkable that scholarly Dr. Henderson should possess such a vivacious wife. They liked her so well that they were always choosing Dr. and Mrs. Henderson as picnic and dance chaperones. Harold considered this a great bore—one of the crosses a professor had to bear—but Carlotta was secretly delighted. Her smooth arms and throat looked beautiful in a party gown. Carlotta taught him to dance, so they wouldn't have to sit all evening, but this was one field of learning in which he didn't excel. His legs moved about as flexibly as stilts, and his patent leathers and the music never seemed to get together on anything. Even when the dance was high he would be thinking about Jonathan Edwards or Emerson or somebody. Nevertheless, Carlotta was very proud of him; he looked distinguished in his dinner jacket.

Sometimes weeks passed without her thinking of Gus, and then a publicity story about his circus would appear and for a few minutes she would feel not really sad but nostalgic. She would remember how young she had been that day she had first gone to Funland Park. Back in 1907 when the papers told of his starting his circus she had experienced a sudden heaviness of heart, and she had retired, ostensibly with a headache, and had cried. But by the time Harold came to bed she was all right. She wouldn't have traded Harold for Gus. She no longer loved Gus, but he had always roused some protective instinct in her. At times he had been very wistful, like a pup that had been abandoned and wanted love and a home. Harold never seemed to need what Gus needed: he was more self-sufficient, possessed of a tougher inner spirit. Yes, of the two men Harold was by far the stronger. Seeing them together, people wouldn't have thought so, for Gus would have puffed up and blustered and laughed and back-slapped, covering up that abandoned puppy soul, and Harold would have looked stiff and socially ill-adjusted. People would have put their money on Gus. Not Carlotta. After her children were born she gave them the love and protection she had yearned to give Gus. That was why she didn't cry any more when she saw his picture in the *Beacon* on circus day, a man grown huge standing by an elephant grown huger.

As a faculty wife you were very busy. There was an organization called the Faculty Dames which met twice a month and promoted benefits to raise money for a new girls' gymnasium. They elected you secretary of this. And you were always being asked to pour at the president's reception or the dean's reception. Once a year you entertained the president and his wife at dinner, and you always talked for days convincing the current maid that food should be served from the left. You attended plays presented by the department of drama and recitals given by senior music students. The old literary societies had gone the way of the Prince Albert coat, replaced by Greek letter societies called fraternities and sororities, and one sorority invited you to join. This was a gesture honoring a faculty wife, and possibly the sisters even hoped it would have a beneficial effect upon grades in philosophy.

So Carlotta joined, but eventually, like anybody growing older, she

believed the old order had been better. In the days of literary societies
the university had been a friendlier, more democratic place. Simpler.
But then America and the social order had been simpler back around
the turn of the century. Bicycles and buggies instead of motor cars.
Waltzes instead of fox trots and bear hugs.

Her being a sorority member had no effect upon the sisterhood's
philosophy grades. Dr. Henderson was widely known as the nemesis
of the apple polisher. With some professors all you had to do was
wear a sweater or a tight skirt and sit on front row, and if you were
asked to discuss the significance of the Magna Charta you looked
pretty and said well, the Magna Charta was something like—ah—well,
you know, like something important and it had been signed by a number of King Arthur's knights at—ah—brilliant smile—ah—Runny—
ah . . . And when the professor said Runnymede you said of course,
that was the place, and when he said it was King John you told him
you meant King John all the time, and when he said it was the English
barons who made him sign and the knights had nothing to do with it
you said certainly, he was absolutely correct there, and as a matter of
course you got a "C." Maybe even a "B," if what was inside the sweater
and skirt was good enough.

But Dr. Henderson was immune to the wiles of peek-a-boo waists
and the hobble skirt. He realized that co-education even at its best
jeopardized scholastic standards, and he suspected that the University
of Tamarack was not co-education at its best. Harold tried not to be
snobbish about his University of Chicago doctorate, but the fact remained that many of the faculty had never attained more than a Master's degree, and those with Ph.D.'s had taken them from odd places
like the University of Wyoming. He hoped some day to lift the standards of Tamarack to those of Chicago. He hoped some day that Tamarack would abolish intercollegiate athletics, but this was improbable,
for winning teams attracted students and besides, there were a great
many six percent bonds outstanding on the new stadium.

Under Dr. Henderson athletes fared no better than pretty girls. He
might have had an all-American tackle in class and never known it.
He might have had a future Follies beauty and never known it. Sometimes his students doubted whether he saw them as individuals at all:
they were just a class. He lectured, mainly, sitting at his desk and
speaking in a voice as dry and colorless as chalkdust. Occasionally he
rose and paced.

Often in those lectures he put forth tentative theories that later he
would rework and incorporate into his *History*. The book absorbed
him more and more, for he realized that in the academic world it is
not the inspirational quality of one's teaching that counts; it is publishing. How could a department head at Michigan or Chicago or Penn-

sylvania know whether one's students were inspired or ennuied? But if one published a sound, scholarly book with an impeccable index and copious footnotes, one's name became known. And some morning a letter would arrive from Michigan or Chicago or Pennsylvania, couched in the involuted prose of the profession. Boiled down to plain English, the letter would say: "We've got an opening. We've tried out your book on a thousand students, and it put every one of them to sleep. You must be smarter than all hell, guy. If you'll listen to reason about salary, we might make a deal."

No matter what Harold said, the class never disputed him. When he mentioned that Francis Bacon perished as a result of stuffing a fowl with snow, nobody asked whether the fowl was chicken, turkey or goose. He might have said Bacon died from sinus trouble or an ingrown toenail and they wouldn't have disputed him. He might have said it wasn't Francis Bacon at all, but Roger Bacon, and that it wasn't a fowl but a rabbit which infected him with tularemia: the class wouldn't have objected. For twelve classroom hours a week Harold's word was Olympian.

This strengthened his self-assurance. On that long-ago afternoon when he ordered Flora Oxenford to leave Manning School, steel had stiffened his spine, and now it was present most of the time. He grew accustomed to respectful listeners. From various teachers at the University of Chicago he had picked up little professorial mannerisms, and he superimposed these on his personality. He had a trick of wagging his forefinger and another of removing his eyeglasses, inhaling and then blowing the air from his lungs. That one he used when some young lady interrupted with a question about some point he had elucidated last week. He was well on the way to becoming a faculty character.

His academic behavior elicited respect from the rest of the faculty. Like Harold, all had borrowed mannerisms from their old preceptors; all spoke with measured dignity, with understatement; all had their stables of favorite jokes, as old as Pharaoh's horses and more circumspect, which they trotted out in class year after year. All were intellectual undertakers; all conspired to convince these concupiscent young Americans that David had reigned in Israel and Copernicus had dreamed the wheeling universe and Shakespeare had written till the Thames was red with dawn just so they could be embalmed in Hebrew History A and Astronomy 1 and English 6.

Occupations brand their followers. In faculty meeting, Harold's colleagues knew he was one of them. His words carried the weight of a Chicago Ph.D. The paucity of "A"s on the records he filed with the registrar convinced them he was a hard teacher, a sound teacher. And he was an academic conservative. He believed in the tried and true curricular virtues of Greek and Latin. The elective system had made alarming inroads. Vocational advocates were menaces. He used words like qualitative and quantitative examinations, like percentile; and what's more, he understood them. He was a stickler for details, decorum, modes of procedure. "Mr. President," he would say, politely but firmly, "I rise to a point of order. . . ." He voted against granting a Monday holiday when the team won from their old rivals. Grades which students received in other courses impressed him, even though he realized all professors did not maintain his high grading standard. He thought of students as possessing "A" minds, "B" minds, "C" minds. When a lad he had flunked became a war hero in 1918, and another made a million in the 1920's, he never understood. He remembered only that the first lad could not spell, the second whispered during lectures.

Without Carlotta, Harold might have carried that sort of thing to excess. And without Harold, Junior, who spoke perfect English till they sent him to school, but who soon thereafter came home saying, "Aw, them guys is crazy. . . ." When Harold pointed out that Kittredge and Fowler preferred, "Oh, those boys are mistaken," Harold, Junior, protested, "Aw gee, Pop . . ."

Yes, he was Pop and Dad as well as Dr. Henderson. And he was Honey or Sweetheart to Carlotta. At home, she wouldn't permit him to maintain his lecture manner for long. She joked him out of it. When she held a Halloween party for the children and their friends, to keep them off the streets, she made Harold don a costume and bob for apples. She kept him human. And with Christmas approaching, in 1911, she insisted that he accompany her and the children to Toyland in Goldstein's Department Store. They started for the car line at midmorning one Saturday, at about the time Mr. and Mrs. A. H. Burgoyne left the Wellington Avenue home with Barbara, also bound for Toyland.

It was a warmish morning of brown grass and sunshine so pale it cast scarcely a shadow.

"Will it snow, Daddy?" Barbara asked. "If it doesn't snow for Christmas how can Santa come?"

"Don't you worry, sweetheart," Gus boomed. "I've been checking up. Fact is, I called Santa by long distance last night. He's bought an automobile."

"As nice as this one?"

"Uh—don't guess it's as nice as this. Not many are."

And that was not boasting; that was fact. This was the fourth car Gus had owned; he had purchased it two months before, after a prosperous circus season. It stood outside what had been Mr. Oxenford's stables. Like Mr. Oxenford, the horses had disappeared.

Motoring was Gus's hobby. Owning a car was as exciting as owning an airplane, twenty years later. The lore of the automobile was vast and fresh. Sometimes Gus whiled away a whole evening leafing through *Motor Age,* dreaming over the advertisements like a boy over a mail order catalogue. Last year he had been elected president of the Tamarack Automobile Club, and in the cause of good roads he was not inactive.

This car was a Haynes, pale yellow and ornamented with brass. At no extra charge the dealer had stenciled a monogram on the door: "A.H.B." And along the sides ran the legend: "Burgoyne's Circus & Hippodrome." Only a ninny could have doubted who owned that car.

Although the machine gleamed and flashed, it was not speckless enough for Gus; he was industriously swiping the hood. He looked as well turned out as the car. The best tailor in town had created his suit from the best imported woolen. It was conservative and yet dashing, with its tiny check in silver-gray. Because of his expanding waist, Gus was no longer so easy to fit, but the tailor had mastered the problem. He wore a derby this morning, and the heliotrope necktie that flowed from his high linen collar was adorned by a single ornament, a very small horseshoe set with diamonds, in the best of taste if your taste ran to horseshoes. Another diamond sparkled on the little finger of his left hand.

Gus loved possessions, rich, showy possessions. A fortnight ago in the *Beacon* he read an account of a speech delivered before the Tamarack Women's Club by Dr. Harold Henderson. The educated fool declared, with Socrates, that those who wanted the fewest things were nearer to the gods. Gus broke out laughing when he read it.

"Just what you'd expect from him," he thought. "Wonder what Carlotta thinks about that. Bet she'd rather have a husband who's going places instead of starving along on a teacher's salary."

Oddly, the statement stuck in his mind, troubling him. It sounded like something Frank might have said. One glum evening Gus grouched about the library, thinking it over. He had to admit that he wasn't actually happier with his new automobile than with his old one. He had a twenty-car show now, and a dozen bulls, but as he looked back it seemed he was happier that first summer with his little wagon circus.

Damn the educated fool, anyway, for saying a thing like that and upsetting you. A half-truth! Wouldn't hold water. Suppose people were converted to that idea. Modern civilization would collapse. If people wanted few things where would that leave the salesmen? Up the crick without a paddle! Where would it leave the merchants, bankers, pickpockets, gamblers, lawyers, car dealers? Same place. Looking at it that way—reducing it to absurdity—Gus had to laugh. Certainly was a shame Carlotta had got stuck with that idiot.

Like her father, Barbara was expensively turned out, and like him she and her clothes maintained a symbiosis whereby each gained in style and flair from the other. Her slender legs were encased in white ribbed stockings, her dainty feet in black-and-white patent leather shoes. Her white coat was of curly chinchilla with big white buttons. A little red hat was tip-tilted on her dark hair.

"Looks better now, doesn't it?" Gus said, stepping back from the car. "Better polish."

"Yes, it does, Daddy. It looks a lot better." She glanced up coquettishly. "You look nice too, Daddy. You look beautiful."

Gus laughed and roared. He inserted paws beneath her armpits and lifted her. She squealed and giggled. But she added:

"Don't muss me up, Daddy. I'm too old for Daredevil Barbara, now. Don't muss me up so I won't look nice and you won't be proud of me."

"Be proud of you if you wore gingham."

"I don't think I'd like gingham, Daddy. I like velvet best. Velvet and silk. I love silk."

"Don't want to wear gingham, don't have to," Gus said. "Guess that's why I work so hard, to buy you velvet."

"I love you, Daddy. Let me kiss you."

She flung her arms around his neck and showered him with kisses.

"You look mighty nice yourself," Gus said, putting her down. "Mighty pretty."

"Am I a pretty little girl, Daddy?"

"Should say you are! Ought to have a yellow hair ribbon with that red hat."

"Why ought I?"

Grinning broadly, Gus leaned over.

"Because," he confided, "red and yellow, catch a fellow. That's why. Red and yellow, catch a fellow."

Barbara laughed merrily and rolled her eyes.

"Red and yellow, catch a fellow. Maybe Santa will bring me a yellow ribbon. Think he will, Daddy? Red and yellow—"

Gus consulted his watch. It was the watch the boys at the *Beacon* had given him when he left newspaper work. He could have afforded a better one now, but he kept this one from sentiment. The old gang had dispersed; when he visited the *Beacon* now he saw strange faces in the city room. Many of the new reporters didn't realize he had once been city editor, till he told them. They were polite and respectful, and that was gratifying, but it would have been even more gratifying if they had yelled, "Hello, Gus, you old reprobate. Where've you been?" Instead, they called him Mr. Burgoyne. They realized he was an important man in town.

The watch was still guarded by the heavy gold chain with the dangling lion's tooth. He returned it to his vest pocket.

"We'd better get started. Your mother's waiting."

"I want to sit with you in front," Barbara said.

He boosted her into the car. Usually when they motored that was the arrangement: Flora behind, father and daughter in front. Sometimes Gus wondered whether Flora noticed how in this and many other situations Barbara preferred her father's company.

Gus didn't crank the car today. Cushions wheezing, he seated himself behind the wheel and tramped a button. The motor exploded into life. Self-starter! Progress! Imagine that educated fool saying those who wanted the fewest things were nearer the gods! Sour grapes!

The car rocked along the drive and paused beneath the porte-cochere. Gus switched off the motor: that way, he would have the pleasure of starting it again. He honked the horn.

Wearing a hat as big as an eagle's nest, Flora opened the door and hoofed it across the porch. Before descending the steps she paused, staring at the car as if she were beholding for the first time a gasoline-propelled vehicle. She always did this.

"You ready?" she asked Gus.

"Ready? I'm Reddy's brother."

She stared at him. "What?"

"Nothing. Just a joke."

"Oh. I didn't get it."

Barbara was giggling fit to kill. "Don't you see, Mamma? You asked if we were ready, and Daddy said he was Reddy's brother. Like Reddy was a man."

"Now Gus," Flora said, preparing to enter the back seat, "I hope you won't drive fast. It's dangerous."

"I'll keep 'er down to forty," Gus grinned.

Barbara giggled again. She was a good audience. With her so appreciative he had fallen into the habit of lightly baiting his wife.

"Forty's too fast, Gus. You drive that fast and Barbara will have to go to the bathroom. Scares her."

"It does not scare me, Mamma! I'd like to drive a hundred. I'd like to drive a million."

"Now Barbara," Flora said.

"I don't know, Barbara," Gus said. "Think a million's too fast. I'll keep 'er down to a hundred."

Barbara was giggling so hard it seemed she really must have to go to the bathroom. But that wasn't true; it was just her father's wit.

Flora appeared a little contemptuous of all that nonsense. At least, she was fairly certain it was nonsense; the car could not attain a hundred miles an hour; anybody knew that. When her husband and daughter went off on one of those silly tangents, Flora withdrew behind the moats and thick walls of her stupidity. Her stupidity even gave her a kind of superiority. She did not despair because she was stupid; she didn't even know it. What she did not understand she dismissed as unimportant, the way a counterfeiter dismisses Gresham's law. Nonsense.

"You can laugh," she said, "but just the same accidents happen. They happen every day."

"Every night, too," Gus said. He was getting warmed up, now. "If they didn't, don't know who'd buy toy balloons at the circus."

That one whizzed over Barbara's head, but Flora comprehended and, to her credit, she blushed.

"Gus!"

"Uh," he said.

"I don't think that's nice."

He was shaking with laughter; he had a great sense of humor.

"Well, I don't," Flora added.

Barbara gazed from the mirth-red face of her father to the shame-red face of her mother.

"Mamma," she said, "I think I want to go to the bathroom."

"See there, Gus? You talk about fast driving and you scare her."

"Uh. Well, don't take too long. We want to get down to Goldstein's before they close."

"Oh, we will, Gus. They'll be open for hours yet. They won't close till six o'clock."

"They might close," Gus said, a little grimly. "They might get bored and decide to call it a day."

"That's silly," Flora said. "I never heard of such a thing."

She heaved herself from the car and accompanied Barbara into the house. Gus ignited a cigar. Almost automatically, his thoughts turned to his circus. He would try to add more cars and animals next season. No longer did he buy all his equipment from Pawpacker. He shopped around. Last spring he stumbled on a great bargain. Arnold's Circus went broke and he bought six railroad cars and a lot of stock for a song. He hadn't seen Pawpacker for more than a year. Ive was a nice fellow but a sharp trader; you had to watch him. The last time he talked to him, Ive had hinted they might hook up in a partnership. Gus wasn't interested; he was doing very well alone. The thing was, Ive saw how much money Burgoyne's Circus was raking in and he wanted to get his hands on it.

Funny the way things went. Eight years ago Gus would have given an arm to go into partnership with Pawpacker. And now when he

didn't need Pawpacker's resources the little devil offered them. Some-
times Gus wondered what life would have been like if he had married
Carlotta instead of Flora. He would have got the *Clayton Junction
Tribune* eventually, and he could have sold it and started a wagon
show. But he wouldn't have been able to expand so fast, without Mr.
Oxenford's insurance money. Still, it was nice to think about, he and
Carlotta starting out in the spring with painted wagons.

Barbara came skipping across the porch and into the car. But Flora,
enslaved by habit, paused at the edge and stared at the Haynes.

"Guess we're ready now," she said.

"We're Reddy's brother," Barbara said.

At that moment, Dr. and Mrs. Harold Henderson with their three
children were crowding into an elevator bound for Toyland.

Gus stepped on the starter and the motor caught. Lot of power in
that motor. It had a rich, liquid, throaty roar.

Tamarack looked beautiful on that morning of pale sunshine and
soft sky. The trees on the Burgoynes' lawn had lost their leaves, but
they didn't look stark with the hazy sunlight mellowing them. Even
the big old house didn't look so bad this morning. Last summer Gus
had hired it repainted a creamy white, and with its flashing clean windows and spacious porches it looked like a rich man's home. It wasn't,
of course, exactly that, but it was the home of a man who would be
wealthy some day if he would only save part of the money rolling in.
The great wooden dunce caps on either corner still slandered Flora and
the memory of Mr. Oxenford, but Gus thought it a nice home.

Steady as a Pullman, the car rolled along Wellington Avenue. A
year before, the street had been repaved with bricks manufactured by a
company in which the streets commissioner had more than a passing
interest. Goodness knew the street needed repaving; the old bricks
had been there since the days when Doll Burgoyne and Gus Phelan
drove a spanking team along the avenue.

Cities grow and cities change, especially when they are full of bustling wholesale houses and fine stores. Especially when they serve a
prosperous section of a prosperous state, and distances are shrinking because of the motor car. Men start insurance companies and establish
home offices. Men invent things like better washing machines and hair
tonics and vacuum cleaners. To begin with, they manufacture those
things in the back room of a barber shop or a plumbing establishment,
but sometimes the thing takes hold and factories are built and people
move to town; and first thing you know it isn't the same city it was.
Some people are nostalgic for the city as it used to be, but Gus wasn't
among them.

He thought of himself as growing with the city, and it delighted him to see how the business district was probing an exploratory finger out Wellington Avenue, how apartments were rising, how delicatessens and bakeries and shops selling a single luxury item, like furs, were fronting the avenue, how some of the close-in old houses had been sold and were being razed to make way for commercial enterprises. Other houses that had been High Society back in the 1890's were now funeral establishments.

Sight of the business skyline lifted his heart. Against the tender sky those spires of commerce stood out silver-gray. His cigar cocked up from his smiling mouth. Those massive buildings represented power and progress. Heady stuff! Great town, Tamarack! In and out of his consciousness phrases darted: on and on, bigger and bigger. His brain basked warm and mellow as a landscape in sun.

Traffic thickened as Wellington Avenue plunged toward the heart of town. A busy pre-Christmas Saturday. And nearly as many motor cars as horses crammed that pulsating artery. Up ahead, Gus glimpsed a white-clad street sweeper with his little cart, industriously brushing manure into a neat pile.

"Won't see those fellows much longer," he told Barbara. "Your grandpa saw them, and his grandpa, and his grandpa. But your children won't know anything about them. Horse will be a curiosity."

"Who won't we see much longer?" Flora called from the rear.

"Street cleaners. Reminds me of the traveling man who said to the street sweeper, 'This is sure a one-horse town.' And the street sweeper said, 'Brother,' he said, 'if you had my job you wouldn't think it's a one-horse town.' "

Flora got that one, but she didn't think it very nice. Gus was laughing, but she thought it improper to mention those fabulous traveling men in Barbara's presence. She said as much. But Gus ignored her protests; he was explaining the joke and Barbara was giggling.

Possibly that was why, at the corner of Wellington and Twelfth, the Haynes journeyed on into the intersection after Sergeant Terence McMullin of the Tamarack Police Department indicated that it should pause.

"Hey! You!" called Sergeant McMullin.

The Haynes tarried then, and Gus scowled around. The sergeant's tone was too raucous for hailing a man like A. H. Burgoyne: former president of the Commercial Club, member of the Greater Tamarack Association, president of the Tamarack Automobile Club.

"Who'd you think you're yelling at?" Gus inquired.

"Yelling at you. Didn't you see me signal?"

One trouble with Sergeant Terence McMullin, he had contracted a head-cold three nights before. Patrick, his fifth and youngest child, had been seized by colic at 2:47 A.M., and Sergeant McMullin had paced the floor with Patrick. In so doing, he had neglected to dress warmly enough. Nor had he opened the draft of the hard-coal burner in his house in East Tamarack. Hence the room was chilly. Hence Sergeant McMullin began sneezing.

In its thirty-five years of inhaling and exhaling, the nose of Sergeant McMullin had never been redder or sorer. This darkened his outlook. All the time he stood directing traffic he was brooding how Sally was pregnant again, how he forever owed bills to physicians and surgeons, how he had thrown in his lot with the wrong faction in police department politics, how the opposing faction had boosted Pud Myra up to chief. And then, when he lifted the majestic palm of the law, ordering Wellington Avenue traffic to cease and desist, this fat rich-guy drove his wealthy car right into the intersection. And so, representing the power of the city of Tamarack and the United States of America, he strode over to the car and bawled out the cigar-smoking driver.

He hadn't spoken many words before he suspected he had selected the wrong man. About the driver there was nothing contrite. A deep flush pumped up his heavy throat and spread to the roots of his hair. The driver swore. At a cop he swore. The driver explained explosively who he was. Sergeant McMullin was now beyond caring who the driver was. The driver maintained that a policeman was the servant —not the master—of the people. Such unheard-of philosophy was tantamount to resisting an officer. Go ahead and give me a ticket, the driver urged. See what good that would do Sergeant McMullin. So Sergeant McMullin obliged, and the driver roared we'd see about this, and the Haynes shot off down the avenue in a bluish cloud of exhaust smoke.

During the next fifteen minutes Sergeant McMullin took it out on draymen and cabdrivers.

The new Municipal Courts Building glistened in the sun on the east bank of the river. It was of that modified Grecian design known as United States Government architecture. Across its white front, cut in stone, ran the legend: "Erected By The People Of The City Of Tamarack." The legend didn't discuss why public buildings cost so much more than private ones.

White-globed electroliers flanked the wide, shallow steps leading to the entrance of the Municipal Courts Building. The door flashed and revolved, and inside the reflections of lights were frozen in marble corridors.

The chief was in conference. The conference was taking place in a remote chamber where electricity glared into the eyes of two woozy, bleeding bums who were willing at last to confess sticking up a grocer Thursday night even though at that time they had been in St. Joseph, Missouri.

The chief smiled into his office with his belly slopping out above and below his leather belt. He heard the complaint. He took the ticket, grinned, tore it up.

"Sorry about it, Gus," he said. "McMullin is a trouble-maker. Tell you what. I'll discipline him. Give him a week's layoff without pay."

The physicians and surgeons whom McMullin owed money weren't going to like that, but it pleased A. H. Burgoyne.

"Have a cigar, Pud," he said.

Pud leaned over for the match Gus held.

"Nothing wrong with this cigar," Pud said. "Um-m-m—Gus. Been meaning to call you. We'd like an act for our annual police benefit ball, and I wondered—"

Anything . . . Sure . . . Elephants . . . Tigers . . . The world was not a whirling globe of stone rotting into soil. The world was a great, ripe melon to be sliced and gobbled by massive men.

"Fixed it up," Gus grinned to wife and daughter. "Guess that will show that cop."

He considered driving back to Wellington and Twelfth and making a left turn and telling the cop he hoped he'd enjoy his layoff. But it was getting on toward noon so, ballooning with good humor again, he drove along streets festooned with Christmas decorations and loud with the bongs from Salvation Army Santas. He nosed into a parking spot a second before a car that had stopped ahead and was going to back into it. The other driver was mad. Hadn't he ever heard about survival of the fittest? What did he think life was—a pink tea party?

The great slabs of Goldstein's plate glass window mirrored two huge figures, A. H. Burgoyne and wife, and a daintier one, Miss Barbara Burgoyne. Little lady, little beauty.

"I want a yellow ribbon. I want a yellow ribbon from Santa. Red and yellow, catch a fellow."

"Barbara! You shouldn't say—!"

"Daddy said it. Red and yellow, catch a fellow. Daddy said it, didn't you, Daddy?"

Into Goldstein's. Vast reaches of commerce: light-painted walls, counters heaped fat with silks from Chinese bazaars and perfumes from France. Throngs jostling, spending, spending. The smell of a department store: dress goods and furs and powders. Three elevators ascending from this section of the store alone. Once Isaac Goldstein had been an energetic little man with a pack on his back and once he had advertised in the *Clayton Junction Tribune*. Good town, Clayton Junction; good town to be from.

Express elevator to Toyland. Up, please. Express to Toyland. Up, please.

Daddy, can we look at yellow ribbons after we go to Toyland?

Uh—ribbons? Sure, sure. Anything. Santa will bring you anything you want. Money rolling in. Once you tap into the big money it's an artesian well, it's a gusher in the oil fields. It's a fat man in a cartoon, wading knee-deep in green-backs, flinging them high, yelling, "Whee!"

Express to Toyland. Back in the car, please.

So A. H. Burgoyne and Flora and Barbara stepped back in the car. And so did Dr. and Mrs. Harold Henderson and their three children. Only theirs was the express from Toyland to street level.

The 1912 season began auspiciously enough for Burgoyne's Circus & Hippodrome. As usual, the show opened in Tamarack, and as usual, the newspapers threw their columns wide to advance stories. Editorials appeared, pointing out that this was "Tamarack's own circus." When the show paraded at noon the Haynes rolled immediately behind the band chariot. Uniformed in blue and gold, a Negro chauffeur piloted that spectacular car. Gus sat in the back seat, wearing a silk hat and formal morning attire.

Honor and position had not, however, gone to his head. He was still the same friendly Gus. Nothing stuck-up about him. It was a sunny spring day, and the curbs were lined with waving thousands. He waved back, as cordially as a presidential candidate. Sometimes when he spied people he knew he even called them by name. "Hello, Fred," he would call, or "How are you, Mayor?" You had to give him credit; even though he rode in glory he was still as common as an old shoe.

During its one-day stand in Tamarack, the show was strictly honest. At the ticket wagon you received every penny of your change. You couldn't have discovered a single game of chance on the lot. You could have attended with a thousand dollars bristling from your breast pocket, and not a dollar would have been stolen. Gus's conscience would have never forgiven him if shady activities had occurred on the lot in Tamarack. Only a crook would steal from his friends.

When Gus suggested that Beryl travel with the circus she declined. Her mother might object. And unlike Ruby—who no more had a mother than an incubator chicken had—Beryl really possessed a mother. A father, too. She dwelt with them in Tamarack. They had no idea that there was any funny business about her working for A. H. Burgoyne.

So when the circus steamed away Beryl remained on duty in the Tamarack office. Having little to do, she went down the corridor to a dentist's office to have her teeth examined. They were such interesting teeth that the dentist wanted to see how they would function at a meal.

He and Beryl took dinner together. They went to Funland Park. In July they were married. Things happen fast, sometimes.

It certainly astonished Gus to receive the letter of resignation in which Beryl told of her marriage. And he didn't like it. If an affair was to be broken off, he wanted to do the breaking.

Early that season, Gus assured himself that everything was going fine, and on the surface this appeared to be true. Week after week the show rolled from town to town, setting itself up and parading and giving two performances, clicking right along on schedule. It was what Gus called a beautifully mounted circus, meaning it had luster and snap and dazzle. Every wagon gleamed with new paint. The horses were sleek and prosperous. Even the baggage horses wore red shakos above their noble Percheron heads. Gus had plowed a lot of profits back into equipment, and the canvas was resilient and snowy, the tent poles sound as boulders, the ropes new and tough.

In May, when the show was playing Missouri, Ivan Pawpacker visited it for two days. Gus heaped a tremendous welcome on him. Nothing was too good for Ive.

Late at night as the train rocked and swayed they sat in the Clayton Junction Pullman drinking Scotch and soda. Wesley Thompson, Gus's Negro servant, waited on their every wish. The car was so opulent, the whole show so magnificent, that Ive had no reason to doubt Gus when he boasted about the blizzard of currency assailing the ticket sellers.

"It's a gold mine," Gus grinned. "It's better than the Klondike. I've struck it rich—nuggets as big as goose eggs. I've got so damned much money I don't know what to do. I'm a nigger that's hit the jackpot. I'm an Oklahoma Indian swimming in oil."

Gus sighed, shook his head in delirious despair at ever finding ways to spend his money. Through the haze of cigar smoke and Scotch, he looked as huge as a bursting-full moneybag.

"Talk about doubloons! The Spanish Main wasn't in it. El Dorado was pin money."

Those comparisons enflamed Ive's imagination. As he grew older and the passions of the flesh cooled, the passions of the countinghouse burned more feverishly. Money was power, making money adventure. It was almost the only fun he had.

Gus had always swayed him, even in the days when Gus was an upstart. But now the upstart days were past. The circus had been mere words once, breath vanishing into air. But no longer was it a windy dream. It was a fact. The power and the glory had come to pass.

The whiskey mellowed the edges of reality, and Ive's mind was a bee-drowsy noon in a land of dreams that came true.

"Gus," he said, "I've done pretty well, too."

"Know you have. Always said you were a money-maker, Ive. Always admired you. Couple of money-makers—that's us. Make the dollars and the pennies will take care of themselves—that's my motto." Laughter shook Gus's chair, and he told Wesley to refill Mr. Pawpacker's glass.

Ive watched the amber liquid swirling as Wesley obeyed the command of Croesus.

"Freshen mine up, too," Gus said.

When both glasses were sparkling full, Gus extended his and tinked it against Ive's.

"To the suckers," he chuckled. "To the golden geese and the golden eggs."

They drank.

The train swayed. The wheels said clickety-clock, clickety-clock. The vestibules drummed and moaned. Against Ive's nose, bright little soda bubbles exploded refreshingly.

"Gus," he said, "what will you take for half-interest in the show?"

"At it again," Gus boomed. "Always wanting to go into partnership with me. Remember back in the Funland Park days. You used to pester me something terrible."

It was meant only as humor, and Ive took it that way.

"But I was in love," Gus said, "and I couldn't be bothered. Girl named Carlotta. Ever told you about her? Wonderful girl. I still think about her, sometimes. Feel mighty sorry for her. She made a mess of her life. Married an educated fool. She's had an awful time of it. Too bad . . ."

"How much, Gus?"

"Uh? How much for half-interest? Not that I want to sell, you understand. Never quit when your luck's running strong—that's my motto. Uh—what'll you give me?"

Ive named a good round figure.

"I'll remember you," Gus told him, "if I ever want a partner. Don't know any man I'd rather hook up with. We'd make a million, Ive. A cool million."

"Then why don't we hook up now?"

"You don't want to get messed up with me," Gus said. "Unhappy man like me."

"Unhappy!" Ive smiled. "Gus, you're quite a card."

"Yeah—the old Joker, that's me. But the fact is, Ive—well—sometimes a man looks back and thinks he would do it different if he had it to live over."

Ive nodded, thinking of Georgiana.

"Yes sir, Ive—a man looks back and doesn't like what he sees. Ah love, couldst thou and I with Fate conspire, to grasp this sorry scheme of things entire. . . . Ever hear that one?"

Ive thought the liquor must be hitting Gus where it hurt.

"Then it goes—let's see. Girl read it to me once. Very sad, Ive. Very sad. Uh—it goes, Would we not shatter it to bits and then . . . Remold it nearer to the heart's desire. . . . Beautiful poem. Wouldn't believe it, but an Arab wrote it. One of those Arabs that folded his tent in the night. Don't know where he learned English."

"A cool million," Ive said.

"Uh? Well now Ive, let me tell you. Money's not everything. What you said once though about being unhappy in comfort. Something to that. On the other hand, here I am coining money so fast I don't know what to do with it. A man can eat just so much. Sleep in only one bed at a time. A man looks back and sees where he might have made a different turn in the road. Know what the trouble with life is, Ive?"

"Not enough suckers."

Gus roared. "Oh, no! Not that, Ive! Plenty of suckers. As Barnum said—and never think he wasn't a showman, Ive!—as Barnum said, there's one born every minute. Uh—what was I saying?"

"That we'd make a cool million."

"Naw, naw—after that. Uh . . . Got it! The trouble with life! The trouble with life is that the view behind is so much better than the view ahead. Here today, gone tomorrow—that's the trouble. And you never know what's just around the corner. Now you take old Vince Fye . . ."

"Don't know him."

"No, guess you don't. Matter of fact, he's dead. Dead and buried and—"

Gus broke off. Frowned. And suddenly, he slapped a palm down on his knee.

"Beats all!" he exclaimed.

"What beats all?"

"How a man will forget! Just remembered how I'd promised to keep flowers on Vince's grave. Never thought of it from that time to this! Remind me, Ive, to make a memorandum of that in the morning. Beats all how things will slip a busy man's mind!"

Gus had exaggerated when he declared the circus was better than the Klondike, although early in the season profits held up fairly well. Gross profits. The net was something else again, because after several seasons of grift city councils demanded a higher pay-off—official and unofficial—for a license to show. Sheriffs had to be taken care of, too, and chiefs of police, and detectives, and other defenders of law and order.

In June, the universal law that troubles never come singly chose

Burgoyne's Circus as a proving ground. Rain fell. For two long weeks it fell, every day and every night, pounding, driving, deluging rain, converting the show grounds into swamps and lakes. And with the rain attendance fell, and profits; and there were melancholy evenings when the pickpockets would have had to pull one another's wallets to show any adequate returns on time and labor.

In June, also two baggage horses contracted pneumonia and perished, and one of the new bulls went on a rampage and did considerable damage to property adjoining the lot, and in the menagerie top some silly girl was bitten by a monkey; and finally, when skies cleared and a good-sized crowd filled the tent, a section of the blues collapsed, breaking several gillie arms and legs; and after such occurrences it is wise to pay cash damages instantly, and get releases, before shysters go into action.

July was hot and bright, but receipts didn't make their expected comeback. Something was wrong. Deep in the vitals of the show some jinx was working. It could have been grift. Not that, of course; but it could have been. It might have been that towners remembered from last year how Walt Ambrose's understanding of mathematics was not in harmony with accepted standards.

It might have been, too, that profits diminished and finally vanished because there were cities from which the show was barred. In past years, because of grift, it had achieved such heights of unpopularity that now some city councils were forced to refuse a license. Otherwise, newspapers and voters might get on their necks, which is not the position city councils approve of in newspapers and voters.

By August, Gus was heavily worried. He considered rechristening the show, next year. Might call it Honest Gus's World Famous Circus. But he didn't want that, because he derived too much pleasure from seeing Burgoyne in big fat letters. Worry drove him to ridiculous extremes, such as contemplating a return to Sunday School policies. But that seemed like going backward.

Several times that season, the show simply had to risk returning to towns where only the year before there had been lively threats of trouble. For this, routing was responsible. One such town was Plains City, North Dakota. The circus reached it in early September, and even Lorenz looked worried.

It was not much of a town. It had tried, but still it wasn't much. Baking sun and dusty wind had saddened it. The lawns never did very well, and everything needed paint. Most of the trees in that town were cottonwoods, shedding gray fluff that collected in gutters.

That was a land flat as a roller-skating rink, but not as gay. As far as you could see the earth ran level to infinity. Up there, it was possible to believe the world flat, and if you traveled to the edge you would tumble off. There was too much sky. You felt exposed and unprotected. All that open space gave you the feeling not of freedom but of vulnerability.

The circus did not pitch its tents within the corporate limits of Plains City, for the council members refused a license. Even when the advance man offered to make it worth their while they refused. They didn't want Burgoyne's Circus. But the circus needed Plains City. Otherwise, it would have to make a two-hundred-mile railroad jump. That was too long. So Lorenz told the advance man they must play Plains City whether or no.

The advance man was not unresourceful. Along the railroad, just beyond the town limits, he discovered vacant ground the right size for a circus lot. It adjoined the wooden tower of a grain elevator. This was owned by the Tri-States Grain Company, and the local manager was willing to discuss business. He was new in Plains City, and he despised the town. Till three months ago he had worked at the home office in Minneapolis, and then the company stuck him away out here in the middle of nowhere. It made him mad enough—nearly—to quit the company.

There was plenty of railroad siding outside the town limits where the train could stand. So all was well. Or was it? As they unloaded that morning, Lorenz wondered. Things didn't feel right. The sparse crowd that watched the unloading seemed unfriendly. The kids made smart-aleck remarks. And as the unloading went forward, little incidents occurred. Kids threw stones at the horses and the bulls. Lorenz delegated a half-dozen roustabouts to chase the kids away. The kids scurried and hooted. They yelled things. Things like "crooks."

"Why in hell did you book us in here?" the twenty-four-hour man growled. "This town's after our hides."

He elaborated. It was a tale full of woe. Much of the billboard paper had been torn down. Other sheets had been mud-spattered. The twenty-four-hour man had encountered unfriendliness at the post office when he called for circus mail. He had found grocers and bakers and butchers unwilling to sell supplies, except at swollen prices.

Not having a license, they didn't parade that day. Late in the morning, Lorenz entered the Clayton Junction car and discussed things with Mr. Burgoyne. Drinking coffee and smoking, Gus sat at his desk in a dressing gown, reading his mail. A letter from his wife disturbed him, for it seemed Barbara had not been feeling so well. She had eaten a lot of things she shouldn't have eaten, and her digestive system objected.

"I've put her to bed," Flora wrote. "Think she'll be all right. If she's not better by tonight I'll call a doctor."

That chafed Gus. That part about not calling a doctor immediately. It was as if Samuel R. Oxenford rode again, apprehensive about a doctor's fee.

Chewing his cigar, Gus listened without more than half hearing. He told Lorenz to handle things as he thought best.

"Don't want any trouble, of course," he added.

Lorenz left. Gus sat scowling. The car windows were lifted and a September-dry breeze sifted through the screens, graying the sills. Gus reached for a Western Union pad and scribbled a message to Flora, telling her to send him two wires each day, reporting on Barbara. He tore off the sheet and told Wesley to send it from the station.

The platform bricks were dusty and the wooden station was bone-dry in the desiccating sun. Inside, the place was silent save for the clacking of telegraph sounders. Wesley put the message on the counter and asked how much.

The station agent shoved it back. His lips were tight, risking a lot of seniority, as he said:

"Can't take it. Wires down."

Wesley belonged to a race that found it wiser not to argue.

But Mr. Burgoyne argued, a few minutes later. How could wires be down, with the sounders clicking?

"Wires down. Can't take it," the agent said.

Anger hung in the station after Mr. Burgoyne left. But the agent was not angry. He grinned. Seniority or not, it was worth it. Last year he had attended the circus. He had presented a twenty-dollar bill at the ticket window. He had been shortchanged and shoved and threatened. In his small way, he was doing what he could to even things up. That evening, he continued doing what he could. When a telegram arrived signed "Flora," he took it off the wire, but he made no attempt to deliver it.

Walking toward the telephone exchange, Gus sizzled with rage. Wires down! Absurd!

Well, he'd call Flora long distance. By telephone, he'd get the very latest information about Barbara's condition. Not, of course, that it was anything to worry about. Children were always getting sick. Little bilious spells. Constipation had always troubled Barbara.

He passed a lumberyard and cut through a vacant lot. At the far edge a shack leaned obliquely, and circus posters had been pasted there. Coming closer, he saw that his favorite lithograph adorned the shed, a sheet bearing the tinted likeness of a stalwart young man. The brow was wide, the jaw sturdy, the mouth and eyes pleasant. You could bank on that young man, and you could bet on his achieving greatness.

Beneath this regal portrait red letters said: "A. H. (Honest Gus) Burgoyne, Owner."

But against that picture, a repulsive abomination had been perpetrated. Hoodlums had desecrated it with a paint brush. Across the chest and the face, scrawny letters crawled: "Crook!"

Outrage burned Gus's ears. He found himself wading toward the shack through weedy debris, to rip down the picture. But suddenly he stopped. Hell with it. This was an imbecile town, anyway. He had a long distance call to put through.

Jaws clamped, he strode along the sidewalk of the business district. The sun burned down on his neck. There was too much sky and it was too full of light. Outside a pool hall, he passed a group of loafers. One hawked and spat and said something insulting about the circus. His cronies laughed. Gus wanted to wheel and plow into them. But he kept walking, feeling their gazes on his spine.

Above a doorway hung a sign of chipped enamel, bearing the likeness of a bell. Gus entered, clumped up bare tan steps. Inside the exchange he drummed impatiently on the varnished fence separating the public from the switchboard. A dried-out woman manipulated snaky, metal-tipped wires. "Number, please. Hello. Oh, hello, Gertie! Yeah. Huh? Well, I dunno. Wait a minute. Number, please. Four five. Thank you. Hello—Gertie?"

That went on. And on.

"I'm A. H. Burgoyne," Gus boomed finally. "Got an important call to put through."

"Wait a minute, Gertie. Some guy wants service."

Some guy! Fine way to refer to the owner of Burgoyne's Circus & Hippodrome.

"You'll have to wait," she said sourly, after Gus gave her his telephone number in Tamarack. "Them long distance calls take time."

He sat on a wooden chair that had been bound with wire to keep it from falling apart. Sometimes he stood up and roamed to the fence. The operator seared him with her eyes.

"I'm working on it," she snapped. "I've got Fargo and they're trying to get through to Minneapolis."

Fargo. Minneapolis. Tamarack. He had a vision of those leagues of thrumming wires, thin lines cutting the pitiless northern sky. And he experienced hate for that flat eternity of Dakota. He sat down, closed his eyes, thought of the rolling hills of his native state, the green meadows, the willows following a sparkling rill.

Ten minutes passed. Twenty. Thirty

"But I *am* trying," the operator snapped. "Can't get beyond Fargo. Don't go blaming me, mister, if them Minneapolis operators is asleep."

Another ten minutes. Fifteen. The afternoon performance would be starting. Well, Lorenz would look after everything.

Twenty minutes. Twenty-five. Gus would never forget the picture on the wall-calendar: a sexless girl with sexless legs, sitting on seashore rocks. A tinsel moon shone, and the sky was a staring, electric blue. A half-dozen lines of waves were rolling in, low and close together, the water stiff and definite.

"All right," the operator said. "I'll keep on trying. When I get it through I'll send some kid after you."

The operator grinned as Gus's thumps receded down the stairs. It gave her a laugh when she thought of how she had duped that fat guy. She had said, "Hello, Fargo," without ever plugging in. Did he fool easy!

Burgoyne! Honest Gus! This town knew better. This town remembered last year.

The worst about last year was the way the circus treated poor old Nick Gieman. Maybe Nick wasn't very bright, but he had made a living with his dray. But somebody at the circus got hold of him and paid him a big price for his dray team, and then somebody else told him he could double his money by gambling. But did he double it? Lost every cent. Cried about it like a baby, when he saw his dray waiting in his back yard with no horses to pull it. Old Nick would have starved last winter, if the neighbors hadn't taken pity on him.

So if Burgoyne thought she was going to put through a call for him he was mistook. This was her switchboard and she'd run it as she wished. Even if the stockholders of the Plains City Mutual Telephone Company heard about it, they wouldn't fire her. Not with her uncle a big stock owner. Not with her husband marshal of this town.

Her husband had said that some of the loafers down at the pool hall were talking about learning that circus a lesson. Ordinarily, her husband would have put a stop to talk like that. But not this time. Her husband felt as sorry for old Nick as everybody else did. Besides, the circus was showing outside the city limits, so it wouldn't be up to the town marshal to maintain order. Let the boys have their fun. That circus lot was outside the law, you might say. Only the sheriff had authority there, and he was busy with his own affairs at the county seat, thirty miles away.

Circus business had been meager that afternoon. Almost nonexistent. Lorenz had never witnessed anything like it. At dinner in the cookhouse he expressed his opinion of Plains City.

"Yeah," Gus agreed, "terrible place."

They were sitting at the management table. On the circus, dinner was served at five, so the cookhouse could be torn down early. The side walls were rolled up and late sunlight shafted in upon the long tables where roustabouts and razorbacks were gormandizing like hogs at a trough.

Usually Gus ate as much as any two people, but now he had no appetite. How could you settle to eating when you kept expecting a small boy with a message that your long distance call was ready? For that matter, how could you share Lorenz's worries about trouble when you kept wondering about your daughter's health? Trouble! What did Lorenz know about trouble? Why didn't that call go through? He'd feel better when he heard Flora's matter-of-fact voice. "What?" she'd say. "I don't get it. Oh. Why, Barbara's all right. What were you worried about, Gus? Oh—about Barbara. Why no, Gus—she's all right. Her stomach was upset, but she's all right. Want to talk to her?"

And Barbara would be lifted to the telephone.

"Hello, Daddy," she would say. "I love you, Daddy. When are you coming home? What are you going to bring me? Are you going to bring me a doll?"

Lorenz was saying:

"And if you think we hadn't ought to show, we'll tear down right away. Whatever you think, Gus. Personally, I think it's bad practice to let 'em scare us out of town. I think we ought to show if there ain't nobody buys an admission. I'll have the boys loaded for trouble, and—"

"Uh—sure. Trust your judgment. Handle it the way you think best."

"Then we'll show. I've told the railroad to have an engine here early, if we want to leave. And I've wised up Lefty about what to do if any guys want a clem. I've—"

Lorenz droned on about his preparations for battle. Gus drank coffee, but he wasn't able to do much with his roast beef and mashed potatoes. The food just didn't taste like anything. He pulled out a cigar and nibbled off the end. He thought he had lighted it, but later he discovered he hadn't. He was smoking it dry. Getting absent-minded. As bad as some college professor, some educated fool. He lighted it and glanced at his watch.

"Know you'll handle it right," he told Lorenz. "I've got a phone call to put through. Important call. Think I'll go down to the telephone office."

He brooded across the lot. Looking west, he could see for a thousand flat miles. He could see distant fence posts and barbed wire; he could see far, tiny trees, ailing, spindling things. Above the ruler-flat horizon the sun hung raw and fiery.

In the telephone exchange, the same dried-out woman still sat at the switchboard, still treated him like a criminal. Under other circumstances he might have thundered his demand for better service, but these were special circumstances. He wanted so badly to get that call through that he was actually meek.

"Uh—it's an important call. Very important call."

"I guessed it was, or you wouldn't be making it."

"Tell you," he said. "You get that through, and there's a box of candy in it for you. Five-pound box."

Her mouth twisted.

"Mister, we don't do business that way in this town. This is an honest town. I'm paid to do my job and I do it. I don't take candy from strangers."

Gus felt himself redden. What was wrong with him? He seemed to have lost his grip. It was this damned town, this damned eternity of flatness, this worry that made his brain feel like snarled rope.

"Uh—were you able to get Minneapolis?"

"Finally. They're trying for Tamarack, now. I said I'd let you know when the call came through, and I will."

"I'm with the circus," he said. "A. H. Burgoyne. Guess you know that."

"I know it right enough," she said.

He left. Dusk was sneaking like a footpad along the street. What was wrong with that operator? Unhappily married, perhaps. Like Aunt Lucy. Only Aunt Lucy hadn't soured. Always good to him, Aunt Lucy. He'd never forget how he felt that day Frank told him she had died. He had ducked back inside his tough crust; but within the crust he had been weeping. Through the years that crust had served him well, by and large. Sometimes he had been afraid, often lonely, often full of misgivings; but nobody knew. They saw the crust. To them, that was Gus Burgoyne. The crust was pretty well trained, like an animal that knew the show must go on despite aches. The crust laughed and boomed and played poker and even made love. Only with Carlotta it hadn't been the crust that made love. With her, he hadn't worn it. Maybe that was why those things she said on their last night together hurt so much. When you really loved and took off the crust you were at a terrible disadvantage, terribly at the mercy of things beyond your control.

He was passing a drugstore, and it occurred to him that maybe if he bought candy and presented it to the operator she would be glad to get it, after all. Experience told him that few persons could resist a bribe. Bribery and graft, everybody on the make—that was how the world went, at any rate the world he knew. He supposed there were people who weren't that way—people like Frank, like the Leslies—but

he hadn't known many. Too bad he hadn't, because he liked them.
Nice folks. But somehow or other, he had got mixed up with the
other kind.

The druggist looked small town and small business. That consti-
pated expression. Those grasping, cash-register eyes. That mouth
puckered from feeding on small-town crab apples.

"No boxes of candy," he said. "Can't keep it in the summer. Gets
wormy."

"Couldn't you keep it under refrigeration?"

"A lot of people know more about my business than I do," the druggist said.

Gus moved toward the door. Suddenly he stopped, staring at a
counter where dolls were on display. Might send one of these to
Barbara. He was always doing that when he traveled, sending her
surprise presents. There was a silken-gowned brunette doll that looked
something like Barbara.

"How much is this one?" Gus asked.

"Four seventy-five."

"Take it. Uh—will you box it for shipping?"

"Don't do that here. I'll wrap it but I can't box it."

The sour-puss! Gus would have enjoyed kicking his hips up to his
shoulders. But he wanted the doll.

"Okay," he said. "Wrap it."

He returned to the telephone exchange, but the long distance call
had not projected itself beyond Minneapolis. He sat for a time, listening to the operator plugging through local calls. Once she said, "Fargo.
Hello, Fargo. This is Plains City, Fargo. About that call to Tamarack . . ."

But it didn't come to anything. There were times in a man's life
when the dice always turned up sevens, and times when you couldn't
roll a seven in a thousand tries. There were times when you could
stand on a busy corner and attempt giving away five-dollar bills and
nobody would have any.

He thought of the telephone exchange in Minneapolis. It would be
huge, with scores of switchboards and trunk-wires spiderwebbing in
from wheat country and dairy country and timber country and the
iron range. He thought of the myriad voices crying over those wires,
and of his own call trying to make itself heard like a lost child in a
multitude.

At last he left the exchange. Night had spilled tons of ink over
North America. Arid scraps of breeze tiptoed after him and sniffed
his ankles. He was tired and worried, and he would be glad when the
season closed. Another month. Then the show would return to its

barns, and in his Tamarack office he would go into conference with himself and figure what had gone wrong this season, and what to do about it.

Street lights burned feebly in the business section, and in the dark doorways shadows stood like Borgian assassins. Tramping through the residential district, he heard cottonwood leaves whispering malicious gossip overhead. Like the gossiping tongues in Clayton Junction, he thought. "There goes Gus Burgoyne. Doll Burgoyne's kid. She never married. She'd sleep with anybody. We ran her out of town. She left her kid. The little bastard. The little bastard. The little bastard . . ."

Usually he could slam a door on those past years, a stout, tight door, such as fire underwriters demanded in ratty buildings. But tonight he was too weary to heave shut the door, and grotesque memories came trooping into his thoughts. He was a little boy in a corner, shaking with terror as he saw that peculiar light in Uncle Tim's eyes. He was a little boy on the first day of school, and he clutched Aunt Lucy's hand as she escorted him to the schoolhouse door. "It'll be all right, Gus. It'll be fine. . . ." Then she kissed him and left him, washed-out blond Aunt Lucy with her thin, pale face and her long, slender hands, and her uncertain, curtsying manner. He watched her wagging her tail away down the street, like a fox terrier that had been abused but was eternally hopeful for pats and pleasant words. And suddenly, backed up against the schoolhouse, he was hemmed in by a crescent of boys; older boys, freckled boys, tough boys. He was all lumpy and tight inside, and they were saying, "Hello, Mistake. Hello, Bastard. Hello, Mistake." And then Dutch Schneider—of the butcher shop Schneiders—snatched off Gus's cap and ran with it, and Gus pursued yelling, "Give me my cap! Give me my cap!" but Dutch Schneider laughed and threw the cap to a Mexican section hand's son, and he threw it to Red Finney, and Gus was in tears now, running from boy to boy pleading, "Give me my cap!" Then a tall pair of pants appeared, topped by a lean chest and a severe schoolmaster's face, and one talonlike hand grabbed Dutch Schneider's collar and the other smacked his cheek. So Gus got his cap back, but school wasn't going to be fun. He had escaped from the trap above the saloon with the terror of Uncle Tim to the trap of the school, with strange, multiple terrors. Clayton Junction was a trap, and since it was his universe he thought life itself a trap. But he would escape, somehow. He would become great, because greatness would give him freedom. Nothing would stop him. Life was a free-for-all on a school playground. If you didn't want to be kicked and trampled, you did the kicking and trampling yourself.

Frank MacGowan had never understood how life was, Frank with dreams of socialism shining in his eyes. He had never understood the

necessity for ruthlessness. But sometimes Gus understood—almost—
what Frank had in mind. Understanding came to him in the most
unlikely situations, such as at a meeting of the Tamarack Commercial
Club. As you stood with the others, all singing "Tamarack the beautiful, We love thy parks and trees," a herd-warm sense of man's brotherhood filled your chest, and for a moment a great wave of affection
flowed from you. They were good fellows who would never call you
bastard, and you wanted to slap their backs and address them by their
Christian names and nicknames. And they must have sensed how
much you liked them for they elevated you to the presidency, and you
stood with humid eyes, meaning every word when you said, "Boys,
this is the proudest moment of my life."

Maybe that was why you joined so many organizations; they were
something you could tie to; and they welcomed that part of you which
was still lonely little boy. They didn't care about your parents; it was
you that mattered; and they gave you something you had missed as
a kid, and that was why you joined them in droves: you were making
up for lost time. In Tamarack, people liked you, whatever they
thought in Plains City. And just thinking how you were a past president of the Commercial Club warmed you tonight. It didn't matter
if the cottonwood leaves whispered behind your back.

Gus could hear the circus band while he was still several blocks
away. And the music told him what was happening in the ring. "The
Blue Danube" and "The Skater's Waltz"—bareback riders. "Yankee
Doodle" and "Turkey In The Straw"—clowns.

He wondered whether any gillies were attending the show tonight.
Not that it mattered. Lorenz was taking care of everything. Good
man, Lorenz. In a few hours the show would be loaded and the train
would roll. And he would sleep. Drink a highball and sleep. Lord,
he was tired. Worried, too. About Barbara. She'd be all right. But
he couldn't help worrying. He'd always been that way about her:
fussy and silly.

The houses thinned out as he approached the edge of town. He
passed dark side yards and garden patches. The air had cooled slightly.
Within sight of the lot he stopped, took off his hat, rested his elbow on
a garden fence post. He felt lethargic with weariness, and he stood
there for several minutes, soaking up what peace and balm drifted
through the evening. The darkness smelled of summer's end and
autumn's beginning, the heavy mingled odors of apples rotting and
fat grapes and tomatoes sagging corpulently on vines. Insects clicked
and sang.

He tramped on. The sidewalk ended, and the smell of vegetation
thickened as he kneed through weeds to the road. His heels sank into
heavy dust. The lot was nearer now, and through band music he heard

the creak of baggage wagons hauling the dismantled menagerie top
toward the train. As he reached the edge of the lot the band stopped
playing. In the middle of a bar it stopped. He wondered why. It was
unnatural, as if all movement had halted in the solar system.

He cut into the lot, heading toward the splash of floodlamps beyond
two baggage wagons. The wagons stood in shadow. As he swung
toward them the shadows spurted forth six or eight men. They weren't
roustabouts. They weren't on his show at all. Gillies! He yelled something. They were in front of him and on both sides and behind. It was
bad, having them behind. He saw an arm go back and something
left a hand and came hurtling. Rock. He ducked, not quite in time,
and pain skidded brilliantly along his forehead. He was a trumpeting
bull now, and he charged. The earth rose and fell, so some of the time
he was running uphill and sometimes down. The man who had
thrown the rock was backing away, but it was very necessary to reach
him in order to smash your fist into his jaw so he would go sailing up
and up and on and on, like the baseball you used to dream of batting
over the fence when you were a kid.

The figure kept backing, backing. And everything seemed moving
very slowly. Your legs pumped with that torpor of legs moving under
water. Beyond the figure you glimpsed Lorenz and roustabouts coming through floodlighted air. And from behind something struck your
left shoulder blade with agonizing velocity. Brickbat, probably. The
backing figure saw Lorenz and twisted and darted away. You would
never reach him. From your right something came at you—a man
reeking with whiskey—and a fist jolted your face and you went floun-
dering into two men on your left. Something batted into your diaphragm and your entire consciousness rushed down there where your
breath had collapsed, and you were on your knees, swaying sickly but
swinging your fists; and then the earth turned upside down, and
turned again, and again.

He thought he rode a crowded streetcar on Christmas Eve, the
windows steamed over. Smooth girls in furs called, "Merry Christmas," but he didn't desire them because he had Carlotta. He left the
car and walked along a quiet street, and it seemed deeply good people
dwelt in every house. Nobody was rich, nobody poor. They slept
soundly at night, because they weren't looting the city and the county
and trust companies. They didn't dread the arrival of the evening
paper, because their names would never be dragged through the gutters of page one.

Christmas packages jammed his arms, silks and perfumes for Carlotta, a doll for Barbara. He hurried along the snow-hushed street and
turned in at his own house. A wreath hung in the window and

Barbara stood with her nose against the pane, watching him; and beyond her he glimpsed Carlotta, heartbreakingly lovely. He hurried faster, but his feet went out from under him as they encountered a patch of slick ice, and he fell heavily, striking his head on concrete.

The doll. Where was the doll? He had fallen and lost it. Carlotta. Barbara. Where are you? I have fallen, I have fallen. . . .

Inside his head dynamite kept going off. He twisted, trying to escape pain; and gradually, laboriously, his brute will to live, to stand erect, asserted itself. He didn't want to open his eyes. It was like waking up after a night of carousing: you thought you couldn't bear to open your eyes and see a bedroom full of ash-colored light, and remember bit by bit the night's corruption. If you shifted your head the least bit the room would reel. Well, get it over with. Have to be up and doing. Have to open your eyes.

Gus opened his eyes and saw the stars. Green stars, blue stars, red stars. He could hear a lot of hell going on somewhere. He elbowed himself up into a world that wobbled.

"Mr. Burgoyne, just take it easy, just—"

Wesley! And a roustabout stood near by, gripping a stake.

"What the hell?" Gus said.

"Gillies," the roustabout said. "They jumped on you. Lorenz left me to see they didn't tromp you while you're down."

Sitting there on the grass like a great baby he felt futile and foolish. His fingers brushed his forehead, discovered a lump. His jaws ached.

"The bastards," he said.

"Yeah," the roustabout said. "But Lorenz has things in hand. They tried to wreck the show, but Lorenz—"

Yells and hoots came mobbing from the other side of the tent. So Plains City had started a clem. The bastards. Gus clamped his teeth and pulled himself erect by will power. Great thing, power of the will. He had read a book about it once, but the book hadn't said what to do when the ground started lifting like the far end of a teeter board. He heard himself saying, "I'd better sit down."

Time and the world went away somewhere. Then, without quite knowing when, he began thinking. He was thinking this was an undignified posture—flat on the grass—for a former president of the Tamarack Commercial Club. And like all great healthy people whose bodies go back on them, he felt ashamed of the weakness that had knocked him flat. Something cool and dripping was swashing his forehead. He opened his eyes. Wesley was dipping a cloth into a water bucket.

"I'm all right," Gus said. "I'm all right."

Lorenz had materialized from somewhere.

"Take it easy, Gus."

Gus gained his feet, and this time he planted his legs apart against the treachery of tipping ground.

"I've got a headache. That's all. Just a headache."

Wesley took one arm and Lorenz the other, and they started walking him toward the train. But he halted, like a balky drunk.

"Doll."

"That's all right, Gus. Take it easy."

"I want the doll."

"You get some sleep," Lorenz said. "Them smacks on the bean ain't good for a man."

"Oh, hell!" Gus said. "I'm all right. But I bought a doll—for Barbara—"

They returned with him then, although he suspected they thought him off his head.

"I can prove it," he said. "I can prove there's a doll."

It seemed very important to prove it, but when he saw the package trampled in the grass he didn't think he'd better lean over. He was erect now; better stay that way.

"Wesley," he said, "that's what I'm after."

So Wesley picked it up, but something tinkled faintly.

"Them damn gillies," Wesley said. "They step on this here doll's face and smash it in."

"I can't give it to her that way," Gus said. It seemed a pretty tremendous problem. But he was all right; he could solve problems. "Might as well leave it," he said. "I'll buy her another one. A better one."

He swayed slowly between them, toward the train. Some roustabouts were working like sixty, and others prowled with stakes.

"We beat 'em off," Lorenz said. "We'll be loaded and out of here in an hour."

Once Gus halted to stare at a baggage wagon tipped over on its side, one wheel smashed as if by a sledge.

"They did a little damage, Gus," Lorenz said. "But nothing that can't be fixed. My idea, we'll pull out as soon as we can. Two towns left to play in North Dakota, but to hell with them."

"That's it," Gus said. "The hell with them."

"Now you're talking, Gus. My idea, we'll cross the state line to our first Minnesota date and rest up and repair."

His body hurt as if from a clubbing. In his stateroom, before Wesley undressed him and ministered to him, he glimpsed himself in the mirror. He looked like a roughneck after a Saturday night brawl.

Twenty hours later, Gus was the first passenger to alight at Tamarack from the Minneapolis-Kansas City Flyer. He carried no luggage;

only an oblong box. In search of a cab, he hurried through the marble echoes of the Union Station. He limped painfully and he wore dark glasses, to conceal the puffy discoloration afflicting his left eye. Patches of court plaster crisscrossed his jaw.

The evening was sultry, and when Gus sank into the cab cushions he removed his hat and swabbed his forehead. His muscles and head still ached from last night's encounter, and he felt weak from worry and lack of food. It had been a dreadful day. All the night before, sleep had been a thin veneer of pain, and at dawn he had ordered the train to halt in a Minnesota village so he could call Flora. This time, the call went promptly through, and Flora told him that Barbara was very ill indeed.

He wanted no breakfast, after that. He swayed back to the station and inquired about the next train to Minneapolis and connections to Tamarack. Then he bought a ticket and emerged to the platform. He was chewing an unlighted cigar, and he stood staring at his circus train on a siding. It seemed unimportant that car windows had been stoned out, that wagons had been smashed and canvas ripped. He heard footsteps and turned to see Lorenz. Gus said, "I've got to get to Tamarack. You patch up the show."

At noon in the Minneapolis station he called Flora again. Barbara's condition had not changed. Two nurses were in attendance, and the doctor called several times a day.

"Have you had consultation?" he demanded.

"Consultation? Think we ought to, Gus?"

"Ought to! My God! Get every doctor in town!"

"Don't swear, Gus. Please don't swear."

After hanging up, he stood in the booth, arms crossed on the telephone, head resting against them. Sweat bathed him, but despite the heat he experienced occasional chills. He thought he should eat, but after tramping to the station restaurant he discovered he could not swallow food. He forced coffee into his stomach, where it swashed hard and sour.

Two hours would elapse before his train left for Tamarack, so he plodded the streets of Minneapolis; and he found himself in the toy section of a department store. He purchased the most spectacular doll in the place, a yellow-haired deb doll wearing a red-velvet gown. The girl who waited on him looked something like the doll, and time was when he might have smiled at her and patted her. Not today. Nothing seemed important today except a sick little girl in Tamarack.

"Keep the change," he told the cabdriver, and he mounted the dark porte-cochere steps. A dim light burned in the hall, and outlined against it he saw Flora.

"Oh, Gus," she said. Her heavy hands fumbled around him and he kissed her.

"How is she?" he asked, his voice as low-keyed as the shadowy hall.

"I don't know, Gus. She's pretty sick." And she asked, "Did you hurt yourself? That court plaster. And why are you wearing dark glasses?"

He removed them; Flora gasped with concern.

"Some gillies tried to get funny with me," Gus said.

"They hurt you! You're hurt, Gus!"

"You ought to see them."

"You shouldn't fight, Gus. I wish you wouldn't fight."

She had momentarily forgotten Barbara; she could never juggle more than one idea at a time.

"Had to," Gus said. "They jumped on me."

"I don't know, Gus. It takes two to make a fight. You should have just walked away."

He gritted his teeth. "Forget it! Damn it, I don't want to talk about it."

"Don't swear, Gus." Flora's gaze dropped to the oblong box. "What's that?"

"Doll. Bought it in Minneapolis."

"It must be awful big."

"Biggest in the store."

"How much did it cost?"

"What difference does that make?"

"Difference? Why, it makes a lot of difference. Papa always said—" She broke off and asked, "Where you going, Gus?"

He had strode off along the corridor; now he stopped.

"Where do you think? Up to see Barbara."

"You can't, Gus. Nurses won't let you. It's past seven. After seven they won't let us in. So she can sleep."

"The hell with that," Gus said, and he swung along the corridor and up the stair. Flora trotted after him, imploring in loud whispers, "Gus. You can't, Gus. They won't like it."

In the southeast bedroom only one nurse was on duty, and when he softly clicked open the door she jumped up and swished toward him. She blocked his way, a battle-ax of a woman.

"No. You can't come in."

He flushed; he took a step.

"No." Her mouth tightened, and she looked as if she were going to pinch his ear and lead him into the hall.

"God damn it," he roared, "get out of my way."

She recoiled, horrified. Who did he think he was, to talk like that to her? A doctor?

Across the room a single lamp burned, and the mammoth old bed was shadowy. It was the bed on which Flora had lain one April morning years ago, sobbing because Minnie Pond had told her about a girl who was stealing Gus. It was the bed from which Flora had observed Gus at his morning calisthenics back in the early days of marriage.

Gus stared down at the tremendous pillows, and as his eyes accustomed themselves to the dull light he distinguished Barbara lying there. She lay very still, but he saw that her eyes were open and she was faintly smiling. He bent and touched her lips.

"Daddy," she whispered, "you came back. I'll get well, now."

"Why," Gus boomed suddenly, " 'course you'll get well. Day or two you'll be up and around." He straightened, gestured. "Ought to have more light in this room. Got a present for Barbara."

"Mr. Burgoyne!" the nurse exclaimed. "I can't permit—"

"Too dark," Gus boomed. "Gloomy. Enough to make anybody sick. Turn on those ceiling lights."

"Mr. Burgoyne. I—"

"Hell's bells! Little light never hurt anybody."

And Gus trundled to the switch and snapped it.

Barbara blinked at this sudden illumination, and Gus was appalled at how pale and thin she looked, at how unnaturally large and luminous were her eyes. But he wasn't going to admit she looked sick. His weight bowed down the edge of the bed, and he tried to untie the package. But his blunt fingers were impatient with knots, so he broke the cord and ripped away the wrapping and lifted out the yellow-haired doll in its red dress.

Once Barbara would have squealed and flung her arms around his neck. But fever had weakened her tonight, just as it had dampened her dark hair. He tucked the doll into the curve of her arm, lying flaccid on the sheet, and he bent and kissed her again.

"Daddy," she whispered. "Red dress. Yellow hair." A tiny smile brushed her mouth. "Red and yellow, catch a fellow."

Those were the words he remembered, later, in the library. He was alone, wandering about the room, as if by keeping in motion he could somehow help Barbara. The night was far advanced; Flora had gone to bed; and he was desperately tired. Much of the room lay in shadow, and on the walls the brilliant circus lithographs were murky: dim, ghostly tigers and elephants, watching him pace. They meant nothing to him now, and the circus meant nothing. He stood at the window overlooking the lawn, and he remembered the night he had stood there jubilant because he had concluded a successful deal about a baby elephant. He remembered how old Sam Oxenford had looked, clawing his yellow whiskers; how Ive Pawpacker had looked, an immaculate, elegant man, romantic because he owned elephants. The room was full of ghosts.

Two nights later she died. And Gus was a man stumbling through rubble and ruin. For days he ate nearly nothing, and his clothes hung loosely on his big frame. He fell into the habit of sitting—just sitting—staring with eyes not focused on anything. When he walked he stumbled over things. When he brought a match toward his cigar he sometimes found it impossible to bring the flame and the tobacco into contact. In that time he wished for Frank MacGowan and Lucy and a woman named Doll, for they might have given him solace. Flora had taken to her bed. She did not give him solace.

Out on the road his circus rambled on, clanking through the fag end of the season. He did not rejoin it. He smoked cigars alone in the library of the great empty Wellington Avenue house, remaining indoors by day. Sometimes at night when he could not sleep he ventured out, wandering along the sidewalks of the city, and when he encountered other pedestrians he kept his gaze lowered. He didn't want to talk to anybody, he who had been so gregarious.

At last the circus limped home to winter quarters at Oxenford; and a week after that Gus drove south to Winchester.

"I'm through," he told Ive Pawpacker. "The hell with the show. I'll retire."

"You're too young a man, Gus—"

But words like that didn't reach him. He sat across the desk from Ive in the livery stable office, chewing a dead cigar, his skin pale, his eyes heavy.

So at last, for a good round sum, he sold Burgoyne's Circus & Hippodrome to Ivan Pawpacker. Not the farm at Oxenford, but the cars and the cat animals and the horses and the bulls.

Driving north from Winchester with Pawpacker's check in his pocket, he watched with slitted eyes as the road rushed under his car. He took corners too fast. He didn't care what happened to him.

13

THEY TRAVELED. Michigan Avenue knew them, and Fifth Avenue and Market Street. They visited Florida once, and Gus waxed tepidly interested in acquiring an orange grove. Escorted by realtors, he crunched along between sunny rows of trees, a sad-eyed man chewing a cigar. But in the end, he decided he did not want an orange grove. He did not know what he wanted.

They drifted. They heard French in New Orleans and Spanish in El Paso. They followed the vagabond sun south in autumn, north in spring. They visited Hot Springs and took the waters. But none of it was any good.

They were bewildered, punch-drunk, a beefy, lugubrious couple who said hardly a word as they dawdled through course after course in the dining room of a famous watering place. They became dutiful sight-seers, wandering along beaches or through the Garden of the Gods, she heavily veiled, he with an expensive cigar that was always going out.

Once in Los Angeles he pawed through the telephone directory to MacGowan, Frank. But he didn't reach for the telephone. He would have enjoyed going to Frank and pouring out his grief, but he couldn't bring himself to that. "Guess he's sore at me for selling the *Tribune,*" Gus thought. "Can't blame him much, at that."

Sometimes during their travels they dropped off in Tamarack for a few days or weeks, and Gus visited his office in the Oxenford Electric Building. No longer did he employ a secretary, and after being closed for months the office was full of dead air. In the reception room he picked up letters the postman had popped through the door-slot. They were never important. Gold leaf on the door still said: "Burgoyne's Circus & Hippodrome, A. H. Burgoyne, Owner." One day Gus ordered those letters removed. After that, he felt anonymous; and oddly, he wanted to feel that way. He was a wounded bear deep in a hillside den, brooding in the dark. Time was unimportant, swirling past outside.

He didn't go to the Chamber of Commerce any more, or to his luncheon clubs. All of that belonged to the brave, bright past. He thought of himself as he used to be, jovial and booming; and it seemed he had been another person then.

People saw him in the corridor of the office building, waiting for an

452

elevator. "Hello, Gus," they would say; or "Good morning, Mr. Burgoyne." Sometimes he would merely nod. Or if he said, " 'lo. How are you?" his voice would be thick, his eyes far away.

Often on the street he didn't speak to men he had known well. They would see him plowing along through thin gray cold, coat turned up, hat low, mouth chewing a cigar, eyes fixed ahead. Nobody thought he meant to be unfriendly. "Poor Gus," they said. "He took it hard, losing his little girl."

Now and then he brooded into the Eagle Cigar Store for a game of poker. But he almost never won. He couldn't keep his mind on the cards.

On occasion he drove alone to the farm at Oxenford, where he went through the motions of checking up on the caretaker. It was lonesome out there now, a place of empty barns, the west pasture buried by February in unbroken white.

And on some afternoons he visited a florist and bought flowers for a girl. Through cold and slush he drove to the west edge of the city, to the place of cypress and marble where Samuel R. Oxenford and Barbara Burgoyne lay in the earth. He placed the flowers, red and yellow roses, on the mound above Barbara, and while the frozen red sun descended he stood there unheeding, in his own bewildered fashion attempting to puzzle out the ancient enigma.

Those were blank years, lost out of his life; and when he gazed back on them he realized he should have treated them as a wise poker player treats a run of bad cards. He should have sat tight, made no bets. He should have said to life, "By me." Luck was running against him, in those years.

But he was not one to live negatively forever; and gradually as the months elapsed he came groping out of gloom. Doll Burgoyne, Carlotta, Barbara—each he had lost, and for each he had grieved; and then at last time had piled up heaps of forgetfulness.

His excursions with Flora grew briefer, the intervals in Tamarack longer; and one morning in his office, more than a year after Barbara's death, he sat reading the weekly bulletin from the Chamber of Commerce, and all at once he decided to attend the luncheon that day.

It was a significant decision; he felt like a patient long bedridden about to take his first steps. Moving through the sunny noontime streets, he experienced a touch of timidity, it had been so long since he had congregated with his kind. It was as if when Barbara died part of him had died, too; and now he was a ghost of the Gus that used to be, returning to the city of the living.

He didn't look like a ghost. His appetite had revived, these last weeks; his shoulders and belly filled out his suit, checked in his favorite gray-and-black. He wore his dove-colored hat pulled at a slight angle; his face had plumped again, and the unhealthy half-moons had vanished from beneath his eyes. Only his gait hinted at his long sickness of spirit. Today he didn't bustle and jostle, as of yore; he moved along easily with the noon throngs; he was almost portly.

As always, the luncheon would be held in the General Grant Hotel; and when Gus was still two blocks away an amazing thing occurred. With other pedestrians he had halted at a busy intersection, waiting for the traffic officer's change of signal. On the opposite corner other pedestrians were clustered, and Gus found himself staring at a pretty little girl of two or three. This was not unusual; he was always noticing little girls. And then, as a matter of course, he would glance at their mothers.

So now he glanced at the little girl's mother, and for a second he thought merely that she was a handsome woman of thirty; and then his joints turned weak as he realized he was staring full into the face of Carlotta. It was quite involuntary, what he did. He swayed forward, out into traffic; and he heard brakes squeal and a horn honk and a driver yell; and just in time he stepped back to the curb, where he belonged. And across the street he beheld Carlotta picking up the child and plunging back into the crowd on her side. Mentally he cried out, "Wait! Carlotta! Wait for me!" But she did not wait.

In those seconds he saw pictures he would carry in memory till the end of his days. Her profile so distinguished; her shoulders so fine; her beauty so smooth. Her waist was still willowy, her bosom and hips womanly, and she was wearing one of those fashionable and daring split skirts. A dark skirt, and as she turned he beheld it parting up her calf, to reveal a flash of yellow-silk underskirt.

Traffic changed, and he lurched forward toward the place where she had been. On the opposite corner he halted, pedestrians swirling against him. He heard the voices of the noon: men saying, "So I put the proposition to him cold," and girls saying, "She said to me, 'I like your hat, but I don't think it's your type,' and I said . . ." And he heard his own voice crying mutely, "Carlotta. Carlotta."

She had vanished; he had lost her; everything was working against him, these days. A department store occupied that corner, Goldstein's chief competitor, and he thought she must have disappeared inside. He even ventured in himself, walking through the smells of perfume and silks; and he saw many women, but none was Carlotta.

He felt angry and hurt. She had no right to snub him. What did she think he'd do, make a scene or something? She was heartless, he thought; she had everything—children to buy presents for at Christmas time—and he was a man bewildered and stumbling because a child had died; and she would not even speak a few civil words to him.

The department store wall-clock impinged on his vision: 12:14. He would be late for the luncheon meeting. Not that it mattered, not that it mattered; but he was trying to overcome his sickness, creeping and crawling toward normal existence again, and he'd better go. He left the department store and strode along the sidewalk, and just inside another entrance to the store Carlotta halted and stepped back, watching him stalk past.

"His hair is turning gray," she thought. "At the edges. He looks harder. He's fat. Once I loved him. I don't love him now. But why do I want to cry?"

They welcomed him back tremendously, at the Chamber of Commerce. They couldn't have been more cordial if he had been a strike-breaker. Following dessert, when the chairman introduced visitors, his eyes twinkled and he said they had another stranger in their midst, A. H. Burgoyne.

"Stand up, Gus, you old rascal," the chairman said.

So Gus stood up and bowed and the applause was thunderous. It warmed his heart. It was just what he needed, after the way Carlotta had treated him.

Following the meeting, many members squeezed his hand and welcomed him back individually; and the president asked whether he would be willing to serve on a committee. Gus said he would. So he was appointed chairman of the Automobile Affairs Committee. Its purpose was to induce motor car manufacturers to establish plants in Tamarack, and although it never achieved any concrete results it submitted many long reports that the meetings heartily approved.

After that, Gus attended the Chamber of Commerce every week, and he returned to his old luncheon clubs. And he resumed his activities with the Greater Tamarack Association. He was seldom happy, but he discovered that by keeping busy he could numb unhappiness.

He and Flora were not much help to each other. The shameful fact was that he dreaded an evening alone with her, she was so lachrymose. Oddly enough, she had grown heavier since Barbara's death, for she had nothing to do and she passed the hours by piecing between meals. She was like a cow grazing out of boredom.

"I don't know what I'd do without Madam Thale," Flora said; and it was certainly true that the Madam afforded her great consolation. Flora was her only client now, and often she spent several days at the Wellington Avenue house, entering the trance state and receiving messages from Samuel R. Oxenford and Barbara. They were, they communicated, dwelling happily in heaven, and Flora should be of good cheer. Residence in a place where the streets were gold-paved had evidently given Mr. Oxenford better perspective about money, for he never accused Flora of squandering the currency she paid Madam Thale.

At that period Gus did not maintain any extra-matrimonial apartments, for like everything else his luck with women had turned against him. He met pretty girls here and there, but he seemed to have misplaced his knack of sweeping them into his orbit. Usually the girls who attracted him were eighteen or twenty, and they were already involved with boys of their own age. He seemed old to them.

Their attitude soured him. Low in spirits, he asked himself whether he had ever been attractive to women. Perhaps they had merely used him to get jobs at the amusement park and with his circus. Then he told himself that after all Carlotta had loved him once, and she was better than all the other women bundled together. He daydreamed about her a great deal.

Leaving the Chamber of Commerce one noon, Gus spied a man he knew sitting in the General Grant lobby. A small, elegant man with a walking stick and a clipped beard. He bustled over.

"Ive Pawpacker! Well I'll be damned! How are you, Ive?"

He expected Ive to spring up and extend his hand. But Ive did nothing of the sort. He stared up coldly.

"Hello, Gus."

"Why didn't you call me?" Gus demanded. "I'd taken you to the Chamber of Commerce. How long you been here?"

"I came yesterday."

"Yesterday! I like that—you being here and not calling me."

"I think," Pawpacker said, "you know why I didn't call you."

Gus stared. He felt as if Ive had dashed ice water into his face.

"Why no," he exclaimed, "why didn't you? Too busy? You here buying horses? That why?"

"I'm here buying horses. But that isn't why."

Gus was nonplussed. He remembered now that he had written Pawpacker several letters during the past year, and had received no replies, but he had ascribed that to laxness. He sat down.

"Look here. Let's get to the bottom of this. Take it you're mad at me. Why?"

Pawpacker regarded him icily.

"Here. Have a cigar. Let's talk things over. Don't want you sore at me."

Ive started to take the cigar, then hesitated, then reached.

"I might as well," he said. "Maybe it will help even things up."

"What do you mean, even things up?"

"For the trimming you gave me."

"Trimming! What do you mean?"

"Gus," Ive said, "there's no need pretending innocent. You gave me a hell of a trimming when you sold me the show, and you know it."

"Trimming! Don't know what you mean!"

Pawpacker smiled sarcastically.

"I mean it," Gus exclaimed. "Don't know what you're talking about. The show was up for sale and I gave you first chance. We came to terms and I sold it. What was wrong with that?"

"Keep it," Pawpacker said. "Keep it for your Chamber of Commerce friends. You crooked me. Well, maybe that's all right. Let the buyer beware. I've dealt in horses long enough—I should have been on guard. But I liked you, Gus. And with your little girl dead, I felt sorry for you. I didn't think you'd take advantage of me."

Gus's eyes turned hard.

"You're crazy," he said. "I never crooked you and you know it. Serious thing to accuse a man of—being crooked. They called me Honest Gus, didn't they? You can't back up that charge."

"It's not so much being slickered out of the money," Pawpacker said. "I can afford that. What I hate is being known as a sucker. Word gets around. They know about it on every show in the country."

"Now listen," Gus growled. "I like you Ive, and I always have. But I don't like you telling me I crooked you when I didn't. How did I do it? If you've got a bellyache, why in hell don't you quit beating around the bush?"

"I'm wasting my breath, Gus—but I'll waste it. First thing, I paid you for good will. For the show's name. And when we tried to book it, what did we run into? A stone wall! Not a town in the country wanted us!"

"Uh," Gus said. "Matter of fact, it never occurred to me you'd have trouble—"

And that was true. When he sold his circus he had been so muddled by grief that he had not dreamed of taking advantage of Ive Pawpacker.

"The equipment wasn't worth half what I paid you," Pawpacker was saying. "But you'd led me to believe you were coining money and I thought the show's name was valuable."

"We were coining money!"

"From grift. And you took the cream off the territory. But that wasn't the worst. The worst was the way you switched equipment and stock on me."

"Switched! What are you talking about?"

For a moment Pawpacker didn't respond. His eyes were furious. Gus thought: "He's mad at me. Terribly mad." It was bewildering, part of the bad dream which life had become.

Pawpacker's voice quavered. "Gus, you have more brass than a cir-

cus band. Pretending you didn't know a thing about it. Trying to
brazen it out. That makes me mad. You must think I'm a simpleton."

"Don't think anything of the sort! Always admired you, Ive. Had
great respect for you."

"Then why do you pretend you don't know about that switch of
equipment? Next thing, you'll be telling me it was all Lorenz's doing."

Lorenz! Suspicion dawned. Gus's brows drew together; and he was
remembering how, after selling the show, he had embarked almost at
once on his travels. He had ordered Lorenz to wind up the business
and deliver the circus to Pawpacker in Winchester.

He exclaimed, "Lorenz! That's it! The guy's a crook—nothing but
a crook. What did he do?"

Pawpacker hurled his cigar into a spittoon.

"You know what he did. When I visited the show it was beautifully
mounted. The stock was good. The wagons. But after I bought it,
what did I get? Junk! Fourth-rate harness. Spavined nags. Nothing
but skin and bones, ready for the glue works. And the cats—"

Pawpacker's words cracked like pistol shots, and he went on and on,
recounting how he had been duped. Gus sat staring. Lorenz! The
thief! He had simply looted the show, substituting worthless equipment and feeble animals.

"Ive! Now listen! You've got to believe me—!"

"Believe you! After a swindle like that? God! I must look a simpleton!"

And Ive stood up and fumed to the elevator.

Gus sat there a long time, cigar ash spilled on his vest. Finally he
heaved to his feet and dragged back to his office. He sat at his desk,
hands big fists. Never before had he bamboozled anybody, uninten-
tionally. He would have enjoyed getting his hands on Lorenz, and
with that in mind he called Honest Jack Dennison.

But Honest Jack didn't know the whereabouts of either Lorenz or
Walt Ambrose. More than a year ago they had dropped from sight.

Gus hung up. He played with the idea of calling Pud Myra, asking
him to telegraph every police station in the country to be on the lookout for Lorenz and Walt. But where would that lead? To court, perhaps; and in court Lorenz and Walt might offer embarrassing testi-
mony about the way affairs had been conducted on Burgoyne's Circus
& Hippodrome.

Of all people, why had Lorenz swindled Pawpacker? Gus stood up,
paced. Pawpacker was his friend. You didn't bunco your friends. And
why hadn't Pawpacker raised a howl before this? Gus stood at the
window, staring down at Harrison Street traffic, and gradually understanding came to him. Pawpacker had been a horse trader. He had

lived by his wits. He was proud of living by his wits. And there was
a code among horse traders. You outwitted the other fellow if you
could, but if he outwitted you, you kept your mouth shut, went your
way. You had pride about such things.

Well, what could be done? Suddenly Gus whirled to the desk,
grabbed his checkbook and impulsively dashed off a check for a good
sum that should reimburse Ive for the swindle. And he wrote a letter
to accompany the check. People had not, he declared, called him Honest Gus for no good reason. He wrote of his grief at the time he sold
the circus; he reiterated his innocence.

He dropped the letter into the mail-slot by the elevators, tramped
back to his office. The check had left a hole in his bank account
through which you could have driven a band wagon, but he did not
regret it. Someday he might want to venture again into the circus
business; he might need Pawpacker.

His letter brought no response. But Pawpacker did not spurn the
check. At the end of the month Gus found it among his canceled
checks, endorsed in Pawpacker's neat copperplate.

In Europe mad people started a war, and an era ended. But Gus did
not think of it that way. "Be over by Christmas," he told Flora; and
she said, "I don't know, Gus. It might not be over by Christmas." It
was not that she had become a student of logistics, but only because
she had formed the habit of contradicting Gus. It was her way of
keeping a conversation going.

He was accustomed to her habit; once it had irritated him; but now
he was pretty well calloused to Flora's ways. Often he conversed with
her without being aware of what they were saying.

"Why are they fighting, Gus?"

"Uh? Fighting? Who?"

"Why those foreigners."

"Oh. Them. I don't know. Just cussedness, I guess."

But that foreign cussedness, as it turned out, was not without its
effect upon America. In Tamarack it halted work on *The History of
American Philosophy,* for Dr. Harold Henderson discovered that war
had turned his thoughts blood-dark, and he was too depressed to continue writing his book. The shells that wrecked the great Continental
libraries filled him with sickness. His *History* shriveled to unimportance, and he locked it away in a drawer. "Man stood at midmorning
in the sunshine," he told his journal, "and sweet reason was his companion. But now we shall not know tranquillity again, nor will our
children."

For two years the *History* remained untouched, and Harold shambled along his academic treadmill. He had always enjoyed routine

tasks, for routine subjugated the disorder of life to a pattern; and now more than ever he worshiped routine. Routine was his way of taming life.

But as the war dragged on, and millions perished, even Harold became anesthetized to violence, and he returned to his *History*. In 1920, when it was completed and revised and impeccably indexed, he showed the manuscript to a traveler for a New York publishing house; and the book burst upon the world in 1922. It created a great sensation, among several hundred persons, and even the reviewers for scholarly journals rendered it the high praise of confessing it to be nearly as good as if they had written it. Instantly it became the textbook for Philosophy C at Tamarack, and as years passed it found its way into many institutions of higher learning. Most students found it dull, and they scrawled comic pictures on the end-papers, never reflecting that those solid paragraphs had been composed by a human being whose children suffered whooping cough and whose pretty wife had once sobbed into her pillow for the love of Doll Burgoyne's son.

The war affected Ivan Pawpacker too, very prosperously. For just as in the time of Alexander and Caesar, horses were still the sinews of war. Mules, too. War had caught short the horse markets of the world, and buying agents for the Allies visited the United States; and from Chicago and St. Louis the news flashed to Winchester that horses and mules were needed to haul the caissons through the mire of France. Ive was a busy man, traveling constantly, purchasing magnificent animals whose destiny now was darker than pulling a corn plow through the meadow-lark songs of June. Money poured into his life. He amalgamated his bank with its Winchester rival; for a time his fingertips possessed Midas magic; and if as a bank president he made mistakes he could not be censured too severely; intoxication was in the air, then.

By the spring of 1915 Gus seemed his old self again. His gusto returned. He was a powerful motor car that had been idling in neutral, but now some spiritual gearshift had occurred and he was impatient to roar toward Big Things.

What these Big Things were he didn't know, except that they would include making piles of money within a short time. He didn't propose, however, to accomplish this by organizing another circus. He told himself that someday, after his finances were in better shape, he might venture into the circus business again; but not at present.

He didn't analyze his emotions concerning circuses, but the truth was they were still as dark and sick as when he sold out to Ivan Pawpacker. To think of his showman years was to experience the bad memories of his photograph on a poster with "Crook!" scrawled across it, of Barbara's death.

So even though he seemed his old self, he was not, wholly. And even though he had abundant energy again, there was a difference. In the old days his energy had been directed not so much toward making money as bringing into reality his circus dream. Money would follow, incidentally. Now he determined to make money for its own sake. He told himself he was feeling fine; but the tides of his luck were still at the ebb; and money can be elusive.

It seemed a fine idea, the Tamarack Speedway. It looked magnificently profitable, on paper. It was one of those things which simply cannot miss, on paper.

Gus became impregnated with the idea as a consequence of his passion for the motor car. The Tamarack Automobile Club had rented space in the General Grant lobby, and Gus was always dropping in to yarn with fellow devotees about the bewitching caprices of the gasoline engine.

His old friend, Honest Jack Dennison, was among those who shared his interest in the motor car. Honest Jack was a gambler, yes; but that did not mean he thought of nothing but cards and dice. He had his hobby, like any man. Gus was always encountering him at the automobile club.

Jason Cadwallader was another habitué of that place. Not old Jason; not the founder of the Cadwallader Medicine Company. This was Jason III. (Tamarack's best families had recently borrowed from royalty this means of distinguishing members of the male line.) Jason III was a slim, blond chap of twenty-two, more or less educated by Princeton University.

When Gus bustled to the Automobile Club, he would often find Jason III lounging in an easy chair, conversing with Honest Jack; and one May afternoon they fell to discussing the races at Indianapolis, to be held Memorial Day, and the upshot was that they planned to attend this event. Gus had recently purchased a fine new Packard, and they accepted his invitation to make the trip as its guests.

"Three of us," Gus mused. "Ought to have one more in the party. Four's better than three if we want poker in the evening. Uh—s'pose Pud Myra would like to go?"

It seemed possible, so Gus called Pud at police headquarters. Pud said he would love to make the trip, but maybe the police commissioner wouldn't like his up and leaving.

"Uh," Gus said. "S'pose it would help if I had Honest Jack call the commissioner?"

Pud thought this would help a great deal, and he was dead right, for Honest Jack had contributed heavily to the commissioner's election fund.

The night before their departure Gus sat studying maps and his Blue Book, and he retired early. Next morning he vaulted from bed with the first belling of the alarm clock. He and Flora had occupied separate bedrooms that night, so his early bustling would not rob her of sleep. Madam Thale was to keep Flora company during his absence, and the two ladies were snoring together in Mr. Oxenford's old bedroom.

He snapped shut his Gladstone and tiptoed downstairs, where in the kitchen he brewed stout coffee and fried bacon and eggs. Their sizzling odors titillated his big nostrils as he sat spooning up heavily creamed breakfast food. He ate leisurely, for he had allotted himself plenty of time. Since he enjoyed eating more than sleeping, he preferred rising early to missing out on a satisfying meal.

He lit a cigar and puffed over his third cup of coffee. He was a man of consequence, about to make a motor trip with other men of consequence; and he was the master of this house. His old sense returned of having done pretty well for a boy from Clayton Junction. Life was good, after all.

It was still early when he emerged to the porte-cochere. The lazy sun had not yet risen, but the eastern sky was bright glory. The morning lay cool and pure on the dewy lawn, and as he trudged through the scents of the garden the wrens and cardinals were singing about the joys of springtime and love.

Springtime and love. He paused when he reached the old stable, with its morning-glory vines and cupola like the spirit of the 1890's, and for a moment he imagined how it would be if Carlotta were his wife, and if Barbara were alive, and if the three of them were starting off on a motor trip. A smile played over his mouth, and his eyes were neither sorrowful nor worldly hard: they were tender, the eyes that might have been his always if events had arranged themselves differently. He felt oddly calm and at peace, and it seemed that Carlotta and Barbara were near him. He thought of Barbara in her grave and Carlotta in her bed across the daybreak city blocks, and he wondered whether the human spirit, when the body lay in death or in sleep, ever broke from its prison house and roamed free, seeking out those it had loved. That was a moment as sweet as the robin songs, as pure as the early dew; and he remembered how in that first year of his circus he used to have the feeling that Carlotta was near him.

Suddenly the sweetness was heartbreaking. An ache stabbed through his lungs. He broke from his reveries and bustled. He rolled back the stable door, hurried to the wheel of his Packard. And all that day and indeed for years thereafter, when he looked back upon that moment in the sweet May morning, he had the delusion that he had been close to Carlotta and to his daughter.

It was a fine trip. It had a splendid masculine flavor, like a duck-hunting expedition. All the voyagers liked women very much indeed, but nevertheless there were occasions when a man liked to get away for a few days with other men. It was as if you were a boy again, with secret societies from which girls were excluded.

Indianapolis was crowded and lighthearted, but they secured excellent hotel rooms, owing to Gus's foresight in wiring for reservations. And their seats at the races were worth the stout price paid for them. It was a fine, balmy day, and Gus splashed into the excitement. Crowds! Thousands! Flags afloat! Band music! Pitchmen hawking souvenir programs! Popcorn, peanuts, hot dogs! The sleeping show-man awakened in his soul. He enjoyed the races too, with men out on the track semaphoring with checkered flags, with reporters in the press box telegraphing a running account to their papers, with the deep roar of the motors. But most appealing was the general excitement, the bustling, the thronged humanity.

Driving back to Tamarack, Gus was sometimes silent for miles, rolling his cigar, pondering. One noon at lunch he said:

"Boys, I've been thinking. Why couldn't we build a speedway in Tamarack?"

It was such a momentous suggestion that they all just stared. Then Jason Cadwallader III exclaimed:

"Ha! Now you've got something!"

Pud wrinkled his forehead.

"Gus, I believe you're on the trail of something there."

"No doubt about it. We'd make a million. A cool million! How about it, Jack?"

That secretive smile played over Honest Jack's lips, as mysterious as lightning flashing silently on a far horizon. His voice was suavely confidential.

"I'd take a flyer in a sporting proposition like that," he said.

All through the meal they discussed it.

"We'd organize a company," Gus said. "Incorporate. Think of the people it would bring to Tamarack. And publicity. Tamarack would be on every sports page in the country. You know, I think I could get backing from the Greater Tamarack Association. And sell stock to men with dough. How about it, Jason? Wouldn't your old man come in on such a deal?"

"Oh, yes," Jason said carelessly. "The old man would come in."

In Tamarack, Memorial Day was hot with deep blue sky and heavy sunlight; and Madam Thale was grateful for the coolness of the spacious house on Wellington Avenue. The evening before, she and Flora had taxied to the cemetery, decorating the graves of Barbara and Mr. Oxenford. Now at midmorning they sat in the library, where the Madam was reading aloud to Flora. The book was *Three Weeks*.

Because of Mr. Oxenford's prejudice, Flora was largely unacquainted with the diversion of fiction. When the Madam suggested reading aloud, she had expected to be bored, but this was far from the case. The novel grabbed her interest and stirred in her what is called the tender passion.

The Madam finished a chapter and closed the book. Still under the thrall of the story, Flora sat chewing gum.

"Read some more," she said.

"I want to rest my eyes," Madam Thale said, removing the pince-nez from her sharp nose. In the decade since she had fastened herself upon Flora, the Madam's body had thinned till she was little more than skin and bones. Mr. Thale, a believer in Whitman's theory that loafing benefits the soul, was long dead; and the Madam's daughter and two sons had married and were regularly presenting her with grandchildren. She dwelt alone in her East Tamarack oracle, and she enjoyed a good life. With Flora her sole client, she had removed the clairvoyant sign from her window, and she no longer needed to pay the police for the privilege of tuning in on the Infinite. She received no stated salary, but when she needed money Flora gratefully shelled out.

With Gus her husband, Flora had plenty of money. Just as in their honeymoon era, he continued flipping her twenty-dollar bills; and most of this currency Flora hoarded. As the years passed she found herself taking pleasure in saving.

Paying Madam Thale was her only fixed expense, and never for an instant did she begrudge a cent of this. Why should she? Value received was stupendous.

"Do you like the story?" the Madam asked.

Flora heaved a great sigh.

"It's wonderful. I think love is so pretty. Puts me in mind of Gus."

"You still love Gus as much as ever?"

"More."

"You're lucky to have such a good husband."

"Oh, I know that."

"He's very attentive, I suppose."

"Attentive?"

"Kissing you, and so forth."

"Well," Flora said, "he kisses me when he leaves for downtown. But not much of the 'and so forth.'"

"No?"

"No."

"Um-m-m," said the Madam. "That is odd."

"I think so, too," Flora said. "Think it's his health. Don't think he's enjoying the best of health."

"He seems very robust."

"I know," Flora said, "but the fact is, he's not. Every night, he goes right to sleep. Maybe he kisses me good night and maybe not. But either way, he goes right to sleep. No, I wouldn't call him robust."

"He used to be?"

Color burned Flora's cheeks.

"When we were first married," she said shyly. "I remember in that Chicago hotel—he kind of shocked me, if you know what I mean."

"Yes," said the Madam, "I know what you mean."

"But I didn't mind," Flora added loyally.

"One doesn't," the Madam murmured.

Flora sat chewing, lost in the past. Finally she opined:

"Yes, think it must be his health. I think it's his liver."

"His liver!" the Madam exclaimed, in some surprise.

"Think so. He smokes too much. Worries me. I've read up on the liver. You smoke too much, and eat rich victuals the way he does, and drink alcohol—it's not good for you. Upsets your liver. Gus has always had liver trouble. Land knows, I've warned him about it, too. But he will eat. And smoke. I think he's undermining his liver, Madam. That's what I think."

"Possible," the Madam murmured.

"I don't like it, anyway," Flora said.

"I can see your point."

"We might as well not be married. There's more to marriage than just living together."

"A great deal more."

"But he will smoke, and he will eat. His liver trouble gives him insomnia, too. He'll sleep a while and then get up and come downstairs. Since Baby passed away. Makes him sad."

Flora began to weep, softly.

"Why," asked the Madam, "don't you point out to him it might be nice to have another child?"

"Have," Flora sniffled. "It won't work. He don't want another baby. Burned child fears the fire, he says. Oh, I've tried everything."

Flora's tears were coming freely, now. Her fat hands clenched, and her shoulders heaved.

Madam Thale sat in speculation, and then her brow cleared and she smiled. She went to Flora and put her arm around the sorrowing shoulders.

"Don't cry, honey."

"Oh," Flora wailed, "I just can't help it! I love him so much and sometimes I think he don't love me any more."

"It's probably only his liver."

"Well then, he loves food and cigars more than me."

"I think I can help you," the Madam said.

"You do? That would be wonderful! Are you going into the trance state?"

"I've been in it. While you were crying. And I think I've found the solution."

"Madam," Flora sighed, "you're the best friend I've ever had."

"The only trouble with my solution, it's very expensive."

"How much?"

"A hundred dollars."

"Kind of dear, all right," Flora admitted. "But think it would be worth it. What is it?"

The Madam's smile grew coy, and she looked at Flora from the ends of her eyes.

"Have you ever heard of love potions?"

"Can't say that I have. What are they?"

"They are very ancient and very mysterious."

"Sound like they'd be hard to come by."

"They are. That is why they are so expensive."

"But once you've come by them," Flora asked, "what good do they do?"

"They stimulate. Gus would be stimulated, once he swallowed the potion."

"Suppose he didn't like the taste?"

"He'll never know."

"I think he'd know, all right. He's a big eater, but he's particular about what he puts in his stomach. If I try to feed him round steak, he won't have it. Sirloin, tenderloin and T-bones—that's what Gus likes."

Madam Thale sighed.

"My dear, the potion is tasteless. You'll slip it into a food he likes."

Flora asked, "How soon could you come by this potion?"

"I don't know. It may take time. And, of course, money. It might cost even more than a hundred dollars."

Flora could take a hint. "Just a minute," she said. "I'll get you the money."

Gus was exceedingly busy that summer, pushing ahead the business of the Tamarack Speedway. He presented the proposal to the Greater Tamarack Association, and the members gave it their blessing. But he wanted more than that. He wanted money. He engaged a lawyer to draw up papers of incorporation, and armed with these he called a special meeting of the association. He delivered an impassioned speech, declaring that if Tamarack did not go ahead it would surely slip backward. Progress! Thousands visiting the city to attend the races!

His audience succumbed. The Greater Tamarack Association bought stock, and individual members risked modest amounts of capital. Jason Cadwallader II bought shares on behalf of his son, in the hope that if Jason III grew fascinated by the Speedway he would cease roistering and amount to something. Honest Jack invested in the company, and even Pud Myra bought a few shares.

But Gus was the most heavily interested; he owned more than half the stock; and presently gold letters appeared once again on his office door. "Tamarack Speedway, Inc.," they said. "A. H. Burgoyne, Pres." He admired those letters tremendously, and if putting them on that door had dangerously inroaded into his capital there was nothing to worry about. He would be somewhat close run for a time, that was all. Next summer after the races he would be swimming in money.

Gus labored so tumultuously that by August the company was prepared to roll, and early one evening he asked Flora:

"Want to take a little drive? I've got something to show you."

"I don't care if I do," she said.

That was her way of expressing delight. She couldn't recall when Gus had asked her to go riding, it had been so long. She marked this invitation down to Madam Thale's credit.

Not yet had the Madam delivered the potion; it seemed it was monstrously hard to obtain, and great expense was involved; but several times a week the Madam visited Flora and counseled patience. Soon, soon. Meanwhile, she was bringing psychic instrumentalities to bear upon Gus, fanning his embers, putting him into the proper state to receive the potion. The invitation, Flora was convinced, had great mystic import.

So her being sang as she emerged to the porte-cochere. The long summer twilight was only beginning to fall, and as always she paused momentarily to stare at the car in the drive.

"Now, Gus," she admonished, "don't drive too fast."

"Uh?"

"I say don't drive too fast. It's dangerous."

"Uh—no. I'll keep 'er down to fifty."

"Now, Gus."

He tramped the starter and shifted gears, thinking of the secretary he had recently employed. A pretty woman, young, but married, alas. She resented his hands; if he merely patted her shoulder she frowned. But he did not take offense at the frown of so handsome a girl; he felt challenged.

Through balmy air they drove west along Wellington. After a dozen blocks the car slowed, for a barricade loomed ahead: sawhorses that said, "Street Closed," and red lanterns. Always the pavement of Wellington Avenue had plagued the Tamarack burghers, owing to the venality of some long-ago streets commissioner, and his successors.

"Have to detour," Gus murmured, turning north.

And so it was that in continuing westward they passed Funland Park. Only Funland was no longer Funland. After the collapse of the Oxenford empire, the park had degenerated through a series of fumbling hands; it had wallowed in receivership; and last season it had closed for all eternity. Some real estate firm had purchased the land, and already houses were building there.

The Packard crept past; and Gus stared.

"You know," he mumbled, "makes me feel kind of bad to have it gone."

"I remember the night we rode the merry-go-round," Flora said. "My, I was excited."

"Always liked merry-go-rounds," Gus said.

"They don't get you anywhere, though. That's what Papa always said. People go round and round, and when it's over they're right back where they started. And their dime's gone."

"Gone forever," Gus murmured.

"That's right, Gus, That's what Papa always said. Their dime's gone forever."

The Packard moved on, finding its way to the hillcrest overlooking Clayton Junction. At this hour the town was a smudge of dusk and coal smoke, jeweled with twinkling lights. As the Packard descended Gus heard a locomotive wailing, and he saw a westbound limited creeping along the valley floor, a black-and-gold worm. Midnight would find it in Omaha, and by daybreak it would be plunging through the high plains, into the dream West of cowpunchers and range wars. He found himself restless to follow; to get away from Tamarack. Although controverted by a hundred journeys, he still believed that by travel he could get away from himself.

"Let's go to San Francisco," he said.

"What for?"

"World's Fair. Ought to be a great experience. I happened to buy a *Billboard* the other day, and they say it's the best midway of all time. Like to go?"

"I don't know, Gus. I just don't know."

She hated leaving Tamarack, when any day Madam Thale might hand her the potion.

"How about your Speedway?" she asked. "Could you get away?"

"Sure. Couple of weeks rest will do me good. Fact is, we're waiting now for the blueprints. But we've bought the ground. That's what I brought you out to see."

He stopped the car and pointed south at shadowy acres of tin cans and ash heaps and weeds. It was the spot between Clayton Junction and Tamarack where, years before, Gus Phelan had gathered red haws for Doll Burgoyne.

So to San Francisco they journeyed, callousing their feet on the exposition grounds, gawking skyward at Art Smith looping his biplane above the bay. Flora, oddly enough, found herself interested in the educational exhibits: in such things as the telephone company's display, where one sat with headphones and heard a man in New York talking as plain as if he were in the next room. Long distance coast to coast! What wouldn't they think of next?

In one building they stepped into an elevator, a replica of a mine-shaft cage, and descended into a mock coal mine. While the guide escorted their party along papier-mâché tunnels, Gus's thoughts turned to the abandoned mine at Oxenford. It troubled him that the property should be idle, merely because the coal was of such wretched quality; it seemed there should be some way to exploit it.

Flora had no interest in what, to Gus, was the best of the exposition: the midway. Hence they parted company, and Gus went strolling through the cries of barkers. And on the midway he encountered two old friends.

The reunion occurred outside an exhibit of female anatomy, which, in its way, was just as educational as anything the telephone company could offer. In that era, America found itself enravished by Hawaiian music, and upon a platform outside this concession, girls in grass skirts were strumming tunes from the Islands. Music lovers, nearly all male, were thronged before the platform, observing a pretty lass dancing the hula. Gus stood munching a hot dog, giving no heed to the ticket seller or the barker who, at the moment, remained silent so the gents could concentrate upon the little lady.

But presently Gus felt somebody's gaze drilling him, and upon the platform he beheld the barker and the ticket seller. Lorenz and Walt Ambrose!

Lorenz grinned and motioned Gus to the end of the platform.

"Stick around," he whispered. "After the suckers go in, we'll have a gab."

The music ceased and Lorenz did a wonderful job of talking. And Walt Ambrose did a flourishing business at the ticket booth.

But Walt's fingers were behaving themselves, Lorenz told Gus, after they had shaken hands and commented upon the smallness of the world.

"No grift," he said. "We're raking in enough without it. Well, Gus! How've you been, you old bank robber!"

"Fine," Gus said. "Everything's great. Just now, I'm building a Speedway."

They discussed that, and Gus was delighted to receive Lorenz's endorsement of the project. And presently the conversation circled to Burgoyne's Circus & Hippodrome, and Pawpacker's purchase.

"Uh—Ive Pawpacker was pretty mad about that. Don't think you should have done what you did, Lorenz. Hardly seems right."

"What are you talking about, Gus?"

"Well now, Lorenz—don't want you to think I'm accusing you, or anything like that, but Ive claimed you ran a whizzer on him. Says you substituted a lot of broken-down animals and wagons and harness for my good ones."

"That little liar," Lorenz grinned. "God, he's crooked!"

"You mean Pawpacker just lied to me?"

"Sure he did."

"Uh—he seemed pretty mad. Hardly thought he was putting it on."

"Well now, Gus—let me tell you. He might have been sore about the condition of the show after that clem in Dakota. You remember the car windows were busted, and the wagons smashed up. I didn't think you'd want me to repair them, as long as you'd sold the show."

"Yeah—see your point. So you didn't make any substitutions?"

"I swear to God I didn't, Gus."

"Uh. Ive's a crook, you say?"

"You've got to watch him, Gus. That's for certain."

Gus flushed as he recalled the size of the check he had sent Ive. It went to illustrate that when a man tried to do the right thing somebody always trimmed him.

Two women in Tamarack were delighted when the Burgoynes departed for San Francisco. One was Gus's secretary.

She was twenty and her name was Marcene, but her moral standards were infinitely higher than one expected in a girl named Marcene. The winter before, in college—the Tamarack Commercial College— she had been voted the most beautiful girl in the student body: she could have gone far as a secretary. But her interest in a business career was temporary. In June she had married Eustis, a butcher at the Tamarack city market, and she intended working only long enough to help pay for their furniture.

She entered Gus's employ while still a bride, and so far as she was concerned there existed only one man of consequence: Eustis. Gus was merely that inevitable nuisance of the employed, the Boss. Marcene possessed a magnificent figure, and her coloring was brunette, somewhat in the Carlotta tradition.

Every evening in their apartment she recounted the day's events to Eustis. It both annoyed and amused her, she said, the way old Burgoyne kept pestering her. He must be thirty-five or forty; why couldn't men act their age?

Her reports infuriated Eustis. He wanted to wrap a meat cleaver around Burgoyne's neck. But his bride counseled against violence. If Burgoyne grew too fresh, she would up and quit.

The other woman who dreaded the Burgoynes' return was Madam Thale. Thus far, the Madam had cajoled more than two hundred dollars from Flora on behalf of the love potion, but she was no nearer acquiring it than on Memorial Day.

She had supposed finding the potion would be simple, but when she broached the matter to a druggist friend he shook his head. Certain ingredients listed in the Pharmacopoeia were said to stimulate, but laws had been passed against their use. He wouldn't touch the business, the druggist said, with a ten-foot pole.

So Madam Thale launched investigations of her own. She visited the public library, searching old tomes for the secret. Here and there in ancient writings she encountered mention of potions, but no formulae.

She was in despair. She cursed herself for promising more than she could deliver. For years she had kept Flora in subjugation and ignorance; but now she had overstepped. If she delivered worthless powders to Flora, and if after digesting them Gus immediately fell asleep, Flora would be disappointed. She would lose faith in the Madam. It would be farewell to the years of living in clover; back to the slim pickings of reading schoolgirls' palms.

Nearly every day that summer Flora had called her by telephone. "Thought I'd ring you to see how you're coming."

"It's almost ready, Flora. But it takes time."

"Well, I thought I'd ring you, anyway. Hope you can get it before long."

So it was small wonder that the Madam breathed a sigh when Flora's train pulled out for San Francisco. She felt she was on vacation. But Flora harried her with post cards and letters, and she always made esoteric reference to the potion.

Like all vacations, the Madam's passed swiftly; and one morning she received a letter announcing the Burgoynes would return within the week. "Damn it to hell," the Madam said aloud; and she paced her living room, that tawdry room with the velour sofa and purple window shades. It did not occur to her that the situation had overtones of comedy and pathos, for living by her wits had hardened her. "I've had a hard time," she thought, when she gazed back on her life; and this was true. Born into the poverty of Chicago, she had secured employment as a parlor maid at fifteen. She had never been beautiful, but her mind was rapid, and her sharp ears picked up the syntax and inflections of the ladies and gentlemen she served. At seventeen she advanced to the post of personal maid. Her employer, a double-chinned, brocaded widow, full of sighs, had fallen in love with a young dandy. Her passion was not requited, and she took to visiting prognosticators. It occurred to the Madam that this was easy money.

So she visited seers herself, not to learn the future but to study their technique. She read everything she could find dealing with second sight, and she was about to launch herself as a clairvoyant when she fell in love with the coachman, Stanton Thale. He was twelve years her senior, a restless fellow who drifted from job to job.

Soon after their marriage he heard of a good opening in a Tamarack livery stable, and he took it; but the job didn't last; and when their first baby was four months old, and Stanton Thale was without employment, the Madam turned psychic. So naive was she that she embarked on her career without first consulting the police, and presently she found herself in jail. The judge offered her thirty days or a fifty-dollar fine, and since fifty dollars was as unattainable as a thousand, she passed a month in the workhouse. There, she struck up a friendship that aided her greatly.

The friend was Tessie Kelly, a girl of nineteen who had been picked up for soliciting. She was a pretty little thing, and she confided to Madam Thale that her workhouse sentence had taught her the futility of the life she had been leading. No more promiscuity for Tessie.

"I'll find me a man who'll set me up," she declared; and surprisingly enough, Tessie did just that. She saved her money, and presently she turned capitalist, operating an establishment of her own. A discreet place, Tessie's, and expensive; the best men in Tamarack could be found there.

Tessie rather well knew all the weaknesses of men, but the one that astonished her most was their failing for chatter. Like Achilles and Hector, the heroes of Tamarack loved to boast of their prowess, of the business citadels they were going to sack. She turned this information to profit. Back in the nineties, she learned in advance that Tamarack & Northern intended buying the streetcar company. She bought streetcar bonds cheap, and when they soared after the merger she sold them dear. Her information did not, however, come from Mr. Oxenford; never did he step foot in Tessie's place. He wouldn't have enjoyed himself if he had. Expense!

Tessie wasn't one to forget a friend, and she passed along to Madam Thale all the gossip she heard. And the Madam, in turn, passed it on as psychic intelligence to the wives of Wellington Avenue.

Now in her trouble the Madam thought of her friend, and she boarded a car for West Tamarack. It was only eleven when she reached her destination, and the house looked asleep. But Tessie was no sluggard, even if her girls were; she answered the Madam's ring herself. The two women kissed and seated themselves in the living room, where from gold frames paintings of Persian houris looked down on them.

The years had turned Tessie's hair hoary, and she wore eyeglasses with a gold chain. She was a thin, precise little woman; and she spoke in a thin, precise voice. You might have thought her a dean of women at a fashionable college for girls, and in one sense you would have been correct.

"I'm worried, Tessie," the Madam said; and she poured out her woe. "I thought," she concluded, "that you might have a recipe for a potion."

"My dear," Tessie smiled, "I'm afraid I must disappoint you. The men who come here aren't in need of that."

Madam Thale smiled thinly, but worry soon returned to her brow. And Tessie frowned in sympathy. At last she said:

"Let's talk to Octavia. She's my cook, and she's colored. She may have some ideas."

Octavia had heard of such love charms, and when the Madam pressed a bill into her palm she promised to make inquiries.

"But these here witch doctors in Tamarack ain't much account," she warned. "Now if this was Memphis—"

Next month, she said, she was returning to Memphis for a fortnight's visit, and if the Madam could wait she would bring back a love charm.

"I can't wait," Madam Thale said.

But in the end she had to wait, and poor Flora, also.

"Like I said," Octavia reported, "these Tamarack witch doctors don't know hell from nothing. But when I go to Memphis—"

So in mid-September Octavia departed, in her purse many of the Madam's hard-earned dollars, and upon the success of her mission depended Madam Thale's reputation and Flora's happiness.

By then, of course, the Burgoynes had returned from San Francisco, and the Madam was hard put to placate Flora for the delays. She upbraided herself for ever embarking upon this venture; after paying Octavia, her profits would be slight. But she was a good psychologist and she managed to string her client along. Her problem was complicated by Octavia's lighthearted decision to remain longer in Memphis than she had intended; the fortnight stretched out to a month; to five weeks. The Madam was beside herself. She felt she was in a race with time.

Gus felt the same way about a different matter. The Speedway blueprints were completed now, and enormous activity descended upon the vacant lot between Tamarack and Clayton Junction. Mules were pulling scrapers; teamsters were unloading sand and cement sacks and lumber; all day you could hear the voices of foremen, the whine of saws, the pounding of hammers. Gus could usually be found there, urging speed. For winter would halt the work, and if next spring were a late one the Speedway might not be ready for its grand opening in July.

Crises were always arising; and it appeared that the great oval structure, seating twenty thousand, was going to cost more than had been supposed. Capitalization would have to be increased. But that involved difficulties: the other stockholders were reluctant to send good money to rescue what might be bad. Gus never lost faith in the project, even when a strike in November stopped work for ten days, but exhort as he would he failed to convince his associates that they must write more checks. Finally capitalization was increased, with A. H. Burgoyne furnishing the additional funds. This left him deeply in debt; the Wellington Avenue house was mortgaged; but he told himself he would be richly repaid next summer, when thousands attended the races.

Octavia returned from Memphis at last, bringing the precious potion, and one afternoon in November the Madam left Tessie's house and caught a westbound streetcar. The day was raw and windy, and now that she finally possessed the love charm she experienced misgivings. She remembered the druggist's telling her that laws forbade such stimulants, and it chilled her to think that the potion, concocted by some ignorant Negro in Tennessee, might contain deadly ingredients.

While the car swayed she opened her purse and brought forth the little box. Inside, soiled tissue paper contained the potion, about two tablespoons of glistening white powder. It resembled crushed aspirin tablets, doubtless because that was what it was; but the Madam thought it looked as sinister as cocaine. She moistened her forefinger and lightly touched the powder. Bringing her finger near her eyes, she scrutinized the clinging grains. She smelled them. And then, impulsively, she licked her finger.

Her imagination was so enflamed that she thought she might drop instantly dead. She sat rigid, waiting. Nothing happened. And by the time she left the car and opened the gate into the Burgoyne garden, a new fear was attacking her: perhaps the potion was worthless.

That brought her to a standstill on the garden path. If the potion had no power, Flora would be furiously disappointed; she might lose faith entirely in things occult. Perhaps it would be better to tell her that after all the love charm was beyond attainment. But she couldn't do that; for nearly six months Flora had been pestering her, and she had promised.

What to do! For a long minute she stood there frowning, a woman as thin and troubled as the gray November wind, as desiccated as the stalks of flowers rattling in the gusts. She felt dispirited and old and beaten, and in that instant she hated herself because for so many years she had been a fraud, false counselor to schoolgirls with crushes, to women sorrowing and desperate because nature had commanded they yearn for love and then had withheld the object of love.

"I'll confess!" she told herself. "I'll tell her I'm a fake," and she hurried toward the porte-cochere.

When the wind blew, the great old house was always hard to heat, but this afternoon a fire blazed in the library and the Madam stood on the hearth, hands outstretched, her thin body soaking up the warmth. Flora watched her.

"Sure glad you dropped in, Madam. I was lonesome. Anything wrong?"

A shiver rattled the Madam's vertebrae, and she said the wind had chilled her.

"I'll fix the fire," Flora said, and she heaved on more wood. "Maybe you'd like a cup of tea."

"Don't bother."

"Think tea would warm you up," Flora said, and she went hoofing toward the kitchen.

The Madam's decision had left her unstrung, and as she watched Flora depart she experienced a sudden affection for that poor mortal. Thick-witted and bumbling she might be, and pedestrian and matter-of-fact, but she was kind.

Alone, restlessness seized her, and she wandered about the room. Framed circus posters still adorned the walls, but the years had faded their brilliant colors. She paused beneath the largest poster, that of A. H. (Honest Gus) Burgoyne, Owner. It had the unreal familiarity that old photographs always possess. The young man in the lithograph had an open countenance, and he looked jolly and actually honest.

She moved on to the window and stared out at the lawn. The grass looked as bleak and gray as the cloudy sky, and dead leaves went sweeping across it in dervish dances. The Madam shivered and returned to the fire.

Presently Flora lugged in a tray of tea and cookies, and the two women sat before the fire.

"Don't suppose you've come by that potion yet," Flora said.

The Madam snapped open her purse and extended the little box. For an instant her thin fingers encountered Flora's plump ones; the hands of both women were trembling.

Flora unlidded the box and stared at the powder. Her eyes might have been an opium addict's, envisioning dreams and enchantment in a drug. Outside, rain was beginning, and through its wind-blown spatter the Madam could hear Flora's breathing.

And suddenly tears started down Flora's cheeks, and her freckled face twisted. Great sobs heaved her massive shoulders and she blurted out:

"Oh, Madam, you're the best friend I ever had."

In the past the Madam would have smiled slyly, but today she was not herself, with chills chasing through her body. Even the hot tea had not warmed her, and she felt old and worn.

"I don't think it's any good," she said.

Trouble returned to Flora's eyes; that old cowlike bewilderment at a world past understanding.

"Maybe it's good," she said. "It's been hard enough to come by."

"I tried, Flora," the Madam said. "I really tried. This powder came all the way from Memphis, but I think it's a fake and a fraud, like so many things are. Like I am."

"You're not yourself," Flora said. "Maybe you're ailing."

The Madam shivered and her lips quivered. Her hands were clenched and all at once she bent forward and began crying. Not for years had she wept so bitterly, not perhaps since Stanton Thale died. She had supposed herself too hard for tears, but now they had begun she couldn't stop.

"I'm no good," she sobbed. "I'm a fake and a fraud who's given bad advice. You ought to throw me out. You ought to have me arrested."

"You're not well, Madam," Flora said. "Maybe you're catching cold." She plodded to a liquor cabinet and returned with a glass of brandy. "Here. Drink this."

The Madam sipped the brandy, and presently her weeping ceased. She dried her eyes. And she said:

"Don't you hate me?"

"Why, Madam! You're my best friend. No truth in what you've been saying. If it hadn't been for you I don't know what I'd ever done. Wouldn't have married Gus, that's for sure. You're psychic. You were born with a caul. I think you're wonderful."

The Madam sat staring into the fire. And she realized it was too late by many years to destroy Flora's illusions about her. It was kinder to let her believe.

"Maybe you're right," she said. "And maybe the potion is good, too." She arose to go.

"Better stay," Flora said. "It's raining hard. You could sleep in Papa's old room."

"No," the Madam said, "you and Gus will want to be alone tonight. I hope everything goes well."

"I do too," Flora said.

They kissed at the porte-cochere door and Flora stood watching the Madam's departure, a thin woman wavering away through the gales of rain.

Flora felt like a bride. After ordering the cook to prepare steaks and French fries for dinner, she hurried upstairs and luxuriated in a warm bath. In her bedroom she burrowed into sachet-scented depths of the dresser and brought out her smoothest lingerie, exquisite garments that had been presents from Gus. She had never worn them; she had saved them for some special occasion.

The perfume she used had likewise come from Gus, and had likewise been hoarded. And the dress she selected was one he had admired in a store window. She had purchased it, even though it seemed much too expensive for such a plain garment.

But its plainness was exceedingly smart. It was of fine black wool with small white buttons, and it flattered her opulent curves. Indeed, after she had worked on her hair and face, Flora did not look at all badly turned out.

While she dressed the rain poured down outside, and by the time she was ready for her man dusk had come. From the dresser she picked up the box of potion and stared at the white powder, wondering how best to introduce it into Gus's digestive system. Sometimes after dinner he drank brandy with his coffee, so now she carried the box down to the library and went to the liquor cabinet. She uncorked a bottle of apricot brandy and sifted into it all the contents of the tissue paper. Then, vigorously, she shook the bottle and replaced it. The tissue and box she tossed into the fireplace.

She sat before the fire, waiting, her ears alert for the sound of Gus's car through the rain. A single floor lamp burned in the library, and the smooth half-light was kind to her skin. Now and then she arose and peered through the window toward the avenue, where homeward traffic spattered along the gleaming pavement. At last headlights turned in at the drive.

She began tingling. She hadn't felt like this since that romantic April night when Gus came with Mr. Pawpacker to discuss business with Papa. Outside she heard the stable door rumbling shut, and she started toward the porte-cochere door. Then she halted. Some obscure instinct took her back to the library fire. She sat waiting, listening.

She heard a door opening, and presently his footsteps came along the corridor. She recognized them the way a dog knows his master's step. And like a dog, she sensed his mood as soon as he entered the library. This had been one of his bad days.

"Hello, Gus. It's raining, isn't it?"

"Raining hard," he said. "Cats and dogs."

"You're soaked, Gus. Your feet are soaked. You'd better get into dry clothes."

"Have time before dinner?"

"Of course. We'll wait dinner."

He glanced at her then, and she could see that something in the day's events had made him angry. But he wasn't angry at her.

"Thanks," he said.

"I wouldn't want you to catch cold."

At the liquor cabinet he poured himself whiskey, and she wished she had put some of the potion into that bottle. He tossed off the drink, poured another. She was tempted to mention his liver, but she refrained. The whiskey seemed to cheer him. He said:

"You're fixed up. We're not going out, are we?"

"Oh, no! I just thought I'd fix up."

"I'll take a hot bath," he said, and he thumped away up the stairs. Flora went to the kitchen and told the cook to be sure to broil his steak brown, with the juice seared inside.

The rain still poured but the wind had died, so the house was warmer, now; and dinner was a cozy meal. Gus came to the table in dressing gown and slippers, and when he beheld his enormous steak, swimming in butter, he looked delighted.

"Guess you know what I like," he exclaimed, surveying the French fries and Vienna bread and Waldorf salad.

It flushed her with pleasure, as if he had told her she was beautiful. She was never happier than when making Gus happy. Dessert was chocolate ice cream, and he loved that, too.

"By golly," he exclaimed, "this is a wonderful meal! Sets me up. I had kind of a bad day."

"What happened?"

Anger returned to his face.

"Oh, I had a fight with my stenographer."

"What about?"

His countenance took on that shuttered look.

"Nothing much. About her work. She wouldn't follow orders. She was too damned independent. We had a showdown this afternoon, and I fired her."

"Did it make her mad?"

"Sure she was mad. We both were."

"Papa wouldn't have women working for him," Flora said. "He thought they were trouble-makers."

They had coffee in the library, and Gus sat smoking, legs stretched toward the fire. Once he patted his belly and spoke again of the satisfying meal. Outside the autumnal rain fell heavily, soaking the city, but there on the davenport it was dry and warm.

"Would you like some brandy, Gus?"

He glanced at her in surprise. "Why, I don't know. Pretty full. But—"

"It will help you digest, Gus. I was reading in a health column that brandy is good after a full meal."

She moved to the cabinet and uncorked the bottle. Her fingers shook as she poured him a generous portion. And she was all atremble as she gave him the glass. Then she switched off the floor lamp and sat by his side in the light of the fire. He drank slowly.

"Does it taste good?" she asked.

"Uh? Oh—bet it does. Good brandy."

He drank more than he would have if he had poured it, and there was youth in the glass and warm dreams. The sound of the rain was hypnotic and he felt soothed. He was no longer so enraged at Marcene for calling him a fat old fool, but although anger had departed passion had not. Staring into the fire, he thought of Marcene's lovely body, and he thought of Beryl and of all the girls he had known. He thought of Carlotta. He slumped lower on the davenport, resting his head against the back and closing his eyes, and presently his wife's fingers were smoothing his hair and his brow. The scent of perfume came to his nostrils. It was the scent Carlotta had always used. Once when he bought birthday perfume for Flora he had sniffed a score of glass stoppers till he had found that scent. It brought to him the memory of a long-ago March. He stirred and encircled Flora with his arms and kissed her, his eyes still closed. She didn't yank away and slap him and call him a fat old fool. With the perfume in his nostrils and the liquid sunshine of brandy in his blood he could imagine he was a young man kissing Carlotta.

Next morning Flora went to the telephone and gave Madam Thale's number. She wanted to tell her how wonderful she was and how mistaken she had been about the potion's inefficacy. But there was no response. Off and on all day Flora attempted to reach her.

She tried again the following day, but not till afternoon did she get an answer. Then it was not the Madam's voice that responded, but that of a stranger, the Madam's daughter.

"Who is it?" the voice asked.

"Mrs. Burgoyne. I'd like to talk to Madam."

"She's sick."

Instantly, Flora felt concern, and it mounted as the receiver poured out details. Like Flora, the Madam's daughter had tried to reach her yesterday, and this morning when there was still no answer she had gone to her mother's home and found her in bed with a fever. A doctor had been called, and he said the Madam was afflicted with pneumonia.

"I'll be right over," Flora said.

She caught a car for East Tamarack. She remembered how the Madam had not seemed herself the other day, how the weather had chilled her, how thin she had looked going away into the rain. Tears came to Flora's eyes and she blamed herself for not insisting that the Madam spend the night on Wellington Avenue.

The weather was still drab and raw, and there in the poverty of East Tamarack the Madam's house looked shabby and very small. Approaching it, Flora experienced outrage against the world because it had not recognized the Madam's genius. The Madam's daughter admitted her, and Flora said:

"I came to do anything I can. She's my best friend."

It transpired that the Madam needed a nurse, but that nurses cost money.

"I'll hire a nurse," Flora said.

For three days and nights Flora did not leave the little house. In the end there were two nurses, and the Madam's sons and daughter and their families came and went, and the neighbors, and a woman named Tessie. But Flora was most faithful of all. And perhaps she was most agitated, although her anxiety was thickly swathed in phlegm. Sometimes on the sitting-room sofa she caught a little sleep, but for the most part she sat in a rocking chair, a floor board squeaking as she rocked, her jaws moving as she chewed her cud, her soft eyes worried. "Anything I can do?" she would ask; but there never was, except foot the expenses.

Through the years the sitting room had not changed, and in the long silent hours of night Flora's thoughts went back to the various occasions when she had gone there for succor. It seemed a romantic room because here she had received advice about winning Gus.

Now and then they permitted her to tiptoe into the little downstairs bedroom where the Madam lay. It was an impoverished room. In a dozen places the wallpaper had come loose and had been glued to the plaster by the Madam. The carpet was worn thin. One door of the commode had come off. The window shades were cracked and torn. White enamel had chipped off the iron bed. No electricity burned here, but an old oil lamp, turned low. Flora could not but contrast it with the fine rooms of her own home, and her throat caught. She wished now she had given more money to the Madam.

Toward the end Madam Thale was unconscious, and in sleep her face looked ravaged and old. All the shrewdness and chicanery had left her countenance, and she was just a poor old woman who had been compelled to make the best of the world as she found it. Flora stood gazing down at her, and then she bent and kissed her forehead where the girlishly blond hair began.

When at last the Madam died, Flora lay on the sitting-room sofa and wept. Without her best friend she felt lost and adrift, and her old sense of bafflement at dealing with the problems of existence returned. If a crisis arose now she would never know what to do. It was as if she were a child again, the fat little girl in grade school who found sums in arithmetic beyond her and who would always bite on a conundrum.

"I want to buy her casket," Flora said, "and pay the undertaker."

The Madam's children did not object. They were very poor, with the poor's terror of the unexpected expenses of sickness and death. They were grateful to Flora and bewildered by her love and loyalty.

Even Gus was saddened by the Madam's passing, and he too performed a last act of loyalty. He wrote an account of her death and sent it to *The Billboard*, mentioning that she had once traveled with Burgoyne's Circus & Hippodrome, A. H. (Honest Gus) Burgoyne, Owner; the same A. H. Burgoyne who was now building a great Speedway in Tamarack which would open next July 2 with three days of breath-taking races.

14

STUDENTS OF history will find that in 1917 the United States declared war on Germany. They will also find that A. H. Burgoyne and Ivan Pawpacker entered into a partnership.

The birth of Burgoyne & Pawpacker's Great 3-Ring Circus astounded those persons who knew what happened behind scenes in the outdoor show world. They simply couldn't comprehend why Pawpacker, so clear-headed and sagacious, would join forces with A. H. Burgoyne.

"Pawpacker will regret it," they said.

Everybody had heard how Burgoyne switched equipment when he sold Pawpacker the Gus-show. They knew it in clown alley; they discussed it on winter afternoons in humble theatrical hotels in Chicago. On that deal, they said, Pawpacker had lost heavily, and he was certainly through with Gus Burgoyne.

And for that matter, they said, Gus was through as a showman. He was broke, for he had blundered egregiously in constructing an oversized Speedway in Tamarack. They remembered he had always liked elephants, and they quipped that he certainly had one now, a white one.

In 1916, despite showmanship and publicity, the Fourth of July races had been unsuccessful. The Tamarack Speedway, Inc. passed into receivership. After the fact, it became apparent that Tamarack's population was too small to put twenty thousand racing fans into the bleachers on three successive days. Moreover, the races failed because of a shrewd counterthrust by Ivan Pawpacker.

On July third and fourth of that year, a circus booked itself into Tamarack. It was virtually the same circus that Gus had sold, only now it was known as Yankee Pawpacker's Trans-American Circus. Its posters were to be seen for miles around; it paraded; the elephant, Molly, traveled in its bull herd; it was without grift; and the Tamarack Speedway was forced to share publicity columns with Yankee Pawpacker. And most painful, the Speedway shared with the circus the dollars of the amusement-seeking public.

There were persons with a sense of irony who smiled at the way Ivan Pawpacker gave the Tamarack Speedway a push toward receivership. They found wry amusement in Gus Burgoyne's going broke at the hands of the circus he had organized and loved and sold.

In September 1916, red flags were to be seen along the street in front of the Wellington Avenue home. This did not mean that communism was gaining ground, but only that Burgoyne had lost it. The flags were an auctioneer's, and throughout one afternoon scores of bargain hunters tramped through the old house. Historical items were sold under the hammer, such as the bookkeeping desk where Mr. Oxenford had schemed, and the bed where he had slept.

And presently Mr. and Mrs. A. H. Burgoyne were living in the country, at the farm which had quartered Burgoyne's Circus & Hippodrome. The farm and the coal mine Gus had not lost, because they had not been worth mortgaging.

For a few weeks the Wellington Avenue house stood empty. On Saturdays small boys invaded its porches and peered through the windows. They saw bare floors, bare walls; and in their minds it was already haunted. The ghosts they imagined, however, were not so commonplace as Mr. Oxenford screeching about expense, or Flora weeping in the cause of love.

And then one morning workmen appeared, with hammers and crowbars, and began wrecking the house. For the bank had sold it to a firm that intended building an apartment hotel on the site. Soon the shingles were ripped from the great dunce caps; the porte-cochère vanished; the yard was littered with bricks and two-by-fours; and people driving past on a moonlit night saw the ribs of the old dwelling bare to the wind.

And people said Gus Burgoyne was through. He never showed up any more at the Chamber of Commerce or at his luncheon clubs. Out in the country, he took long walks over his sterile estate, mooning through the empty barns. He walked to the ridge, staring off into the misty distances where Tamarack existed, or gazing speculatively at the inactive tipple of the coal mine at Oxenford. As the days passed the mine occupied his thoughts more and more; and finally, carrying an empty suitcase, he went to the settlement and prevailed upon a miner to put the cage machinery into operation. The miner was an ancient Slovak from Mr. Oxenford's time, and he spoke almost no English. But at last he conducted Gus down into the black shaft and along the dripping tunnels. When they emerged, the suitcase was heavy.

Lugging that suitcase, Gus journeyed to Chicago, where he had the samples assayed. The coal, he was told, was too full of foreign matter to be mined profitably. But this did not leave Gus downcast. He asked many questions, and he prowled through book stores, buying volumes dealing with coal.

And after he returned to the farm a perfectly amazing thing took place. From a village ten miles away, trucks hauled coal to Oxenford and dumped it. And thereafter, the mine was put into operation. Several Slovaks were employed, but instead of blasting coal from the earth's innards they descended into the depths with the coal that had been trucked to Oxenford. And down there in the tunnels secret things took place, but what they were no man knew save only Gus and the Slovak miners who would not tell.

Then one October morning when the land sparkled with hoarfrost Gus drove from the farm to Tamarack, and thence southward. Arriving at Winchester, he checked in at the hotel, and next morning he called at a certain livery stable.

He remained in Winchester three days. His reception was cold, but he was so full of good humor and warmth that the icicles Ivan Pawpacker hurled in his direction melted before they jabbed him. Was he broke? A ruined man? Gus laughed. Did Ive fancy for an instant, he asked, that he would sit in on life's poker game without an extra ace up his sleeve? A black ace. Coal-black.

Ive became curious. And less angry. He recalled how Gus had once told him that some of the richest coal in America was to be found in the mine at Oxenford, and he remembered the sizable check Gus had sent in repayment for the switched equipment. On Gus's second evening in Winchester, he was a dinner guest at the house where Pawpacker lived alone save for his Negro servants. His wife, of course, dwelt in St. Louis.

It was exceedingly difficult to remain angry at this great, good-humored fellow. As of yore, he had the knack of making the world seem a romantic place. He painted the future in intoxicating colors. He pictured the Ringlings becoming worried. He talked of power, and it was heady talk. After dinner they sat smoking and drinking, and Ive envisioned himself as the circus czar of America, every show under his control. He imagined wealth flowing in, and part of that wealth he could use in other enterprises. He saw himself buying into oil, into railroads. He didn't commit himself that evening, for he recognized he was under Gus's spell, but next morning he was still excited.

After all, what could he lose? Gus was offering him the farm and the mine for half-interest in Yankee Pawpacker's Trans-American Circus. He would have the coal assayed, of course; indeed, Gus insisted upon that.

"You know how slick old Sam Oxenford was," Gus grinned. "Well, for reasons of his own he closed the mine and spread the rumor that the veins had petered out. I don't know all the ins and outs, but I guess Sam had some stockholders in the mine he wanted to wash out. Anyway, the fact remains that the mine's full of rich coal."

"Why don't you work it yourself, Gus?"

"Me? Do I look like a coal miner? Or a coal baron? Hell, I want to get back into the circus game. That's my field. We'd make a million, Ive. I'm a showman if I do say so myself."

True, true! And Gus was still comparatively young. He still had pounding energy, tremendous enthusiasm. Busy as Ive was buying horses for the Allies, he couldn't give Yankee Pawpacker's circus the attention it deserved. Piloted by Gus, its profits should triple.

Another thing: Ive's business had grown so rapidly under the impetus of war that his barns in Winchester were crowded. If he acquired the farm near Tamarack, the Yank-show could winter there.

And yet another: American factories were working day and night on war orders. That meant coal consumption. And it looked as if the United States might get into the war. That would mean prosperity, rising prices, lots of money, soaring markets for coal.

"Why don't you drive back with me and look over the mine?" Gus urged, on the third afternoon. "We'll go down in the tunnels and you can see for yourself. You can pick up samples and have them assayed, and you can look over winter quarters. Hell, Ive—the setup is perfect."

So that was how Gus made his comeback. Yankee Pawpacker's circus became Burgoyne & Pawpacker's Great 3-Ring Circus, and the mine and the farm were deeded to Pawpacker, and the partners agreed that Gus should live at the farm. Returning to Winchester, Ive felt quietly satisfied at the way things had turned out. It seemed exciting and dramatic that he should own the winter quarters at Oxenford as well as his Winchester business. He was a little Napoleon of capitalism whose dollars had captured a province to the north.

And now once again after the silent years the circus farm bristled with activity. From Winchester railroad cars began arriving, the old Clayton Junction car and boxcars full of horses and elephants, and flatcars loaded with cage wagons. Molly arrived, ecstatic to be with Gus again, and men in sweaters came; and in the Blacksmith Shop the anvil played merry music.

Gus was happier than he had been in years. He seldom thought of Carlotta now, or even of Barbara. He was a man born again. His appetite became huge and so did his waistline; every morning he awakened early, rejoicing that here was a new day in which he could do the work he loved; life was enchanted again, and he exuded optimism and cheer. Once more he was to be seen in Tamarack, in newspaper offices and at his luncheon clubs. In March they even invited him to deliver the noon address at the Chamber of Commerce, and it was the most moving speech they had heard for many a meeting. He loaded them all onto a magic carpet and piloted them into a future where Burgoyne & Pawpacker's circus was America's greatest. They thought him a colorful and glamorous man.

One thing alone troubled Gus at that period: he suspected Pawpacker might be irked when he discovered that the coal was not of the best quality. But he counseled himself not to cross that bridge till he reached it. And he was wise there, because not for several years did Pawpacker try to mine coal. He was too busy, after America entered the war. For suddenly the army wanted multitudes of horses, and Ive was the man to buy them. Mules, also. Never had there been such a booming market for horses and mules. The coal could wait.

A fortnight after war was declared the circus opened in Tamarack, and the patriotic motif was in evidence. Flags and bunting were everywhere, and one clown resembled Kaiser Wilhelm and he fared very badly at the hands of a clown garbed as Uncle Sam. In the parade that day Gus rode in an open car heavily flag-draped, and the band played "The Stars and Stripes Forever."

It was a wonderful season. Everybody had plenty of money. And the next season was even better. After long hours in factories and long nights of worry about those in the trenches, people were glad to forget their woes at the circus. The band played "K-K-Katy" and "Rose of No Man's Land" and the war news was good. Hindenburg's big spring push had failed and the submarine menace was licked. It wouldn't be long now, and every afternoon and evening the band knocked the Heligo out of Heligoland, and the money rolled in. On Armistice Day the circus was back at winter quarters, and Gus was so elated at the good news that he telephoned for Tamarack & Northern to send out an electric engine, and this hauled to town a boxcar containing Molly and she marched the streets with the other merrymakers, waving a flag in her trunk.

Yes, Gus was back on his feet now; and again in 1919 money was common as dirt. Plasterers and carpenters attended the show wearing silk shirts and everybody drove motor cars, and the band played "Ja-Da" and "Take Me To The Land of Jazz." Music like "After The Ball" seemed ridiculously old-fashioned. The war had speeded things up. A great new era had been born. Prosperity would be perpetual and war abolished. People felt that in some obscure manner the world would be richer after years of destroying wealth, and that men would be kinder after years of hating and slaying.

Everything was changing, swiftly, swiftly. If a woman wore short skirts and bobbed hair it didn't mean she was a chippy; and cigars had yielded in popularity to cigarettes. But Gus could never enjoy a cigarette. You couldn't roll it around in your mouth in the satisfying way you could roll a good cigar. To that extent he resisted change; in that, he was a child of the 1880's.

After the war the boom in horses collapsed, but Ive Pawpacker didn't worry because a new boom was gathering force, and as a country banker he was in an excellent position to soar with it. This was a boom in land.

In the past years, prices of wheat and corn and beef and pork had risen spectacularly, and so it was quite natural that the price of the land producing these should also rise. With much of the world hungry, nobody doubted that food from the Mississippi Valley would bring fat prices for years to come. Farmers who had contentedly tilled 160 acres now lusted for 320 because they would make twice as much. And the farm boys who had marched away to glory and gay Paree were returning now, desiring marriage and farms of their own. The amount of land was fixed. When people demanded more shoes and B.V.D.'s the factories made more, but only God could make more land and He seemed in no rush to do this.

So farms were bought and sold, always at loftier prices, and the desire for land and easy money swept the middle states like a contagion. In small towns the real estate agents who for years had scraped along, writing hail insurance on the side and still barely making ends meet, suddenly found themselves garnering enormous commissions; and they wanted more commissions, and more, so like fever-carriers they drove along willow-lined country roads and urged that farms be put up for sale. And much of the business was transacted on money borrowed from banks like Ivan Pawpacker's. The loans were secured by first mortgages and second mortgages upon the land, and that looked safe enough because the value of land was so great, and ever increasing.

But then in the Ukraine and upon the plains of Hungary swords became plowshares and warriors became sowers; and the wheat ripened and was harvested; and the starving ate. And the vast fertility of Middle America yielded astronomical bushels of corn and wheat, and the sows farrowed and the little pigs grew; and suddenly on the great exchanges in Liverpool and Chicago corn futures and wheat futures sagged.

It was a great sagging. And as the products of the land shrank in value, so did the price of the land itself; and the people sorrowed. The real estate men turned back to hail insurance, and instead of money in their vaults the bankers beheld mortgages upon land that could no longer be sold for five hundred dollars an acre, or four hundred, or even three hundred.

These were events of the early 1920's, and although the lush money days had departed the people thought they would return. The real estate men thought so, and the farmers and the bankers. Things were a little tight just now; that was all. All through the twenties they waited and hoped, and not till a decade had passed did they realize they had been bankrupt all the while without knowing it.

"You'll want a cab, sir?" asked the bellhop.

Ive Pawpacker nodded.

It was a summer morning in the reign of Warren G. Harding, and they were descending by elevator toward the lobby of Tamarack's newest hotel, the Commander. It was an apartment hotel, finely appointed, rising from landscaped grounds that bordered Wellington Avenue. Once the grounds had been the lawn of Samuel R. Oxenford's mansion, but Tamarack had changed during the years and old landmarks were vanishing.

Always Ive Pawpacker had stayed at the General Grant Hotel, but three months before it too had vanished. A salesman had drowsed while smoking in bed, and by 2 A.M. the old sandstone structure with its wooden floors had been a mass of flames. The *Morning Chronicle* published photographs of the conflagration, as well as a feature story about the old hotel. The story said it had been the scene of festive gatherings and informal political meetings where history had been made.

The Commander lobby was less ornate than the General Grant's. Instead of brass spittoons there were vases filled with white sand. Gold leaf and curlicues were absent; planes and geometric designs were present. With his old-fashioned beard and cane Ive Pawpacker had looked more at home in the General Grant.

On the circular drive his cab waited, and he told the driver to take him to the Union Station. He was bound for North Platte, Nebraska, where tomorrow the show would play and where he would join battle with Gus.

Ive had reached his early sixties now, and on this corn-weather morning he looked tired. In his hair and beard more gray showed than cinnamon-brown, and his movements were not quite so rapier-resilient as they used to be. As ever, he was immaculately dressed; his linen suit and Panama hat were crisp; but instead of looking like a dandy he looked like those neat old men who are scrubbed and starched because on the side lines of life they have plenty of time to attend to such grooming.

Not that Ive had retired to the side lines. His money-mind was still keen, and when he told bank customers that land prices would go up again they believed it. He believed it, too. Because his knowledge of horses was so profound it seemed to follow that his knowledge of economic law should be profound also.

Where horses were concerned, his erudition was now in obsolescence. In these days farmers drove Model-T's to town. Trucks were replacing lumber wagons. And on farm after farm tractors were appearing. His livery stable in Winchester had become anachronistic: no longer did the young bloods rent a fine rig on Sunday afternoon and go driving with their sweethearts. The young bloods had cars, and their sweethearts were their babes and their red-hot mammas, and they thought nothing of driving thirty miles to some dance, where saxophones mourned out the music that had traveled up from the honky-tonks.

Yet Ive kept his livery stable open. In its office his mind seemed to function better than in his bank. A solitary hostler worked for him now, and his horse-buying trips were few. Occasionally some firm in St. Louis wanted horses; not often.

With the collapse of the land boom he had lost heavily, not only on his bank's behalf but on his own. At first he had dabbled, not intending to become deeply involved; but after he turned easy profits on a few deals the fever infected him wholly. He was no longer wealthy; but of course he was no pauper, either. He told himself that in business there were always ups and downs.

His circus brokerage business wasn't doing so well, either. With money scarcer, new circuses were not taking to the road; and instead of adding equipment the established shows were cutting down. So a few weeks ago he had decided to open the coal mine at Oxenford, and that was why he was angry at Gus.

Where the West begins is a question hotly debated among the cities of the Plains. Kansas City believes itself the gateway to that never-never land of smoking six-guns, and so does Fort Worth, and so does Omaha. But to Willie Krummer the West began in North Platte, Nebraska, in the window of a store specializing in cowboy boots.

On that July afternoon Willie had brooded from the circus lot immediately after Captain Philip Latcher entered the arena, and now he was honoring the downtown streets of North Platte with his presence. Captain Latcher would be annoyed to discover that his cage boy was not on hand to administer a rubdown, but he would have to make the best of it. Thinking of the Captain's annoyance, Willie smiled obliquely.

In the years since entering the Captain's employ, Willie had grown and muscled-up. He had become a fine specimen of Teutonic manhood, a big, upstanding fellow with blond hair clipped tightly against his squarish skull. His hands were squarish, too, with heavy fingers, and it was amazing how many creatures were afraid of him. The cats were afraid of him, and the roustabouts, especially the Negro boys. Now and then, in order to keep in fighting trim, and to express his soul, and to teach the inferior race a lesson, Willie accosted some black roustabout and beat up on him. Any excuse would do, or no excuse. Recently he had attained Man's Estate, but he was more interested in attaining Captain Latcher's estate, complete with the Captain's wife.

There was, however, one obstacle between Willie and the Captain's estate. Not the Captain: in imagination Willie had removed that man from the earth's face dozens of times. No, what stymied Willie was the Captain's brother in British Columbia. Long ago the Captain had remarked that if he died his possessions would go to his brother, and Willie's mind was like marble to retain. It did not occur to him that the Captain might have altered his will in favor of Marybelle Monahan. She was merely a woman, a possession like a cat. To Willie the world was a man's world. He enthusiastically endorsed the good old German proverb that woman should limit her interests to children, kitchen and church. And, of course, to Willie Krummer.

But Marybelle ignored Willie. Possessing woman's nice sense of social distinctions, she treated him as if he were a buck private and herself a real captain's lady. Often days passed without her uttering a word to him. If they met in the circus back yard, he tried to be friendly. He halted, shoulders squared, hands yearning to explore her blond skin and learn whether it felt as cream-smooth as it looked. Smiling obliquely, eyes violating her, he said, "Looks like a nice day."

So there they were together; a dramatic meeting. He thought her unutterably beautiful, so blond that a fine golden haze always shimmered about her lovely head. She was not a large girl, but her calves and breasts and hips were deliciously rounded. Her throat was smooth. And ever upon her mouth lingered that half-smile, as if she were mocking Willie's lustful breathing and his dry tongue.

"Yes," she said impersonally, "it is," and passed on.

Damnation! Color surged up Willie's heavy neck.

She was never far from his thoughts. Because of her he kept his pants pressed, his shoes shined, his fingernails clean. Because of her he beat up Negroes, even though she wasn't present to observe. She brought out the best in him.

He was thinking of her today as he swaggered along the North Platte streets, chewing gum. And he was thinking of his situation with Captain Latcher and his future. After years with the Captain his cash wages had risen to ten dollars per month, and that wasn't getting on very rapidly. The Captain, of course, still bought his clothes, and fed him during the winter, and lodged him; but the whole arrangement filled Willie with discontent. Often he dreamed of leaving the Captain, but that would mean leaving Marybelle and the cats.

Years of practice had made him a pretty good man with the cats. As good as the Captain. Better! Right now he could take over the act. Except he couldn't, because the Captain owned it. Or he could organize his own act. Except he couldn't, because he had no money to purchase animals and cage wagons and an arena.

He drifted to a halt before a shoeshop window and beheld the cowboy boots. They were beautiful boots. Of gleaming tan leather, they had high, slanted heels, and they were adorned with large white stars and white stitching. In North Platte, Willie had seen ranchers wearing such boots, but these were fancier than any. His mouth watered and he had an impulse to march into the shop and order the clerk to ensconce with them the Krummer feet.

But he didn't enter the store, because of a card propped beside the boots. The card said $27.95. Willie scowled.

How masculine he would look, wearing those boots! Willie Krummer of the Lazy V Ranch, a mustang between his knees, a lariat coiled handily, chaps protecting his shanks, two faithful six-guns in his belt! There he went, riding hell-for-leather, pursuing the head of the rustler gang, who resembled Captain Latcher, and rescuing the ranch owner's daughter, who looked like Marybelle. He saw himself dismounting at the lonely cabin and advancing as implacably as a cinema hero.

"Latcher," read the subtitle, "if you don't come out I'll shoot my way in."

Picture of Marybelle bound and struggling. And the villain scowling and pulling his shooting-irons.

Bang-bang-bang!

And Latcher died like a dog and Willie and Marybelle went riding slowly into the sunset.

Abruptly, Willie turned from the window and strode angrily down the street. $27.95. Nearly three months' wages! He felt put upon.

But although he admired movies depicting the great West, he worshiped no Western star the way he worshiped that man with the high haircut and the monocle and the stern mien. Eric Von Stroheim! There was an actor! Willie never missed the cinema when it recounted his exploits, and usually he remained for the second show. And upon emerging into workaday streets, Willie assumed the harsh demeanor of his hero. He paced, and he imagined a monocle in his eye. But in the end he had to return to his duties as cage boy, and if Captain Latcher observed him moving in that Prussian manner he flicked him with barbed humor.

"What's the trouble, old chap? Did you sleep in a draft and get a stiff neck?"

Willie growled and muttered, eyes murderous.

Boots and Marybelle and cats and fine clothes were not the only things Willie wanted. On any stroll through a business district he beheld dozens of items for which he yearned. Possibly this was natural in a lad reared in a North Woods shack without toys or even enough food. Today, for instance, he wondered about the time. But he didn't consult his wrist watch, for he owned no wrist watch. And how he wanted one!

Willie found a jewelry store and glared through the window at a clock. It was later than he had thought. Later in the afternoon, and later in his era of cage-boy duties. The horizon of his life had never been blacker, but a glorious dawn was in preparation. Yet when he reached the circus lot, and discovered that an accident had terminated two lives, he did not see that it concerned him. If Captain Latcher had no brother, and if death had struck at the Captain—! But it hadn't. The Captain was safe and sound. Shocked, yes, like nearly everybody. So shaken, in fact, that he neglected to upbraid Willie for not being on hand to rub him down.

Then how could the deaths of those acrobats, Sebastian and Orika, possibly serve Willie's advancement, and ultimately leave Marybelle Monahan a widow?

Steel is a trustworthy metal. You can depend on steel. Usually its molecules cling to one another the way Mr. Oxenford clung to a penny. But on rare occasions steel becomes temperamental, and its molecules quarrel, and it crystallizes. If this happens to a steel ring, high in a tent-top on a summer afternoon, and if you are Ned Sebastian gripping that ring, and if your wife is gripping your ankles, then the results can be disastrous.

Unless, of course, you are working with a net beneath you. But you aren't. Long ago you discarded the net because Mr. Burgoyne believed your turn would thrill the public more without it. You wanted to please Mr. Burgoyne and the public. You wanted to get ahead. Some afternoon, you thought, a scout for the Big One might be in the audience, and if the public gasped at your turn the scout might offer you a position with the greatest circus in the world. That would be getting your break. But you received a break of a different sort.

It was over very quickly. One moment you and Lily Orika were young and healthy and as full of life as a pair of thoroughbred horses. You were in love and the future looked fine. Your eyes were clear and your brains were clear. Away up there in canvas heights you felt as much at home as two strong-pinioned birds. Far below the band was playing a soft, lovely waltz.

The next moment it happened. But hazards were part of your profession. Neither of you screamed. Good troupers to the end. Lily's fingers never unclamped from your ankles, while the end rushed up through band music to receive you.

Those molecules shouldn't have done it. That steel ring should have chosen another time to crystallize. Breaking when it did, it altered too many lives. Apparent to all was the immediate disaster resulting from its treachery. Women screamed and little boys and girls looked sick, their jolly afternoon ruined. People surged across the hippodrome track, toward the two figures lying in the ring, and somebody rushed to the red wagon to interrupt an important conference between Mr. Burgoyne and Mr. Pawpacker. And somebody else found Eloise Sebastian playing with her dolls in the dressing tent.

Oh, yes, everybody agreed the molecules were villainous. But nobody could see the seeds of further disaster sleeping in present disaster. It is like that, always. The consequences of an event go on to infinity. Cast a stone into the sea and its ripples change the course of the solar system. Two people make love in Corsica and forty years later Bonaparte rides through the ashes of Europe. A slave trader visits Africa and in the 1860's America wars with itself. A steel ring breaks in Nebraska and it alters the life of a St. Louis woman named Georgiana Pawpacker. The ripples from the stone never cease; they only widen till they can no longer be seen.

At noon that day, Ive Pawpacker arrived unheralded in North Platte, tired and peevish. But despite himself, when the taxi discharged him at the circus lot, his anger at Gus began dulling. He would give Gus a piece of his mind, but he would not break with him. For of all his enterprises, the circus was the one making money. And without grift, too! Not so much as last year, but still it wasn't doing badly. Gus had the knack.

Ive stood there at the edge of the lot, and his eyes were mellower. He even smiled. Such activity! Such bustle! He saw wagons with "Burgoyne & Pawpacker" in huge letters. Roustabouts were setting up bleachers in the big top, and from center poles flags were flying. He saw Molly ponderous in work harness. He smelled hot dogs sizzling.

And as he paced into the lot, he knew he would be recognized and word would fly about that Mr. Pawpacker had arrived. The other owner! It made him feel consequential.

They had paraded early, and now they were eating in the cookhouse. His entrance created a sensation. Gus jumped up and came roaring, hearty paw extended.

"Ive Pawpacker! Well I'll be damned! Glad see you, Ive!"

Oh, he was a great red-faced rogue, but you couldn't help liking him, with his overpowering good humor.

Words were exploding from Gus's lips like firecrackers. His laughter filled the tent. The wave of his arm was gigantic as he gestured that a place should be prepared at table for Mr. Pawpacker. And while the Burgoyne lackeys scurried to obey, Ive paced over to the performers' table to say hello to those nice kids, Ned Sebastian and Lily Orika. And to their daughter, Eloise. Always since that morning in the Tamarack Union Station he had liked them, felt almost their sponsor.

Ned Sebastian sprang to his feet and shook hands. A firm handshake, but not bone-crushing, like Gus's. There was something so clean-looking about him, so—well—wholesome. His teeth were from a dental ad.

And Lily Orika had that same fresh health, and Eloise was a little girl with curls, and she had grown. She and Ive were great friends, and she told him that one of her dolls was to be married next week and she was sewing a wedding costume. Ive was much interested, very courtly.

And then Gus blustered over.

"All ready, Ive. Food's all ready. Bet you're hungry after your trip."

So Ive told them good-by. He would talk to them again, he promised, following the afternoon performance. But there are promises no man can keep.

He did, however, talk to Eloise. All through the late afternoon and evening he talked to her. His purpose in coming to North Platte seemed petty, by then. She had wept till no tears remained, and when the evening performance began Ive suggested that they walk together into town and find a drugstore and an ice-cream soda. They trudged along for blocks, till the circus music was dim, and you could hear the quiet tapping of his walking stick on the concrete. He told her that love was a very great force, man's best contribution to the universe, and that love did not die merely because somebody who had been loved died. She was silent beneath her curls, and whether his words gave her comfort he could not tell.

And he recounted what an interesting town was Winchester, with barns full of tigers and mules, and a house with two Negro servants, and he asked whether she would like to go home with him and dwell in Winchester and be his little girl.

She found his hand, then, and clasped it tightly. And for an instant it seemed that she was his daughter, and he was appalled at how life had cheated him, because he had married badly and because his house had never known the voices of children. And he thought she was delicate and lovely, and he vowed he would strive to replace the love that had departed from her life, and because his impulse was selfless and deeply good he experienced a sudden happiness such as he had never known.

This was one of Captain Philip Latcher's worst evenings, and hence in the dressing-van as he prepared for the performance he was more than usually debonair and British. Being by nature a facile talker, he sought courage in speech.

"A bit of a bad break for the Sebastians, eh?" he said, as he worked ground-tone into his face.

"Oh, yes," Marybelle said. "Very bad."

"Not a bad chap, you know, Ned Sebastian. And Lily Orika— plucky little thing. I'm glad we didn't see their finish."

He dipped a powder puff into a can of brown theatrical powder, closed his eyes and patted it over his face. While he smoothed it with a rabbit's-foot, he could hear the early evening sounds from the lot. Spielers, squawking toy balloons, voices of early customers.

"The beggars," he thought. "Oh, the bloody beggars! How they'd like it if the cats would muss me up a bit!"

He surveyed himself in the mirror. He was nearly forty-five, but it was a lean, hard forty-five. His juvenile-lead make-up had subtracted years from his face. He might have been thirty-five, save for a head that was no longer baldish but undeniably bald. But he thought it a youthful baldness. Yes, he looked dashing. Not at all frightened.

Yet his long body housed fright, and inside his lean stomach cool little breezes were whirling. Those handsome teeth felt on edge. Twice a day, dressing for the arena, he suffered this torment.

He lived with two great fears. His fear of the cats was the lesser, although heaven knew it was bad enough. In the arena anything might occur. You never could tell what a cat was thinking. But the other fear was worse because it was fear of himself. He was afraid that some day in the safety cage his nerves would at last rebel, and instead of brave Captain Latcher the audience would see a man going all to pieces. And he would be through as an animal man.

Through! And then what could he do? It left him in an icy sweat. So he had to go on. By jolly, he was a chap with a bear by the tail. Life had jockeyed him into a desperate spot. If only he could have shared his fears with Marybelle it might have helped. But one had pride. How would she react if she discovered that the elegant chap who had swept her off her feet was scared of the cats?

She was scared of them, of course, but she was a woman. She had never pretended otherwise. Early in their relationship he had suggested that he might work her into the act.

"Oh, no," she trilled. "I would be so-o afraid."

He had not insisted. He laughed and kissed her behind the ear. He loved her ears, they were so dainty, so crisp, so translucent. He loved her brilliant blondeness, her faint smile, her silences. In his bachelor years he had known many women, but never one with such a capacity for stillness.

She looked beautiful this evening, sitting there watching. Her delectable body was clad in a fresh linen suit, and her ankles looked lovely in high-heeled pumps.

He glanced at his watch. Time was implacably passing, bringing nearer the moment when he must enter the arena. He finished dressing, stood with legs apart, hands on his belted revolvers. A stance like that helped drive off the fear. But tonight it didn't help much. He kept thinking of Sebastian and Orika, how this afternoon they had dressed for the show. His act had come before theirs; when they plunged he had been back in the van, waiting for Willie to rub him down.

That reminded him. He had intended chiding Willie for his absence, but in the confusion following the accident he had forgotten. So now he went to the door.

"Willie! I say, Willie! Come in, old chap."

Willie entered. The Captain stood observing him, feeling braver all the time. Marybelle sat watching.

"Old chap, what happened to you this afternoon? I don't pay you to fade away as soon as I enter the arena. Where were you?"

"I didn't feel so good."

"Ah, Willie—your adverbs. You were ill?"

"I had a gutache."

A grimace crossed the Captain's face. And he exclaimed:

"Willie, Willie. Have you no sense of delicacy?"

"Aw, lay off. Can't a guy be sick?"

"You weren't here for my rubdown, you know. Do I pay you to yield to these alarming pains in your intestines?"

Willie's gaze was on the floor, his face full of heat.

"What are you looking at, Willie? My boots? They are very dusty, you know. Where's your alertness, old chap?"

Willie rummaged for a cloth, knelt, rubbed the boots. They were not dusty, save in the Captain's imagination. While he worked he sneaked glances at Marybelle's crossed legs.

"Very well, Willie. Dismissed. And see that you do better in the future."

Willie arose, replaced the cloth in the box of shoe-shining equipment. He heard the Captain saying to Marybelle:

"Well, little bug, the time approaches. And Ned Sebastian, poor chap, will not be with us tonight."

"You will be careful?" Marybelle's low voice asked. "After that terrible accident this afternoon—"

"Careful?" The Captain laughed. "Why, my little chick, I thrive on danger. And an accident never strikes twice the same day. But if I should ever die you will be provided for. I am a man the insurance underwriters will have none of, but the cats will be yours, and the cages and this van. They should bring a tidy sum."

He spoke lightly, rapidly. And though it was all bravado, at least the words had a gallant sound, and perhaps they infused him with desperate courage. Nor were they lost on Willie.

In the arena that evening nothing untoward happened; the Captain snapped through his act with great address; and afterward, in the van, he noticed a change for the better in Willie. In recent months the cage boy had grown more surly, till sometimes the Captain exclaimed to Marybelle, "By jolly, the chap is becoming impossible! Really, I believe I'll have to replace him."

But tonight Willie was more the way he used to be after he had frightened poor Cecil out of his wits. It was "Yes, sir," and "No, sir," tonight. And he administered an excellent rubdown, his strong fingers kneading the Captain's muscles till they felt blissfully supple. This change the Captain ascribed to the dressing-down he had given Willie before the show, and lying there on the table he thought:

"I must knock the chap about a bit more. He respects nothing but brutality."

In the last year he had ceased knocking Willie about, physically, for the cage boy no longer accepted beatings as if they were part of his wages. One winter day in their quarters at Blue Island, when the Captain warmed up to his not unpleasant task, Willie had suddenly rebelled, smashing out with his enormous fist. The Captain hadn't ducked in time, and Willie's knuckles cut open his lip. This was humiliating, for Marybelle stood watching.

Moreover, Willie kept blurting his fists toward his employer; one blow in the solar plexus was especially distressing. Panic came to the Captain, and he had a humiliating vision of himself knocked flat, and Willie swaggering over him. He didn't know how Marybelle would react to that, but he very well knew how Willie would react. He would become insufferable; it would be necessary to dismiss him.

And the Captain didn't want to dismiss him. The fellow had virtues: a passion for cleanliness, for order. Moreover, the Captain was both fascinated and annoyed by Willie's square-headed disposition; he always hoped to conquer him in spirit as well as in body. He had grown to dislike Willie intensely, even to fear him; and hate bound the two men together.

That day it was a very rum go, but in the end the Captain's boxing knowledge brought him victory. His legs weakened and his lungs were agonized, and he knew he couldn't stand it much longer. Then, luckily, he landed a blow that sent the fellow sprawling; and once Willie was down he kicked him in the face. Willie cried out. So the Captain seized a whip and on the floor Willie writhed and howled. At last the Captain flung down the whip and dusted his hands.

"Old chap," he said, "you made a mistake when you struck back at me." And to cover his fear-inspired decision to battle no more he added: "By jolly, sometimes I doubt whether it's worth the trouble to beat you."

And turning easily to Marybelle he said:

"Well, little chick, how about dinner in the Loop and the theater?"

"Oh, yes, I would like that."

As always, her serene little smile was enigmatic; but inasmuch as that day's beating had resulted from Willie's heavy attempt to steal a kiss, an intuitive flash told the Captain she might have been flattered because the two men had fought over her, and that now she was like a medieval Swedish maiden bestowing the accolade of her smile upon the Viking who jousted victoriously for her favor.

On his flatcar pallet beneath a cage wagon, Willie lay sleepless for a long time after the train steamed westward from the North Platte yards. He was grinning secretly, and his brain blazed with excitement, for now after years of mortification at the Captain's hands, and years of frustration and despair at ever becoming an animal trainer, he envisioned a course of action that would bring him fame.

Marybelle would inherit the cats. The Captain had said so. And if a fatal accident should overtake her husband, what would be more suitable than for Willie Krummer to take over the act and marry the pretty widow? Willie breathed hard.

While the wheels clicked and the cinders rattled he lay there scheming, and he wished he might sponsor an accident the very next day. But his old woods caution whispered he had better wait till they returned to winter quarters in Blue Island. On the circus there were always people about, and somebody might detect foul play. Moreover, Willie could not forget the Captain's brother in British Columbia. Perhaps the fellow had died. Perhaps that was why the Captain was leaving the cats to his wife. Or, he realized now, it was possible that such a brother did not exist. For among his other attainments the Captain was a lighthearted liar; often he said anything that popped into his head, if it seemed amusing or pat; and perhaps he had simply lied about possessing a brother. This outraged Willie. He thought of all the years he had wasted as cage boy, when he might just as well have owned the act. On the other hand, there might be a brother, and if so he wanted to be certain the scoundrel was no longer heir.

After that, action! But crafty action! Willie told himself he must plan the Captain's death with all the cunning he had learned in the woods, setting snares. With even more cunning! For if Marybelle ever suspected he had killed her husband, she might be prejudiced against marrying him. She might refuse him anyway. What then?

His hands twitched and his breath coarsened. She wouldn't refuse. All these years she had ignored him, and mocked him with her smile, but he was convinced this was a mask disguising the attraction she felt for his overwhelming virility. Once the Captain was housed in a coffin, Willie anticipated no difficulty with Marybelle. He would dominate her as if she were a pliant, yellow tulip in his fingers. None of this little Viking, little chick nonsense! Women were like cats; they needed to know who was running the show.

It heated Willie, dreaming about being her lord and master; and as the train hooted and clanked, swaying through the ghost herds of buffaloes and the ghost Indian warriors, his imagination blossomed with blond light, and he made love to Marybelle in his fashion.

Wearing a dressing gown, unable to sleep, Gus sat in the Clayton Junction car, alone except for a highball and a cigar. What a day!

"That's how they come, sometimes," he told himself.

When Ive turned up in North Platte, Gus had suspected what was on his mind. And he didn't know how he would answer Ive's accusations.

"I want to talk with you privately," Ive told him at lunch.

Gus kept finding things to do, but the dreaded hour could not be postponed forever; so when the matinee was well under way he and Ive retired to the red wagon.

"Uh—something on your mind, Ive?"

"A great deal. I've opened the mine at Oxenford."

"You have? Glad to hear it. Ought to take a fortune out of there." Ive's voice was chilled.

"Gus," he said, "I don't know why I put up with you. I'm not ordinarily a fool."

"Should say not! You've got a head on your shoulders, Ive. Always have had great respect for you."

"Cut it out," Ive said. "You salted that mine, and you know it."

Gus was about to protest innocence, to accuse Mr. Oxenford of having perpetrated the foul deed; but suddenly the humor of the situation got the better of him. He broke out laughing. He didn't want to make Ive madder, but he couldn't help it.

And it did make Ive madder, naturally. He lifted his cane and banged it on the floor. Gus must have been nervous; perhaps his laughter was partly hysteria; but much of it was pure humor.

"Damn you, Gus! How did I ever get mixed up with you!"

"Now wait a minute, Ive. Don't get mad. Maybe I did take you on that deal. But you'll have to admit it was pretty cute."

"Cute! Why you damned crook—!"

"Wait a minute, Ive. Look at it from my shoes. There I was, busted wide open. Had to do something, didn't I? If I'd gone to you without anything to put up for half-interest in the show you'd have kicked me out. You know you would. Suppose I did salt the mine. I'm making you money on this show. She's rolling in—rolling in—the good old long green. Why, hell—what do you care about that coal mine? I'll make you a mint of money on this show."

An element of truth there!

Gus stood up, laid a hand on his partner's

"Tell you, Ive. Think it's your pride that's hurt. But don't look at it that way. Why, that deal would have fooled any financier in the country. Now if I'd just sold you the mine that would have been pretty bad. I'll admit it. But I didn't. I was working in your best interests, Ive. I knew I could make you a pot of money. And I will! Before we're through we'll own every show in the country. They can't stop us!"

Gus talked on, recounting how when he was a young man the very name of Pawpacker had excited him.

"I spotted you for a great man, Ive, the minute you walked into the city room to tell me about Molly. Right then and there I knew I wanted to hook up with you. I knew that with your brains and my brass we'd clean up the world. Why, hell—"

It was then that the conference was interrupted by news of the accident.

And it was never resumed. Too much hell popping. When Gus saw Eloise he felt all choked up, and he was glad Ive was on the lot to take charge of her. Himself, he was too busy talking to newspaper men, to undertakers, and calling a Chicago booking agent about a new act. He hadn't talked to Ive again till the show was almost loaded. Then, with Eloise, Ive came down to the yards and the trio sat in the Clayton Junction car.

And Ive was much different from the angry man of the afternoon conference. And so was Gus. The accident had given tenderness to their voices.

"Eloise and I have been talking," Ive said. "And we've decided she'll be my daughter and go back to Winchester with me."

"Uh—yes," Gus rumbled. "Nice place, Winchester. You'll love it there, Eloise, I'm sure."

She had sat red-eyed and silent. Now she began to cry.

"Uh—now wait a minute, honey. Don't cry. Know you feel like it, and all that, but don't think I would."

She looked up at him, eyes glistening. She whispered, "All right."

"That's better. Sure it is. Uh—maybe you think I don't understand your position. But I do. I've been through it too, honey. Had a little girl once, myself."

For a moment he looked derelict, standing there, fumbling out a cigar, absently biting off the end. Then he pulled himself together and boomed:

"Yes, sir! Winchester's a wonderful place! All kinds of elephants there!"

Eloise sat with her head back against the huge chair, and presently she closed her eyes. Gus and Ive talked about circus matters, and from outside you could hear locomotives steaming and the shouts of razorbacks. Presently the train was loaded, and the men stood up. Eloise did not move. Her body had relaxed and she was fast asleep.

Gus sighed heavily.

"Kind of a shame to wake her up," he said.

But they had to, of course.

Gus accompanied them to the rear platform and down the steps. When he shook hands with Ive he knew he had been forgiven for the coal mine deal. Ive looked tired and Gus felt that way; and he felt mellow, too. He felt sorry for Eloise and, oddly, for everybody in the world. He didn't often experience moments like that, driven as he was toward some misty and shining goal that he thought of vaguely as success and greatness.

"Well Ive, take care of yourself. And you, Eloise. Be a good girl. See you in the fall."

He watched them trudging away down the long line of cars.

After Cheyenne, the circus swung southward through Colorado, then east through Kansas, then south again. Twice daily the Captain entered the arena, and twice daily he left it unscathed. To Willie's eyes, the act looked very tame. And his eyes were correct. The Captain took no unnecessary risks; from time to time he had singled out and sold the actually vicious animals; so now his galaxy consisted of lions that had long since abdicated as kings of beasts, and tigers scarcely more alert than hound dogs. Willie considered this disgusting.

And so did the customers, for that matter, and so did Gus. You couldn't get around it: the act wasn't going over. One day near season's end, on the Gulf coast of Texas, the Captain and A. H. Burgoyne discussed the matter, and the upshot was that both men lost their tem-

pers and that Captain Philip Latcher would not travel next year with
the B.&P. show.

"Odd chap, Burgoyne," the Captain mused aloud in the dressing-
van. "I don't understand these Americans."

Word leaked out about the quarrel, and from Burgoyne's show, performers wrote friends on other shows, mentioning that the Captain was
slipping, and so it was that when the Captain visited his booking agent
in Chicago the following October, that practical man told him something must be done.

"You're good—sure, you're good," the agent said. "Greatest in the
business. But word's got around you've lost your grip."

"Oh, come now!" the Captain smiled.

"That gossip's hurting us," the agent said. "Unless we put more life
into the act, I can't guarantee a thing as to next season, or even as to
indoor bookings this winter."

"What would you advise, old chap?"

"You've got to scare the pants off them. Buy some unbroken animals and work them into your routine. People pay to see danger.
They pay to see you escape death—or maybe not to escape it."

"Right you are, old boy," said the Captain lightly; and when he left
the office, swinging his stick, he didn't look like a man frightened sick.

In a speakeasy, he sat drinking Capone liquor, his thoughts circling
the cage of his dilemma. He thought how wonderful it would be to
make a fortune painlessly, on the stock market or by winning the
Irish Sweepstakes. Then he could rid himself of his cats and his fear
and live like a gentleman with Marybelle in some Lake Shore apartment. Life was too sweet, he thought, to risk it in the arena.

But since winning a fortune was unlikely, the old question mark
hung in his thoughts: if he quit show business what could he do to
make money? He had nothing saved. His fine clothes and elegant
manner were all front. He would have to take a job. What job? By
jolly, he wouldn't even know how to secure one, let alone how to fill it.

In the end he did what he must: he bought six unbroken animals,
three lions, three tigers.

Having made the purchase, he experienced relief and even optimism.
He knew what he had to do now, and that was better than indecision.
He called on his booking agent and assured him the act would surpass
any in America.

Then the animals arrived at the old factory building, and as he
studied them his distress returned. Last summer he had dreaded entering the arena with even his sluggish cats. Now he must master these
hissing fiends. They were mainly two-year-olds, of recent African
residence, and their opinion of civilization seemed low. Willie Krum-

mer stood by his side, admiring the way their muscles rippled, commenting upon their sharp claws, their splendid fangs.

"When do we start?" Willie asked.

"We? Don't you think it a bit presumptuous, old chap, to employ the personal pronoun in the plural?"

"Aw, quit it," Willie growled.

Every night the Captain resolved to begin training the next morning, but when morning arrived he decided to wait another day. But that couldn't continue, for on the strength of the rejuvenated act the booking agent had secured indoor circus dates, beginning after Christmas. So one morning, accompanied by Marybelle, the Captain appeared at the factory, where Willie slept in the office.

"This is the day," he exclaimed with great gallantry, "when the kittens enter kindergarten."

And presently, booted and belted in his training costume, he strode through the gloomy old factory to the arena.

"Lights, Willie!"

Above the arena, high-powered bulbs flashed on. Gripping his whip he called:

"Bring them in, Willie! The lions, this morning."

From the animal chute they came pouring into the arena, where they padded about, snarling and spitting. Willie joined the Captain in the safety cage.

"Don't you want the tigers, too?"

"Do I look a fool, old man? I shan't mix the breeds for a time yet."

He gripped the kitchen chair, stepped inside. The safety door clanged. And although the factory was cool on this late autumn morning, his shirt was already drenched. Once in the arena, he felt better, for his worst battle was the one with himself in the safety cage. He didn't try much that morning; he merely accustomed the cats to his presence. His fear yielded to the habits of years; he ducked and side-stepped with matchless footwork. His concentration was intense; he forgot everything but the cats. Willie was far from his thoughts, and the fact that of all animals man is most dangerous.

Every morning thereafter he came to the factory, and now his light-heartedness was no longer spurious. For he had discovered that courage feeds on itself. Brave Captain Latcher had won battle after battle with timid Captain Latcher, and it looked as if he would also win the war.

Having dawdled so long, he would be unable to use all six cats in his old act when he filled his first winter engagement, but he had hopes of working in one or two, even if all they did was to sit snarling on their pedestals. And as the winter went on he would continue training, and by next summer his act would be spectacular. His new confidence was so contagious that his agent spoke optimistically of securing a contract with a really first-rate circus.

He thought his new confidence even infused Marybelle, although with a girlie like her—placid waters!—you couldn't be sure. Nothing ever seemed to ruffle the little Viking's composure. A jewel of a wife, she! But by jolly, something of a mystery woman. She was passionate —nothing to the old fable of cold blondes—but in spirit she seemed always remote, as if her soul had never left the snowy northern forests of her ancestors.

"What are you thinking, little gosling?" he would ask.

"Oh-h—nothing."

And her utter serenity would make her an enchanted person within a circle drawn by a wizard, and her tiny smile would mock him just a little, so it seemed, as if it were taunting, "Break through the shining circle if you can."

Jove! Fascinating little chick!

It didn't trouble him, feeling excluded from the land behind her smile, for being a tremendous egotist he was more interested in himself.

Her smile troubled Willie, even though he too was an egotist. But he was not a romantic like the Captain, with the romantic's habit of endowing women with traits they do not possess. Willie simply concluded she was mocking him. It vexed him, and in due course he intended to erase the smile, but his practical mind believed in putting first things first. At present, the Captain's demise stood high on his agenda of chores to be done.

His plans were laid. Nothing could go wrong. Nobody would suspect him. Weeks ago he had discovered that Captain Latcher had no brother, in British Columbia or anywhere. One day while administering a rubdown, Willie craftily launched into reminiscences of his boyhood, inveighing against his old man for being so fruitful.

"Maybe the old fool had so many because he wasn't no good at anything else," Willie speculated irascibly.

The Captain lay smiling, amused as ever at the Krummer personality.

"Willie," he exclaimed, "I perceive that with your other attainments you are a psychologist. Do you know Krafft-Ebing, old chap?"

"Naw," Willie growled, and he mumbled that the Captain was making fun of him.

"Furthest from my thoughts, old lad. How many little children blessed your happy household?"

"A litter of 'em!"

"You keep in close touch with them, I fancy? All sorts of festive missives flying back and forth between you and the brothers Krummer?"

"Never heard from them and never want to," Willie declared. "Do you write your brothers and sisters?"

"Quite impossible, old boy. I had no brothers, and my one sister died in infancy."

A liar! A detestable liar! It certainly outraged Willie, when he thought how the Captain had duped him all these years. Perfidious Albion!

Willie's rage poured down his heavy arms, into his thick fingers, and the Captain protested against the vigor of his masseur.

"Hold! Enough!" he cried. "My muscles aren't steel ingots, you know. By jolly, old chap, if fingers were brains you'd be a college president!"

But a career like that was not what Willie wanted. An animal trainer!—that was what he longed to be. Already he had selected his professional name. The Baron Karl Otto Von Krummer!

When the Captain purchased the new cats, and announced his intention of breaking them, Willie congratulated himself. The whole affair would be simplicity itself. The world would learn that one morning the Captain had fallen victim to these vicious newcomers, and the world would say, "Yes, animal training is a dangerous calling." No embarrassing investigation by the police.

"You will find out, Mr. Smart Aleck Captain," Willie muttered, pacing the factory office at night. "Always beating me up and using big words against me before *her*. You will find out and she will find out."

But plans are one thing, effecting them another. And Willie's plans had not included Marybelle's coming to the factory every morning with the Captain. Why did she not stay at home, where a woman belonged, darning socks and sewing? She would need a great deal of schooling, once she became the Baroness Krummer.

Always it was the same. Willie awakened early and sprang from bed, thinking perhaps this would be the morning when he could execute his plans and the Captain. The factory office was cold and dark, but an old iron stove stood in the corner and soon Willie had a fire roaring. The kindling he had laid out the night before, arranged neatly. The coal bucket stood at attention; the office was as orderly and clean as a Prussian barracks.

He was wonderfully efficient. While coffee brewed he made his bed, and after breakfast he swept the floor and dusted. In the makeshift closet his shoes, although old and few, were lined up like soldiers at inspection. His suits were ranked on hangers. He was full of virtues.

After household duties, he marched into the factory and cleaned the cages. It was routined so well that you could have set your watch by what he was doing at any moment. No lost motion. An efficient German.

When he returned to the office, the waiting began. An exasperating business. For the Captain was not punctual. He slept till he wakened, and if it amused him to lazy in bed he lazied. With Marybelle by his side. Thinking of their occupying the same bed, Willie growled out all his old lumberjack and road-kid oaths.

Then at last the Captain arrived, a trace of shaving-powder on his cheeks, the morning paper—unfresh from his reading—in his pocket.

"Good morning, Willie old man. Just out of bed, I fancy."

That always made Willie mad. He wasn't the one who slept late.

"I've been up a long time," he growled.

"Now, now, Willie! No before-breakfast grumpiness! You'll feel better, old chap, after tea and crumpets."

Tea! The sissy!

"You can't get me to drink tea," Willie growled. "That pale puke!"

And then the Captain grimaced and pretended shock.

"Willie, Willie! Ladies are present, old chap."

On that great day in Willie's life, the two of them arrived as usual, and as usual the Captain needled his cage boy about late rising, and as usual—even though he knew the Captain was riding him—Willie rose to the bait. But after that the usual became the unusual. The Captain kissed his wife lightly good-by, and it transpired she was making an excursion to the Loop, because of Christmas shopping.

"Good-by, little chick," he said. "And I say, if you should meet Marshall Field give him my best."

He escorted her to the door, waved farewell, and Willie experienced an almost voluptuous satisfaction, knowing he had the fellow all to himself.

There in the office, dressing, the Captain hummed lightly. The song was "Chicago," and once he even sang a few phrases.

"That toddling town, that toddling town . . . All ready, Willie?"

"Yes, sir."

" 'Sir!' I say, Willie! You haven't employed that term of respect much of late. And I like it, you know."

"Yes, sir."

"Very good, Willie! What are you smirking about, old chap?"

"Huh?"

" 'Huh!' How I detest that monosyllabic interrogation! Say 'Beg pardon,' Willie."

"Beg pardon."

"Better! Yes, you're learning. A few more decades and we'll graduate you from eighth grade. Well, to business, old boy."

As Willie strode into the factory toward the animal chute, he could hear the Captain singing again.

"On State Street . . . that great street . . ."

For several days the Captain had been working all the new cats together. Battles had ensued between tigers and lions, but these had been broken up when Willie seized a heavy hose and directed a stream of water into the arena.

Now he called, "All six of 'em together, sir?"

"Certainly, old boy. Progress on the march, eh?"

His voice had a hollow, ghostly quality, echoing among the dusky reaches of the old factory.

The arena lights blazed and the animals poured from the chute, hissing and feuding. Gripping a training stick of hardwood tipped with steel, Willie joined his chief in the safety cage.

"This is the most dangerous moment of all, Willie. If you're ever a trainer, remember that. When the cats have just entered and are mill-ing about." The Captain hitched up his belt, seized his whip and the kitchen chair. "Here goes, old man."

He pushed open the door into the arena, stepped over the sill. And then he collapsed to the floor, the reason being that Willie had cracked his skull with the hardwood stick. The force of his fall sent the kitchen chair hopping across the arena, where a tiger pounced on it. Willie clanged shut the door and waited. A strange light showed in his eyes, and he was grinning. He was also breathing hard.

The Captain lay prone, motionless; and the cats were interested. A lion came prowling toward him, ears back, tail switching; and Willie expected it to spring and bury its claws in the Captain.

Instead, when it was a couple of paces away, it halted. Its teeth gleamed and it snarled softly. Here was a situation without precedent, and a million years of jungle suspicions were roused. Its nose twitched, and it did not smell death. The Pain Giver lived. It backed away.

"God damn you," Willie urged. "Get busy!"

The lion's gaze met Willie's and it snarled. Then it sat down and yawned nervously.

The next instant it whirled, meeting the attack of a tiger. They were rolling over and over, and the uproar was terrible. The Captain was forgotten. Willie cursed his way from the safety cage and grabbed the hose, directing water through the bars. It broke the cats apart. They shook themselves, licked themselves. The other animals were remaining close to the chute on the far side of the arena. The Captain lay alone.

Willie twisted off the water, flung down the hose. He wasn't grin-ning now, because panic was touching him. He was swearing con-stantly, doggedly, desperately. He had planned so exquisitely! By now, according to plan, the Captain should be in ribbons. But unconsciousness was protecting him! Presently he might awaken and save himself. And he would remember that the blow from behind had fallen from no cat. Willie could hear him telling the police:

"My cage boy attacked me and left me at the mercy of the kittens. Odd chap, Willie. Twisted in his brain, you know. I say, don't you think Joliet is the spot for a lad like that?"

Joliet!

Willie's throat felt as if some guy were choking him. His heart was laboring. He snatched up a feeding fork and strode to the far side of the arena, poking through the bars at the animals. They roared. Snarled. Then a lion swatted the fork, almost lazily, and it was torn from his grasp.

Willie screamed out oaths. The cats swore back. There was sickness in his stomach; his face was pasty; and his heart thumped his ribs. Oh, damn, damn! He had never felt so unstrung, and all at once he began to cry. He kept stamping about, cursing the cats, and all the time the tears streaked his face.

It passed. The weeping; not the panic. The panic remained. So did the sickness in his stomach. All at once he knew with terrible clarity what he must do. His pores were running with sweat and a queer lightheadedness afflicted him. His breathing was choppy. For he must enter the arena.

His tongue felt swollen and he was trembling dreadfully. He weaved like a seasick man as he forced himself toward the safety cage. Just outside, he grabbed an extra kitchen chair. Behind his Adam's apple something throbbed. He was in the safety cage now, and his knees were swinging.

"God damn it!" he howled, as if he were suffering the torments of hell.

Then he opened the arena door, and he attained a plane of super-fear, so lofty and thin-aired that it was almost like courage. His thoughts clicked precisely, and his nerves and muscles regained co-ordination. And never had he known such strength. He put down the kitchen chair, grappled the Captain's heavy belt, lifted him and heaved him toward an advancing tiger.

He glimpsed the tiger springing but he couldn't observe the Captain's finish, for he saw something else. A lion. It was in midair, and its target was Willie. He screeched. He flung himself aside, grabbed the chair. It seemed a white-hot prong was tearing the flesh of his left arm, his side, his left leg. The chair crashed into a mass of fangs and tawny fur. Willie jumped backward, and as he revolved he glimpsed another form slithering toward him. He tensed. It sprang. He leaped. He saw a door. The safety-cage door. He grabbed.

He was on the safety-cage floor. The universe had been black but now it was a whirling thing, full of agony. He ground his teeth, sat up. The floor was sticky and scarlet. Blood! Panic returned. His blood! Monstrous! Inconceivable!

He didn't walk to the office. He dragged; slowly, slowly. Once he passed out. He left a trail of crimson. He had never known such weakness and such pain. He was no longer Willie Krummer. He was a determination to live.

On a table in the office a telephone stood. He watched it swaying back and forth, creeping laboriously toward him. It would never reach him. Oaths thundered in his brain. Not from his lips. Lips were —too tired.

And then he summoned all his forces. All the strength of the tough years. The Wisconsin woods. The road-kid days. He crept and dragged.

He was lying on the floor, a transmitter at his lips. He was croaking, "Accident. Help. Help."

After an eternal blankness he opened his eyes and found himself between sheets. White walls. Medicinal smells. A starched uniform. His arm and leg and side were burning and throbbing. He closed his eyes.

Later still he awakened feeling stronger. A man in a white bib told him he would be fine in about a month.

And after more sleep he felt better yet, and several men were in the room, pencils poised above copy paper. They congratulated him upon his heroism. They wanted to know all about him.

"My name," he said, "is the Baron Karl Otto Von Krummer."

News was a bit dull, just then, and the papers splashed it. The wire services sent it all over the country, and it even traveled by cable to foreign lands.

It seemed Captain Philip Latcher had been attacked. And his assistant trainer tried to save his life. Greater love hath no man. The assistant's name was the Baron Karl Otto Von Krummer. Descendant of Central European nobility. Maybe in the city rooms they doubted the part about his being a baron. But they didn't check it. After all, when a guy's a hero and claims nobility it makes a hell of a good story to say he's a baron.

The papers said that the Baron, after his recovery, intended continuing with Captain Latcher's act. Some said there was a movement on foot to award him a Carnegie Medal. That, of course, was pure fancy.

But the wires arriving at the hospital were not imaginary. Several circus owners offered the Baron Von Krummer attractive contracts. After the glowing publicity he received, it would have been un-American to do otherwise.

15

"Get married, you two," the late Captain Latcher's booking agent said. "That's my best advice."

"See there—what did I tell you?" said the Baron Karl Otto Von Krummer, addressing the Captain's widow. *"Mein Gott!* In this waiting there is no sense."

Marybelle smiled, but she did not respond. One of her silences! Those silences vexed the Baron.

It was a February afternoon, and they were sitting in the booking agent's office. Except for her leopard coat, which she had removed, Marybelle's clothes were black. But widow's weeds only accentuated her beauty.

"Well, what do you say?" the Baron demanded.

"I do not know what to say. I have not decided."

Willie cursed. But they were mute curses. Outwardly he was as stiff with nobility as an iron statue in the Tiergarten. Like all effective actors, he had stumbled upon the great truth that to convince others the actor must first convince himself. This was not difficult for Willie, because with all his shortcomings he had native intelligence and a vivid imagination. Years before he had convinced himself poor Cecil was a villain. When he viewed cowboy boots he was virtually the grandson of Buffalo Bill, and when he watched Eric Von Stroheim he was a Prussian nobleman.

His admiration for Herr Von Stroheim had stood him in good stead when the newspaper men interviewed him in the hospital. Also to his aid had rushed childhood memories from Wisconsin: German phrases and mannerisms. Even though sizzling with pain, Willie put on a fine act. He said, *"Ja,"* and "So?" He told them his grandfather had been a baron and had fled the Fatherland.

Under Captain Latcher's tutelage, Willie had scorned nice shadings of grammar, but as he lay answering questions that very tutelage came to his aid. He avoided "ain't" and double negatives, and if he made a few minor slips it didn't matter, because the accent he assumed flavored these with quaintness. The reporters were eager to believe him a nobleman, anyway—a better story—and the enormity of his lie helped. His claim to nobility was so massive and impertinent and vigorously repeated that they had to believe. Like an advertising man, he employed repetition to establish truth.

When the newspapers appeared containing the interviews with "the hero of Blue Island," the Captain's booking agent rushed to Willie's bedside and arranged to represent him. And when telegrams from circus owners flashed to the hospital the agent took charge and arranged a contract with Vendee & Gonzaga's Circus.

After the pain quieted in his wounds, Willie enjoyed the hospital. He spent long hours with his press notices, and he meditated endlessly about how to consolidate his position as a nobleman. He remembered more and more of Captain Latcher's advice, and one day he sent out for an English grammar and a German one. He studied these. It was difficult going. At first, it was nearly impossible going. Like most grammars, these had been written with incredible stupidity, and Willie cursed the authors. But he was nothing if not methodical and persistent, so he lumbered and butted through the books. And day by day in every way his German accent became better and better.

He had been a week in the hospital before Marybelle visited him. Her neglect enraged him, and when she entered the room he growled:

"Well! It is about time!" His words sounded more like, "Vell! It iss about time!"

"I am so-o sorry," she murmured, "that you got yourself hurt, Willie."

She seated herself by his bed, and as they talked he feasted his gaze. She looked innocent and unprotected. Her legs were crossed, her ankles delicately shaped as a doe's, her calves snugly filling the flesh-colored hosiery. She wore a black dress, and as her breath rose and fell he observed the stirring of her bosom. She set him wild.

"I did not know you were of noble blood," she said. And she smiled faintly, and fell silent.

This discomfited Willie. Was she mocking him? Did she doubt him? And he found himself wondering whether she suspected what had actually taken place in the arena. A chilling thought! He said:

"It was too bad about the Captain. I did my best."

"Oh-h, I am sure of that."

The smile lingered on her pretty mouth. More mockery? Hell and damnation!

Presently she bent her lovely head and wept quietly.

"It was a great shock," she murmured.

"No good to cry over spilled milk," Willie consoled her. And he asked, "How are the cats?"

"They are well." And she told how the booking agent had hired a man to look after them, and how the agent had arranged with her for Willie to use the cats and equipment during the coming season.

"You will travel with us?" Willie asked.

"I do not know."

"The sensible thing," he said, "would be for us to get married."

"Oh-h," she breathed, "no."

"Why not?"

"I could not do that."

"We could be married here—today."

Her eyes were wide and she shook her head.

"Oh-h, no. It has been hardly a week since Philip kissed me good-by."

"God damn it to hell!" Willie shouted mentally, "what has that got to do with it?"

"I must go," she murmured, "I must go."

And she hurried from the room.

One night when he had been a fortnight in the hospital Willie had a dream. It took place in the factory office. In the dream, Willie was sweeping the floor, and then the door opened and Captain Latcher came in. He looked jaunty and dashing, swinging his cane.

The dream produced a peculiar effect upon the sleeping Krummer brain, for Willie was both participant and observer. When he beheld the Captain, who was supposed to be dead and buried, Willie dropped the broom and stood gaping. His tongue was dry and his knees were quivering.

"What is it then that you want with the Baron Karl Otto Von Krummer?" Willie demanded.

The Captain smiled. And he said tauntingly:

"She knows, old chap, she knows. The little Viking knows."

And then the Captain lifted his cane, as if it were an orchestra leader's baton, and loud, weird music flooded the office. The song was: "Chicago."

"Don't!" Willie cried. "Don't play it!"

But the music continued, all the time louder, always "Chicago," and suddenly Willie found himself running down State Street. *And State Street was a great street,* except in the dream there was no traffic and no people except Willie and the gaily pursuing Captain. And the orchestra kept playing and the street looked like the street in a mad city, the buildings leaning crazily, everything distorted and grotesque. Willie ran faster and faster till his throat strangled shut and he awakened writhing in the hospital bed.

Only a dream; only a dream; but the horror of it sickened his blood and poisoned him with terror.

"She knows," he thought, "the little Swede knows!"

No! She couldn't know. She had been shopping in the Loop that morning.

Willie slept no more that night.

And from that day forward Willie grew guarded, and fear became his companion. And suspicion. He suspected everybody, but especially Marybelle. Now and then she visited him, but no longer could he gaze on her with pure lust. Fear, the enemy of lust, was present. He was afraid the Captain had warned her that Willie might bring about his death, and that her smile and her silences were complex with suspicion. Somewhere he had heard that a wife could not be forced to testify against her husband, and he thought this meant she could not even though she wished to; so he grew wilder than ever to marry her. Presently he left the hospital and set about wooing her, but caution deterred him from pressing marriage too impetuously. So he urged the booking agent to advise marriage.

She was not complex. She was not mysterious, to herself. It never occurred to her that her little smile and her silences veiled her with enigma in men's imaginations. She was silent because she had nothing to say, and she had nothing to say because at the moment her thoughts were empty. Her mental processes were sound, but they were slow. She had the phlegmatic mind of a Swedish peasant housed in the lovely head of a beautiful Swedish princess. Had she been less delectable the world would have recognized her smile as akin to the vacuous smile of students in a school for the simple-minded.

Not that she was simple-minded! But simplicity she certainly had. It was the simplicity of forestfolk or fisherfolk back when the world was young; the charming simplicity of a fisher maiden on some wild northern coast where the blue-black forests marched down to the sea. You could imagine her mending the nets and dancing on feast days and worshiping the northern gods. She was like some maiden in *Beowulf,* afraid of the dragon that came out of the forest and adoring the warrior who slew the dragon.

No dragons came out of the forests to threaten the Minnesota village where she was born, possibly because there were no forests. The town was New Stockholm in the wheat country, and she was the fifth child of Anna and Peter Swanson. At the edge of town they lived in a house with linoleum on the dining-room floor and a heavy Bible in the parlor. The town was Swedish. If you were Norwegian or Danish, and wished to go broke fast, you could have found no quicker way than to set up business in that town.

In the land of his fathers Peter Swanson had been a shipbuilder by trade, but in New Stockholm the business of constructing ocean-going vessels was slack, so he was a handy man. He could—and would—do anything, and he almost made a living at it. He thought of himself as a God-fearing man, and on Sunday mornings you would see Anna and Peter and a whole row of tow-headed Swansons in a pew. The church called itself Lutheran, and generically this was correct, although it belonged to an archaic synod that long ago had broken away from the rest of American Lutheranism. The synod was small and so exceedingly fundamentalist that it considered all members of every other Lutheran synod bound for perdition, along with the Methodists, Baptists and Catholics. The church in New Stockholm was usually cold, just as the bedroom where Mabel slept was usually cold. In that country, autumn came early and the winter snows were deep.

As a girl, Mabel did not enjoy the advantages of travel. Till she was sixteen, when she boarded the evening local for St. Paul, she had never stepped inside a train. She did not kiss her family good-by, because they were unaware of her departure. To run away from home was not her idea; she was not a girl who thirsted for the merry lights of cities; she would have been content to wed in New Stockholm and produce tow-headed children. Her leaving was Mr. Christianson's idea.

Chris Christianson owned a store where you could buy golden oak furniture and satin-lined coffins. One day he hired Peter Swanson to install a new pane of glass in his store, and that evening Peter told Mabel she was a lucky girl, for Chris Christianson had offered her a job to work after school and on Saturdays. Peter did not mention salary, because since Chris would pay him direct it was not Mabel's concern.

Mr. Christianson was a massive man of forty-five, with a heavy neck and a heavy nose. Like Peter he feared God; he never missed Sunday services; he thought the Almighty had given man passion with the idea of tripping him up and sending him headlong into flaming hell. He took religion so hard that probably he never realized his offer of employment to Mabel was the work of the Serpent. Or perhaps he realized it and couldn't help himself. Perhaps his blood stirred when he saw her at church, so golden and maidenly, and perhaps her mysterious little smile sent thoughts through his stolid head that were hardly proper for a married man with children, New Stockholm's leading furniture dealer and undertaker.

If wicked thoughts were absent when he hired her, they soon visited him once Mabel became his employee. When he viewed her delicious blondeness he felt like a farmer who sees a field of ripe wheat and wishes to reap it. She had a clean scent of soap and water and young girlish skin and hair, and when she passed near him his stout heart labored. He took sex the way he took religion, very hard. He had not the Latin's lightheartedness in such matters, quaffing young lips as if they were wine. If he had to sin he would sin, but he would be damned if he would enjoy it. His wild Viking heritage commanded him to plow into wild storms, to burn cities and pillage and carry off the wives and daughters, but these pagan recreations had, many generations back, been hedged about by the precepts of stern northern pastors. The poor fellow suffered terribly.

When at last he surrendered to impulse, it was as if a glacier on some northern mountain had at last succumbed to the sun and gone berserk down the slope, roaring and crushing. It surprised Mabel. Till then, he had kept himself so sternly under control that she had no hint of his purposes. A Frenchman would at least have patted her hand. An Italian would have purloined a kiss. Not Christianson. It was Saturday evening, and after locking the store he asked her to help him move some furniture in the back room. One minute he had been as respectable as a church fence, and then she was in his mighty arms.

She struggled. But she did not scream. And the entire experience puzzled her. Slow of thought, she did not know what to say about it. She did not know her inalienable rights about preventing men from the pursuit of happiness. She was nothing. She was Peter Swanson's daughter. And Mr. Christianson was a leading citizen. She was bewildered. She suspected that if she reported him to her father her father would accuse her of wickedness. Indeed, she felt wicked.

And so did poor Christianson, by then. He realized he had been mad, and he begged her forgiveness. She was silent. He begged her to tell nobody, to have pity on him. He remembered his wife and children. Disgrace! Imprisonment, perhaps! The fires of hell!

"We have sinned," he groaned. "We must think what to do. Do not tell till we have thought. You will not tell?"

"No," she promised. "I will not tell."

Christianson did not sleep that night. Nor did Mabel.

Next day, both she and Christianson attended church. Their gazes did not meet. She could not guess what would happen when she went to the store after school on Monday,

An amazing thing happened.

"I want to talk to you," he said sternly.

She felt frightened, following him to the back room. And she was more frightened when he launched out with a terrible diatribe. He accused her of wickedness. She had tempted him. She was bad. He was an upright man who had been seduced. She must leave town at once.

She wept. She begged his forgiveness and promised not to do any more whatever it was that had tempted him. She was feudal. He was authority; a businessman; a council member. Her ignorance was appalling. Her sense of sin was intense. Christianson demanded:

"Have you told anybody?"

"No," she protested. "No. No. I have held my tongue. Please believe me. I have said nothing."

She was like a child.

He lumbered back and forth, scowling. Sweat stood out on his brow. At last he said:

"Well, well, well—it will be all right. But you must leave. You must run away and say nothing to nobody."

"But where can I go? I am afraid."

"To St. Paul. A job there—you can find a fine job. I will give you money. I will give you thirty dollars. No! By heaven—I will give you fifty!"

"But—but—?"

"No more nonsense! I will tell you what to do!"

He instructed her. After supper she was to ascend to her room and tie her clothes in a bundle. Toss them from the window. And then make some excuse to her family and leave the house. Bring the clothes to his store. He sold suitcases; he would give—give!—her a suitcase. And fifty dollars. The evening local left at a quarter of ten. She could steal along alleys to the station. She was not to buy a ticket. She was to wait in the station shadows and just before the conductor called all aboard she was to hurry to the train. Pay the conductor on the train. St. Paul. A fine job! And never write so much as a line to anybody.

She obeyed him. Acting fugitive, she felt fugitive. She felt a sinner, an outcast. She felt Mr. Christianson had helped her. She vanished into St. Paul. Her disappearance caused quite a stir in New Stockholm, till the station agent reported glimpsing her boarding the train. The town speculated why she had acted as she did. Mr. and Mrs. Peter Swanson felt vaguely disgraced.

She knew nobody in St. Paul. The train arrived at eleven on that April night, and when she descended to the platform in her countrified clothes she was assailed by terror as well as homesickness. Already New Stockholm seemed a week behind, and she was dreadfully lonely for her brothers and sisters and all the familiar things of the little town.

She put down her suitcase and stood wondering what to do. She saw people being greeted by other people. Those not greeted went striding along through the coughing noises of locomotives. She longed to board a train and go back, but Mr. Christianson would be furious. He was an important man, and in her ignorance and sense of sin she didn't know what he might do. Spread the tidings, perhaps, that she was bad. And the lot of a bad woman in New Stockholm was not joyous.

And so at last she mingled with the people hurrying along the platform to the stairs leading up to the station. When she emerged into its marble vastness she was taken aback. Beneath its vaulted ceiling she beheld more people than dwelt in the entire town of New Stockholm.

It seemed everybody in the station was staring at her and speculating. In New Stockholm everybody would have stared at a strange girl and speculated. She had no inkling of how cities dull humanity's curiosity. She found a bench and sat down. Once there, she was afraid to move. She realized that by and by she would have to leave the station, but the prospect terrified her. Through the windows she could see the office buildings of St. Paul and hear the honking of taxis and the clanging of owl cars, and she experienced panic.

Mabel spent the night in the station. Almost never before had she sat up later than ten, and by 2 A.M. she was woozy for sleep. Yet she dared not yield. Somebody might steal her grip or her purse. She sat with her gaze lowered, and you would not have supposed her a girl frightened and bewildered. She had endurance, stoicism. She looked like a country girl waiting for a train. She even managed that faint smile. Sometimes she prayed, explaining to God she hadn't meant to rouse the devil in Mr. Christianson and that she was very sorry.

Toward dawn the station crowds thinned, and a few seats away she saw an abandoned newspaper. It occurred to her she might find in its columns the notice of a room for rent, but she didn't know whether it would be right to appropriate the paper. Whoever left it might return. But at last she reached for it.

The swarming ads astounded her, they were so many. They suggested the vastness of the city. She was afraid, and she wanted to cry. But crying might attract attention. So she smiled. Her smile was becoming her defense.

The prices asked for rooms confirmed her superstition that everybody in St. Paul was wealthy. She selected an ad with the lowest price. It said, "Walking Distance." She did not understand what was meant by that.

Daylight came. Back in New Stockholm she would be missed. But with bleak northern resignation she told herself the past was over. She could not go back. She had sinned and she must suffer. She acquiesced. Life was harsh. She was like the wife of some northern seafaring man lost in a storm.

She dreaded picking up her suitcase and walking, but one did what one must. Again she felt everybody was staring and she flushed. Passing a lunch counter she smelled coffee, and she realized she was hungry. She paused, gathering courage. Her good sense told her the counter was there to sell food, but her shyness was so imperious that when finally she made herself sit upon a stool it was a deed of courage.

"Toast and coffee," she said in her low voice.

"Right away, honey," the waitress said. She was middle-aged and Mabel wanted to burst into tears of gratitude.

She had the Scandinavian passion for coffee; always a pot had simmered on the Swanson cookstove; and now it gave her strength. As she ate her eyes were downcast, but her ears picked up the voices of St. Paul. She did not always understand the wit of the lunch-counter badinage, but she admired the ease with which it was tossed off. When the waitress brought her check Mabel performed another act of courage. She showed her the newspaper and asked how to reach the lodging house.

The waitress rattled off directions. They were too complicated for easy comprehension. The waitress asked:

"You new in the city?"

Mabel nodded.

"Well now, wait a minute, honey. My shift will be over at eight. My car goes within a block of that address. You wait till my shift's over and go with me."

"Thank you," Mabel whispered.

There was nothing wrong with the waitress, she told Mabel as they left the station, except her feet. The arches. Except for her arches, her health was impeccable.

"Oh-h?" Mabel said. "That is too bad."

You would not have supposed her weeping dry tears of gratitude. Her face was serene and composed. You would not have thought her a girl experiencing a miracle. Nor did the waitress resemble a Samaritan. She was just an ordinary woman, doubtless full of human faults. Yet extraordinary, now. She sensed it vaguely, bathed as she was in Mabel's current of invisible gratitude. She felt elation as she escorted Mabel to the streetcar. It seemed unlikely that an act of simple kindness could be so refreshing after a night's hard work.

After they boarded the car and it banged along the grim old streets the woman asked:

"You have friends in the city?"

"No."

"What'll you do here?"

"I will have to find a job."

"Any experience?"

And although Mabel had had quite amazing experience, clerking for Mr. Christianson, she shook her head.

"Now you listen to me, honey. The thing for you to do, you go to an agency."

Mabel gazed at her with that serene, inquiring look that could mean anything.

"I got my job through this agency," the woman said. "It ain't much of a job but I ain't much of a looker. Now with a beauty like you, honey, you ought to pick off a lot in tips. I'll write down the name and address of this agency and you go there."

At the last moment, upon impulse, the waitress left the car with Mabel and helped her find the lodginghouse and deal with the landlady. It was one of those smoke-colored old dwellings into which society jams healthy young people from the country. Mabel's room was small, but it had a window with an unexcelled view of an alley and junky back yards, and she felt lucky to have it. When she had been left alone, she lay on the bed and closed her eyes. She slept like a child.

Late in the afternoon she awakened hungry, and that meant she must venture forth for another encounter with the city. She dreaded it and yet, perversely, anticipated it. Sleep had given her strength. Homesickness was a weight on her heart, but she so fully accepted the impossibility of ever returning to New Stockholm that she achieved tranquillity. And despite her loneliness and apprehensions, she took a simple pleasure in her own beauty as she stood at the mirror pinning up her hair. It had never been bobbed, for New Stockholm considered bobbed hair depraved, and as she wound it about her head in simple braids it was radiant with complex shadings of flaxen and sunny straw and candle-flame yellow. She stepped back from the dresser, and in the mirror her face with its high cheekbones was grave and composed.

Outside, the spring afternoon was mild with late sunshine. Mabel's timidity returned, but no longer did she experience the panic of last night in the station. With her rent paid in advance, she could think, "Well, I have at least a roof over my head." And gradually the wonders she beheld jostled aside her shyness. Passing the statehouse, she thought: "That is where the governor works." It awed her. Heretofore the governor had been a legendary half-god in a civics textbook, somebody like George Washington, and all the machinery of state had operated in some remote fourth dimension. Staring at the Capitol, she felt in the center of things, as much at the hub of empire as a girl from some English village gazing upon Buckingham Palace. And although she realized her unimportance and rusticity, still she could not but feel a momentary vanity and superiority over most residents of New Stockholm.

She mingled with the crowds on Wabasha Street, bombarded by multitudinous new impressions; streetcars loaded with home-bound workers; traffic policemen; show windows displaying fish packed in ice; puppies tumbling in a pet shop window; lurid posters outside a picture theater; the gassy city smells flowing from alleys. She stared through the window of a florist shop, consumed by wonder at a business as frivolous as that, for men in New Stockholm would as soon have flung currency into a stove as buy posies.

Opulence! Luxury! Passing a hotel she beheld a Negro doorman in a green uniform; a man and woman, laughing, emerged and stepped into a taxi. Mabel trudged on, and when she reached a boulevard overlooking the Mississippi River she paused, bewildered by all she had seen. Her prudent northern soul could not approve of existence thus embellished, and the stern religion of her fathers told her that St. Paul must be as wicked as Nineveh. And even though a sinner herself, even though she intended lying and naming a fictitious town when people asked where she was from, she nevertheless felt an evangelical superiority to the primrose-path treaders she had seen.

For a long time she lingered on the bluff above the river, while twilight darkened the great sweeping curves of the water and lights winked on in South St. Paul. Far away she perceived a network of railroad tracks and she recognized the Union Station: that she knew a landmark added to her courage. Once a man smelling of liquor swayed near her and doffed his hat and suggested dinner together. To Mabel his mentioning dinner when noon was long past indicated how drunk he must be; her refusal was prim, and she left the river. His accosting her had not frightened her, as might be supposed after her experience with Mr. Christianson, for he was outside the self-righteous barricade of the little church in New Stockholm. It was Mr. Christianson's Swedish blood and prominence in that church that had robbed her of the ability to cope with what happened and its consequences; their being within the barricade together had tinged the situation with almost a father-and-daughter flavor, and that was why she had shared his conviction of sin and obeyed him.

Returning along Wabasha Street, she thought about the back room of the furniture store and she relived her sleepless terror of that night. And from the wicked whisperings of high school companions she knew enough biology to realize that her flight to St. Paul might not be the last of the consequences. The possibility blew like an icy wind across her mind. Her countenance did not reveal her fear. In the lighted street she looked tranquil and beautiful and she was smiling gently. "I will know next week," she thought, "and I will cross that bridge when I reach it."

By now she was very hungry, and she entered a wondrous place called a cafeteria, with acres of terrazzo. She filled her tray with good, solid northern food; roast beef and mashed potatoes and pie; and as she sat eating it occurred to her that a girl might very well get a job here even if she were without experience. She watched girls going from table to table, gathering up empty trays and soiled dishes, and she thought: "I could do that." So after paying her check she lingered by the cash register, and when the cashier had a free moment she asked for a job.

"You'll have to talk to Mr. Costello," the cashier said; and she beckoned a dapper man of thirty with eel-slick black hair. He ushered her into his office, and from his air of destiny you would have supposed him a theatrical manager hiring an actress for some great role. And his black little eyes suggested this too, the way they darted over the beauty of her face and figure. At last, in a confidential voice, he said: "It's bad, you not having experience, but maybe I could start you gathering trays."

And so next day she went to work there, and presently she advanced to a job of rolling silverware in napkins so they would be handy for customers; and at the end of a month she stood behind the counter dishing up food. Sometimes business took Mr. Costello behind the counter and he brushed against Mabel, and from the way he eyed her she realized he was up to no good. She had experience now, so in August she secured a job as a real waitress in the restaurant where Captain Latcher found her.

By then, after several months in St. Paul, the city had veneered her with what many persons so veneered like to call sophistication. The wonders which had sharply impressed her senses were now commonplace. She knew her way about the city and about Minneapolis, too; she was aware of which bargain basements really sold bargains; and with the advice of the other girls in the lodginghouse she dressed to look like St. Paul instead of New Stockholm. Nevertheless, underneath it all, she was the same Mabel. Her worries about bearing a child had proved groundless, but her sense of sin persisted. Every Sunday she attended church, shocked at first by the advanced ideas held by members of this metropolitan congregation. They attended movies, played bridge, golfed on Sunday afternoon; and the minister smoked. In his sermons he sometimes hinted that hell was not precisely a pleasure resort, but he did not elaborate upon the wails of sizzling souls.

Sometimes the young people held parties in the church basement, and these were gay affairs. Mabel met many large pink-and-blond boys of her own age, and they took her to moving pictures and to amusement parks. She learned to dance. Now and then she was embraced and kissed good night, and twice she verged on falling in love. And hastily backtracked.

For only now did the real mischief of Mr. Christianson's rashness become manifest: he had impregnated her with a sense of sin that had grown monstrous in the dark cellar of her mind where she tried to keep it locked. She tortured herself with the conviction that she was not as other girls, and she believed that with a past like hers she could never marry a nice boy. And without marriage, what could the future hold?

Growing more adult, she argued with herself, trying to convince her tenacious little mind that the fault had been all Mr. Christianson's. But her emotions disbelieved. She recalled passages the New Stockholm pastor, with great lip-smacking, had read from the Bible, wherein neurotic old prophets railed against wicked women; and she remembered conversations in the lodginghouse when the girls, talking shop, discussed how to handle fresh guys and agreed that rare was the man who could not be handled unless the girl wished otherwise.

So in secret her worry grew, feeding upon its own absurdity, thriving in sunless soil, abnormal and ghostly, as unhealthy as the tainted mushrooms that luxuriate in dankness and darkness. Captain Latcher was exactly the dashing fellow to fling open that cellar door of her mind and usher in the sunlight and sweet air.

The café where Mabel worked was owned by a Danish woman, Mrs. Justesen. A few New Stockholm prejudices against Danes still clung to Mabel—they were pretty mercurial and vivacious, most of them hardly likely to sneak past St. Peter—but at least Mrs. Justesen wasn't always brushing against her like Mr. Costello.

Her working day began at seven, and being conscientious she always arrived on time. On the morning when she met Captain Latcher, she left her lodging at six-thirty and hurried toward town. Street lamps were still burning, although the east was scarlet, and the sharp autumn morning silvered her breath as it left her lips.

She was a strikingly pretty girl, clattering along on high heels. In sheer hosiery her ankles were as beautifully cut as diamonds, her calves richly curved; and her woolen coat from a cheap store gained distinction and symmetry from her figure. The crisp air brought a faint color to her smooth skin.

Few people were yet abroad. Off toward the river, Mabel could see thick mist rising, and although the dingy old city, encrusted with coal smoke and corruption, looked surprised by the dawn, like some old roisterer caught at daybreak leaving a house of ill fame, yet it had a certain smudgy freshness too, like a morning paper.

The wall-clock said five of seven when Mabel entered the café. It was all window glass and white walls and steamy warmth. She changed to her uniform, wondering about today's tips. Soon the breakfast rush began, and as she hurried oatmeal and wheatcakes to the famished, aware of the city outside growing busier by the minute, she did not feel like an unimportant corpuscle in the economic bloodstream; she felt in the midst of things and consequential. It gave her a sense of duty faithfully discharged when she perceived how the food she carried to some salesman changed him from a grumpy bundle of desire to go on sleeping into a wide-awake go-getter.

The first rush had subsided when Mabel saw two men enter and select one of her tables. Oddly enough, her interest was not snared by the lad of her own age. Pimply-faced, his nose thick-bridged, his mouth an oblique gash, he looked a queer mingling of arrogance and sneakiness. His body seemed uneasy in his new suit, and after he sat down he ran his forefinger around under his collar.

The other man attracted her notice. He swung a light stick, like some high-born Englishman in the movies, and after hanging up his hat and topcoat he surveyed the café with an altogether lordly air. He was Clive of India and Wellington. Her study of history having been interrupted by Mr. Christianson, Mabel did not realize this; but she thought he looked romantic. His lean countenance with its clipped mustache and browned skin hinted of encounters with tropic suns, and his high baldish forehead did not suggest the dullness of middle age but rather the bare power in the head of a high-velocity bullet.

Although she denied it later, it was actually her fault about Willie's eggs being cooked turn-over style instead of sunny-side-up. She wasn't heeding Willie's orders as she should, for awareness of the Captain filled her consciousness. As he told her what food he wished, his gaze was not fresh or lustful but alert and friendly and interested. She felt her cheeks warming. She kept saying, "Yes, sir," but she was thinking how pleasant it would be to go out with a man like that instead of Swedish boys. Upon reaching the kitchen, she remembered Willie had spoken of eggs turn-over style, but she did not recall that he had sneered his hatred of eggs thus prepared. So she told the cook to fix them that way.

Waiting for the food, she busied herself about the café, but she managed to steal glances at the Captain. She couldn't see his face now, for the morning paper concealed it, but his whole attitude had poise and a careless Oxonian grace.

Then she set down the eggs before Willie, who bristled like a Prussian haircut, and mortification flushed her throat. But the Captain put down his paper, shaming the vicious-looking fellow; and the verbal punishment he so soundly administered stirred instincts in Mabel that had been buried under centuries of ice and Lutheranism and frock-coated decorum.

She thought the Captain was courage and strength, and she felt weak and docile, and these elemental sensations were so confusing and yet voluptuous that she thought they must be wicked. After he had gone, leaving a twenty-five cent tip, she kept looking at the sheet of paper he had given her, which would admit her to the indoor circus; and she even rummaged through the kitchen wastebasket, vainly seeking the old newspaper in which his picture had appeared.

"But why am I thinking about him?" she asked herself. "He will never give me another thought."

Yet think about him she did, during the noon assault of the hungry, during the afternoon lull. She felt awakened and more alive than usual, and at the same time delectably happy and sweetly sad. As she waited on customers her smile had never been more shyly mysterious, her serenity so pristine.

She entertained daydreams, too; they flowed through her thoughts like a slow stream of honey. She imagined going out with the Captain to some fashionable restaurant. And strangely, as she imagined her association with him, Mr. Christianson's wicked deed did not loom as an obstacle but rather as a force behind her, pushing her into greater wickedness. For she realized that all along she had thought of the Captain as a man who must be wicked. He was a circus performer; he had a worldly air; doubtless he had made love to many women. All wicked. But how attractively so! His wickedness must exceed hers; she would not be wronging him by falling in love, as she would be wronging nice Swedish boys with that northern fetish for intact bridal maidenheads.

"I am outside the gates of the Kingdom," she meditated, her thoughts phrasing themselves in the scriptural imagery she had heard on dozens of Sundays. "Perhaps it is God's will that I should fall among tares and thistles."

Captain Latcher didn't look very thistlelike when he strode jauntily into the café at midafternoon.

"I say," he exclaimed, "this is a bit of luck, finding you. I fancied you might have toddled off home."

"Oh, no. I do not leave till four."

"Could you bring me a spot of tea, Mabel?"

When she put the tea before him he smiled and said:

"By jolly, I don't know where my manners were this morning. Beastly of me to invite you to the performance and not arrange to see you home. May I count on your waiting for me at the entrance, after the show?"

"Yes. I will be there."

Her lips seemed to mold themselves about her words, so that the vowels in her low voice were as round and true as notes of music.

A colossal sports palace. Thousands of cigarette tips glowing in the murk. A mauve cloud of tobacco smoke hanging under the roof. A band playing. A ring, glaring calcium-white. An arena. A lean man, snapping together booted ankles and bowing.

Mabel sat in the first balcony, first row. She had never witnessed a circus. She had never beheld sand-colored lions, or tigers striped in flame and night. She bent forward, intent. Her fingers were clenched.

"I served him breakfast," she thought, "and I served him tea."

Into the arena he strode, so brave, so hard-bitten, so the master of his beasts. Fear for his welfare lumped her throat. Her lips were parted, her eyes wide. She was with him in the arena. His dangers were hers. His mastery was hers. Nothing had ever stirred her that way. Somewhere in her mind she was crying mutely, "Our Father who art in heaven—protect him—please God—do not let him be hurt."

And when at last he nimbly gained the safety cage, escaping the wild beast crashing the door, and when he bowed amid the band-blare and the roaring surf of voices, Mabel sank back in her seat, limp, and she whispered, "Thank you, God. Oh, thank you."

She did not even notice the cage boy, standing so valiantly at attention.

The band played comic tunes and clowns came tumbling in. She did not remain. Anything in the ring would be anticlimax now; and besides, she feared that if she lingered till the show was over she would be delayed in the throngs and he might not wait for her. When she reached the foyer she cast a swift glance around for him, although her good peasant sense told her he could not by this time have changed into street clothes.

She stood against the wall, serene-looking, patient. But her heart was beating fast and her blood tingled. That barnlike place with its littered concrete floor enhanced her beauty. Once a trio of sporty-looking men left the circus and ogled her loveliness. She ignored them; and she thought: "If he were by my side they would not look at me like that."

Presently applause thundered inside and she heard the rumbling of the spectators leaving. The doors banged open and they came pouring out. The torrent swelled, and then she glimpsed Captain Latcher, a white muffler at his throat, edging in from the street. When he saw her he lifted his cane, and he cried out to the mob, "I say, let a chap through, eh?"

He was recognized. People nudged one another. It did not in the least embarrass him. When he reached Mabel he exclaimed:

"By jolly, what a current! Nothing like it since I swam the Hellespont!"

And although the only time the Hellespont had dampened his toes

was when he read Lord Byron's biography, it sounded very romantic.
Nor did he really mean to lie. So mercurial was his imagination that
often he almost believed he had performed the exploits of his fancy.
He lied as easily as he breathed, and he had no difficulty breathing.

Never having heard of the Hellespont, Mabel did not comprehend.
But her eyes were shining with admiration, and her gentle smile was
magical. She always smiled when she did not understand.

He took her arm, but before he could pilot her through the crowd a
group of high school girls accosted him with out-thrust autograph
books. They were about Mabel's age, but they seemed years younger.
Her slow temperament gave her poise.

Flourishing out his fountain pen, he dashed off his signature, the
large letters covering half a page. He smiled charmingly at the girls.
This troubled Mabel. But it did not nick her surface serenity.

"Great bore, autograph hunters," he said, as they emerged to the
sidewalk; and her jealousy left her.

He lifted his stick and called, "Cabby!" And he named a restaurant
in Minneapolis.

Minneapolis! It startled her. The cab meter would tick off a fortune. Moreover, because she dwelt in St. Paul, she harbored prejudice
against Minneapolis. Prejudices veined her nature the way granite
veins northern mountains.

"Anyway, I will try to enjoy myself," she thought.

"Well, little Viking," the Captain was saying, "did you enjoy the
show?"

"You were wonderful," she murmured.

"Eh? By jolly! Surely not that good!"

"Oh-h-h, yes! I was so-o afraid for you. How can you be so brave?"

"It's nothing."

"Oh-h, you are too modest. It gave me a fright in my heart. All
around me people talked about your bravery."

"I say, now! You're not pulling my leg?"

A street light flashed across her face and showed him her bewilderment.

"Sorry, old girl," he chuckled. "A bit of slang, you know. I mean
you're not having one on me. Not kidding me?"

"I would not do that. I think no man is so brave as you. All those
people watching with their hearts in their mouths—"

"By jolly," he chuckled, "I believe you mean it."

"Oh-h, of course I mean it."

The conversation flowed in this channel for some time without
boring either.

Promptly at seven next morning Mabel left the café kitchen and
hurried about her duties of feeding the hungry, precisely as if she had

spent last evening rinsing stockings instead of in the company of a famous animal trainer. But she had changed.

Her eyes and smile had a dreaming quality, and she felt the way a springtime flower feels on a warm hillside when after the delectable agony of swelling into bud it at last bursts open. Her movements were as graceful as a flower's in sunny wind, and like a flower she existed at the center of her own bright nimbus.

"I am in love, then," she told herself. "This is what it is like."

How it would all end she did not know. Saturday would come and he would finish his engagement and leave St. Paul; and what then? She tried not to speculate, to live in the ecstasy of the moment only. She was a little tipsy, like some golden-winged midge that had fluttered into a glass of sweet wine, slowly drowning but too deliriously intoxicated to care.

Nothing had happened last night; nothing remotely similar to her experience with Mr. Christianson. The Captain had not kissed her or even held her hand, except when they danced in the festive restaurant. A time or two he had called her his golden kitten, and perhaps he was employing his usual prudence in breaking a fresh cat.

He had, however, urged her to attend the circus again tonight and to meet him afterward.

"Yes," she whispered, "I will be there."

He had not mentioned seeing her this morning, but she expected that of course he would come to breakfast here. When the rush of customers thinned she glanced at the clock, and for the next hour she expected him. He would stride into the café, swinging his stick, and she would humbly serve him.

What she did not realize was that an English gentleman has a sense of the fitness of things. A chap who—in imagination—had prepared for life upon the playing field of Eton simply couldn't permit the girl of the night before to serve him breakfast.

"Maybe then he has changed his mind about me," Mabel thought, as the clock showed noon; and her blood turned leaden. "Yet—he invited me to the circus again."

And so all through the luncheon hour and the afternoon she was, by turns, miserable and keenly happy. Remembering the autograph seekers of last night, she tormented herself, imagining other idolatresses storming his hotel. Perhaps one would be a beautiful heiress, wicked at heart, and the Captain would succumb.

That reminded her that she too was wicked, and the old horror filled her mind, as if the occurrence in the furniture store had left her unclean and unfit for Captain Latcher. She told herself she had been incorrect in supposing him wicked, because he performed in a circus; and so again her past heaved up as a barrier between her and happiness.

"But I would not need to tell him," she thought; but at once she added, "Oh, I would have to, I would have to, and he would cast me aside."

But at ten minutes of four all these tortures vanished, for Captain Latcher entered the café.

"Mabel," he exclaimed. "I say, you're looking fit!"

She wanted to burst into tears of joy. She said smoothly:

"You have come for your tea?"

"Not at all, old girl. You're off at four, right? I'll wait for you and stroll along with you."

Always before, like a peasant giving good measure, she had waited till four to change from her uniform; but now she hurried through the swinging doors. The clock hands lacked thirty seconds of four when she left with the Captain. She felt like royalty, walking beside him.

"You know, Mabel," he said, "you're a beautiful girl."

A flush tinted her cheeks.

"Maybe you are only flattering me," she murmured.

"Not at all, old bug! You know, I fancy you're rather like a Swiss watch, small but finely made. What makes you tick, Mabel?"

Shyly, she glanced up.

"Do I tick?"

He laughed lightly.

"Tick, tick, tick—yes, old Viking, you tick. And so do I, when I'm with you. By jolly, you've been ticking in my thoughts all day."

"Oh?"

"Rather! As the Bard says, in the spring a young man's fancy . . . Only it's not spring, you know, and I'm not young."

"I do not like young boys," she said. "They are so-o—young."

He laughed again and exclaimed:

"By jolly, you turn a neat phrase!" And guiding her toward a florist shop he added, "I have a bit of business to transact."

Mabel did not for a second imagine they had entered the shop so he might buy her a corsage, and even when the lovely violets were in her hand she was unbelieving. Then he said:

"For you, Mabel." And to the clerk: "I say, do you have something like a pin we could use to fasten them on?"

A sudden moisture threatened her eyes, and she buried her face in the flowers and drew a long breath.

"Oh-h," she told him, "they are wonderful!" And on the street she asked, "How did you ever think to buy me such a present?"

"Why, Mabel old girl, can't you guess? Flowers speak, as the Bard says, a language one's tongue does not dare employ. Can't you guess, Mabel?"

She felt dazzled.

And so after the performance that evening they met again in the foyer, only this time he did not give the cabdriver a Minneapolis address but instead named his hotel, the best in town.

"Last night," he said airily, "we danced and supped in a gay company. I thought tonight we might go to my diggings, eh? Order food brought in, and talk."

"Do you think," she asked slowly, "that is proper?"

"Oh, quite. Quite. Well, old girl, how did the act go tonight?"

"It was so-o thrilling. You were wonderful."

"Eh? Was I now, really?"

"Oh-h, yes," she said, almost somberly. "So wonderful. I was frightened for you."

The Captain thought Mabel the best theatrical critic he had ever encountered, and they were still discussing the act when they reached the hotel. In his room, while he lifted the telephone and ordered food, her gaze wandered from the dresser, with its military brushes and leather traveling case and tiny scissors for clipping his mustache, to the writing desk where three framed photographs stood. She studied them with admiration. They depicted the Captain mastering his cats. Presently he joined her and shared her admiration.

A knock fell on the door, and after the table had been laid he tipped the waiter handsomely and said:

"By the bye, old chap, don't bother returning for these dishes tonight. Pick them up in the morning."

To her it seemed luxury attained its apex with this private supper. The night outside had been raw, but here in his room everything was coziness and soft light. As they ate the Captain yarned on prodigiously, and if many of his stories were fanciful it didn't really matter, because his manner was so charming and worldly. Mabel's slow mind did not attempt to absorb the details of his experiences, but the total impression was highly flavored with valor. She was like a country girl on a station platform at night, with a luxury train whizzing past; she was aware of the locomotive scintillating sparks and power, and she glimpsed scenes of wealth and urbanity in the dining car and Pullmans.

Sometimes when he paused for breath she put in a word or two. "Oh?" she said, or "I think that is so-o interesting." And she smiled. This provided the Captain ample encouragement to talk on.

"Old girl," he said once, "what are your plans for the future?"

"I do not have plans."

"Come now. One must have plans. Surely you don't intend working in that café forever."

"It is a good enough job."

"Aren't you planning marriage with some lucky chap?"

"No-o. I have no plans."

"By jolly, Mabel—I'm going to miss you when I leave."

"I will miss you, too. It is sad to think about."

"Sad! Righto! By jolly, little bug, I have a notion to pack you into my luggage and carry you away with me."

She smiled. It might have meant anything.

"How about it, Mabel?"

"I think you are having fun with me," she said.

"No! Never more serious! Come to Chicago with me, eh?"

"Why are you inviting me to do that?"

The Captain sprang up, rounded the table, seized her hands and pulled her to her feet.

"Because I love you, old bug. I love you."

He embraced her and kissed her, again and again. Her arms went around him, but presently she pushed him away, and she was sobbing.

"Mabel! I say, old girl! What's wrong?"

She turned away and sank to the bed.

"Come, come, Mabel. Don't you love me?"

"I will never love anybody else."

Exhilaration flashed through him like electricity.

"Mabel! By jove! A great love, eh?" He paced the carpet as if springs were coiled beneath his insteps. "To think," he exclaimed, "that a chap like me—getting along in years—to think—like Heloise and Abelard, eh?—God's own mad lover, as the Bard says, dying on a kiss!"

"You are not old. You are wonderful. You are too good for me. I have been bad, and—and—"

She flung herself down, weeping copiously now, her hands clenched on the counterpane.

"I say, I say," the Captain exclaimed.

He lay by her side, stroking her hair, whispering endearments, and he told her that whatever she had done she could never in his eyes be bad.

"Tell me, old girl. Tell me about it."

"I can't."

"Come, come. Bad? Nonsense. What did you do, old child? Steal a stick of chalk from school?"

"Oh-h, no! I never did that."

"What did you do, Mabel?"

"I worked," she said slowly, "in a furniture store."

The Captain was taken aback. "You did what, old bug?"

"Mr. Christianson," she whispered, nearly choked. "It was in the back room. He—he—"

She buried her face and sobbed heartbrokenly.

"Christianson? What did he do?"

"He—he—oh, I cannot tell you!"

"Come, come, old girl. You must. He—ah—this Christianson blighter rather took you unawares, eh? By force, eh?"

"He was very strong," Mabel admitted slowly. "I was surprised. I did not know what to do."

"By jolly! You had the gendarmes at him, I trust?"

She looked bewildered. "What?"

"The bobbies. The constables. You brought him to justice and all that, eh? The police."

"Oh-h, no-o! He made me promise to tell nobody! He made me leave town."

"Eh? How was that?"

And so slowly, bit by bit, the Captain pried the whole story from Mabel, and the enormity of Christianson's villainy set him pacing again, this time in rage.

"By jove!" he exclaimed. "The bloody rascal deserves to be caned! By jolly! I should like to challenge him. Run a rapier through his heart!" And after dueling in his imagination, and wiping his blade clean of Christianson's blood, the Captain asked:

"But why do you say you are bad, little bug?"

"Why? Because—he said—he said I was temptation. He said he could not help himself—he—"

"Mabel!" The Captain sat down, took her hand. "Don't you see, old child, the fellow was trying to pass the buck?"

"You do not think it was my fault? You do not think that God will punish me, then?"

"God? Not a bit of it, old Viking. I daresay God is as outraged as I am about the whole matter."

And although the Captain had never studied theology in military school, he launched into a discussion of the religious aspect of the affair. The God about whom he talked was created in the Captain's image, a broad-minded, rather jolly chap, something of a man-about-town. Mabel listened wonderingly, and although the Captain's words seemed faintly blasphemous they were exceedingly convincing. And now she had unburdened herself she found her sense of sin diminished.

As he talked he slipped his arm about her, and he murmured:

"You must forget all this, Mabel. Come to Chicago with me."

Then he was kissing her, and she thought:

"I will do what he wishes. Anything he wishes."

That was not quite true. As they lay there the Captain made two requests of Mabel: that she stay the night with him, and that she quit her waitress job at once. To one request she acceded, but she refused the other; for after all she was a good, steady, conscientious girl, and she thought it would hardly be right to quit her job without giving more notice.

"I will finish the week at the café," she said.

"Oh, come now. No need at all to do that."

"I think I had better finish the week. Besides Mrs. Justesen owes me wages and if I do not go back at all how could I collect?"

"Bother the wages!"

"But the money is mine and owing to me."

So in the end the Captain yielded, although it seemed not quite decorous to permit his inamorata to wait tables.

Those next months were lavishly happy. There are always hazards when a girl chases off with a man twice her age, and a lion tamer in the bargain. The Captain might well have turned out a rake who would have brought about a delicate condition in Mabel and then abandoned her, but this didn't happen. After all, Captain Latcher was a gentleman in the great tradition of honor on the playing field and Trafalgar and the long week end; and besides, Mabel was so toothsome a morsel that abandoning her never entered his head.

He enjoyed her companionship. With her silences, she was a wonderful audience, and his tongue felt as uninhibited as a phonograph needle. He loved escorting her about Chicago, his walking stick pointing out the many wonders of that up-and-coming metropolis; indeed, his manner suggested that responsibility for these wonders was about ninety-five percent his. When he explained such marvels as how the Chicago River had been reversed she seemed greatly impressed, and she said:

"Oh-h?"

But this enthusiasm was spurious. Mabel secretly believed St. Paul surpassed Chicago as much as it surpassed Minneapolis. However, she never argued. The closest she came to disputing him was the day he quoted statistics to prove that Chicago harbored more Germans than Hamburg, more Finns than Helsinki, more Ethiopians than Addis Ababa.

"I think there are more Swedes in St. Paul," she said.

"Eh? Oh, yes. Quite. Quite."

He rather doubted this, but realizing that companionship between men and women is a matter of give-and-take he didn't dispute her. His statistics were shaky anyway; he had just been talking to amuse himself; so he scrambled to safer ground and related his experiences on an animal-trapping expedition into Central America, where neither of them had been.

During that winter they journeyed to a score of cities, presenting the act; and if Mabel's intelligence quotient did not soar, at least her knowledge of the world increased. Unlike Willie Krummer, who had struggled and squirmed when the world tried to veneer him with its conventions, Mabel was so passive that *savoir-faire* slipped over her as gracefully as sheer hosiery over her legs.

Her supply of hosiery had increased, as well as her stock of pumps and frocks and pretty lingerie. She was so lovely that the Captain

enjoyed seeing her smartly dressed, and he was always suggesting that
they go shopping.

"But I have more clothes now than I need," she said.

"Oh, come, come, little Viking. The world accepts one at one's own
valuation. Clothes make the man want to make the woman, eh?"

He broke out laughing and exclaimed:

"Not bad, eh? Rather good, don't you think?"

And although such flashes of wit always bounced off Mabel's bright
head like a light ray off a mirror, she smiled and said:

"Oh-h, yes. Very good."

And so in a city like Dallas they went to a store like Neiman-Marcus,
where in showrooms of thick-carpeted luxury the Captain leaned on his
stick or lounged in a chair, almost desperately British, while Mabel
tried on frocks. His thin, pleasant face lighted as the unfamiliar dresses
pointed up afresh her luminous hair and clear skin, and gave new
piquancy to the richness of her bosom and hips.

"By jolly!" he told himself. "The female form divine! A Swedish
Venus! How all the other chaps must envy me!"

Perhaps because he was so concerned with her bodily charm, the
Captain never discovered Mabel's great simplicity. Because she endowed his existence with dazzling magic, he assumed there were enchanted glens in her mind, as full of witchery as Grieg's music. Those
silences! Those opulent, half-smiling silences! Her low voice, her
vowels as rounded as her breasts!

In their hotel rooms, he loved to while away the time lounging back
on the pillows, smoking an English Oval and watching her dress. Perhaps she would be clad in the scanties he had bought her once, a brassière and panties of expensive black satin and spider-web lace. To his
nostrils came the sweetness of her powders and colognes, mingling
deliciously with the scent of his Turkish tobacco; and his gaze delighted itself following the seam of her stockings up to the smooth
creaminess peeking through the frivolous lace.

"By jolly, old chick!" he exclaimed. "You have a maddening
beauty!" And although he wasn't watching her face he added, "Like
Helen of Troy. Was this the face that launched ten thousand jolly
old ships!"

She turned from the mirror, rewarding him over her pearly shoulder with that tantalizing smile.

"I love you," she said, the delicious timbre of her voice tingling his
spine. "You are so-o good to me."

Sometimes she surprised him, not often enough to discomfit him,
but often enough to keep his interest alert. Perhaps some afternoon
when she had not accompanied him to the auditorium, where the business of setting up the arena engaged him, he would return to the hotel
and find her absent. And instantly, he felt as lonely as an actor on the

stage of an empty theater. Restless. Sometimes a tiny, foolish panic came to him. What if she had left him?

"Oh, rot!" he told himself. "The little chick loves me."

At those moments he seriously considered marrying her. After all, why not? It was more dashing this way; an affair appealed more to his romantic nature than matrimony; but, all in all, marriage offered certain advantages, such as immunity from arrest for whisking the little Viking across state lines.

"It's something to consider, marriage," he meditated.

When she returned he was immensely relieved; he took her into his arms and kissed her; and casually he asked:

"Where were you, old girl?"

"Oh-h, I was just walking."

Did her smile conceal something? A rendezvous with some caddish chap?

"I missed you," he said.

"Oh-h? I missed you too, Philip."

Their gazes met; the innocence and serenity of her eyes convinced him he had misjudged her.

But she had her secrets. One was a passion for chocolate sodas. As a child in New Stockholm ice cream had been rare as hummingbirds in January; and now she was making up. In their early days together, when she invariably ordered sodas, the Captain made light fun of this appetite, not in an unkind spirit, but because he was tenderly amused and charmed. Mabel, however, had feared he really disapproved; so now when opportunity offered she slipped into a drugstore and enravished her tongue with cool, delicious mixtures.

Once in Kansas City she was gone for so long that he was really alarmed. This was shortly before Christmas, and when she returned the packages explained her absence.

"I have been shopping, Philip," she said. "You must not ask questions."

It was but half the truth. She had spent her time in a department store, right enough; but in Toyland. In childhood, Christmas had brought sadness to Mabel. Being practical people, Anna and Peter Swanson always decided it was more sensible to fill their children's mouths with food than their stockings with fripperies. And Christmas mornings without the dolls you had hardly dared hope for—and yet had hoped for—can leave scars on the heart.

Toyland enchanted Mabel. Her eyes shone like a child's as she observed the little trains clattering into make-believe tunnels; she looked on the verge of clapping hands in delight. The sleds, the coaster wagons, the play houses and play furniture—she saw them brighter than they were. But the doll section held her longest. She wanted so badly to buy a doll that she ached with it. Well, there was money in her purse. Useless for her peasant thrift to remonstrate! She yielded.

"I will show you one gift," she told the Captain. "It is not for you. I bought it to give to some poor child."

She unwrapped it and sat cuddling it.

"A doll!" he exclaimed. "A sweet notion, old girl. *Noblesse oblige,* and all that."

For several days Mabel played with it; indeed, December twenty-fourth arrived before she could bring herself to leave it with a Salvation Army Santa.

Often on Sunday morning the Captain awakened to find his pretty bedfellow gone, but these absences he understood. Mabel was in church. His religious instincts were not overpowering, but he had the good sense to realize that attending to the welfare of one's soul is a highly personalized occupation.

"Odd," he told himself. "She seems hardly spiritual. And yet— those northern races are serious-minded chaps."

The truth was that Mabel's sense of sin had revisited her. Not about Mr. Christianson, but about living in iniquity with the Captain. Every evening she prayed that he ask her to marry him. She knelt not in the bedroom, because she was too shy to beseech God in the Captain's worldly presence, but in the bathroom, her elbows on the tub.

And as the weeks of their association multiplied she sometimes dropped hints about marriage. One day she was overjoyed when he said:

"Little chick, I'm thinking of changing your name."

"Oh-h?"

"Righto. If you could just overcome your fear of the cats, I'd break you into the act, and as a professional name Mabel Swanson isn't— well—very *chic*. Let me see, old child. How would Marybelle strike you? Marybelle—Marybelle—ah—Monahan. Marybelle Monahan. Rather unusual, eh? Like it?"

"If that is what you wish," she said quietly.

And then at last, one glorious spring day in Tamarack, the Captain burst into her room and exclaimed:

"Marybelle, old Viking, the hour has struck! Ring out, sweet bells, and all that!"

"What is it that you are saying?" she asked.

"A blushing bride, Marybelle! Let's toddle to the courthouse and buy a license, eh? And find a parson to tie the knot."

"Is it that you wish to marry me?"

"Why not, old girl? Beastly of me not to have thought of it before."

He embraced her, and she whispered:

"Oh-h, Philip—you have made me so very happy."

16

AT THIS late date, everybody knows that an artist of great talent and perhaps genius was working in the Middle West during the 1920's. But when Willie Krummer became a hero and a baron, few persons knew Alex Kerry, and of those who did almost nobody thought he was working. He spent his time painting. Not houses or barns. No. He painted pictures.

His fellow townsmen of Millborough might have tolerated this odd occupation if only it had supported him. It didn't. Never did his pictures achieve the immortality of magazine covers; never were they reproduced and sold in dime stores like the great canvases of Maxfield Parrish. Nor did he get a newspaper job like a practical fellow and draw cartoons.

Alex Kerry had served in the first World War, using his brush in camouflage, and after the Armistice he was stationed in Paris. For him, those were months of intense artistic and intellectual excitement; and upon returning to America he enrolled at the Chicago Art Institute. Years later, one of his instructors told a biographer:

"Alex was nearly thirty when he came to us. He had sketched since he was four, but his only formal instruction had been a course in art by correspondence. He told me that as a farm boy in Iowa he always carried a pad and pencil when he went into the fields, and I suspect he did more sketching than plowing.

"Alex was of medium height with a tendency toward plumpness. He had reddish blond hair, a wide mouth, a funny little upturned nose, and he wore steel-rimmed glasses. His blue eyes were usually amused, and he laughed a lot. He was the most deliberate person I've ever known. You could no more hurry him than you could hurry the sun. He spoke slowly in that flat—almost feminine—voice, and he worked slowly. He'd brush on a few strokes and then step back and stare for five minutes.

"He smoked incessantly—cigarettes he rolled from brown paper. His hands were small and exceedingly deft. After he became famous and had money, he stopped rolling his own and smoked Camels. That was the only visible evidence of his prosperity.

"Alex loved Chicago and the central states. I remember when his paintings caught on. Their calm satire was something new, and when the newspapers reproduced them the readers were furious. They thought he was insulting us. Yet Alex always maintained that the Chicago River was a better subject than the Seine, and he preferred the Near North Side to the Latin Quarter. He liked the raw strength of Chicago and the corn country. He hated the merely picturesque or arty. But he saw our faults too, and because his mind was full of comedy he didn't hesitate to depict them.

"When he studied with us, Alex was very poor. He and another fellow rented an abandoned farmhouse away out north of the city, and he told me later that once he lived for two months on twenty-seven dollars, and most of it he spent commuting. In the winter he slept under his overcoat and old newspapers.

"Finally he went broke and returned to Iowa. I thought that would be the end of Alex. But he had a third cousin in Millborough—a dentist—who believed in him, and Alex fixed up a studio apartment above the dentist's garage. It had an alley entrance. And that's where Alex painted his way to recognition."

Millborough was a pleasant-appearing town with big old houses and maple-shaded streets and so many churches that one would have supposed only godly persons dwelt there. The surrounding country refused to conform to the superstition that the great Mississippi watershed is flat and drab. It was a lovely land of rolling hills and green meadows and wandering creeks and woodlands.

In the early 1920's Alex went much into the country, carrying his easel and stool and his lunch; and all day while the meadow larks whistled he would paint, slowly, methodically. At that period his work was interesting enough, but scarcely unusual. Conventional landscapes. He was happy then. He was still a youngish man and fame was a faraway city which he couldn't see but toward which he was trudging. Sometimes after lunch he lay on the grass, staring into the sky, permitting the rich earth to send its strength into his body. He had a peasant's love for the earth.

And he had a pagan's love for the sun—those early landscapes were flooded with airy yellows—and because he loved its warmth he would strip off his shirt and trousers and lie soaking in golden light. His body was as well covered as if he had been clad in a swimming suit, but in those days sun-bathing had not become fashionable. Farmers plowing corn, upon reaching the end of a row, would see him lying there, not only virtually nude but loafing as well; and one farmer named Hanke, who worked his daughters like mules, compelling them to plow corn, beheld Alex one day lying thus beyond a fence in a meadow. Hanke did not want his daughters to behold a near-naked loafer and get ideas.

So he shouted at Alex to don his pants and be decent, and why wasn't he working? Alex had been pondering how to depict June sky without having it look like a souvenir post card, and he sat up, startled, blinking at the red-faced rustic. And in his slow voice, as flat and dry as desert, he said:

"I beg your pardon."

Instead of mollifying Hanke, this angered him more. He did a lot of guttural talking, and at last Alex asked:

"Is this your land?"

It wasn't, the meadow. But Hanke wished it were—indeed, he had tried to buy it—so naturally he felt insulted. By this time Alex's anger was mounting, and he said:

"You can go to hell."

And he lay down and resumed sun-bathing. Hanke yelled more insults and even threats before he drove away. He plowed no more corn that afternoon. He hopped into his Ford and chugged to Millborough, where he reported Alex to the sheriff.

Fortunately, the sheriff was a young man whose horizons had been broadened by service in France, so instead of arresting Alex for indecent exposure he passed along a friendly warning. It bewildered Alex. He saw nothing vile in the human body. A columnist on the *Millborough Star* heard the story and printed it. He used no names, but when he referred to "a certain local artist" the readers knew he meant Alex.

That was the first of many brushes with the community. Yet Alex lived on there, and few suspected that beneath his calm, heat was generating. He made some friends, of course. In towns all over America there are persons with ideas whom life has stranded. They gravitated to Alex: a high school athletic coach who had studied drama in college and had dreamed of revolutionizing the American theater; a spinster librarian who had once sold a poem to Harriet Monroe; a Congregational minister who read *The New Masses*. And Alex found less likely persons who were kindred spirits up to a point. There was a big fellow named Schmitz, a garage mechanic, whose passion for natural history had led him to accumulate numerous volumes by Gilbert White and W. H. Hudson. There was a used-clothing dealer named Rosenbaum who had been born in Vienna and who had the Jew's sad hatred of injustice. And there was Alex's patron, Dr. George Massingham, a little man of fifty with a round bald head and a round belly and ingenuous eyes. His wife had died a few years before, so now if he wished to spend his money helping Alex whose business was it? Although not an intellectual, Dr. Massingham had hopes of becoming one, and he was as proud of Alex as if he had been his son instead of his cousin thrice removed. As a boy Dr. Massingham had wished to study piano and go on the concert stage, but his father, a dentist also, had thought it wiser for his son to learn how to torment human beings. By sponsoring Alex, Dr. Massingham felt obscurely that he was evening things up with his father, and the more the town contemned Alex the more resolutely the doctor supported him.

So that Alex would not feel an alms-receiver, the doctor "bought" his paintings, hanging them on the walls of his home and his waiting room and even in his star chamber, and perhaps some of the town's feeling against Alex was a result of staring at his work while Dr. Massingham applied the buzzer. After Alex became famous, Dr. Massingham's life was lighted by the reflected glow: connoisseurs were always migrating to Millborough to examine those early paintings.

Every Friday evening Alex held open house in his studio, and there was good talk and good music and not very good liquor. The little group enlarged as the years passed, and some evenings you would find twenty persons there, boys and girls home from college and that new reporter on the *Star* and a truck driver who did not think it inconsistent to be simultaneously a Communist and an Anarchist. Sometimes when Alex found himself going stale he caught a train for Chicago, and if he happened to be gone on Friday the group met anyway. But those evenings without Alex were unsuccessful. In his absence they realized how vital a rallying point he was.

Always he had been glad to show them any canvas on which he was working, but in 1928 an exception took place.

"You'll see it when it's finished," he smiled. "It's a departure for me, and I want your reaction to the completed work."

Those who were present on that hot July evening never forgot the genial air of mystery hovering over Alex. When they climbed the outside stair and entered the studio they noticed that his eyes were merrier, and they saw on the easel a canvas wrong-side-to. By now they knew him sufficiently well not to try hastening the moment when he would show the painting. They sat on the studio couch and on the floor, and somebody played the broken-down piano and they sang, "I've Been Working on the Railroad," while against the window screens insects pinged. The place smelled of oils and turpentine, and against the bright pastel walls silhouetted figures from Alex's brush cavorted in humorous and faintly bawdy poses. Finally, Alex announced he was ready to exhibit his new canvas.

He stood by the easel, stockier now, a round bald spot on his head, looking like a plump and worldly little friar. He wore his wide, calm smile, and he told them the painting was called "Corn Plowing."

When he turned the canvas they understood why he had been secretive. They realized that heretofore all his work had been practice. This painting was unlike anything he had done or anyone had done.

He had been searching for a way to express the uniqueness of Alex Kerry, and now he had succeeded.

In smooth oils that glazed the canvas with the brilliant hardness of pottery, a farmer sat on a corn plow. He was sixty, perhaps, and he glared out at you as if enraged because you were sun-bathing. The big horses stared at you too, and they also expressed disapproval. Even the highly stylized rows of young corn had an unyielding primness, and in the background far away the farmhouse looked as if it would stand no nonsense.

The painting was brimming with comedy, and it was full of June, too. You could almost smell the rich loam and hear the thrushes and feel the warm sun. But always your gaze returned to the man. Embodied in him was the community's disdain for Alex Kerry. He was the old-fashioned farmer of the American midlands. He was to-bed-with-the-chickens-and-up-with-the-roosters. He was high tariff and avoiding foreign entanglements and keeping cool with Coolidge. He was of straight old American stock, like Mr. Oxenford. He was this year's Sears, Roebuck catalogue on the lamplighted knees, and last year's in the backhouse. He was the Sunday afternoon nap after the heavy chicken dinner. He was the big red barn and the small house. He was the man who drained marshes and plowed steep hillsides and worked his land and his wife to death. He was the hero of the Iowa picnic in California. He was the buggy whip and the shaving mug, the new manure spreader and the telephone with the crank. He was a great American.

For a moment nobody spoke. Those on the floor stood up and crushed nearer. Then Dr. George Massingham expelled a long breath. He said, "My God!" And he laughed. He laughed himself into hiccups, and the others laughed, too, till it seemed the dark sky outside must be full of this titanic laughter rolling out of Iowa.

Four months later the painting won a three-hundred-dollar prize at a Chicago exhibition. And because it was a winner, the newspapers reproduced it, in black-and-white, at first, and only three columns wide. Then, because angry readers protested, the papers brought it out in Sunday roto. They were rewarded by a blizzard of envelopes to the readers' forum departments. Alex's fan mail was terrific. About one letter in fifty was admiring. It was a bonanza for the lunatic fringe.

Even citizens not actually angered were uncomfortable when they beheld the painting. And they were uncomfortable because they were uncomfortable. Why should a mere picture rile them so? They felt vaguely that the man who painted it lacked the right attitude.

"Corn Plowing" angered other artists, too, but for a different reason. They roared like old bulls spying a new head of the herd. The critics were divided. Here was an American Hogarth. Here was a mere cartoonist in oils. Here was a fresh eye, a sure hand. Here was a vulgar showman.

Alex smiled and painted.

Several salient events took place in Alex Kerry's life in the spring of 1929. Late in February he shipped off a new painting to the Marbury Galleries in New York. The Marbury people had become his dealers, and when they exhibited the canvas Alex was news again. You would not have thought that inanimate oils applied to inanimate canvas by a man in an Iowa garage could have stirred up such a furore.

When "Corn Plowing" appeared the Middle West was angry, but the new picture affronted persons in cultural citadels like Boston and New York. Editorials were printed, accusing Alex of wretched taste and even unpatriotic impulses. Resolutions condemning him were passed by such bodies as the Young Republican Club of Albany and the Daughters of the American Revolution.

The painting was entitled "Relay," and it depicted a race held in a stadium. One athlete was passing the baton to another. Your position as spectator was a dozen feet above the ground, so that the athletes looked foreshortened and not too significant. Early in March a new president had been inaugurated in Washington, and what disturbed people was the strong resemblance of the athletes to Messrs. Coolidge and Hoover. In his track suit Mr. Coolidge's limbs appeared thin, and his face was full of caution and thrift. You could almost hear him ordering the Marines into Nicaragua and saying, "They hired the money, didn't they?"

Mr. Hoover, on the other hand, looked as if he had eaten too much lunch and had neglected to swallow soda mints, but he was smiling bravely, nevertheless. He looked younger than the little fellow thrusting out the baton; in fact, he was undeniably a Wonder Boy. His limbs were pleasantly plump, and instead of a track jersey he wore a white shirt with a very high linen collar.

You could see a few faces in the first tier of the stadium: a cotton senator with a passion for lynching in his eyes; a man in a brown derby who was so little interested that he had averted his head and was drinking a stein of beer; and the countenance of the greatest Secretary of the Treasury since Alexander Hamilton.

Had he been concerned about his career, Alex would not have painted it, for it certainly stocked the arsenal of those critics who maintained he was only a cartoonist. Republicans couldn't enjoy the canvas; nor could the Democrats, because of the cotton senator and the man drinking beer. The Socialists and the Communists, being without humor, chided Alex for wasting his talents within the framework of capitalism. They called his garage studio an ivory tower, and they wished he would paint grimly of everyday occurrences, such as state troopers murdering coal miners.

But Alex had no interest in propagandizing. He was that vague thing, a liberal, but not a passionate one. He had painted "Relay" as a high lark, that was all. He believed in being himself, in telling the truth as he saw it, and this was so unheard of that he became famous.

When a Hollywood actress, upon press-agent advice, purchased "Relay" for a good sum, the *Tamarack Beacon* perked up. Any artist who made that kind of money must be a genius, so to Millborough it sent a photographer and a reporter for a feature story. They found Alex hard at work on a new painting, "Independence Day." It was the canvas of which the Chicago Art Institute was later so proud, an aerial view of the Millborough courthouse, with tiny figures on the lawn, holding picnics and exploding firecrackers. Although the painting was far from complete, you couldn't miss the Kerry touch. It was as if you were viewing the scene through the eyes of a high-flying, sardonic crow.

Instead of a smock, Alex wore mechanic's coveralls, and the reporter thought this would lend human interest to his story. Alex explained that coveralls were a wonderful garment for a man working with paint, and although this was true other artists, rigidly unconventional, said that Alex wore them as a pose. They accused him of showmanship. This didn't sadden Alex greatly: he realized it would be difficult ever to please his competitors.

Studying the painting, the reporter asked:

"But how do you get your perspective so right on a picture like that? Have you ever seen the courthouse from that angle?"

The laws of perspective, Alex said, were the same for a courthouse as for a box. And he added:

"To get an idea of the view, I hired an airplane. And I snapped pictures to refresh my memory. Although they aren't much help—we flew too high."

The photographer became interested now, and when Alex produced his camera they discussed lenses and film.

"I've used a camera for years," Alex said. "After I finish a painting, I always take a picture of it. That way, I have a complete record of my work."

Following the interview, the photographer flashed shots of Alex, and one showed him with a camera, taking a picture of a completed painting. That seemed harmless enough. And when the feature story with this photograph appeared in the *Beacon,* nobody expected the storm it raised.

The *Beacon's* circulation was regional, but since Alex was in the news other papers picked up the story, and they wired for illustrations. And when unfriendly critics beheld Alex with a camera, they cried out.

They accused him of first photographing his scenes, and using the prints as models. Whereas painting from life was proper, painting from photographs exceeded all wickedness. A photographer! They had a new epithet for him, now.

To the Friday evening group, Alex presented his usual smiling calm, and when they commiserated with him about the vicious publicity he stated it was unimportant and voiced the opinion that the critics were donkeys. But underneath, he was wounded and disgusted. When "Corn Plowing" and "Relay" appeared, he had convinced himself that the angry letters had not chafed him, just as earlier he had pretended invulnerability to Millborough's jibes; but this tempest unnerved him. Perhaps after all he was concerned about his career. He imagined people saying, "Alex Kerry? Nothing but a photographer with a copyist's knack." It sickened him and robbed him of enthusiasm for work.

In his studio he gazed with aversion at "Independence Day." It no longer seemed amusing, and he told himself he would never finish it. Through the windows he could see the trees leafing out, so instead of mixing paint he left the studio and wandered toward the edge of town, keeping to alleys because alleys suited his mood. He told himself he had gone stale.

Ordinarily at such a time he would have fled to Chicago, roaming along Halsted Street, soaking up the noises in the Loop, dawdling through the galleries at the Art Institute, till the city's rank life invaded his blood. But now the last thing he wanted was to encounter his friends there. Even though the charges against him were untrue he felt disgraced, and he thought he would like to go a thousand miles away, changing his name, getting a job driving a truck.

Every evening Dr. Massingham came to the studio, and he grew concerned about the lack of progress on "Independence Day."

"I can't paint," Alex told him; and the more the doctor urged him to take himself in hand, the more certain Alex became that he was stalled forever. Perhaps refusing to paint was his way of fighting back, for he suspected himself a genius and by sulking he was depriving the world of pictures without which it would be poorer. One evening he said:

"I'd like to go on the bum. Get away from it all."

Dr. Massingham felt as troubled as a parent with a difficult child.

"You can't get away from yourself," he said. "No matter where you go you'll take Alex Kerry along."

"I don't like Alex Kerry," Alex said. "I'd like to lose myself the way a drop of water does when it falls into a river."

That went on for several weeks. Dr. Massingham grew deeply worried. Being Alex's patron was the greatest thing that had ever happened to him. He tried all sorts of dodges to coax his protégé back to work, but the more he tried the sicker Alex became, in spirit. His depression fed on itself and at last affected him physically: he lost his appetite and sighed heavily and dragged his feet. The poor doctor tried to diagnose the malady in the light of his experience, and he suggested that possibly Alex's teeth were infected and he should have them x-rayed. Alex's only response was "Oh, hell."

One evening late in April the doctor said:

"I've bought tickets for the circus tomorrow afternoon. We'll go."

"I don't want to go."

"Well by God!" Dr. Massingham exclaimed, his temper snapping; and although ordinarily mild he gave Alex a dressing-down. From the depths of his gloom Alex did not respond. At last the doctor tramped out of the studio, despairing. He was halfway across the back yard when he heard his name called. On the landing outside the studio door he saw Alex standing.

"I'm sorry," Alex said, in that deliberate voice, "if I have been difficult. I'll be glad to go."

Next day Alex regretted yielding, for he had discovered a negative pleasure in cutting off one's nose to spite one's face, and since he was enjoying sympathizing with himself for the kicks his genius had suffered he feared the circus might do what Dr. Massingham hoped it would: snap him out of it. Like a sulking child he even enjoyed the discomfort his dark mood inflicted on the doctor.

He supposed he would attend the circus, since he had promised, but he hadn't promised to dress up, so that afternoon when the doctor came to the studio he found Alex unshaved and wearing coveralls.

"You're not ready," the doctor said.

"I'll go this way."

And hence when they walked through the sunny afternoon to the circus lot Alex did not look like somebody from *Who's Who* in his paint daubed coveralls and old hat.

The circus was Burgoyne & Pawpacker's Great 3-Ring Circus, playing its second date of the season; and Alex had not been long on the lot before he was asking himself how he would render on canvas what he saw. It was as if he had been wearing somber glasses and had now removed them. There were grifters on the lot that day, and gamblers, for once again Gus had forsaken Sunday School; but the presence of these rascals delighted Alex, for he was an artist and wholly amoral. The depression lifted from his brain, and on the thronged midway he reveled in the smells of human bodies and frying pork, and all the noises of shrilling children and raucous barkers and a band playing ripely. He found joy in the villainous faces of ticket sellers and roustabouts; he smiled at the crude art of the midway banners; and in the side show with its midgets and monstrosities preserved in alcohol and its reptile charmer he derived pleasure from wallowing in the lowest common denominator of human entertainment.

"Are you glad you came?" Dr. Massingham asked.

"I think I'll be painting again," Alex smiled.

On the midway, as they jostled toward the Main Entrance, Alex perceived a man standing beside the ticket taker. He was a large man of about fifty with a great hog belly and a gross scarlet countenance. He wore a suit checked in gray, a lion's tooth dangling from his watch chain, and a diamond ring sparkled on the little finger of his left hand. His hat was shoved back on his noble head; pouches hung beneath his shrewd gray eyes; and a corpulent cigar traveled from side to side of his grinning mouth. Alex found him so fascinating that he halted, staring.

"That's Gus Burgoyne," Dr. Massingham said. "He spoke to us at Rotary this noon."

"I want to meet him."

Dr. Massingham, shy by nature, looked dubious.

Then Alex noted the outsize lodge symbol flashing in the Burgoyne lapel.

"You belong to the same lodge," Alex said. "Go ahead—give him the secret handshake. I want to meet him."

And so, somewhat timidly, Dr. Massingham approached the man, and Alex watched them shaking hands. But the doctor need not have been timid, for Mr. Burgoyne was simply overwhelming him with brotherhood. Then Alex was beckoned.

Mr. Burgoyne grabbed his hand. There was momentary confusion among their fingers, for Mr. Burgoyne assumed that Alex was also a lodge brother and he was attempting the secret clasp; but Alex's failure to respond did not in any way detract from the heartiness of the handshake.

"Kerry," he boomed, "I'm mighty glad to know you. Understand you paint."

"I daub away at it," Alex said.

"Uh—yes. Great thing, painting! Wonderful gift for a man to have!"

"Alex is a great genius," Dr. Massingham said. "People will be admiring his paintings a hundred years from now."

"That so? Well now, isn't that wonderful! A hundred years! We need more geniuses. Always have said that. Good for a country!"

Before they moved on, Mr. Burgoyne crushed their hands again; and in the menagerie top Alex said:

"I ought to join some lodges. You meet such interesting people."

"He meant well," the doctor said. "And you asked to meet him."

"I think he's terrific," Alex grinned. "I'd like to paint him. He—"

But then the doctor nudged Alex, for he sighted Mr. Burgoyne shoving toward them.

"Uh," he puffed, "you boys got reserved seats? Here—give 'em to me!" He seized the pasteboards from the doctor, tore them up. "No good, today," he laughed. "Want you to be my guests in the owner's box. Got a mighty fine performance waiting for you. I was fortunate this season to get the Baron Karl Otto Von Krummer and his wife. Animal people. Hired them right out from under John Ringling's nose." Mr. Burgoyne laughed jovially. "John was pretty mad about that, but he got over it. Nice fellow, John. Couldn't ask for better competition. Uh—think you'll enjoy the Baron. Imported him from —uh—Germany. Famous European impresario. His wife's good, too. Beautiful little piece. Her performing name's Marybelle Monahan, but she's really Swedish—uh—royalty. Her act will kind of get you. Does something to you. Blond flame—that's what she is. Absolutely blond flame!"

Owing to its proximity to the band, their box was noisy, and conversation below a shout was impossible. This, however, did not prevent Mr. Burgoyne from conversing. His vocal cords seemed well-developed, and as host he felt it his duty to comment upon the performance. Favorably. Huge and jubilant, he sat between Alex and the doctor, energy pouring from his body as bounteously as from some great natural power source.

"It's like watching Niagara Falls," Alex thought, "or the aurora borealis."

The band was Negro, because Negroes could be hired more cheaply, and with one's partner always complaining about expense it was necessary to cut corners. This was not, however, the explanation given by Mr. Burgoyne.

"Got a coon band this season," he boomed. "More colorful, don't you think? And a nigger can get more out of a horn or a drum. Their playing's got a lot of pork chops and watermelon in it."

Alex enjoyed the show, although not in the way Mr. Burgoyne had intended. Watching the clowns, he realized he hadn't been thinking of the newspaper stories; and then into his thoughts there flashed an idea blazing with adventure.

"I'd like to clown for a while," he told himself. "Lose my identity in a shabby little circus. I've been in a rut."

And instantly he determined to do just that.

17

O<small>UT ON</small> the North Side, when they left the manse in the late afternoon, oyster-colored rain was peppering down from the early March sky. Wearing a raincoat cut in military lines, the Baron Karl Otto Von Krummer took such long strides that his bride found it difficult to keep pace.

"Maybe we should have called a cab from the minister's," Marybelle observed.

"A cab! Who said anything about a cab?"

"Aren't you looking for one, then?"

"*Mein Gott!* Are we made of money?"

"It was only that I thought—"

She had been going to explain that inasmuch as a cab carried them to the wedding she supposed one would haul them back to the Loop.

"It is not your place to think!"

And he machine-gunned her with a glance compounded of triumph, lust and contempt. The contempt was only natural, for after yielding at last to his battle for her affections Marybelle was like a fallen foe.

As they hurried along the street, crossing running gutters, Marybelle told her spouse:

"I am getting so-o wet."

"Is that my fault? Didn't I tell you to bring a raincoat?"

"Why are you cross?"

"You do what I tell you after this and everything will be fine."

The Baron had indeed advised her to wear a raincoat. When he called for her at the Blue Island apartment, he had plainly stated that March weather could not be relied upon, that before dusk the windy clouds might release moisture. But she had been vainly reluctant to intrude a tan raincoat upon the smart effect of her new spring suit. It was sky blue, beautifully pointing up her golden hair.

"I do not believe it will rain," she had said.

Insubordination! Infuriating! But the Baron swallowed his fury. He did not want her to change her mind about matrimony. Now, however, she was his wife. With satisfaction he noted that her thin slippers were drenched, her hat woebegone, her suit darkened by water. Except for the rain, he would have called a cab; but the cold downpour offered opportunity to give her a fine lesson.

An elevated station loomed through the rain-slant, and the Baron hurried across the street. Clutching his arm, Marybelle kept up as best she could. They ascended the steps and found shelter on the platform.

"I am so-o wet," she said, "and cold."

"I will warm you in good time," the Baron thought. He said, "What did I tell you? I said it would rain."

"Yes, Willie."

Blood darkened his neck, and he would have shouted, save for the presence of others on the platform. As it was, he seized her wrist, and his voice was low, coming through his teeth.

"How many times must I tell you not to call me Willie! Call me Baron!"

"Please," she whispered. "You are hurting my wrist."

He released it, but not before a final loving squeeze.

Downtown, on an old street beneath the "L," she hurried along by the Baron's side to the restaurant of their wedding feast. On the windows, dusty Gothic letters spelled out the proprietor's name, and the legend that German food was served within. Sawdust covered the floor; a rathskeller odor of hops and pigs'-knuckles steamed the air; and a waiter with a boiled shirt and a Doberman pinscher face escorted them to a round bare table.

After hanging up hat and coat, the Baron stood surveying the place in a manner borrowed from Captain Latcher. Yet the effect was not the same, for whereas the Captain's pose suggested Oxford and White-hall, the Baron's reminded you of Heidelberg and the Wilhelmstrasse. In honor of his wedding, he had visited a barber, and the close clip of his blond hair revealed the foursquare construction of his thick skull. He was clad in a herringbone suit, and he stood with shoulders squared and belly sucked in, so that you might have thought him a young major whose admirable military bearing could not be softened by mufti. Of the slippery road-kid Willie nothing visible remained, except his smile. It was still oblique and raw-looking, as if a layer of skin had been stripped from his lips, and it was not so much a smile as an insolence.

Having seated himself, the Baron scowled at the menu with a dominant silence, and its effect upon his bride and the waiter was tyrannical.

"The spareribs are very nice, sir," the waiter said humbly, at last.

Even when the Captain lived, and held Willie on a checkrein of wit, it was an error for an underling to address him as sir; for it roused in the Krummer breast an overbearing quality that was almost sexual. So now the Baron ordered:

"Shut up and let me think."

Marybelle colored, for it seemed possible a scene might ensue; but the Baron's rebuff did not stir rebellion in the waiter, but a huge and almost patriotic respect, as if the words had been a band playing *"Deutschland Uber Alles."* He bowed, delighted to find in decadent America a *Markgraf* who knew a waiter's place.

"Bring me kraut and pigs'-knuckles," the Baron said. "And the Baroness will have the same."

Baroness! This was an occasion the waiter would not forget already so soon!

"Yes, Your Highness," he murmured soothingly. "And beer, yet?"

The Baron looked as if he were about to swat the fellow with the flat of a saber.

"Did I say beer? Coffee. Two coffees! And see that it is hot."

The waiter scampered to the kitchen; and even though pigs'-knuckles and kraut was a dish Marybelle detested, something prevented her from voicing that fact.

The Baron's bad temper was not wholly a pose. It blossomed from worry and fear. He feared the past, especially that portion concerning a December morning in the old factory.

"There is nothing whatever to worry about. Nothing. Nothing," he kept telling himself; and although this was true he continued fretting. His excellent imagination tormented him endlessly. In his daydreams he kept imagining scenes that ended on the gallows. Useless to tell himself that nobody suspected he had killed Captain Latcher; his imagination found ways to bring him to justice.

For instance, the Baron was a young man of exemplary habits: no smoking; no drinking. But now, absurdly, he worried lest someday he turn to alcohol, and in a drunken stupor reveal facts detrimental to the Krummer neck. So he hated alcohol; but so insidious and convoluted was his fear that he found himself tempted to sip a drink. This was only one of the many tensions resulting from his fear.

Back in the cage-boy era, his slumber had been solid, but in the last weeks insomnia had usurped his couch. Upon leaving the hospital he had resumed housekeeping in the factory office. He had never been troubled by nerves, but an odd uneasiness afflicted him that first evening. It was January, with snow falling and wind blowing, and as he sat by the stove, reading the sports pages, an eerie sense that he was not alone snaked along his spine. He tried to ignore it, but presently he realized he had been reading the same paragraph over and over.

He stood up and tried the door. Locked. He went to the stove and idly spat upon it: the resulting sizzle sounded as noisy as frying bacon. He dumped coal into the fire, and in the midst of this commonplace activity he was smitten by the sense of being observed. He whirled. Nothing. And then he grew aware of the windows. They were tall and narrow, uncurtained, and tonight their many panes gleamed blackly. He gazed from one to the other, while the fire hummed and crackled; and suddenly he thought he glimpsed movement beyond one pane. Somebody spying!

"What do you want?" he shouted, lunging angrily across the room. At the sill he stooped to peer out, and when he beheld his countenance mirrored darkly it gave him a start.

"I'll fix the bastard," he muttered, so he seized a flashlight and plunged out into the storm. But he saw nobody. And the snow beneath the window sparkled smooth, unbroken by footprints.

He was shivering now, probably from the cold night; and he hurried inside and stood by the stove. He could have sworn he had seen something moving beyond the pane. But that couldn't be, because there were no footprints. Unless—

He wouldn't admit the thought. But it was there just the same, on the threshold of consciousness. Then, with ghostly ease, it floated into consciousness.

"Maybe it was him," Willie thought. "Maybe he's wandered back to haunt me."

He tried to laugh, but his throat produced only a dry croak. And his spine tingled. He told himself he did not believe the dead could rise and return to harass the living. He told himself he did not believe in ghosts. Yet his throat was tight and his thoughts kept going morbidly to Captain Latcher, long and cold and waxy skinned in a coffin.

"God damn it!" he exclaimed. "I'm going to read!"

Firmly he sat himself down and picked up the evening paper. He was much interested in the story about the University of Wisconsin's standing among the Big Ten basketball teams; but he couldn't get much out of it. For again he felt he was being watched. And he heard the wind screeching about the cornices of the old factory. At last he flung down the paper and said aloud:

"I'll go to bed."

But he had chores to do first. He must go into the factory and fire the stoves, so the cats would not freeze during the night. When the Captain lived, Willie had never thought twice about opening the inner door into the factory. Tonight he thought twice about it; yes, and a dozen times!

He made himself do it, finally. He yanked open the door and snapped a switch. Lights glowed weakly in the vast gloom of the place. It looked cavernous tonight and thickly shadowed; and there were many windows through which eyes could peer. Willie started to whistle, to buck himself up; and then, in the middle of a bar, he broke off in horror.

He hadn't thought about what he was whistling. His lips had pursed automatically. And they had whistled "Chicago."

It all rushed back then: that pre-Christmas morning. He heard the Captain's voice, playful with self-mockery: "And I say, if you should meet Marshall Field, give him my best." In memory he beheld the Captain, debonair and British, striding toward the arena.

And yet another fear came to Willie. Several times his sleep had been tormented by the Captain's leading some invisible orchestra playing "Chicago." Now he thought how awful it would be if some time when he was awake he should hear that music and see the Captain.

He halted in the factory by one of the thick wooden pillars, and the old wood-rat shiftiness returned to his body. His fists opened and closed. Then all at once he squared his shoulders, and at the top of his voice he roared:

"You can't! You can't come back, you son of a bitch! You're dead as a stuck pig! If you think you can get my goat I'll show you, you lousy—"

And he rattled off a string of lumberjack epithets.

As he shouted he paced, waving his fists; and then the echoes of his voice died away in the uncanny reaches of the factory, and the only sounds were the rich thrumming minors of the wind, and the flutelike high notes, and a sleepy lion muttering. Willie stood scowling. Finally he shouted:

"I guess that showed you, you English bastard! I fixed you once and I'll fix you again!"

He felt more courageous now, and hurriedly he stoked the fires and returned to the office and undressed. But in bed he was wakeful. His tendons were tight as he lay in the dark, hearing the snow whispering against the windows and the wind mournful in the chimney and screeching along the eaves. Minutes went by; he could not relax. Maybe a light sleep coated his mind, for when he thought of the University of Wisconsin basketball team he was astounded to note that the referee was Captain Latcher, and the whistle in his mouth called fouls with three notes. *Chi-ca-go.* Like that.

Willie found himself bounding from bed and groping for the light. He stubbed his toe before finding it, and he swore copiously. Then he returned to bed with the office brightly lighted.

He thought of Marybelle and his campaign to wed her, but the memory of her body did not tonight stir him with rapacious impulses. For she had become an object of danger. What did her silences mean? What did her knowing little smile mean? Willie surmised that a married couple kept few secrets from each other, and again it occurred to him that the Captain might have suspected that his cage boy intended killing him and confided his suspicions to her. Once long ago the Captain had said: "Not thinking of buying me out, are you? And certainly not thinking of sponsoring an accident!"

Willie's brow oozed sweat. A deep one, that little Swede! Biding her time, perhaps! Maybe tomorrow she would appear at the factory with a squad of police. In imagination he saw her smiling and pointing at him.

"He did it. My husband warned me about it."

And lying tensely in bed Willie saw the scene like the climax of a crime movie. He saw himself heaving a chair at the police and plunging through a window and fleeing wildly, while bullets snapped at his ankles the way they had that night in the Worcester railroad yards when he was a road kid. And then he fell, wounded; and the scene changed to a gallows and the trap opened and he was dangling, kicking, mouth wide for air that the tight rope wouldn't permit to enter his lungs.

His fists were tight. And he told himself:

"My God!—she's got to marry me! Got to!"

Every night it was like that. Because of losing sleep, Willie's temper shortened; and sometimes when he tried to convince Marybelle she should marry him, and she said, "I do not think I should remarry so-o soon," it was all he could do to refrain from slapping her.

He struggled pluckily against revealing his fears to the world, so his manner grew sterner, more baronial, but it was all cover for the terror within. And worst of all, that terror interfered with business. He had to have the act routined and polished, the new cats worked into it, when he opened with Vendee & Gonzaga's Circus in April; but his progress was slow. He found himself lingering in the safety cage. This was not because of the arena shell shock the Captain had talked about, but because he feared he would have an accident and be given an anesthetic in a hospital. And while under the ether he might talk! He might reveal his secret!

One day the booking agent came to the factory to watch the act, and he groaned:

"Great God, Baron—it's awful! It stinks! They'll try to break your contract!"

Willie wanted to drive his fist into the fellow's mouth, but he only sighed.

"I know it," he whined. "I know it's bad. It's because I'm worried."

"Worried the man is! And you should be, the way it stinks!"

"Naw, naw—not about that. About my situation. Where do I stand, that's what I want to know. Marybelle owns the act, but I'm the trainer. Maybe she'll can me. God damn it, we ought to get married. More businesslike. Then I can quit worrying and go to work on the cats!"

The booking agent nodded thoughtfully.

"Baron, I see your point. Well—why don't you marry the little broad?"

"What did you call her!" Willie thundered.

"Now wait—wait! Don't get yourself mad with me, Willie. I mean Baron. I just mean to say, why don't you ask Mrs. Latcher—?"

"Have," Willie spat out. "She says it's too soon since the Captain died."

"Soon! Soon, she says! Maybe she thinks he will be any deader after a year or two! Soon, she says, and upsets an artist like you Baron and ruins the act!"

"Yeah," Willie said, "it upsets me, all right."

"I'll talk to her," the booking agent said. "You bring her to my office and I will talk to her. I'm administrator of the Captain's estate, ain't I?"

Marybelle's apartment occupied the second floor of a dwelling a couple of blocks from the factory building. It was an old square house, its vivid burnt-orange paint dulled by years of soft-coal smoke; but inside, the apartment was cozy. The Captain had rented it back in 1917, furnishing it in a style befitting a London clubman. The landlady, a Lithuanian, possessed a mind as broad as her purse was narrow, so as long as the Captain paid the modest rent she did not object if late at night he escorted ladies up the private stairs from the side entrance; and it never occurred to her to ask about a marriage certificate when Marybelle arrived from St. Paul.

The landlady thought so highly of the Captain that she even took the afternoon off and attended his funeral. This was held several days before Christmas in a South Side establishment, and the mourners were few. The booking agent was there, and a scattering of circus performers, wintering in Chicago; not more than a dozen in all.

The afternoon was damp and raw, and they buried the Captain in one of those metropolitan cemeteries with an iron fence. Except for Marybelle, nobody grieved deeply, and she did not show her grief. Her face was white and her eyes dazed, but centuries of northern stoicism held back her tears. She wore a black veil, and as the minister said dust to dust, and the coffin slowly descended into the earth, she found herself unbelieving. It seemed incredible that her dashing husband, in whom life had burned so joyously, should now be shut away in the ground.

"God is punishing me," she whispered, back in her apartment. "I should never have lived with him in sin before marrying him."

And she sank to her knees and implored God to be kind to Philip, out there in the awful vastnesses of eternity. She asked nothing for herself. That would have been impudent. For she had been bad and bad. Her flesh had tempted Mr. Christianson, and wickedly she had

not insisted upon a wedding ceremony before departing from St. Paul
with the Captain.

"I have been a wicked girl, oh Heavenly Father," she whispered, "but
I will try to be better."

Then she sat on the davenport, meek and silent. The living room
was so full of her husband's possessions that it was possible to imagine
his spirit there. The walls were covered with his photographs: in circus
costume; as a lad of five on a rocking horse; with his class in military
school. His books were there: a small case with open shelves. They
were travel books chiefly, and memoirs, and most of them dealt with
the British Isles, bearing such titles as *London Nights* and *Round
About Kensington Gardens*. And in that corner stood his Victrola,
the turntable still holding the record he had played during breakfast
on their last morning together. The record was "Chicago."

At last Marybelle changed into a house dress and prepared dinner.
It comforted her to work with her hands in the tiny kitchen. Heretofore she had not thought of the future, but now she wondered what
was to become of her. Yesterday the booking agent had called, telling
her that the Captain had deposited his will in the office safe, and that
she was his sole heir.

"Yes," she said. "He told me he had done that."

"And I'm the administrator. That means a lot of legal stuff. Till
the estate's settled I'll handle the funds. There won't be much left
except the cats and equipment, after expenses."

"No," she said dully, "not much."

The complications brought about by death bewildered her.

"You turn the bills over to me and I'll pay them," the agent said.
"Willie Krummer will be working the act. Till he can buy it, maybe
we could work out some way where he could rent the cats."

"Whatever you decide," she said.

"But I'd better warn you, Mrs. Latcher, that the whole shooting
match won't amount to much of an estate. You'll have to get a job."

So now in the kitchen Marybelle wondered what she could do to
support herself. The abilities she did not possess were many. She could
not type or scribble shorthand; and her moral degradation had cut
short her career as a furniture store clerk, so she had no retail experience. There remained a job waiting tables.

But after years of luxury, she felt reluctant to resume the occupation
she had abandoned in St. Paul. It would, she realized, wound her
pride; and she told herself:

"Oh-h, I am vain. It is not enough that I should sin. I must have
vanity, too."

But recognizing the sin of vanity and eradicating it were two different things. As the days passed she studied the help wanted ads in the

papers, but she could not bring herself to apply for work. And then Willie proposed marriage, but she recoiled from that occupation, too. It shocked her that he should wish to marry her so soon after Philip's death; and besides, some instinct warned her away from the fellow. When he gazed at her she felt frightened. She could never bring herself to marry him, even if now he did call himself a baron.

Following his release from the hospital, Willie visited her apartment. It was the day after his first dreadful night in the factory, and he was so changed that Marybelle in her simplicity told herself that possibly she had been misjudging him.

"I have been worrying about you," he said. "That's why I came."

"Worrying?"

"Living all alone. It's tough. Here. I brought you something."

He thrust a florist's box into her hands, and when she unwrapped it she found roses.

"Oh-h," she trilled. "This is so-o nice. Thank you so-o much."

"Like 'em?"

"They are very lovely. I will put them in water."

While she hurried to the kitchen, Willie sat down and ran his forefinger under his collar. His soul rebelled at the role he had chosen for himself: that of an old family friend, full of sympathy and solicitude. He felt like a pansy, carrying flowers to the little Swede. But better to feel that way than like a gallows bird! In the horrible deeps of night he had decided to do anything—even to humiliate himself by being pleasant—in order to marry her.

He had never before visited this apartment, for the Captain had not considered a cage boy his social equal; and now being alone here with a tantalizing widow stirred manly instincts in his libido. But he had resolved to refrain from any attempts at lovemaking.

And then while he sat there alone an odd experience visited him. His gaze roved the walls, where photographs of the Captain hung, and it occurred to Willie that without doubt the man he had killed had often sat in this armchair. His skin prickled and his body jerked uneasily. And all at once he had the vivid sensation that somebody was standing behind the chair, somebody lean and dashing and smiling. Willie's teeth tightened and he swore he would not yield to last night's mood and look around.

"Oh, *won't* you, old chap?"

He thought he heard it! The Captain's voice!

Willie's spine was acrawl with icy footed ants, and involuntarily he jumped to his feet and whirled. And he saw nothing, of course, except the wall with more photographs of the Captain, smiling out mockingly; but he was badly shaken. He told himself the voice had been only in his brain, that he had associated with the Captain for so many years that he could imagine what he would say on any occasion; and although this was the true explanation Willie couldn't quite rid himself of the feeling that the Captain had been standing there.

"My God!" he thought. "Am I going nuts?"

At that moment Marybelle returned, the roses in a vase, and she stared.

"Why, Willie! What is wrong? You are white as a sheet!"

He would have enjoyed striding over and knocking the vase from her hands and slapping her. Instead, licking ashen lips, he sank into the chair.

"I don't feel so good."

"Willie! What is it? Maybe you left the hospital too soon!"

"Yeah, I'm still kind of weak."

"Maybe some coffee would be good for you," she said, with her Swedish faith that coffee could accomplish miracles.

"Yeah, maybe it would."

"I will go and make it."

Before he knew what he was saying he blurted out:

"Wait. Don't leave me alone."

She looked so bewildered that he added:

"I mean, don't bother. I'm no good. Don't go to no trouble on my account."

"But if you feel faint—"

"Naw. I'm better now. Don't go to no trouble."

She sat down across the room and crossed her lovely legs, but sight of their curves stirred no passion now in his breast. He wanted to marry her more desperately than ever, but only to preserve the Krummer species, not to perpetuate it.

After that Willie was always dropping in at the apartment. And although he felt it was vitiating his manhood, he labored strenuously at being courteous. He discussed with Marybelle the problems he encountered with the animals, even asking her advice. Since it was impossible for him to treat anybody as an equal, he humbled himself in being pleasant to her, and this charmed her vanity. She never knew the answers to the training problems he posed, so she smiled mysteriously and murmured:

"I would have to think about that."

Her smile seemed to taunt:

"I know many things, Willie Krummer. Oh-h, many things. I know you are not a baron, and I remember how Philip used to say you might try to kill him some fine day. You think you are a smart fellow, Willie Krummer, but I know, I know. And if you are not careful I will go to the police and tell."

Whereupon Willie would redouble his efforts to be pleasant; but stamping back to the factory he growled to himself:

"You wait! You just wait! You are top dog now, but if I ever marry you—"

Almost imperceptibly Willie's role changed from that of an old family friend into that of suitor. Marybelle was lonely and presently she found herself looking forward to his visits. One evening he invited her to accompany him to the movies, and she gladly accepted. Presently they were going out together often.

Willie found one trick very effective: to commiserate with her about the Captain's death.

"I miss him," Willie said. "I miss him and need him."

"Oh-h, so do I. I miss him and need him so-o much, Willie."

"He was a wonderful fellow. He taught me a lot."

Marybelle sighed. "I think I will never love again. He taught me so-o much, too."

In Willie's soul, great racial reservoirs of bathos were sequestered; in him, brutality and sentimentality were Siamese twins; and one evening in the apartment, in discussing the Captain's virtues, he even shed a few tears. Nor was this mendacity; just then, he was as sincere as a Schiller poem. Remembering the past, how the Captain had hired him as cage boy and bought him clothes and whipped him and humiliated him, a great sadness oozed and dripped like fog through his thoughts; the past seemed mournfully beautiful. It was gone and dead; it was the golden age, as full of *Weltschmerz* as a Wagnerian hero. Small wonder that tears came to Willie; in that mood, he would have wept over the death of a sardine he had just swallowed.

Moreover, although Willie did not believe in supernatural phenomena, he had the comforting feeling that Captain Latcher was overhearing his words of praise, that perhaps they would dupe him into concluding that Willie after all had not brained him and tossed him to the cats.

It was an enjoyable experience, but it ended badly. Marybelle did not weep; her eyes took on that dazed expression and her lips that slight smile; and when through his tears Willie beheld her smile it filled him with terror. It seemed to say:

"I'm on to you, Willie Krummer. Your crying doesn't fool me. You murdered him."

And through his brain oaths marched like lumberjacks, and he thought:

"All right, laugh at me! Here I've been crying because the bastard's dead, and you laugh! But we will see. Some day you will laugh from the other side of your mouth!"

It was a romantic courtship.

And it was a platonic courtship, too. Never did Willie so much as touch her glorious hair. As a boy in the North Woods he had learned the ways of wild creatures; how easily they could be startled; how much craft was needed to ensnare them. And hence, as if she were a lovely doe, he sneaked up on her from the downwind side.

Once it would have been impossible for him to restrain his strong appetites; he would have yielded to her lure the way Mr. Christianson had. But now, when Willie's wrists began pounding, he reminded himself that she was the widow of the man he had killed, exceedingly dangerous to be running at large; and instantly this divested her of passionate glamor. He was learning that impending danger and lovemaking are incompatible.

Several times, almost casually, he brought up the subject of marriage, but she always shrank back.

"It is too soon, Willie. It would not be proper."

Significantly, she did not declare, "I will never marry you." This was because the idea of marrying him had at last gained a toehold in her thoughts. When she said it was too soon she meant that and nothing more. In New Stockholm custom dictated that a widow should not remarry for at least a year, and in Marybelle's head folkways had a habit of becoming religious precepts.

On the other hand, Marybelle had a practical nature, and she realized that it would be sensible for them to marry. By living together and pooling the proceeds from the act, they would do better financially than if each tried to exist on half the income. And by now she was sure she had wronged Willie, when she used to contemn him as a scoundrel and a boor.

"He is very nice," she thought. "He brought me flowers and he does not get fresh with his hands."

Now and then she wished—guiltily—that his hands would be less circumspect. She was young and healthy and the Captain had taught her the beauties of passion. She was not the first widow who, after the shock of death, had changed her mind about never remarrying. And quite aside from her strong passion, she thought it would be very nice to have a man around the apartment again. It was a dreary business, cooking for oneself alone, sharing with nobody the gossip that accumulates during the day in any neighborhood. And more than most women, because of her simplicity, she needed a man to stand between her and the world. In her heart she was still the New Stockholm girl who had desired nothing more from life than a good husband and a kitchen and humdrum. If to men she gave the impression of being

mysterious and seductive and adventurous, it was not her fault. She
did not yearn for adventure. All she wanted was another husband;
and Willie was handy.

"Baron," said the booking agent, that day in his office, "will you step
outside? I want to talk to Mrs. Latcher alone."

"*Ja*—okay," said the Baron, goose-stepping to the door.

"My God, but she's stubborn," the booking agent thought, smiling
across the desk. "What have I done to deserve that blockhead Krummer calling himself a baron and now this Swede!"

Marybelle returned his smile, serenely, sweetly.

"You say," he said, "that you ain't made up your mind about marrying Willie. Just what do you mean by that?"

"I will tell you," said Marybelle, in her low singsong. "I mean I
have not yet decided."

"I see," said the agent.

"That is right," Marybelle smiled.

"Do you think you might marry him someday?"

"Oh-h yes, someday I might."

"Ain't you ever heard the slogan eventually, why not now?"

"I do not believe I have heard that."

"A good slogan."

"Oh, yes, very good."

"Gold Medal Flour people use it."

"Oh-h? I do not use that brand. It is made in Minneapolis. I use
the Pride of St. Paul Flour."

"That so?" asked the agent. And somewhat absently he added,
"Nice town, St. Paul."

"Very nice. I like it much better than Minneapolis."

"This ain't getting us no place, Mrs. Latcher. If you're going to
marry Willie someday, why not right away?"

"You think I should?"

"Certainly I think so! He'll make you a fine husband. If you don't
marry him, what'll you do?"

"Maybe I can find a job."

"A job! What do you want with a job! You marry Willie. That
boy's going places. He'll be famous."

"But it is too soon. Philip has not been dead a year. Only two
months—"

"A year? What has that got to do with it?"

She explained.

"Um-m-m," said the agent. "That's a very fine sentiment, Mrs.
Latcher. But suppose I'd tell you that Captain Latcher wanted you to
marry sooner than a year. Would that make any difference?"

"But how could you know that?"

"Because he told me so himself."

"Philip told—?"

"In this office. When he gave me his will to keep. I can hear him like it was yesterday. He said, 'I've appointed you administrator, old chap.' And he said, 'If I should ever shuffle off, old chap, I wish you'd urge Marybelle to remarry as soon as possible. Tell her not to wait.'"

Marybelle looked impressed.

"Philip told you that?"

"It's the God's truth. And he told me he thought Willie Krummer would be a good husband for you. He wanted you taken care of, Mrs. Latcher. He said you was a beautiful woman, and he could never rest easy in his grave if he thought you had to go to work. Now Mrs. Latcher. Are you going to go against his wishes? Willie tried to save his life—you owe a great debt to Willie—and Willie loves you. He worships the ground you walk on."

"I did not know that," she murmured.

"He does! And Willie's a catch. If you keep going against Captain Latcher's wishes, and keep putting Willie off, do you know what will happen?"

"What will happen?"

"He'll find someone else, that's what. There're a dozen girls who would marry him at the drop of a hat. So don't you think you should be sensible and do what the Captain wished? Don't you think you should marry Willie?"

"I will think it over," she said.

She wanted time to sort out all this new information. The Captain's wishes! Willie besieged by a dozen girls, but preferring her! Willie worshiping the ground she walked on! It warmed her wicked vanity, roused her tenderness toward him. And she thought he had never touched her because his love was too pure for that, too spiritual. It was like being courted by a minister.

Upon leaving the restaurant on their wedding night, full of pigs'-knuckles and kraut, the Baron relented and engaged a cab, possibly because the rain had stopped. All the way to Blue Island he sat erect and mainly silent, thinking how the adventure-path upon which he had embarked had already been explored by Captain Latcher. This troubled him. In everything the Captain had been expert—doubtless including being a husband—and the Baron wished Marybelle were without experience. From road-kid days he recalled the proverb that it is better to surprise an old maid than to disappoint a widow.

And so his anticipation of the hours ahead was marred by misgivings. He told himself he would feel differently once they reached the apartment; his absence of ardor, he thought, resulted from his considering Marybelle dangerous since her husband's death.

After paying off the cab, he felt as skittish as when he stood in the safety cage, bucking himself up to enter the arena. His heart was hammering. He did not, however, reveal his anxiety. As they mounted the steps his manner was brave and soldierly.

A dim light burned in the hall, and after the Baron unlocked the door Marybelle stood with ankles together, smiling.

"Well—why are we waiting?" he asked.

"Aren't you going to carry me across the sill?"

He hesitated, then swept her into his arms and carried her in. It was like carrying a bouquet of flowers, she was so fragrant. Her arm slipped around his neck, and her warm breath whispered:

"You are so-o strong."

He was breathing harder than the exertion seemed to warrant, and inside he kicked shut the door and put her down and embraced her deeply. Her lips were as hot and sweet as notes from a jazz trumpet, and again her fragrance engulfed him, as if he were caught in the branches of a flowering locust tree. Her body was infinitely seductive, and he was no longer fretful about disappointing her.

Then suddenly he broke away and whirled.

"What is the matter?"

"Thought I heard something."

"But what could it be?"

"I—I don't know."

The blood had left his face and the road-kid shiftiness had returned to his body. He looked ready to twist and squirm like an eel from a railroad detective's grasp. He scanned the room, and everywhere he beheld the Captain's photographs.

"God damn it," he muttered.

"But what—what is wrong, Willie?"

Savagely he turned on her, seizing her shoulders.

"How many times must I tell you not to call me Willie?"

Her cheeks pinked.

"I am sorry, Baron," she whispered.

His hands fell; he flung himself into a chair.

"All right," he growled. "See that you remember it."

She looked bewildered, and she asked, "Did I do something wrong?"

"Shut up and let me think."

His brow was furrowed, his knuckles white.

She whispered, "My clothes are still damp. I will change to something dry," and she slipped away to the bedroom.

It was almost physical, the horror he had experienced, as if the pigs'-knuckles had been tainted. There he stood, sweetly smothering in her loveliness, when he heard the voice. The Captain's voice.

"But old chap, you can't, you know. The little Viking belongs to me."

So Willie whirled, sick with dread that this time he would actually see the dead man. He could imagine how he would look, leaning on his cane, his teeth gleaming in a death's-head grin, his skin the lifeless white of a dead fish belly. His clothes would be shredded by tiger claws, his flesh bleeding. An abomination that would not stay buried, his bones exuding dank air.

But he did not behold the specter. Of course not! The dead were dead for all eternity. The voice had been nothing but bad imaginings. Yet Willie's throat felt choked shut, and his legs were weak.

So now he sat trying to regain control, to return to the mood of passion he had experienced when embracing Marybelle. But horror remained. And the Captain mocked him from the photographs on the wall.

"God damn!"

He snapped shut his eyes. But if the darkness hid the photographs, it had terrors of its own. He remembered a December morning in the old factory, with the Captain singing "Chicago." And then suddenly, inconceivably, Willie was actually hearing the strains of that song. It wasn't a dream. He was wide awake, but still he heard it. He thought wildly, "This is it! My God, it's happening like in the dream, the bastard's after me, it's the music—!"

He leaped up. Then rage boiled through him, for he saw Marybelle in blue-silk pajamas winding the phonograph. She it was who had filled the room with horror-music. Playing that corpse-awful piece on the machine!

He sprang to the phonograph, jerked up the playing arm, grabbed the record. He lifted it in shaking hands, breaking it like a potato chip, flinging it down, grinding it under his heel. And he thundered:

"You know, don't you? You know!"

She had never looked so dazed.

"Why—what—?"

"That God-damned piece! Why did you play it?"

"You did not—feel well. I thought—maybe music—would make you feel—better."

His was nearly a tiger lunge, taking him to her. He grabbed her shoulders.

"Never play it! Never! Never hum it! Never!"

Frightened out of her wits she murmured:

"I thought—only—that you might like it. Philip liked it."

"Philip!"

His raw lips expelled the word as if it were rattlesnake venom. And his rage and horror flashed into his fingers. They closed on the neckline of her pajamas and jerked. So much strength was in the gesture that the blue silk ripped like paper, and there she stood, naked to the waist.

Once the sight would have set him wild, but now before his passion could accumulate he had the prickly feeling that eyes were drilling the back of his neck.

"Get out of here, you bastard!" he yelled, wheeling around. And again he beheld no specter, but his spine had malaria shivers, and he flung across the room to the davenport and lay with fists tight, knowing he could never be alone with Marybelle, not if they fled to the ends of the earth, for always Captain Latcher would follow, whispering playfully barbed comments that would render him an insufficient husband.

"Oh-h, you are not well," Marybelle murmured. "You are sick—maybe that food was spoiled." And she added, "I will make you some coffee."

The coffee steadied him; but he was so shaken he was in no mood for love. Yet when the apartment was dark he was foolish enough to make demands of himself. And the more he demanded the more difficult and embarrassing everything became.

Willie sensed his bride's disappointment, and he burned with shame. She was not his first woman; he had proved his manhood many times; but with her he was not a man. It was humiliating and anguishing, for of all the lovely girls in the world she was the one he desired most. He lay awake for hours, telling himself it would be different in the morning or tomorrow night; but it was never different.

The owners of Vendee & Gonzaga's Circus considered themselves lucky to get a famous man like the Baron for their 1924 season, but after the show took to the road they soon suspected their luck had been bad rather than good. The Baron was their headliner; his brave countenance could be seen on lithographs from Illinois to California; but when he entered the arena the only person frightened and thrilled was the Baron himself.

Gonzaga urged the Baron to invigorate the act, but nothing came of it except the addition of many lumberjack oaths to Mr. Gonzaga's already ample vocabulary. Mr. Gonzaga even wrote the Baron's booking agent, imploring him to prevail upon Von Krummer to improve the act, but nothing came of that, either.

The shameful truth was that the Baron still feared injuries and a tongue loosened by ether. Hence, instead of breaking the new cats into the act he worked the old ones, sending them through the ancient routine that had seemed lifeless and stale even when the Captain presented it.

Yet with his long experience and dashing manner, the Captain had at least given the act color and polish and even an occasional sense of danger; but the poor Baron looked like a bungling amateur. Things dragged. Even the cats yawned. When their trainer cracked his whip into their seedy hides, or fired his revolver, they merely snarled and balked. Critics for the trade papers used skinning knives in reviewing the Baron's performance. Upon reading the notices, the Baron wadded the papers and flung them into a corner of the dressing-van; and he stamped about swearing while Marybelle stood frightened. Catching sight of her, he thundered:

"That's right! Laugh at me!"

She had not laughed; but her lips wore that habitual slight smile.

"Oh-h no," she whispered. "I am not laughing."

To have a woman dispute him—and his wife at that—fueled the Baron's rage; so three or four sharp reports, like those from a light-caliber pistol, sounded in the van; but they were not pistol reports but only the Baron slapping his wife's face. He had taken to abusing her. It was as if his passion for her, unable to fulfill itself in a normal way, had found an outlet in punishment.

In October, when they returned to Blue Island, the future looked gloomy.

"Willie," said the booking agent, "the act stinks. There ain't a show in the country would have you as a gift."

"I was just hitting my stride."

"You ask me, Willie, you ain't got no stride."

"I'm going into rehearsal," the Baron said. "You come out to Blue Island in a month and you'll see how good I am."

But it was all braggadocio; and on a home-bound bus dejection oozed from his pores. He looked more subdued than in cage-boy days. More mature. Worry and responsibility had seasoned his countenance, and he had acquired the nervous mannerism of clamping and unclamping his teeth so that you could see his jaw-hinges working beneath his skin. With great effort he maintained his soldierly demeanor, but he was jumpy inside, and if somebody jostled him in a crowd his head would snap around in terror that it was a detective. And occasionally in his brain he would still hear the Captain's voice, chiding him about his fear of the cats or his insufficiency with Marybelle; and all those things added together can be unsettling even to a valorous Baron.

The factory office was now home, for to save expenses the Von Krummers had given up their apartment and moved here. Today he found Marybelle peeling potatoes, but she did not greet her husband, for she had been taught that a wife should be seen and not heard. Ignoring her, the Baron stood scowling, turning over in his thoughts the booking agent's words, and at last he moped into the factory where he stared at the empty arena. It was as somber as his brain, and from long ago he heard the Captain saying: "You're young now, old son, and you think nothing will ever break you. But it will, it will. If you keep on the jolly old cats will get you. . . ."

"The hell they will," the Baron muttered. "I'll show the bastards."

He had fallen into the habit of replying aloud to the Captain's re-membered comments, and although this was not precisely talking to himself Marybelle considered it that, and it frightened her even more than his rages. Sometimes she ventured to think he was not quite sane. Certainly his wild jealousy of her was unreasoned; if she glanced at another man he was furious; and once he had promised to kill her if she were ever unfaithful or if she should seek a divorce.

"But I have never thought such things," she protested; but this was a lie and she could not meet his gaze.

"Don't give me that stuff," he growled. "I know you, you little—"

And he assailed her with many foul synonyms for an unfaithful woman.

She colored, but she took his verbal abuse as she took his physical; meekly, stoically. There was nothing else to do, for by now she knew him well enough to believe that if she appealed to the police against his beatings or went to a lawyer about a divorce he would carry out his threats. She might have freedom for a few months but in the end he would trace her.

Nor was Marybelle the only human being who feared him and con-sidered his mind poisoned: a whole series of cage boys shared her opin-ion. But they could quit his employ. And they did, fast. So the Baron was compelled to clean the cages, and this exacerbated his grudge against the world.

Now in the factory he shuffled to the cages, returning the bitter glares of the unbroken cats, and he told them:

"Tomorrow I will start on you. I'll break the hell out of you."

For like the Captain before him he had reached a desperate decision: if he wished to remain an animal man he must vanquish his fear. Standing there with legs apart, he felt better; and next morning he abided by his decision and went to work with a will. And although Marybelle had a tender heart and a mortal fear of the cats he compelled her to assist him, poking a feeding fork through the bars or sending in water from a hose; and during the next weeks people passing the factory heard terrifying sounds issuing through its walls, roars and shrieks of wild beasts in horrible agony, as if from hot irons and noses and eyes squirted full of ammonia; and this was odd because the summer before, in newspaper stories on circus day, the Baron was always quoted as averring that the only way to train wild animals was by patience and kindness.

One morning after six weeks of this the Baron appeared in the booking agent's office.

"I've got an act now," he stated, "that will scare the socks off you."

"I'd have to see it to believe it, and then I wouldn't believe it."

"You come out to that factory and I'll show you. You come out this afternoon."

"I should waste my time, but I will waste it. Once. Just this once. But if it ain't good—"

"It ain't so bad but it ain't so good, either," the agent said, six hours later, in the factory.

"What's wrong with it?"

"It needs something, Willie."

"What does it need? You tell me just one thing it needs and I'll—"

"Let a man think, Willie. I almost got what it needs and you run off at the mouth and I can't think."

The agent tipped back in his chair, and his gaze roved past the arena bars to Marybelle. As the Baron's assistant, she was wearing an old training costume, light tan pants and a tan shirt. The agent contemplated her, and then his chair came down and he stood up, grinning.

"Willie, I've got it. You fix up the act like I tell you and I'll book you with a carnival."

"A carnival!"

"What do you expect? Can I book miracles? After the way you flopped with Vendee & Gonzaga—"

"Never mind that. What does the act need?"

"Sex."

"Sex, for Christ's sake!"

"Sure, Willie. Ain't you heard of sex? The act needs sex. You give the act sex and I'll book you with a carnival and after a season or two I'll find you a nice circus."

"I don't like the idea of no God-damned carnival."

"Maybe you think I should book you with the Ringlings. Maybe you think I'm a miracle man. You'll take what I get you or I'll toss you out on your can."

"How can I give the act sex?"

"The man asks that," exclaimed the agent, "when he's got a wife that will knock 'em in the snoot. You put your wife into the act like I'm going to tell you, and—"

He waved a hand, and they both looked at Marybelle. Her smile might have meant anything, but her eyes were those of a tribal princess hearing she must appease the gods by jumping into a volcano.

"Oh-o, no," she murmured. "I do not think—"

"That is right!" the Baron thundered. "You do not think and you will be all okay! You do what we tell you and everything will be fine!"

From that day forward being the Baron's wife was less than ever like being the wife of Captain Latcher.

"I was like the poor monkey," Marybelle told herself, early one evening the following May, as she stood on a carnival lot in Kentucky. Soaring up from the throng a great balloon wobbled, leaking hot smoke, and dangling below the bag a monkey swayed on a trapeze.

As she watched, balloon and monkey diminished with altitude, and then the monkey cast itself loose and plunged. A parachute blossomed against the green twilight and the crowd cheered the brave monkey.

"I am still like the monkey," she thought, for she knew that Jocko had no stomach for his work. Performing the free balloon ascension terrorized him so abjectly that he would have refused, except that his trainer whipped him each evening till he preferred the danger of the sky.

"Still like the monkey," she thought, climbing into the dressing-van, where her trainer waited.

It was a very fine carnival, as carnivals went. Its name was Lorenz & Ambrose's Universal Shows, and its owners were the same Lorenz and Walt Ambrose who years before had accumulated a snug nest egg on Burgoyne's Circus & Hippodrome by following the dictate that honesty is the next-best policy.

At a good pitch on the midway the Baron's tent stood, and all that season and for several seasons thereafter the denizens of rural America gathered before the platform outside the tent, listening to the barker's fanciful predictions of what would occur within. A great tawdry banner proclaimed: "Baron Karl Otto Von Krummer & His Jungle Beasts." And beneath, in smaller letters: "With Marybelle Monahan."

Thrice each evening the Baron and his wife mounted the platform, and the barker thumped a bass drum and shouted, "Eee-yo! Eee-yo! Eee-yo!" These noises were designed to snag the crowd's attention. And once snagged, Marybelle held it.

She looked ravishing in the tight hussar's coat, scarlet, with gold braid and black frogs; and her creamy silk tights and black Roman boots were pleasantly filled. Upon her hair, glorious in the bright electricity, she wore a scarlet cap with a gleaming black bill, and to hide her dread of the arena she smiled. She looked serene and composed, a mysterious lady from the great world beyond the carnival lot. And to the creek bottom farmers and the grocery clerks it never occurred that her valor in entering the arena was inspired by the animal whip in the Baron's hand.

He was a valiant figure, too. Impossible to imagine that those shoulders, broadening with the years, had ever darted and squirmed to the rods beneath a boxcar. Incredible that he had ever groveled and howled before Captain Latcher!

Yes, a fine, brave figure! But an angry one, because Marybelle rather than he drew the crowd's gaze. Yet his ire was understandable, for he had become an artist now, with the artist's professional jealousy. And if there were inconsistency in his jealousy that too was understandable, for it abraded his masculine pride to have a woman surpass him in anything. Small wonder he had grown slowly to hate her! The hate had planted itself on their wedding night, as if, being an extremist, he must hate what he could not love, and it grew with the years as her performance in the arena evoked more applause than his. And if he realized that without her the act would fail, this did not warm him with gratitude but only with more hate.

He still suspected her, too, of deep, crafty thoughts. Sometimes inadvertently she said something that brought his old fears to life, and he told himself that she was waiting—thinking out some cunning plan to turn him over to the hangman. Well, he thought, she would have to divorce him before she could testify; and that was one reason why he watched her when other men were about, and threatened to kill her if she ever left him. The other reason was because he did not intend to let another man have what he could not himself enjoy.

So she was virtually his prisoner, but he was also hers. They were chained together. And she irritated him, being always about. The fox in the fable at last slunk away from the grapes it could not eat, but the Baron was tantalized and mocked always by her beauty. He had given up attempting to enjoy her beauty, because even when he thought that this time he would be successful the memory of old failures intruded. And shame crawled over his skin. So he abused her because she was desirable and dangerous and necessary to the success of the act, and she cried out and begged him to desist and promised to do anything he wished. But she could not turn her mind inside out and show him its great simplicity; she could not tell him she had never suspected him of murder, because she had not.

Traveling with the carnival gave them a living, but that was about all. During the winters they were without income, and by spring their funds had sunk desperately low. Once, in the hopes of pleasing him, and getting away from him for a few hours daily, she offered to secure a waitress job to tide them along, but the suggestion angered him—he lived in constant fury—and he announced he would not have a wife of his working. And although he sincerely believed that a woman's place was the kitchen, his refusal was complicated by his fear that as a waitress she would pick up some man as she picked up Captain Latcher and run away. Nor did he seek winter employment. If he were gone all day, who knew what his wife might be doing?

Her appearance changed as the years passed; she was a woman now; and her bright hair would have darkened had she not employed a golden rinse. But his changed more. Life in the open leathered his skin; his muscles became heavier; his face was completely mature. And other indefinable changes slipped over him. The brutality of his spirit extended itself to his countenance. And discontent stamped itself there, for the Baron was an ambitious fellow, the equal—nay, the superior!—of any animal trainer alive; but where was all that ability getting him? A carnival! Starving along! It made him furious!

And then after so many years there came puffing across his orbit the trajectory of A. H. Burgoyne.

This fateful meeting took place in the fine little city of Maplewood, in southeastern Kansas. It was August, 1928, and the carnival had booked itself there for a week. And meanwhile, Burgoyne & Paw-packer's Great 3-Ring Circus was attempting to drain off some of the riches of the oil town of Bartlesville, Oklahoma.

Unfriendliness had never been successfully charged against A. H. Burgoyne, and upon realizing that a carnival owned by his old cronies, Lorenz and Walt Ambrose, was doing business within a few hours' drive by fast Packard, he loaded himself behind the wheel and went whizzing across the plains.

Arriving at the lot in the early afternoon, he drove up to the office wagon and held his thumb on the horn. Lorenz and Ambrose thought at first it must be some gillie getting smart, and they came striding out with blood in their eyes, but when they saw who it was they whooped and celebrated the brotherhood of man.

"You God-damned old thief!" Lorenz exclaimed. "Knew you was playing Bartlesville, but—!"

"Hello, Gus," the side of Ambrose's mouth said. "The Oklahoma cops after you?"

And Gus exclaimed well, well, well, it was a pretty small world after all; and people a half-block away could hear him laughing.

"Haven't seen you boys since Frisco," Gus exclaimed. "Neither of you look a year older!"

This was false, for Lorenz had lost all his teeth, and he was a round-shouldered, wolf-eyed old man, but it was one of those things that costs nothing and pleases an old friend, and Gus loved to please people.

"You've got a nice layout here," he said. "How's business?"

"We're getting along," Lorenz admitted. "Making an honest dollar one way or another."

Gus laughed harder than ever at that.

Owing to hot weather, Gus wore not a checked suit but a Palm Beach one today, and he had removed the coat. That way, you had an unexcelled view of his Santa Claus girth. Both a belt and suspenders guarded his trousers, and as he talked he removed his hard straw hat and mopped his brow.

In the office wagon the three friends reminisced about old times, and Lorenz inquired concerning Flora.

"She's fine," Gus said, "except she's taken on weight. Her corset bills are terrible." And he laughed and patted his belly. "Guess I could use a corset myself."

"How did you come out with your Speedway?" Lorenz asked. "Heard you didn't do so good with that."

"I went broke," Gus admitted. "Mistake of my youth. But let me tell you how I made my comeback."

And as he recounted how he had salted the coal mine and duped Ive Pawpacker, the office wagon rocked with their laughter. Tears of mirth rolled down Gus's cheeks, and Lorenz kept saying:

"If I could just have seen the little devil's face when he found out! If I could just have seen it!"

Then Gus sobered.

"I really didn't grift him, though. Knew I could make him a pile of money with the circus, and I have."

"Business is good, eh?"

"Not so good as it used to be. But we're managing. I don't know— the gillies don't tumble to a circus the way they did twenty years ago."

"It's these God-damned moving pictures," Lorenz declared. "And autos. The gillies are wised up, now."

Then through the windows there drifted the music of a merry-go-round organ, and as always those joyous notes and the beats of bass drum and snare drum stirred Gus's blood.

"Kind of like to look over your layout," he said.

So they sauntered along the midway, and presently they stood before the tent dedicated to the Baron and his beasts. The barker thumped his drum, and Marybelle and the Baron mounted the platform.

"I know those folks!" Gus exclaimed to Lorenz. "Von Krummer. Used to be Latcher's cage boy. And Marybelle Monahan! Gave her a wedding dinner when she married the Captain."

"Sure, Gus. And ain't she a pretty little plum?"

"Uh," Gus said, his gaze lost in her loveliness. "I'd kind of like to see their act."

The Baron recognized A. H. Burgoyne, so that afternoon in the tent his demeanor was that of a good soldier under inspection by a field marshal.

"I'll show the fat bastard," he thought. "His circus ain't much, but at least it's not a carnival."

But the Baron's valor and precision were wasted, for while he performed A. H. Burgoyne focused his attention on the Baron's wife, standing outside the arena with shapely legs together, awaiting her turn. At last the Baron retreated to the safety cage; and then Marybelle, who had been so composed and feminine and mysterious, turned toward the arena. A sharp observer might have noted in her a half-second's hesitation, and the Baron snapping his whip against his boots, as if she had been trained like the cats to respond to this cue.

Her manner altered as she entered the safety cage. Beneath her uniform you could sense her nerves tightening and her muscles growing taut; and when she clanged open the arena door her soft femininity was overlaid by swift litheness. Her footwork was graceful and precise, like a dancer's. And the whole act took on a flowing ballet quality. The lions undulated and the tigers were sinuous; and Marybelle, cracking her whip, was suddenly not so much Venus as Diana: a vivid Swedish Diana with the cunning of the stalker and the ruthlessness of the huntress. Because her fear was so primitive the act became primitive. It was as startling as gazing unexpectedly upon a naked woman.

"Beauty and the beasts," Gus thought. "By God! Give her act music, and—"

There was a great hoop through which a tiger must leap. And the tiger balked.

Gus found his breath coming faster, his heart pounding. Her body curved like Diana's bow, and her tendons were bowstring taut. And the contest of wills between the silky butter-and-black cat and the woman with the cracking whip seemed to generate an elemental energy that glittered like light-flashes through the arena bars.

And then the cat's muscles rippled and up it soared, flying lightly through the hoop, and the woman's heels were winged, carrying her backward.

The applause was spontaneous. And the Baron's mouth twisted, for his own applause had been as sparse as firecrackers late at night on July Fourth.

Gus didn't offer the Baron a contract that day, naturally. After all,

Lorenz and Walt Ambrose were his friends, and as their guest it would have been scarcely honorable to try hiring their featured act. He did, however, renew his acquaintance with the Von Krummers.

"Great act, Willie!" he exclaimed. "Not a dry seat in the house!"

And to Marybelle:

"I want to congratulate you on a thrilling performance! Got a lot of heat!"

She smiled.

He thought about her smile, driving back to Bartlesville, and during the next weeks he remembered that afternoon as a happy one. It was a blond-colored afternoon and charmed. His adventures with pretty women had grown few as the years passed and his youth receded; and never except with Carlotta had he been in love. And she was so·far in the past that he almost never thought about her, and when he did even the poignancy was gone.

But now as the season closed and he returned to winter quarters the memory of Marybelle persisted. On bright autumn days or autumn days of soft rain he would find himself thinking of her sweet face and that queer little smile that promised so much. And he would remember how her composure had burst into flame, once she entered the arena, and he wondered how it would be to make love to a woman so smooth and cool on the surface but so hot with passion beneath.

And then he would think of her husband. And tell himself, "Whoa! That Dutchman looks meaner than hell. Good way to get bullets in your pants, making a pass at his wife."

Nevertheless, he continued thinking of her. Her savage husband flavored her with danger. And he didn't dislike the flavor. Gus had attained the dangerous age in man. Nearly fifty. He had lived longer than he would live. Life was so brief, so brief, with its silken surfaces and cozy restaurants and smooth liquors and juicy steaks. Still in the prime of life; but over the hilltop sixty waited, and seventy if you were lucky; and after that there would be city streets full of people and theater marquees blazing but you would be shut away in the dark ground and forgotten.

"God, but I love it all," he thought, "but how it's flying past!"

And he wondered whether her smile when she looked at him had been something special. An invitation?

And across the dinner table at winter quarters he beheld Flora, her double chins quivering, full of sighs and solicitude about his liver, apt to break into mourning for Baby or Madam Thale, and he thought:

"I let life cheat me once. Let Carlotta get away from me. I won't let life cheat me again."

And so in December when he visited Chicago he called on the Baron's booking agent; and that was how it came about that when

Alex Kerry joined the circus as a clown the Baron Karl Otto Von Krummer (with Marybelle Monahan) chanced to be a headline performer.

Till mid-July Alex traveled with the show. He received no salary, and although his intent had been to clown every day he did not, actually, enter the ring more than two dozen times. The circus heaved into his artistic hopper so much material that his fingers yearned for brushes and oils, and you were always encountering him in the back yard or beneath the menagerie top, making sketches.

Gus liked him well enough, but he never fully understood him. He always had the uneasy feeling that Alex might be smiling at him. The fellow had an oblique way of saying things that troubled Gus, who felt more comfortable when the obvious was insisted upon.

Nor did Gus realize for many years just how famous a guest he had entertained. This was natural; Alex's talent was appreciated by only a few thousand Americans; not till he died did he become really respectable. Moreover, Alex's appearance did not square with Gus's ideas of fame. Gus liked to have a famous man look famous, the way Warren G. Harding had looked statesmanlike. He wanted fame to don a plug hat and a Prince Albert coat, as it had in the eighties and nineties.

Nevertheless, since Alex was a notoriety, Gus welcomed him on the show, quite disregarding his request that his joining be kept secret. Gus tipped off Pinky Connor in the publicity department, who tipped off the press; so once again Alex broke into the newspapers. ARTIST BECOMES CIRCUS CLOWN. That sort of thing. And Alex's enemies cried gleefully that at last this upstart Kerry had revealed himself for what he was: a vulgar showman.

Alex was pretty cross about that publicity, but when accused of betraying a confidence Gus denied everything, maintaining that Pinky Connor had broken the story without consulting him. This didn't fool Alex, but he let it pass. He was planning to do a portrait of Gus, and he felt the incident gave him valuable insight into the man's character.

"Don't know why you want to paint my mug," Gus said, one afternoon while posing. "Ought to paint Marybelle Monahan. She's a beauty. Why don't you paint her?"

"I didn't bring along enough gold oils," Alex smiled.

Despite his show of modesty, Gus was delighted that Alex wished to do his portrait, and he was especially delighted that Molly was to be included on the canvas. For several afternoons they posed in the menagerie top, Gus stalwart by Molly's side. She was so huge now, with such a tough old hide, that it was hard to imagine she had once been a baby elephant in Funland Park.

"Ever tell you how I got Molly?" Gus asked, and he told the whole story about the children contributing dimes. And Alex was such a good audience—he wanted to know everything about the subject of a portrait—that Gus elaborated and relived those days of youth, even recounting how Carlotta came to the park and how he fell in love. His face was heavy and sad.

"What happened?" Alex asked.

"Happened? Uh—I let her get away from me. Lovers' quarrel. I married Flora and she married an educated fool. Guess she's had a bad time of it. I met her and her husband on the street three or four years ago. He looked about the same, only dried up. A stiff wind would have blown him away." Gus laughed. "She'd changed. Hardly knew her. You know—gray hair and all that. We talked maybe five minutes and then they walked on. She still looked pretty young, from the back. Still walked the way she used to. And you know, it left me feeling kind of blue. Sort of in the dumps. Well, guess we can't stay young always."

"You're a philosopher," Alex said; but he realized instantly that was a mistake, for Gus's eyes became shrewd and guarded.

"He's no fool," Alex thought. "At first you think he's just a bag of wind, but he's intelligent."

After three sessions of posing, Alex announced that their work was at an end.

"I'll finish it in my studio," he said, "and send it to you. It'll take me weeks of work."

Gus was disappointed, for by now he was eager to see himself in oils. And at this point the canvas looked like nothing at all; just smears.

"Glad to keep on posing if you want me to," he said.

"That isn't necessary. I have a good memory. And I have my sketches. Besides, there are a couple of other pictures I want to do."

And so before returning to Millborough Alex blocked out two more paintings, and when at last he shipped them east in 1931 his dealers were enthusiastic and sold them at splendid prices even though times were hard. Carlton Briggs Trelawney, Esq., the Cleveland industrialist, bought the picture called "Funny Man," depicting a broken-down old clown. Another dealer, working through a stooge, bought "The Animals" and held it for a price rise, selling it finally to Mrs. Gilbert Folawn, who gave it to the Metropolitan. This was the canvas showing the Baron Von Krummer in the arena, a disturbing thing, for Alex had the satanic ability to strip outer layers off his subjects. Fear floated out from that canvas, and cruelty; and connoisseurs said that not since Toulouse-Lautrec had such a countenance been painted.

In the world of art there were rumors that a third painting had crossed Alex's easel as a result of his travels with the circus, but it never reached the galleries. When asked about it Alex merely said: "I gave it away."

And he had. When he completed it late in 1930 he shipped it off to Gus. Dr. Massingham told him he was a fool to give away what might well be his best portrait, but Alex said he had promised it to Gus, and he intended abiding by his word. He had a mournful lack of money sense, anyway; he painted for the same reason that a lark sings. Till his death in 1938, he lived on very simply through success, with an Aristotelian disregard for possessions. Once he told an interviewer that when a man owned the sunrise and the new moon and cumulus clouds and the songs of dusk frogs, it seemed absurd to lust after Packards and electric refrigerators. It was not difficult to understand why many persons in Millborough referred to him as that nut painter.

The painting, "Gus The Great," arrived at winter quarters in December, while the Burgoynes were making their traditional Chicago visit; and not till early January did Gus uncrate it. By then, he had nearly forgotten Alex's traveling with the show. Since 1929 many worries had lodged themselves in his brain.

Despite the billboards announcing "Business Is Good" and "Nothing Can Stop Us," and the wistfully rosy speeches at the Chamber of Commerce, and the Greater Tamarack Association's sponsoring a "Prosperity Week," and merchants' saying that if only people would ignore the depression it would end, Burgoyne & Pawpacker's Great 3-Ring Circus had lost heavily in the summer of 1930.

"Tell you, Ive," Gus boomed, in April of that year, "way I look at it is this. People will always want entertainment. If they're worried about money they'll come to the show to forget."

"I hope you're right," Ive said.

They were sitting in the office at winter quarters, and Ive looked tired and worried and old. He was still immaculately dressed, but inside his clothes his body had shrunk like a wrinkled bean in a pod; and he was having trouble with his eyes. He had spent considerable, visiting specialists, but the malady was exceedingly odd.

"Mr. Pawpacker," a famous St. Louis doctor had told him, "I can find nothing wrong—organically—with your vision. So I'm going to ask you a question, although it's really out of my field. Have you suffered any great shock?"

"No more than any businessman. I was in the market."

"Did the crash affect you emotionally?"

In recent years Ive had grown testy, and he snapped:

"No."

"The reason I ask is this. You tell me you have moments of complete blindness. Then your vision clears. I venture to believe that your blindness may be—and pardon the term—psychic."

Ive laughed shortly.

"It sounds absurd," the specialist said, "but it's the only explanation I can offer. We have found that some men shell shocked in the war have been afflicted with such blindness. To simplify a complicated subject, I'll say that their eyes had gazed upon such horrors that the brain recoiled and refused to grant admittance to the impulses of the optic nerves. Now if you could remember just where and when you were first afflicted with loss of sight—"

Ive stood up.

"That's nonsense. How much do I owe you?"

The specialist sighed.

"My secretary will give you my bill."

Old men sometimes become crotchety, and Gus had his hands full with Ive.

"Why," he groaned to himself, "am I always mixed up with bankers? He's worse than Sam Oxenford!"

And while this was exaggeration, certainly in these bad years Ive found fault with every penny Gus spent.

"You're hauling too many cars," he fretted, toward the end of the 1930 season. "Send some back to the farm."

"We're down to twelve now. The Ringlings have a hundred.

"Damn the Ringlings! Forget the Ringlings, can't you?"

Gus grinned ruefully.

"Always kind of thought we'd run them out of business."

"Well, we never will. We'll be lucky if we keep afloat. If we don't show a profit in '31, Gus, we'll close down."

"Now wa-a-ait a minute, Ive—!"

"We've got to look facts in the face," Ive snapped. "You don't have any money to pour into deficits and I'll be damned if I'll keep dipping into my personal fortune. If you can call it that—and you can't."

"Tell you," Gus said. "My idea is, we'll lean a little heavier on grift. Don't like to do it—when I think how they used to call me Honest Gus—but a man's got to do what he's got to do. My idea, Ive—we'll clean up in '31 and then change the name of the show in '32 and go out with a clean slate. Uh—make it strictly Sunday School, in '32. Times will be better then. You can't tell me a little crash in Wall Street can keep the old U.S.A. down on its pratt forever. Prosperity's just around the corner. Don't you think so?"

"No."

"You think this thing's going to last?"

"They'll call it the depression of the thirties, Gus."

Gus laughed, but it chilled him.

On that morning when Gus first viewed the painting, January lay brightly white on the earth and brightly blue above. The overnight train from Chicago relieved itself of the Burgoynes' weight in the Tamarack Union Station, and they waddled to a nearby garage where Gus had stored his Packard. During the prosperous twenties he had purchased a new car every year, but this was the same sedan that had carried him from Bartlesville to Maplewood back in 1928.

In the garage Flora paused momentarily and stared at the car.

"Now, Gus. Don't drive too fast."

"Uh—I'll keep 'er down to a hundred."

Only the integrity of the Packard Motor Company prevented the car from collapsing when Flora mounted the runningboard, for she was even heavier than her husband. Her legs would have given solid support to a grand piano, and her movements were about as nimble as a grand piano's, too.

Gus did not pay the storage bill, for this was one of the many business establishments where he maintained charge accounts. They were all in arrears. His old policy of strict honesty and good credit in Tamarack was aiding him now.

"Had a tough season with the show," he told creditors. "But next year—"

They understood. Times were hard for everybody.

They left the garage and cruised through the business section. On this cold morning traffic was light, and Gus didn't need to employ his horn as much as he did. Few pedestrians hurried along the sidewalks, and with his love of crowds this depressed Gus.

"The turn will come in the spring," he said cheerfully. "Ive's a pessimist, that's his trouble. Being a knocker never got a man any place. Look for the silver lining! That's my motto."

"What turn will come?" Flora asked.

"The turn in business. This is just temporary. Bet we'll rake it in next summer. You don't think Hoover and all those big fellows in the East will let this go on, do you?"

"I don't know, Gus. The turn might not come. People spent their money awful fast, that's sure. It's like Papa always said. You spend a dime and it's gone. Gone forever."

"Uh," Gus replied.

They passed the Oxenford Electric Building. It looked soot-coated and out-of-date; no longer did it soar up from the best business corner. Not that it had moved: the business district had edged westward through the decades, block by block.

"Wouldn't even want an office there now," Gus thought, "if I could afford an office in town. Nobody offices there but shyster lawyers."

To him, fresh from Chicago, even the best of the business district looked inconsequential; but he harried that disloyal thought from his mind. He began whistling "Tamarack the Beautiful," and he summoned up the memory of a map the Chamber of Commerce had once issued, showing the United States with Tamarack at the crossroads, lines radiating out to every corner of the country.

"Great future," he thought, "here in the Mississippi Valley, the garden spot of the world."

But those catch phrases from luncheon speeches on long-forgotten noons did not comfort him today. What was wrong with him, anyway? Was he going to permit financial worry to poison his system?

"It'll be all right," he thought. "Bet we'll have a great season. We'll have the Baron again, and Marybelle—"

She smiled mysteriously in his imagination, as he drove through residential streets and gained the open country. The Burgoynes had entertained the Baron and his wife at dinner in Chicago, and now he remembered the suppressed excitement he had felt as he watched her across the linen and silver. Always something unspoken hovered between them.

"You ask me, Willie, and I'll say your wife's the best animal woman in the country."

That was the nearest to a compliment he dared go, and when he glanced at her he could see her cheeks warm with pleasure.

"If I could only get her alone!" he moaned inwardly.

But he couldn't. Or at least hadn't. The damned Dutchman was always present! Terribly jealous of her, so the gossip ran. On the circus the Von Krummers lived to themselves; unfriendly! And yet now and again, behind her husband's back, Gus caught her gaze, and her smile sent warmth through his arteries.

"Terrible thing—a jealous man!" Gus thought.

At that Chicago dinner, there had been a dancing floor and an orchestra; Gus had planned their dining at such a place; for it seemed that if he could only hold her in his arms he would attain supreme happiness. And so between courses he had suggested:

"Good orchestra, don't you think? How about it, Mrs. Von Krummer? Like to shake a hoof with me?"

He thought a light came on behind her face, but before she could respond that damned Dutchman glared at Gus and announced:

"We do not dance. You go ahead and dance with Mrs. Burgoyne."

One of those social crises!

"Uh—tell you. Wouldn't want to leave you sitting alone."

"That is all right. You dance."

"I don't know, Gus," Flora smiled. "I think maybe I would like to dance."

"Uh—well—sure." And then to the Baron, hopefully and humorously he suggested: "Sure you don't want to dance, too? Might trade off wives, huh?"

At that the Baron really looked angry, although anybody would have known that Gus's words were spoken in levity.

"We do not dance, I told you!"

Heat was burning Marybelle's throat; her gaze was downcast.

"Uh—guess you did, at that. Didn't mean we'd really trade wives, naturally."

So out on the floor he danced with Flora, who had never been expert in a ballroom but who welcomed this opportunity to nestle in her hero's arms. Gus found himself perspiring, and he suspected that people were smiling at their cumbrous progress around the floor.

"Flora ought to act her age," he thought.

"What is it, Gus?" Flora asked, when they found the narrow crate in the kitchen at winter quarters.

"No idea. I haven't ordered anything."

Still in hat and overcoat, he leaned over heavily and scrutinized the return address lettered on the wood: "A. Kerry, Millborough, Iowa."

"Uh. Bet I know. Bet it's my picture."

"What picture?"

"Didn't I ever tell you how Alex Kerry traveled with us a couple of seasons ago?"

"Who's Alex Kerry?"

"Artist. You know. Paints pictures."

Gus pried at the crate with a hammer, and Flora asked:

"Why did you have your picture painted? I think a photograph's more lifelike."

"Matter of fact, so do I. A painting's kind of old-fashioned. But this fellow wanted to paint me."

Nails squealed from wood; the painting was heavily wrapped with brown paper; from its excelsior nest Gus lifted out the wrapped canvas and lugged it into the living room. Despite what he had said about preferring a photograph, he was oddly happy. It aggrandized one's ego, having an artist paint one's portrait. He had discovered that sometimes trifling things brought unexpected happiness, and now for the moment he had forgotten his grinding financial worries.

He cut the cord, unwrapped the canvas, perched it on a chair, stepped back.

"Uh," he said, and a flush swept his neck.

Flora blinked.

"I don't know," she said. "I don't think he's much of an artist. It don't look much like you, Gus. Why did he paint Molly so big?"

"Because he's a damned fool."

The painting was smooth and brilliant with sharp color, like all Kerry's work. Overhead the menagerie top spread its bright brown, and on the right side of the picture stood a huge man in a checked suit, his watch chain sporting a lion's tooth, his lapel announcing his lodge membership. With one heavy hand he held a silk hat upon his chest, but as Gus told Flora this was imagination because he had not posed with such a hat.

The man's countenance was big and imperial, and feature by feature it certainly resembled Gus. And yet the face, taken as a whole, didn't look like the Gus the world saw. The noble elevation of the wattled jaw was slightly too noble, the mouth too kingly. But the pouched gray eyes disturbed you most, for they harbored a queer mingling of reveries and ruthlessness and bitterness and ambition and regret. Their total effect was sadness, not jovial brotherhood. They looked at variance with the beefy face.

Beside the man stood an elephant, and she towered to a height that must have been exaggerated. Her trunk was coiled aloft, as if she were trumpeting, and her head was twisted slightly, so that with one sapient eye she gazed down, regarding the man with amusement. You felt it was more than the amusement of an elephant at a man. For the great beast had a tantalizing dreamlike quality, as if she were something the man was imagining, or as if she were his soul briefly made visible. She loomed so big that the man, for all his corpulence, looked inconsequential.

"Uh," Gus scowled, "don't see anything in it. More you look at it the less it looks like me. Doesn't even look like Molly. Never saw a bull turn its head that way."

Bumbling to himself, he left the house, slogging through the snow from barn to barn, gruffing admonitions to his reduced staff of maintenance men. The mood of the picture clung to his mind like fog, and he had a notion to destroy it. But he couldn't bring himself to that; maybe, he told himself, it was better than it seemed in this time of depression and woe; so he wrapped it in its paper and slid it back into the crate and carried it up into the attic, where it gathered dust.

In times of inflation, the stupidest entrepreneur makes money and believes himself sagacious; in deflation the shrewdest loses, and blames the economic cycle. The summer of 1931 was not inflationary. It was such a bad season that to Gus the losses of the previous year looked almost like profits.

"Never thought I'd see the time," he told himself, "when a good grifter couldn't hustle a living."

But that time had come. Once the three-shell men and the monte men and the dips had made a good thing out of the show. Now they garnered dimes and quarters, when they garnered at all.

"People had money. Where did it all go?" Gus demanded of high heaven.

Somewhere, somewhere. Into the banks, perhaps, but now the banks were breaking open like rotten melons, and the money was not inside. Where was it? Button, button—who's got the button?

"This thing can't go on," Gus announced; but of course it went on, and on. Yachts had long since been sold and great houses closed; waiters were courteous and thankful for ten percent tips; and you were always being surprised when a man you thought wealthy put a bullet through his temple. Wall Street moped and Main Street sulked. There was too much of everything except money, people said; and the factories that made shoes and ships and automobile wax closed down; and the cows were annoyed because nobody would buy their milk, and the pigs depressed because nobody would eat them; and the bales of unsold cotton burst the seams of warehouses, and the corn was burned in stoves because it was cheaper than coal; and in general it was a perfect hell of a time to be clanking about the country with a circus.

But even with Ive Pawpacker announcing that they would close the show forever at the end of the season, economic matters didn't occupy Gus's entire thoughts that summer. There was Marybelle. In June opportunity came to extend his acquaintance with her.

The circus train arrived in Alliance, Minnesota, soon after sunup on a morning that promised a sweltering day, and one of its passengers awakened in a furious mood. He was the Baron Karl Otto Von Krummer; and when with his spouse he left the sleeper and strode toward the lot, the reason for his temper could plainly be seen: he had a black eye.

A fortnight earlier, the Baron had erred by hiring a cage boy named Mike Murphy, a fellow with carrot-colored hair and Irish blood. Murphy was twenty-five, older than the usual apprentice, and before entering the Baron's employ he had driven trucks, labored in foundries and carried hod. And in the evenings, for recreation and side money, he had entered the ring in various boxing clubs and demonstrated the possibilities for self-defense inherent in a pair of hard fists.

Only bad times could have induced Murphy to accept a position as cage boy, for the wages were low, and he took an instant dislike to his employer. But at least there was food in the cookhouse.

Murphy ignored the Baron's request that he be addressed as sir, and he further annoyed the Baron by smiling at Marybelle and attempting conversation. His first day on the show he said:

"So your name's Monahan! A fine Irish name, if I do say so. Were you born on the old sod?"

It frightened her, the Baron being present. And before she could reply her husband squared his shoulders, and every short blond hair bristled from his skull.

"You will not talk to the Baroness!"

"Why not?"

"Because I say you will not!"

And he escorted Marybelle into the dressing-van and slammed the door.

Relations between the Baron and the cage boy disintegrated swiftly. Murphy took a lot of lip, because of the cookhouse; but after all, food or no food, an Irishman can stand just so much; so on the night before the show reached Alliance, following the performance, Murphy stood outside the dressing-van, grinning in anticipation. Presently he climbed the steps and said:

"There's something I want to see you about, sir."

It amused him to throw the Baron off guard, calling him sir.

He led his employer to the dark edge of the lot, where he told him a thing or two; and then, feinting with his left, he drove his right into the baronial solar plexus. The battle terminated with the Baron sitting on the grass, his face writhing in the light from distant floodlights, and he swore like a lumberjack and told Murphy he was fired; but this was redundant, since Murphy had quit before launching out with his fists.

"Hoch der Kaiser," Murphy laughed back. "Be seeing you—I hope not."

And that was why, on this June morning in Alliance, the Baron walked more stiffly than usual. That was why his right eye was swollen nearly shut.

Breakfast in the cookhouse failed to palliate his mood. People glimpsed his black eye and smiled and whispered. And after breakfast, because of his cage boy's desertion, the Baron was reduced to menial labor: in the menagerie top he had to clean the cage wagons. And in Wagon Number 23, a tiger attacked him, clawing his shoulder and ribs. Although Marybelle and several roustabouts were present, nobody could state just how the accident happened.

Bleeding profusely, the Baron managed to squirm from the cage wagon. There was great excitement; A. H. Burgoyne was summoned; and while waiting for an ambulance the Baron lay on the grass, swearing what he would do to the cat when he recovered. The ears of the

Society for the Prevention of Cruelty to Animals must have burned. And the Baron kept screeching also:

"I won't take ether! I won't have no God-damned anesthetic!"

That afternoon, Marybelle presented the act alone. And in one sense the accident was lucky, for the publicity department went into action, and the evening paper printed her picture, elaborating upon the devotion between husband and wife, quoting her as saying many things she did not say, such as that the show must go on.

And that evening the train left without the Baron. This he did not like but he was in no position to forbid it, with fever roasting him and blood poisoning likely. It set in, too, and for weeks the Von Krummer vitality fought the infection. Till August he lay in the hospital, and he was always asking nurses whether he talked in his sleep. They told him he muttered a good deal, but they couldn't make sense from it.

"You're always talking about Chicago," one nurse said. "What do you have against the place, anyway?"

It could not be said that Marybelle regretted the tiger's attack upon her husband. Nevertheless, he was her man; and when she beheld him swaying from the cage wagon she was frightened and bewildered.

"If he should die what would I do?" she thought.

Like all accidents this one both sharpened and distorted reality, and while the roustabouts thronged around her cursing husband, and his blood ran red instead of blue, Marybelle simply didn't know what to do. So she stood smiling slightly.

Then into the menagerie top stormed A. H. Burgoyne, booming:

"What's wrong, Willie? Did you get hurt?"

The question caused the Baron to curse louder than ever.

"God damn you for a tub of lard from a sick pig!" he screamed. "Of course I'm hurt, you gutty kangaroo!"

And many other inaccurate but refreshingly vivid oaths.

Mr. Burgoyne took charge of everything, booming out orders that sent the roustabouts scurrying. And to her he said:

"Better go to the dressing-van. This is no place for a lady."

She hesitated, fearful that the Baron might be annoyed at her leaving, but he was too occupied with other matters to notice. So she obeyed Mr. Burgoyne, and it warmed and comforted her to submit to his will. After living with the Baron, obedience had become her normal way of life.

In the van she sat with hands clasped loosely in her lap, her thoughts slowly arranging themselves. How would the accident affect her? Would she become a widow once more? If so, what then? She was still as religious as ever, so now she closed her eyes and prayed, asking

God to provide guidance in a troubled situation. She made no suggestions, and she finished by whispering, "Thy will be done."

Presently Mr. Burgoyne appeared in the door.

"Uh—sent him away in an ambulance. Hospital. He'll be okay."

"You think he will get well?"

"Willie? 'Course he'll get well! Take more than a few scratches to make Willie kick the bucket."

She felt relieved, but queerly let down, too.

"Uh—you'll carry on, of course, with the act?"

"I do not know."

"Now look here, Mrs. Von Krummer! Of course you'll carry on! Wonderful artist like you wouldn't let a little thing such as this stop you!"

Wonderful artist! The words warmed her. Always the sin of vanity had afflicted her. As the Captain's wife she had received compliments daily, purring softly like a kitten full of cream; and the years with the Baron had left her starved.

"You think I will be able to handle the act?"

"Able! You're too modest, Mrs. Von Krummer. Uh—mind if I call you Marybelle? Seems more friendly."

"Oh-h, no, I do not mind. You think I am too modest?"

"Should say you are! Modesty's your middle name! Understand your point of view, though—I've always been that way myself. But there's no cause for you to be modest! I think you're the best animal trainer in the world."

"Oh-h, no!"

"It's a fact! Act wouldn't be any good without you."

"My husband is very good, too."

"Not as good as you! Willie's a fine fellow, and all that, but it's your work that puts their hearts in their throats."

She glowed and basked. But, oddly, she missed her husband's authority. She had decided to enter the arena, but she wanted to be compelled to enter it. So she said:

"I do not know. Maybe I had better not work the cats."

And she lowered her gaze.

"Now look here, Marybelle!" He strode over, and she felt his big forefinger beneath her chin, lifting it. "You've got to do it! Show must go on! You've got to!"

"If you say I must, I must," she whispered, and her heart beat faster under the sway of his authority.

They would parade at eleven, despite the Baron's hospitalization; and as Marybelle dressed she found herself enjoying her husband's absence. Her thoughts kept returning to the interview with Mr. Bur-

goyne, and her smile was happier than it had been for years. He had
made her feel necessary and important to the show's welfare.

"Willie never told me I was a wonderful artist," she thought.

She could not agree with her husband about Mr. Burgoyne's being a
tub of lard. He was the owner. In his bulk she saw dignity and authority. He had a paternal quality that she liked, because it suggested
protection and benevolent despotism. Always as a girl she had enjoyed
obeying her father, and as Mr. Christianson's employee she had liked
being told what to do. A virtue in a woman, obedience. Of course, it
could lead to excesses.

In the dressing mirror she saw her reflection, and she was astonished
at its happiness.

"Oh-h," she whispered, "I am wicked. Poor Willie is so-o hurt, and
I am thinking about Mr. Burgoyne. He thinks I am a wonderful artist
and it is turning my vain head."

But the happiness persisted on her countenance, and the richness of
her coloring made the mirror blond. She was twenty-eight, but her
placidity had protected her from the ravages that her experiences might
have eroded upon the face of a less tranquil woman. She had few
wrinkles, and they were almost invisibly delicate. Her hair was glorious, and summer suns had tinted rather than burned her creamy skin:
it was evenly and faintly golden, as if warmed by peach-colored light.
Her brow and eyes were serene.

And struggle against vanity all she would, she could not but admit
that she looked dreamily lovely this morning; and she wondered
whether her beauty influenced Mr. Burgoyne's opinion of her work
with the cats.

"Perhaps some day he will tell me I am beautiful," she thought. She
wished he would. It was only the harmless yearning of her vanity for
peacock-colored words.

She turned from the mirror and regarded the gown she would wear
in the parade when she sat upon the silver sleigh drawn by the yellow
wooden horses. Freshly cleaned, it hung from a wire hanger. It was
of bridal satin. Mr. Burgoyne furnished two such gowns, and he always insisted that they be fresh and spotless. She stood thinking about
how she would look wearing it amid the silver calliope music.

This was part of her new freedom: to dawdle as she dressed. Willie
would be thundering for her to hurry. But Willie was injured.

Getting ready for the parade, she had sponge-bathed from a pan and
a bucket; and then, obscurely impelled, she had attired herself in filmy
underthings she had bought long ago while the Captain's wife: a lacy
brassière and lacy briefs. She wore no stockings—none would be
needed with the satin gown—but her feet looked pretty in silver slippers. She was all graceful curves, her skin as smooth as the gown.

And while she stood stroking the gown before putting it on a knock fell upon the door, and somebody said:

"Uh—Mrs. Von Krummer. Marybelle."

Later, she upbraided herself. She should have called out, "Wait, please. I am dressing."

But she said only, "Yes?"

The word was not precisely an invitation to enter, and yet in a way it was, too. Perhaps she had wanted him to enter. Wickedly! Oh, that dreadful vanity! Perhaps knowing how fetching she looked, she had wanted Mr. Burgoyne to see her thus, and to titillate her insatiable vanity with lovely words.

However it was, the mischief was done and he opened the door.

And oh, what a bad thing her vanity was! She knew what she should do. She should exclaim and snatch something around her. But what? Her dressing gown was hanging on the other side of the van. And besides, the expression on his face—the admiration and genuine interest—held her inactive in her revealed loveliness.

And she smiled, although her cheeks burned with shame and wickedness. Still not too late for modesty!—she could still make a dash for her dressing gown!—but vanity, vanity!—she knew she would look embarrassed and flustered, trying to cover herself.

"You wanted to talk to me?" she asked, in that low, modulated voice.

"Uh . . ." His face had gone scarlet, and she could almost see his brain racking itself, trying to remember what had brought him. And now he was the one flustered, and suddenly she felt cool and in command, and although usually she preferred submission she enjoyed that sensation, too.

"Uh—yes. Just wanted to tell you we're ready to start parading."

"Oh-h, I am late! I am so-o sorry."

"That's all right. Think nothing of it." And suddenly he smiled and the embarrassment left him and he was in command again. "You're a beautiful woman, Marybelle. Always knew you were, of course, but I'd never—uh—realized just how beautiful. You'd win a beauty contest any day!"

"Oh-h," she smiled. "You are flattering me!"

"No, no!—no flattery about it! Beautiful woman! Beautiful!" He pointed at her legs, swelling up from her dimpled knees. "Hurt yourself, I see. What happened?"

She looked down at the dark parallel marks.

"Willie."

"Uh?"

"Oh-h, he was furious last night. The cage boy gave him such a bad black eye. He was so-o angry that he whipped me."

"Did what!" Gus thundered.

"He punished me."

"Why that's—that's a terrible thing! Sweet woman like you! Why that's—that's—why damn that ornery Dutchman! Serves him right the tiger clawed him!"

"You should not say that! And you must leave now and let me dress. The parade!—we must not keep it waiting!"

She shooed him out and closed the door, and while she slipped into her gown and arranged a tiara upon her golden hair she found herself smiling and her heart beating excitedly, as if she were standing upon the verge of great adventure.

Gus felt that way, too. Following the afternoon performance, he drove Marybelle to the hospital; and since he had no wish to commiserate with Willie, he remained in the car while she went inside.

He watched till she disappeared. She was wearing a blue linen frock with a large hat of pale yellow straw, garlanded with field flowers, and she looked June-like and lovely. He had shared with her his appreciation of her radiance, and although she accused him of flattery he could tell she was not displeased.

"Prettiest legs in the world," he thought, as he observed them conveying her up the hospital steps; and he heaved a sigh and relaxed behind the wheel.

For this occasion he had dressed elegantly. Vanilla flannels enclosed his powerful legs; his white oxfords were spotless, his yellow socks snappy, his dark blue coat unwrinkled. He had visited a barber, and like a harbinger of returning prosperity he had taken the works: haircut, shave, massage, manicure. His cheeks were velvety with talc, and from beneath his hard straw hat a scent of hair tonic emanated.

He sat smoking and sighing, enravished by lunacy in its most pleasant guise. The sky was unbroken blue and the warm air carried the perfumes of flowers. He felt young, shot through with all the delicious aches of enchantment. He was smiling, and the colors of earth and sky—all the hot summer golds and blues and tranquil greens and passionate reds—vividly stained the surface of his mind.

"Think she likes me," he thought. "Always have thought so, the way she smiled. And then inviting me into the van—"

So he sat with his fever; and when he beheld her coming from the hospital, her high heels making castanet music, he bounced from the Packard and hustled around to open the door.

"He is asleep," she murmured, her low voice almost conspiratorial. "He was in so-o much pain they put him asleep."

Asleep! Her husband helpless under opiates!

"Uh," Gus smiled, "I've been thinking. Let's not eat in the cookhouse tonight. Let's you and me find a little café and eat where we can talk. Like to do that?"

She gazed up at him, close enough to kiss; her eyes serene, her parted lips bright.

"Oh-h," she whispered, "I think that would be so-o nice."

He was the happiest mortal alive.

The café was enchanted, although it was the ordinary café with leather booths to be found in any small city. Negotiating the booth, Gus attempted to pull in his stomach so it wouldn't jostle the table, but his stomach was a proud and outstanding part of his anatomy, and it refused retreat. As he squeezed in, he mutely excoriated restaurateurs for failing to consider the interests of fat men.

Never till now had he so regretted his obesity; and never till now, when in heart he was so young, had he been so conscious of his half century upon the earth. More than twenty years difference in their ages! For a moment he was desolated, and his brain cried out in anguish at the tricks of that old bunco man, time. Into his thoughts he summoned all the newspaper stories he had read of septuagenarians and octogenarians who had taken brides in their twenties or their teens. Things like that did happen. And he was only fifty. And such a young fifty! But maybe she was being pleasant only because he owned the circus; maybe behind that inscrutable smile she was amused at his beef.

Then across the table their gazes met and his misgivings dissolved. The edges of things softened and they were sitting at the heart of a soft blond haze. At the boundary of the magic somebody was shifting impatiently. The waitress. Dull girl with no understanding of finer feelings!

"Uh—like a steak, Marybelle?"

"That would be very nice."

"Bring us the two biggest T-bones in the house," Gus ordered. "Broil 'em on the outside with all the juice seared in."

The waitress departed; the soft haze enclosed them again; and the minutes were drenched with romance.

"You know, Marybelle," Gus said once, "I've always thought you were a beautiful woman. Remember the first time I saw you. You simply took my breath away."

She looked almost tipsy with pleasure, so he rumbled on, dealing in the fluffiest of sweet nothings, and presently he said:

"Tell me about yourself, Marybelle. You know all about me, but I hardly know you."

"But I do not really know you, either."

"Me? Oh, I'm just an old guy who—"

"Oh-h, you must not call yourself old! You do not seem old!"

"I don't?"

"Oh-h, no! You seem very wise and very successful but not old!"

Gus put the torch to his bridges.

"I was fifty my last birthday. Bet that seems old to you."

"Oh-h, no!" she crooned. "I do not think fifty is old!"

"Uh," Gus beamed, "guess you've got something there, at that. Man's as old as he feels—that's my motto."

"I do not like young men," she said. "They seem—so-o—so-o young."

Vast cheerfulness flashed over his countenance.

"That's a good one! Neat way of putting it! Marybelle, you've got a clever head on your shoulders!"

Clever! Nobody—not even Captain Latcher—had ever called her clever. Her vanity entered a land of milk and honey.

After dinner the Packard rocked into the circus lot and halted boldly by her dressing-van. Possibly it would be dangerous to be seen much in her company; lot of damned gossips on the show and word might reach Willie; but to hell with danger!

They lingered at the van steps. The west was blazing gold, and in that warm light her flesh was rosy and her hair miraculous in its sorcery. Gus quaffed her beauty like champagne, and he thought, "I'm in love. I'm in love with the Dutchman's wife!"

"Want you to be careful in that arena tonight," he said. "I'd never get over it if something would happen to you."

"Nothing will happen. You have made me feel very brave."

Each drew a long breath. The air smelled of green grass and of the menagerie and of popcorn. On the midway barkers were shouting, and a band was playing. It would be an evening of dew and stars and moths with moon-powdered wings.

"Uh—just thought of something. Let's you and I drive to our next town."

"Drive?" she murmured dreamily.

"Uh—yes. Be hot and stuffy on the train. But it ought to be a great night for driving."

"Oh-h, I do not know. Do you think we should?"

"Sure we should. Right after your act I'll call for you. Will you be ready?"

"If that is what you wish," she whispered.

At the door, over her shoulder, she gave him her smile.

18

In the summer of 1923, Mrs. Ivan Pawpacker, nee Georgiana Kelvin, returned to her native habitat.

Between Winchester and much of the outside world, train connections were as wretched as ever, so the trip from St. Louis consumed nearly a day, with several changes at junction points to trains that became successively shabbier. At last she was riding in a motorized train with a single passenger car.

Although having progressed far into her fifties, Mrs. Pawpacker did not look—or even act—her age. You would have placed her between forty-five and fifty. For this miracle—virtually stopping the sun—much hard work, self-denial and expense were responsible. So that a plastic surgeon might be paid for a little job upon her countenance, a great many horses and jacks had made love in Winchester.

Wisely enough, Georgiana had not attempted to retain the golden coloring of her locks. With the years her hair had darkened to brown, and henna rinses now concealed any silver strands among what had once been the gold. She wore it bobbed, and it was richly auburn.

Her face was the fortune of beauty operators. The skin had lost its youthful bloom, but creams and lotions kept it soft, and although an artificial face it was a smart one. And it was pleasanter, too, than in her girlhood. Now, to prevent wrinkles, Georgiana would not permit herself the luxury of scowls and a downturned mouth. Even in rage she tried to smile.

And she still had her rages and her times of sulking. Till his death a few years ago, she had made life hell for Stuart Kelvin. He had known she would if he ever succumbed, but he did succumb; and after that her threats of tattling to Eulalia kept him faithful. And Georgiana—with legislative ability inherited from W.C.—passed an income tax law, so Stuart helped Ive Pawpacker support Georgiana. However, a Southern gentleman to the last, he never mentioned this to Ive.

With Stuart's death the income from him ceased, but Georgiana did not like to lower her standard of living. Ive had come to St. Louis for the funeral, and afterward in her apartment she told her husband that her monthly check must be increased. Ive objected to giving her more money, but she threatened a divorce and whopping alimony, and at that time—the farm collapse had just occurred—he could not afford having some judge direct a huge cash settlement upon a wronged wife. So he yielded. She was as willful as ever, and just as resourceful and happy at making others uncomfortable as in the days of her youth.

The motorized car jolted and clattered, and Georgiana brooded. In that country of hills and tangled valleys everything looked the same. Although the train drowned the sounds, sheep bells were tinkling among the brush, and as twilight thickened hound dogs were yelping far away. Supper smoke curled up from distant farmhouses; the corn grew lush on the bottomlands; and at the little stations the train crew visited leisurely with the agents.

Georgiana felt deeply troubled. A few days before, the *Winchester Enterprise* had arrived at her St. Louis apartment, and a news story had told of human tragedy and human kindness. Beneath a circus tent in North Platte, Nebraska, a steel ring had crystallized, sending Lily and Ned Sebastian plunging to death; and this had orphaned a ten-year-old girl named Eloise. And Ivan Pawpacker had brought the little girl to Winchester, where she would dwell with him.

As Georgiana, in her apartment, read that story, her mouth hardened and she cast the paper to the floor. Oh! If she could have got her hands on Ive she would have given his beard a good hard yank.

She stamped to the window. Ive, she told herself, was doing this to annoy her and make her the laughing-stock of Winchester. People would say that since she had never given him a child he was adopting one.

Adopting? She whirled, grabbed up the paper, smoothed its crumpled pages.

Nothing in the story about Ive's adopting the brat. But no statement, either, that he was not adopting her. And if he did—?

She sat down, anger yielding to the problem of self-preservation. Suppose the brat insinuated herself into Ive's senile affections, and he adopted her. That would make her his legal heir, sharing his estate with his wife. Sharing? Perhaps more than that. Old men were old fools, and Ive might draw a will leaving everything to the brat!

It chilled her.

"I'd sue!" she thought. "I'd break the will!"

But the law was slow. Till she won the case, what would she live on? And perhaps she wouldn't win! The simpering little brat might craftily ingratiate herself with the jury.

She had the alarming sense of things happening behind her back. The brat must be wily to have inveigled Ive—who was becoming stingier every year—to pay her fare to Winchester and buy her food and dresses. A girl! A young female! Georgiana imagined her perched on Ive's knee, her fingers entwining his whiskers as she cajoled expensive gifts from him. Oh! There were places for young ladies like that!—orphanages and reform schools!

Georgiana decided it was high time she returned to Winchester to mend her fences. She began packing at once.

Darkness had come by the time she alighted at Winchester, and she waited while her luggage was unloaded. She felt tired and queerly depressed, as always when returning, for all the departed years were here. It was as if the mellow old town had managed to trap time; but the human beings who peopled time had slipped from the trap and vanished. She felt almost ghostlike, wandering back this way.

"I'm Mrs. Pawpacker," she told the agent, after the train chugged on. "My husband's nigger man will get my baggage in the morning. I'll just take this light bag."

The wooden station looked the same, except for electricity; and the worn bricks of the platform had known Stuart Kelvin's feet, and W.C.'s, and Eliza's, when they boarded a train for a St. Louis wedding. Georgiana sighed, and started up the hill toward the Square.

The darkness was heavy and sweet, with fireflies in vacant lots and moths at the street lamps, and she heard children playing summer games. Everything was the same; nothing was the same. Her nostalgia sharpened to loneliness, as if the ancient buildings and the humid earth released the past and it was soaking into her bones.

The Square. Concrete walks now instead of board; Fords at the hitching posts; but among the heavy trees the courthouse was the same dank building where W.C. would have argued brilliantly, if only he had had a case. Loafers were clustered outside a pool hall, and although they lapsed into speculative silence when she passed they didn't whistle after her. This disappointed her, till she told herself that Winchester was a country town without up-and-coming young men.

At the northeast corner of the Square she saw Pawpacker's Livery Stable, dark tonight, and across the street his bank. Old red brick. Gold letters on the windows announcing capital and surplus. It looked infinitely shabby and small, compared with the great St. Louis banks. It looked, she thought, somewhat like Ive; a grim, tight-fisted, calculating bank.

She walked on north, along the uneven brick sidewalk, her body heavy with the melancholy she had absorbed from the town.

When she sighted Pawpacker's house she paused, considering the business at hand. She had decided upon her strategy: to pretend surprise at finding Eloise there. She would tell Ive that she had wearied of St. Louis; and in his presence she would be sweet to the little girl, at least till she learned the lay of the land.

She gazed at the lighted house. It stood on the west side of the street, its grounds spacious. It was of Georgian architecture, and she remembered how during the eighties and nineties, in the curlicue age, it had seemed old-fashioned; but now the newest city houses were planned on the same model, so its simplicity and pure lines made it seem modern again.

Georgiana picked up her bag and moved on, but before turning in she stopped again. The land sloped gently north to the street marking the town limits, and beyond she could see Ive's farm, with the great barns housing mules and elephants. He would never tell her how much he was worth, but she thought the figure must be very large. At the possibility of his willing everything to the child she experienced renewed outrage.

Georgiana had not spent five minutes in the living room before she realized how shrewd she had been to return.

It was a pleasant room, aglow with reading lamps, quietly furnished in warm shades of beige and rose. Ive's books were there, the Dickens and Shakespeare and Montaigne he had read as a boy upon Major Redmond's urging; and there were modern authors who had written upon economics and etiquette and English usage. It was the library of a man who had educated himself. Tonight he had been reading Boswell, and now the fat volume lay on the end table by his easy chair.

"What were you reading, honey?" Georgiana asked. It was the first time she had called him honey in years. And after he told her she exclaimed, "I do declare. Just like Daddy, always reading those *old* things."

"You'll find the drugstore has a fine stock of confession magazines," he said.

She glanced at him sharply. His mouth was ironical, his eyes hard. No love in those eyes, after her coming all the way from St. Louis to visit him! It ruffled her. She felt like yanking his beard. But being on her good behavior she resisted the temptation, seating herself and chattering about St. Louis.

"I'm surprised you left."

"Why honey, I just felt all lonesome to come back and see you. And now tell me, *who* is this child?"

She indicated Eloise, sitting quietly on the davenport. Ive had briefly introduced her to Georgiana, without explanations. Now he said:

"You must have read about Eloise in the *Enterprise*."

"Read about her? No, I didn't. That old *Enterprise* is so uncertain about reaching me."

"But I'm sure you read about her."

"I like that!" Georgiana exclaimed. "You're going to make me put out, honey, practically accusing me of lying."

So Ive told his wife what both knew she already knew; and she studied the child. Eloise had a sober, still face, and she wore her hair in curls. Doubtless some persons would consider her pretty, but Georgiana knew from her own girlhood that beauty was only skin deep. A sly little sneak.

"I do declare," she told Ive, "it was *mighty* nice of you to bring her here for a *visit*."

"She's going to live here. She has no relatives, and her parents are laid to rest here in Winchester."

"Live with you! Why that's a mighty nice sentiment, I'm sure. And she'll need a mother, too, so I reckon I ought to stay and help you out."

Eloise was studying her sandals. Ive was lighting a cigar. Neither said a word, nor did they look at each other. Yet Georgiana had the uncomfortable feeling that each was thinking the same thing, and each knew what the other was thinking. Leagued against her! She determined never to leave Winchester till she had made life so miserable for Eloise that the brat would implore Ive to put her in some nice institution, such as an orphan's home.

Next morning she slept late, and when she awakened her brain was teeming with plans. She had passed the night in the guest chamber at the northeast corner of the house, and this gave her a fine opening for attack.

The guest chamber! As she flounced into her clothes she flagellated her anger. The guest chamber! Just as if she were not Ive's wife, as if she didn't belong here. And where had Eloise slept?

Eloise—if you please—had slept in Georgiana's old room at the southeast corner. Plain evidence that the brat had supplanted her in Ive's affections.

Ive, oddly enough, still occupied the small back bedroom whither Georgiana had moved his possessions long ago, when she returned from St. Louis with the newfangled notion of wives and husbands sleeping apart. He was comfortable there, and used to it.

Well! This fine summer day would see a change or two in this household!

Descending to breakfast, she glanced through the front door and beheld the brat in the yard, visiting with Emancipation who was mowing the lawn. Ive's Negro couple, Aunt Acacia and Uncle Meredith, were long dead, so now Blossom and Emancipation, rumored to be man and wife, occupied the servants' alley quarters. Emancipation! A Yankee name!

"Mornin', Mis' Pawpacker," Blossom called cheerfully, as Georgiana seated herself in the dining room.

"Good morning. Tell Eloise and Emancipation I want them to come here at once. Quickly!"

"I'll tell 'em, Mis' Pawpacker, though that man of mine ain't much fo' movin' quickly."

And indeed, most of Georgiana's grapefruit had slid down her gullet before Eloise and the two servants stood awaiting her pleasure. She decided her discipline would be more effective if she let them wait, so she ate in silence. But then the little drama was spoiled by the brat's asking:

"You wanted us?"

Georgiana flushed. And she snapped, "Yes, I wanted you, you little nigger-lover. Hereafter, if you *must* simper with the servants, *please* do it in the back yard."

"You mean I'm not to talk to Emancipation? That's crazy. Uncle Ive doesn't care."

It was before breakfast coffee: that was why Georgiana lost control and screamed, "Oh!" That was why she jumped up and stamped her foot and acted indeed more like a crazy woman than a Southern lady. At nearly the top of her lungs she informed Eloise that henceforth she would take orders from the mistress of the house. And when Eloise turned to go, she ordered, "Wait! I'm not through with you!"

Next she turned attention to Emancipation.

"Where are my trunks?"

"What you mean, Mis' Pawpacker?"

"My trunks! They're at the station with my other luggage. Two trunks."

"I ain't hear nothin' about no trunks."

"I want them at once. Now go."

And after Emancipation shuffled out, and Blossom fled to the kitchen, Georgiana told Eloise:

"I see you enjoy my room."

"Your room?"

"Yes, strangely enough, I do have a room in my own house. You've been sleeping in it. I want you to move your things out at once. You're not wanted here, but if you *must* impose on us you'll sleep in what has been Mr. Pawpacker's room. And you'll move his things into the southeast bedroom. That is where we'll sleep from now on."

Eloise looked stricken by bewilderment.

"Well, you little nigger-lover—move!"

And Georgiana started toward her.

Eloise whirled and ran. But not upstairs to work. She ran out the front door and downtown to Ive. Twenty minutes later they returned, and a very terrible quarrel ensued between Mr. and Mrs. Pawpacker.

There was considerable cane-thumping by Mr. Pawpacker, and foot-stamping by Georgiana. Blossom heard it all, from beyond the kitchen door, and cackled silently. And the brat heard it. At last in fathomless rage Georgiana ran upstairs and slammed the door of the guest room, where Mr. Pawpacker had decreed she should continue to sleep. Oh!

Nobody was happy in the Pawpacker household during the next week. Certainly not Georgiana. Her spirit was a mass of boils. She considered herself a wronged wife. Not only had Ive established another female in his home, but in every controversy he took Eloise's part.

This enraged Georgiana, but it alarmed her even more. She was convinced Ive would draw a will leaving everything to Eioise. Perhaps he had already drawn it! She could not believe that Ive's bringing Eloise to Winchester was an act of simple kindness, because kindness was outside her experience. She could not believe Eloise a grief-stricken little girl. Because Georgiana, even as a child, had been crafty and grasping, she thought Eloise a schemer.

Ive baffled Georgiana. For many years she had held him in contempt: an ungentlemanly Yankee with money-making knack. She had not supposed this knack implied shrewdness and tenacity and judgment; she considered it about on a par with the ability to wiggle one's ears. She had always got anything she wanted from him, if she raised enough hell. She had not realized he increased her allowance and winked at her affair with Stuart because he was so delighted to have her live in St. Louis and leave him in peace.

So now he was a stranger. Against her assaults he turned his Vermont granite. She couldn't nick it. His face had strength and hardness, with its gray beard and thin nose knifing from between wiry gray brows. His eyes were unyielding. And contemptuous. He knew her. It was a terrible knowledge.

Often as the years gathered grayly about him he had yearned for life as it might have been if he had met a girl with a body as pretty as Georgiana's but a better disposition. Companionship! Children! Through the decades he had been a lonely man, adding columns of figures in his livery stable. When he walked home in the evening he wished he had a family awaiting him; a wife who cared, children who cared. Sometimes it chilled him to realize that not another human being actually gave a damn whether the day had gone badly or well, whether he had a headache, whether he wore rubbers when it rained. He was like an old bachelor.

And then, Eloise.

It was a warm new experience to be depended upon, not for a monthly check but for affection, for protection. It was wonderful to have somebody else at the dinner table, somebody else in the living room while you sat reading. Sometimes in the evening, glancing over his book, he saw tears on her face, and he took her on his lap and she sobbed into his shoulder.

"Everything will be all right," he murmured. "I'll never let you down."

And although he felt wrung by her grief, those were high moments. Her tears, her vulnerability, her complete dependence gave him a sense of strength and power. His spirit was a warrior with a shining sword and shield, pacing the ramparts of some ancient city, guarding the sleep of the innocent and the beautiful.

Small wonder Georgiana found him obdurate and strange! His mind had been honed sharp by his occupations: horse trader, circus broker, country banker. It was his habit to rip aside the habiliments with which men cloaked their motives. Before she had been in the house ten minutes he deduced what had brought her. And he thought: "You're up against a different proposition this time."

That first morning when Eloise ran downtown, finding him at the livery stable, his eyes flashed when he heard her story. He said:

"Sit down. We'll talk it over."

Then he closed the doors.

"It's war," he said. "But if we stand together we'll lick her."

Till Georgiana's arrival, Eloise had known only vaguely that there was a Mrs. Pawpacker living in St. Louis. And till that morning, when Ive snapped out a brief history of their marriage, she had seldom seen him in any but a gentle mood. His bitterness surprised her.

"She's fired the first volley," he said. "Now we'll go home and open up with the field artillery."

He looked almost happy, as if during all his years of marriage he had been waiting for an issue which would warrant a fight to the finish. As they walked homeward, his short beard jutted and his step was resilient. His cane crepitated on the sidewalk like musketry. In the quarrel, his words were vitriol. And although he emphasized them with his cane, he did not seem angry. Sometimes he even smiled. And he was keenly conscious of Eloise's presence: he fought better because she was there, as a schoolboy is a better fighter when his best girl is watching.

One afternoon Georgiana, on tiptoe, crossed the hall to Eloise's bedroom. Her large fingers with their showy diamond rings were curled about a pair of sewing scissors; and although the house was empty, she moved with the stealth of a plump old cat. Her breathing was shallow; a slight smile parted her sensual lips; and her eyes glinted with that carnal and almost salacious expression they had always shown when she was up to mischief. She paused and peered over the staircase. Listened.

At Eloise's door she listened again, then moved swiftly inside, crossing to the south window. Beyond the lawn she spied Eloise in the orchard, helping the servants gather plums. Tomorrow Blossom would stew plum butter on the kitchen range.

Georgiana turned back into the room. A fortnight had passed since her return to Winchester, and she was as far as ever from shattering the Eloise-Ive combine. She had employed all her old tricks and many new ones: storming, wheedling, smiling, weeping. She had stamped her feet, broken dishes, locked herself in her room, threatened to kill herself, threatened to leave, threatened to stay forever. Ive remained unmoved.

He and Eloise had developed a singularly effective defense: they ignored her. Oh, she knew what they were about, but it was acid in her entrails, nevertheless. At dinner they pretended she wasn't there. They looked right through her. If she said pass the salt they didn't hear, and she had to reach. She endeavored to employ the same weapon against them, but it was no good. Such subtle warfare wasn't in her line. She liked to plot, raid, gallop, shoot, despoil. So usually before dinner was over she blew up. Once, before raging upstairs, she hurled a chicken drumstick at Ive. It was like a second honeymoon; and just as in honeymoon days he ducked. The drumstick whizzed harmlessly past his ear. And to Eloise he said, "The Rebels never were good shots." Oh! Insulting her father's memory! She dashed a glass of water into his face. And ran. Not, perhaps, the most effective way to replace Eloise in his affections, but a Southern lady had pride and spirit.

At dinner next evening, there was no water tumbler at her place. And just as sweet as you please she requested one from Blossom. The Negro laughed and said:

"No, ma'am! Mr. Pawpacker he say wine goes to some people's head but when you have water it go to his head!"

And Blossom cackled. And the brat giggled and Ive guffawed. Mad? Certainly Georgiana was mad! Who wouldn't be mad? Guyed, picked on, humiliated! Even the niggers had entered the cabal against her. Could she be censured for sailing her dinner plate at Ive? He dodged, but of course the plate was shattered. A very nice Haviland plate, too. And all the conspirators' fault: if they were going to ridicule her they should have laid the table with cheap crockery. She rushed upstairs, shaking with anger, and flung herself to the bed, assailing it with her fists, madder than a cat streaking from a rain barrel. Oh!

For more than twenty-four hours she sulked behind her locked door, taking it out on Ive and Eloise by not eating. They didn't mind, but her stomach raised hell. Late next evening she sneaked down to the pantry and gorged. And she decided her approach was faulty. She would try being pleasant to Ive. It went against all her principles, but she was desperate! Even that didn't help. She had always known, of course, that if you were nice to people they only took advantage. So she tried something else.

She decided to concentrate on Eloise. Heretofore she had not really neglected the brat; she had kept assuring her that Southern hospitality did not include the daughter of circus acrobats; but something more was needed. Not physical abuse, for although Georgiana longed to inflict it she suspected this would only bring Ive to the brat's defense. Besides, Georgiana had a pretty high opinion of her tongue as a weapon; when she got warmed up she could think of the damndest things to say. With Ive downtown she was always cutting loose and making Eloise cry. Yes, all in all, her tongue was very effective; and although abused flesh might heal she knew that words festered in the soul and left lifelong scars; and that was all to the good, also.

Nevertheless, although she could see she was getting under the brat's hide, she felt this was picayune progress; she needed to discredit the brat in Ive's eyes. So three days ago she hid her cameo pin in Eloise's dresser, and that evening in Ive's presence she asked the brat:

"What were you doing in my room this afternoon?"

"I wasn't in your room."

"There's no need to lie about it, honey. I saw you sneaking out as I was coming upstairs. You're very welcome, I'm sure, to come to my room just any time you wish, but I sure enough would like to know what you were doing there today."

"I wasn't there."

Georgiana sighed significantly. *Such* little liars, these Yankee circus brats.

Next evening she missed her cameo, and although she searched high and low she couldn't locate it; so she came downstairs where Ive and Eloise were sitting.

"Eloise honey, are you sure you didn't pick up my pin when you were in my room yesterday?"

"I wasn't in your room."

Georgiana was very sweet about it, but one remark led to another, as remarks sometimes do, and presently Eloise was flushing as guiltily as if she *had* stolen the pin. And Georgiana said it sure enough didn't matter too much, but she would feel better about it if they searched Eloise's room. And she was joyous when Ive, looking stern, announced:

"That's the only course to take."

So they searched, and as certain-sure as colored folk liked pork chops they found that cameo pin in Eloise's dresser. And while it *really* didn't matter, since they were all more or less one happy family, *still* it did give one pause, having a thief in the family, and Georgiana reckoned that a spanking might well be administered just to *teach* the child —for her own good—that those old stealing ways she had learned from her parents on the circus were contrary to the decalogue of Southern gentility.

Ive said:

"I want to look in the mirror."

At the dresser he peered at himself, and then smiling he turned to Georgiana and said:

"I thought I must have been looking simple-minded tonight, but I can't see that I do."

Oh!

Georgiana couldn't really be blamed for stamping her foot and flying angry. For she knew now that Ive had just been giving her plenty of rope; leading her on to humiliate her. Her nose tip turned fiery, and she screamed:

"You don't love me any more!"

Of course, she hadn't really supposed he did, men being the filthy old goats they were, but just the same it was heartbreaking and maddening—especially maddening—when he said:

"Why no. I haven't loved you since you left me for Stuart Kelvin."

Oh!

Accusing her of a thing like that with her own *cousin!* And poor Stuart dead and unable to defend himself! Georgiana never had been so insulted. She ran screaming to her room and slammed the door with such force that it startled poor Blossom down in the kitchen, who rolled her eyes and murmured, "Lordy-Lord. That woman meaner than cat juice!"

Georgiana had persistence. Even though she had failed to discredit Eloise in the cameo affair she was still of good heart. So now in Eloise's room she had high hopes of convincing Ive that the brat suffered from naughty and freakish impulses. If she failed, nothing would be lost. At the very least the brat would be miserably upset.

Clutching the scissors, she moved toward the clothes closet. Her route led past the dresser, and she could no more pass a mirror without stopping than an old puss could ignore a plate of sardines. The face in the mirror would have sent seventeenth century villagers hunting for the ducking stool, because of its witchery. Georgiana smiled at her reflection, and then her gaze slid down to the dresser where two framed photographs stood. Her mouth twitched its contempt. Eloise's mother and father. Acrobats! One photograph depicted Lily Orika and Ned Sebastian, bedizened in shameless tights, their smiles incandescent. The other, a close-up, showed Lily and Ned with heads together, still smiling. They looked as clean with youth as a new bar of white soap. Thoughtfully, Georgiana turned over the photographs. Steel brads held them in the frames. She considered prying loose the brads and despoiling the pictures, but at last she decided to let that wait till another day.

So she went to the closet, where she spent a profitable fifteen minutes working on Eloise's frocks. In some she cut little triangles; from others she removed great full moons of cloth; and in the rest she scissored long zigzags.

She returned to her room and behind the closed door lay on the bed, full of satisfaction. By and by she heard Eloise skipping upstairs. Georgiana sprang up, listening. Presently an outcry came from Eloise's room. Georgiana's lips were working, and when she heard Eloise hurrying into the hall she hoped—oh, how she hoped!—that the brat would pound the door and assail her. But the brat fled downstairs and out the front door.

Georgiana lay on the bed again, nearly hugging herself in congratulation. Ive and Eloise couldn't get the better of her. Her resources for mischief were unbounded; she would stay on and on in Winchester, making life increasingly unbearable for the brat and for Ive. If she couldn't break the combine she could torment her husband into begging for a divorce and agreeing on a huge settlement.

An hour passed before she heard Ive and the brat ascending the stairs. Georgiana remained on the bed. She caught the murmur of voices, and presently a knock struck her door. She pretended sleep. The knock struck again; then the door rattled open. She sat up, startled from slumber. She demanded crossly:

"What do you mean, breaking in and waking me up?"

"You weren't asleep," Ive said. "You snore when you sleep and I didn't hear any snores."

Oh!

She scrambled to her feet. Snore! The very idea! No gentleman would accuse a lady of that!

Ive was holding one of the mutilated dresses, and he accused her—her!—of cutting it. She bridled. Her nose tip reddened.

"Why do you always pick on me?" she demanded. "I get blamed for everything. Eloise must have done it just to be naughty. And she's trying to put the blame on me."

It was a rousing fight. Ive told her she would have to return to St. Louis, and she replied she would never leave unless he agreed to divorce her with a settlement of a hundred thousand dollars.

He broke out laughing.

"You're crazy. I don't have a hundred thousand."

"You do too. You're rich. You're a rich man."

"I was once."

"I'll never leave! Never!" Her foot stamped. "Never till I get that money!"

"You're raving like a lunatic," he said.

"I'm not!" Georgiana raved. "I'm not raving! I'm just trying to be your wife."

"Something queer in your blood," he said. "You're worse than your sister May."

Oh! *Oh!*

She pivoted to the dresser, seeking something—anything!—to snatch and hurl. She seized her hand-mirror, flung it with all her might. It wouldn't have done Ive any good, getting hit with that, so it was fortunate he anticipated her intention and dodged into the hall, yanking shut the door. The mirror struck the jamb, shattered.

Georgiana stood frozen as the realization of what she had done iced over her.

She had a bad night. She did not dine with Eloise and Ive, but after the household was dark she stole downstairs for a solitary snack. But the food was tasteless; and because of her worry and rage it lay hard on her stomach. Presently she wandered outdoors.

The darkness was thick and moist. Her legs felt heavy and her feet dragged through the dewy grass of the garden. She sank into a lawn chair and lounged inert and miserable.

"What can I do?" she asked herself. "What can I do?"

More than she liked to confess the broken mirror troubled her. Not that she was superstitious! Not the way a nigger was superstitious. Nevertheless, the broken pieces of the mirror gleamed derisively in her consciousness, and she almost wished she were nigger-superstitious, for then she would have known of some countercharm. She wondered what Maggie would have done to ward off disaster; and as she sat there with her eyes closed her thoughts wandered back and back through the dead years, and she was a little girl again in the Kelvin kitchen where Maggie was vigorously stirring batter.

"You broke de mirror, you broke de mirror," Maggie chanted.

And Georgiana screamed, "It wasn't my fault! It's that circus brat! She—"

Maggie whirled, pointing the batter spoon, her eyes rolling.

"Seven years' bad luck! Seven long years—!"

"No! It was the brat's fault!"

"Unless you do what I says. Seven is a hex number. Seven, seven—that's the devil's number. You find you a grave of a loved one when the Big Dipper is shining. And you walk across that grave seven times. Once fo' each Dipper star. That the only way you can ward off bad luck!"

"No! That's—"

Georgiana was on her feet. But she was no longer a little girl and no longer in the Kelvin kitchen. She was in the Pawpacker garden, and she tossed her head and tried to laugh. She must have lightly dozed; and the scene with Maggie had shaped itself in the misty frontier between imagination and dreams. But why had that odd conversation floated into her thoughts? Had Maggie once mentioned such a countercharm, in the moldy long ago?

Nonsense! Nigger nonsense! Georgiana sat down. She swept the shattered mirror out of her mind. She thought of other things: of Ive's telling her she must return to St. Louis. Her fists clenched. The nerve of him, ordering her to leave! Turning her out! She would never go. Never! Not unless he paid her a hundred thousand. But he had said he didn't have that much. Her mouth curled. The tightwad! She would see a lawyer, that was what she would do. A wife had legal rights.

Her gaze was on the northwest sky. There it hung blazing, the Big Dipper, beyond the dark farming land. And Georgiana was counting the stars. Nigger nonsense. And yet—

"I'm not going," she thought. "It would give me the shivers."

Seven, seven—the devil's number.

She stood up suddenly and crossed the lawn. It was this town, she thought; this old, dank town. A haunted place. In St. Louis she was a woman of the world. She could have laughed off a broken mirror, in St. Louis. And she would laugh it off here! She wasn't going to the graveyard. She was taking a stroll, that was all.

Winchester slept. The ancient houses were heaps of shadow on lawns of shadow. Older than the War Between the States, older than Andrew Jackson and "Oh, Susannah" strummed on a Negro's banjo. She hurried along the brick sidewalk. Decades had thickened the boles of the maple and locust trees, and their branches swept low overhead. She smelled the night odors of damp earth and fecund vegetation.

Late, late. The Square was an abandoned place, thinly illuminated by street lamps. Not a mule there now; not even a watchman. But the past had accumulated there like stagnant water in a pond. The streets were rivers of time past, emptying here, where the store fronts walled in all the departed years. Façades of wood and yellow brick. The decorative cornices. Grove's Store. The Vickery Block, 1871. Drenched with age; oozing age like a wall oozing moisture.

Georgiana crossed the Square and plodded along a street that tunneled through the murky vegetation of antiquated trees. The infrequent street lamps sprayed down watery light; and then she reached the town's end, her slippers sinking into the voluptuous dust of the cemetery road. On a starlit hilltop a quarter of a mile away, she descried the dark shapes of yew trees, sentinels at guard. She paused, then pressed on, for she was not afraid.

Not afraid; but when she gained the hilltop she remained for long and long outside the iron fence. The countryside lay black beneath the late stars. Humanity slept, and all the sounds of humanity were quelled. Not a car motor did she hear, not a railroad whistle. But summer insects were abroad, fluttering and clicking, and the birds that hunted in darkness. In the next valley a whip-poor-will repeated his call with idiotic monotony; down the road an owl hooted softly; and from far, far away—from the next township or the next county—hound dogs were yelping and yelping. And their voices were indescribably mournful, as if they were sobbing out an elegy for the lost South, lamenting Appomattox and gray valor dead in tangled ravines.

And suddenly a shiver passed over Georgiana as she thought of the transience of existence upon the planet, and for an instant she glimpsed herself and everybody who breathed on that night as poor itinerants sharing the hot hurly-burly of life for a brilliant flash in eternity. And she experienced a sudden horror at the undug graves waiting for her and all who lived and all who would ever live, and a brief compassion for all pitiful beings, driven by life a-sizzle in flesh.

At last, she marched to the cemetery gate. She was without fright, because dead people couldn't hurt you; and she was without superstition. She was following Maggie's advice about counteracting the evil of a broken mirror only in the half-humorous spirit of intelligent persons who knocked on wood. Nothing to it; but on the other hand it did no harm to go through the rites, just in case.

She lifted the latch; and the gate, in swinging toward her, sagged and scraped on the concrete sill. An awful, clangorous sound, like the iron ringing of a harsh bell. Georgiana stopped. And she found herself listening. She had the eerie sense that the gate had clanged a summons through that population of tombstones. Every pine needle was alert, every grass blade. Then the broken silence mended itself and was immaculate, save for the trilling of insects and the monotonous whip-poor-will and the lonesome baying of hounds. Georgiana crunched along a path whose gravel lay pale in the starshine.

The path branched into a network. Her eyes were habituated to the darkness now, and she found her way to the plot where a block of

marble bore the aristocratic letters, "Kelvin." Ive had bought that
stone twenty years before, when W.C. departed to the eternal hall of
fame reserved by the Republic for its statesmen. It was one of the
nicest tombstones in the cemetery, the final encomium in W.C.'s path
of glory. The Kelvin lot was very fine, also. One of the cemetery's
best. It had an evergreen tree of its own, which doubtless pleased May
—poor May—who lay in the earth beside her parents. And as she stood
there Georgiana fancied the tree's roots seeking out May, so perhaps at
last she had been united with the one manifestation of nature which
she admired above all others.

"I'm not afraid one little bit," she thought. "It's just nice and peaceful here."

Yet she was keyed up, slightly; for when her gaze sought the Big
Dipper she fancied for a moment that she beheld in a yew tree a black
figure, cowled, with wings outspread. She nearly screamed. But immediately she saw it was only something she had imagined in the
complexity of inky tree branches. So she located the Dipper and decided to begin counting off stars at the tip of the handle. "One," she
murmured; and she walked across W.C.'s grave.

But that little journey brought to her attention something she had
supposed mere shadow before. A heap of fresh earth. She ventured
toward it; and then she discovered a second heap. Two new graves.
On the Kelvin lot. She was astonished. Then suddenly comprehension
came, and with it fury.

Those acrobats! Who else? Ive had said they were buried in Winchester. And the tightwad—oh, the Yankee tightwad—had insulted
Southern gentility by burying them on the Kelvin lot! Ive's money,
of course, had paid for the lot. No matter! An insult, nevertheless!
Rage boiled in her wrists. Not satisfied with establishing Eloise in his
household, Ive had crowded a pair of acrobats into her family's resting
place! Oh!

Fury hurled her forward.

"You've no business here!" she screamed. "Why couldn't you stay
where you belong?"

And she kicked one mound of clay.

It was not, possibly, an ideal place for losing one's temper, but Georgiana didn't realize this till something—she never quite knew what—
halted her in the act of delivering a second kick. Probably nerves. At
any rate she desisted. And a shiver streaked her spine. She whirled.
And she saw nothing, really, save the massed shadows and the massed
imaginings that cluster in such a place. She saw nothing, nothing; but
before she could stop herself she screamed. It was such an icy outcry
that it curdled her blood, and she ran. And running made her scared
—she fancied she heard the slither of pursuing shrouds—so she

screamed again, and screaming scared her the more. Perfectly ridiculous, she realized later, for what could be safer than a cemetery with everybody good and dead? Nevertheless she ran through the gate and down the road to town. And not till she paused, nearly strangled by the exertion, did she realize that her fright had prevented her from carrying out the countercharm. This troubled her, and she determined to go back, but she didn't go back. So her journey had come to naught, and it was all Eloise's fault. At least her parents' fault. Oh! The brat! The brat!

Georgiana did not sleep the rest of that night. Dawn found her very cross. And when she descended to breakfast, long after Eloise and Ive had eaten, her lost sleep and her worry about the mirror and her future poisoned and barbed her like a lady porcupine. Her disposition had never been worse, so perhaps she couldn't be blamed for what occurred that morning. Certainly she didn't blame herself, although everybody else blamed her.

Blossom was stewing plum butter on the cookstove that morning. She was very happy, because tomorrow she and Emancipation were going on an all-day fishing expedition with four friends. After serving Georgiana, Blossom returned to the kitchen and went outdoors to find Emancipation and jog him at his duties. As Blossom left the back door, she met Eloise entering.

Just what happened in the dining room remained obscure. Georgiana maintained that Eloise insulted her, while Eloise said that scarcely a word passed between them. Quite without warning, she said, Georgiana jumped up and grabbed her wrist and dragged her to the kitchen.

At any rate, when Blossom approached the back door she heard screams, and in the kitchen she discovered a struggle. Georgiana was gripping Eloise's wrist with both hands and pressing the child's right hand against the hot cookstove.

During the rest of the morning great activity took place in the household. It began with Blossom's screech and her seizing Georgiana's shoulders and yanking. The noise in the kitchen was considerable, what with Eloise crying and Blossom's excited remonstrances and Georgiana's stamping her heel in rage because a nigger dared lay hands on her. Finally she exclaimed, "Oh!" and ran upstairs and locked herself in her room.

Blossom telephoned Ive and Dr. Bennett—the grandson of old Dr. Bennett who had so brilliantly diagnosed poor May's malady—and Emancipation shuffled in to learn what all the excitement was about; and then Ive and the doctor arrived; and after Eloise's hand had been treated and bandaged and the doctor left, Ive ascended the stairs and demanded to be admitted to his wife's boudoir. He was ashen-angry, and when Georgiana did not unlock the door he lifted his voice and laid down the law. He mentioned the camel's back and the last straw, and he informed her she was leaving next morning for St. Louis. If she didn't, he said, he was certainly going to have the law on her, for abusing a child.

It was a pretty good fight, despite the locked door between them; you could hear stamping from within the room; and Ive repeated that if she didn't leave town she would be arrested. He said Blossom and the doctor were ready to stand as witnesses, although they had promised to keep mum if Georgiana left Winchester. It might have been a bluff and again it might not; in any event, it worked; although Georgiana maintained she couldn't possibly prepare to leave tomorrow morning; she wanted to wait till day after tomorrow. Ive agreed to that, at last.

And for a time it looked as if the fishing expedition of Blossom and Emancipation might be ruined, for Ive had reached the conclusion that Georgiana's emotional equilibrium was out of adjustment, and he certainly wasn't going to trust his wife alone in the house with Eloise. However, Blossom looked so disappointed that Ive hit upon a scheme whereby she and Emancipation could go fishing after all. So the next morning, when Ive left for the bank, Eloise accompanied him, her hand in a sling. And Georgiana was all alone in the house. Ive had really thrown a scare into her camp the day before, with that talk about having the law on her; but she was a resilient woman, and during her hours alone the scare wore off. And outrage poured through her. And hate. She decided that she would not leave Winchester, after all.

At midmorning she entered Eloise's room and with a crayon desecrated the photographs of Lily and Ned Sebastian. By the time she had finished, those photos looked like the crudely obscene pictures scrawled on the walls of public washrooms by degenerates. Georgiana smiled to herself and returned to her room, happily looking forward to the moment when Eloise beheld that bawdy art.

The noon was brilliantly hot. Georgiana stood on the sun porch, gazing at the walk leading from town. She had reached a decision. She would tell Ive she was remaining in Winchester. She was his wife and this was her home. Just let him try to have the law on her for burning Eloise. She would telephone St. Louis for a lawyer to defend her. She would start divorce proceedings. She would stop at nothing. The case would burst open like a stink-bomb on the front pages of newspapers. She would sue him for every cent he had; she would break every financial bone in the little devil's body.

This decision gave her sinister calm. Her eyes were cold as a coiled snake's. She would not fly to pieces this noon. She would tell him what was what.

She kept glancing at her watch. When it showed 12:17 she sighted Eloise and Ive coming along the walk. Georgiana glided into the living room, seating herself and taking up a magazine. She tried not to smile, but she couldn't help it; and her heart was beating rapidly. She felt in command of herself and of the situation.

As they entered the house she put down her magazine. For a moment they stood side by side, staring at her. She stared back. They did not speak, nor did she. Ive, she thought, looked old. Much too old to be her husband. His linen suit had wrinkled in the heat, and the hand gripping his cane was an old man's hand, mottled by liver-colored spots.

Ive and Eloise went into the dining room and on to the kitchen, where Blossom had left a cold lunch in the refrigerator. Georgiana picked up her magazine. She could hear them puttering around out there, talking in low voices. Evidently they were eating at the kitchen table. It occurred to Georgiana that she could spoil their meal by joining them, so she jumped up and hurried thither. When she opened the swinging door they broke off talking. She pulled up a chair and sat down.

Eloise ate with difficulty, because her right hand was in a sling. Georgiana fixed her gaze on the child, as if by staring vindictively she could shrivel her into oblivion. At last she told Ive:

"I want to talk to you."

In his eyes she saw chilling contempt. He didn't speak. She felt herself getting angry. But no anger this noon! She held all the cards. She smiled.

"I said I wanted to talk to you. Alone."

"Everything has been said."

"Oh no it hasn't."

"You're leaving in the morning," he said. "And that's the end of it."

"I'm not leaving. I'm staying. If you want to talk it over, I'll be in the living room."

She saw his skin turn crimson, at the roots of his whiskers. She stood up and left the kitchen. In the living room she sat down and took up the magazine. But she couldn't read. She glanced at advertisements and as she turned the pages they rustled harshly in the silent room. Her ears were cocked toward the kitchen, but all she heard was an occasional tinkling of silverware against crockery. Her heart was beating with excitement. She couldn't believe that Ive would accept her announcement without a fight.

At last she heard movement in the kitchen, and she saw Ive and Eloise coming through the dining room. In the central hall Eloise

mounted the stairs, but Ive came thumping into the living room. He
sat down and brought out a cigar. His mouth looked tight and ashen.
He snipped the end off the cigar and stuck it into his mouth, where it
angled up bellicosely. He said:
"You've misjudged me. I'm not going to give in to you, this time."
"I'm staying."
He didn't light the cigar. It remained motionless, jutting upward.
The lids of his eyes were almost together. On his cane his hand looked
tight and lean. A hard man, she thought. Breed of the carpetbagger.
It seemed incredible he was the same human being she had met first
on a night of spring mist.
"I'm staying," she repeated. "I'm your wife. This is my home."
He didn't respond. She wondered what he was thinking. She didn't
understand Yankees.
Then from upstairs came a low outcry, and this was followed by
long, melancholy sounds, as if somebody were half weeping, half moan-
ing. Ive's head jerked, and he looked belligerently alert.
"What have you done to the child now?"
Then she remembered. The photographs! She wanted to break into
hysterical laughter. And she wanted to see Eloise's face. She ex-
claimed:
"What have *I* done? I declare! I get blamed for everything."
She soared to her feet and hurried toward the stairs.
"Georgiana! Stay where you are. I'll see what's the matter."
His dictatorial tone enraged her. He had stood up, gripping his cane,
and she flung back a poisonous glare.
"I'll thank you," she said frigidly, "not to speak to me like that!"
As she climbed the stairs she glimpsed Eloise in the upper hall. In
her left hand the brat clutched one photo, and her face was a contorting
mass of rage and grief. Georgiana glanced behind, saw Ive starting up;
so she hurried on and met Eloise on the landing.
It was like meeting the embodiment of primitive rage.
"Oh, you—you—you mean old *thing!*" Eloise screamed.
And she tried to kick Georgiana.
A brat, a vicious circus brat. She needed teaching. So Georgiana
grabbed her right hand—the one in the sling—and dug her fingers into
the bandaged flesh and twisted. Eloise screamed. Georgiana thought
perhaps she should desist, but she couldn't. It was as if all her hates
and frustrations were there in her fingers, digging and hurting. Then
suddenly some elemental instinct caused her to glance around. She
saw Ive's face. It was terrible. And she saw his cane lifted. Georgiana
screamed. Then an explosion of bright pain struck her skull and
flashed blindingly through her cranium. And then a surge of darkness.
She fought the darkness. Her hands flung out and she took a step.

But when her foot descended there was nothing under it and she knew then that she had stepped off the landing on the way downstairs. And she was pitching through nothingness. That much she knew, in terror. Then her head struck something and she knew nothing at all.

She tumbled clear to the bottom of the steps in the central hall. She lay still. It was Appomattox all over again; the Yankees had won the war.

The first thing Ive did was to close the front door. Then he stood gazing at Georgiana.

"Is she—dead?" Eloise whispered.

"I don't know. Don't touch her. Let me think."

He stood for perhaps thirty seconds. Then he turned to Eloise and put both hands on her shoulders.

"Are you with me?"

She whispered, "Yes."

"Can you keep your nerve? Can you lie and lie?"

"Yes."

His gaze seemed to be scraping the bottom of her soul.

"I understand that little girls have a hard time keeping secrets. But this is a secret you'll have to keep." His hands were tighter on her shoulders. Her eyes were wide and staring. "Some day you'll grow up. You'll fall in love. You'll want to tell him everything that ever happened to you. But this is one thing you'll never tell."

"Never. I'll never tell."

He kept staring. Her voice rose:

"Honest! Honest I won't. Cross my heart and hope to die, I won't."

His hands fell. He said:

"I'll leave now for the bank. In fifteen minutes you call me there. Tell me that Mrs. Pawpacker tripped on the landing and fell downstairs. Can you remember that?"

She nodded.

"I'll bring Doc Bennett. He's the coroner. Your story will be that you were in the lower hall and looked up. You saw Mrs. Pawpacker trip and fall. That's all you know."

"That's all I know."

And suddenly his eyes that had been so hard showed tenderness. He patted her head. He kissed her. And his mouth softened.

"We'll pull it off. We're old partners, aren't we?"

Her eyes were wet, but she smiled.

"Yes. Old partners."

And that was all there was to it. The coroner found that Mrs. Pawpacker died because of a broken neck suffered in a fall. At her funeral the minister elucidated her many wonderful qualities, and the *Winchester Enterprise* gave her a splendid send-off. They buried her in the cemetery south of town, and nobody ever saw her again. The Lord giveth and the Lord taketh away. And the grass grew as sweetly above her grave as above W.C.'s or Eliza's or poor, poor May's.

Her good must have been interred with her bones, for the evil that she did lived after her. Yet not for a long time did it manifest itself, and when it did it chose a peculiar, oblique way—typically Georgiana-ish—of revenge.

Her ghost never stalked through Ive's mind, as brave Captain Latcher's stalked through Willie's. He never heard her voice. Nor did Eloise. Georgiana was good and dead. Ive and Eloise never spoke of her, never mentioned what had occurred on the stairs. Their life seemed very happy, as the 1920's filled the newspapers with flagpole sitters and bathtub gin and Marathon dancers and the Charleston.

Yet there were times under the reading lamp in the living room when Ive's book lay on his lap and his cigar smoldered. And he sat staring. But who knows what another human being is thinking? His thoughts might have been concerned with Gus and the show. Or with his livery stable. He had closed it at last, and men had torn it down, and the lot had been sold to an enterprising young fellow who built a garage and sold the products of the Ford Motor Company. If you wanted to buy mules now, you went to Ive's farm at the edge of town. Not so many lions and elephants dwelt on the farm, now. Circus business was not brisk. Too many movies, too many radios.

As Eloise grew up, Ive grew older, although neither noticed the changes in the other till they had taken place. His hair and beard were white now, and his cane was really a cane, not a dandyish walking stick. And he lost weight, as if his body were retrenching and conserving.

Twice a day he walked to and fro from house to bank, but his step was not as elastic as it used to be, or his figure as erect. Winchester people said that Yankee Pawpacker was failing. And like his body, his financial empire was retrenching and conserving. No longer did he plan brilliant financial forays, or dream of becoming a director of railroads and a czar in oil. Yet his brain remained alert, and in his office at the bank he studied the financial journals, figuring out which were the coming industries and which stocks were likely to rise. He edged gradually into the great bull market of the twenties, and his judgment was shrewd. He thought of himself as an investor, not a speculator, for he always bought outright, never on margin.

His horse-buying trips had long since ceased; he spent most of his time in Winchester, now. Seldom even did he visit the circus. Letters arrived from Gus several times a week, always bloated with optimism, always mentioning how worried the Ringlings were.

Occasionally business took him to St. Louis or Tamarack or even Chicago, and Eloise accompanied him. People thought them grandfather and granddaughter. She was a good girl, bearing the brunt of traveling: seeing about luggage, engaging cabs, registering at hotels.

For a long time after Georgiana's death, his mind had tried to worry about the incident on the stairs, but he wouldn't let it. He dismissed those worries gruffly, the way he dismissed a deadbeat who wanted to borrow money. But at odd times the worry returned, maybe flashing into his thoughts as he tapped homeward through November wind, an old man in a whirlpool of dead leaves. "I'm a murderer," he would think; and it startled him. Then he laughed shortly, harshly. Nonsense. He had hit her, certainly; but the blow hadn't killed her. The fall had killed her.

In the autumn of 1929 stocks descended, quite rapidly and in considerable disorder; and after that he had a new worry, for he had increased his holdings more than was perhaps wise. Yet there were financial prognosticators who wrote that this was no more than the market passing through a technical correction, so Ive disregarded his old maxim that one's first loss is the best loss. He held on. In the spring stocks would soar. He had concentrated so much on the market that he had grown to think of it as a separate entity, something with a notional life of its own, not simply a reflection of the hopes and fears of men's checkbooks.

The following spring he sold his farm and pulled out of the circus brokerage business. He took a loss, but he needed cash. After all, his bank was not unconnected with the country's financial system.

It was the day after the sale when the appalling thing happened. He was sitting at his desk figuring, and suddenly he couldn't see. It was as if it were night and the lights had gone out. But it wasn't night; it was a bright March morning. He blinked; he closed his eyes; he opened them. He held his hand before his eyes. He was frightened.

Then, as oddly and suddenly as blindness came, it departed. He sat there shaken. He was thinking not so much of himself as of his bank. The examiners were young smart alecks—bureaucratic know-nothings —who had never met a payroll in their lives, and they liked nothing so much as locking up a bank. They didn't understand the local situation. If they would just leave him alone to run affairs in his own way, he would pull the bank through this flurry and nobody would lose a cent. He knew what he was about. He had been handling money since before they were in diapers. He thought of them as gratuitous meddlers; governmental sticklers for the letter of the law; spinners of red tape.

They were fair game, and if he juggled things a bit and threw dust in their eyes it was only because he wanted to keep the bank going till this financial typhoon blew itself out.

That very day he visited Dr. Bennett, mentioning he was having trouble with his eyes. The doctor gave him a thorough examination and told him he was in pretty good shape for a man of his years. And as far as the doctor could see, his eyes were all right.

But next evening it happened again. And just as suddenly, as if a switch had been snapped off. It lasted nearly thirty minutes. And a few days later it happened as he was approaching the door of home, and he called to Eloise to help him. Till then, he had not told her.

Finally, that St. Louis specialist put forth the theory of shock. Ive laughed. But inside he was not laughing. He talked it over with Eloise and she wrote to city stores for books on psychology. And she found cases such as the specialist had mentioned, of men blinded by shell shock and of men blinded by hypnotic suggestion. It outraged Ive. He felt like a victim of stuttering who is told that his speech organs are impeccable but that his stammer results from some mental block.

Shock? What shock? Georgiana? He would not admit it. Modern nonsense! That specialist had reminded him of the bank examiners; young, sure of himself. The world was being appropriated by youth, and it was going to hell. Youth! Jostling, pushing, shoving, trying to steal the country from the men who had built it up. And they had caused a boom and a depression. Ive's mouth was scornful. And he thought of the giants who had walked the American earth in his own heyday: Jay Gould, Jim Hill, Morgan the Elder, Andrew Carnegie, Grover Cleveland, Mark Hanna, William McKinley. Those old swashbucklers, he told himself, would have taken hold of this business depression and straightened things out in a hurry. But they were dead.

In 1930, Eloise went away to the University of Tamarack, and Ive looked forward to Thanksgiving and after that to Christmas and after that to summer vacation. It was not a good year. She wrote regularly, but he could tell she didn't miss him the way he missed her. That was natural, of course; he told himself he would have had it no other way. She had pledged a sorority and she was very busy with studies and boys. His eyes were troubling him more and more; the interludes of blindness were afflicting him oftener and lasting longer; he was accepting blindness as his natural state. At the bank he used the cashier as his eyes and at home Blossom read Eloise's letters aloud, interjecting many comments of her own.

Winchester knew about his blindness, and it was a common sight to see Yankee Pawpacker tapping from home to bank, guided by Emancipation's hand. As the months passed those journeys consumed more time, for the Yankee's step was slower, and his shoulders sagged.

He was often tired, and at his desk in the bank or in his chair at home he was likely to slump more than he used to, and sometimes he dozed. Or if he was awake his thoughts roamed back through the years, and he remembered how he used to play checkers with Etta, before she died, and how much money he had made on this deal or that. He was really more aware of the past than of the present.

When Eloise returned to Winchester for vacation in the summer of 1931 he couldn't see her at all. But he could listen to her. He loved the sound of her voice, and often she read aloud. And now instead of Emancipation she accompanied him to the bank, and he *would* go, even on the most sweltering days. They trudged along slowly, for the heat made him feeble.

But presently the mornings were crisper and the noons cooler, and as they walked he would say something to Eloise but Emancipation would reply, and then he would remember that she had gone away again to the university. He missed her, sitting alone in the evening; and then one evening late in September the telephone rang. He made no move to answer: central ought to know he wasn't spry about answering telephones. But it rang and rang, as if central were telling him this was important, so at last he creaked up and groped to the telephone table; and it was important. It was Corpus Christi, Texas, calling. Some man whose name he didn't get was on the wire; somebody with the circus.

"Well, what is it?" Ive snapped.

The man talked fast; the receiver crackled with a poor connection; something about the Baron Von Krummer badly injured when the lights went out while he was performing in the arena.

"Who's the Baron Von Krummer?" Ive demanded testily, but then he could have bitten his tongue because he remembered who the Baron was. So he added: "Why are you calling me? Have Gus—"

So the man repeated, and this time Ive understood. Gus had vanished. Likewise the Baron's wife. Likewise all the cash in the office wagon.

"We're stranded, I tell you," the voice said. "It's a hell of a mess. You'll have to come."

Ive was going to say, "Why, you damned fool—I can't come. I'm an old man and I can't see." But then it occurred to him that he could call Eloise at the university and ask her to accompany him, and for a moment he was exceedingly happy at a trip with her.

"I'll be there as soon as I can," he said. "Where did Gus go?"

"How do I know where the son of a bitch went? He ran away, I tell you, with the Dutchman's wife."

"He shouldn't have done it," Ive said. But he realized this sounded banal and lame, so he added, "I knew it. I knew it. He's got a crooked streak. I knew it that first night when we talked about Molly. He's young, that's his trouble, and impulsive. Interesting fellow, though. But crooked. Who did you say you were?"

But Corpus Christi had hung up.

The South.

Not the unreal, romantic South of Winchester now; not the George W. Cable South; not the sad, distinguished Sidney Lanier-W. C. Kelvin South; but the genuine article, flashing past the windows of a rapid train. Arkansas; Texarkana; East Texas. Black peons in the fields of cotton; the stilted unpainted cabins. Not the South of the Mammy songs; not the I-wanna-go-back, I-gotta-go-back South. No; this was a vast, still, lugubrious land, cotton giving way to the turpentine forests.

Down, down, down into wet heat and hot light, and buzzards circling above the treetops. The chain-gang South, the station platforms peopled by fugitives from Faulkner novels.

They sat together in the Pullman, Ive and Eloise. He was tired; he hadn't slept well; it was too long a journey for an old man. He couldn't see what was going on, and he didn't understand it very well, either. His dry, thin old hands kept clenching and unclenching on his cane; and sometimes, querulously, he ruminated about what had happened. Gus leaving the show . . . running away with another man's wife . . . he shouldn't have done it. The heedlessness of youth. It was as if his memory of Gus had skipped back to those early years when Gus was a city editor and manager of a place called Funland. Such an energetic young fellow, he would mumble, so full of promise. A born showman.

"A fascinating man, Eloise. A jolly fellow. People liked him. He could put things through. Did I ever tell you about the time I sold him an elephant? Molly, her name was . . . and this fellow Burgoyne hatched a scheme. The children gave dimes. And oh, the crowds at the park. Amazing. But—well—the fellow was crooked. I knew I should avoid him. But I couldn't help liking him. His personality. Colorful. When you were with him life had more meaning."

The Houston station. Eloise tipping the porter and engaging a Red Cap, Eloise at his side, guiding his slow steps through crowds; Eloise wearing an Empress Eugenie hat.

The South. But not even the sunny South, when they reached Corpus Christi. Clouds had scuttled in from the bay that some Spaniard had named for the body of Christ; and it was pouring rain. A cab carried them through spattering streets of Mexican bazaars, of windowless store fronts and heaps of fruit; and they went to one of those tall cream-and-tan resort hotels overlooking the palms of Ocean Drive and the quays and the rainy bay.

And men were drilling for oil hereabouts; and there was oil money in town; so you would scarcely know that elsewhere capitalism was in distress. They were both drenched, but it was already midafternoon; so it was necessary to find the circus grounds.

Another cab, and rain pouring. A Mexican driver. *Si,* the rain. *Si,* the rain had been falling since yesterday. The circus? But *señorita,* the circus had closed . . . two days, three days before . . . Still, if one wished to go there . . .

One wished. So the cab honked and slithered along streets that were gleaming mirrors; and beneath wooden awnings brown men in bright serapes smoked brown cigarettes. And the gutters were running water where spoiled oranges bobbed; and the rain dripped from the leaves of orange trees and from the petals of luscious tropical flowers and rattled among the fronds of palms.

The circus had pitched at the edge of town, on a lot where cactus prickled and yucca bristled and scrubby mesquite twisted thin limbs like contortionists. From there you could see the great sweeping shore of the bay, and the water with a fishing boat losing itself in gray rain; and far beyond you could imagine the tankers and the banana steamers plying the Gulf.

The driver declined to maneuver the cab into the lot, lest the tires mire in drenched loam; he smiled and shrugged but declined. So they descended to the pavement and plowed and sloshed toward Burgoyne & Pawpacker's Great 3-Ring Circus; the show that had been born in wagons as Burgoyne's Circus & Hippodrome, A. H. (Honest Gus) Burgoyne, Owner; that had suffered a clem in Dakota and had become Yankee Pawpacker's Trans-American Circus; that had worried the Ringlings when Burgoyne joined forces with Pawpacker.

But now, pitched amid the Spanish bayonets, a collection of slatternly tents in the gray deluge, it didn't look especially imposing. You expected to see a swarm of Southern buzzards above it. The wagons stood silent and mournful, sunburst wheels bogged. The great lurid midway banners sagged, drenched through. Nobody seemed to be about; not even small boys; and certainly not A. H. Burgoyne booming toward you to pump your hand, and without him it was a body without a heart.

"We'll try the red wagon," Eloise said. Her voice was low now, as voices are low in a room of death.

The ticket window was closed. But the rear door stood open, and as she mounted the steps she roused from moody contemplation of the weather and the vicissitudes of humanity a youngish man with vivid socks and tie, and a cigarette in a long holder. His name was Connor, Pinky Connor, and his occupation was press agent, and his spirit had been long adrift on the infinities of cynicism.

"Hello," he said. "When did you blow in?"

"An hour ago."

"You see how things are."

"Yes," she said, "I see."

And standing there soaking in rain Ive pounded his cane into the sodden earth and demanded testily:

"Who is it? Did you call me? Are you the man?"

Connor shook his head, and Eloise said, "You'll have to speak. His eyes, you know."

"I didn't call you," Connor said. "That was Mike Higgenbotham. Your general manager."

"My general manager! I don't know him. Never heard of him. Gus attends to those things. Has Gus come back?"

Connor laughed. It was a laugh compounded of wry mirth and boundless weariness and measureless disenchantment and even a touch of indulgence for the weaknesses of man.

"He won't come back," Connor said. "He killed the Dutchman."

"He shouldn't have done it," Ive murmured, and then he demanded, "Dutchman? What Dutchman?"

"Von Krummer. Oh, the fellow's not dead yet. But he probably will be. He's unconscious in the hospital. The cats shredded him when the lights went out. Gus did that—turned out the lights. He went to the dynamo wagon during the Baron's act. Sent the fellow in charge on an errand and yanked the master switch. The lights went off all over the lot. The cats did a nice job on the Dutchman."

Ive stood with his head cocked forward, like some ancient, rain-pelted water bird in a marsh. The big drops pearled his hat rim and dripped into his beard, where they glistened like tears. He looked confused. His lips kept twitching, and a sigh came from his concave chest and he shook his head, slowly and sorrowfully, as men shake their heads as they rue some appalling cataclysm of nature.

"Impulsive," he muttered. "An impulsive fellow. Always buying elephants . . . Where did you say he went?"

Connor shrugged. They were sludging slowly now across the lot, toward the performers' entrance of the big top, as people wander aimlessly through the ruins after a tornado.

"Nobody knows where he went. It took us a while to piece together what happened. There was a lot of confusion with the lights out. Somebody went to the dynamo wagon and found the switch open and threw it on again. The Dutchman lay there in the arena, looking like he'd got the worst of a ketchup fight. Most men would have been dead, but he's a tough customer. We were busy, driving the cats back through the chutes and getting the Dutchman loaded into the ambulance. After it was over we missed Burgoyne. His car was gone. And the Dutchman's wife wasn't around. Then we found there wasn't a dime left in the office safe. You ask me, I think Burgoyne and the Dutchman's wife are in Mexico by now."

They shambled into the big top. Everything was motionless there, and silent except for the steady drumming of rain on canvas. In places it leaked, and trickles of water fell through the dull light, spattering the reserved seats, forming puddles on the hippodrome track and in the rings, splashing upon a blue-painted wooden barrel with white stars, even violating the steel arena where once Captain Philip Latcher had demonstrated the bravery of which a human being is capable.

"Where's everybody?" Eloise whispered.

"The kinkers are on the train, keeping dry. The roustabouts are out panhandling. Higgenbotham's seeing some guy about a job in the oil fields. Everybody's broke. Burgoyne hadn't paid salaries for a month."

"He'd planned it, then. He knew Uncle Ive was closing the show and he planned it all."

"Closing?" Ive piped. "Oh yes, we'll close. We're in a depression, you know. It's been getting worse for a long time, and it will keep getting worse. The depression of the thirties, that's what it will be called. We had a panic back in '07, and a washout in '21. But nothing like this."

They were moving into the menagerie top, and the humid air enclosed by the saturated canvas reeked with the smell of uncleaned animal cages and of filth collecting along the line of elephants. Their entrance was greeted by an uproar: yelps and barks from the dog wagon, squeals from the monkey cages, pacing and roaring from the big cats, trumpeting from the elephant herd. A single attendant was there, an old man without teeth, without a shave, without the spryness to panhandle perhaps, and he limped toward Ive, announcing in a high voice:

"They drive a man nuts. They're starving. No God-damned meat, no hay, no nothing. We got to get supplies."

"We've got to move the show, too," Connor said. "The health department is raising hell."

"And how about wages?" the animal attendant shrilled. "By God, you can't do this! By God, I've worked for more God-damned gyp outfits than a bastard could shake a God-damned stick at, but by God I ain't never—"

Ive's cheeks showed crimson, at the roots of his whiskers. He gripped his cane. He squared his shoulders.

"Shut up!" he ordered. "Shut up!" And he added, "What kind of language is that, in the presence of a lady? You'll get your money. I brought my checkbook, didn't I? I'll move the show. I'll pay the bills. I'm Ivan Pawpacker of Winchester, Missouri. I'm a partner in this outfit. You'll take your orders from me."

And for a moment, despite his blindness and his rain-soaked clothes and the years heaped heavy upon him, he looked his old self again, the rapier-keen little Napoleon of banking and land and circuses and horses and mules. His beard jutted, and authority made his frame rigid. But he was tired and old, and presently, involuntarily, a painful sigh heaved his shoulders, and he looked confused and uncertain, as if the enormity of Gus's deeds had pummeled him into bewilderment, as if the labor of prying into motion a derelict circus were too much for him, and the complexity of the situation beyond his ebbing strength.

"Eloise," he whimpered, "I can't see."

19

I N SAN ANTONIO, Texas, the sunshine is brilliant and the air smells of flowers and the sky is a dry, polished blue. In San Antonio, Texas, there are soldiers and *señoritas* and wide boulevards lined with amusement parks where merry-go-rounds whirl and tinkle far into the soft, blue night. It is a city of love and music and light hearts and pleasure. There are little winding streets thick-walled by adobe, and there are the great famous plazas with palms and *palacios* and Spanish urchins polishing the high-heeled boots of cow men and statues in bronze and girls selling tamales.

It is neither South nor West, but both; and it is Spain, and it is the memory of O. Henry and Santa Anna and Sam Houston and James Bowie. There are concerts by military bands and fountains splashing in the lavish sunlight, and there are *fiestas* where girls with rose-beige skins dance in green skirts, and there are grilled windows and patios scented with jasmine and scarlet with poinsettia. Once men seeking refreshments rode their cow ponies up to the bar of the Buckhorn, and through the center of town a small, smooth river winds, mirroring skyscrapers and live oaks and swans and little boats carrying lovers. In San Antonio, Texas, life is not such a serious matter after all, and if you planned to elope with another man's wife you would be well advised to consider carefully the many advantages offered by this gay capital of Spain in America.

All one night in September 1931, a pair of headlights flashed along the highway that races through the mesquite and chaparral between Corpus Christi and San Antonio. A powerful Packard owned those headlights, and a fat man with more than three thousand dollars upon his person owned the Packard. Dawn was breaking over Texas by the time the Packard sighted San Antonio, and when it reached the city's outskirts rosy sunlight was flushing the dome of the Mission San Jose and the walls of a Texaco filling station.

The Packard's driver looked a man of consequence, with his bold senatorial countenance and his cigar and his suit checked in gray-and-black. In the daybreak his eyes were bloodshot, owing to the strain of all-night driving, and it was possible to imagine worry lingering in the corners of those eyes. But it might have been only the weariness of driving. In any case, the expression vanished as he heaved air into his great chest and grinned and boomed to his companion:

"Uh—we're getting here. San Antonio! Beautiful city! Think you'll like it?"

"Oh-h, yes. It looks very nice."

"Picturesque! Remember the Alamo, and all that. Spent a few days here in 1912. My daughter had died, and I was trying to pull myself together."

"Oh?"

"Uh—yes. Had a sad time of it."

Marybelle waited to hear more, but he fell silent, staring through the windshield, chewing his cigar.

She looked serene as the fresh morning streets, and she greeted that city of flowers and music with her faint smile. Her blond brow was smooth. Her eyes gave no inkling of her thoughts. She was deciding that in municipal grandeur San Antonio fell far short of St. Paul, and she was disapproving of the cathedrals, for among her prejudices was a lively one against Roman Catholics; and she was wondering whether the wounds inflicted upon the Baron Von Krummer had been so serious as to widow her. Possibly Gus wondered about that also, for in the Alamo Plaza he parked the car and got stiffly out.

"I'll get a morning paper."

She watched him bustling across the street to an old Spanish news vendor. Even before returning he opened the paper and stood scanning it, his cigar cocked up, his pants wrinkled, his hat shoved back.

"No news," he said, upon his return. "Thought they might have a story about Willie."

"Perhaps it is too soon."

"Uh—yes." He sat with hands clamping the wheel. "You know, it never entered my head the cats might go for him."

"No? But they hate him very much. With the arena dark they saw their chance."

"Uh—s'pose they did. Funny I didn't think of that. My only idea in jerking the switch was to give you a chance to leave the tent while Willie was performing without him seeing you."

"They hate him very much," she said.

"Uh. Well, no use worrying about it. We'll find a good hotel. Feel better after breakfast. Best meal of the day. I've always said that."

He tramped the starter and cruised slowly on. Last night's events seemed unreal. Early morning in this strange city seemed unreal. By now, he supposed, Ive Pawpacker would know what he had done; and perhaps Flora. He thought of her back on the circus farm near Tamarack, and he hoped she wouldn't blame him too much.

Gus chose a hotel overlooking a block-square plaza, with a fountain and a heroic statue and benches for lovers. Palms and pecan trees grew there, and there were flower beds and doves.

He didn't wish to register as A. H. Burgoyne; so, since his luggage was gold-stamped A.H.B., he gave his name as Arthur H. Buckman. This incognito lent a clandestine flavor to his adventure; it was as if he were a monarch in romantic exile. He would have been completely happy, had his conscience not troubled him about Ive and Flora and Willie. Except for the trifle of stealing his wife, he had meant no harm to the Dutchman.

The hotel was done in the *circa-1910* manner that Gus liked: gold frescoes, pink marble pillars veined with wine, an occasional cupid, lobby alcoves where marble women fingered the heads of marble lions. Having reached maturity in an age of plaster embellishments, he found modern decoration too severe for his tastes. He didn't feel he was getting his money's worth, unless the *décor* were gaudy.

The bellhop escorted them to a suite overlooking the plaza, and presently Room Service in the person of a dapper Spaniard arrived, and Gus ordered a huge breakfast. He had prophesied correctly: breakfast indeed elevated his spirits. Over their coffee they dawdled for a long time, while the early sunshine bedazzled the snowy linen and vivified all the shimmering wheat-yellows and flax-golds of Marybelle's face and hair. Smiling serenely, she listened to him rumble and puff, and once he said:

"A penny for your thoughts, snookums."

"Oh-h, I was not thinking anything."

But this was a fib, for she was asking herself what God thought of her elopement.

After breakfast they went to bed, partly because they had been up all night. However, they didn't go to sleep at once; and slumber closed Marybelle's golden eyelids before it touched Gus. Her head lay on his shoulder, and up into his big nostrils there drifted the scent of her hair and skin. They smelled the way honey tastes. He took a long breath, drawing the fragrance deep, and he closed his eyes and lay smiling, for he was in love.

At heart he had ever been an adventurer and a romantic, and now after many years he had found romance and adventure again. Eloping with her had demanded a certain boldness, but he had been equal to that, and he felt he would be equal to any other bold necessities the future might demand. The money he had taken from the show would last for a comfortable period, and he knew that after it was gone he could make more fast. Just how, he hadn't considered, but with Marybelle by his side the world was his to take what he wanted.

Till this morning, weeks had elapsed since he had made love to

Marybelle without worry about Willie's interrupting, for in August the hospital in Minnesota had discharged the Baron and he rejoined the circus. In Gus's stateroom, on the evening before her husband's arrival, Marybelle said:

"This is the end of everything, then."

She looked somber.

"Uh—s'pose you mean we can't see each other, because Willie's coming back."

"He would be furious. He might kill us both."

Gus chuckled.

"Hardly think he'd do that."

"Oh-h, but he might. I think he would stop at nothing."

"Why don't you divorce him? And I'll divorce Flora. Then we'll get married."

"If I did such a thing he would kill me."

"He wouldn't dare."

"He has told me he would kill me if I ever leave him. I think he would do it. If I left him and started divorce action he would find me and kill me."

"Dog in the manger!" Gus declared. It outraged him. For little by little from Marybelle he had learned the facts of their marriage.

"He will come back and my life will be miserable again," she murmured. "He will beat me."

"Not when I'm around!" Gus stood up in the swaying compartment and smacked a fist into his palm. "Terrible thing. A sweet, beautiful little lady like you!"

She was sitting on the berth, hands clasped loosely in her lap, and she smiled faintly. Her emotions were exceedingly complex. At Gus's adoration her vanity purred like a golden kitten, and that same vanity was pleased that she disturbed Willie so much that he beat her, and that this outraged Gus. She did not dread her husband's return as much as Gus did, for ever since she had yielded to passion she had been burdened by a conviction of sin. In her imagination hell crackled brightly, and she often thought how unfortunate it would be if she were to be killed in the arena while in the midst of these sinful weeks with A. H. Burgoyne.

More than once she had determined to cease sinning, and make her peace with heaven. But she was a passionate woman, and A. H. Burgoyne had not spent all those light-o'-love years without learning a great deal about bringing happiness to others. He might be a weighty lover, and a fiftyish one, but he was tender and passionate and adoring and lavish with praise of beauty. Moreover, he loved her. That alone would have turned her vain head.

Hence, although she had struggled against sinning, she had pro-

ceeded to sin. Nearly every evening, up in heaven, a clerical angel
rustled to her page in the Book of Life and made another black mark.
It worried her. She prayed for assistance. Still she sinned. She told
herself she had always been bad, tempting Mr. Christianson, living
with Captain Latcher before matrimony.

The trouble was, she had to struggle against twin temptations: passion and vanity. Passion alone she might have conquered. But vanity!
He called her Snookums. He commented favorably upon her curves
and the apricot coloring of her skin. He told her she was the most
beautiful woman alive. He declared he loved her, and she knew he
meant it. Without her, he said, life would not be worth living. It was
an extravaganza of vanity. Her self-esteem soared and she was amazed
that a great, successful businessman like A. H. Burgoyne should
plunge head-over-heels in love with her.

In addition to her specific sense of sin, she entertained a general sense
of guilt because her hours with Gus made her happy. The theology
she had heard as a child had convinced her that happiness in itself was
to be suspected. In a way, she was never unhappier than when happy,
and never happier than when unhappy. She was like a Pilgrim Father.

Sometimes she thought Willie's impending return was God's answer
to her prayers for aid against temptation. Hence, although happily
sorrowful about that return, she thought it was for the best. She would
sin no more. And perhaps her suffering as Willie's wife would erase
some of the black marks against her.

Following his release from the Minnesota hospital, Willie had rejoined the circus in Wyoming, and after that Gus and Marybelle no
longer spent pleasant evenings together. A fortnight passed. Then,
one hot afternoon in Colorado, the Baron approached Gus in the back
yard and declared, "I want to have a talk with you." His words sounded
more like "I vant to haff a talk mit you," for after years of practice
he had gradually grown into his role. Aided by his ebullient imagination, his inborn sense of superiority, and a mystic racial gift for
inductive reasoning, Willie had become as truly aristocratic as any
Prussian peer.

"Sure, Willie," Gus said cordially. "What's on your mind?"

The Baron's neck became stiff as the spike on a helmet. With the
sun gleaming on his black boots and flashing about the gold braid
on his scarlet coat, he looked as military as a court-martial.

"We cannot talk here. It iss confidential."

Gus experienced alarm. Had Willie somehow learned of his affair
with Marybelle? Unlikely! They had been most discreet.

"Uh—why don't you drop into the Privilege Car after the matinee?"

"Ja—goot."

And the Baron executed an about-face and departed to his dressing-van.

Gus stood frowning. If Willie suspected he loved Marybelle he might want to settle matters by physical combat. Gus was suddenly conscious of his stomach's vulnerability; so he moved over to a baggage wagon in whose shadow a roustabout lay dozing. With his toe Gus nudged this stalwart's ribs and asked:

"Want to make five bucks?"

The fellow wanted to, so Gus instructed him to go to the Privilege Car and wait.

He felt better after that, although only relatively so. For during his conversation with Willie his emotions of the past weeks epitomized themselves: his love, his jealousy, his growing frustration. He missed Marybelle; since her husband's return they had spoken scarcely a word.

He felt a little wounded; she might at least, he thought, have sent him love missives on the sly. But perhaps she was waiting for him to make a move. Waiting and yearning and grieving. But what move? Dozens of times, in the cookhouse and in the back yard, he had accosted her and her husband, trying to make conversation. And always he had encountered the bristling fortifications of the Baron's personality. At such times Marybelle kept her eyes lowered, and if he addressed a remark to her the Baron broke in and replied.

Yes, undoubtedly she was expecting him to act. How, how? Always those fortifications around her!

During these meditations Gus was patrolling the back yard, and his gaze never strayed long from the Baron's dressing-van. Inside the big top the band started playing, and presently his vigil was rewarded: the Von Krummers left the van. First the Baron appeared, whip in hand, glaring about the lot. Having descended the steps he glanced impatiently around, and Marybelle appeared in the van door, all honey and curves in her arena costume. Gus's heart thumped, and his gaze arrowed toward her, finding her eyes for a moment. She was smiling. That tormenting, challenging smile. What was it saying? Take me if you dare? Are you brave enough and resourceful enough?

The Baron spoke curtly. Her boots and tights flashed down the steps. The Baron strode toward the performers' entrance, his *frau* hurrying to keep pace. She didn't glance toward Gus again. He was chewing his cigar. She never looked more luringly feminine than when in the company of that brutal Dutchman.

Gus joined them at the entrance. He didn't look directly at Marybelle, but her presence swayed him.

"Well," he said, "see you're all ready to give 'em a thrill."

Marybelle studied the ground. The Baron stared straight ahead.

The hinges of his jaw clamped and unclamped. Possibly he didn't mean to be boorish; possibly it was the habitual attack of nerves that assailed him before his act. But Gus felt rebuffed. His pupils narrowed. And the flanges of his nose quivered slightly, for he picked up the delicious scent of the powder Marybelle used.

Gus harried the frogs from his throat and slapped the Baron's shoulders.

"Uh—when you come to the Privilege Car, Willie, why don't you bring the missus? Have a cold drink. Kind of hot today."

The Baron's face snapped around. Viewed at close range, it looked startlingly big and ugly and furious. The skim-milk eyes had cruel clarity. The oblique lips looked freshly stripped of skin. The thick-bridged nose showed large pores, a couple of blackheads, a sick-yellow pimple.

"We vill talk business. No place for a woman."

"Uh. Just thought—pretty hot day—cold drink—"

But the Baron's face jerked away; the jaw-hinges were working again. Marybelle's eyes were still lowered, but under the cream of her skin Gus detected a warm, passionate pink.

He turned away. By God! He almost hoped the big Dutchman would try to start something in the Privilege Car. With the roustabout's help, it would be a joy to beat him up and kick him down the steps.

The roustabout needed a shave. A crescent of scar tissue ran from his ear to his nose. From his good ear; the lobe of the other had been chewed in an argument. He wore a green jersey that exuded a stench of sweat.

"You wait in the middle section," Gus ordered, gesturing toward that part of the car devoted to games of chance. "Fellow's coming here who might want trouble. If I need you I'll holler. What's your name?"

"Memphis Jack."

"Uh. Tell you, Memphis, I'll yell if I want you."

Alone, Gus mixed a drink and sat gazing through the open back door where the sun burned hot on the brass of the observation platform and on the flashing railroad yards. The vault of sky was fiery. The dark-purple cinders soaked up the sun's rays, and far down the tracks a switch engine expelled snowy puffs as it wavered through the heat-devils. The stuffiness of the car was intensified by the old-fashioned interior with its red steel and its window shades and upholstery in that weary railroad-train green. Gus mixed another drink and from the misted glass the alcoholic genie floated up and touched his eyeballs. And the problem of breaching Willie's fortifications and reaching Marybelle no longer seemed insuperable. He would manage.

He rested his head on the chair back and closed his eyes, remembering how she had looked this afternoon; desirable, desirable. He sighed and thought how delectable it would be to run away somewhere with her, leaving behind the circus wobbling toward bankruptcy, and Willie, and tight little Ive Pawpacker. His hand dangled over the chair arm and the glass found the carpet. He dozed.

"Vell, I'm here," somebody said harshly.

Gus stirred.

"Uh. Must have dropped off. Well—Willie. 'Lo. Have a drink?"

"No!"

Willie looked cruelly offended. He could not permit a cool concoction to lave his tongue, lest his tongue speak of Captain Latcher. With booted legs apart he glared down at Gus, and then his fingers brought out a single eyeglass and screwed it into his eye. He had ordered it from the hospital and practiced with it. A baron! Like Eric Von Stroheim!

"What in hell do you want with that thing, Willie?"

The Baron stiffened, seated himself erectly.

"But you're on the right track, Willie. If you're going to be a baron, be one! Nobody'd ever think you'd been a cage boy."

"Please!" The word snapped out like a bullet. "I have two matters to discuss mit you. First, salary. During my absence you did not pay the Baroness. You have paid me nothing since my return. I am here for my money."

"Now looky here, Willie," Gus exclaimed; and he elucidated the dreadful condition in which the economic system found itself. "But you'll get your salary. Had a letter from Ive Pawpacker. He's promised me a draft at the end of this week, and I'll pay everybody."

This didn't satisfy the Baron. He argued. Gus argued right back. At last he asked, "What was the second matter you wanted to bring up?"

"My wife."

"Uh?"

"My wife. The *frau*."

"Fine woman," Gus murmured.

The Baron's raw lips drew back, revealing powerful teeth. They gleamed; the monocle gleamed; and upon Gus's brow sweat gleamed. He added:

"Took hold of your act in fine shape, while you were gone. Show must go on, and all that."

"*Ja!* But what did she do in the evenings?"

"Evenings? Why, she presented the act same as in the afternoons. Went over big. Not a dry seat in the house."

"Stupid *schweinhund!*" the Baron muttered under his breath. Aloud he said, "I mean after the act. I have reason to think she kept company with other men. Maybe with several, yet."

"Other men?" Gus exclaimed in astonishment. "Why now, Willie! Sure you must be mistaken! The Baroness—uh—strikes me as being a mighty faithful little woman."

The Baron's teeth gleamed. And he spat out his opinion of women. It was low. Schopenhauer-ish. All women were faithless. Marybelle was a woman. Ergo—

"Oh, no! No! Think you must be misadvised. Sure the missus kept her heels together while you were gone. Don't believe she looked at another man. What does she say about it?"

"I have not yet been able to get a confession."

"Uh—no. Don't s'pose you have," Gus rumbled, but his blood ran chill. Get a confession! By physical abuse? How long would Marybelle be able to keep her counsel? "Think you're mistaken. Sure of it, in fact."

"We will see." The Baron arose. "I thought you might have heard gossip or maybe have seen her mit another man."

"Oh no! No! Nothing like that!"

"If I can break her silence," the Baron said, between his teeth, "I vill find the fellow and work on him fine and fancy."

"Uh—how'd you mean? Kill him, I s'pose, and all that?"

The Baron snorted. For such a fellow killing would be too good, already. He brought out his knife. That same toad-stabber with which he had threatened poor Cecil.

"I would—"

He explained. His voice was level and cold. And Gus thought:

"My God! The Dutchman means it! He's crazy with the heat!"

Gus accompanied the Baron to the rear platform. He poured out reassurances as to Marybelle's faithfulness, and he was sweating liberally. The reassurances bounced off the Baron's skull. At the bottom of the steps he saluted and marched away. Gus meditated back into the car, where he found Memphis Jack grinning.

"Ain't that God-damned Heinie a stiff radish!" he opined.

"Uh—you heard what he said?"

He nodded. "Knew a guy once in Little Rock that operated on another guy like that, and—"

But Gus had no stomach for such surgical details. He broke in:

"Uh—Memphis. Think the Dutchman may cause some trouble. Mean about his back salary, naturally—not about his wife." Gus laughed heartily. "Uh—think he's a little touched. Wearing that monocle, and so on. Uh—how'd you like to work for me permanently?

Five bucks a day—cash salary. Kind of a—well—" Gus laughed.
"Well—call it bodyguard, if you want to."

Memphis held out his hand and scratched the palm.

Eastern Colorado, western Kansas, Oklahoma—through those sad
lands with their gray soil and red soil and rainless soil the circus
limped and clanked, migrating slowly southward. Business remained
poor. Sometimes a thin beggarly wind dimmed the sunshine with
dust, and pitched beneath the immense sky the poor little show looked
like a gray photograph from a weak developing-solution.

During those weeks Gus's head felt like a wasp's nest, full of buzzing worries with stingers. He worried lest the show continue losing
money, and lest at Willie's hands he suffer a loss even more grievous.
Would the Baron back up his threat with action? "No!—of course not!
—terrible thing!" Gus consoled himself; but on the other hand the
Dutchman was notoriously ornery. At any time Marybelle might
break down and confess her lover's name. And then Willie would
come striding into the Privilege Car. That was why Gus took care to
remain in Memphis Jack's company; they were nearly as inseparable
as the Siamese Twins in the side show.

The circus played four days in Fort Worth and a week in Dallas;
and, for a change, it made money. Gus's optimism surged back. He
told himself the business depression was lifting. Spring would see
prosperity's return. He was like those traders in stocks who, when the
market flurried upward during the bad years, discovered cheerful
omens in the entrails of a ticker. He had wild hopes of finishing the
season with a loss small enough to convince Pawpacker the circus
should be continued.

It was wonderful to see Gus there on the lot in Dallas, so like his
old self. Even in hard times it was a wealthy city, and among the best
people, attending the circus caught on as a fad. And Negro Society
imitated this fad. The lot was thronged with white nabobs from High-
land Park and chocolate potentates from Deep Elm Street. Money
flowed easily, and that was how Gus liked things.

So cheerful did he feel that toward the end of the week he even paid
a few performers a little back salary. The Baron was among these.

"I'll clean up the rest soon, Willie," Gus promised.

Much of the profits, of course, he retained in his own pockets, for a
roll of currency gave off a glow that warmed his bones.

He regretted leaving Dallas, and on the final night he was the last
man to board the train. It was very late, and after Memphis Jack went
to bed in one of the Privilege Car compartments Gus sat in a huge

chair in the observation end, his shoes off, drinking beer and eating roast beef sandwiches.

At last, sleepy-eyed, he pushed up from the chair, looking not at all like a great lover. Slowly he bent over and picked up his shoes, grunting slightly, and trudged to his compartment.

In pajamas, bending over the washbasin, brushing his teeth, he made a noise like an angry bumblebee, for Gus believed that anything worth doing was worth doing vigorously and audibly. Then he turned toward his berth, enjoying its invitation to repose. The seat of his tent-huge pajamas sagged, and despite his size he looked almost like a sleepy three-year-old, needing to be tucked in.

The springs of the berth sighed, and so did he. He switched off the light, said "Uh-h-h . . ." He stretched his toes and his head made a comfortable nest in the pillow that smelled of fresh laundering. Uh-h-h . . . Tired. Bed felt good. And sleep came; deep, deep sleep. Only the sounds of his breathing now, the endless thirst of a living organism for oxygen: primal, inexorable, pitiful. And the train clanked and clattered, vestibules jolting, a little universe of mortal hopes and cruelties and passions. Southward, southward—through the cotton and the corn, past black cabins or some cabin showing a feeble light, announcing imminent birth or imminent death. Southward, southward —toward the live-oak land and the humid flood plains of the Gulf. Toward Corpus Christi, ultimately.

And then in Gus's compartment a change took place. The door had been closed, and the future was a road leading God-knew-where. Then the door opened, softly, and the future became a different road, still leading God-knew-where, but different, more dangerous. The door closed once more, and the lock snapped; and into Gus's nostrils there poured a dry, sweet scent, like a warm summer current off a field of ripe wheat. Lips touched his forehead and murmured warmly into his ear.

"Gus," the lips said, "are you asleep?"

"Uh?"

His returning consciousness was a rhinoceros staggering from a confused jungle.

"I should not have wakened you," she whispered.

"That's all right. Glad see you." The thickness on his brain was evaporating, and he added cordially, "Well! Quite a surprise! Uh— where's Willie?"

"He is sleeping. Back in our car."

"Take it he doesn't—uh—know you're here."

"Oh-h, no!"

"Just as well," Gus said.

"Oh-h, yes! Better!"

"Anything wrong?"

"No-o. It was just—that I had to come."

"Well now—that's mighty nice! Great idea! I've missed you, snookums."

"You have?"

"Night and day! All I've thought about!"

She was silent, waiting to hear more. His words were the first gentle raindrops upon the Sahara of her vanity.

"I've missed your beauty. And your company. Heart has been aching." He was wide awake now, and warming up. "Missed your conversation. Let me get a look at you."

He snapped on the berth lamp.

"God!" he exclaimed, as her vivid golds and apricot coloring burst upon his vision. "Beautiful! Most beautiful woman alive!"

She wore a negligee of summer-sky blue, and silken blue pajamas, and in the peach-warm light she looked exquisitely serene and utterly desirable. Her eyes were innocent as spring dawn. Yet the innocence was subtly disputed by the complexity of her high cheekbones and her smile.

"My God, honeybunch!" Gus exclaimed. "You're lovely—ravishing—"

She listened ecstatically. When he paused she said:

"Maybe you are just saying those things."

In denial, he launched out again. And inasmuch as Gus always yielded readily to enthusiasm, his own included, he became convinced that since Willie's return he had thought of nothing but Marybelle.

"Without you, life's no good," he declared. "If I can't have you I'd just as soon curl up my toes and die."

"But what can we do? This is very dangerous."

That recalled Willie's threat, and Gus pointed to the door.

"Better lock it."

"Oh-h, I locked it when I came."

"We're safe, then. Uh—what would Willie think, if he'd wake up and find you gone?"

"I would tell him I had gone to the ladies' dressing room."

"Great idea. Most natural thing in the world." And he asked, "Why did you come?"

"Because I have missed you so-o much."

"Uh—mean you—you love me?"

Her warm hand touched his.

"I think you are so-o wonderful and interesting and kind. And I love you."

He squeezed her hand.

"Uh—better get in here under the covers. Might get a chill."

"Oh-h, no! I must go. I must not be gone too long."

His hand hardened on hers. Authority! She submitted.

Later, very softly, Marybelle slipped from Gus's compartment and stole through the swaying darkness of the train. Now that her vanity and passion were satiated, she was alarmed about her welfare. Willie might be awake. Punishment! Her pretty legs cringed. But more than earthly punishment she was worried about eternal agonies. Picture to yourself, the preacher in New Stockholm had said, the hottest fire imaginable. And picture eternity. A mountain of rock. Once every thousand years a bird came and carried away a pebble. When the bird had carried away the whole mountain one second of eternity would have elapsed. Picture, then, yourself in that hot fire for all eternity.

"Oh-h," she moaned silently, "I am wicked and I am vain. I will never do this again. Never, never!"

And she wondered which had betrayed her, passion or vanity? Both! For weeks her blood had seethed with yearning. If only Willie had been capable of quenching that yearning! But he had not. Since his return he had tried and failed. Yet his masculine presence fueled her yearning. Even when he punished her. Especially then!

Oh, it was all torment and madness, her marriage to Willie.

But even so she might have been faithful, if only he had understood the demands of her vanity, overwhelming her like secondary desire. Never did he say he loved her, or that she was beautiful and wise. Her association with Captain Latcher had been a warm incubator hatching the peacock egg of vanity; and during her weeks with Gus the bird had preened and strutted and flaunted spectacular plumage. Willie had cooped up the bird in a dark poultry house; it molted and clucked sadly.

Outside her stateroom Marybelle paused, her heart racing like the clickety-clock of the train wheels. She slipped inside. In the dark she listened. And presently through the groan and creak of the train she made out Willie's breathing, regular in slumber. She crawled in beside him, lying rigid. Presently his body stirred and he spoke, but it was a mumble, the unintelligible speech of one who dreamed.

She did not sleep. The first tired tint of daybreak found her worrying still about her soul's welfare. Once she sneaked a look at Willie. In slumber his raw mouth was atwist. It was as if agony burned forever in his bowels; a driven, furious, hating, twisted man. If he ever learned what she had done he might kill her. And Gus, also. She started, appalled. For if Willie killed it would be her fault. Murder! She had hopes, somehow, of getting right with God about her vanity and her passion. But if she should be suddenly killed—in the midst of sin—and if it were her fault—she would never have opportunity to seek heavenly forgiveness. She saw herself, a figure in a gloomy illustration from *Paradise Lost,* pitching with flaming hair toward the fiery pit. Oh-h-h, she thought, I must never, never go to Gus again. And she didn't, for several nights.

Daybreak found Gus wakeful too, and he was worried. Not about God but about that devil, Willie. With Memphis Jack as bodyguard he felt fairly safe, but fairly safe wasn't enough when so much of value was at stake. Lying in his berth he pondered further protection, and he thought of a revolver that for years had been kicking around in the red wagon. Theoretically it was supposed to protect the ticket seller against holdups. He determined to find it and carry it.

That palliated his worries, and he lay in a golden mist of memory, thinking of Marybelle's visit. It was delicious to realize he could attract and satisfy a beautiful woman twenty years his junior. She loved him. And he loved her. A great romance! He smiled and sighed.

Yet—well—there were complications. Complications in addition to Willie's dastardly threat. Where was it all leading? Such a relationship did not remain static. Change! The law of love as well as of life. He had wanted his affair with Carlotta to continue forever the way it had been during those first lovely weeks, but life had intervened and forced him to a bitter decision. Would life intervene again?

That very morning he armed himself with the revolver, and that night in a state of intense excitement he waited for Marybelle to visit his compartment. She did not come. It depressed him, whetted his love. Nor did she pay a call the next night or the next. What was keeping her? Willie? Damn Willie!

During the day when he beheld her on the lot, in her husband's company, her innocent eyes and mysterious smile told him nothing. Willie continued boorish, curt. By the fourth night Gus had given up expecting her, so of course it was then that she opened the compartment door. He was dozing when he sniffed her fragrance, and instantly he forgave her all previous disappointments. "Darling!" he whispered, and then she was in his arms. Later she told him she had desired to come but that Willie had been wakeful. This was not wholly true; her fear of sin had kept her; but this fear was so terrible that it was sacrosanct; it was as if she dreaded voicing it lest it become blacker.

"It is so-o dangerous, what we are doing. Willie might kill us both."

"Why, snookums—I wouldn't let him do that."

"How could you help it?"

"I'd shoot him."

And he told her of the revolver. It iced her nerves. Willie with a knife, Gus with a gun! From such an encounter one could not expect pleasant results. And it would be her fault! Thou Shalt Not Kill. She could virtually hear the hell flames crackling.

"Oh-h," she moaned softly, "I am wicked, I am wicked."

"Uh? Wicked? Should say not! You're the sweetest, most beauti-ful—"

Those lovely adjectives pouring off his tongue anointed her like sweet oil. Her vanity soaked them up and thirsted for more. Passion could be quenched; vanity, never.

"I am wicked, wicked. Causing so-o much trouble—"

"No trouble at all. Uh—that is, unless Willie starts something."

"We mustn't let him know! I must never come here again."

Gus argued that point, earnestly.

She held out for more than a week, after that. September was nearly gone; in the North the mornings were frosty wine, the dusks a-smolder with leaf smoke; but now the circus had reached the Gulf, playing Houston and Galveston and crawling westward; and down here it was subtropical. Passionate bright noons; moist, passionate nights. On some days the circus showed a profit, and Gus's roll of currency fattened. He was paying no salaries; something told him he might need the power that throbs in money as in radium.

His nerves were kicking up. A strain, always thinking that tonight Marybelle might visit him. The uncertainty! A strain, beholding the furious Dutchman! Again, uncertainty! In a few weeks the season would close, and then what? Arguments with Ive Pawpacker about reopening next spring. Good-by to Marybelle. Back to Blue Island she would go, out of his existence. And he would return to Flora. And if Ive closed the show, what would the future hold? How could he gain a livelihood? Unemployment rising; money tight; a bad time. He had a vision of himself brooding along the gray winter streets of Tamarack, bucking hard times. Without Marybelle, all the fight would be gone out of him. Life was ganging up on him, he thought; he lived at the center of concentric circles of trouble.

Yet in her presence he felt young and resourceful. He thought he could lick the world, with her beside him. He played with the idea of running away with her, into a daydream land where a little business depression could not stop him. Even in hard times there were always men who coined money; men who made such brazen demands of life that life rewarded their impudence. He would be like that. Money would pour from the horn of plenty his personality would construct, with her, with her.

But after all, when you were married to a woman like Flora, for whom you had a comfortable fondness, and when you were involved with a shrewd little devil like Ive, of whom you were also fond, and when she was married to a fellow like Willie, half-crazy with meanness, you considered twice and thrice before actually skipping the coop. Whenever a man acted, vast complications followed. Likewise when you did nothing, which in itself was a form of action. Oh, damn life! A Chinese puzzle! No wonder a pitch like Madam Thale's had been so popular. You never knew what to do. Even the old proverbs laden with racial wisdom were contradictory. He who hesitates is lost. Look before you leap.

At 2:57 A.M., while the train was smoking and hooting en route to Corpus Christi, the Baron Karl Otto Von Krummer had a bad old dream. He was darting along State Street, pursued by an Englishman and the strains of "Chicago." He awakened in cold horror and jumped from his berth, cursing freely. Stumbling and pawing, he finally located the light switch and snapped it.

"*Ach, Gott!*" he muttered, sinking to the edge of the berth.

Mouth twisting, eyes terrible, big hands opening and closing, he fought for reality. Nearly eight years since the Captain had passed away, and still the dreams! Would the English bastard never cease molesting him? A long string of curses, deliberate and foul, squirted through his clenched teeth.

Uttering them improved his outlook; and the old arguments goose-stepped through his brain. Nobody could prove he had killed the Captain; he was a hero, a baron; so many years had passed that even if Marybelle tipped off the cops there would be no evidence. He was convinced that she suspected him, and that only by beating her regularly did he prevent her betraying him.

He had been so absorbed by his dream that he had not remarked her absence, but now he missed her. He stood up, eyes suspicious. During the last weeks his doubts as to her faithfulness had subsided, for she had seemed sincere when she screamed her innocence, and A. H. Burgoyne had declared her conduct impeccable. But what was this? Faithful wives did not sneak from the marriage bed in the middle of the night. Willie yanked open the door.

He really welcomed jealousy, because it crowded the nightmare from his mind. Scowling, he advanced along the car, past the staterooms of other featured performers. Those closed doors he did not suspect, for married people slept behind them; but she might be in somebody's arms in the front vestibule.

She wasn't. Beneath a dim bulb he stood there on the checked linoleum. This was the first Pullman on the train, and immediately forward he could see a huge boxcar swaggering, the coupling jerking and creaking. Behind its orange-painted wood, elephants drowsed; she wouldn't be there. He pivoted, strode back past the staterooms and into the next car. As always with Willie, to imagine a thing was to believe it, and now he was convinced his wife lay in somebody's embrace.

He stared down the length of the night-lighted Pullman, where green curtains billowed with the car's rocking. He pretty much knew where everybody slept: the girls, the performers who were bachelors. Methodically, he parted the curtains of berths occupied by the latter. In one he thought he had found something, for two persons lay there, and he uttered a curse. It was echoed by the occupants, a clown and a girl who, upon closer scrutiny, proved a brunette. They were outraged, and Willie backed hastily away.

He reached the Privilege Car. Any use proceeding? Certainly she wouldn't be with that tub of lard, Burgoyne: even in his jealousy he realized the absurdity of that. Then he remembered the roustabout who had been much in Burgoyne's company, Memphis Jack. Willie strode past the galley and through the gaming section. Ignoring Burgoyne's door, Stateroom "A," he kicked his way into Stateroom "B" where Memphis slept. It was black, but Willie was so convinced his wife was there that he plunged toward the berth.

A moment later a great commotion could be heard within Stateroom "B." For Memphis was dreaming he was in solitary, with a couple of guards beating him up, and when Willie grappled him he snapped awake and let fly. Realizing his error, Willie yowled and retreated. As he reached the sill Memphis landed a good one, and Willie found himself on the corridor carpet, gazing up at Memphis Jack's face, where the scar tissue gleamed in the subdued light.

Memphis was swearing, and for good measure he drove his bare heel down into the baronial mouth. Willie cursed bloody murder and begged Memphis to quit.

"Get up and fight, you Heinie son of a bitch," Memphis urged.

But just then the door of Stateroom "A" opened, and A. H. Burgoyne stepped out, closing the door behind him. It was a bold course, for the Baron's wife was hidden within, but Gus was fortified by the revolver in his paw.

"What the hell's going on?" he inquired.

Both men talked at once. Memphis explained he had been peacefully asleep, dreaming of his old mother, when this Heinie—

And the Baron explained he had missed his wife and had searched for her in likely places.

"Willie, you damned fool," Gus boomed. "She's probably in the can."

The logic of that, so prosaic, so probable, took all the fight out of the Baron. He realized he had made an idiot of himself, threshing through the train. He scowled, looking as baronial as one could in such a circumstance, with one's lip bleeding, and he admitted:

"Ja, ja—maybe you are right."

"Then what do you mean, waking everybody up?"

"Ja—okay. I vill go."

He scrambled to his feet and retreated on the double-quick.

"The damned fool," Gus muttered, and returned to his compartment.

But Memphis Jack did an odd thing. Loudly, he slammed the door of his compartment, but from the corridor side. Then, grinning, he folded his arms and lounged outside Gus's door, waiting.

When Gus returned to his compartment he found the Baroness huddled on the berth, her innocent eyes wide, her smile very faint indeed.

"You—sent him away?"

"Nothing to it. Now listen to me, snookums. You sneak back to your car. Tell Willie you ate something last night that made you sick. You've been in the ladies' room throwing up. Get it?"

He whispered rapidly; the instructions were very complicated for her quick comprehension.

"It is all a lie," she murmured, stricken by the thought of her sins compounding.

" 'Course it's a lie! Do you want him to kill us?"

"Oh-h, no-o!"

"Then do what I tell you. You'd better scoot!"

He kissed her briefly, and she opened the door. But instead of slipping away she uttered a little gasp and ducked back inside.

"Uh? What's wrong?"

"There is a man outside," she whispered, all the peach and apricot tints washed from her frightened face.

"Man!"

Gus too was startled, but in his huge pajamas he looked dynastic, steering his bulk into the corridor. He gripped the revolver, but when he spied Memphis Jack he said merely:

"Oh. 'Lo, Memphis. Thought you'd gone to bed."

Memphis grinned.

Over his shoulder Gus called:

"It's all right. You go. And remember what I told you."

Marybelle was a blond-and-blue rustle of silk, disappearing along the corridor.

Gus filled his chest; his chin was up; he looked very dignified.

"Uh—Memphis. Baroness and I were—uh—having a little—uh—

conference—uh—about a private matter. Willie might have misunderstood—"

Memphis kept grinning. Gus didn't like his attitude. The train
swayed and clattered, and far ahead the locomotive hooted derisively.

"I get it," Memphis said.

"Uh—naturally—it would be better for all parties concerned to—uh
—not mention the matter."

Memphis lounged against the corridor wall, his gaze on the black
window, past which you could imagine the Southern night racing.
When he spoke his voice had a gentle, reflective quality.

"Gus, I've never had no good breaks, to speak of. My mother was
a whore, Gus, and I've been on the bum since I run off from reform
school. I never had a decent drink till I was twenty—just this God-
damned canned heat. I never had more than fifty bucks at once—even
when I was sticking up filling stations. I always kind of hankered for
a thousand bucks all together at once, Gus. I'd spruce me up in new
clothes, and get me a juicy broad, and smoke two-bit cigars. Yes sir,
I've always wanted the feel of a thousand bucks, and it looks like
you're my banker."

Gus cleared his throat. Memphis gave him a sidelong glance, forehead crinkled almost whimsically.

"Now don't pull that revolver stuff on me, Gus. Guys like you
don't shoot. That's for guys like me. Yes sir, I could use a thousand.
I've got you over a barrel, Gus, with your pants down, and you know
it."

"Uh," Gus said. The network of blood vessels in his nose and cheeks
were ablossom with rose and purple, but he wasn't really angry.
Alarmed, yes, but not enraged. He understood Memphis Jack; in his
shoes he would have acted the same.

Memphis sighed.

"I kind of like you, you old cuss," he grinned. "I'd hate like hell to
see that Heinie Baron go after you. But winter's coming and times are
tough." He stretched, yawned. "Think it over, Gus. I don't want to
crowd you. Know a thousand bucks is a nice little piece of change,
to come by all at once. Let's say tomorrow night—after we're loaded
—here in the car. Pay me then."

"Uh—well now, Memphis—"

"Take it or leave it," Memphis said.

And he disappeared into his compartment.

It was a warm, beautiful morning, in the city named for the body
of Christ. The weatherman predicted rain for tomorrow, but at 11
A.M. the bay was bright blue with whipped-cream rollers foaming on
the golden beaches.

On the lot the parade was forming. No longer did Gus lead it astride a white horse; he was so bulky it was too hard on him, and the horse. Nor did he always ride in his Packard, amid the imaginary roses flung from the throngs. This morning he smoked his cigar along the lined-up parade, countenance jovial beneath his Panama. Far ahead the Negro band was playing "Dixie," and soon the bright wagons would start moving. Waddling vigorously toward the end of the parade, Gus exclaimed, " 'Lo, Willie," to the Baron Von Krummer, booted and mounted on a fine steed. The Baron glowered straight ahead, and Gus hurried past the animal wagons till he reached a snowy equipage like something frosting a huge wedding cake. There were yellow wooden horses, leaping hotly into nowhere, and silver harness and a silver sleigh. And in the midst of this powdered sugar a lovely lady rode the sleigh, exquisitely composed, smiling faintly, a tiara flashing in ripe-wheat hair.

Nobody was within earshot, so to her Gus said:

"Be ready to leave tonight. Read this. It will tell you what to do."

He thrust an envelope toward her.

She murmured, "But Willie—"

"He won't stop us. I'll handle everything. You do as I say."

The driver hurried to mount the equipage; wheels were turning; and behind the sleigh the calliope showered forth a snowstorm of silvery notes: *In a little . . . Spanish town . . . t'was on a night like this . . .*

She looked bewildered, but obedient; and Gus stood watching the parade winding from the lot, Marybelle's hair in the sun the brightest thing in all that flash and sparkle.

I murmured . . . be tru-u-ue to me . . . and she sighed, Si, Si . . .

He knew he would never see that parade again; he wanted to cry.

That afternoon Gus wandered to the wharves and gazed for long and long at the bay, as if by contemplating the timeless ocean he could read the future. His plans were laid; it was very simple; during the Baron's act he would yank the master switch; and in the confusion he and Marybelle would depart.

Eyes slitted against brilliance, he sat staring at the indigo rim of sea. He didn't look so very happy. Life forcing him. But he knew if he paid Memphis a thousand the fellow would be back for more. And a thousand was a lot of money. Depression. A bad season. Ive would close the show. And again he saw himself, shambling through freezing light, through the falling plaster of capitalism. No, no, times would improve . . . but Ive had said it would be the depression of the thirties. Trouble, trouble. Lord, he was tired . . . up all night . . . my mother was a whore, Gus . . . well, Memphis, guess mine was, too . . .

He heaved a sigh. The water splashed about the piling, and the little fishing boats bobbed up and down, because a wind was blowing on the other side of the earth, or because the moon was tugging out in endlessness. He was fifty; soon be fifty-one. Might think a man would learn something about the chess game of life, in fifty years. What were those lines from that poem Carlotta had read aloud? Something about . . . the checkerboard of days and nights . . . An Arab wrote it. Amazing, the fellow's command of English.

He was staring at a hunk of driftwood, washed in from infinities of ocean, having been carried, perhaps, on the currents that flowed like rivers through the sea. He thought of those leagues, of the life teeming in the waters, the billions and billions of slimy forms, all children of Jehovah, like himself. What was existence all about, any-way? Thinking in that large way made his own life seem inconsequential, anything he did unimportant. And there by the sea, by the great warm mother that once upon a time had sent life forth to invade the lands, Gus experienced the sadness for which there is no balm, and the loneliness that had swept Sophocles upon Aegean shores.

20

THE NEWSPAPERS were full of it. Not only the Corpus Christi papers, either: it was a feast in nearly every city room in America. Of course! It had everything; sex, violence, romance, glamor, mystery; oh God, it was wonderful.

Consider:

You are a news editor and you've been giving them the ordinary stuff: Herbert and J. Edgar Hoover, bank failures and love nests, car smashes and tornadoes, legs and Lindbergh, everything that has put the American press away out front in world leadership. Then this!

A circus. Color, romance, tinsel, the happy animals, the kind trainers, the roustabouts with hearts of gold: it has appeal.

A baron and a baroness. Now this is a democracy; that's well known; everybody born free and equal; but despite this Utopian social order the average American is interested in nobility. Look how the Prince of Wales captured the hearts of dime store clerks, back in 1924.

Now then, not only a baron, but a baron about whom clippings already are in your morgue, for once in Blue Island he risked his life trying to save Captain Philip Latcher. And not only a baroness, but a baroness who is an animal tamer. Moreover, she's what the more intellectual reporters call pulchritudinous. This means that when you dig her publicity photos from your files, and make a nice art layout, the resulting cheesecake helps your paper fulfill the great aphrodisiac mission of the Fourth Estate.

See the setup?

And now then further: this Baroness tumbles for A. H. Burgoyne, and he's a colorful figure in his own right. Rags to riches; poor boy makes good; a true American success. And Burgoyne, it is suspected, and deduced, and hinted, yanks the master switch, plunging the tent into darkness, while the Baron is in the arena. And Burgoyne and the Baroness turn up missing, so there's the mystery of wondering where in hell they are.

The beauty of this yarn is that there are so many follow-up angles. In a Corpus Christi hospital the Baron is lying in critical condition; doctors consult; it is announced that his left arm and right leg must be amputated. Great stuff! And there stands the circus in the rain, flat broke, and the Corpus Christi health department is making statements; and the newsreel cameramen are flying thither, so one of these nights in your neighborhood theater you will hear a sound-track voice, funereal and orotund, commenting upon what is fairly obvious: that this circus isn't doing so well.

The press does a bang-up job; really covers the story; and in Tamarack Mrs. A. H. Burgoyne is interviewed. She takes it very calmly. "Think there's some mistake," she says. "Don't think Gus would do that." In print, of course, you zip up the interview slightly, commenting upon her fortitude, and her smiling through her tears, and her saying, "I still have faith in my husband."

Well, a good story can't last forever. After the amputation the Baron battles death, and is winning the battle; and Ivan Pawpacker, Burgoyne's partner, rescues the show, paying bills, sending it back to winter quarters, selling off the animals; and on the farm an enterprising reporter and photographer pay the roustabouts to scatter equipment, tipping over a wagon or two, in order to get a last sensational yarn about the sad end of the glamorous circus.

The thing peters out. There's no proof, after all, that A. H. Burgoyne yanked the switch, or that, if he did yank it, he yanked it with malicious intent; and the Baron, when he's convalescing, looks upon the affair with a truly noble attitude: he does not, he says, believe A. H. Burgoyne was responsible for the darkness. He looks awfully mean when he says it, but say it he does. There's more mystery there: possibly the Baron has his reasons for not wishing charges filed against Burgoyne; and in your future book you make a note of that ornery look, just in case the Baron intends settling the score in his own way.

Well, that's about all. The story diminishes and travels from front page back through the paper, landing finally on the market page, with the rest of the doleful news. Days have passed, and it's all over.

And then—splash!

You had thought every angle exhausted. You had devoted some attention to Pawpacker, but what with the Baron, and Marybelle Monahan's legs and bosom, and A. H. Burgoyne, you hadn't given that Missouri banker the attention he deserved. So what happens?

So one day the wires chatter out how the examiners have closed Pawpacker's bank. Moreover, there has been crookedness in its operation. Juggled records, deposits received after the management knew the bank was broke; and it appears that Pawpacker, in rescuing the stranded show, drew heavily from the bank, using the funds of widows and grass widows and even an orphan or two in order to move the circus from the bogged lot in Corpus Christi. So this story, which ordinarily wouldn't have attracted much attention, because Pawpacker's deeds are virtually standard banking practice, connects up with the earlier story and explodes all over page one.

But it doesn't last long. Pawpacker's attorney confers with government attorneys, and it is agreed that Pawpacker shall plead guilty to one of the charges, which he does, receiving in due course a stretch in the Federal clink in Leavenworth, Kansas.

The story seems really played out, now. It's still a mystery where the Baroness and Burgoyne are; but Thanksgiving is approaching, so it's time for some turkey art; yesterday's news is dead news; nobody is excited about Burgoyne any more, except maybe his creditors, and his wife, and the Baron and likely Ivan Pawpacker. Yet, with a big yarn like that you never know. A story like that has endless ramifications; sometimes it will sleep in your morgue for years, and then burst out again in great glory.

It startled Gus, that first day in San Antonio, when he bought an afternoon paper in the lobby and saw how the press was playing the story. He told himself he should have known they would splash it, for he had been a newspaper man, but when you're so close to a story, one of the principals, you might say, you're not as objective as you might be.

Standing there by the tobacco counter, he felt a good deal like a jungle elephant observed by hunters with rifles. Or like a sleepwalker who awakens in public without his pants. Not an especially pleasant sensation, either way.

First thing he did, upon glimpsing the headlines, was to fumble out his reading glasses, big horn-rimmed things, thinking they would provide a disguise. Then, trying not to look like anything but a traveling salesman, he retreated to a far corner of the lobby and slouched into a heavy chair. He was mighty glad he had possessed the foresight to register as Arthur H. Buckman.

There he was, smudged into newsprint, two columns wide; and there was Marybelle, legs and all, in her arena costume, smiling mysteriously out at the paper's circulation; and there was the Baron in the midst of his act, with two big cats snarling at him. In those days wirephoto was a recent thing, and the press associations grabbed any excuse to play with their new toy.

The story began two columns wide, narrowing to a column that ran down the right side of page one and then jumped back among the ads for toothpaste and trusses. It was beautifully done. Nowhere did it come right out and say that A. H. Burgoyne had yanked the master switch and eloped with the Baroness, but the implication was there.

Gus let his glasses slide down his nose, and over the rims he peered at other persons in the lobby. Nobody seemed interested in him. Several had afternoon papers, too, but they didn't connect him with that newspaper drama. And it occurred to him that newspaper readers looked upon what they read as semi-fiction, something taking place in a bigger-than-life existence of sugar daddies and state secrets and gangsters, so that office workers would have something with which to while away their strap-hanging homeward treks. Nobody would expect to encounter this latest sugar daddy, A. H. Burgoyne.

He felt unreal, being such a large mote in the public eye; and he thought how in newspaper offices all over the country desk men had been fitting his name into heads, and printers setting it up, while he and Marybelle made love. And that fact more than anything else made him feel uneasy and debauched.

He reread the story, paying special heed to the paragraphs devoted to the Baron. They had unearthed the fellow's earlier heroism, and they were slanting things to rouse public sympathy for him. Yes, Willie was the hero of this scandal, with Marybelle no better than she should be, and A. H. Burgoyne decidedly worse. With that viewpoint Gus couldn't agree. He couldn't believe he had acted like a villain. He had done what he had to in the circumstances.

Soaring in the elevator, he pondered the wisdom of showing the paper to Marybelle. Might upset her. Still, the newsboys would be howling the headlines, and she might grow curious: best to do the forthright thing.

His countenance was sober, as he plodded majestically along the corridor, but when he entered their suite he was jovial. And when he beheld her at the mirror, her delicious coloring and sweet curves the personification of witchery and desire, all his regrets vanished. She was worth it.

"You bought a paper?" her low voice asked.

"You bet I did, snookums. Gave us a great play! We're all over page one!"

"Oh-h-h?"

Her brow was smooth, her eyes serene, her lips smiling. She took the paper and seated herself, following the type slowly, lips moving, for in school her grades in reading had been low. He could not deduce how it affected her. When she put down the paper he exclaimed:

"Well, we kind of busted into print, didn't we?"

"Oh-h, yes." She lifted the paper and stared at her picture. "I wish they had used a different one. I have never liked this picture as well as some of the others."

"Now, now," Gus chuckled. "Don't want to be vain about it."

It sobered her. She looked almost stricken.

"Yes," she murmured, "yes. You are right. I am a vain woman. It is a great sin."

"Don't know as I'd say that. Never saw a woman worth looking at who wasn't a little vain. Kind of a charming trait."

"Oh-h, no. It is very wicked. That is why we must bring forth children in agony."

"Uh—guess you're right, at that," Gus said, for he had no wish to engage in some deep theological discussion. "Uh—just occurs to me, snookums—we'd better move from this hotel."

She gave him that open, inquiring look.

"Uh—well—you see, we might be recognized. Just as well for us to lie low, till this blows over. Won't last long. Newspaper scandals never do. Think we might find a quiet roominghouse somewhere. How does that strike you?"

"If that is what you wish."

"Well now, I don't exactly wish it, but think it might be better, everything considered."

"Oh-h, yes. Whatever you decide."

She was as plastic as creamy clay in an artist's fingers.

He rumbled on, telling her what a romantic city San Antonio was, and how happy their life would be there. She listened, but she busied herself, too, going to a suitcase and fetching her scrapbook, along with scissors and paste. And while he extolled San Antonio, and the sweetness of flowers drifted from the plaza across the way, she clipped the news story and pasted it into the scrapbook. Perhaps it was wicked, that scrapbook, for it was a monument to vanity, but she was so far gone in sin it didn't seem to matter; and besides, it helped to work with her hands. She was like a housewife scrubbing the floor to forget worry.

But she didn't forget. When you're at the edge of a fiery pit you don't forget. She had yielded to the sin of elopement to avert the sinful calamity of Willie's murdering them both, and her responsible. But now Willie lay at death's door. If he died it would be her fault. So while Gus boomed on about the Alamo, and she clipped and pasted, smiling and looking so placid, she was frantically beseeching God to save Willie's life, and to show her a way to save her soul.

Next day they found an apartment on a lost little street that was narrow and twisting but didn't care because it was going nowhere, anyway. Locusts and pecans grew there, and live oaks and palms, and it was near enough to the center of things so that if you listened at night you could hear the low mutter of traffic from the great avenues. Monterey grill-work decorated the balcony opening off their quarters. The slate-colored house had dozed into a siesta a century before, and with a Latin understanding of such matters nobody had awakened it.

Vines festooned the balcony, and the yard below with its low wall topped by ironwork was a garden where flowers with scarlet throats formed entangling alliances with all sorts of gay, flirtatious vegetation; and on sunny mornings, when Gus dawdled on the balcony in pajamas, drinking coffee and blowing smoke at the complex interlacing of light and shadow, there floated up a blend of scents as sweet as the fragrance from Marybelle's dressing table. The plumbing was in poor repair, and the gas range leaked.

Their landlord was an old Irishman with Spanish blood, married to a Spanish woman with Irish blood; and whether they suspected Arthur H. Buckman of being A. H. Burgoyne remains unknown. They possessed that Old World indulgence for human peccadillo of all true San Antonians, and if a prompt-paying tenant wished to emigrate from a foreign land like the United States and set up residence in Texas, who were they to inquire into a relationship that was after all highly personal?

Their pleasant indifference was fortunate, because during those first weeks Gus and Marybelle were often mentioned in the press. The Baron, also. Daily he loomed more heroic, and after the surgeons pruned him of two limbs all North America followed his gradual recovery. The Republic felt as compassionate toward him as toward his defeated Fatherland after 1918, and like his Fatherland the Baron wallowed in this pity and profited thereby. For good causes and good men never lack a champion, and when a Corpus Christi newspaper set up a fund to rehabilitate the noble fellow contributions arrived from every state in the Union, as well as Alaska, Hawaii, the Canal Zone, Puerto Rico and the Virgin Islands; and often letters accompanied the checks, written by lonely women, hinting that the Baron would find them interesting companions.

Oddly, one of the anonymous five-dollar bills was dispatched to the fund by Marybelle. She didn't tell Gus, because he might have asked why she sent it, and she could not have made him understand her motive for she didn't herself clearly understand it. It was very mixed and misty: she felt sorry for poor Willie; she always believed the newspapers, so now she half-believed her husband a wronged hero; and possibly she hoped the five spot would eradicate one of those black marks on the Book of Life. The chances were it didn't, for the fiver was intercepted by the reporter in charge of the fund, who spent it with a bootlegger.

Gus and Marybelle had a fine life in San Antonio, so it seemed. Except for an occasional Norther, the autumn weather was halcyon, and they could be seen strolling along Military Plaza in the bright afternoon, or consuming peppery dishes in some smoky café near Milam

Square, or boating on the river like lovers in some old hammock novel, Marybelle trailing her fingers in the mirroring water. They slept late into the bird songs of morning and breakfasted lazily, and they attended concerts and the theater. Sometimes in the Packard they drove into the country, and Gus was always freshly amazed that this city with its Continental flavor should be beleaguered by endless miles of Wild West country.

"Big state, Texas," he often commented.

"Oh-h, yes. But it does not grow such fine crops as Minnesota."

"Uh? Guess you're right, at that." And he added gallantly, "Doesn't produce such beautiful women, either."

She was as pleased as a farm wife discovering an egg with a double yolk.

They never quarreled. This might have indicated that their lovers' souls were in complete harmony, or it might have meant that their interests were so far apart that they had no common territorial boundaries of the intellect over which to declare war. Either way, it was very nice. Life with Marybelle was like the placid existence on some lovely island in warm seas, where the seasons never changed, where day after day the sun shed its golden beneficence, where you drowsed beneath a tree and when you were hungry a tepid breeze stirred and loosened ripe, luscious fruit that fell into your hands.

Gus bought the newspapers regularly, and in the evenings Marybelle clipped and pasted the stories into her scrapbook. He watched her through his cigar smoke, taking pleasure in the blond halation of her hair. If his desire had been recently quelled he could gaze upon her almost with objectivity, and sometimes his vigorous mind forced him to admit that she wasn't the liveliest companion imaginable. When he waxed enthusiastic about anything except her beauty and Minnesota's wonders, she did not contribute much to the discussion. It had been different with Carlotta. And as the weeks passed, Marybelle except for her beauty reminded him more and more of Flora. This astonished him at first, and he believed he must be mistaken, but gradually he accepted the fact that Marybelle was a bit dull. Often he wondered what thoughts were plodding between her temples, and like Captain Latcher he asked her.

"Oh-h," she responded, "I was not thinking of anything."

But this was untrue, for she was meditating upon the welfare of her soul, and upon the wickedness of San Antonio. To her it seemed the city was sinful because its climate was so good. To be saved one must suffer, and she missed the early freezes and bitter snows that were so beneficial to the soul of St. Paul. Flowers in November seemed ungodly. And the lightheartedness of the town convinced her that on a theological map it would be located astride the primrose path with road signs announcing, "Hell, Four Miles." The numerous Roman missions and churches strengthened this conviction. Moreover, many of the citizens looked like foreigners and jabbered in a foolish language, and she had always believed foreigners wicked, especially foreigners with Latin coloring.

Sunday after Sunday, Marybelle attended various Lutheran churches, but although the congregations were tow-headed she believed their souls lost, for the sermons were frivolous, often being concerned with worldly matters. Feeling sinful, she even ventured to attend Baptist and Methodist churches, afterward beseeching God's forgiveness. Then quite by chance she discovered a group that called themselves the Genesis Faithful. They had no church but congregated in a bare-walled store room at the edge of the business district. The preacher had the seductive voice and mellow countenance of a hammy old Shakespearean, and when he led the singing he played an accordion. Of that instrument Marybelle disapproved, but when the man launched into his sermon she gave a soft sigh of homecoming and content, for he inveighed against the wickedness of San Antonio and mankind, and from his graphic description of hell you would have supposed he had visited the place.

Like Fabius Thompson, he was self-ordained; one of those wild men of God who are to religion what quacks are to medicine and shysters are to the law; and he was still mad about Darwin and the higher criticism of the nineteenth century and movies and cards and hard cider and mammillary glands; and in his opinion there would never be any traffic problem in the streets of heaven, because nobody except the Genesis Faithful would be dwelling there.

Every Sunday morning and every Wednesday evening Marybelle listened to him preach, depositing a dollar in the collection plate; and sometimes she thought the minister was talking directly to her. And this was correct, for the poor man was not immune to the wiles of golden flesh, and besides he had shrewdly deduced the source of that collection plate dollar. One Sunday she lingered and told him she had enjoyed his sermon, and haltingly she even mentioned her personal problem: vanity. He promised to touch upon this the following Sunday, and he was better than his word; he fondled the problem, and lashed it, and cuddled it lasciviously; from the way he castigated thighs and breasts you would have thought he hated them, although quite the reverse was true.

However, he was never able to do anything about Marybelle's, for when she remained to talk with him his wife was there also. He did get his eyes full, though. And he recounted the history of the Genesis Faithful denomination, telling how, naturally, it had originated in

southern California, and how it needed money to carry on its great
work. Marybelle thought idly that some day she would like to visit
the original church in Los Angeles, and she hinted to the pastor that
she was wrestling with a sin even greater than vanity. He advised her
to continue attending church and praying, and presently God would
tell her what she must do to be saved.

So, as she walked homeward through the bright Sunday noon, along
streets full of misguided, doomed people who had attended other
churches, Marybelle prayed for guidance. Once it occurred to her that
she might leave Gus, that worldly man. But instantly, conflict was
joined in her soul. Her conscience would hurt her, leaving him in the
predicament which she accused herself of bringing about; and her
passion would miss his embraces and her vain ears his endearments.
She was sorely troubled.

He was troubled that day too, for he had read in the papers about
the calamity that had overtaken Ive Pawpacker. His eyes were sad,
and he brooded a good deal about it. In his dejection Marybelle wasn't
much help. That afternoon, in order to forget his woes, he suggested
that they visit one of the amusement parks along Broadway, but since
this was the Lord's Day she declined. He went alone. But the laughing people and the merry-go-round organ failed to cheer him. He sat
on a bench, scowling, and his cigar went out.

Gus gave little thought to money that autumn, because the sum he
had taken from the circus was holding out very well. Everything
could be purchased at depression prices, so the cost of maintaining
what the press would have called a love nest was not excessive. And
Marybelle was thrifty. She liked to buy food at open-air markets, and
while she did not really haggle it amounted to that. "Oh-h," she
would trill to a tradesman, "that is too much." She had never heard
the Italian proverb that a woman should be a lady on the street, an
economist in the kitchen, and a demi-mondaine in the bedroom, but
she lived in accordance with it.

Money interested her more than it did Gus. Preparing for bed, he
would dump his roll and his loose change on the dresser, and sometimes Marybelle asked:

"How much money do we have?"

"Uh—don't know, exactly. Why don't you count it?"

So, sitting on the edge of the bed, looking as pretty as a maiden
weaving a garland of vines and daisies, she counted it to the last penny.
Gus watched with amusement; in many ways she reminded him of a
little girl. It was her childlike quality which restrained his possible
annoyance, for after all her pecuniary concern was not unlike Mr.

Oxenford's and Flora's, and some day she might develop as intense and degrading an interest in small change as all the other tightwads with whom life had thrown him.

Like a child reporting the correct solution of an arithmetic problem she said:

"We have twenty-eight hundred and ninety-one dollars and seventy-seven cents."

"Uh—sure it's not seventy-eight cents?"

"Oh-h, yes—I am very sure. It is seventy-seven."

Then he roared with laughter and she looked puzzled.

"What will we do," she asked, "when we have no more money?"

"No need to borrow trouble. Enjoy life as you go along, that's my motto. But as a matter of fact, I've several ideas under consideration."

She waited, but he did not elaborate. Once she suggested:

"We might go to Los Angeles."

"Uh? What do you want to go to L.A. for?"

"I have heard it is very nice."

"Too many other grafters out there," Gus roared. She looked disturbed; she was thinking how fine it would be to worship in the original church of the Genesis Faithful; so he comforted her by adding, "Just joking, of course."

It was true that in a vague way Gus was considering the future. Every week he bought *The Billboard,* chiefly to follow the news about such old friends as Willie, but he also read the pages devoted to outdoor shows. He told himself he could always join a small circus in some capacity. Technically, this was probably true; actually, not; for somebody would recognize Arthur H. Buckman as A. H. Burgoyne, and word might reach the Baron. Gus was not eager for further encounters with the Baron; better lie low. But even though he knew he could not return to the show world he kept telling himself he would do so. Consistent he may not have been, but optimistic he was, as ever.

In that magazine he read that although Ive Pawpacker had lost everything else in the bustup, he had retained control of the circus farm at Oxenford by deeding it to Eloise Sebastian. Some legal shenanigans. Gus was puzzled. He couldn't fathom why Ive had wished to keep that worthless land. Did he think he would start another circus, someday? Gus shook his head. Ive was old; probably he would die in prison.

It never occurred to Gus that he was responsible for the farm's going to Eloise. Long ago he had announced that some of the richest coal in the country veined that land. Ive had discovered this was exaggeration, but toward the end, in all the worry and confusion, he had grown forgetful, as if his pride, about to suffer a catastrophic blow, had obliterated the memory of old business deals in which he had been

bested. With queer trickery his mind had washed out the memory of
the salted coal mine, and it comforted him to believe that although
he was leaving Eloise alone she would at least possess land wealthy in
coal. Once long ago he had promised her he would never let her down,
and by deeding her that land with its fabulously rich coal he was keeping that promise. He always kept his promises, man of shining honor
that he was.

Through thick and thin, through her abrupt affair with Mr. Christianson and her long affair with the Captain, Marybelle had been
religious. But now that she had surrendered to the influence of the
Genesis Faithful, she was simply running religion into the ground.
Always she had believed what any minister said, so now she swallowed
whole all the outlandish utterances of the Genesis Faithful rector.
Once in a spirit of self-torment she suggested that he preach upon the
consequences of a man and woman living together in sin. This was
the sort of topic he liked, and he did a good job. You would have
thought it the Fourth of July, the way the brimstone popped. His
sermon startled the congregation, and before he was through the poor
fellow even scared himself.

That was in early December, and while she listened Marybelle decided she must leave Gus. Living in sin, she might fall into a manhole
or be killed by a motor car, and there would be hell to pay. Possibly
all along she had known she must make this decision, but it was a
dread one and she had postponed it. And even now she postponed
mentioning it to Gus. Where would she go when she left him, and
what would she do to support herself? She prayed for guidance, and
she kept expecting divine intelligence to manifest itself.

Just how this would come about she did not know, whether by a
bush crackling into flame and broadcasting the voice of God, or by
some less spectacular method. She waited, her mind blank as a wall
waiting for the ghostly writing. But nothing happened. In her more
worldly moments the devil whispered that such a phenomenon would
never take place, that heaven meant for her to dwell with Gus. She
wanted to believe this, for she shrank from leaving his protective
authority and trying to support herself; she might starve; and certainly her vanity and passion would starve unless she found another
man. And if she were going to do that, she might as well remain with
Gus. She could never get a divorce because if she took that action
Willie would learn her whereabouts and kill her. That would be a
great sin, unfortunate all around. Oh, it was a very bad tangle! Knowing the demands of her vanity and passion, she realized she would ever
be tempted by men, but her indissoluble marriage would forbid her
living with them save in wickedness. The future looked bleak.

Then in mid-December she underwent an experience that a less religious person would have called a dream, but that she called a vision. As she slept she beheld herself in the starched uniform of a beauty operator, administering a permanent wave. Perhaps her visiting a beauty shop the previous afternoon was responsible, but since she was waiting for a heavenly message she convinced herself, next day, that this was a hint from God. He must mean for her to learn hair-cutting, like Delilah in Scripture. As a beautician she could earn a living while she battled against her sinful impulses.

So she returned to the beauty shop and asked the operator how one learned that profession, and she was told that there were schools devoted to the subject. And with some astonishment Marybelle heard herself saying:

"I am going to Los Angeles. Are there such schools there?"

She was told there were many such schools there.

Why had she said she was going to Los Angeles? On the street she pondered the question. Certainly she had not been conscious of such a destination. Strolling past shop windows, vainly admiring herself, she at last concluded that God had put those words into her mouth. He wished her to visit Los Angeles. Why? Because the original church of the Genesis Faithful was there. It was all becoming clear. He was indicating that if she went there and attended the original church she could wash her soul clean of sin.

It was such a genuine religious experience that she felt exalted. She decided to leave on the last day of December, thus beginning the New Year right.

Having settled the matter, she gave herself over to a last fling of temporal enjoyment. To Gus she had never been more loving. He gave her money for Christmas presents and she shopped happily, passing many hours in Toyland. They bought a turkey and she roasted it to a juicy golden brown; she baked Swedish pancakes and meltingly sweet cookies from recipes her mother had taught her. Gus boomed his appreciation, comparing her to the cookies: small, deliciously shaped, sugary. Certainly she looked beautiful in a dainty apron, basting the turkey.

Christmas dinner she set upon a table in the living room, before the open doors to the balcony, and Gus ate all he could hold, which was a great deal. Outside, birds were singing and flowers perfuming the benign air. Happiness overwhelmed him, but he experienced a few sad twinges, too, for he remembered Christmases when Barbara was alive, and he wondered where Flora was eating today, and what kind of fare they were serving Ive Pawpacker. For a moment he wondered if he were not living in a fool's paradise, but this misgiving evaporated when he glanced across the steaming food at Marybelle, so smoothly lovely, more desirable in her starched apron than she had ever been in arena costume.

She too had misgivings. A week from today was New Year's, and she would be—where? On a Los Angeles-bound bus, probably. Soon she must tell Gus of her decision and ask him for money to see her through the beauty college. He would want to know why she was leaving, and it would be difficult to put into words the spiritual imperatives that were driving her. He might argue, and she dreaded that. He was exceptionally persuasive, and she would be tempted to yield to his authority and continue living in the tinted quicksands of sin. She would miss him sadly, for she had grown to love him as much as she once loved Captain Latcher. He was good to her, and tender, and cheerful as a rooster crowing up a fine morning. He whistled when he shaved. With him she felt wonderfully sheltered and protected; and sometimes she who had never borne a child felt motherly toward him, too. After they made love he put his head on her breast and she brushed her lips across his hair and patted him. He sighed and sighed again, drifting into a doze. Those were such poignant moments, so beautiful, that it was difficult to remember they were sinful.

In a meteorological mood Henry Wadsworth Longfellow, an American poet always full of baked beans and wisdom, once declared that into each life some rain must fall, an observation holding true even with such a brilliant city as San Antonio. After Christmas a cold wind blew, and big hoggish clouds wallowed in the sky. Rain poured, and Gus returned from a cigar-buying expedition with drenched feet and chilled bones.

Like most people of habitual sublime health, he regarded threatening illness as an outrage that should be ignored. Instead of changing into dry clothes, he sat in the living room observing the gales of rain blowing against the windows. Sometimes he stood staring down at the flower garden shivering in its icy drenching.

The room was dank, its high cool walls heated only by a portable gas burner, for in warm climates architects are stoned if they suggest central heating. Gus's corpuscles battled heartily, but the flu germs were making love fast and giving birth to more warriors. Shivers chased along Gus's spine; his tonsils swelled and felt sprinkled with pepper; aches lodged themselves in his joints and behind his eyes. He ate scarcely any lunch and at midafternoon he surrendered to bed, and even after Marybelle piled covers on him his teeth chattered. He grunted and groaned, and when she took his temperature and discovered that it had risen above a hundred he considered himself a goner.

Reinforcements for the corpuscles arrived in the person of a doctor.

He swabbed and wrote a prescription and looked wise, predicting recovery for the patient but ordering him to remain in bed a few days. Marybelle paid him from the currency on the dresser, and after his departure she trudged through the downpour to get the prescription filled. The drugstore was several blocks away, and on her return journey she examined Gus's seizure for celestial significance.

Darkness had fallen early, and the rain flashed down past street lamps. Her breath left her mouth in silvery effervescence, as if her pretty lips had a wandlike power to beautify all they encountered. Rain sparkled in her hair. She enjoyed the cold evening, for generations of Vikings had thickened her slow northern blood. It reminded her of the autumnal rains in New Stockholm and St. Paul. Her feet were soaked, but that was nothing to a girl whose ancestors had waded in cold breakers, attending to the nets.

Tonight she had planned going to church, for during the holidays the Genesis Faithful assembled every evening. Now she could not go. That was unfortunate, because often in church she understood God's will more clearly. Certain she was that Gus's illness was a manifestation of God's will, but the meaning was cloudy. In her self-centered little mind, she reduced the staggering mystery of ordered planets to a size she could comprehend, and hence she decided that God had sent rain to San Antonio and flu germs to Gus in the spirit of somebody sending a telegram commanding a course of action. But the telegram was in code. She couldn't unravel its meaning. In a few days she planned to leave, but now Gus was sick, and that might mean God intended her to remain. On the other hand, she wanted to remain, so this interpretation might be inspired by Satan.

Upon reaching her own gate she was as undecided as ever, so she told herself she would wait for further heavenly intelligences. Rain flung itself after her as she mounted the veranda steps and entered the lower hall, a sepulchral place this evening, with a feeble gas flare wavering at the tip of a bracket. As she mounted the stair her shadow wobbled enormously on the wall.

She found Gus lonesome and groaning, but the medicine contained a sedative and presently he slept. In the dim light she sat sadly by his bed, in a world silent save for the steady rain and his breathing. In illness he looked older. The tremendous good humor was absent from his usually animated face. His closed eyelids were veined in violet, his bristling brows white. Fever had heated his cheeks and dried his lips. They were parted and sometimes he expelled a long breath with a little blowing sound. She experienced the superiority of the waking to the sleeping, the healthy to the sick; but it was a superiority tender with compassion and the womanly desire to nurse the weak. She stood up and placed her palm on his forehead. She drew a sigh and tears glistened in her eyes. She seldom wept, but now the thought of leaving him wrung her. And she knew he was a sinful man, lost beyond redemption. He never attended church. He would never save himself; only God's mercy could save him. She knelt and prayed a long time, for his soul and hers, for guidance. The rain droned on. After prayer she felt as baffled as before. Well, tomorrow night she would attend church.

At the dresser, she picked up the currency and silver, and to pass the time she counted it. What a strange man he was!—carrying his fortune about with him instead of banking it. Tossing it to the dresser instead of hiding it. And how generous! Trying to help him save, she had learned not to admire a hat she did not need, or a trinket in a window, because he always insisted on buying it. Willie had not been thus. Even Captain Latcher had been less openhanded. He stirred in sleep, grunting softly, and she smiled. Gus. She loved him. She would always love him. In the beginning, perhaps, it had been vanity and passion, but now she loved him because he was so uniquely and wholeheartedly Gus. He needed her, she thought, he needed her terribly. "Dearest God," she whispered, "please do not send me away from Gus."

Next day the physician returned, and the next, and the next, for times were hard and cash patients scarce. The weather turned fine again, but Gus remained in bed, his diet restricted. This repose deflated his tonsils and harried the aches from his bones. He slept a great deal, because of the sedative in the pills.

On the last day of the bad old year he dozed off late in the afternoon, and by the time he awakened darkness had filled the apartment. "Snookums," he called; but she was out. The house was quiet. In the distance through the open windows he could hear children at play and motor horns. He grunted into a more comfortable position, remembering that this was New Year's Eve. And he was unwell. It would have been fun to dress up tonight and go places where lights and champagne sparkled. He lay thinking of other New Year's Eves. Once the boys on the *Beacon* threw a farewell party for him, and Frank was there. He smiled tenderly. In retrospect that period of his life seemed drenched in romance, because his meeting Carlotta lurked just over the hilltop of time. He sighed; and he wondered about Frank. He was undoubtedly dead by now, like so many people. "Best man I ever knew," he thought.

Again Gus called, "Snookums," and again there was no response. She'd be back soon, but he wished she were here now, for remembering Frank and his youth made him lonesome. Presently he grunted from bed, feeling a bit weak when he stood upright. No wonder!—

eating scarcely enough to keep a bird alive! His legs were hollow. He groped into the living room and snapped on lights.

He sat there for a while, and he found himself listening for her return. Probably she had gone to church. Odd about that: prior to their elopement he had never thought of her as the religious type. Well, he guessed church never hurt anybody.

His body grew tired, lacking food as it did, habituated as it was to bed. He arose and waddled slowly to the bedroom. Snapped on the light. Then he noticed a sheet of notepaper propped on the dresser. He fumbled on his reading glasses, and his stance was middle-aged: paper held up to catch the light. The note said:

> Deerest Gus, I think it is best this way, please do not try to find me, we have been sinfull. I have taken most of the money but it is not for myself Gus but to give to the Church to help save Souls, you can make more. Working will help you save yourself Gus, the Devil finds mischef for idle hands, you will find cold meat and hard boiled eggs in icebox, also milk. Take care of yourself, I will allways love you, Gus.
>
> Yrs, Marybelle.

He was chilling, and his lips were dry. Laboriously, he turned to the dresser. His hands were shaking; they fumbled among comb and brushes and a pin dish; and he found a little silver and currency, but only a little. Weakness was running through him, and in the mirror he stared at a huge, wide-eyed, open-mouthed man in pajamas.

Fully dressed, weak as a puppy, his hatband slick with sweat, he was propelling himself along a lighted avenue. Cars tore past in both directions. Whenever a cab blurred yellow through the brilliance he had an impulse to hail it. Then he remembered his almost empty pockets.

It was early yet; early for San Antonio on New Year's Eve; but already revelers were abroad. Soldiers with pretty girls; soldiers alone; groups of pretty girls stagging it; M.P.'s; and outside a hotel on Houston Street taxis disgorging couples in boiled shirts and party dresses. The surface of his brain was numb, but under the numbness his voice was crying, "Marybelle. Marybelle." He had some large, ambitious scheme of visiting all bus and railroad stations, but it was doomed to fail, for the city was big, the stations scattered, and he had little money for cabs.

But he attempted the project; afterward, he remembered transportation terminals as from a fever dream: bright magazines arrayed on newsstands, people with luggage. But he didn't see Marybelle. Once he was sitting on a varnished bench, as bogged as a big motor car that had run out of gas. He was fumbling for a cigar; none was in his pocket; and he didn't think that he should buy one, being almost broke. Presently he was on the street again; a warm night with stars mellow overhead; and then he was drifting about the Menger lobby; it was crowded with people laughing; men wore paper hats and the women had confetti in their hair. His legs were weak beneath him; he swayed; guessed he needed fresh air; and by now Houston Street was a mob of people; celebrating, celebrating. Beggarly old women were selling noisemakers and bouquets of paper streamers on sticks; and people who were not almost broke purchased these gay things and the air was full of racket. Outside a movie house people were waiting for the midnight show; Gus shoved on; and sometimes he rested, leaning against building fronts, while the merrymakers trooped past, swirling like autumn leaves, leaping and cavorting and giggling; and by now you could smell alcohol and hear alcohol when the girls shrilled and squealed in that silly way of women who had been drinking.

Marybelle, he kept thinking, Marybelle. You wouldn't do this to me. It's a joke. You wouldn't leave a man nearly flat; you wouldn't leave a man with only a few bucks.

And suddenly he was convinced it was indeed a joke, or a mistake, something he had imagined in his sickness. He would go home and find her.

So he started homeward, through the noisy throngs, bumping along, and once he heard a girl yelling, "Happy New Year, Grandpa. Happy New Year, Gramp." He stared. And she giggled and shrieked, "Yes— you! It'll soon be midnight. Haven't you heard of New Year's?"

He didn't reply; just swayed on; and the group she was with howled with laughter, and somebody said, "Pie-eyed. Blind drunk."

And he hadn't had a nip.

Then all hell cut loose, whistles blowing and horns blaring, people screeching and laughing and dancing on the sidewalk; another calendar tossed into the wastebasket; a fresh calendar on the wall; everybody starting the New Year right; the year that would fix everything up, bringing prosperity back; the sweet naked little baby wearing a ribbon stamped 1932; and Gus plodded and hurried and swayed. He was trembling when he reached his own door; and he hurried so fast up the stairs that he whistled and wheezed. But he did not find Marybelle in the apartment.

A couple of days later he sold his car. And it was a crying shame to let it go at the price he got, a fine big Packard like that, but the used car lots were jammed with cars that nobody had the money to buy. Besides, he needed cash; and he was still too sick in body and spirit to turn on the old up-and-at-'em and bludgeon a better price from the dealer. His old fight had departed. Probably the dealer sensed that this fat man, shuffling and moping like a promoter in an era when all promotion schemes had gone sour, needed the dough.

Gus remained several weeks in San Antonio, sticking pretty close to the apartment just in case Marybelle should return. He was always listening, and this was something of a strain; he grew jumpy. All morning he sat on the balcony, smoking cigars, dolefully turning pages of *The Billboard;* and in the afternoon he napped in the bedroom. Maybe he would dream she had come back, and he would jump up and hurtle into the living room, but she wasn't there. Late at night he took long walks about that gay city which didn't seem so gay any more.

He ate alone; he slept alone; and he fell into that forlorn habit of the lonely, talking to himself.

Presently his bewilderment lifted, and he saw very clearly what had happened; she had pretended to love him to get his money. "Played me for a sucker," he muttered.

He could not know that Marybelle had acted upon a clear command from heaven, reaching her through the Genesis Faithful pastor. One evening the fellow had elaborated upon the story of the rich young man who was told to sell his goods and give to the poor, and Marybelle thought of Gus's money. It occurred to her that she might wash away her sins, and Gus's, by giving away the money on the dresser. After the services she spoke of this to the pastor, hinting at her sinful state; and the man licked his chops at the possibility of receiving a couple of grand. So he lectured her upon the discomforts of hell, and she was frightened sick. She knew, then, she must leave Gus and help him attain salvation: suffering and hard work would benefit his soul. But the pastor never smelled a cent of the boodle, for she carried it off to Los Angeles and gave most of it to the original church of the Genesis Faithful, retaining only enough to see her through a beauty school. Of all the students she was the most intellectually brilliant; she became an excellent operator; and regularly she gave a tenth of her salary and tips to the church, so that the Genesis Faithful could continue its good work.

In February, Gus left San Antonio, drifting westward by day coach. With money running low he sought employment in El Paso, but what with all that cheap labor from Ciudad Juarez he did not succeed. He departed from El Paso without redeeming his watch and chain—that nice watch the boys on the *Beacon* had given him; that chain with the lion's tooth—from a pawnbroker.

A bus deposited him in Las Cruces, New Mexico. No work there. So on he drifted, up through dry scenery, through a land of bright sky and beige infinities and mountains swimming like mirages. In Albuquerque he sold his diamond ring and finally his extra clothes and his luggage; he didn't work in Albuquerque.

He rode the Santa Fe to Denver. Santa Fe freights. But he wasn't a tramp, any more than the scores of other seedy men on those trains were tramps. In these times railroad dicks didn't slug you, nor did the shacks kick you off; capitalism was caring for its own, most railroads permitting men seeking work to ride free. The journey took a long time, what with stopovers in the trackside jungles for food; there were no dining cars on the freights. And sometimes the food was pretty good, for from back door to back door the ragamuffins went begging, returning to the jungle with their hauls. Coffee bubbled in a blackened pot, and the mulligan stew simmered.

Buckman, that was his name; Arthur H. Buckman. Used to be in real estate, he told them. Sometimes he almost believed that story, for the days when he piloted a circus seemed long ago. The days when he bathed and shaved every day seemed long ago. He didn't talk as much as he used to; like most of the older men he was morose; the kids could take it better; they had faith things would improve and they would still beat the system, marrying the boss's daughter, if they ever got a boss and he had a daughter, and end up rich.

From all over the mountain states surplus labor had drained into Denver, but the sons and grandsons of gold prospectors and silver prospectors and ranchers whose cattle had eaten themselves fat on the public domain believed that the rich should be nice to the poor, so soup kitchens had been set up on back streets, and there were well-appointed flophouses.

He survived, somehow, just as a lot of people survived. But he changed: when society has no use for you, you feel useless, and that isn't such a good feeling. It was a long, hard summer; a long, hard autumn; a long, hard winter. He kept losing weight; he was always hungry and often cold. But the public library was warm, and as the months passed he formed the habit of going there to thumb and sigh through the current *Billboard*. Needing a shave and haircut, wearing a thin Salvation Army overcoat, he looked like an old bum. You would not have thought him a man who had once electrified headwaiters. His fingernails were dirty.

Yet in his suffering, hope kept burning. Down but not out; that was the way he thought of himself. Times would improve and his fortunes with them. Then one winter morning in 1933 he found a brief item in *The Billboard*: a Denver man named Thornton was organizing a carnival. Gus put down the magazine and shuffled over to the city directory and looked up Thornton's address. He dwelt away out in South Denver, and Gus had no carfare.

His jaw hardened. He would get carfare. Outside, he lingered on the library steps, teeth tight, bucking himself up, and when a seventeen-year-old kid in a camel's-hair coat emerged, Gus bore down on him. And at the last moment, instead of begging a dime, Gus asked for a quarter.

"I've got to have it," he said. And he thought: "Give it to me, you punk! Damn you, give it to me!"

It was really miraculous, what happened. The kid's hand went into his pocket, and a moment later there Gus stood with twenty-five cents shining in his palm. He was astonished. The kid hurried off down the steps toward a parked coupe. Gus expelled a long breath. And his spirits soared. He felt rich. His luck was turning. At a drugstore he selected the best cigar a nickel could buy before catching a streetcar.

It was indeed a turning point, even though Thornton shook his head when Gus hit him for a job, any kind of job. They were standing in what had once been a garage out in the seedy subdivisions, but the garage had gone broke, like a lot of enterprises.

"Full up," Thornton said.

Gus covered his disappointment. The cigar helped. He had saved it, smoking it dry, but now he struck a match and puffed deeply. It made him feel capitalistic, standing there blowing out smoke.

He could see the carnival was a crumby little outfit; Thornton had been painting merry-go-round horses, and many had broken ears. Head up, cigar jutting, Gus paced over to shelves along the wall where advertising posters were stacked. He pulled one out. The red letters did not advertise Thornton's carnival but Archibald's Gigantic Shows.

"Picked those up cheap," Thornton said. "Archibald went busted."

"Uh." Gus was staring at white space at the bottom of the poster; space which would announce the dates when the carnival would play a certain town.

"See you don't have your paper printed yet," Gus said.

"Can't do everything at once."

"Uh." Gus was scowling. And suddenly he swung on Thornton. "I'm connected with a printing firm. I'll give you a bid on the job that will save you a lot of dough."

Thornton looked interested.

It was nothing but nerve, of course; nerve and wind and blow-hard; for Gus didn't even know any Denver printers. Yet he virtually closed the deal then and there; and a couple of hours later, down near the Union Station, he ascended dirty wooden steps to the third floor of a rattletrap building and entered a printing shop. He had chosen it carefully; he wanted a non-union, one-horse little business that smelled of bankruptcy.

This one smelled that way; and it also smelled like the *Clayton Junction Tribune* and all printing shops. The grimed windows stained the light seeping in, and the presses were silent. At the dilapidated desk an old man was sitting. He had rumpled gray hair, and he looked up vaguely through bifocals.

"Buckman's the name," Gus boomed. "Arthur H. Buckman. Want to make some money?"

Out of that deal Gus made twenty dollars. It looked a huge sum. And out of the deal Gus pulled himself up from the world of flop-houses and panhandlers, into the world of chiselers and making an honest dollar any way possible. The printer's name was Jesse Martin, and he had been nearly as broke as Gus; rent unpaid; bills, bills; no printers to help him.

"Hell, Jesse," Gus said, that first day, "I'm a printer. Brought up in a print shop. You furnish the equipment and I'll do the work. And we'll split the profits. And after this job's done I'll rustle up more business. We'll underbid every printer in town and make a million. Uh—well, anyway, we'll make us some dough."

So next morning, after all those years of glory and greatness, Gus became a printer again. And presently at secondhand he bought a cot and blankets, and slept in the shop. Martin was so vague and fumbling that without actually intending to he let Gus adopt him.

But soon after the carnival posters were paid for the bank holiday came, and for a fortnight even Gus could not scratch up printing orders. And a queer sensation it was, walking past those huge financial institutions on Seventeenth Street and seeing them closed. It was as if men like Mr. Oxenford had got their hands on the country and ruined it.

Then the banks opened, and people felt that bottom had been scraped at last; and one day Gus talked a greasy café owner into a deal whereby ads on the menu would pay for the printing and make the printers any extra profits they could reap; and he sweated and boomed and sold ads; and then he set up the type and did the printing.

So he was making money again. Some weeks he cleared twelve or fifteen dollars. But he worked for it. Worked harder than ever in his life. Just as well he was so busy; kept him from brooding. But sometimes at night he brooded, lying on his cot in the shop, with the lilac light from street lamps casting shadows.

After a few months he became sufficiently prosperous to rent a room in a cheap hotel, and as times improved Jesse Martin hired a printer and Gus devoted his energies to selling job work. He made a living, but that was about all. He specialized in selling cheaply to humble little business establishments, so his world shrank to that area of used clothing stores and pawnshops and honky-tonks within a few blocks of the Union Station. On Sundays he spent most of his time in the hotel, dozing in his room or staring through the plate glass windows of the lobby.

Eating regularly again, he regained some of his weight, although not all by a long shot. And in many little ways he changed, as if his personality were adapting itself to his new name. He wasn't as boisterous as he used to be; he didn't laugh as readily or as much; and he worried more, probably because he had fallen into the habit of worrying when he didn't have the price of a bed or a meal. Being alone in the world, he fretted about what would happen if he should get sick, or when he grew old. His health bothered him, for perversely enough, in a climate supposed to be beneficial to asthma, he developed asthma. Not a severe case, but bad enough to keep him awake some nights, propped up on pillows.

Pretty girls didn't notice him any more. Nobody much noticed him, for he didn't bustle along exuding optimism and surplus energy. He was just a portly man moving sedately along the street, a briefcase under his arm; another salesman; not anybody special; one of those men you see at noon in the Baltimore Dairy Lunch, eating with his hat on; somebody with sound opinions about who would win the World Series, and what was wrong with the country. Arthur H. Buckman.

And an odd thing happened: he grew tight-fisted. Oh, not as ridiculously stingy as Mr. Oxenford; but he was no longer the old free-spending Gus. He smoked nickel cigars and made them last a long time; and he didn't buy the evening paper because he would probably find one somebody had left on a leather chair in the hotel lobby. He postponed haircuts. He was trying to save money, maybe enough to buy his way into an old people's home, in a dozen years or so. He no longer trusted life and his high destiny.

The months slipped along, and the years. And since the present was pretty drab, and the future scared him, he spent more and more time back there in the past, when he had been quite a guy, quite a guy. But it was painful to think about, as well as sweet; and when he remembered how Marybelle had played him for a sucker he concluded that women were all unreliable.

Because of the expense, he didn't buy *The Billboard,* although usually he managed to get to the library once a week to read it. And in 1935 he found an interesting little item about an old friend, the Baron Karl Otto Von Krummer. Having lost an arm and leg, the Baron could no longer exhibit his valor in a steel arena; so in Tamarack he had set himself up in a business where dogs were involved. He operated commercial kennels, breeding and selling dogs, boarding them, and even training pups for rich people. For capital he had used the money from the sale of his circus cats and equipment, and the money people had contributed when he lay in the hospital. The magazine published a picture of the Baron, looking not only the same as ever but more so; and it gave Gus a start. He had been so involved with the woes of making a living that he had not given much thought to that Corpus Christi affair, from the Baron's viewpoint.

But now as he thought it over it seemed reasonable to suppose that Willie wasn't especially joyous about losing an arm and a leg and a wife; and there was even a possibility that he blamed A. H. Burgoyne. Remembering Willie's old threat, Gus felt uncomfortable. He was very glad then that he had vanished from the outdoor show world and had lain low in Denver.

That day, saving carfare, Gus walked back to his hotel; and suddenly on the busiest part of Sixteenth Street he thought how unfortunate it would be if chance should bring Willie to Denver, and if Willie should see him. And before he could talk himself out of that fear, Gus glanced back. He didn't see Willie: just a lot of strange pedestrians. "'Course not," he thought. "Nonsense!"

Nevertheless, after several blocks, he felt impelled to glance round again. This time he fought the impulse. Hell, what would the Dutchman be doing in Denver? But just to make sure, Gus looked back. It became a habit.

The night clerk at the hotel was an alcoholic, and in 1936 the manager fired him and out of a clear sky offered Gus the job. Sixty-five a month and a free room. Gus grabbed it. He was on his way up again.

And all in all, he liked it. The money was certain, and no longer did he have to pep himself up, as was necessary in a selling job. He guessed selling was a young man's game, like newspaper reporting and running the Ringlings out of business. And if the weather was bad, or if that silly worry about Willie was troubling him, he didn't have to venture from the hotel, except to grab a meal at a café next door.

He worked from 8 P.M. to 6 A.M. That was all right, too; helling around at night was also for young men. After about 11 P.M. he had the place to himself, except for couples who checked in without baggage, and they never lingered in the lobby. Sometimes the cop on the beat dropped in, but mainly Gus was alone with the switchboard and the clock that gave the correct Western Union time. There were no bellhops at that hotel; the clerk showed guests to their rooms; and maybe on a good night you picked up a little extra in tips.

But for the most part Gus passed the time reading the newspapers and magazines people left in the lobby. And thinking. A man alone will think; remembering all the people he's known and wondering what in hell ever happened to them. Wondering about Ive Pawpacker and Flora and Carlotta. Looking back on his own life and trying to discover some pattern, some meaning. But not getting anywhere with it, except a case of the blues. Once he even wondered how such people as Ive and Willie and Flora and Carlotta would have fared if he had never been born, but he didn't like thinking such deep thoughts and he changed the subject.

One October night in 1938, Gus got the surprise of his life. Somebody had left a national picture magazine in the lobby, and leafing through it he came upon a section devoted to an American artist who had died the winter before. The artist's name was Alex Kerry, and that magazine had a very high opinion of him, giving over several pages to reproductions of his work. And on one page Gus found himself. That picture Kerry had painted of him and Molly. Above the cut the overline said, "Lost Treasure," and the underline told how Kerry had once traveled with a circus and painted this picture and given it away and now it was lost. His habit of photographing his finished paintings, the magazine said, had preserved this black-and-white copy of the picture. If it were as good as the photograph suggested, and as his old sponsor Dr. Massingham maintained, why then, some dealer would doubtless pay upwards of five thousand dollars to acquire it.

Five thousand! It took Gus's breath. A fortune! A sum like that would put a man back on his feet. With five thousand you could buy into a printing business, or a carnival, or—oh, the possibilities were unlimited! Five thousand! Great God!

Gus paced over to the windows. He was grinning; he looked younger. For he owned that picture. He had packed it away into the attic at winter quarters. Was it still there? Undoubtedly! Nobody except Flora knew he had put it there, and she had probably forgotten.

He remembered reading that the farm now belonged to Eloise Sebastian. Perhaps she had rented it. Unlikely, the land was so poor. But even if tenants were living on the farm he could contrive to get into the house for the picture. He could do a lot of things, for five thousand.

Next day he told the manager his sister in Chicago was ill, and he must go. And that night, dressed in his oldest clothes, he caught a freight train east out of Denver. He wanted to save the price of a railroad ticket; and besides, with Willie in Tamarack it was risky returning, and he figured he could best manage the affair by traveling as a hobo.

21

Hard by a highway leading northwest from Tamarack stood the Von Krummer Kennels, Dogs Boarded & Trained, Puppies For Sale. Give A Living Gift, Baron K. O. Von Krummer, Prop. By 1938, it was a thriving enterprise. A crushed-rock drive looped in to a low Colonial building, white and green-shuttered; the grass was close clipped; and in spaded plots young trees stood at attention.

Inside, all was sanitary, the air perfumed by disinfectants and excellent flea soap. To the establishment was attached a young physician, tiny mustache, white bib and all, who had recently been graduated from an outstanding veterinary school; and an elderly couple also worked there, the husband cleaning kennels, the wife performing such chores as cooking breakfast for the Baron (with eggs sunny-side-up). The Baron's office and living quarters occupied one wing, and they were bright and clean. Framed photographs adorned the knotty-pine walls of the office, depicting the Baron in the arena; and there were also certificates announcing his membership in the Chamber of Commerce, the Tamarack Humane Society and a popular luncheon club.

Willie had done well. When he entered the dog business, the newspapers excavated all those old stories about his heroism and his nobility, and this interested Tamarack Society, for in Middle Western cities barons do not grow on bushes. Willie became the vogue. Likewise his kennels. It was rumored he had studied at Heidelberg, although he was too modest to confess it. His grammatical lapses were pardoned on the grounds that English was not his native tongue; and sometimes he was to be seen at tea in the best homes of the city. His opinion of tea remained low, but he no longer described it as pale puke, for like most men Willie had learned to guard his tongue, for business reasons. When a matron invited him to some function he said, "*Ja, ja*—I vill be delighted."

As years passed, Willie had toned down and refined his performance as a baron. His monocle he had long ago discarded, and his accent was not so thick as in circus days. His demeanor was stiff and quietly stern, and he had learned somewhere—perhaps from Marybelle—that silence is an excellent camouflage for ignorance. He dressed well; and although it was difficult for him to move about, now that his left arm and right leg were artificial, he managed to impress people as a hero who had lost those limbs in a good cause. If asked an embarrassing question about his origins, he said simply, "I cannot discuss that." This rejoinder gained him a reputation for modesty. Moreover, since human nature abhors a vacuum in its knowledge of fellow human beings, people imagined all kinds of romantic events in his past. It was supposed that as a young man in Germany he had fallen in love with a peasant girl and had come to America and joined a circus to forget her.

Willie looked older than a man in his thirties. Years of scowling had embedded a deep, vertical wrinkle above his coarse nose, and a patch of hard, bald skull showed through his bristles. He was not in very good health, mentally or physically, for his encounter with the cats in Corpus Christi had shaken up his insides, and he had lost, among other things, a kidney. His face was thinner; and owing, perhaps, to faulty irrigation his skin looked muddy. Suffering—and he really had suffered, in that Corpus Christi hospital—had left its mark on his countenance. His eyes were still skim-milk blue, but it was not the milk of human kindness. And when he was alone they were eyes neither tranquil nor brave.

The dreadful truth was that Willie had never been able to erase the memory of that December morning in Blue Island, when Captain Latcher passed away. He had tried, but it had eaten into his brain like engraver's acid. Occasionally, he still dreamed about it, and he would awaken in a sick sweat. In his maturity, he cursed the Willie he had been as a young man, the brutally reckless Willie who had saddled upon him this galling anguish. He told himself he was a different person now from that swaggering, egotistic young squarehead who had murdered the Captain, and while this was not wholly correct, still it did seem unfair that there was no statute of limitations on murder. There were days, of course, when Willie nearly forgot the entire business, but then in the papers he would read of somebody hanged, or he would be jostled in a crowd and imagine a detective's hand falling on his shoulder, and all the old terror ran through him like poison.

But if he lived with fear, he also lived with hate. He couldn't forget Corpus Christi. He couldn't forget how A. H. Burgoyne had duped him into believing Marybelle a faithful wife, and then had eloped with her. The black abyss of Burgoyne's villainy overwhelmed and staggered him. For the fat old kangaroo had not been content merely to steal one's *frau*. Oh, no! He had to yank the master switch and leave at the mercy of the cats the man he had already cuckolded.

Sometimes as he was dropping off to sleep Willie would relive that night in Corpus Christi. He beheld himself, sound in wind and limb and kidney, saluting the audience and entering the arena. He saw the cats, hissing and snarling. He saw himself at the center of the arena and he heard the band playing. Then—blackness. Utter. Terrorizing. And his nerves twitched and his brain screamed, for he knew what was coming. The cats were coming. After years of torment their hour had arrived. Willie's raw mouth twisted, and then something crashed against him and knocked him down, and his flesh was torn, and he was yelling, "My God, they'll kill me!" And then, for long and long, nothing. And after the nothingness, burning suffering. And after the suffering he was a broken, battered fellow, injured inside, his great career as an animal trainer in the dust.

It was small wonder that, sitting at his office desk, Willie often speculated about what had happened to Burgoyne and Marybelle, that he even built castles in Spain, with inquisition torture chambers into which he flung that old tub of lard, A. H. Burgoyne. He passed many happy hours imagining the man he hated on the rack.

In his desk drawer, Willie kept a pistol. It was an instrument both of defense and offense. He told himself that if a police siren ever sounded in his drive, and men came in and said, "The jig's up, Willie—we've got the goods on you about Blue Island," he would use the pistol. And he also told himself that if ever he learned the whereabouts of Marybelle and Burgoyne, he would seek them and shoot them. But possibly this was all megalomania and bombast, for the mournful fact was that conscience had made a coward even of the valorous Baron Von Krummer.

Afterward, had you informed the barber named Lon McMorrow that he was responsible for certain happenings at the ruined quarters of Burgoyne & Pawpacker's circus, he would have been nonplussed. Nor could he have been blamed; his responsibility was obscure. Mr. McMorrow tipped the first in a wandering line of dominoes.

At fifty-five, Mr. McMorrow was a tallish man, slightly stooped, with horn-rimmed spectacles hooked in front of mild blue eyes and over a heroic nose. He was a kindly man, hard-working and charitable; and he believed himself the most expert barber in Tamarack. His work was not to be compared with that of these young squirts whom the Tamarack Barber & Tonsorial College was graduating so profligately. His razor left the roughest cheek smooth as a babe's, and when he finished with his shears only God could further improve upon the appearance of the customer in question.

Otherwise, if he veered from the ordinary, it was toward sartorial elegance. A careful dresser, Mr. McMorrow; for, as he told his wife, the world's respect for a man began with self-respect, and self-respect originated with fresh linen, pressed pants, shined shoes. Mr. McMorrow was the pride of the Tamarack branch of Foreman & Clark.

On that October morning, at 7:45, as he walked toward his garage, Mr. McMorrow did not look a figure of destiny; but existence is complex and one can never know which of one's actions will alter history. Backing out his Chevrolet, Mr. McMorrow's entire mental processes were absorbed with the problem of Charley Sinbad, the Negro porter in his neighborhood shop. Charley Sinbad dwelt in the back room, cooking there, sleeping there, and occasionally, if the truth were known, entertaining Lucille Le Claire there. It was that back room which troubled Mr. McMorrow this morning.

Driving along through frosty sunlight, Mr. McMorrow reflected that he did not wish his shop to acquire a bad name. He did not wish it to become known as an immoral place. Yet there was peril of this happening. Several nights ago Bert Parks, the druggist next door, had beheld Charley Sinbad entering the shop accompanied by a girl; by Lucille Le Claire. And very early yesterday morning the milkman on the route had perceived two persons departing surreptitiously from the shop, a colored man and a colored woman. The milkman had reported his observations and his deductions to Lon McMorrow.

Mr. McMorrow was not a narrow-minded man. He even harbored a dash of worldliness. Nevertheless, it alarmed him to imagine the whisperings that would rustle among his clientele, if Charley continued entertaining Miss Le Claire in the back room. Young matrons might send their male offspring elsewhere, for haircuts. Plainly, business would not be aided by Charley Sinbad's confusing the purposes of an upright barber shop with those of a seraglio.

Still, Mr. McMorrow disliked broaching the matter to Charley, for interfering in such affairs is always a delicate venture, and often an unpopular one. Doubtless Charley would be abashed and perhaps piqued. And Mr. McMorrow did not wish to abash and pique Charley. For Charley was not just any old colored man: he was something special, a human being, a friend. Moreover, since he moved in last spring, life had shaped itself into a very pleasant pattern. With Charley occupying the back room, Mr. McMorrow could don hat and coat at day's end and walk out without ever a thought about locking up. He liked that. It warmed him with a sense of overlordship. And when he arrived in the morning the linoleum was always shining from Charley's mop, and if he were a bit late and some early customer had anticipated him the door was unlocked for business. And with Charley asleep in the shop, he never wakened in the night to wonder whether the place were on fire.

Nevertheless, with the welfare of the business hanging in the balance, Mr. McMorrow realized he must issue a ukase: no more philandering amid the razors and hair tonic. He determined to issue it this very morning. But he would soften it by slipping Charley two or three dollars, and urging him to take the day off and go fishing with Lucille.

Charley Sinbad was brown, and he was not the molasses-footed Negro of vaudeville but a nimble, wiry little man. Nobody knew his age. Speculation put it as high as fifty-five, as low as forty-five; and this was a tribute to his verve and the dye he employed on his hair, along with Magic Moon Hair Straightener. He told Lucille Le Claire he was forty-two. She protested he didn't seem that old; he was a better lover than these strapping young bucks. Besides, she added, he gave her things. Money, and pretty things. These young bucks wished to take and take, never to give. Charley's quick mind realized this was appreciation, but also a veiled warning. If the money stopped and the presents stopped—!

So that was why in the sixty-third year of his life his fingers yearned for silver coins and the crackle of currency. That was why his cloth beat such a vigorous tattoo on customers' shoes, why he brushed so enthusiastically, why he mopped and ran errands so willingly, why he sought odd jobs washing windows and scrubbing walls when business grew dull in the shop. For Lucille Le Claire, who was a delicate lemon color with a divine figure, represented youth to Charley Sinbad, just as he represented romance to the little neighborhood business district at Thirty-Ninth Street and Milton Avenue.

Yes, romance! There were only three business establishments there, the barber shop flanked by the drugstore on one side and a grocery on the other, and life could be pretty routine there, what with haircuts and shaves and prescriptions to be filled and some housewife calling to say her groceries hadn't yet arrived, and her having company for dinner. Then, with the springtime robins, had come Charley Sinbad, popping into their lives with the gay suddenness of a jack-in-the-box. Charley Sinbad, who could clog dance and sing and play the guitar and crack jokes like peanuts between his teeth. Yes, and he harbored other talents! He could sign-write. In the back room he kept a case of brushes and paint and strange-looking pens and colored inks. On Fridays he covered the grocer's windows with curling red and blue letters announcing week-end specials, and when the druggist held a one-cent sale Charley went to work on the drugstore panes, drawing a letter and then stepping back and judiciously contemplating his handiwork.

He was theirs. He belonged to Thirty-Ninth Street and Milton Avenue; and they were proud and fond of him with the pride and fondness of men who have been charitable and generous. Lon McMorrow would never forget that soft March morning when he was standing outside his shop, getting a breath of air, and saw Charley bustling along the walk. He remembered Charley's pearly spats, his green trousers, his green tie. At that moment, Charley spied Lon's necktie. A flowered job, that day. The brown man's eyes met the white man's; Charley grinned.

"Boss," he said, in his best minstrel show manner, for once he had been an actor, "them windows look like they was just waiting attention from Charley Sinbad. Them windows say to me, 'Charley, let's have some soap and water.' "

Lon hesitated; so Charley cracked some old kerosene-circuit joke, and called him Boss again. He always called him Boss, in humor and irony, as if they were the comedian and straight man in some village Opera House.

"There's a pail and rags in the back room," Lon said; and Charley, rummaging there, eyed the place speculatively. He could imagine a cot snug against the wall. And amid the junk stored in that room he beheld a chair enthroned on a wooden platform, with metal foot-rests. Charley did not comment upon this shoe-shining equipment, but his opportunistic brain churned.

After his ministrations the windows gleamed like gems, and Charley asked:

"You got a porter here, Boss?"

Lon shook his head. Too small a shop. A one-man shop, really, although on Saturdays an extra barber appeared to assist with the traveling-men trade. A busy day, Saturday. Traveling men got in off the road on Friday evening, and they all wanted haircuts and massages and shampoos to look well for the Saturday night bridge parties, the Sunday morning golf links.

"You need a porter here, Boss. It'd class up your shop."

A porter! A vision of grandeur came to Lon McMorrow: with a porter his little shop would take on a metropolitan air. Stepping down from the chair a customer would find a smart lackey armed with a whisk broom; there would be a great brushing, a lavish employment of the word, sir.

Lon sighed. "Too small a shop. Afraid you couldn't make enough, Charley."

"Don't worry 'bout me, Boss. On Saturdays I porter here. Rest of the time I wall-wash an' house-clean an' lawn-mow. This is a good neighborhood, Boss, an' the ladies that want a handy man can phone for me here. Maybe I could slip a cot into that back room, an' kind of headquarter here. Gentleman like you hadn't ought to rassle coal into no furnace. Need your hands kept smooth for that expert work with the scissors and razor. I'll fix the furnace and sweep up the hair and mop. Then I could sign-write for you, too. I could pen-write you some fancy calling cards . . ."

That was how it began, and Lon never regretted coming to terms with Charley. No salary was involved. All Charley desired was opportunity. He knew he would never starve. Not with a grocery next door, where he could do odd jobs and receive lettuce that had become wilted and a shop-worn end of watermelon and possibly a ham bone.

He reckoned shrewdly, established himself as an institution on that corner, a jester and jongleur at the court of Lon McMorrow. The barber shop loafers found him entertaining. They were spruce, retired old men, mostly, living with sons or daughters in the neighborhood; and on the long, dull midweek afternoons Charley would bring out a guitar, strumming and singing the melancholy old songs about Negro men confined in jail-houses, and cowboys who desired nothing less than to be buried on the lone prairie. And sometimes he dipped into his past and yarned of his experiences, taking them into a world of grease paint and one-night stands. For back in the gaslight era he had been end-man with Alabama Joe's Chocolate Drops; he had traveled with carnivals; yes, and with circuses. A few years ago he had played the cornet with the colored band on Burgoyne & Pawpacker's show; fact was, he had been on that show when it died in the rain in Corpus Christi.

"Burgoyne & Pawpacker," a loafer would muse. "Didn't they used to winter out near Oxenford?"

"Yas, suh! The same."

"Understand Burgoyne went broke."

"Oh, yas suh! He went broke, right enough. An' with both hands full. Robbed the show. Robbed it stone barefoot. Plenty men like to get hold of old Burgoyne. 'Cept he ain't to be found. Earth swallowed him."

"What happened to him?"

"Ain't no one know what happen to him. First he is, then he ain't. Just vanish. I hear tell the Baron Von Krummer like to get hold of him. Account of, he vanish with the Baron's wife. The Baron, he's in the dog business, now. But he use to be quite a man with the cats. Lions. Taggers. Yas, suh!"

Barber shop talk, drifting on to other things when a customer wanted a shoeshine.

On that October morning, Lon McMorrow arrived in his shop at eight; and three hours later, in a 1926 Cadillac from the Lincoln Rent-A-Car establishment, Charley Sinbad and Lucille Le Claire drove north from the city on the old river road. Fishing poles were tied to the car, and in the back seat reposed a picnic basket.

"How come he give you three dollars?" Lucille asked.

Charley equivocated.

"Account of I need a day off. That what he say. He tell me to take my girl and go fishing. How do I know how come? I don't ask how come of three dollars."

"Charley," Lucille said, "you snaked yourself into a very fortunate situation."

The road curved tan and mellow in the sunshine, along low banks where autumn had left red and yellow stains. Charley turned into the timber, following a sandy lane, and when the lane humped itself over what had been the embankment of an electric railroad, he glimpsed somebody who had plodded to a halt on the roadbed, to let the car pass.

At first glance the man looked an old hobo. Charley caught the impression of a greenish overcoat, a dusty hat; and then, as the car rocked over the embankment, he stared momentarily into the hobo's face. And Charley exclaimed under his breath.

"What you say, Charley?" Lucille asked.

In the rear-view mirror the hobo was moving, and then a twist in the lane obliterated him. Charley stopped the car.

"Where you go?" Lucille demanded. "What's the matter with you, man?"

"Right back," Charley said.

With some caution he returned along the lane. Near the crossing sumac grew, inked a deep scarlet, and with the leaves screening him Charley peered north along the roadbed. The man's back looked huge, and he carried a club that aided his progress on the decaying embankment. Once he halted and gazed back. Charley ducked. And when he ventured to look again, the man had passed from sight.

It was a very nice picnic, there by the brown river in the golden weather, but Charley seemed abstracted.

"What you thinking of?" Lucille asked once. "That man Burgoyne?"

"If it was Burgoyne. Maybe was, maybe wasn't. Looked like him, though."

"You forget that white man, Charley. What you tell me about him, that man mean trouble. Don't you mess in."

But in his thoughts, Charley had already messed in. With ten dollars, or even five, he could buy a very nice present for Lucille; and it seemed not improbable that the Baron Karl Otto Von Krummer would pay ten dollars to learn that A. H. Burgoyne had returned from oblivion.

22

It was odd that on this of all evenings, while she was finishing her kitchen work, it should have occurred to her that they were very vulnerable. She was not a person given to premonitions, but later she wondered whether the human spirit could sense the gathering of events, the way old Judge Griggs back in Winchester had sensed in his rheumatic bones the distant gathering of storm.

She was drying the dishes when it happened. She was thinking of trivialities, and then all at once she was aware of the kitchen windows, their black panes uncurtained, and before she could halt herself she was imagining how simple it would be for somebody to stand outside and watch. She assembled all the usual arguments against such a possibility, but she kept thinking about it. This was remote country, and here they were—she and Ivan Pawpacker—without so much as a bean shooter for protection. Protection against whom? Nobody. But of course now she had started flirting with such ideas, she was able to dream up all kinds of absurdities.

They had no telephone, no electricity. Back in Burgoyne's time a dynamo used to generate current, but it had disappeared long since. A kerosene lamp burned on the table, and when the dishes were cupboarded Eloise picked it up and lighted her way through the sad old rooms to a downstairs bedroom, where Ive slept. In the doorway she halted, holding the lamp high. He was already asleep. The bed looked gigantic tonight, and lost in its shadows he looked small and inconsequential and infinitely old. She tiptoed away.

In the kitchen she tried to read, but she couldn't concentrate. Everything was silent, save for the humming lamp, and the unexpected noises that any old house will emit: a snap here, a creak there. Nothing unusual. But at last she stood up.

She looked attractive in the lamplight, with the rays bringing out the bronzes and shining oak-leaf reds of her hair. She wore it in a long bob. Her mouth was vivid, and as she stood listening, not for anything special, she looked as alert as a red squirrel in the timber when it stops suddenly, all ears.

"Maybe it won't work out," she said aloud. She spoke low, and her voice had that dry, astringent quality—missing the metallic by a hair

—that suggested disenchantment and a guarded mind. She added, "Oh, hell—it's got to work out."

She was thinking of their retreat to the farm.

She wore a sweater and slacks, and her body had both slimness and roundness, like a young cat's, and she moved with the easy flexibility of a cat too, but without its smugness or hint of the predatory. Now, she slipped on a sport jacket, and outside on the porch she stood with hands in the slash pockets.

It was a fine frosty night. There would be a moon presently, but now as she moved to the gate the earth lay in shadow, save for the starlight and the smudged luminosity of the Milky Way. She crossed the carriage yard and climbed the hill, past the Baggage Stock barn and the Animal House. Since childhood this had been familiar ground, and already the uneasiness she had experienced in the kitchen was fading. At the crest of the ridge she sat on a boulder and smoked. Only a few dim lamps glimmered from Oxenford, but along the southeast horizon a pale fan of light announced the existence of Tamarack, that city of power and dreams where in years gone A. H. Burgoyne had boomed so heroically.

Once she had owned this land, all these acres stretching darkly to Oxenford, and she had owned the mine, but that did not mean she had ever been well-to-do. Water had seeped into the mine shaft, and the timbers had rotted and the galleries had caved in; and when, a few years ago, she paid experts to assay the coal their reports were full of slag and slate. It would never yield anything worth the digging. So she let the mine go, and most of the land, by the simple expedient of not paying taxes. But she retained the house and a few sterile acres for elbow room. She had thought that some day, when society was finished with Ivan Pawpacker, she would want a place where they could go. Not a walkup in some city, either. So ten days ago they had come here.

But it was not as she had imagined it would be. Perhaps unconsciously she had expected it would be like a return to childhood, with the remoteness and stillness bringing tranquillity; and although she should have known better, perhaps she hoped for that protection an adult gives a child. But Ivan Pawpacker had changed. He had been a proud man, and his pride would not admit that the Winchester bank had collapsed, and that he had been taken away to Fort Leavenworth and locked in. His pride had paced haughtily through the house of his brain, extinguishing lights in room after room; so now he lived in the moment only, or in the far, great past. Yet the solution evolved by pride was not entirely successful, for he was always afraid. He listened. For what, God alone knew. Perhaps it was a habit of the blind, to listen.

The great thing, of course, was to prevent his uneasiness from infect-
ing her. Lately she had found herself glancing out at the road, and
tonight in the kitchen that feeling of vulnerability had been sharp.
One could so easily become jumpy, living with a man blind and old
and befuddled.

Eloise had crushed out her cigarette when she discerned a pair of
headlights on the road down the valley. Till they halted, some distance from the farm, and went out, she didn't even speculate about
them. And then she thought idly that the probable couple in the car
had driven a long distance from Tamarack, to find a necking spot.

At the University of Tamarack she had joined a sorority, and in the
fall of 1931 her sophomore year looked pretty fine, stretching ahead.
Perhaps she was no great, ravishing beauty, like some of the girls in
that sorority house, but she was young and striking, full of surge and
joie de vivre, and she had brains enough to conceal her brains. She
knew all about forks and hats, and she employed the slang of the moment, and in her dry, droll voice she was likely to come out with some
remark considered witty.

Boys liked her. She had some tantalizing quality that interested
them. In fraternity bull sessions they tried to tag her, but their vocab-
ularies were limited and she was subtle and unique; so they employed
such phrases as she's a hot number, a mean number. One boy
tried to sum her up by saying she was like a jazz trumpet along toward
midnight, playing something deep blue and heartbreaking and low
down, while couples in love danced and the cigarette smoke drifted;
but this was a description entirely too poetic for those future vendors
of legal decisions and debentures and tonsillectomies.

In those days she intended that her life should follow a pattern not
uncommon among girls who had joined a fashionable sorority. As a
senior she would fall in love with some boy who had a good future
doing one of those odd and rather dull things men do, to make ten
thousand a year; and there would be a house with a recreation room
and a son and a daughter who would attend the university and thus
continue the upper middle-class pattern ad infinitum. She might not
have liked it, if she had tried such a life, for there were restless calls
in her blood. She was one of those people things happen to, and not
dull things, either; so maybe if she had made a deal for bridge teas and
a two-car garage the thing wouldn't have coalesced. Anyway, she
didn't; for A. H. Burgoyne abandoned the circus in Corpus Christi.

On that trip with Ive to rescue the show she should have surmised
what was ahead, with times wretched and his signing whopping
checks; but he had always had money, and like most people she considered the *status quo* a fairly permanent arrangement. She returned

to school, working hard to make up classes she had missed, going to dances where the bands played "Please Don't Talk About Me When I'm Gone," and then one evening a call came from Winchester and it was Blossom, reporting excitedly that the bank had failed and Mistah Pawpacker was under arrest. Transportation into Winchester being what it was, she didn't arrive till the second morning following.

It was a wet day, and beneath heaped autumnal clouds the Square looked small and rural and shabby, but not somnolent, for groups of people stood here and there, lanky farmers in rubber boots, loafers, even merchants, discussing the monstrous news. They broke off talking as Eloise picked her way along the sidewalk; nobody said hello. The largest group lingered outside the bank, the ancient bank with curtains pulled and a notice on the door; and as she passed she felt their hostility, and she knew they must be thinking that some of their money had been spent to turn out this smartly dressed young woman, their money painfully accumulated on lonely hill farms.

Ive was not at the house. A United States marshal, Blossom reported, had taken him away to Kansas City. The house would be sold. Everything would be sold.

" 'Cepting that circus farm up Nawth. That's yours. He done deeded that to you, and they cain't touch it."

Eloise went to Kansas City. And she arrived none too soon, for he had already pleaded guilty and received sentence, and they were going to take him away within the hour. It didn't seem she was calling on him in jail; she entered a white building and found her way along marble corridors with doors lettered Collector of Internal Revenue and Collector of Customs. The marshal's office was like almost any business office, with typewriters and files. Only there was a cell at the back. A deputy marshal with a bronze Legion button took her there.

They had given him a rocker, and he sat with his cane loosely between his legs, sprucely dressed even now. But he looked tired and bewildered and small. She had not remembered him as such a small man. She told him it was Eloise, and he asked, "Who?" She bent and kissed him, and he said, "It's Eloise. I thought you were away. I thought you were in school." No, she said, she was here; and she sat on the floor by his chair, as she used to in childhood, and his hand rested on her shoulder.

There had been trouble, he muttered, in Winchester. Oh, trouble all over the country, for that matter; it was not a good time to be a banker; but he had sought to protect the funds in his bank against young men who had attended schools of business administration, where they had squandered their best years while schoolmasters poured foolishness into their heads.

"There's nothing to business but making a profit," he gruffed, and his lips were sardonic. "Buy cheap and sell dear. And hire dollars the way you hire men. When I was their age I had three bank accounts."

And the government, he told her, had engaged these whippersnappers to journey about the country to lock up banks. He had given them short shrift, but at last he couldn't see and they had hornswoggled him, locked the bank. And Winchester people were disturbed.

"You can't blame them," he said. "It's their money. All tied up in red tape."

He sighed and rocked and his lips moved soundlessly; and then he was muttering about what had occurred that first afternoon, when a lot of hoodlums and hotheads came to his house.

"Blossom told me," she whispered.

"Deadbeats," he said.

Oh, he knew their sort! Livery stable loafers. Years before he had cleared them out of his stable, and they said he was a money-getting Yankee. That was all right. A man didn't conduct business for pins. Let them call him Yankee Pawpacker. He liked it. Proud of it. Named a show that, once.

Well, on that afternoon he went to the porch. He couldn't see them, but he could hear them, and they yelled and called him Yankee and carpetbagger, and it seemed some idiot had brought rope and they were trying to yell themselves into a frenzy so they'd have the courage to use it. He had never been less afraid, standing there alone and blind. The fools! But then something struck his temple and spattered, and something else struck his mouth. Tomatoes, frost-rotted. That made him mad. No telling what he would have done, except Blossom came storming out and grabbed his cane and he could hear her taking after those deadbeats, scolding as only a Negro woman could. Some ruffian jerked the cane from her grasp and broke it—that was why he was using this cheap wooden thing—and then the sheriff arrived.

They scooted then. Deadbeats. Soreheaded because he had deeded Eloise that farm where the show used to winter. It was a valuable piece of real estate, that farm. Coal underneath. Some of the richest veins in the country.

"Swapped it from a man named Burgoyne. A. H. Burgoyne. Interesting fellow."

"I know," Eloise said. "I know."

"You know him? A colorful man—isn't that right? Of course, he's young yet. Impulsive. And you'd never believe it, but he's got a crooked streak. He ought to get over it, a fellow with his promise. He'll go far."

On the street it was raining, one of those steady, cold rains that pour down when autumn is setting in. The pavement gleamed and traffic cops wore rubber hats and slickers, and on the sidewalks everybody hurried. When she was a child Sebastian and Orika had played Kansas City, and once after closing in Tulsa they had passed through on their way to glory with Burgoyne & Pawpacker's circus.

Eloise entered a drugstore, and in a booth with a coke and a cigarette she tried to arrange her thoughts. You could tell she had been crying, because her eyelids were red; but although her face was white she was not a girl you would bust up to, if you were a masher, thinking to take advantage of her grief, because you would sense she could take care of herself without great trouble.

She sat there a long time, wondering what she would do. Irrelevancies kept idling through her mind, such as vague surprise that in this store people were laughing and buying, as if it were any ordinary day. Ivan Pawpacker was nothing to them but a name in the newspapers.

Once she opened her purse and brought out her checkbook, leafing through the stubs. In a Tamarack bank she had more than eight hundred dollars, for when she left for school in September Ive had given her a draft for twelve hundred, to cover tuition and books and living expenses. It had been his idea that it would be beneficial for her to learn to keep an account of her own, instead of yanking his financial apron string when she wanted a nickel.

She supposed that if she were a girl of high and noble purpose she would return this money to the Winchester bank; but to hell with that. She was on Ivan Pawpacker's side of the fence, and those on the other side hadn't shown much altruism, arresting a man blind and mixed in his thoughts and sending him to prison.

Continuing at the university was out of the question, now. She would return to pack, then go away somewhere and enroll in a business school for intensive training. Times were falling apart, but she thought an expert secretary could always get a job.

And so it was that a few days later the poor old Chicago, Tamarack & Pacific, which had missed the great future Augustus Phelan expected of it, limped into Chicago two hours late and discharged Eloise in the LaSalle Street Station. And she enrolled in a business school there, and got a job there, and fell in love there; and she was married for a while; but all in all those years were nothing to brag about, from the standpoint of happiness.

Now on the ridge Eloise didn't want to think about those years, or about the future, either. She stood up. Beyond the dark eastern hills the moon was rising, lopsided with age, and red. It looked like October, the way corn shocks and pumpkins did. She watched it turn to rich apricot and then frosty white; and this was the kind of night you expected to see wild geese crossing the moon.

She started back. The valley was all India ink and quicksilver, now; and at the south end of the Animal House the old monkey cages were intricate with slim shadows and strips of brightness. The roof of the Baggage Stock barn was shining, and its wide door exuded soft, deep darkness. It was stabling ghosts tonight, all those heroic Percherons and Clydesdales.

The dust of the carriage yard had never looked whiter, or blacker where the trees projected shadows. Eloise had almost reached the gate when that feeling she had experienced earlier returned; and this time it was sharper. She was being watched. No, she thought, being a fool. She paused and stared. But there were so many spots where the moonlight didn't pry. She moved on, slowly.

In the kitchen the lamp was a dim red smudge; she turned up the wick and lighted her way to Ive Pawpacker's bedroom. He was awake now, and he said:

"Eloise?"

"Yes."

"A stump-sucker," he said. "My, but he was mad. He couldn't abide a stump-sucker."

"What?"

"I've been dreaming. Are we in Winchester?"

"We're at the farm."

He thought that over, then smiled.

"If you see Gus," he said, "tell him he's wrong. The Ringlings aren't worried."

"I'll tell him."

"He'll be put out. I'd like to see his face. But tell him, anyway."

"I'll tell him. Good night."

She went upstairs, and after she had prepared for bed and blown out the lamp, she creaked up the sash of a south window and stood gazing out at the silence. The moon was high now, the valley bright. Once far away she heard a small owl hooting, the notes wavering cool and liquid, and she thought of the field mice abroad tonight. Her gaze moved along the silvered pines of the drive, and then full in the moonlight down near the old Ring Stock barn she beheld a figure standing. A man. She was more surprised than startled. He stood watching the house, and with the silence and the shadows and the haunted quality of the moonlight he looked shrouded with secrecy. Presently he turned, walking with difficulty because of a bad leg, and upon reaching the white road he moved down the valley. Some minutes later a car motor

started and lights came on. The car turned around without coming
up the road; she heard it receding. Then she went to bed, but not to
sleep, immediately.

The car was the Baron Von Krummer's.

That afternoon, Willie had disappointed Charley Sinbad. In the kennels office Charley had found him at the desk, stern and baronial, but
he had not paid Charley ten dollars or even five for the news of Burgoyne's return.

"Vot does Burgoyne mean to me?" the Baron demanded. "Now get
out." And when Charley hesitated, still hoping for a greenback, the
Baron repeated his command. He repeated it with some vehemence,
fist clenched, and he employed several oaths of lumberjack derivation,
and he reminded Charley of a fact which, living in America, Charley
was unlikely to forget: that he was a nigger.

"Now get!"

So Charley got. Without even a fin for his pains.

Yet the Baron considered Charley's tidings of more than average
consequence, but he thought it unwise to let Charley suspect he so
considered them; and besides, the Baron was not one to scatter currency improvidently. Among other virtues, he possessed a great deal
of good German thrift; and the probabilities were that if Charley had
brought advance tidings of the Second Coming the Baron would not
have tipped him more than a quarter.

Alone at the desk, the Baron heard Charley's rented car leaving the
driveway; and after that he sat for a considerable time in meditation.
The afternoon was far advanced, and a bar of golden sunshine ventured through the window and shone upon the bright coppery hairs
that flourished on the back of Willie's fist. The fist was clenched painfully tight, on the desk. Presently it relaxed into a hand, and the hand
opened a desk drawer. Inside, a pistol reposed. Willie did not touch
it. But he stared at it, with that Teutonic veneration for any instrument of destruction. A peculiar light glinted in his eyes, and in the
silent room his coarse breathing could be heard. At last he exclaimed,
"No! The bastard is not worth it!" And he slammed shut the drawer
and shoved himself erect.

He repaired to the window, where he stood in thought; and sometimes his oblique mouth moved. His fist was clenched again, also.
Presently he swung from the window and paced, right leg dragging,
left arm swaying useless. Back and forth, back and forth. Once he
halted and gazed at a cluster of photographs on the wall. They
depicted a brave man with jungle beasts. A strapping, healthy *karl*, in
possession of both arms, both legs, both kidneys. In one photo a
woman could be seen. She was also in possession of legs, not to men-

tion breasts, blond hair, and a tiny smile. The smile might have meant anything. If one were in a certain state of mind, the smile might have been thought mocking.

The veins in Willie's ears swelled, and when he pivoted from the photo he looked unhappy. He thumped resolutely to the desk, where he jerked open a drawer and brought out the pistol. He stood gripping it. But then, oddly, a tide of pasty white oozed under the skin of his face, and he dropped the pistol and sank down at the desk. He appeared to be suffering. It might have been a toothache. It might have been the memory of a joyous Christmastide in Blue Island. Or it might have been that his soul was torn between the desire to administer a fine lesson to a wife-stealer and the desire to avoid all the spiritual and corporal consequences that might backfire against the teacher of such a lesson.

"The nigger is a liar," he muttered. "Why would that tub of lard come back?"

Yet the nigger's lie was so singular, so outlandish, that it might have been a truthful lie. The nigger declared he had seen the tub of lard, dressed like a hobo, on the abandoned roadbed of Tamarack & Northern. Walking away from the city; in other words, toward the farm. Why would he be going to the farm, after all these years? And where was Marybelle?

Vast, perplexing questions. They roused one's rage; also one's uneasiness. One felt something was going on behind one's back. One disliked it. And one also felt distressed, because for so many years one had promised oneself what one would do to the tub of lard if one ever caught this tub. But now one sat, assailed by the womanish fear that if the police should discover a tub of lard riddled by bullets they might grow curious. They might question everybody who had reason to inflict a fine lesson upon the lard. And the whole world knew that the Baron Von Krummer had just and excellent reasons.

The sun was lower. Presently it would set. If one were going to that crossing on the old roadbed, where the lying nigger had seen A. H. Burgoyne, one should be about it. The Baron continued sitting. But at last, his manly instincts asserted themselves. He slipped the pistol into his pocket. He stood up.

"I will give him a great scare, anyway," he thought.

In the driveway, his Ford V-8 waited. Not, possibly, the most aristocratic means of transportation extant, but still pretty good for a fellow who used to travel by bumming on railroads. The Baron liked to say it had been custom-built, tailored for driving with one arm and one leg and one kidney; but he had in fact purchased it used and had it remodeled by a garage near his kennels.

He drove, now, in deep thought. Usually when he piloted his car he discussed aloud the annoying presence of women behind the wheels of so many cars. He believed a lack of rapport existed between women and motor cars. He was a romantic, putting woman on a pedestal in the kitchen. "Drive it or park it," he would mutter, adding, "And I bet her breakfast dishes are still in the sink!"

Twilight was falling when he reached the crossing of which the lying nigger had spoken. The car halted; the Baron creaked out. In his pocket he gripped the pistol. He stood on the crossing, in gloom. The faint memory of sunset was dying in the west. The air was cooling and in the underbrush blue color was sneaking on soft rabbit feet. Off in the timber a flock of crows were cawing sadly about a day that had died and a year that was dying. Otherwise, silence. The Baron glared along the decaying roadbed, but in the mystery of dusk he did not behold A. H. Burgoyne. Possibly he had not expected to behold him, so many hours had passed since the lying nigger encountered him. But in any case, the Baron's manhood felt vindicated, now that he had come searching.

And he made a decision. This evening he would drive to the farm and nose about. It seemed unlikely the tub of lard could have reached the farm by now, hoofing over those slow miles, but this probability did not dissuade the Baron from his plucky decision to go there; indeed, it strengthened it.

In the deep darkness of evening, the Baron halted his car some distance down the road from the farm. Even a valiant man has his moments of prudence, and this was such a moment. If the tub of lard were at the farm, the Baron did not wish to announce his arrival by driving in.

He left the car, touched the pistol in his pocket. Typifying as it did the augmentation of man's barehanded power, it comforted the Baron, especially since he had only one hand, bare or otherwise. Not that he intended shooting Burgoyne! No, no. Ancient man-to-man justice had departed from this decadent earth. But certainly, if by some long chance Burgoyne had arrived—if possibly he had cut over to a highway after the lying nigger had seen him, and hooked a ride—then, *ja,* he would give the fat kangaroo a fine scare. Jab the gun into his porky ribs. Make him kneel. Make him beg. Make him answer a few questions, such as where, then, was the Baroness. And perhaps whack him upon the skull with the pistol, knocking him out, and after that beat his face till it resembled beefsteak. *Ja!*

Dragging along the road in the dim starshine, the Baron derived a warm, voluptuous pleasure from these visions; but possibly they were only after all the vaporings of a reluctant combatant, for suddenly the

Baron halted. His gaze was fixed on the distant farmhouse. Through the quiet evening he saw a light.

What was this? Had Burgoyne actually reached the farm? Had he indeed hitched a ride? Was he in the house now, sprawled hugely in a chair, patting his belly and laughing at how he had ended the great career of the Baron Von Krummer? And again Willie asked himself why the old tub had returned. That was the great question. Some tremendous force must have driven him back to the Tamarack area, where his creditors composed half the population. Where the dangerous Baron Von Krummer waited.

And then it occurred to Willie that in returning, the tub of lard would certainly not have been so rash as to come unarmed. And such a thought was not comforting to a man alone on a dark road. Such a thought could retard one's progress to the vanishing point, along that road.

Yet, one had manhood. One was not a woman, already! One also had a gun. *Ja!* Then why did one not proceed? *Ja,* on to the farm! Damn the torpedoes! Proceed! Forward!

Some minutes later, in the carriage yard, he paused. The light was burning in the kitchen, smudging the windows red. He listened. He envisioned Burgoyne in that kitchen, and he reminded himself that Burgoyne was a low wife-stealer. He thought also of the police. Also of Captain Latcher. Oh, that was a bad old dream; one awakened drenched and shaking. It would be unnerving to dream both of Captain Latcher and A. H. Burgoyne. It would be difficult to meet the level gazes of the police. Sometimes, so Willie understood, they sought the aid of rubber manufacturers to obtain confessions. Stop, stop! *Ja, ja*—I done it! But he stole my *frau. Ja, ja*—the Captain, also . . .

Willie took hold of himself. He crossed the carriage yard, squeaked open the gate, moved to the north kitchen window, peered through. And he saw nobody. Only the low-turned lamp. What did it mean, a lamp burning and nobody there? Perhaps Burgoyne was in another part of the house. Well, if the tub of lard had lighted the lamp he would be bound to return.

In the shadows close to the house Willie waited. Presently the eastern sky reddened and the moon peeked over the hills. But the side of the house remained in shadow, and so did Willie. As minutes passed his good leg ached, and the stump of his bad leg ached. That reminded him of Corpus Christi, and his thoughts prowled like morose tigers through the rank vegetation of his brain.

Suddenly he stiffened. Somebody was coming. Somebody moving down the moonlit slope. From the shadows he stared. What was this? A girl! She had halted now, in the bright carriage yard, and he recognized her. Eloise Sebastian! What did this mean?

The gate squeaked, and presently through the window he beheld her entering the kitchen. She lifted the lamp, and for an instant its rays backlighted her attractive profile, so that her hair was running flame and her forehead and firm chin were gilded. Then she turned, and in the complex interplay of light and shadow she looked watchful. Carrying the lamp, she left the kitchen.

Willie made his way along the outside of the house, following her. The moving lamp shafted yellow through the windows of the dining room, the library. At the west corner of the house the rays splotched the ground outside a bedroom, and Willie crept to the window. He could see her in the bedroom door, lamp aloft, and he thought that in the falling light her countenance looked sober and guarded. Then he glanced at the bed.

It astonished him, seeing a man there among the strange angular shadows cast by the lamp. A wizened old man, his hair and skin silvery. Then suddenly Willie knew the man. His beard had been shaved off, but it was Pawpacker. Pawpacker! When had they let him out of prison?

The lamp departed, but Willie remained, puzzled and obscurely disturbed. At last, with great stealth, he limped back to the carriage yard and down the drive. Near the Ring Stock barn he halted, staring at the house. Light glowed in an upstairs window, and once he glimpsed the girl's moving figure. Then the window went dark. In the moonlight the white old house was softly luminous, save where gable-shadows and tree-shadows printed themselves in blackish purple. Finally, Willie returned to his car, telling himself the nigger had concocted the whole story about Burgoyne's return. Burgoyne would not be at the farm on this night, or any night. Not with Pawpacker there. For Burgoyne had ruined Pawpacker, just as he had ruined the Baron Von Krummer. The nigger had lied. Willie felt relieved. For now to satisfy the demands of his valor he would not have to seek out Burgoyne and scare him and possibly lose control and actually shoot him. Burgoyne was far away, lost in anonymity among the millions of the great world.

And yet, back at the kennels, as he undressed and lumbered into bed, Willie found himself profoundly troubled. The nigger had lied—*ja,* sure; but it was such an odd lie. And it was strange the girl and Pawpacker should be at the farm. Could Burgoyne and Pawpacker have patched things up and arranged a meeting at the farm? Concerning what? Who could know? Possibly after all the nigger had not lied. Perhaps Burgoyne had indeed returned; the past had sent him back like a bad penny. Why?

Willie lay sleepless. Now and then he heard a car tearing along the highway past the kennels, but presently even late traffic ceased. The city slept. All but Willie and men in police stations; the police, alas, never slept. Sometimes Willie turned and groaned.

It was exceedingly late, and he was lying on his back, eyes open, staring at darkness. His tired brain had at last given up trying to un-riddle Burgoyne's return; his thoughts drifted; he was thinking of Captain Latcher. Possibly a light doze had crawled across his brain, the way dirty yellow fog sneaks through the alleys and over the cobbles of a wicked old city. In any case, in his mind's ear, Willie heard words. They were spoken softly, with playful malice.

"Why is Burgoyne back? Simple enough, old chap. The little Viking must have tattled about that affair in Blue Island, eh? You've a nice dog business here, old boy, and you could sell it for a tidy sum. Burgoyne and Pawpacker must both need cash. But Burgoyne could hardly approach you personally. So Pawpacker will, or Eloise. Jolly old blackmail, eh?"

The ceiling bulbs blazed; their glare revealed a man in pajamas at the wall switch; and the man's face had the bloodless appearance to be seen on a face in a coffin. The eyes were peculiar, and one corner of the raw mouth curled. You could hear the man breathing. Presently he labored over to a rocking chair. The world was a silent world. Then, from the kennels outside, a dog lifted its voice in a long mournful wail. The man's nerves must not have been in first-class condition, for that doleful sound caused him to wince.

"*Ja,*" he whispered, "it is all clear, now."

Like a solved geometry problem it lay sharp and lucid in his thoughts. From the beginning Marybelle had suspected how the Cap-tain died. And perhaps, after she became the wedded wife of the Baron Von Krummer, she had listened while her husband slept, and had heard him talking in his sleep, muttering words that clinched her suspicions. But with a deep, villainous Norse craft, she bided her time. Then after eloping with Burgoyne her serpent's tongue hissed out the story. And Burgoyne was a schemer. He had written a letter to Eloise or to Pawpacker, suggesting they all join forces to bleed white the Baron Von Krummer.

They were all against him; everybody had always been against him. "But I will pay," he thought. "*Ja, ja*—anything if it will only bring me peace."

For a moment that decision soothed him; he felt beaten and drained, but at peace. It was the sad, tired peace of defeat; and he wondered how he would ever earn a livelihood, without the dog business. Squat-ting on a sidewalk, maybe, with a hat full of pencils. He sighed.

But even the peace of the vanquished did not assuage him long; for he found himself thinking that after ruining him Burgoyne might go

right ahead and report him to the Illinois authorities. For a full second
Willie did not breathe. On the chair arm his fist clenched. Then he
lifted it and swatted the chair. *Ja!* Of course! Certainly! A vicious
character, Burgoyne! Full of abysmal treachery! Just as when the
Judas stole Marybelle he had yanked the switch in uncalled-for malev-
olence, so now he would bleed the Baron Von Krummer of every cent
and then toss him to the hangman! No, not the hangman! In the
papers he had read that Illinois was now killing murderers by electricity. Willie went rigid, as in imagination his body received a million
volts.

The dog howled again, and in his mind Willie saw the slow march
to the death chamber. With Teutonic morbidity he lingered over such
details as the black hood they slipped over his face and the black hearse
with the black coffin waiting in the prison yard.

Daybreak found him desperate; he could eat no breakfast.

It was a beautiful morning, October at its best. Yet when the Baron
drove away from the kennels he did not appear to be enjoying the
weather. His destination was Charley Sinbad's picnic spot. In his
pocket he carried the pistol, and he had virtually tormented himself
into a mood for using it. Not by batting Burgoyne over the head,
either.

He tried to convince himself his worries were silly. Suppose Burgoyne did report him to the Illinois police. What then? Could they
prove he had tossed the Captain to the cats? Of course not! Unless—

Well, when one has lost sleep, and one's imagination is flaming, it
is possible to conjure up a vision of authorities exhuming a body long
in the earth, and examining the skull, and discovering the skull had
suffered a hard blow, such as might have been delivered by a training
stick. *Ja,* that was how it would come about. Then, an arrest. And a
confession, secured by means unpleasant to contemplate. And once one
was safely locked up, the tub of lard would produce Marybelle, from
where he must have her hidden, and she would recount how Captain
Latcher had always suspected his cage boy of bloody designs. And
one's baronial credentials would be scrutinized, and it would be discovered that the Baron had once been Willie Krummer, and before
that Willie Parr; and it would be learned that Willie Parr had fled
home to avoid reform school. Thinking such thoughts, one feels like
a tiger in a net.

Willie drove along the river road, and the sunshine was warm on
the tan gravel and on the burning scarlets and the leafy yellows. Again
today he halted where the sandy lane crossed the old embankment, and
again he left the car and stared. And again, no Burgoyne. So he returned to his car and drove farther along the river road, cruising slowly,

scrutinizing the timber and the right-of-way; and when the road and the embankment parted company he halted the car and got out, scanning the weedy roadbed where it curved off into the woodlands. He beheld nobody beneath the tipsy trolley poles.

At last, with difficulty, he waded through a ditch and negotiated a fence and mounted the embankment. He stared down at its ruin, hoping to detect some trace of Burgoyne, but he failed to decipher a man's passage among the blue-and-cinnamon ties or in the gravel. He muttered to himself. And he scowled at the roadbed vanishing into the woods, a figure of wrath knee-deep in frost-withered weeds, the tall autumnal sky towering over him, a cloud of migrating blackbirds chattering about him from the brilliantly stained timber.

"Ach," he thought, "if I had my leg . . ."

If he had his leg! Then, oh then, he would go racing over the weed-tips, into the timber and on and on, swift with winged heels of vengeance, till at last he overtook Burgoyne. But he did not have his leg. He sighed, labored back to his car, wondering what to do.

Well, Burgoyne was going to the farm. *Ja.* So the logical place to find him would be the farm. Again, *ja.* But not by daylight! Wait till evening and go out there. And spy and listen. But to what purpose? Burgoyne would already have outlined the devilish plot of blackmail. Yet, would he? Possibly not. Perhaps he had only written Pawpacker that he had a great, fine scheme to make money. Perhaps before disclosing the scheme he and Pawpacker would dicker about how to split the money from the fine dog business. If one could intercept Burgoyne before he disclosed the scheme—

Following breakfast, after settling Ive on the porch in the frosty sun, Eloise went to the carriage yard and examined the dust. Its beige softness bore the delicate claw-tracks of sparrows, and the evidence of a man who had dragged one foot. The right one. She found several sharp prints of a left shoe, big, soldierly. On the drive there were no prints, for the ground was rutty and hard and sifted over with pine needles. She crossed the interurban, going to the west entrance of the Ring Stock barn. There was dust here, and she found more shoe marks.

It must have been Willie. In the moonlight she hadn't been certain, although when he moved, his left arm swinging dead and his right leg erratic, she had surmised his identity. She hadn't seen him for years, but she knew he had lost an arm and a leg, and he lived in Tamarack. So what? Why in God's name had he come out here to prowl?

She wasn't afraid, or even uneasy, exactly; but baffled she certainly was. He had always been a queer one. She remembered how he had looked that first spring here at quarters: pimply and insolent-eyed, with an oddly corrupt grin. Sometimes he sneaked along with shoulders twitchy and spine snaky; and at other times, as if he were in evolution toward nobility, his backbone cracked to attention and his shoulders were absurdly brazen, and he swaggered ridiculously. Captain Latcher used to guy him unmercifully.

Well, to hell with him. She returned to the kitchen; she felt quite up to handling Willie. Nevertheless, it was undeniable that beholding him there in the moonlight left her jittery. Nobody liked to be spied on. She remembered her sense of being watched when she returned from the ridge: probably he had been skulking somewhere, gaze drilling her. Raping her, likely, in his thoughts.

She didn't mention the matter to Ive. But strangely enough, she had the impression that Ive's nervous system, antenna-like, had received delicate radiations of something out of the ordinary. Through the window she observed him on the porch, and he wasn't dozing in his rocker, but sitting with fragile hands on his cane, listening.

Early that afternoon she left for the store at Oxenford, going to the ridge and cutting across the autumnal fields; and back in the house Ive lay in the bedroom, taking his nap. Only today he didn't really sleep. A light doze coated his consciousness, that was all. And he kept feeling guilty about taking time out for rest, he was such a busy man. Mr. Kronkmeyer would be expecting him at the livery stable, and possibly Major Redmond would drive in to Larkin Corners; only Ive knew very well he wasn't in Larkin Corners: he was in a bedroom belonging to some people named Kelvin, laid up with a sprained ankle, and it so happened the Kelvins had a daughter named Georgiana, and he was going downtown with her to purchase a bracelet. Girls liked such trinkets. He chuckled.

Blankness washed over his consciousness; and then he was telling himself he must be up and doing, for the dinner hour was approaching and here he was, napping in the General Grant Hotel, and that young man named Burgoyne would be entering the lobby to discuss buying a baby elephant named Molly.

Ive opened his eyes but nothing happened; it startled him, till he realized he wasn't in the General Grant but in the bedroom at winter quarters. He said, "Eloise?" Again, nothing happened. No, of course not; she had gone for groceries. And he was alone here. There was no longer a circus, and sometimes he wondered why. He must have sold it, although why a man would sell a business better than the Klondike was puzzling.

He sat on the edge of the bed, slowly groping into his shoes; and then gripping his cane he shuffled from the bedroom. The air in the house smelled faintly musty and it had a shut-up coolness; he would be glad to reach his chair in the sun. A time or two he stopped, on that journey through the downstairs rooms, head tilted as he listened. And he was afraid. That was humiliating and foolish. A leading citizen with money in the bank had nothing to fear. On the other hand, lack of sight was something of a handicap, increased the hazards in life.

As he reached the kitchen he heard the gate squeak. That would be Eloise. He paused just inside the door to the porch, listening, thinking what a good girl she was, looking forward to hearing her voice, wondering whether she would bring him some of those hard peppermint candies he liked so well. An anticipatory trickle of saliva watered his tongue, as he thought of the candy; but then suddenly he had forgotten the candy and he was afraid again, for the footsteps were not hers. He stood very still. The footsteps halted. He waited, and on his tongue the saliva had dried; and it occurred to him that he was not exactly unassailable, standing there alone and blind. And he was ashamed to realize that something a great deal like panic was running in his blood. Beneath the skin of his temple he could feel a vein beating. His speech organs were numb and arid. He said, "Eloise?"

There was no response. And that was scarcely a state of affairs to allay panic, knowing somebody was standing a few paces away, ominously mute. The trouble was, he was pretty certain there was a batch of years, recent years, when unpleasant events had taken place in his life. What these events were he could not recall, but he was of the opinion that if he could recall what they were he would be willing to forget them again. And it might well be that this person who stood so close and so silent had come tracking out of those void years.

"Eloise?"

The silence was pure.

Resolution poured through him. His life had not been without courage, but this was audacity beyond imagination, this edging through the door to the porch. He inched to a halt, feeling the sun, and feeling also, more palpably than ever, the presence of another. He kept a tight grip on his cane and a tight grip on himself, too.

Then, exquisitely delicate, the noise of somebody on tiptoe, retreating, brushed his ears. The gate squeaked. And from some distance away he thought he heard feet in the dust of the carriage yard. After that, silence.

He eased down the steps, along the path, through the gate. It was necessary to find Eloise. She had gone to the store and he must find her. Underfoot he felt the softness of the carriage yard, and he warned himself not to give way to panic, because then he might lose all sense of direction and wander in circles. He made himself take it slowly, up the hill, his cane swording ahead of him; and presently his cane struck something with a loud clang. His hand groped. Bars. For an instant he fancied himself in jail, but that was a silly thought for a leading citizen to entertain; and then he knew what the bars were. They were the monkey cages at the south end of the Animal House. He pushed on, feeling his way along the side of the building, never knowing but that the next moment something hot and quick might happen to him.

All in all, it was not a good journey. Not an experience one wished to repeat. In a way it was like what a lyceum lecturer had once called the journey of life; full of blindness and the unknowable, with strange things jabbing at you and the ground underfoot yearning to trip you up. It seemed to be lasting a considerable time; and the trouble with life wasn't that the view behind was so much better than the view ahead. Gus had been wrong there. The trouble was that there was no view at all.

Barbed wire bristled against his palm, and the age of miracles returned and permitted him to crawl through without getting caught and hung up on that fence. He was searching for a girl. She had gone to a store at a place called Oxenford, and her name was Eloise. At the moment her last name didn't matter. She was a good girl and she would take care of him. She would never burn his hand with a lantern. He wanted to find her but although he kept walking and walking, uphill and down, he didn't seem to be getting anywhere significant. At last he paused.

"Eloise," he whimpered, "I am lost."

And indeed he was lost, there in boggy ground on the far side of the ridge, in a tangle of burdock and thistle, such a little man staring up blindly at such an immense amount of sky.

In the loft of the Ring Stock barn, a man who might well have been an old hobo lay on a pile of hay. But appearances are so often deceptive: he was not an old hobo, at all. He was a man who in his day had been of considerable consequence, booming orders from a city desk, getting himself married in a mansion, even making speeches at the Chamber of Commerce. And American life being what it was, so full of opportunity, there was a good chance he would once again be a man of consequence. Always provided, of course, he raided the attic successfully and carried off a painting by an artist named Alex Kerry.

He was dozing now, hat over his face, belly rising and falling. And there was that about his breathing which suggested he was about to drop down into the wonderful oblivion of deep sleep. But then, from far away through the stillness, a low drift of voices reached him.

He sat up, listening; and presently he went thumping in his socks to a slit in the north wall of the barn. He saw nobody, but he remained there, kneeling. Then he heard the gate squeak. Through an orifice in the pines he could see the kitchen porch, and presently two persons trudged slowly into his range of vision. They were Ivan Pawpacker and Eloise Sebastian. Ive looked exhausted, leaning on Eloise. She helped him climb the porch steps, and they disappeared into the house.

Minutes passed. Although his knees ached, Gus remained steadfastly at the slit. Then presently he descried Eloise emerging from the house. The foliage hid her as she strode along the path; Gus heard the gate squeak; and a few moments later he beheld her on the drive, coming toward the Ring Stock barn.

He heaved to his feet, tiptoed to the aperture leading below, and he stood there listening. He heard silence and the distant cooing of pigeons. Then by and by, from down there on the passageway through the barn, he sensed the presence of somebody.

He stood like a statue, ear drums straining; and he hardly permitted himself to breathe, lest his asthma choose this moment to begin whistling. Time was a smooth, slow whirlpool, with him at the core. At last, with infinite caution, he knelt at the edge of the aperture and peered below. He did not see Eloise. He saw only the afternoon sun invading the passageway, and the empty stalls.

He returned to the slit, but Eloise was not visible from there, either. Finally he went back to the pile of hay and lay down. Outside, the afternoon lengthened, but he did not doze again.

Eloise had her hands full. Both ways: literally, figuratively. Literally with the groceries; it was a heavy bag, and she had wrestled it all the way from the store. And figuratively with Ive.

He had been scared white, of course; and he kept babbling about some citizen who had sneaked in and spied on him and then sneaked away. Willie, probably. Well, enough was enough. She decided to find the fellow and learn what he had been up to, prowling about the farm last night and again today.

All the way down from the north pasture she kept reassuring Ive, telling him not to worry, she would handle everything; but his lips were tight and sometimes he stopped, holding up a hand for silence and listening, as if he believed the ears of the blind could detect more than the eyes of those who could see.

"Come on, darling," she kept saying. "The hell with this. It was probably a tramp."

So at last she soothed him, and persuaded him into the house; and then she marched down the drive, past the Ring Stock barn, to the road. It was empty. Returning, she ventured into the barn, but only a few flies were there, buzzing in the autumnal warmth. She glanced at the ladder climbing to the loft, and she even considered mounting it; but then she told herself Willie would not have dragged himself up there, with his bad arm and leg. Finally she went back to the kitchen.

And as the day waned and she prepared dinner, she decided on a course of action. She would put Ive to bed early and then go to the ridge. Up there last evening she had seen the lights of a car that must have been Willie's. Tonight she would watch for those headlights, and if they halted she would know Willie had returned and was on the prowl again; and she would sneak down and surprise him at whatever mad business he was about.

In the month of October when the year is old the days draw in early; the hot fire of sunset cools fast; and in that season of frost and smoke the twilight comes swiftly. Now it was dusk on the farm where once the horses of Pawpacker had crunched their supper oats, and the elephants of Burgoyne had swayed at their hobbles; and there were shadows on the land.

The loft of the Ring Stock barn was black, and a shadow existed there, too. A fat one. It was moving, now; a board squeaked; and then briefly a pocket flashlight torched the ladder leading below. There were grunts. Rusty nails complained, for the shadow was descending.

"Uh-h," Gus whispered, as he grounded; and his asthma wheezed.

He waddled softly through the door and crossed the drive, advancing watchfully up the interurban embankment. The kitchen windows glowed orange through smooth indigo air. He felt his way along, at last groping down the embankment and through a ditch. Along the west edge of the yard bushes had rioted wild, and they screened him from the house. He fumbled north, halting presently and intruding into the thick growth, parting the branches, staring at the kitchen windows.

He had no plans now, except patience. Five minutes or five hours, it was all one. At some moment on this still night opportunity would come, and he would act promptly, boldly.

Some distance down the road the Baron Von Krummer switched off the motor and the lights. A black evening, so he too was a shadow, at the wheel.

"Well, I am ready," he thought. "I will see what monkey business is going on."

He checked his revolver and his small flashlight, but he did not immediately leave the car. He sat there trying to heat up his valor by remembering Corpus Christi. But unfortunately, other thoughts kept icing his brain; such thoughts as Marybelle's tattling and district attorneys and electric chairs.

At last he left the car and moved along the road. He would try to find Burgoyne, but beyond that he had not decided what to do. It was only that his sanity would crack if he remained at the kennels doing nothing. Hence, action! *Ja!*

During the minutes when the Baron lingered in his V-8, screwing up courage, Gus maintained a strict vigil in the bushes, his gaze fixed on the kitchen windows. The stars were shining now, sharp and frosty, and through the quiet evening he could hear a dog barking in some distant farmyard. Nearby a cricket chirped out a feeble little song, mourning a summer that had departed and the death that would overtake it in the frosts of 3 A.M.

Once the kitchen door opened and the girl stepped to the porch. Gus stiffened. But then his nerves eased, for he saw that her errand was only to drag the rocking chair inside. Through the open door the sizzle of frying hamburger drifted faintly and aromatically. Gus's mouth watered.

The door closed, and he stood in the dark, thinking of the future. Before leaving Denver he had sewed fifty dollars inside his vest lining, and his plans were made. With the painting he would proceed by back roads to the nearest town with an express office, and ship the painting to Arthur H. Buckman in Denver. Then he would buy a shave and an enormous meal and a bus ticket. And in Denver, he would write various art dealers and sell for the best price offered. He could envision the check he would receive. A pale-golden slip of paper. Pay to the Order of Arthur H. Buckman. Five thousand and no one-hundredths dollars. Perhaps even a greater sum, art addicts being obviously mad people, where Kerry was concerned. He would deposit the check. His checkbook would be plump and virginal. He would stride into a tailor's, smoking a rich cigar. He would invest in a lucrative business. Opportunity knocked constantly, if you had loose capital. Somebody had said that once.

But first he must get the painting.

On the kitchen window the lamp rays shifted, as if the lamp were being picked up, and the window darkened. The lamp was being carried through the house. Presently light was shining through the window of the downstairs bedroom. Then, after a time, the lamp traveled back through the house, to the kitchen, and the girl opened the door. She stood for a time on the porch, then moved along the path. The gate squeaked. Silence.

Where had she gone? And for how long? Was this opportunity?

Gus waited several minutes. Then, after a last moment of listening, he tiptoed swiftly to the porch.

Again tonight she wore the sport jacket, and again tonight, as she ascended the slope toward the ridge, she found herself thinking that perhaps after all it wouldn't work out, her coming to the farm with Ive. From Chicago this place and this manner of life had looked peaceful, but it was not peaceful. It was all bogged and tangled.

She was thinking now not only of Willie Krummer's odd snooping, but of her entire situation, and she did not like herself. She did not like herself because Ivan Pawpacker got on her nerves. She was in her middle twenties and he was old; and already, after less than two weeks, she wanted cities again, the harsh, sweet jangle of traffic and the sight of mauve Neons.

"I'm a heel," she thought. "Lord, but I'm a heel. A steel ring crystallizes and a nice man takes me in. And he gets old and they put him in stir and when they let him out he's dim and he gets on my nerves. Just a heel."

She reached the boulders on the ridge and sat smoking, her gaze on the road where last night she had seen the headlights of Willie's car.

Once she had been a girl in a philosophy class at the University of Tamarack, and there had been a teacher named Dr. Harold Henderson. And he was a dryball, this Doc Henderson, but now and then he came forth with something that stuck in your thoughts, and once he had said that the only peace was inner peace. And she had never had that.

Probably it was too much to expect, inner peace, with the things that had happened to her. Things like an afternoon in North Platte and a hot noon in Winchester with Mrs. Ivan Pawpacker tumbling down the stairs to the central hall. Her marriage hadn't contributed to inner peace, either. He had been a drummer in a honky-tonk, and why she had married him only God knew. Because she was young, probably, and lonely. His name was Freddie and he had possessed all the usual sins.

So of course it hadn't lasted long, that wedded bliss; and after that she had been a secretary, working and saving against the day when Ive Pawpacker would be released. Well, that day had come; and now she was following the way of life she had planned, and it wasn't working out so well.

She had been a hell of a good secretary. They had hated to lose her, and she could go back, if she ever wanted to. And if she ever did go back then someday, unless the law of averages had been repealed, she would probably meet somebody who wasn't a drummer in a honky-tonk, somebody who would be a good guy, somebody you could have a lot of fun with, during the remainder of your allotted span upon the earth.

Only of course you were not likely to meet such a good guy, stuck away on a farm with elephant ghosts and an old, old man. And thinking such thoughts generated queer tensions in you, and you resented the man who had been kind and generous to you, who had treated you better than any man ever had, except an acrobat named Ned Sebastian. That was why you held a low opinion of yourself. That was why you thought you were a heel.

But she told herself that even if she were a heel she wasn't going to act like one. She would stick by Ive, the way he had stuck by her. She had a modern mind, and words like duty didn't mean much to her, but the concept behind a word like that had not fallen into rust and decay. Once he had said they were partners, and she guessed that summed it up: you didn't let a partner down. You kept his mortal secret locked forever in your head, and when he was old you stuck around to be helpful.

She sat smoking, thinking, and all the time she watched the road for headlights, but no headlights flashed. And then, despoiling the quiet, she heard a voice from the farmhouse. It was a loud voice, coarse and brutal, thick with the accents of Prussia. Willie! He must have driven to the farm earlier tonight. Eloise jumped to her feet. And then she heard another sound, and she hurried to the fence and ran fast through the shadow of the Animal House and down the slope.

From the kitchen Gus came on tiptoe, through the dining room, into the living room, a watchful, moving bulk. His hands were cupped round the burning end of the flashlight, lest its rays on a window announce his intrusion; and its bulb was glowing red through his flesh, as if he were carrying live coals. He halted, wheezing softly, while all the memories of his years of glory wafted from the walls and swirled round him. He knew then how a ghost feels when it steals back through the clockwork of the stars.

He unmasked the light, flashed it round the room; then moved on to the stairs.

Dankness hung thick in the black upper hall; dankness and mildew and must. In spots the plaster had bulged, cracking the wall paper.

"They've let the place run down," Gus thought; and he experienced sadness and outrage at human shiftlessness. But of course Pawpacker had been in prison, and times had been wretched. And he had a melancholy vision of the old house standing empty and silent during the long chaos of the thirties, assailed by moths and mice and spiders and creeping damp, by gales tearing its shingles and frost prying its foundation, by all the ravaging forces of nature that labor so endlessly and enthusiastically to demolish the edifices of man.

His light found the door to the attic; it rasped open; and he saw that the steps were thick-coated with dust. He closed the door after him and wheezed upward. The ascent was steep and narrow.

"Nobody's been here for a coon's age," he thought, as he creaked to the upper landing.

It looked gray and forgotten, that attic, save by the mice that had tracked its floor and the spiders whose webs festooned the rafters. A long-necked chimney rose through the roof; and all the sweepings and rubbish of the years had accumulated here, crippled chairs, a rusty flat-iron, a corset ample enough to engirdle Flora, a scabrous leather suitcase, gaping open. Inside, Gus glimpsed something yellow and he bent heavily and fished it out.

It was a doll. And once it must have been a very nice doll, with its golden hair and red dress. The dress was filthy now, of course, and the hair scraggly. Nobody had ever played with that doll; she had been too sick; she had just lain with her arm around it.

"Kind of a shame," Gus thought. "Some kid would have enjoyed it. Should have given it to some poor kid."

He held it clumsily, as might be expected of an aging man with thick hands. Once he smoothed the hair away from its face. "Kind of a shame," he thought. "Kind of a shame."

Then he remembered why he was here. He put down the doll, gently, on a stack of ancient magazines, and flashed his light on the chimney. He had stored the painting, in its box, beside an old trunk beyond the chimney.

He fumbled over there, around the chimney, remembering how the box looked, with Alex Kerry's name lettered on the wood. But when he reached the spot where he had left the box he didn't see it. He saw the trunk, but not the box.

"Must have got moved," he thought; and he flashed his light in search.

One attic window could be seen—and was seen—from the driveway shadows where Willie Krummer scowled. And to him the light looked eerie, flashing with soft secrecy on the small, lofty window.

"What goes on?" he asked himself; but instantly he knew what went on. The knowledge froze the very fluid in his spinal canal. And his mind was a dark town, stricken with pestilence and fear.

They were searching the attic; that was what went on. They were all up there, Eloise and Pawpacker and Burgoyne and possibly Marybelle. They were ransacking the place for something harmful to the Baron Von Krummer. What? Unimportant; his imagination had carried him far beyond the frontiers of logic. Maybe a letter. Maybe Captain Latcher had written a letter once to Burgoyne, mentioning his suspicions of his cage boy.

On the window the light kept flashing, mysterious, cabalistic, baleful.

"By God," he thought, hysterically, "I will not let them do this."

And rage poured through him and he went swaying toward the house, his manhood regained, a very frankfurter and steaming kraut of a warrior, plunging valiantly into his Götterdämmerung.

It wasn't here. The painting simply wasn't here. Gus had searched high and low. He had divided the attic into sections and searched each one. He had emptied the trunk. He had moved things. He had flashed his light across the walls and sent it into the rafters. It wasn't here.

His quest had raised dust, and now in the torch beam the motes swarmed amid the cold silver of his expelled breath. And the motes surged up his nostrils and down his throat, cutting into his bronchial tubes harshly; and he wheezed. He flashed the light once more over the disorder he had produced. The slim beam wandered halfheartedly; at last he snapped it off and stood in the blue-windowed dark.

It wasn't here. Where? God knew. Gone, vanished. He guessed he should have held on to it when he had it. And he had the obscure feeling he should have held on to a lot of things, precious things, when he had them. He was very tired, suddenly. Not as young as once. Soon be sixty.

Once more, with that human reluctance to abandon hope, he flashed the light. But the painting wasn't here; it really wasn't. He shuffled toward the steps, then returned to a stack of magazines and picked up the doll. Then he descended. At the bottom step he switched off the light and opened the door, softly. And it was then he heard something.

From downstairs he heard it, somebody coming. From the living room. Thump, drag, thump. Like that. Somebody moving, it would seem, on a good leg and a bad one. Thump, drag, thump. Climbing the stairs, now.

He thought of Willie. Willie had a good leg and a bad one. And thinking of Willie gave him a scare. It would not be Willie, but nevertheless he would have preferred not hearing what he heard. Gus was in the upper hall, now, and he saw a light bobbing up the steps, preceding the intruder.

And Gus was wheezing. It was the asthma. The asthma would betray him. He gulped a mighty breath and on tiptoe moved swiftly into a bedroom. At the far wall he knelt behind a bed and stared toward the hall.

And then the light came into view, and the person holding the light. Before ducking, Gus glimpsed the person's countenance, weirdly uplighted by the flashlight; a countenance thick-nosed and raw-mouthed and blond; the Goth; the warrior; the barbarian from the terrible North. And crouching there like a Roman senator behind crumbling ramparts Gus thought, "My God, it *is* Willie. It's the Dutchman."

His lungs were nearly bursting with his breath held against the asthma. He had to breathe. His lungs were shrieking.

So, slowly and cautiously, he permitted a trickle of sweet oxygen to slide through his bronchial tubes. And his head inched up and he peered over the bed. The hall was dark. And steps sounded on the attic stairs.

Gus soared to his feet. He gained the hall, and risking his flashlight against a tumble he plunged down the stairs. Into the living room, the dining room, the kitchen. He didn't stop till he had pushed through the bushes at the west edge of the yard.

And then he paused for only a moment. He told himself he should wait, search further for the painting. But where? He turned, picked his way through the darkness to the interurban. He crawled under a fence, crossed the pasture, heading for a patch of woodland beyond the road. There he would spend the night.

He had failed in his quest, but he was alive. He was Arthur H. Buckman, clerk in a seedy hotel, but he was alive. And oddly enough, as he bumbled through the darkness, putting space between himself and Willie, still holding the doll, a wave of optimism buoyed his spirits. Alive. And almost sixty did not seem so old. Times would improve. Maybe be a boom, some day. And he would find means to ride it and soar with it. He'd done pretty well. He had scraped bottom in '32, and now he was on his way up. He would get there, yet. The world would know about Arthur H. Buckman, before he cashed in. He turned his face toward the American West.

Ivan Pawpacker was awake now, and he didn't like it. He didn't like it at all, the noise. In the house people were moving. A fine hour of the night to be moving about! Maybe Blossom and Emancipation? But why? Besides, they didn't walk with a thump and a drag. He lay listening, exasperated. Sleep was so beneficial, but how could one sleep with all this noise? Somebody rumbling down a flight of stairs, now. What did it mean?

He creaked thin legs over the edge of the bed. It was a dark night; no light coming through any windows. He blinked. Then he remembered. His sight was no longer with him. And he was no longer in Winchester. He wondered why. He found his cane and stood up. In his nightshirt he tottered from his bedroom, tapping through dankness. When he reached the kitchen he said, "Eloise?" No response. He wasn't, however, afraid. In the center of the floor he stood with lips pursed, head cocked. Far away in upper reaches of wherever it was he lived he heard that thumping. But he wasn't afraid. Again he said, "Eloise?" She wasn't here, because if she were here she would answer.

The thumping sounded closer, now; it was coming from the downstairs rooms; and one's fortitude was not without limits. He began to shake. Perhaps after all he should have remained in bed.

"Eloise?"

And then the thumping entered the kitchen, and all at once, from a mouth he could not see, there poured forth a stream of swearing. He had heard swearing in his day—in livery stables and on circus lots men were not above profaning God's name—but this was thicker, more savage swearing than he had ever heard. He stood with lips working silently, not in the least afraid now, for barking dogs seldom bit. And gradually he realized the fellow was swearing at him. Accusing him of all sorts of insane things. The fellow was evidently a fool. Ive said, "Shut up."

The fellow didn't like it. He was really yelling, now; disgusting, disgusting; some roustabout drunk, probably. He sounded as if he were working himself up to some hysterical pitch. And then, incredibly, Ive's cheek smarted, and he realized he had been slapped. That, of course, was carrying drunken rage too far. He'd have Gus fire the brute. He'd fire him, himself. Ive said, "You're through. Your goose is cooked."

The fellow slapped him again, yelling louder; and Ive thought it would be just as well to give him a lesson. So he lifted his cane and whacked toward the sound of the voice, but his cane didn't strike anything. It did, however, bring a perfect torrent of profanity from the roustabout, and then another sound. An explosive sound, such as a gun might make, going off.

And still Ive was not afraid, although he disliked the stab of heat in his stomach, as if a hot poker had jabbed him; and then there was another explosive sound, and another; and all at once it seemed there was nothing solid in the world; just blackness; and you were swimming in this insubstantial blackness; and your body was burning.

But then suddenly everything was very nice. Everything was really fine. You could see again, and you were young again, your body a willing servant instead of a burdensome master; and it was a very wonderful morning in spring, in New York State. And the eastern sky was pink glory, and you were driving along the road that led from Larkin Corners past Major Redmond's place, toward the West. The dew sparkled and the springtime birds were singing and it was wonderful to be alive, even though, strictly speaking, you were not alive.

It was all over with him now. He had done it. He had shot a man. He had shot a man through the belly and the shoulder and the heart.

The man's name was Pawpacker and the swine had insulted him and struck at him. He was a blackmailer and better dead. So he had shot him.

Willie stood in sickness and heat, staring down at what he had done. His hand was shaking and he dropped the gun. Then he swayed to the porch and along the path. He had done it. He had shot a man and it was all over with him now.

As he squeaked open the gate he heard somebody coming down the hill, coming fast; and all at once the red rage he had experienced in the kitchen returned and he wished he had not dropped the gun. It was the girl and he would have shot her too if only he had the gun. But as it was, when she rushed up to him and screamed something, he could not shoot her. He could only call her pig names; and then she whirled and ran to the house and he was swaying along the drive.

And now abruptly he felt sick again because he had shot a man. He swung along faster. There was no help. The girl had seen him. No possibility of blaming the cats, this time. He would run but they would catch him. He was cold in his veins and sick in his stomach. The night was cool but he was sweating. They would catch him and beat him and hang him. It was all over with him now.

He staggered against the Ring Stock barn. He leaned there, shaking. He would have to crawl to his car and drive fast to get away for a little while. But they would catch him in the end. This was not like running away to avoid reform school. They would take a more serious view of this than of his cutting up dogs and cats. They would get him. He began to cry.

He reeled on, and all the way along the dark road to his car he blubbered and wept. Everybody had always been against him.

He creaked inside his car and the motor caught. Gears clashed and the car kicked up gravel as it leaped away. He was not returning to Tamarack. He would drive along back roads to a main highway, fleeing on and on through the night. He did not know where he was going. He did not know much of anything, except that everybody had always picked on him, making fun of him before her and stealing his wife and planning to blackmail him because of a murder the cats had really committed. Well, he had shown that swine, Pawpacker. He had fixed him good. He had shot him and it was all over. It was all over now with the Baron Karl Otto Von Krummer.

The car weaved along wildly. Maybe it was dangerous driving so fast with only one arm and one leg and one kidney, but it did not matter. Nothing much mattered now. They would hang him if they caught him and Marybelle would get the dog business and marry the tub of lard.

Presently the car reached a concrete highway and he turned west and the miles raced under him, fifty of them each hour racing under him, sixty of them; and the car swayed and weaved but it didn't matter. By and by there was a town, and he intended slowing down as he passed through it, because he did not wish to be arrested for speeding. He did not wish to be arrested at all. But he would be, he would be. He had shot a man and he would be.

But although he intended to cut his speed he did not, at the last minute, because he was so eager to be far away from the farm and the man he had shot. Then as he lurched crazily past a filling station in the town he realized it had been a mistake, not cutting his speed, for a car of the state police stood in the filling station. And two uniformed cops were there and when they saw the car driven by the Baron Karl Otto Von Krummer they hurried into their own car and gave chase.

Willie jammed the accelerator to the floor. He did not wish to be arrested just yet. They would get him in the end but *ach, Gott,* not yet, not yet. So west from town he gave them a chase. Their lights were behind him and he heard a siren and the speedometer showed sixty and then seventy and then even eighty; and through the windshield the Baron saw a curve coming which he could never make; but he did make it; but the car was swerving so badly that he found it impossible to avoid crashing into the concrete abutment of a bridge. For an instant he was frozen motionless in time and space, and he knew he would never hang, they would never get him now; and then he broke out of that frozen moment and he was rushing through the universe where lights blazed as a couple of major planets crashed; and he was spinning in darkness; and then indeed it was all over, quite over, with the Baron Karl Otto Von Krummer.

23

It was gray, next afternoon, the fine Indian summer weather over; and in Tamarack the Commander Hotel, situated on what had once been the grounds of Samuel R. Oxenford's mansion, looked gray and no longer so very new. The thirties had not been a good decade for hostelries, what with the invention of trailers for traveling, and motor courts; and the management of the Commander was happy to rent apartments at modest sums.

In one apartment, by a window overlooking the garages and garbage cans that had once been stables and gardens, a woman was sitting. She was huge. The light from the pearl-colored sky revealed her hair to be more gray than red; much more; and she wore glasses. She was not reading, or even meditating; she was just sitting. Her name was Mrs. A. H. Burgoyne; and although not a wealthy woman, still she had means of support. She was thrift triumphant; for during her years of marriage her husband had often flipped her a ten or a twenty, and this money she had not squandered. In a quarter of a century the sum had grown; and when, a few years ago, her husband had been kidnapped by a lion tamer, the woman had visited an insurance agency and asked whether it wished to sell her a policy. As it happened, the agency had so wished. Hence, the woman had plunked all her considerable savings into an insurance company's treasury, and every month till death intervened the company would send her a check for a nice amount. She almost never spent all the monthly check.

At the door of her apartment, something thumped. She sighed, arose, opened the door, picked up the afternoon paper. A paper called the *Beacon*. Today its banner was not concerned with turmoil in foreign parts, but turmoil and death in domestic parts. The banner excited Flora. She sat reading.

Certain things had happened. At the ruined quarters of Burgoyne & Pawpacker's circus, a man named Pawpacker had been shot and killed by a man named the Baron Von Krummer; and then the Baron, pursued by the state police for speeding, had crashed into a bridge abutment, with the to-be-expected consequences.

Why the Baron had voyaged to the circus farm remained a mystery. Eloise Sebastian, daughter of acrobats, had been living at the farm with Pawpacker, but she was unable to enlighten the authorities as to why the Baron had visited the farm. Eloise, the paper said, was leaving the farm soon for Chicago.

So the Baron Karl Otto Von Krummer was a villainous fellow. Or was he? Through the lines of the news story seeped a bit of doubt as to the Baron's villainy. For after all, Ivan Pawpacker had been a crooked banker, an ex-con, while the Baron had behind him a long, spotless record of heroism and community service. There were implications in that news story that perhaps the Baron had not been wholly at fault. For upright men seldom become murderers without great provocation, such as self-defense, and the Baron was an upright man.

An editorial appeared, composed by a fellow luncheon club member of the Baron Von Krummer. It ignored the violence that marred the Baron's last hours among the living. The Baron, it lamented, would be missed. And as a member of the Tamarack Humane Society, he would be missed not only by Tamarack bipeds, but also by the quadrupeds. He was called one of the best friends of man's best friend.

The paper descended to Flora's lap. She sighed. Mention of Burgoyne & Pawpacker's circus farm reminded her of Gus. She sighed again, and her gaze went to the apartment wall, where hung a memento of Gus. It was not much; not a very good painting; but years ago upon leaving the farm she had rescued it from the attic and brought it here. Staring at it, she studied the color of the man with the elephant. His countenance, she thought, did not look any too healthy. But this was not astonishing, in view of the long-standing defectiveness of his liver.

THE END